Book One
The Chains Trilogy

Breaking Chains

A novel by
Rob Cherville

Copyright © 2013 Rob Cherville

First published in paperback December 2013
First available as a Kindle edition September 2014
This edition published November 2014

All Rights Reserved

No part of this work may be reproduced or transmitted in any form (without exception) unless the express permission of the author has been obtained in writing.

Rob Cherville asserts his moral right to be identified as the author of this work in accordance with the Copyright Designs and Patents Act 1988.

All characters depicted in this work are, with one significant exception, creations entirely of the author's own imagination. Any resemblance to real persons, living or dead, is wholly unintentional and purely coincidental.

ISBN-13: 978-1493694525
ISBN-10: 1493694529

Published by
Aullton House Books, Derbyshire UK

Printed by
CreateSpace, Charleston SC

robcherville@aulltonhouse.org.uk

To Jan

My dearest friend and loving wife of so many years who has patiently tolerated my quiet mutterings and faraway looks.

He brought them out of darkness and the deepest gloom and broke away their chains.
Psalm 107 v 14

"Is not this the kind of fasting I have chosen: to loose the chains of injustice and untie the cords of the yoke, to set the oppressed free and break every yoke?
Isaiah 58 v 6

"For to be free is not merely to cast off one's chains, but to live in a way that respects and enhances the freedom of others."
Nelson Mandela

Prologue

St Helena Island
South Atlantic Ocean

10 years earlier

Prologue

The Lammermuir Hills, Scotland – May 2005

It felt heavy in my hand. Black and warm. Over three kilos of lethal metal. I'd never held one before that day and hoped I never would again. But right now, on that lonely veranda with its long view over the meadows to the trout stream, the power in that awesome weight was my only hope of staying alive.

The magazine was nowhere near full. I'd watched him count the bullets as he loaded it. Twenty-five shiny brass tubes. But I'd already fired several. Though I'd lost count of how many, I knew I must have some left. If their plan had worked out, it would eventually have been me looking into that black muzzle waiting for one of those shiny tubes to explode and send a bullet blasting through my skull.

But he couldn't resist a pretty face. I'd often seen his eyes ablaze with desire for my body, which had been bought and paid for so many times, and now he had his opportunity. Whatever he imagined he was going to do as he tried to force me into that bedroom, it caused him to overlook the danger of getting too close. And now it would cost him his life because I had no other way of overpowering him. He would die, and I would live.

He knelt there moaning on the wooden boards clutching at his eyes, while beyond him the grass stretched away over the stream to acres of Scottish woodland.

As I watched him, my heart pounding and my breath coming in gasps, my mind jumped back over ten years to the day this nightmare began.

To a different veranda with an equally long view, on a small island over eight thousand miles away.

To a day when I was eight years old and immortal.

Saint Helena Island – February 1995

The day it happened began like any other. I woke with the sunrise as usual, washed without enthusiasm, dressed quickly in my blue school skirt and white blouse, grabbed my sewing, and went out onto the veranda where I sat for maybe half an hour working on the cross-stitch design which Mum had drawn out for me. I loved setting the stitches and watching the picture grow on the fabric, but I wasn't much good at drawing the initial design. On a clear day the colours, in that early morning light, seemed so vibrant, and the silk threads resonated with a mystical vitality. I could hear Mum and Dad moving about inside but I didn't pay them much attention. While they went through their own morning g routine, they usually left me alone with what they jokingly called my "morning meditations" for which I was grateful, except when I felt in need of a bit of attention. Then I'd go in search of the hugs and kisses which cemented our family together.

I loved to eat breakfast out there on the veranda. It was just wide enough for the necessary table and chairs, and continued in an unbroken run around all four sides of the house, with stout posts at the corners to support the overhanging roof. I don't really know why, but I have always loved the open air. I don't just mean the fresh, clean, scented atmosphere of the island, although that was always part of it. I just loved being outdoors, and almost every morning the view from our veranda held me enthralled until I was summoned to help set the table with shreddies or wheaties or whatever other healthy goodies the latest ship had brought out from the UK or the Cape. The trees fascinated me. They didn't grow in abundance on this side of the island, but I really treasured the ones I could see as I looked out over the plain to Prosperous Bay and the grey-blue of the South Atlantic. This was the scene which Mum had sketched for me to create with my stitches.

Usually, my mum and dad would come and sit with me during breakfast and we would talk about what we had planned for the day. My contribution was often quite short. There wasn't a lot I could say about school, not because I didn't enjoy it, but because I rarely knew what was going to happen until it did. My teacher had been trained in the UK, at Bristol I think, and rarely did she let slip what she had planned for us to do. She kept most of us in her class in a state of eager anticipation from one day to the next and, because she was truly skilled at what she did, we were rarely disappointed. Next to my mum, Miss Shirley Thomas was my ideal role model. She was young, mid-twenties probably, with coffee-coloured skin, dark hair and laughing brown eyes. She was attractive in both looks and personality, confident and capable, and through all the terrors that followed that morning, I never forgot her.

The small breakfast table was pushed right up against the veranda rail to allow us to sit around the other three sides. The sun was not yet high enough in the sky for us to be protected by the overhanging roof, and we could feel its warmth both directly and also reflected off the white wall of the house. I just took it for granted then but, looking back now, the peacefulness and safety of that remote place seem to belong more to a fairy tale than to reality.

It was Friday and I can remember our excitement as we talked about the British warship which had anchored in James Bay the previous afternoon. I now know that a Type 42 destroyer is not huge, as warships go, but to me she had seemed massive when I had gone down to the wharf to see her with my friends after school. Dad had met some of the sailors in Jamestown that same evening and already there was talk of a football match between the Saintes and the crew of HMS Selkirk on Saturday morning. The ship was due to sail again on Sunday, but on Saturday afternoon would be open to any who could beg, buy, or otherwise coerce a passage out to her. In the evening, there would be a party on board for invited guests. Dad was confident he and Mum would be among the select few, partly because of his job, and also because he was meeting one of the officers later on to help him out with something which Mum seemed to understand but which meant very little to me.

My dad was pretty clever. I know that because he worked for Cable and Wireless and was responsible for the project to bring TV to St. Helena Island. We were all hugely excited at the prospect and I was really proud that it was my dad who was helping to make it happen. From what I could make out, it seemed that this officer needed Dad's help to send a message to some people in the UK and he needed an immediate reply by fax. It never occurred to me at the time to wonder why the message could not be sent from his ship.

The officer's name was Gordie, which is how my dad introduced him when he came to dinner on that Friday evening. I never did know his last name. I played with my friends after school as usual, only this time it involved a certain amount of ogling of the sailors who were allowed ashore, while I waited for my mum to finish her shift at the hospital in Jamestown, the only town on the island. She now worked as a midwife on the very ward where I had been born. She loved her job in spite of the fact that she knew could never have any more children herself. She had explained it to me when I had asked about the chance of having a brother. I met her that evening about five o'clock and we walked up together from the hospital to The Briars, the headquarters of Cable and Wireless to see if Dad was ready to come home.

We found Gordie also waiting there. He and Dad had finished their business and, when he commented on how much he was growing tired of ship food, Dad had invited him to dinner. Mum was a bit concerned until Dad reassured her that he had already rung Joyce, our housekeeper, to ask her to "throw something extra in the pot". I often heard him use that phrase when he asked someone home on the spur of the moment which, I suppose, is why it sticks in my mind.

Gordie was fun. He had a full beard, jet black and neatly trimmed, not bushy. And he had smiling eyes, all crinkly at the corners. He told amusing stories as Dad drove us in his Clio Williams along the narrow, winding road that led up country from Jamestown. Dad loved that little car which was so well suited to the island's narrow roads, and was pleased when Gordie commented on how easily it pulled up the steepest of hills, even with the four of us on board. He also said nice things about our house as it came into sight, and when I showed him my favourite view, he seemed as thrilled by it as I was. He played catch with Dad and me for a few minutes on the grass in front of the house while we waited for Mum and Joyce to finish off preparing the dinner. When all was ready, we all sat down in the dining room and I remember feeling quite grown up as I took my seat and placed the carefully folded napkin on my lap. Gordie didn't talk down to me like so many adults do. I didn't contribute much to the dinner table conversation but, when I asked a question, Gordie would explain in a way that was simple and didn't make me feel as though he thought I was too young to understand.

If I'd had a list of my ten favourite adults, number ten would have been bumped off the bottom and Gordie would have come in about number nine. He might have been higher except for something strange that happened towards the end of the meal. Dad filled our wine glasses - I had a small one, a very small one - and proposed a toast. He congratulated Gordie on the new job that awaited him back in the UK. As Mum and I were saying, "Congratulations", a strange look came into Gordie's eyes. It was only there for a moment and then, before I could be sure whether it was fear or anger or just a trick of the light, his eyes were smiling again. He asked my dad how he knew about the job, and Dad told him he'd caught a glimpse of the fax as it came through that afternoon from the UK in response to Gordie's phone call. I sensed a bit of awkwardness, as though Dad was embarrassed at having seen something he wasn't supposed to, and Gordie was annoyed but didn't want to show it.

The moment passed and we all settled down to play Monopoly. It was now dark outside, the sun having set about six o'clock. We didn't have time to finish the game before Gordie said it was time for him to be getting back to the ship, so Dad said we'd better count up our assets to see who had won. Surprisingly, it was me and, as Gordie said, "Well done," I gave him a hug, partly excitement, partly goodbye. He gave me a quick hug back, and I noticed that strange look again as I pulled away from him. Mum said she'd go with Dad to drive Gordie back down to Jamestown and they could then call in at the Consulate Hotel for a drink before driving back.

Joyce stayed to keep me company - it hadn't been called "babysitting" since I was about five. We stood on the veranda and watched them drive away. I had no sense of premonition, but I remember refusing to go back inside the house before the lights of the Williams had completely disappeared.

I had just finished washing and changing for bed when we heard the explosion that signalled the end of my fairy-tale existence. At that moment my life disintegrated, and every minute of that last fateful day became forever etched in my memory.

Saturday

30th April 2005

Aushra Paulauskaitė – Day One

Vilnius, Lithuania – 6:00 am

Aushra lay still, staring blankly through the gloom of her bedroom at the cracked and peeling ceiling above. A light from the communal courtyard outside peeped lazily between the curtains to cast a tired glow into her room. She had no idea how much alcohol had invaded her system last night, nor did she care. Her only worry was that the numbing effect was wearing off and soon the memories would return with a stark, bleak reality that she feared might overwhelm her.

The flashing lights and exuberant, pounding rhythms in the club had deadened things for a while the evening before, until somewhere in the small hours the drink had taken over and anaesthetised the pain. As her mind emerged slowly from the safety of its alcoholic haze, she wondered how she had managed to get home? Perhaps Jolanta had brought her, but surely her friend had been pouring in the booze with even more enthusiasm than she herself.

So, what had happened?

She reached down to her waist, and the movement sent a jolt of lightning through the front of her skull. She relaxed, hoping the sudden pounding would die down, but the effort had been reassuring. Her underwear seemed intact.

She hoped Jolanta was OK too. She was an attractive girl. In fact, they both were, and they knew it. Eighteen years old, with birthdays only days apart, they drew in the boys like magnets, so how could they not know?

But one boy would not be responding to their charms ever again.

Mykolas Kubilius had lived across the courtyard with his mother. A student at the university, in his second year, he had been quietly studious, more of a brother than a suitor to Aushra or Jolanta. He had known the girls since they played together as toddlers among the flowers of the ragged courtyard garden. If he'd been there last night, he would have seen her safely home and, if there was a possibility that he might have liked to remove her panties, he would never have done so without her knowing and willing consent.

But he had not been there.

Two days ago, in a desperate response to what his classmates were calling the bleakness of a future without hope, he had stepped off the Zaliasis Bridge to fall without a sound into the Neris River.

He had been the twenty-seventh person to kill themselves that week, the latest casualty of Lithuania's suicide epidemic.

So Aushra lay and cried for her friend, a prey to guilt that her own future, once as bleak as his, was now looking safe and secure, thanks to the generosity of a British company somewhere in the English Midlands.

In just a few more days, she and several other carefully selected recruits would be flown out of Vilnius airport to good jobs with guarantees of a first-rate business training and wages beyond anything she could previously have imagined.

It was a crying shame that Mykolas could not have been chosen to go with them but the company representatives, though sympathetic, had been adamant. Females were seriously under-represented in their lower levels of management and, for that reason, they were only recruiting girls.

One

Heighley Woods, Staffordshire - 6:00 am

Quietly, reluctantly, the dark tendrils of the night let go their fleeting grasp of the trunks and twigs of my temporary shelter. Early morning twilight, pale and tranquil, eased its way down through the canopy overhead, reaching inexorably into the shadows.

My eyes, wide and staring, saw it all and registered nothing.

I lay absolutely still, struggling to calm the pounding in my chest. My breaths came fast and shallow, yet almost inaudible, as I listened intently for some repetition of the sound that had disturbed me. Something was out there among the trees, I was sure, though not even the faintest whisper could now be heard in that peaceful summer's dawn.

I was flat on my back, fully dressed, lying on a cushion of moss and leaves in the hollow centre of a cluster of holly bushes, in a wood some thirty miles or so north of Birmingham. It was a strange place for a nineteen-year-old girl to be resting in the gloom of that soggy dawn. A few hours earlier, it had seemed like a good idea, but now I was beginning to wonder if I'd made a serious mistake.

I started to take deeper breaths, trying to slow my rapid heartbeat and calm the pulse pounding in my ears. At that moment, I longed to hear the cheerful twittering of birdsong, to reassure me that nothing large and threatening was disturbing the peace of the woods, but the treetops remained obstinately silent. Nor could I detect the rustling of small animals making their way home through the tangled undergrowth after a night of foraging. In spite of the silence, or perhaps because of it, the longer I lay there the more certain I became that I was not alone in those woods.

I tried telling myself that there was nothing to be afraid of, but I couldn't quite make myself believe it. In fact it was the total absence of sound that was at the root of my fear. The natural noises of the night had not troubled me in the least when I made my way into the wood under a bright full moon around two-thirty that morning. I was used to them. In my nineteen years I had probably acquired more experience of living outdoors than most people in England build up in a lifetime. The calls of neither owl nor vixen had caused me any qualms as I had settled down by the aid of a small flashlight in the heart of this overgrown clump of holly. So, I asked myself reasonably, why was I now filled with such an overwhelming sense of dread?

I couldn't believe that they had found me.

Not so soon. I was sure I had left no trail, no clue as to where I was going. Not even Angie, who had first told me about the farm, had any idea that I actually intended to go there. As the silence stretched from seconds into minutes, my breathing became more regular, my pulse steadied and panic slowly gave way to a reluctant reassurance that all was in fact well. I was safe.

I had to be. I had taken a great deal of care to make sure that there wasn't any way their many tentacles could reach out to drag me back into the life which I had, with such determination, left behind.

The sudden click and snap of oiled metal parts drew the breath from me in renewed panic. Out there among the trees, over to my left and not many yards away, someone was moving. I rolled onto my side trying desperately not to make a sound as I reached into the side pocket of my light denim jacket for my only weapon. The penknife with a locking 3" blade was normally used for cutting string or tape. On one occasion I had used it to slice through the hand of a would-be mugger, but it wasn't a serious weapon. It was only good at close quarters, and close was what I definitely intended not to get. And then I stopped, my hand still gripping the knife but not withdrawing it. Whoever it was out there, he certainly wasn't after me, not unless the Birmingham low-life had taken to hymn singing, which was about as likely as Ashbourne United winning the Cup.

Very faintly, but with a deep resonance that carried clearly to my prickly refuge, a male voice hummed the tune to *Amazing Grace*. No words, just the tune, verse after verse to the accompaniment of more clicks and the rustle of leaves and twigs.

The pale rays of that April dawn, now strong enough to penetrate the burgeoning canopy of oak and chestnut, gave delicate substance to a tall shape moving in the darkness. As I peered out of my stronghold of holly, I could actually distinguish the outline of a figure between me and what seemed to be a small lake which I hadn't noticed earlier in the night. He was silhouetted against the faint light entering the wood through the break in the trees and reflecting dimly from the water's smooth surface. I could see he was standing, his sheer size left me in no doubt, but at first I couldn't make out in which direction he was looking. Then he turned slowly from side to side and I could see that he had his back to me with his hands up in front of his face apparently holding something.

Still humming quietly the hunter, for that's how I thought of him, scanned the clearing at the edge of the small lake through what I took from their size to be a pair of powerful night glasses. I couldn't really make out any detail, but against the lighter background of the lake's surface, they seemed large and business-like in his steady hands. What he was looking for, I had no idea. I could make out nothing but the shapes of trees and bushes around the lake. Nothing out of the ordinary. As the clouds in the sky above the clearing began to drift away, I found the shapes around me developing depth and detail, colours beginning to emerge from the greyness.

The hunter had stopped humming now, and I waited with more curiosity than fear to see what he would do next. He too seemed to be waiting for something, just watching and waiting, with no sign of unease or impatience. His movements were all calm and unhurried and I wished I could see more clearly just what he was doing. Whatever it was, I knew he hadn't come for me, just as certainly as I knew I had never seen him before in my life. He was big, very big, and taller than anyone I knew. As the minutes wore on, and nothing happened, I became aware of a growing need to find a bathroom. It's surprising what effect fear has on the bladder. I had been perfectly capable of peeing in the bushes when I had known myself to be alone, but the presence of this bulky stranger was altogether too inhibiting.

After several minutes during which the light gradually improved, he knelt down and reached for the silenced rifle resting on the old trunk beside him. I hadn't noticed it before, but its shape as he raised it to his shoulder was quite unmistakable. Having watched the right movies, I was able to work out that it was fitted with some kind of high-powered night scope. I assumed it was already zeroed on the centre of the clearing thirty-five metres away because, having looked steadily for several moments, he put it down again without making any adjustments. What was he hunting? If this was the highlands of Scotland, a man with a rifle would be stalking deer, but I'd never heard of it happening in Staffordshire. With a shotgun, he might be after pigeons, or maybe grouse, partridge or pheasant. But weren't there open and closed seasons for those? Well, probably not for pigeons, but what did it matter? Shotguns didn't have telescopic sights and silencers as this man's weapon most certainly did.

Then I thought of paintballing. I knew about that because a year or so previously I'd been enlisted in the entertainment party for some visiting Lithuanian businessmen. Paintballing had occupied most of the afternoon, in which I faithfully played my part along with eight other girls as "prey" being hunted through the woods of some country house, corporate function place. Whichever businessman/hunter "shot" us, we were his for the night, after their business discussions over dinner in the evening, to which we had definitely not been invited. Yes, I knew all about paintballing. I knew the guns, the clothes and the sounds as inexperienced stalkers thrashed about in the undergrowth trying to make like the SAS. But that rifle was not a paintball gun, and the woods remained utterly quiet. So, what was he hunting? Or whom?

It seemed as though he was completely unaware of there being another person in the wood. My dark holly-shrouded eyes penetrated his hide with a clarity increasing minute by minute, at times boring so fiercely into his back that I felt he must sense my presence. But the hunter just waited, apparently oblivious, relaxed and patient, for his quarry to appear.

In other circumstances, I would have found the quiet of the woods to be very soothing, but this morning there was something ominous in that stillness. It was also very restricting as any movement on my part was likely to generate sound which the hunter couldn't fail to hear. I just hoped that the occasional rustle to his rear as I changed position would be taken to be small animals foraging in the early dawn. I adjusted my legs slightly, trying to relieve the discomfort of a full bladder, and desperate not to snap a twig in the process, as anything big enough to do that would be sure to attract the hunter's attention.

A moment later I froze, bladder problems forgotten for someone else, making far more noise than I had, was approaching through the trees. I saw the hunter lift his head and stiffen as he caught the sound of feet padding on the path, running not walking. A figure came into view on a path leading to the water's edge, moving quickly at a steady jog, clearly following a familiar route for which the scarcity of light was no hindrance. The hunter reached out for his glasses but then laid them aside in favour of his rifle. He seemed to be aiming at the centre of the clearing some way ahead of the jogger and thirty-five metres from the hunter's position. Here, for several paces, the jogger would be moving directly towards the hunter's hide, thus showing clearly in his sights before veering right to follow the contours of the lake.

In the pallid light seeping into the clearing, I could make out a pale face topped by dark hair dampened by drizzle and sweat, eyes wide and staring and lips drawn back as his mouth sucked in large gasps of cool air. To the hunter, that face must have appeared huge in the scope's lens as he readied himself for the shot that would blow it to extinction. Then he sighed. I actually heard it, a long breath of exasperation. At least, that's how it seemed to me. Then, as if in confirmation, he sighed again as he shook his head slowly and rested his rifle back against the log. I started breathing again. I hadn't realised that I'd stopped until that moment of relief when it dawned on me that I wasn't actually going to see someone shot to death after all. At least, not yet.

The jogger's head jerked suddenly to his left, and his pace slowed. The hunter panned slowly to his right searching for whatever it was that had caught the jogger's attention. Then the runner slowed to a stop in the clearing, just a few feet from the crumbling earth shore. He turned his back to the lake and leaned forward slightly, hands on hips, breathing hard.

The panting jogger waited, peered into the bushes almost as though he expected someone to appear. Then he lifted his hand and I thought he was going to call out, but I didn't hear any sound. I tried to follow his line of sight, and at first could see nothing in the shadows of the bushes, but then I saw that his gaze had settled on a crouching figure obscured from the lake by one the clumps of willows which fringed the clearing. The wood was proving a popular place this morning. Our little drama had now acquired a fourth character, whose shadowy figure seemed to be clothed in some sort of dark camouflage smock, the head obscured by a black balaclava covered by the hood of the smock. Where the stranger had come from there was no telling. I certainly hadn't noticed him a few moments before when I had watched the jogger enter the clearing.

In my den of holly, I decided I had little option but to wait it out. I was the only character who had a clear view of the other three, and probably the only one with a clear line of sight to the newcomer in the balaclava. I was also probably the only one who didn't have the faintest idea what was going on. I eased forward slightly, both to improve my view and to relieve my right knee of the sharp stone which seemed to be trying to bore a hole into it. As I gently lowered my knee to its new location, it pressed down on a dry twig and the woods resounded with an explosive crack. Once again my heart stopped, but apparently the shattering of the twig was not as violent an explosion as it had seemed to my highly sensitive ears.

The hunter glanced around and for a moment seemed to gaze directly into my eyes which I immediately clamped tight shut. It really was only a moment but it seemed to drag on for ages until curiosity prised my eyes open once more. I noticed my heart was beating again about the same time as I saw the hunter turn his attention back to the clearing and to the jogger who was still gazing uncertainly around. Then suddenly, everything was panic. The shadowy figure had vanished. The hunter leapt to his feet just as the jogger fell to his knees, doubled over as though in great pain his right hand clutching at the upper part of his chest.

I almost leapt up myself to try and get a better view of the action. It never even crossed my mind that this was probably my best opportunity so far of creeping away unobserved while the other characters were fully engaged in playing their parts. The hunter was moving forward now, crashing through bracken and brambles with a speed I would not have credited to so huge a figure. The jogger was clearly now in acute distress and before the hunter could reach him he fell backwards into the lake and lay still, his face submerged beneath the muddy water. The hunter waded into the lake and, lifting the jogger's face clear of the water, hauled him quickly onto the bank with no more difficulty than he would a feather pillow.

The hunter seemed to be feeling the jogger's neck for signs of a pulse, but when his head lolled to one side, I could see even at that distance the blood oozing from a ragged gash above and behind his right ear. The hunter continued to search for some sign of life, but there was no doubt in my mind that the jogger was dead. It was then, as he crouched there by the lake, clear of the shadows, that I had my first clear sight of the hunter's face. He looked back into the trees to where he had left his rifle and presumably other equipment, and there was such shock and sorrow in his expression that I knew I had been completely wrong in assuming he had any intention of harming the jogger.

I still wasn't happy about letting my presence in the wood be known. Something bad had happened and I didn't want to be part of it, not even as a witness. Witnesses have to give details about themselves, and I had good reason for not wanting anyone, let alone the police, knowing who I was or where I was. I realised I should have gone, slowly and quietly, while everyone's attention was diverted, but the chance had passed.

I watched the hunter rise and look all around him as though his brain didn't register what his eyes were seeing. At last, his gaze came back to the body on the ground. He stood looking down as though in thought, or perhaps still in shock, then he took a deep breath and turned to make his way back to his hide. He stumbled a few times as his foot caught in a bramble, and once he walked straight into a young oak that bent and then snapped under the pressure of his great bulk. I watched him all the way back to his hide and then, confident that he was coming no nearer, I looked around for that camouflaged figure who had come and then disappeared so mysteriously. I listened to see if I could hear any sound of him - I had assumed from the first that it was a *him* - but all I could hear was the hunter searching through the backpack which he had rested on the fallen tree. I breathed slowly and listened harder wishing I had the hunter's glasses in my hands. Nothing. I concentrated hard as I scanned that area of the woods most likely to be hiding the camouflaged figure. Still nothing. Either he was as good as me at playing the silent watcher, or else he had gone. On balance, I decided he'd gone. I would have. It was likely to get pretty busy around here before long which made me realise that, however difficult it might be to achieve without detection, I too had better leave.

Then I heard the hunter's voice. Not the gravely rumble I had subconsciously expected from a man his size, but pleasant, even cultured, rather like Peter O'Toole in "How to steal a million". I loved that movie.

"Police......James Montrayne, The Dower House, Abbot's Newton. I'm in Heighley Woods. There's a dead man near the lake at the top end of the wood…… Yes, I am sure he's dead…… Yes, I know him very well. His name is Phil Simmons…… Yes, I'll be right here."

His voice grew fainter as I retreated from my refuge, still keeping a wary lookout for balaclava man, just in case. I had no idea what had taken place that morning, and I was absolutely certain that I wanted no part of it, but I had an awful feeling that my life had just taken another turn for the worse.

Two

Heighley Grange Farm, Staffordshire - 8.00 am

The gap in the hawthorn hedge separating the sheep pasture from the lane was quite narrow and the weathered timber of the old stile neatly filled the opening. The hedge itself had been trimmed not very long ago, so I had been able to climb the steps without getting scratched by any of the long thorns. Now, I sat on the cross-step of the stile looking across a field of lush, green grass towards the distant farm buildings. Sheep were dotted around the field, some solitary, others in small groups, but they seemed as little interested in me as I was in them.

For the thousandth time that morning I asked myself why I had been so foolish as to take shelter in that wood the night before, and I still came up with the same answer. Given the circumstances, it hadn't just *seemed* like a good idea, it *was* a good idea, and on any other night of the year would have caused me no problem.

My cooperative lorry driver had made a slight detour to drop me at the end of the lane, helping me down from the cab with no suggestion of favours needing to be repaid, for which I was heartily thankful. I had felt slightly guilty for having misjudged him as I walked up the lane. He really had been a decent guy, helping for no other reason than a desire to lend a hand, without seeing what he could get for himself out of the situation. Once I'd walked up the lane in the dark and got as far as the trees, I realised I had no idea how the folk at the farm would react to being woken by a stranger at that early hour, and I was desperate enough for a place to stay that I didn't want to risk annoying them at the outset. I had to admit to myself also that I was influenced by what Angie had told me about the dogs that were allowed to roam the farmyard at night to deter foxes, and I had no wish to be mistaken in the dark for an unwanted intruder. I had also been aware that if my tampon didn't get changed pretty soon, I would be in trouble. So, I had opted for the dark privacy of the wood, not as scary an option as you might think, since I was used to the outdoors and had been from a child. No, it really hadn't been a stupid decision given the circumstances. It was just unfortunate that someone else had picked the same wood as a convenient place for a murder. Still, I was out of it now, and almost at my destination.

For months, I had been building up a picture in my mind of Angie's farm. Not that it was hers in any possessive sense but once, aeons ago, as a fifteen year old runaway she had stayed here for the better part of a year. She had described it to me, one rare evening when neither of us was working, and my own imagination had done the rest.

I had no doubt this was the place. The old brick farmhouse was some distance away, but there was no mistaking the three tall, patterned chimneystacks, one at each end of the steeply-pitched slate roof, and the third exactly central over the main entrance which was invisible to me, being on the far side of the building. The rear of the house presided over a three-sided courtyard with symmetrical wings, also in brick, projecting towards me left and right. At this distance, I couldn't make out the detail, but I knew what I should find.

For some reason which I didn't understand, the farm had some kind of status with the Social Services and Angie had been allowed to stay and celebrate her sixteenth birthday in a small apartment in one of the courtyard buildings. Apparently there were several of these small units, usually occupied by young people who'd managed to get themselves into some sort of trouble and needed help in getting straightened out. Well, I could manage my own straightening out, but I did need somewhere to stay where I wouldn't be easily found, and this had sounded like the right place. Assuming Angie ever guessed that this was where I'd run to, I was confident she'd never tell, not unless Bruno and his friends decided to get very persuasive which, though I didn't like to admit it to myself, was quite possible.

The nearer buildings, which looked like big barns, were probably the chicken sheds. I knew there were thousands of birds here, allowed to range free within the fenced enclosures surrounding each shed. I wasn't quite sure how it worked but, according to Angie, the young . . . . residents? delinquents? whatever, were involved in some way in managing this enterprise, or at least in working their keep. Their quarters were presumably in the long, right-hand wing leading off from the main farmhouse, behind and to the left of the sheds. The other wing which I could see more clearly appeared to have large doorways which I assumed were for vehicles.

I've no idea how long I sat there looking at the buildings, waiting for someone to appear, someone I could go up to and say, "Hi. I'm Lizzie. I've come to stay." It had seemed so easy back in Birmingham, but now I was here I wasn't so sure. Would they have a spare place for me, or even want to take me in if they had? I didn't know how they'd feel, taking in a stranger, once it became known what had happened in the woods that morning. And did I really want to stay if the police were going to be crawling around asking questions? This farm wasn't going to be quite the anonymous refuge I'd been hoping for. And what about reporters? They were bound to come snooping around with their notebooks, cameras and prying questions, and the last thing I needed now was my picture in the paper. But where else had I got to go?

My thoughts were interrupted by the growl of a heavy vehicle easing up the narrow lane in low gear. I stood up and looked back over the stile to watch a large creamy coloured milk tanker crawl past from right to left. I continued to watch its slow progress, as I could still see the top of it over the hedge, and an idea suddenly erupted in my mind. A few hundred yards further up the lane the tanker slowed almost to a stop and made a sharp right-hand turn, presumably onto a farm track leading to one of its daily milk collections. I was pretty sure it wouldn't be calling at Heighley Grange Farm as there was no dairy herd, or there hadn't been during Angie's stay. I believed I could now see how to avoid arousing the interest of either police or reporters.

I watched the top of the tanker for a few moments more, before turning to make my way, with some hesitation, to follow the footpath across the field to the farmhouse. I had only gone a few paces when I heard the sound of footsteps coming along the lane, accompanied by the whines and yelps of a dog scuffling about in the hedge. I would probably have heard them earlier if I hadn't been concentrating so hard on the tanker. I turned back and waited to see whether the newcomer would climb the stile and enter the field, perhaps en route to the farm. He didn't. I saw a tall man in a dark overcoat glance quickly over the stile as he passed, obviously intending to continue his walk up the lane. When he saw me, he stopped and fixed me with such a piercing stare that I was terrified for a moment that he had come in search of me. The thing was I was absolutely certain that I'd never seen him before. He looked to be in his forties, dark haired with bushy eyebrows and a very belligerent expression on his thin face. His steady gaze made me very conscious that I was far from looking my best that morning. He took in everything, from my stained Reeboks, up my faded jeans, over my Robbie tee-shirt and denim jacket, to yesterday's make-up and tousled chestnut hair.

"So, you're another of them," he said, in a cultured middle-class sort of voice. He seemed to deduce something from my back-pack and my rather dishevelled appearance, as he went on to add, "I take it you've just arrived from whatever cesspit you normally inhabit."

I wasn't frightened anymore, just puzzled and resentful of his obvious antagonism, and it must have showed on my face since, before I could say anything, he came right up to the stile and, pointing a gloved finger at me over the top, said, "Let me tell you that we can well do without your sort around here. My neighbours and I have children of our own and we certainly don't want to see them corrupted by the likes of you. Go back to where you came from, because I swear that if you stay around here I'll make sure you live to regret it."

His dog had by now finished his business in the hedge and was prepared to turn his attention to me. The face of a black Labrador gazed good-naturedly at me through the stile before glancing inquiringly up at the tall man as if to ask what all the fuss was about. I wanted to ask the same thing. It was as though this total stranger was familiar with all the lurid details of my recent life story and yet it was perfectly obvious that he couldn't have the faintest idea who I was.

I was still puzzled, but anger was beginning to take precedence now, and I was tempted to respond with some of the juicier language that I had picked up in the gutters of Birmingham, but I knew that would only confirm his opinion of me, and I still wanted to draw as little attention as possible. Then it dawned on me that perhaps his arrival could be put to good use so I asked, as politely as my fiery emotions would allow, "Could you perhaps tell me the time, please?"

If I had actually let rip with the verbal abuse that was simmering in my mind, he couldn't have looked more startled. He did look at his watch as I'd thought he might, but it was clearly instinctive and instead of responding to my query he just said, "Remember what I told you. You're not welcome here." Then, after glancing away in the direction of the farmhouse, he turned aside and, with a quick, "Come on boy," he strode off up the lane.

Wondering what had caught his attention behind me, I turned slowly to see another male figure ambling down the footpath towards me. In contrast to my recent acquaintance, the newcomer was casually dressed. In fact as he drew nearer, I could see that 'casual' described just about every aspect about him; Wellingtons caked in mud, and probably worse, brown corduroy trousers, a blue and red checked shirt under a green waxed jacket from which most of the wax had disappeared long since. He was tallish, I thought, though probably under six feet, and comfortably rounded. Much of his face was hidden behind a full beard, and shadowed by the large brim of a green bush hat.

After my recent encounter, I was a little nervous about meeting this fellow, a feeling which escalated rapidly at the sight of the huge, tan-coloured animal bounding over the field behind him. My first horrified thought was that a lioness was on the loose, but since the unkempt figure ambling towards me was clearly unconcerned as the creature drew abreast of him, saner thoughts prevailed. It had to be a dog, but I had never in my life seen anything as big as the animal surging towards me. I stood absolutely still, desperate to run, but completely unable to encourage my legs to take the necessary action. I guess I was both amazed and petrified in equal proportions, and I suppose the owner must have sensed my fear as he yelled something unintelligible and the animal skidded to a halt. It looked back at him just once, as if to enquire why its fun was being curtailed, and then sank down to lie on the grass about ten feet away, with its head resting on its forepaws, and an incredible amount of dribble oozing from its jaws.

If raising your heart rate really is good for you, then I was having a particularly healthy morning, though at that precise moment I felt utterly wretched. Flushed and breathing fast, with my whole body trembling slightly from the accumulated emotional assaults of that day, I gazed into the dog's benevolent black-rimmed eyes and, to my absolute horror, burst into tears.

Ten minutes later, I was sitting in the large and pleasantly cluttered kitchen of the old farmhouse. There were three of us seated at the long, oak table. At least, I always assumed it was oak, for the wood was dark and grainy, and bore the chips and blemishes of a long and interesting life. I sat at the end, and along the side to my right, quite close to me, sat the farmer, still casual but now without the jacket and hat, and with a concerned and kindly look in his eyes. He leaned his folded arms on the table and looked from me to his wife who sat opposite him, to my left. There seemed to be some kind of silent communication between the two of them because, after a moment, she smiled and nodded slightly and they both turned their eyes on me.

We hadn't spoken much, the farmer and I, on our way up to the house. On seeing my tears, he had pulled a white, neatly folded handkerchief from his jacket pocket and handed it to me saying, "My name's Rick, Rick Childers, but most folks call me Chick. That brute there is Simba. Brave as a lion, when occasion warrants it, but daft as a brush, so don't let him worry you."

He had picked up my backpack, which somehow I'd allowed to slip to the ground, and said, "Why don't you come up to the house and meet my wife? Her name's Rachel. We've had breakfast, but I don't doubt she's got some coffee on the go."

I had mumbled some kind of thanks, and managed to mention that I was more in need of a bathroom than I was of coffee. He had just smiled and nodded, and followed him back up the path while the dog careered around us, shooting back and forth in enormous bursts of energy. I did notice, however, that he kept clear of the sheep, never getting close enough to cause any of them to panic, in spite of his obvious exhilaration. Perhaps he wasn't quite as daft as his owner claimed.

With a coffee mug steaming on the table in front of me, and a successful bathroom visit behind me, I began to relax and think that maybe things just might work out OK after all. I could see why Angie had spoken so warmly of Chick and Rachel. I don't know what chores they'd had planned for that Saturday morning, but we sat round that old table as though there was nothing else in the world that they'd rather be doing. It felt warm and cosy and safe, and somehow the drama in the wood only hours earlier faded like a barely remembered nightmare on a sunny day. Now it actually came to the point, I realised I had no idea just how much I should tell them about myself. I knew they had at least one child and I wondered if they'd actually let me stay if they knew the whole truth about my life.

So I started with Angie and kept it brief. I told how we'd met in Birmingham soon after Christmas, how we shared an apartment and occasionally worked together. I told how my boss wanted me to do stuff at work that I wasn't happy with and so I'd left and needed a place to stay while I sorted myself out. It all sounded a bit lame put like that, and I was sure that they sensed there was a great deal that I wasn't telling them especially when Rachel asked me how Angie was doing. Was her job OK? Where was her apartment? What was it like? She spoke of Angie as she'd last seen her, bright-eyed, optimistic, full of health with her whole life ahead of her. How could I tell these folks that Angie was now the main attraction in a massage parlour, not yet HIV+ but coming closer to it every day, high on drugs much of the time because she couldn't face the reality of what she'd become. I said she was OK, was earning good money and the apartment was nice, which I suppose was true enough as far as it went.

Chick just looked at me steadily as my story limped to an end, but Rachel reached out and laid her hand on my arm.

"So, Angie told you to come and stay with us, did she? Well, she's quite right, though I don't know where we're going to put you."

I glanced at her quickly and my anxiety must have shown because she gave my arm a little squeeze and said, "Now, now, don't you worry. We'll think of something," she smiled at her husband, "won't you, Chick?"

"Sure," he nodded, "but while I'm thinking I have an idea our young friend here might appreciate the chance of a shower and," he raised an eyebrow, "perhaps a sleep?"

He was right. Now the tension was draining away, drowsiness was beginning to creep up on me, so much so that I felt like reversing his order of events; sleep first, shower later. Chick's next words, however, had me fully alert.

"You didn't say how you managed to find us. Angie's directions must have been very good."

I was ready with the lie. "I scrounged a lift with the milk tanker. The driver said he knew all the farms around here so I just left it to him. He said he wasn't calling here so he dropped me in the lane by the stile and went on to some farm a bit farther on."

That established my time of arrival, just in case the police should start showing an interest in strangers in the area. Enquiries at the neighbouring farm would determine exactly what time the tanker had called, and if further verification were needed, there was always the unpleasant man with the Labrador. If ever he was asked, the driver would obviously deny having given me a lift, but that might be interpreted as self-defence, him not wanting to get in trouble with his employers. The only other possible flaw in my story was the driver of a 4x4 which had raced down the lane shortly after I had emerged from the wood. It had been going so fast that I had been forced to jump onto the verge to get out of the way. This had been some time before the tanker had turned up so I would just have to take my chance that the driver wouldn't think to mention to anyone that he'd nearly run down a young female walking up the lane soon after dawn. Now, I just hoped Chick wouldn't ask where the tanker had picked me up, as I had not the least idea where it had come from.

He didn't ask, just stood up saying, "Right. That would be the Harveys' place. They've got a lovely herd of pedigree Holsteins."

I was sure he was right, though Holstein to me sounded more like some kind of German lager. Maybe they were German cows; I couldn't really care less. I think Chick noticed since he stood up and said, "You can have Abby's room. She's a friend of our Debbie. Stayed over last night but her dad will be picking her up later today."

I guess I must have been looking a bit puzzled because he went on to say, "I'll bet Angie told you about the flats in the old barns." I nodded. "Well, if one of those was free, you'd be welcome to it. But it just so happens that every single one is taken at the moment, so, if you think you can bear to put up with us, you'll just have to settle for a bed in the main house."

That almost brought on the tears again, but I fought them back as I stood up and reached for my backpack. Chick beat me to it and led the way out of the kitchen with all my worldly goods dangling from his right hand.

"I'll show you the room while Rachel sorts out some clean linen for the bed."

Without checking to make sure Rachel had heard his implied instruction, he led me out into the hall. I was surprised at how big it was, for I hadn't seen it when we'd come into the house because we'd entered by way of the kitchen. Had we used the front door, something which I later learned would have been a most unusual occurrence, we would have been faced with a wide staircase ascending the left hand wall to about head-height before turning to continue up the rear wall. After making a second turn, it continued to rise up to the landing which ran across the front and left side of the upper hall. The stairs were enclosed by wooden banisters, simply carved and now dark with age. I assumed they must have formed part of the original structure.

I followed Chick up the stairs and round the landing to a room at the back of the house over the kitchen.

"This is our spare room, but it's mostly used by Abby. She's a regular visitor."

Opening the door, he looked around at the rumpled bedclothes on one of the twin beds and the hastily discarded Winnie-the-Pooh pyjamas decorating the other.

"Just ignore her stuff for the moment. Rachel will tidy up presently when she brings the sheets and towels."

He pointed to a door in the further corner.

"That's your bathroom, so just make yourself at home and I'll see you later."

He pulled the door shut as he left and I sat down on the end of the rumpled bed and looked around the room. I don't really know what I'd been expecting, but Angie had said these were religious people, so I suppose I was looking for pictures of Jesus or holy sayings on the walls. Instead, staring at me from the wall by the door was an almost life-size poster of Robbie Williams in bare-chested full-tattoo mode. I smiled as I looked around at several other, albeit smaller, examples of a young girl's pop-idol fantasies.

I couldn't understand it. I had always wondered if Angie had slightly over-iced the cake when describing life at Heighley Grange Farm. What was in it for these people? I had never met anyone who appeared so unselfishly accepting and generous as this family, so what was their angle? It was possible, maybe, that they were just what they seemed, but life had taught me that something that seemed too good to be true usually was. So I'd accept their hospitality, and make use of it, but I couldn't afford to lower my guard.

At that point, Rachel knocked on the door and came in with the towels and bed linen. She asked if there was anything else I needed, but when I told her no thanks, she stayed only long enough to gather up a few dirty, eight or nine-year-old size clothes before telling me to take as long as I needed, and come down again when I felt ready.

I started to empty out my backpack, and froze.

Spilling out onto the bed was, amongst other things, a small pack of moist wipes and a half empty packet of tampons. My last change had been many hours ago, in the middle of my den of holly. Having no way to dispose of them, I had left the old tampon & wipes under a loose covering of earth and leaves. Biodegradable, I'd thought. A few months and there'd be nothing left. But that was before the killing, and the police, and their dogs and their meticulous search of a crime scene.

I had left my DNA in the wood, which was not in itself a disaster. But I had every reason to believe that my DNA profile was in some Derbyshire police computer, the result of another killing some three years before; a killing in which my part had been more than just spectator; a killing for which the police, I was sure, still wanted to find me

Three

Defence/Trade Liaison Office, London – 9.50am

"You realise I'm supposed to be on the golf course at ten o'clock this morning. Just tell me what tight-arsed sheep-brain cocked this one up, and I'll have his balls served up on toast."

"Don't be vulgar, George. Calm down and drink your tea." Alistair Montrayne surveyed his irate second across an ocean of polished oak, dotted with neatly sorted islands of paper. He smiled somewhat ruefully. "Besides, I'm not entirely sure he has any."

The thirteenth Marquess of Thurvaston, currently Director General of the DTLO, was no less angry than his less polished colleague but, from long habit, he repressed the emotion in order to focus clearly on the matter at hand. Of no more than average height, rounded rather than lean, with thinning brown hair showing signs of grey, Alistair Montrayne would still make his mark in any sort of crowd. Especially if you knew him, in which case your eyes would seek him out, as his was the lead you needed to follow if you valued your job or your social standing.

He had begun his Civil Service career as the second son of the eleventh Marquess, and his natural abilities ensured that he moved quickly up through the ranks. When an unfortunate plane crash in Scotland killed several members of his family in 2003, he found himself unexpectedly occupying the shoes of his elder brother, then the twelfth Marquess. To the surprise of many, his sudden inheritance did not knock him off his intended course, and his power in the Civil Service continued to grow as he entrusted others with the management of his newly acquired estates.

George Holborn breathed out heavily through his nose whose red hue owed more to malt whiskey than his present temper. He pursed his full lips and started to relax.

"All right, Alistair. What say we drag young Riddings in here and wring his nuts … … sorry, get him to fill in some details?"

"Good thinking, George. He's already on his way up. In fact," looking to the door as a firm knock sounded, "this should be him now."

The young man who entered, tall, late twenties, good-looking in a craggy sort of way, was clearly ill at ease. A nest of pit vipers was more congenial company than old Thurvaston on a bad day, and this promised to be worse than most. After a brief spell at the Foreign Office, Paul Riddings had transferred to the DTLO four years earlier when it had been set up by the previous government to monitor overseas trade agreements which had a defence dimension. The public, or at least the media, had seemed to become strangely concerned about who might be in the market for Britain's defence technology now that the country's reduced defence budget limited opportunities at home. For the last year, Riddings had headed one of the two teams in George Holborn's investigations section. He hovered behind a straight-backed wooden chair in front of the massive desk, unsure whether he was sufficiently in favour with his boss to be allowed to sit.

George Holborn's anger was obviously still simmering. He snapped at Riddings, "Sit down and stop pratting about."

"Sorry, sir."

Riddings sat, rather stiffly, anticipating the inquisition and not relishing the answers which he knew he would have to give.

"Right, now tell us what the hell you were pissing about at to let . . . ."

"Thank you George," Thurvaston interrupted. "Let's not condemn the man without a trial. Very well, Riddings, tell us as concisely as you can why our only source of inside information in this investigation is now lying dead in a Staffordshire wood."

Riddings took a deep breath and licked his lips as he wondered just where to begin. His last report had been filed early yesterday. Assume they've read that, and take it from there.

"Simmons went into the office rather early yesterday morning. It's unusual for him to be there before eight thirty but not unheard of, and he had a marketing seminar at FerroTech at ten thirty so it looked as though he was just in to get some work done before driving down to Redditch. He logged on to the system soon after seven and started to search for the information we asked for."

"I thought he already had most of it."

"Yes, sir, he did. But that was before his hard drive failed last week, sorry, week before last now. He had it saved in an encrypted file on his hard drive but hadn't made any back-up copies."

"Stupid prat, you should have told him to make back-ups right at the start, insisted on it."

Riddings looked at Holborn with as much indignation as he dare.

"Actually, sir, I did, but he seems not to have listened. Anyway, when he tried to find the information again yesterday, it wasn't there. The access codes hadn't altered, but the files had been moved. At that point, Simmons had no way of knowing whether this was simply a precaution on their part unconnected with his prying, or whether they had actually become suspicious that someone was looking into things he shouldn't. He started checking through different directories, but didn't even know if he was looking for the same file names. Then when the head of security popped in around eight to check if everything was OK he panicked, closed the system down and left the works."

"Just remind me, Riddings." It was Thurvaston this time, frowning as he spoke. "Would there be any record of his searches left on the system?"

Riddings almost sighed. He knew this was covered in an earlier report, and then he saw the intense look in Thurvaston's eyes and realised this was a crucial point and worthy of double-checking. "No, sir. Simmons believed not, or I don't think we'd ever have got him to agree to look. The system they use is not all that sophisticated. His logging on and off the system would be recorded, and if he accessed or modified any files the date and time would be recorded but not directly attributed to him."

"Very well. When did you last speak with him?"

"Late yesterday afternoon, sir. He was back home and outside in the garden. He called me on his mobile. He was still afraid the house might be bugged, even though we've now swept it twice."

George Holborn sat forward on his chair, his stubby forefinger pointing at Riddings chest.

"Listen carefully, sonny, and think twice before you answer this. Was there any reason, apart from the switching of the files, to believe Simmons might actually be in danger?"

Riddings reddened, his earlier embarrassment turning to anger. This was the first occasion when he had lost a subject through violence and he had not yet had time to come to terms with the raw emotion seething within him. He boiled over.

"If you seriously think that I'd have left him without protection if I thought there was any possible threat to his safety then you're a bigger old fart than I thought you were."

He immediately regretted his imprudence but Holborn merely raised his eyebrows and smiled grimly as he glanced towards his boss.

"You were wrong, Alistair. He has got some after all."

Thurvaston nodded slightly but with no trace of a smile in response. For several moments he looked hard at Riddings who sat stiff and motionless, puzzled and a little calmed by Holborn's placid response to his disrespect.

"Young man," Thurvaston spoke quietly, but his tone was anything but reassuring. "I have yet to decide whether you bear any responsibility in not anticipating and therefore failing to prevent Simmons' death. So let us for the moment keep emotion in check and stick to the facts. Did Simmons at any time ask you to provide protection?"

"No, sir, he didn't. He was afraid of being caught, but he didn't seem to think that anyone at Lichfield Tube or FerroTech could have found out what he was doing."

"What about the missing files?"

"By the time he called me, he'd got over his first panic and had time to think it through. He reckoned it was probably just the routine archiving of old files. Lichfield Tube have always been pretty sloppy about that and probably wouldn't bother at all if FerroTech didn't insist. He was pretty sure he knew where to look for them, and was going to go in early on Monday to check."

Thurvaston and Holborn both digested this in silence. Finally, it was Riddings who spoke again.

"Look, sir. I'm not trying to wriggle out of any blame for what happened, if blame is due, but we have to consider another possibility."

"Quite right," snapped Thurvaston, "and I'm not yet so senile that I haven't already considered it."

"Sorry, sir." Riddings reply was almost drowned by a grunt from Holborn which turned quickly into a cough. "I ought to have realised."

Thurvaston's hand flapped as though to brush the apology aside, and when he spoke there was more than a hint of tiredness in his voice."

"Yes, you ought, but no matter." He sat back in his red leather swivel chair and stared at Riddings in so disconcerting a manner that the young man was about to apologise again when it dawned on him that his lordship was not looking at him but through him to some point in infinity where inspiration lay.

"It's possible, just possible, that Simmons' death was a random event perpetrated by some psycho entirely unrelated to the investigation, something which could have happened irrespective of our interest in Simmons and his business affairs. It's possible," he repeated. "Coincidences do happen, we all know that, but," his voice grew firmer to emphasise his point, "we have to proceed for the present on the assumption that there is a connection, that Simmons gave himself away and that someone believed him to have, or have access to, information so damning that he had to be removed."

The silence that followed was eventually broken by Holborn's grumbling voice.

"Ruddy tea's gone cold. Mind if I break out the scotch, Alistair?"

Thurvaston sighed, "If you must, George."

While Holborn busied himself with the elegantly carved drinks cabinet in the corner of the office, Thurvaston asked Riddings, "Have you had any contact yet with the local police?"

"Not directly with the investigating team, no sir. But I understand they'll be out in the woods for the rest of this morning, perhaps the whole day."

His lordship nodded, and then his expression changed to one of slight puzzlement as a new thought struck him.

"You haven't explained yet how you came to learn of Simmons' death so soon after the event."

"Damn it, that's right," said Holborn returning to his chair with a glass brimming with scotch diluted with just a small dash of soda in deference to the length of time still to go before noon. "What made you so quick off the mark?"

"Simmons was going to call me around eight o'clock this morning. He said yesterday he needed to think about things some more, and he'd call me. It was going to be at 8 because his wife was getting a bit funny about him taking his mobile out into the garden to make calls, and at that time on a Saturday she's usually still in bed. When it got to half-eight and still no word from him, I decided to give him a call. He'd been a bit er . . . well excitable, yesterday and I was . . . .concerned. A woman PC answered the phone. They'd just broken the news to his wife and I could hear her," he paused and looked down at his hands. He swallowed before continuing, "I could hear her crying in the background." Another pause. "The policewoman asked who I was, and before I could answer a man's voice came on and said he was Detective Chief Inspector Morrissey and would I please identify myself. I told him I was a friend and Phil had been going to call me this morning. I asked if it was true, and Phil was really dead, and then said I was going to be sick and hung up."

"Damn good, that. Fellow's actually got a brain." Holborn set down his empty glass on Thurvaston's desk. His Lordship frowned and slid a coaster across which Holborn slipped under the glass. "So the police don't know your name, and they know nothing of our interest in this?"

"Not yet, sir, no. But they'll no doubt check phone records and in due course will turn up here wanting to know who was using a mobile listed to this department at 8.30 this morning."

"In that case," said his lordship, "we must make sure we have a good story ready for them."

"Shouldn't be too difficult," said Holborn, and proceeded to demonstrate why, in spite of his unorthodox manners – for a civil servant – and his affinity for scotch, he held the responsible position that he did. "OK, let's say I'm Chief Inspector What's-his-name. Where did you first make contact with Simmons?"

"At a stamp exhibition in Derby."

"Are you interested in stamps yourself?"

"Not really, but my father has quite a fine collection. I got him to show it to me before I went to the exhibition. I didn't pretend to be a collector, but just someone with a not unnatural interest in knowing what stamps might be worth. That was the initial cover for my relationship with Phil."

"Why did you go to that particular exhibition? Derby is quite some way from your flat in Crawley."

"Killing two birds with one stone. I also wanted to visit a friend in Lichfield."

"Who was the friend?"

"As you know perfectly well, sir, it was Lord Thurvaston's son, James Montrayne."

"As a matter of interest," said Holborn, policeman no longer. "Is James Montrayne really a friend?"

"Actually no, sir. But his lordship arranged that James would acknowledge the friendship if asked."

"And your relationship with Simmons?"

"We got on well together; he's – was – only a few years older than me, and he offered to tell me what I would need to know about stamps."

Holborn grinned at Riddings. "Not bad. I really do begin to think you might actually be of some use in this department after all."

"What do you think, Alistair? Will the story hold up?"

Thurvaston pursed his lips and nodded slowly. "I don't see why not, but it won't do any harm to go over it again before Chief Inspector Morrissey starts his questioning for real."

Riddings looked from Thurvaston to Holborn and back again, wondering whether to jeopardise his newly acquired credit with his boss, and ask the question that loomed in his mind. Deciding that his need to know the answer justified the risk, he asked, "Why should we not simply tell the police the truth? After all, we may be concealing information crucial to their investigation."

Holborn sighed. "Will you tell him, Alistair, or shall I?"

"Go on, George, but don't be too hard on him."

"Look laddie," Holborn spoke slowly as though to a child. "We don't know why Simmons is dead. As you suggested yourself, it may have nothing at all to do with our investigation. In which case, we don't want to go giving policemen more information than their tiny intellects can cope with. We don't want them clumping round FerroTech or Lichfield Tube in their hobnail boots telling all and sundry that their affairs are under investigation and turning all our efforts thus far to a steaming pile of sh . . . ordure. We may have lost Simmons, but we're still going to nail these villains. It might just take a bit longer, that's all."

"OK, sir. That makes sense," replied Riddings.

"Of course it ruddy well makes sense," growled Holborn.

"Thank you, George." His lordship's tone was quiet, speculative. "I want you to follow the investigation, Riddings. Make a nuisance of yourself, if necessary, as a concerned friend, but don't give away the department's interest. If it appears in time that this was not after all an unconnected event, then of course I shall have to reveal our hand."

"Very well, sir," said Riddings wondering if the new question forming in his mind would irritate his boss even further.

"If, in due course, we do have to explain to the police our interest, will they not be justifiably aggrieved that we kept quiet, even misled them, for so long?"

Holborn's mouth opened, but Thurvaston beat him to it.

"Unhappily yes, but I don't think I shall allow myself to lose any sleep over it. If they become too unpleasant, I shall make sure a word is dropped, very tactfully, in the Chief Constable's ear."

"I see, sir."

"And Riddings," Holborn couldn't resist offering his own rider. "It will be up to you to make sure the police don't get too far off the scent if, after all, it does look as though our foxes are at the bottom of this. We can't really ask for copies of their reports, so it's up to you to keep us in touch with their progress. Don't cock it up, there's a good lad."

"I'll do my best, sir."

"Then we shall just have to hope that's enough, shan't we?"

Four

Heighley Grange Farm - Midday

I woke to the faint but delicious smell of baking bread wafting up from the kitchen situated directly below my bedroom. Whether that mouth-watering aroma found its way up through the corridors of the house, or wafted in through the open window I had no idea, but it was so amazingly restful that I just allowed myself to drift in limbo in the luxury of the soft duvet. I don't know whether exponents of aromatherapy list warm bread amongst their more successful potions, but I know it worked for me that morning. Perhaps it was because of its association in my mind with the happy times in my mum's kitchen, when I'd come home from school and learn to knead bread, and then bake it in time for tea. Whatever it was, I lay there for a few moments in complete tranquillity, until the sound of voices in the yard outside my window, followed by a car driving away, brought home to me the precarious security of my present situation.

    I rolled my head on the pillow and looked towards the window. The sky was now a deep blue with just a few thin wisps of cloud drifting lazily across that small patch of infinity visible through the glass. I watched one line of white edging obliquely towards the top of the frame and told myself that I would get up once it disappeared from sight. Inch by inch it shrank to nothing and I toyed with the idea of selecting another to watch out of sight, persuaded that nothing disagreeable could possibly happen that day until I stirred from the bed. But events that would affect my life were, I knew, already set in motion and would continue their course whether I lay still and ignored them or got up to meet them. So, I got up.

    I sat on the bed and looked around my room. Or was it still Abby's room. I wasn't sure, and couldn't remember exactly what Rachel had said. The contents of my backpack were neatly laid out on Abby's bed just as I had left them, with the pack itself propped against the foot of the bed. There was a green, knee-length skirt with shades of leaf patterns, which I had chosen for its amazing ability to resist creasing, and a paler green, embroidered, short-sleeved top which I thought complemented the skirt rather well. I had also slung in a long black cardigan for warmth, which looked rather good with the green, possibly due to the hood which, apart from looking cool, I had found to serve no useful purpose. A pair of light shoes and a couple of changes of underwear and that was my wardrobe.

    I wondered if it was expected that I would put my things away, but I had a suspicion that the wardrobe and chest of drawers were stuffed with items of pre-teen girl attire. Feeling thoroughly exhausted, I hadn't bothered to check their contents earlier, but had just laid myself down fully dressed on the bed that obviously wasn't Abby's and fallen rapidly asleep.

I got up and opened the wardrobe. Not stuffed, maybe, but other than that, my guess had been correct. A warm coat with furry hood, a couple of dresses, jeans, jodhpurs and sundry boots and shoes. I didn't bother with the drawers. I knew what I might to expect to find. I felt uncomfortable, an intruder, tolerated but not belonging. I moved over to the dressing table where some towels lay, neatly folded, and I noticed for the first time a framed photograph standing in front of the mirror and almost hidden by the towels. Picking up the pile and tossing it onto my bed, I then lifted the picture and tilted it to the window to get the best light. The photograph seemed to have been taken at one of those stately homes that open to the public. It showed a man and a young girl, maybe eight or nine years old, sitting on a bench in front of a billiard-table lawn around which swept a gravel drive leading to the imposing arched entrance to some kind of mansion. The man had his arm around the girl's shoulders, and she snuggled into his side with that look of happiness that comes from knowing you are totally safe and secure.

My dad had used to cuddle me like that, and I had loved it, part of me wanting never really to grow up. But I had, and fast when my parents died and my uncle had come to bring me to England. I had lived with that man, the husband of my father's sister, for seven long years. No safety or security there. His cuddles, though meant to be tender, were unwelcome, even though in the beginning I hadn't really understood their meaning. He had tried to bribe me with presents and eventually had got what he wanted because I was ten years old, an orphan, scared and confused, and his was the only home I had. In the end, I had lost count of the number of times he came to my room.

At first, it had been very infrequent, and only on evenings when my aunt was out. I had no idea whether it was usual for that sort of thing to happen. I only knew that my father had never done that to me, and I hated it. I hated my uncle too, as time went on, and these events that were "our secret" became more frequent, especially as I began to develop into womanhood, and the range of his activities increased. Then shortly after my fifteenth birthday, my aunt became sick and died quite quickly. For some months he didn't come near me, and I think in spite of his abuse of me, he actually did love my aunt and grieved bitterly for her. I actually dared to believe that it was all over. But then, just after I had taken my mock GCSE exams, he came again to my room one afternoon, and his approach was quite different. He had been drinking and there was no attempt at any sort of tenderness, just a kind of fierce expectation that I would service his need. For the first time, I actually resisted but he was much heavier than I was and I only succeeded in turning his approach into a forced and brutal rape.

The memory of that night brought me back to my present troubles and I sat on the stool in front of the dressing table and forced myself to consider various possibilities. The police may not find it necessary to conduct a thorough search of the wood, and even if they did they may still not find my buried debris. If they did, they probably wouldn't decide immediately to send it off for DNA analysis, since there would be no way of knowing whether it was in any way relevant to their investigation, and DNA testing costs money, or so I'd heard. And even if the head cop was a spendthrift type, they may still not get a match. True, I had left traces of blood and vaginal fluid at a previous crime scene three years earlier, but I never did know how far the police had gone in analysing their samples. On balance, I reckoned I should be safe at least for a few days, which would give me time to plan the next leg of my escape route.

Time for a shower, I thought, and then go and make some proper introductions. I grabbed the towels and tampons and headed for the bathroom. Emerging some twenty minutes later, damp and wrapped in fluffy beige robe I'd found hanging on the back of the bathroom door, with my hair wrapped up in a towel, I was surprised to find a girl, maybe eight or nine years old, standing just inside the door and looking curiously at the clothes and other items laid out on her bed. I thought of it as *her* bed since I assumed this must be Abby whose room I had invaded.

"Hello, Abby," I said, hoping that I'd guessed correctly.

"Hi." She looked at me steadily, not smiling, not hostile, and I wondered what opinion she was forming of me behind those expressionless brown eyes. As she stood there, head slightly lowered, watching me from under long lashes, I was reminded strongly of pictures I'd seen of Princess Di when she was a girl. Angie had stacks of them. She had even tried to cultivate the Princess Di look herself, but it never really worked, and even less so in these last few months.

"Look," I said, "I'm sorry about all this stuff on your bed. I'll move it."

"It's OK. I don't usually sleep in the day." Still no smile, and her eyes glanced at the rumpled duvet on the other bed.

"Right," I replied. "Me neither. Usually. But I had an early start this morning and that bed just felt so comfy."

She nodded, gave a little sigh, and turned to look out of the window as though unsure what to say or do next. Her brown hair was long, well below her shoulders, and the sides were brushed back and held by a blue, elasticated band. She was well below my height, maybe 4' 6", and very slender in her jeans and knitted top; no trace of puppy fat.

I took the towel from my head and shook my hair loose. I watched her for a moment as I rubbed the towel over my hair. She seemed tense and I thought I knew why.

"I've invaded your private space, haven't I?" She didn't reply. "Look, Abby, I'll ask Rachel if she can find me somewhere else. I don't want to take your room."

I knew what it meant to a child to have a den, a place to escape to, away from grown-ups, and I knew what it felt like to have your den invaded. I didn't know that Rachel had anywhere else to put me, and I didn't want to leave, not yet, but for some reason buried deep within me I didn't want to do anything to hurt this child. It was crazy. I didn't even know her, but I could sense her vulnerability and that was something I understood.

"Just let me get dressed, Abby, and you can have your room back."

At that, she turned away from the window, and I was amazed to see her eyes glistening with tears.

"It's not that," she sniffed, and I could tell she was struggling to hold the tears in check. "It's Mr. Simmons. Rachel says he's dead."

Oh, shit! I thought, but thankfully not out loud. It must be the jogger in the wood. Not knowing what else to do I gestured to the bed saying, "Come on. Sit down."

She sat slowly, back erect, knees together, hands clasped in her lap and her head bowed, staring at the carpet, but probably seeing nothing but pictures in her mind. Tears dropped on her legs and made little dark splotches on the blue denim. I didn't know her well enough to put my arms around her, though I very much wanted to comfort her, unreasonably feeling somehow responsible for the grief that seemed to be intensifying by the minute.

"Who was Mr. Simmons?" I asked as gently as I could.

For a moment, I thought she wasn't going to answer but then she took a deep breath and said, "He comes to our church. But Mrs Simmons .... she's a teacher ....she works at our school sometimes. I like her, and ...."

She broke off, and now began to cry in earnest. I wondered where Rachel was, and thought of calling for her or for Debbie her friend, and then decided it didn't matter. At that moment, I was all she had, so I took a chance and put an arm around her shoulder. That was all it needed, and she turned her face into my chest and sobbed desperately. She clearly wasn't concerned about the dampness of my robe, so I reached out my other arm and hugged her to me, just holding her and gently stroking her hair until the sobbing subsided to a few convulsive gasps and then stopped.

I was puzzled over the depth of her misery. A member of her church however kind, or a schoolteacher however tolerant and understanding, could surely not generate such an intensity of emotion. Could they? Well, perhaps they could. After all, I didn't know either her church or her school, and individuals can inspire great loyalty and affection, though none save my parents had ever done so for me.

She eased herself away from me and pulled a crumpled tissue from her jeans pocket. She wiped her eyes, blew her nose, and looked up at me from under those lashes.

"You must have liked Mr Simmons a lot," I tried.

"He was all right."

All right? Not exactly the accolade I was expecting. There was definitely something more going on here, and I was just wondering what to ask next when I heard footsteps on the landing outside the door and Rachel appeared.

"I'm sorry, Abby. I was trying to get rid of some reporter. Are you OK, love?"

She came into the room as she spoke, and crouched down in front of us, resting one hand on Abby's knee.

Abby nodded but didn't speak. Rachel looked at me.

"Has she told you what's happened?"

"Something about Mr Simmons being dead, but that's about all."

Rachel got up and sat on the other bed facing us.

"Phil Simmons was a good friend of ours, and something happened when he was out jogging this morning. There was some sort of .... accident by the lake in Heighley Wood .... but, of course, you don't know where I mean. Anyway, Phil died, and the police are trying to find out what happened. They've just been here to ask if we've seen or heard anything which, of course, we hadn't."

I shook my head slowly, considering carefully how I should respond. It couldn't do any harm to do a bit of fishing.

"Have they no idea at all what happened?"

"Well, you know what the police are like. They didn't actually tell us very much. Just asked a lot of questions."

She paused then, looking very thoughtful.

"James probably knows – that's Abby's father - but he didn't get a chance to tell us. He was down in the wood this morning, doing a job for us, and may have seen Phil." She paused again, looking carefully at Abby before continuing. "He's still helping the police. He was up here with them just now, but only to make arrangements for Abby to stay on. He was going to pick her up this morning and take her shopping for some new shoes, but I guess that's going to have to wait."

She leant across to take Abby's hand.

"Do you want to come on down and have some lunch, love? We've got fresh bread."

"I'm not hungry. Can't I just stay here?"

Rachel looked at me for support, and I felt really awkward. This was not my home and these folk were neither friends nor family, but here I was, right in the middle of their tragedy. Absolutely dead centre, and I was the only one in the world who knew it. I shrugged and smiled.

"I don't mind."

Rachel managed a slight smile in return, but still hesitated and I could understand why. Abby was very dear to her, and I was still a stranger. So I just waited while politeness struggled with protectiveness until, eventually, one side won and she stood up. She looked directly into my eyes her mouth open slightly as though she was on the point of saying something, but then thought better of it. Instead, still keeping firm eye contact, she smiled again, and I knew she had decided to trust me, at least for the time being.

"If you need anything, just call me. I'll be in the kitchen."

I wasn't sure whether that was meant for Abby or for me. Probably both, I thought, and nodded. Rachel turned and left pulling the door closed behind her.

There was silence which neither of us seemed inclined to break so, after a minute or two, I took advantage of Abby's distraction to slip into my clothes. I was more or less dry by now, except for my hair which always seemed to take ages, so I slipped on my panties under the robe. I wasn't embarrassed about getting dressed in front of her, but I didn't know how she'd feel about it. She didn't seem to mind. I had just put on my top when I noticed she was watching me.

"Don't you wear a bra?" she asked, distracted for a moment from her sorrow by genuine curiosity.

"Not usually," I replied, as I reached for my skirt.

"Oh." She looked down at her still flat chest. "I can't wait til I get one."

"That time will come soon enough."

"Yeah, that's what Rachel says."

Picking up my hairbrush from the bed, I wondered suddenly where her mother was. Divorced? Dead? Maybe just temporarily away from home. I wasn't going to ask. Too easy to put my foot in it, especially just now.

Abby looked me up and down.

"You look nice," she said, almost shyly.

I smiled down at her. "Thank you, ma'am."

"You haven't told me your name."

I sat down on the bed opposite, to bring myself down to her level, so she wasn't continually having to look up at me.

"It's Lizzie," I said. "Lizzie Burleigh, and I'm very pleased to meet you."

"I'm pleased to meet you too," she said. "I'm Abby Montrayne."

At that moment reality flooded back into her mind, and her eyes clouded. "I'm specially glad to meet you today."

"Oh, and why is that?" I asked, surprised at how much pleasure that brought me. It didn't last long because her reply horrified me.

"Because the police have taken Daddy away. Helping their enquiries, they said. I know what that means coz I've seen it on TV. They must think he killed Mr Simmons."

I was stunned. Abby's face was back to being expressionless, but she was watching mine very carefully as though she was trying to read my thoughts. I couldn't immediately think of anything to say. Her eyes were unblinking, wide and dark, glistening, and full of expectation. It felt as though she was sucking me in to a situation that I desperately wanted to keep well out of. I needed time to think, but she needed a straight response. I needed to be non-committal, but she needed reassurance. Over her shoulder, on the dressing table, I saw the photograph which had so stirred my memories. I nodded towards it.

"Is that your dad?" I asked, trying to break the intensity of her gaze, "In the picture."

She turned slowly and reached for the frame. She didn't answer directly but, looking at the photo, she answered the question I hadn't dared to ask.

"My mum's grave is in the churchyard near there. Dad and I go visit sometimes."

"Your dad's very big isn't he?"

That brought a glimmer of a smile.

"Yeah. The little kids at school call him a giant." Then, after a thought, "But they like him. Everybody likes him."

The hunter. It had to be. There couldn't have been two men as big as that in the wood this morning.

"Right," I said, coming to a decision. "In that case, we'd better see what we can do to make sure the police like him as well.

Her eyes were still wide and dark but, as she blinked away a tear, I could now see a gleam of hope.

Five

Piazza San Marco, Venice - 3.15pm

John Salisbury rested his arms along the back of the bench, stretched out his legs and sighed in contentment. The water-bus from Marco Polo Airport was not due for several minutes yet, assuming there were no delays, but he didn't mind the wait. After all, he had nothing else to do, and the last couple of years had taught him the virtue of patience. His hotel was an unassuming 3-star former palazzo, lurking in one of the narrow streets behind the Piazza.

It had been a good plan, and it had worked. It was just a shame about Phil Simmons. He had never intended that Phil should suffer when his company's financial base was found to have evaporated overnight. Indeed, he had done his best to shield Phil from the worst of the inevitable fall-out, but there were bound to be some very angry people about and there was no telling how vigorously they may react. He sipped his drinking chocolate and smiled. He'd grown to like this rich, dark, sweet liquid, almost thick enough to hold your spoon upright. It was nothing like the thin, pale runny stuff he'd tried in England. His smile widened as he remembered his pleasure when he'd heard that Phil had been offered another job within the group. He deserved the opportunity. John had realised not long after Phil had come to work for Salisbury Marine that the young man had the brains, the expertise and the stamina, though maybe not the ruthlessness, necessary for business success. Yes, Phil deserved the opportunity to make his mark within the FerroTech group. John wondered which company in the group had found a place for him, and he hoped very much, for Phil's sake, that it hadn't been Lichfield Tube.

John sighed. He had always believed that he himself had the qualities he valued in Phil. It had never occurred to him that his feet were far too small to fill his father's shoes until Peter Salisbury succumbed to a fatal heart attack, and Salisbury Marine Components Ltd. found itself in the hands of a new managing director. It wasn't entirely John's fault that he was ill-equipped for his new responsibilities. Peter had played too many cards too close to his chest, mainly to prevent John getting his hands on them and causing a total cock-up. So it was not surprising that his son soon found himself in deep water, literally, when a diesel submarine which the MoD wanted to sell to a foreign government ended up on the bottom of the Irish Sea. True, there had been no fatalities, and the boat had been quickly brought to the surface and towed to the dockyard, but John had found himself unable to face the subsequent inquisition at the hands of the Royal Navy engineers. He had sent Phil instead, and was delighted when he had been able to demonstrate that the pump failure was actually due to incorrect installation, rather than defective components supplied by Salisbury Marine. Phil's confidence increased while John's went into decline.

This had not caused him to like Phil any the less, but it pushed him steadily towards a decision whose consequences he could not possibly have foreseen. He recognised that he had no chance of running the company successfully, as his father had done, and was therefore unlikely to be retained for long by the board of FerroTech who had bought his father's company eighteen months before his death. It had been a condition of the sale that John should succeed his father as MD, assuming Peter retired within five years of the sale taking place. Significantly, the agreement had not specified how long he should remain in that position.

He had racked his brains for a solution before what he now acknowledged about his own abilities became apparent to the board. He had inherited a substantial sum from his father, but not enough to support him indefinitely. A significant cash injection was required. It was just the last in a long series of misjudgements that he chose as his unwitting benefactors a most powerful and unforgiving client: the government of Saudi Arabia.

When he had first been asked to tender for the supply of various components for the newest and soon-to-be largest desalination plant run by the Saline Water Conversion Corporation of Saudi Arabia, he had thought it must be someone's idea of a joke. Then he heard that FerroTech Heavy Industries had been awarded the contract for construction of the new plant, together with an integrated oil-fired power station, and all began to make sense. On the back of that, he was also asked to tender for the supply of air conditioning units both for the plant, and for other Government installations, including the King Abdul Aziz Brigade Headquarters of the Saudi Arabian National Guard.

After two days on the phone to various suppliers to Salisbury Marine, he arrived at a final figure for the joint contracts. For a long while he just sat and stared at the complex array of figures on his laptop. He couldn't believe what he was seeing. He'd reworked the calculations several times and he knew they were right, but he still didn't believe them. At £5.8M over twenty-four months, it would be the largest contract he had ever landed and it scared him to death.

Salisbury Marine components simply didn't have the capacity for such a contract, but if he muffed it that was probably the end of his not very auspicious term as Managing Director. He even began to wonder if Sir Vernon Laycock himself, the chairman and CEO of the FerroTech group, had arranged for the tenders to be pushed his way, so that the failure to snare the contact would provide an excuse for his early dismissal. John knew he wasn't up to the job, but it was the only one he had, but he'd prefer to keep it if at all possible. Unless .. .. ..

It wasn't exactly a flash of inspiration, he had never been troubled by many of those, but it was the gradual dawning of an idea. Suppose he put in a tender based on the manufacture of components within Salisbury Marine's own works, using the best materials from their A1 suppliers, all certified where necessary to current BSEN and Naval Engineering Standards. Then suppose he ordered materials and components from India and China, maybe even Mexico or Brazil at far less than A1 prices. And suppose he could persuade his quality systems engineer to produce false certification for all the products which would pass muster both with FerroTech and the Saudi SWCC. And finally, suppose he could siphon off the difference between the projected costs for the purpose of the tender, and the actual costs to the company. That would provide a very tidy top-up to the substantial nest-egg left by his father.

Against all the odds, it had actually worked. Bill Keegan, his quality man, had been surprisingly amenable once reasonable compensation had been agreed. Bill's wife was seriously ill and probably wouldn't last more than a couple of years. Bill was desperate to give her something she'd always longed for but which they'd come to believe she'd never achieve: a month's cruise of the Caribbean, Panama and South America. They'd had the money once, but private doctors' bills, and exotic treatments, had made severe inroads into their savings. Their house was fully mortgaged and they were just about making ends meet. John Salisbury's plan would give her what she wanted, and just about in time, if they acted quickly.

For fifteen of the twenty-four months of the contract, everything went smoothly. Since only John knew the exact details of the contract, and Bill issued all bogus test certificates personally, no one knew that anything untoward was taking place. Peter Thornaby, the company's finance director and not the brightest light in the heavens, did wonder whether the company really needed a separate bank account, the Saudi Contingency account, but he didn't see any real reason to make a fuss if it kept the boss happy. He probably wouldn't have been quite so laid back about it if he was aware of how closely John was observing his electronic transfers, learning every detail of the process.

Then Phil Simmons had caught on. Bill's presence in the works was becoming rather intermittent as, with the cruise now long in the past, his wife's condition reached a stage of rapid deterioration. Bill was still handling all quality certification for the Saudi contract, but his mind increasingly drifted into dark areas far removed from the job in hand. And so it was that, in transcribing the stress analysis results in a test certificate for air conditioning tubes, he entered the wrong values. FerroTech's onsite

QA inspector missed the error, but his Saudi counterpart did not, and he immediately sent an email to Bill querying the figures. In Bill's absence, his deputy opened the email and took it in some confusion to Phil.

From there, things unravelled fairly quickly, but not so fast that John was caught unprepared. He had known that this would happen eventually and as soon as Phil had left his office, placated but still puzzled, John had begun to dump all the liquid funds he could access into the Saudi Contingency account. That done, the total was transferred immediately to an account in the Caymans where his father's nest-egg had been sitting quietly for several months. The Saudi Contingency account was then closed. As of that moment, Salisbury Marine Components was effectively bankrupt, but it would be another two days before Peter Thornaby became aware of the fact.

The account in the Caymans was in the name of his brother-in-law, Josh Barnett who had died in a car crash about a year before John's financial arrangements began to unravel. In helping his sister, Janet, to clear up Josh's affairs, John had come upon a number of documents including Josh's passport, not long renewed. He was not exactly a double for Josh, but the two had a certain similarity; even moreso, after John decided to lose a couple of stone, change his hairstyle, grow a moustache and begin wearing glasses. It would never have crossed John's mind to dispose of his brother-in-law for the sake of obtaining his passport, but when opportunity struck, he was not slow to take advantage of it. Fortunately, his sister decided to use Josh's life insurance to buy a small hotel up in the Grampians, so she never became aware of his transformed appearance.

The day after his confrontation with Phil Simmons, John Salisbury flew to Brazil where he stayed for one night in Rio de Janeiro. In the morning, Josh Barnett caught an American Airlines flight to Miami from whence he flew British Airways to Owen Roberts International Airport on Grand Cayman. Here he took a taxi to a bank in George Town where he accessed his account and transferred the funds to several banks in different European cities before flying to Madrid to begin what he considered to be a very well-earned holiday relaxing in the Algarve. His net worth at that point was £5.4M, insufficient perhaps for a perpetual life of luxurious extravagance, but more than enough for the moderate comfort that was all Josh required.

So now, John Salisbury, in the form of Josh Barnett sipped drinking chocolate in the Piazzo San Marco and waited for the water bus from Marco Polo airport. He had wandered the cities of Europe for long enough, and it was time to settle down. In the passenger soon to arrive, he thought he had found the ideal partner.

He thought again of Phil, wishing he could have found a better way of dealing with his former colleague. Phil was a good man and didn't deserve to have got caught up in the Saudi scam. But John, never one to suffer from flashes of inspiration, hadn't known what else to do.

That was not the only thing he hadn't known.

When he first saw the young, dark-haired girl with the sad eyes, for whom he now waited so patiently, he had no idea that for several years she had been working for the Saudi security service.

Six

Heighley Grange Farm – early afternoon

I had no idea just how long that afternoon was going to be. Abby continued to insist that she wasn't hungry but I finally managed to persuade her to come down with me to the kitchen and to try some of Rachel's fresh bread with homemade soup. We were just sitting down when, in response to a shout from her Mum, Debbie came in to join us from the stable. She had been grooming her pony, cleaning tack, and generally tidying up, all of which, I was told over lunch, was a condition of being allowed to have a pony in the first place. Abby should have been helping her, being party to the same conditions, but the arrival of her father with the police had distracted her, and when he'd left, all she had wanted was the solace of her own room.

Chick didn't join us for lunch, so I just assumed that he was off doing farm stuff, until a casual enquiry to Rachel brought out the information that he was down at the mobile police incident room, which had been set up in a dirt lay-by near to the wood. Rachel, I think, was wishing he was home. She was cheerful and kind, sitting us down and bustling about with bowls, ladle and a massive saucepan, but every now and then she would catch my eye and I was sure that she was more worried than she was letting on. After we finished eating, Abby asked if she could go over to Heighley Wood to try and find her dad and Rachel's expression became fixed as her mind struggled to frame her answer. I wasn't sure I could see her problem. Then she explained.

"I really need to get over to see Natalie this afternoon." She must have noticed my blank look so she went on to clarify. "Natalie Simmons, Phil's wife. I tried to speak to her on the phone this morning but all I got was a policewoman. She said that Natalie was still too distressed to talk to anyone. They were waiting for the doctor to come."

She paused, and I must have looked slightly puzzled for she went on to explain again. "Natalie's pregnant, you see. No telling what the shock might do. Poor kid."

Rachel sighed and turned away to stack the pots in the dishwasher, but not before I saw the sheen of tears on her cheek.

Abby and Debbie looked at each other across the table

Letting them go down to the woods was not a good idea as Rachel and I both knew, but it wasn't going to be easy trying to convince Abby, especially after Debbie joined in, offering to go with Abby to keep her company. I knew why she didn't want them to go. It was highly probable that the police wouldn't allow Abby to see her dad, even if he was still at the wood and not in an interview room in whatever police station they'd come from, and Debbie was hardly old enough to cope with Abby if she became really distressed.

I looked away, at the yard beyond the kitchen window, trying to distance myself from the argument that was brewing. I really didn't want to get involved. This was not my problem and, friendly and well-meaning as they were, these folk had no claim on me. I had no more idea than Charlie Brown how to handle pre-teen girls, and I was pretty sure I didn't want to learn. I wondered if they would think I was ill-mannered if I just left them to it and went back to my room. Then I wondered if I really cared what they thought and was surprised to discover that, actually, I did. I glanced at Abby, and that was my mistake.

Rachel was telling her that her dad would come as soon as he could, and that it would be best to wait for him here, where he knew he would find her.

"And Chick should be back soon," Rachel said with an excess of optimism. "He'll know what's best to do."

Abby wasn't convinced, but she didn't argue. No pouting, yelling or tantrums. Just big brown eyes, wide and pleading, as they gradually filled with tears that trickled slowly down her cheeks.

I had seen girls not much older than these sobbing their eyes out after their first session with some piece of lecherous filth who could only perform with young unspoilt kids. It hadn't troubled me greatly. After all, it had happened to me, so why not them?

This was different. These girls were young and definitely unspoiled and the distress I saw in Abby's eyes most certainly did trouble me. I remembered how much it had hurt in those first few days when, suddenly, my dad wasn't there any more to protect me, or reassure me that everything would be all right. I felt cold and sick, and wished with all my heart that these past ten years could have been different.

"Look," I said, wondering what on earth I thought I was doing. "How would it be if Abby and Debbie showed me round the farm this afternoon. Explain how things work, introduce me to folks, that sort of thing. Maybe, while we're looking round, we could wander over to the wood and see how Abby's dad is getting on. We could tell someone here what we're doing, or maybe leave a note, in case he or Chick comes back before we do."

There was silence as three pairs of eyes bored into me.

"It was just a thought," I said. "If you don't like it then . . . . . ."

I broke off because it's hard to talk when you're being strangled. Abby had almost fallen into my lap and flung her arms around my neck. It was her bony shoulder that was causing the problem, digging into my windpipe as she hugged me tight. Over her shoulder, I could see Debbie grinning and nodding, but Rachel wasn't quite so enthusiastic. Her eyes looked straight into mine, hard and questioning, her lips slightly pursed, and her thought processes in overdrive. In that moment, as we stared at each other, I guessed that she had a pretty shrewd idea of the kind of life I had recently been living, and was uneasy about releasing Debbie and Abby into my care. Then there was also the little matter of my being an almost total stranger. I understood her reluctance, but I didn't give way. Just held my gaze and waited. It was her decision.

Then she smiled, and the warmth came back into her eyes. And something else too, I thought. Was it trust? Probably not. I always did have a vivid imagination?

"I think that's a great idea," she said, and as Abby relaxed I was able to begin breathing again.

"I'll take care of them," I said.

"Yes," replied Rachel, that look still in her eyes. "I rather think you will."

"What do you mean *take care of us*?" asked Debbie. "It's us showing you around. Remember? And anyway, there's always Cherry"

Cherry? I was about to ask, when they all started bustling around tidying the kitchen, assisted by Simba who seemed to think it was his duty to inspect every item that went in the dishwasher. I tried to help, but since I didn't know where anything went, I was pretty useless. Once it was all tidy, we watched as Rachel left in a rather throaty old Land Rover to visit her friend Natalie. Shortly after that, my tour of the farm began.

As we came out of the kitchen door, my trainers now replaced by a pair of oversized wellies, I noticed a group of lads standing beside a gleaming black 4x4 which even I recognised as a Jeep Cherokee. I knew it hadn't been there when I'd come up to the house earlier in the day. The lads in the little group were laughing about something but looked across as we came out into the yard. It was then that I realised that although two of the lads looked to be in their late teens, the third was no lad at all. A grown man, well in his thirties, he was casually dressed in brown leather blouson jacket, blue jeans and walking boots. Although not particularly tall, he was broad shouldered and stood very erect. The shoulders and the way he let his arms hang a little away from his body reminded me of the weight-lifting hard men who kept the punters in order when the lap-dancing got a little too much for them.

As we walked down the yard, he carried on joking with the two lads while glancing across at us every now and then. I wondered who he was. The lads were wearing well-worn and rather grimy coveralls and muddy rubber boots, but his clothes were as clean as the Jeep which I assumed must be his. He didn't have the look of a farm labourer. If it weren't for the fact that he seemed to know the lads quite well, I'd have been worried sick every time he looked across at us.

First off, we went to the newest of the chicken sheds which I'd seen from the lane that morning. It was bigger than I'd thought. Maybe twenty metres wide by eighty long. A grassy field to one side was surrounded by chicken wire topped by an electric fence. This area seemed full of reddish brown hens, clucking, scratching, occasionally squabbling and generally looking busy.

Debbie saw me watching them. "They're all free range here," she said proudly.

"So I see," I replied, and then to demonstrate my powers of observation I asked, "And the electric fence, is that to keep them in?"

"No, silly. They couldn't escape if they tried. It's to keep foxes out."

"Ah, of course," I said, trying to sound half-way intelligent while feeling decidedly foolish. "Do you get many foxes?"

"Some. But Simba usually sees them off."

"Sometimes one gets through," Abby joined in. "Do you remember that one last summer?"

"Sure." Debbie pointed to one of the older sheds. "An old dog fox got in there one night. It was really gross cleaning up in the morning." She gave an exaggerated shudder.

I was a bit surprised, considering her age, that she'd been asked to help with such a task.

"So . . . er . . . do you often have to do things like that?"

"No, not really." She hesitated, as though there was more to be said, but it was Abby who filled in the details.

"It was Pete's job really. He was in charge of that shed, and Debbie sort of fancied him, so . . ."

"I did not!" Indignant. "Well, only a bit. Anyway, it was no more than you fancied Nathan before he went weird."

I thought it was time to move the conversation on and, since we had by this time arrived at the door of the shed, I asked if I could have a look inside.

Abby stuck her tongue out at Debbie who replied with equally vigorous good humour before opening the door and leading the way inside. I was struck immediately by a pungent smell of ammonia which seemed to scour the inside of my nostrils. I put my hand up to my nose and saw Abby watching me with a smile on her face.

"It's always like that, first time you come into the shed," she said, "but you soon get used to it."

I wasn't sure that I wanted to but it was their tour, so I breathed shallowly and tried not to think what I was breathing in. I had expected to get a view of the entire shed but I found that we were in long, narrow room which ran the full width of the building. There was some kind of machine in the centre with tables at either side of it. A conveyor belt appeared to run from the machine through an aperture in the interior wall but, after I'd studied it more closely, I could see that perhaps it would be more accurate to say that the belt came through the wall to the machine. The belt was moving slowly and every few seconds eggs emerged through the wall to be collected by a young woman about my own age who placed them carefully in standard cardboard egg-trays. I hadn't seen her at first as she was standing on the further side of the machine, but our entrance must have disturbed her as she took a step back and looked up to see who had come in.

Abby gave her a wave and a quick "Hi, Sue" as she drew me towards a door at the left-hand end of the interior wall. As she opened it the smell intensified but I was too curious to draw back now, so I followed her through. There seemed to be thousands of small, brown, feathery bodies; squawking, sitting, walking, fluttering everywhere I looked. There were so many it wasn't easy to avoid treading on them. I jumped back as one overly adventurous hen pecked optimistically at my shoe. I was beginning to feel claustrophobic and wondered how the hens put up with living in such cramped conditions. And how on earth did they tolerate that ammonia stink? Maybe hens don't have a sense of smell. At that moment, I wished I hadn't either. Remembering what Debbie had said, I raised my voice over the squawking and asked, "Didn't you say these were free-range hens?"

"They are," said Debbie. "They come and go as they please. Look."

She pointed to apertures low in the left-hand side wall which was adjacent to the fenced off area outside. I could see a number of hens doing just as she said, coming and going. I was about to ask whether the hens laid their eggs outside the shed as well as inside, when I noticed that neither of the girls was any longer giving me their attention. They were looking back to the door where we had come in. Sue was standing there. I hadn't heard her speak, but the girls obviously had.

She raised her voice, presumably repeating her question, but looking at me.

"Are you here to help? I'm trying to get these graded, but it's taking forever doing it on my own."

Almost in unison, Abby and Debbie both asked, "Where's Nathan?" I just looked blank and shrugged as though to suggest *I'm just new here. What do I know?*

"How the hell should I know where he is? I'm not his keeper, though he sometimes behaves like he damn well needs one." There was more frustration than anger in her tone, and I wondered what it was that Nathan got up to that might make a keeper necessary.

Debbie took my arm and started to draw me over to the door. Abby followed, looking around as though she expected to see Nathan, whoever he might be, leaping out from the central mass of hens.

"Hey, Sue," said Debbie soothingly. "Does Dad know he's gone missing again?"

"Probably not," replied Sue with a long drawn out sigh. "I was going to tell him at lunch but I didn't see him around."

She kept looking at me, obviously waiting for someone to explain what I was doing there. The two girls appeared not to notice. They didn't seem to know what to do, and all Sue was bothered about was getting her eggs sorted, so after listening to them all dithering for a few minutes, I made a decision.

"Look, let's get out of here, then we can talk."

No objections, so we retreated to the smaller room where we had first come in and, when the door was shut, the noise reduced and the smell almost bearable, I said, "How would it be if you give me the tour another time, and for the moment we just concentrate on finding Nathan. If he's got some sort of problem we can sort him out, and if he hasn't, you can just kick his backside and send him along here to Sue."

Sue nodded, "Sounds good."

The two younger ones looked immensely relieved, but I was still no clearer why Nathan being missing was such a big issue. As we turned to leave the shed, we found the man from the Jeep standing in the doorway, quietly watching. True I'd not been listening, but I'd not heard a sound as he'd come in behind us. He'd obviously been watching me since my eyes met his as soon as I turned round, and he was clearly unembarrassed, as he made no attempt to look away. I'd been right about his age, mid-thirties at least, not exactly rip-your-pants-off gorgeous, but pleasant-looking enough, his looks enhanced more than anything by a small scar on his left temple. I'd had men look at me in all kinds of ways, most of which made me want to reach for the nearest nutcrackers and squeeze very hard, but his expression was just a kind of curious interest, like he was weighing me up somehow, and not for the usual reason.

"Nathan gone into hiding then," he asked, his deep voice only slightly tinged with a west-country accent.

"Oh, Cherry, there you are," said Abby. "You'll help look, won't you?"

"Well, I might." His eyes shifted from me to her, curiosity changing to amusement, maybe even affection. Who was this guy?

"Are you planning on making it worth my while?"

"Hey, Cherry, don't mess about," said Debbie, definitely not amused, but Abby didn't seem quite so uptight.

"OK," she said, "how about I let you off watching *Neighbours* for a week."

"Done," said . . . . strange, I couldn't quite think of him as Cherry. Surely that wasn't his real name. And as for *Neighbours*, I couldn't picture him somehow, curled up with an Australian soap that made even me cringe.

Before I could ask Abby for an explanation, we were all outside, except for Sue who was still trying to get her egg mountain into some sort of order. We were looking vaguely around and I knew that at least one of us didn't have a clue where to start.

"OK," I said, "why don't we split up? Debbie with Cherry and Abby with me."

"Sorry," responded Cherry, not looking the least bit apologetic, "I have to go with Abby."

"It's true, Lizzie," said Abby, seeing I was on the point of questioning Cherry's assertion. "I'll tell you later."

As it happened, we did not have to split up at all. When Cherry asked where Nathan usually went when one of his moods came over him, Debbie suggested, "the old shepherd's hut".

"I don't think he always goes there," she said, "but that's where Dad found him last time."

That's where we found him too, about fifteen minutes later, just outside the doorway of what had once been a small stone hut. There was no longer any roof, and I guessed the walls stood to about half their original height, their scattered stones lying all around. It was in the corner of a field on rising ground about half a mile above the wood where I'd spent the night. A small stream trickled down past the hut in the direction of the trees where it presumably emptied into the lake. It was a tranquil scene, the sort of thing that crops up time and again in watercolours of the Derbyshire Dales. I could understand why a troubled mind might find some sort of temporary peace here. The trouble was that none of the watercolours I'd ever seen had included a body draped picturesquely over the stones.

Moving very close to Abby and resting a hand on her shoulder, Cherry told us all to stand still, which we did, while he scanned the landscape all around us. Once he was satisfied, he moved in close to where Nathan lay and bent down reaching out his right hand to the boy's neck checking for a pulse. Having found one, he took off his jacket saying, more to the girls than to me, "Don't worry. He's just unconscious, but we need to keep him warm."

He slipped his mobile phone from an inside pocket of his jacket, before spreading it over Nathan's chest. He then called for an ambulance, giving very precise directions to our location, though how he expected it to reach us over the fields I had no idea. He then moved two large stones close to the boy's side left and right, and told the girls to sit down and hold Nathan's hands. "That will help to stop him getting cold." Maybe it would, but I suspected that the real reason was to give them something useful to do. It was a good move. The girls obeyed without question, apparently glad not to be left just standing around.

Then he started examining the ground close by. It was mostly grass both inside the walls of the former hut and in the surrounding field. Mostly, but there were two muddy areas. One was in the doorway itself, and the other was close to Nathan's feet. He looked carefully at them both but it was the one by the boy's feet that really caught his attention. I could see two long scuffmarks presumably left by Nathan's trainers when he slipped, but there were several other footprints clearly visible as well. They meant nothing to me. A heavy tread pattern, obviously some sort of work boot or hiking boot, and not Nathan's as the soles of his trainers were worn almost smooth. I suppose I wouldn't have thought much of them if Cherry hadn't stepped into the mud and quite deliberately obliterated the prints, carefully avoiding the scuffmarks. I watched him do it which didn't seem to worry him in the least.

When he'd finished substituting his own boot prints for those he had erased, he looked across at me eyebrows raised as though daring me to question him. Maybe I should have done but, whatever was going on, I just wanted to keep well out of it. When I didn't speak, he smiled and said, "Quite right. Always best not to get involved." His smile broadened. "Unless you have to, that is."

Seven

Heighley Grange Farm – early evening

We were a pretty solemn group as we sat around the kitchen table. The girls and I were there, nursing mugs of hot chocolate. Rachel was back from her visit to Natalie Simmons, and although she tried a smile occasionally, it was clear the visit had taken its toll. It hadn't gone well. How could it? Cherry had decided to join us this time, in response to what seemed to be a desperately pleading look from Abby, and I wondered yet again just how he fitted into this family. Although Chick had returned from whatever he'd been doing, even his presence brought no lightening of the mood.

The only individual unaffected by events was Simba, who wandered round the table, nuzzling each of us in turn, enquiring after the food which he knew must be around there somewhere. We were going over the events of the afternoon, trying to work out what must have happened to Nathan, and all of us wondering whether his accident was in any way connected with the death of Phil Simmons.

I mostly kept quiet and listened, still feeling too much of an outsider to contribute greatly to the discussion. I wasn't even sure whether I should be there. It really wasn't any of my business after all. But the two girls seemed to take it for granted I would stay, and no-one raised any objection, so I had accepted my mug, sat down and listened.

Nathan was still alive, or at least he had been when the paramedics had carried him away. For that, I was very relieved, not because I cared a jot about Nathan, but because it had meant I hadn't needed to preside over the girls' first introduction to a
corpse. His main injury, according to the paramedics, was probably a severe blow to the back of his head. Everyone seemed to be hoping that this had been caused by Nathan slipping on that patch of muddy ground, that it was just an accident, nothing more. Well, maybe not quite everyone. I was convinced that Cherry placed quite a different interpretation on Nathan's injury. I was sure that he knew far more about what had happened than he was letting on.

Since there was not much information to go on, the discussion was beginning to falter when speculation was revived by a sudden and very loud knock on the kitchen door. It went on long enough to make it seem as though the caller was expecting that we might all be fast asleep. Surprisingly, it was Cherry who moved to open the door, holding up his left hand in a signal for everyone else to keep seated. He took a quick look out of the window facing the yard, and then seemed to relax slightly as he reached for the door handle.

The young woman who entered was about ten years older than me. She was tall and athletic looking, but with a cynical weariness on her otherwise pleasant features. She pulled out her ID, but there was no need. I could tell. It was like she had plain clothes police stamped on her forehead.

"Detective Sergeant Hayford," she said, slipping her ID back into the side pocket of her navy jacket which had probably started the day looking quite stylish, though it was a moot point whether it would ever do so again. Similarly, the matching skirt with its splashes of mud, above a pair of oversized green wellies contributed nothing to the impression of professional elegance which Sergeant Hayford had clearly set out to cultivate.

"I understand that there was an accident here this afternoon which nobody," and here she paused to look around, making sure we all felt included in her condemnation, "nobody thought important enough to report."

"On the contrary," drawled Cherry. "It was reported immediately we found the boy, to the ambulance service who, I must say, responded remarkably quickly."

"That, as I think you know, was not what I meant." Hayford's schoolmarm snappiness showed she was definitely unimpressed, and wanted us to know it.

"Am I to understand that it was you who found Nathan Campion?"

I don't think, from the lazy contempt on his face, that Cherry was much impressed by her stilted official language, but he decided to cooperate.

"I rather think we all did. That is myself, the two girls over there, and," he gestured towards me, "this young lady at the end of the table."

"I see." Hayford reached into a serviceable black handbag for a notebook and pen. "Could I have your names please, starting with yours, sir?"

"Robert George Cherville-Thomas."

She looked at him steadily for a moment before beginning to write.

Cherry continued helpfully, "That's C.H.E.R.V.I.L.L.E hyphen T. . . ."

"Thank you, sir. I think I've got that."

I couldn't help smiling. At least that was one mystery solved. I looked around the table. Everyone was engrossed in the two key players, and no-one seemed inclined to interrupt.

"And do you live on the farm, sir?"

"Actually, no." and Cherry gave his address, which meant nothing to me, but it caused Sergeant Hayford's interest to click up a notch. She started to write it down, then paused and flicked back a couple of pages in her notebook. She read something, pursed her lips and tilted her head slightly as she looked back at Cherry.

"That, sir, is the home of James Montrayne."

"So it is," replied Cherry, not in the least put out. "He's my boss," and he looked across at Abby, "as well as being this young lady's father."

Sergeant Hayford glanced at Abby and then down at her notebook. She was thinking hard and I wondered just what it was that had caught her attention. In the momentary silence, Chick stood and moved over to fill the kettle and switch it on saying, "Anyone feel like another cuppa? Sergeant Hayford?"

There were some mumbled replies, but the detective completely ignored him. Perhaps she hadn't heard. Cherry seemed to have her whole attention.

"So was it you, sir, who instructed the ambulance to approach through the north gate of the farm."

"Of course," said Cherry, still amiably helpful. "That gave best access to the field where we found Nathan."

"Did it?" replied Hayford, clearly doubting it. "And I suppose it never crossed your mind that approaching from that direction ensured that the ambulance would not be seen by the police officers down in the wood."

"Is that so?" answered Cherry. "Do you know I never gave it a thought?"

I thought suddenly of Cherry obliterating the footprints in the mud, and I had no doubt that he had deliberately taken steps to keep Nathan's accident from the notice of the police for as long as possible, but I couldn't work out why.

Sergeant Hayford suddenly changed tack and looking over to me asked for my name. I gave it. My real name. The one I couldn't now change because I had given it to Chick and Rachel when I had first arrived. The name I hadn't used for about three years. The name that was buried in the police computers along with an unsolved murder.

I waited for some sign on recognition but Hayford just wrote it down along with the fact that I was a temporary resident at the farm. She should have asked me when I'd arrived, but she didn't. She should have asked me whether I'd seen anyone in the woods that morning, but she didn't. She was fixated on Nathan's accident and merely asked me to confirm what Cherry had said, and whether I had anything to add. I knew Cherry was watching me carefully, but it wasn't that which made me decide not to mention the footprints. I just didn't want any more police attention. I shook my head without catching her eye.

After that, it was all plain sailing. She lost a bit of her stiffness as she told us that Nathan was stable but still unconscious, and his mother was with him at the hospital. She reminded us that we were very remiss in not notifying the police of the incident but unbent enough to explain that it had only come to their attention because officers in a patrol car on their way back to Lichfield had seen the ambulance coming out of the farm gate. Wondering what had happened they radioed it in, and then followed the ambulance all the way to the Queens Hospital in Burton on Trent. They hadn't tried to stop it as the blue lights and siren showed that haste was crucial.

She made sure that Cherry would be available in the morning, around 11.00, to show her exactly where the accident had happened since it was too dark now to take in the scene. With that, she turned to leave but paused in the doorway to look back at Chick, still standing by the now boiled kettle.

"I nearly forgot. We're packing up now. We got a good start today and there's little more for us to do in the wood, but I'd be grateful if you could make sure that all your people respect the police notices, and keep out of the area until further notice."

She waited for Chick's acknowledgement and then transferred her attention to Abby, who sat watching her, quiet and wide-eyed.

"Your father's been helping us today but he should be here in a few minutes."

Glancing back to Chick she smiled.

"I should get on with making that tea. I think he's going to need a cup."

She then left, rather more quietly than she'd arrived.

Eight

Heighley Grange Farm – early evening

It had suddenly dawned on Rachel that, in all the strain and busyness of the day, she had completely forgotten about preparing anything for an evening meal. By dint of vigorous arm-waving we were ushered out of the kitchen and told to amuse ourselves while she rustled up toad-in-the-hole with onion gravy. I'd never heard of it but it sounded good, whatever it was. The ushering out didn't seem to apply to Cherry and Chick as they ignored the waving arms and stayed put in the kitchen, maybe to help, but probably to talk over things the rest of us didn't need to hear. That I understood. Abby and Debbie were too young either to be confided in, or to have their opinions sought, and I was an outsider. I was much happier not being involved. I had enough problems of my own already without taking on somebody else's. The more they kept me out of this, the better I liked it.

I drifted after the girls into a large room across the entrance hall from the kitchen. It ran the full width of the house, with a large bow window at the front and patio doors at the rear. It was comfortably furnished, settee and armchairs with slightly faded covers, a couple of beanbags and plenty of bookshelves. A stuffed Winnie-the-Pooh occupied one end of the settee, and we appeared to have disturbed his reading as a copy of Farmers Weekly lay close beside him. A large, but not very new, TV set occupied a niche to one side of a wide, open fireplace. It was a room where a family could enjoy relaxation and the comfort of being together. Not that there was much in the way of relaxation that evening.

The girls were tense, perhaps Abby more so than Debbie, and although they tried to settle to some kind of TV dancing competition, it was clear their hearts weren't in it. I watched Bruce Forsyth cavorting with his pretty assistant, but I found my mind wandering easily from the figures on the screen. I had hoped to be able to stay at the farm for some time while I worked out a real plan for my future, but I could see now that wasn't going to work. There was suddenly far too much interest being taken in the local area and, even if there wasn't, I couldn't really believe this family would be happy to have me living indefinitely in their house. I'd been rather surprised at their readiness to take me in at all, not having much experience of uncomplicated, unrestrained, no-strings-attached hospitality. I certainly hadn't anticipated finding myself being expected to fit into a family. I'd hoped for some measure of independence; a quiet room in the converted barn, self-contained and out of the way. But it hadn't worked out that way, and now the police had my name. No, this was not the safe place I had thought it would be. I needed to leave. Soon!

But I had nowhere else to go. No job, no money, no home, no family and, now I'd left Angie, no friends.

I'd been this way before, but this time there was a real desperation that, even now, I find hard to put into words. I felt sick to my stomach, so much so that I wondered whether I ought to sneak off and find the downstairs cloakroom. I couldn't stand the thought that, three years after descending to the gutter which I was now trying to climb out of, I could see myself heading right back to where I'd started. How else is a girl supposed to scrape a living when she's hiding from the police and daren't use her real name to get a job?

I took a deep breath, summoned up what little resolution I had left, and decided that this time it was going to be different. Maybe. After all, I had information the police would sell their grannies for. Three years' worth, picked up in clubs, hotel rooms, massage parlours, discreet country clubs. Sometimes the guys I serviced, or the guys who sold my services, liked to boast, as if that would somehow boost their performance, or mine; sometimes they talked as if I just wasn't there, of less account even than the furniture. Yes, I knew stuff the police would want, but it was also stuff that could get me killed. Maybe I could do a deal. Give what I knew to the police and they'd forget what happened three years ago. But it didn't work like that did it? Back then, I had killed a man and, despite what you see in American movies, they don't let you walk away from that.

I tried to work out how to leave without raising too many questions. That police sergeant had my name, but she probably wouldn't do anything with it as long as she thought I was unimportant. If I were to leave now, she might just be interested enough to run it through the police computer. The result of that would certainly start them jumping about and, if they then searched the wood thoroughly enough, they could easily place me at the scene. Maybe they'd go for a quick closure and pin it all on me. I was mulling this over when the room was suddenly flooded with light causing Abby to leap up and dash to the window. For a few moments, the headlights of a vehicle coming up the drive from the road shone directly into the room before sweeping aside to follow the curving tarmac around the side of the house and into the yard. Abby was out of the door before I had even made it to the window. Debbie was close on her heels, the TV dancers completely forgotten.

I wasn't sure what to do. Probably best to stay and keep Bruce Forsyth company, and leave the others to their reunion. But discretion didn't stop me searching for the TV remote and lowering the volume. I wasn't going to intrude with my presence, but I could listen. Couldn't I?

There was that voice again. Slow and weary, but still Peter O'Toole at his sexy upper-class best. No doubt of it. Not that I had expected otherwise. Abby's dad was my hunter friend from the wood.

That huge bear of a man in the photo upstairs, hugging his little girl to him, was actually in the kitchen, and I felt distinctly nervous about meeting him. Well, at least the police had let him go. I was surprised to find how relieved I felt, more for Abby's sake than anything else. She needed her dad, and couldn't bear the thought of losing him. Well, I could understand that.

I muted the TV completely and tiptoed to the doorway from where I looked diagonally across the hall to the half-open kitchen door. I hated the thought of being caught eavesdropping, but I needed to know what had happened. I could hear the voices, but had difficulty making out all the words, especially now that the initial excitement had died down. As I stood listening, I could feel a slight draught washing around my feet. I had left the muddy, green wellies by the door of the kitchen when we'd returned and, not possessing any slippers, had preferred to wander round barefoot. The stout, wooden door was no doubt very old and no longer fitted snugly at the bottom of the frame, if indeed it ever had done so. Curled to one side of the door was a kind of long, chestnut coloured, canvas sausage with two ears, one eye and a red tongue at one end, and a plaited wool tail at the other. Taking this elongated dachshund to be the draught excluder, I bent down to move it back into place.

Just as I was straightening up, I heard footsteps behind me and I swung round so quickly that I knocked my elbow on the large brass door handle. Abby's dad was just a few feet away watching me curiously. He was still dressed in the heavy boots, camouflage jacket and trousers in which I'd first seen him and, even in that substantial entrance hall, seemed menacingly huge. I held my left arm across my body as I rubbed vigorously at the sore elbow. I had no idea what to say so I kept quiet and waited for him to speak first which, after a moment, he did.

"I'm sorry I startled you. On the other hand, you could apologise for startling me." He gave a tired smile. "I had no idea there were any other visitors in the house."

I still kept quiet. He gestured towards the cloakroom under the stairs.

"I was just heading for the ... ... er"

I still kept quiet. I wondered what he was going to call it. Lavatory? Toilet? Little boys room?

"It's been rather a long day. Too many cups of coffee."

As he turned away, Abby came out of the kitchen. She ran to her dad and grabbed his hand.

"Hey, Dad. So you found Lizzie."

"Ah, is that who I found? Well Lizzie will have to excuse me for a moment. And you too."

With that, he left us standing there and retreated to the cloakroom. Abby took my left hand and I winced as she pulled me towards the kitchen. Rubbing didn't seem to have done much to relieve the pain in my elbow. Bruce Forsyth and his glittering dancers seemed to have slipped from Abby's mind in the excitement of knowing that her dad was not, for the moment, going to be banged up in jail.

Nothing much seemed to have changed in the kitchen, except perhaps for the delicious smells coming from a large, heavy skillet on the hob. Oh, and Cherry was missing, which somehow struck me as rather odd.

The small stereo system on the top of the old dresser was tuned to a local radio station, so the clatter of Debbie setting the table was accompanied by snippets of sports results, music and local news. I bent slightly to Abby and asked her what had happened to Cherry.

"Oh, he said he had to go and check on something." I must have looked puzzled, as she went on to add, "It's OK. He can go now Dad's here."

That mystified me even more. There was definitely something here that I was missing. I was about to ask her just what she meant when her father came back into the room. Abby turned to him, rested her cheek against his chest and put both arms around his waist to give him a big hug. He looked down at the top of her head and I saw again that tired smile. As he raised his head, just for a moment his eyes met mine, and I saw an enormous tenderness there.

"No sense, my girl," he said. "She goes right on loving me no matter what I get up to." He extended his right hand. "My name is James, by the way."

My hand disappeared in his. He shook it gently but firmly. "Lizzie," I said. He let go. "Yes, I know."

Abby pulled away from him as a knock sounded on the back door and it opened slowly to allow Sue's slightly apprehensive face to peer around the edge.

"Sorry to bother you but … … …"

She was interrupted by Chick who pulled the door fully open saying, "Don't be daft, Sue. Come on in."

"No, really." She jerked her head in the direction of the converted barn. "It's just that the guys were wondering about Nathan. Is he going to be OK?"

"Yes, yes," he said. "Well, as far as we know. Tell you what. I'll come over and have a quick word. Set their minds at rest."

"Thanks," replied Sue, as she turned away.

"Don't be long," called out Rachel, as the door started to close behind him. "I'll be dishing up in a minute."

James pulled away the chair from the end of the table and sat down, occupying the place I had taken at lunchtime. "Don't worry, Rach. If he's not back in time, I'll eat his."

Rachel smiled. "You might have to. Once he gets talking to those youngsters, he loses all track of time."

The two girls took their places at the table, sitting just where they had before, which placed Abby at right angles to her father. I was left feeling slightly awkward until Rachel pointed to the seat opposite Abby saying, "Why don't you sit there, Lizzie?"

I did as I was told, feeling awkward now for a different reason. I could have saved Abby and her father a lot of grief that day if only I had been prepared to speak up and tell what I'd seen. But I had chosen not to, for what seemed to me to be very good reasons and, even though he could still be in trouble, I was determined to keep quiet. That knowledge made me feel uncomfortable, so I just sat quietly listening to the radio as Abby peppered her father with questions.

A gush of warm air flooded the kitchen as Rachel opened the oven door and removed a massive earthenware dish containing a huge, golden-brown batter pudding. As she placed this on the table, I could see that the base of the pudding was filled with succulent, sizzling sausages. The aromatic mixture from the skillet was poured into a large sauce jug which she then placed on the table next to a bowl of buttery mashed potato flecked with pieces of spring onions. Peas and carrots followed in another bowl and we were all set, though there was still no sign of Chick or Cherry.

The radio continued to play quietly even while Rachel said grace before starting to serve out the food. Elaine Page was singing *I dreamed a dream* from *Les Misérables*. The tune was somehow familiar, but I don't think I'd ever listened to the words before. Those haunting words struck a cord so deep within me that, in my present humour, I could easily have burst into tears. Rachel broke the mood by handing me a plate of the sausage batter pudding, toad-in-the-hole, and telling me to help myself to the rest of the vegetables. I let James and the girls go first and then I spooned some peas, carrots and mashed potato onto my plate, finally helping myself to a good portion of the onion gravy. For the second time that day, I found myself tucking into a delicious family meal in a way I hadn't done for years. The buttery mashed potato was light and creamy and, in combination with the onion gravy, was truly delectable.

Opposite me, Debbie was asking her mum about Mrs. Simmons, and wondering how she was going to cope with a baby on the way. Listening while I ate, I learnt that Natalie Simmons was Abby's and Debbie's Sunday School teacher, as well as teaching occasionally at their school, and that she was very highly rated by both the girls. At the end of the table, James was suggesting a trip to town with Abby during the coming week to try and find the shoes she needed. I had nothing to contribute to either conversation so I just concentrated on eating while trying to devise a workable plan from the muddle of conflicting ideas flitting through my mind. I became vaguely aware of Johnny Cash's *Walk the Line* playing in the background and I started to listen, savouring the words whilst at the same time acutely conscious of the impossibility of anyone ever addressing a song like that to me. As the song finished, the programme moved into a local news update and I stopped paying attention until the newsreader announced a story that held me frozen with shock.

Nine

Heighley Grange Farm – early evening

Police have still not released the name of the young woman who fell from a bridge over the A38 Aston Expressway in the early hours of this morning. Initially it was thought that the woman was trying to throw herself from the bridge, as two men were seen by a motorist travelling south on the motorway apparently trying to pull her back over the railings. However, a witness has now come forward to say that the two men actually forced the woman over the railings and held her suspended before dropping her onto the northbound carriageway of the motorway below. The witness reports that her fall was broken when she landed on top of a lorry passing under the bridge, before rolling off onto the road. The lorry did not stop, and police believe that the driver may be unaware of what happened. Police have issued brief descriptions of the two men they would like to question. One is thought to be over six foot, heavily built, slow moving and with a full beard. The other is much shorter, slimmer and very agile. They are believed to be driving in a dark coloured BMW saloon. The young woman was seriously injured as a result of the fall, but police have been told by doctors that some of her injuries were probably caused by a severe beating prior to her fall from the bridge. She is still unconscious in an undisclosed hospital in Birmingham.

I stared at the radio as though I could somehow will it to give up more information, but the newsreader moved on to another story. I couldn't move and I couldn't speak. The warmth of that marvellous onion gravy had totally dissipated. I was chilled to the bone.

As if aware of my exclusion from the conversation at the table, James chose that moment to ask me a question. Something about how long I was staying, and whether I had any plans. When I didn't answer, he reached out and touched my arm, asking me if I was OK. I still didn't answer and, by this time, everyone seemed to have realised that something unusual was happening and I was conscious of them all looking at me, puzzled but not yet overly concerned.

I could still feel James's hand resting on my arm, squeezing slightly as he tried to attract my attention, but it was actually Abby who spoke next.

"Lizzie? What's the matter?"

James must have noticed where my eyes were focussed since he now glanced over at the radio and began to listen, but the news had now shifted to a bulletin on the possible reopening of the MG-Rover car plant at Longbridge. I know that, because I remember thinking, "How can they possibly be talking about cars when Angie's just been dropped from a bridge?" I knew it had to be Angie because I knew those two men, and I'd even been driven in that BMW. It was Bruno's car, the massive guy with the beard, and the smaller man with him had to be the kick-boxing Indian we all knew as Satish. I also knew why they had tried to resurface the A38 with Angie's battered body. They must have asked her where I'd gone and she had, at least for a while, told them she had no idea. Then they would have become more persuasive, and Angie would have begun to hurt, and she may still have told them nothing. But she did know about the farm; and she knew that I knew; and she might, to try and stop the pain, have told them where it was.

Which meant that they could, even now, be coming to find me. I had to leave right away, and get as far from the farm as I could. It no longer mattered whether the police might wonder where I'd gone and why, and possibly run my name through the computer to see whether there was any reason for taking a closer interest in me. I no longer had a choice. Nor did I have any time to spare.

I started to push my chair back from the table so that I could stand up, but James was still holding my arm. Since his hand was about twice the size of mine and refused to budge, I couldn't easily move. I wanted to scream at him to let go. I had so often been held by my arms, and forced to do things which I hated but couldn't avoid. I had only recently been badly bruised in the very place he was holding now. The bluish-purple had faded, but the yellowish tinge was still visible if you knew where to look.

I turned to glare at him, opening my mouth to tell him to get his bleeding hand off my arm. Yes, I did use words like that, many of them far worse, but I didn't have a chance to shock them with my bad language because James spoke first.

"Lizzie, what's happened?"

Before I could even begin to think of an answer, Rachel intervened.

"She's scared, James. Something on the news. I didn't catch what it was, but something on the news has frightened the living daylights out of her."

I looked down at James's hand on my arm and he slowly released me, gently sliding his hand over mine and squeezing it before letting go. I wondered if he was trying to convey to me that he had no desire to hurt me. Now I was free to stand up, I suddenly found that I didn't want to. It felt safe here, and I really had no idea where to go.

Then I heard footsteps approaching the back door and I jumped to my feet and stood petrified as Chick strolled into the kitchen. He started breezily enough.

"Well, that's them sorted out."

But then the stillness in the kitchen caught his attention and he stood looking at each of us in turn, his eyes wide and eyebrows raised, as if asking what was going on. James gestured to one of the spare chairs at the table saying, "Come and sit down, Chick. Seems we may have a bit of a problem."

As Chick came round the table to take a seat next to Rachel, James looked up at me. Not that he needed to tilt his head very much as he was almost as tall sitting down as I was standing up.

"OK, Lizzie, it's obvious to all of us that something's upset you. Now you don't know us very well, and we certainly don't know you, so there's no reason you should tell us anything. But we're willing to listen if you want to tell us what's the matter, and if we can do anything to help, we will." He paused as something occurred to him, and he glanced at Rachel before adding, "If you'd rather just talk to Rachel, that's OK. We can all go into the sitting room."

As he was speaking, Rachel got up and came to put her arm around my shoulders. It suddenly dawned on me that these guys who were offering to help had already got a whole mess of problems of their own. A friend murdered; another grieving and expecting a baby; one of their young residents in hospital; and James had just spent the whole day being grilled by the police. They were good people, probably; or at least as good as people ever get these days. But they were just a farmer and his wife, two kids and an oversized schoolteacher. There was nothing they could do.

But they had known Angie, so maybe it was right that I at least tell them what had happened. Angie had no other family to be concerned for her. Perhaps one of them could then drive me to a train station and maybe buy me a ticket to . . . . somewhere.

I took a deep breath, and breathed out slowly, my eyes closed.

"OK."

Rachel took her arm from my shoulders and, as I sat down again, settled herself in the chair next to mine. I didn't know whether the girls should be sent away to watch TV or something, but they were both watching me with such large eyes and faces full of concern that I just couldn't exclude them. They'd be hurt and offended and I could see no reason to do that to them. I would just have to be careful how I explained things. I sorted my thoughts and then began.

"OK, you know I've been working in Birmingham. I already told you that. And I was living with Angie."

James interrupted, "Sorry. Who's Angie?"

Rachel answered that one for me. "You probably won't remember, James. She was one of the kids who was here about three years ago. She helped organise the barn concert that summer."

"Hmm. I think I do though. Was she that mixed-race girl, skinny, always trying to make out that she looked like Princess Di?"

As Rachel nodded agreement, I could feel my eyes welling up. Even then, it seemed, Angie had fancied herself as the world's most famous princess. And where had it got her? Almost bashed to death, and I was responsible. I really didn't want to tell this story, but I couldn't see any way of avoiding it. So I carried on.

"The place where we worked was taken over. The new guys seemed nice enough at first, but then after a while they started putting the pressure on. Just threats to start with, but then things just went to crap. A couple of girls disappeared, and we didn't dare ask questions. We knew by then that these guys were connected to some seriously bad people. When they told us to … … er … … do stuff we weren't happy about, we were too scared to argue."

So far, so good. Keep it bland; don't give any details. Debbie started to ask, "What work were … … …" but she stopped, and I could see, from the corner of my eye, Rachel shaking her head at her daughter. I thought, "That's right, Rachel. Don't let her go there."

I told them how Angie had mentioned the farm and explained about her time there. I said that I'd wanted to get right away from Birmingham and had tried to persuade Angie to come with me, but she was too scared. She believed we'd be caught and brought back, and punished for running away, as an example to the others who worked for them. I couldn't get her to change her mind, and in the end I told her straight that if I got the chance I was going to run. Eventually, I met someone who was prepared to help me, and give me a ride out of the city. Finally, I told them how I'd made my way to the farm to rest up and plan what to do next.

I didn't tell them I'd arrived early, and was in the wood that morning.

Then I recounted the news story, as much of it as I could remember.

"The girl they dropped from the bridge was Angie. They did that to her because they want me back, and they thought she might know where I am."

There was quiet around the table. The girls were watching me, wide-eyed with their mouths slightly open, still trying to make sense of what they were hearing. as though they couldn't quite translate this movie-plot tale into real life. The adults were different. They believed what I was telling them, and I could see they didn't like it. I glanced over at James, and immediately looked away again. His expression was very serious, angry almost, and I could feel his eyes probing my mind, willing me to look at him. In the end, with a rather pathetic show of defiance, I sat up straight and looked him directly in the eye.

When he spoke, I was surprised to detect neither anger nor condemnation in his tone, but only a slight hint of puzzlement.

"A couple of things, Lizzie. Would Angie have known you were coming here? And why would these folks be so desperate to get you back?"

"I never told her I had any plan to come here, but she might have guessed. Or she might have told them about the farm just to get them to stop hurting her."

I didn't answer the second question, and I didn't look away as his eyes continued to search my face. I was sure that, behind those brown eyes of his, he was understanding a lot more than I was telling. Maybe teachers weren't so dumb after all. He glanced at the girls, and I was fairly sure he was wondering whether it had been a mistake to let them stay. I looked across at the pair of them, but they didn't appear frightened. There was just that look of concern again. He looked back at me.

"Why do they want you back, Lizzie?"

How was I to put this. Plain and simple, that's the way.

"I'm not really sure, so just accept I'm guessing a bit here... ... There was talk of a project or deal of some sort being worked out, and Bruno said I was needed."

James interrupted. "Sorry, but who's Bruno?"

I looked at the two girls, still listening intently.

"He was my... ... my manager... ... but I think it was him who threw Angie off that bridge."

"Your manager," said James, putting a lot more meaning into the word than I had. "OK. Is that it?"

I thought about the number of times I'd seen runaway girls being brought back and then savagely beaten as an example to the rest of us.

"It's the way they do things," I said. "It's bad for business if girls can just walk off and get away with it. And there's another thing... ... While I was working for them, I learnt something, well, quite a lot of things, about how they worked, and who they worked for. Things that could cause a lot of trouble if I spoke to the wrong people. They need to be sure I won't tell anyone."

"And will you?"

"No. At least, not right now."

There was more silence. James and the girls looked at me. Rachel and Chick looked at James. Chick hadn't said a word since his entrance had scared me rigid. This was his house, but it was as though he and Rachel were deferring to James. I didn't understand it, but I had little doubt who was going to break the silence.

"Lizzie," said James. "Are you in trouble with the police?"

"Daaaaad." Abby's drawn out protest was somehow reassuring, and it also gave me a moment to think. I once heard someone say that you don't need a good memory if you always tell the truth; you can't get caught by the lies you've forgotten. Of course, that doesn't mean that you always have to tell the whole truth, does it?

"I ran away from home when I was sixteen. The police probably looked for me for a while after that. That was about three years ago. I shouldn't think they're still looking."

James was giving me that look again. Was he wondering why I hadn't just said *No*?

In that moment of quiet while they wondered what had driven me to run away, the phone started chirping out in the hallway. James's eyebrows rose slightly, but on other faces I saw various degrees of apprehension. After the events of the day, there seemed something ominous about this intrusion. In the end it was Rachel who stood up.

"I'll go. It could be news about Nathan."

The rest of sat quietly, listening to what we could hear of her end of the conversation. There wasn't much; just *Who, Are you sure,* several *No's* and a couple of *I'm sorry's* plus a few words so quiet I couldn't make them out.

She came slowly back into the kitchen, left hand digging through her mop of dark hair to scratch lightly at her scalp, a slightly bewildered look on her face.

"It was some guy from Social Services called Brian Holmes." She looked at Chick. "Do you know him?"

He shook his head. "Can't place the name. Where is he from? Which office?"

Rachel sat down again, still looking puzzled. "I don't think he said or, if he did, I didn't catch it. He said they're trying to find a girl who's run away from the community home where she's been living. Apparently she's only sixteen, but could be taken for nineteen or twenty."

"Did he say which home it was?" asked Chick.

"No, he didn't. But he said that someone there mentioned Heighley Grange as a place she might have run to, so he was just checking to see if any girls matching her description had turned up here today."

She was looking at me now, and I could read in her face the questions buzzing through her mind.

"Did he describe her, then?" asked Chick.

74

"Yes. Her age, well, I've told you. Height, about five foot eight; about a hundred and ten pounds; slim; hazel eyes; brown hair; tanned complexion; very pretty."

Everyone was looking at me now. I could see it clearly in their eyes. No doubt at all who the man was enquiring about. My mouth was dry and I felt sick.

"Did he give this girl a name?" asked Chick.

"He called her Diane Thomas."

I gasped. I couldn't help it. I tried to get some saliva back into my mouth, and finally managed to croak around the hand covering my lips, "What did you yell him?"

"I said that no sixteen-year-old girl called Diane Thomas or anything else has called here today."

I dropped my hand to the table and closed my eyes, breathing out heavily. I felt so grateful. Then I became aware of Rachel's hand covering mine.

"But it is you, Lizzie, isn't it?"

I opened my eyes and looked around the table. I took in the five pairs of eyes fixed on mine; questioning, confused, wondering, but all showing some strange mixture of sadness and compassion. I took in a deep breath.

"Yes, it is me. Or, at least, it was. For three years, since I ran away from home."

I paused, saving the really bad news. "That's the only name by which Angie has known me."

I let them grapple with the implication, and this time it was James who spoke up.

"Do you have a mobile phone, Lizzie?"

I stared at him wondering what he was getting at?

"If you do have one," he went on, "especially if they gave it to you, they could be tracking the GPS."

I shook my head.

"I did have one but I left it behind. I was only allowed to use it for work. Just a few special customers had the number. I didn't want it anymore."

"OK," said James. "Looks like this is what happened. Angie had to give them something, so she told them about the farm. That was them checking to see if you came here. Question is, will they believe what Rachel told them? Are they likely to come here?"

I couldn't answer that with any certainty, and said so.

"All right, Lizzie. One last thing. Do you think Angie's still in danger?"

"Surely not!" Rachel sounded horrified at the thought. I had to disillusion her.

"Oh, yes. Once they've decided they want you dead, that's what happens."

As soon as I'd said it, I wished I hadn't. The girls weren't looking concerned anymore. They were positively frightened. So was I because, even now, having explained everything, I still didn't see how these people could possibly help. Except, of course, for that lift to the station. James had seen the change in the girls, and he reached out to lay his hand over Abby's. Chick had noticed as well, and there was a little growl as he cleared his throat before speaking.

I knew what he was going to say. *We'd better call the police.* In that situation, who wouldn't. Any normal, sane, law-abiding person would do that. Which meant I needed to leave this place and very soon. I was surprised to find how very much I really wished I didn't have to. I hadn't trusted anyone for over half my life, and it made me feel so empty. I wanted to be able to trust these guys, but didn't know if I should, or even if I could. But with the threat of the police getting involved in my life, I wasn't going to have a chance to find out. If only these guys were not as sane and normal as they seemed. I held my breath, waiting for Chick to speak, while at the same time wondering how easily I could get away.

"This is pretty heavy stuff, James. I think we need to take time to commit this whole thing to the Lord before we go any further."

Rachel agreed, and I saw James nodding.

I was stunned.

I thought I knew what Chick meant, but I must have looked completely lost since Debbie piped up, "It's OK, Lizzie. We're just going to talk to Jesus."

I couldn't believe it. I simply couldn't understand what they thought might possibly be achieved by sitting round a table talking to Jesus. I knew about prayer, of course I did. But I never bothered with it, not since my mum and dad died. I couldn't see the point. If there was a god out there somewhere, he or she clearly wasn't interested in what went on in the world. There were simply too many bad things allowed to happen which any god worth his salt would want to do something about. If he couldn't put things right, or chose not to, why bother with him?

Chick prayed, but I wasn't really listening. I was getting quite screwed up over all the time being wasted. It was all so useless. I caught vague phrases about *power* and *Holy Spirit* and *wisdom* but it was all nonsense. Eventually, after what seemed like hours, it came to an end with a chorus of *Amens*. At last, we could start doing something.

I was amazed to see that the girls were actually smiling. Chick was sitting back in his chair, looking more relaxed than before, and

Rachel was holding his hand which rested on the table. I was almost pleased to see that they were not smiling; at least they were still taking this business seriously. James was motionless, forearms resting on the table, his lips slightly pursed, and with small furrows creasing his forehead. His eyes were fixed on some spot way beyond the wall of the kitchen. We all waited, and again I knew it would be James who would break the silence. My heart rate seemed so fast and loud that I thought everyone else in the room must hear it. My nails were digging into my palms, and my skin felt hot and clammy.

"OK, folks. Lizzie could certainly have picked a better time to bring us her troubles, since we seem to have acquired enough of our own today. But that's really beside the point. I don't see we've got any choice but to do what we can to help her out."

I breathed out in a long drawn out sigh, surprised to find that I'd been holding my breath. I seemed to have done that a lot today. I relaxed and found that I could no longer hear the blood pulsing in my ears. It was amazing. That's all it took. I don't know how he did it. Facial expression? The confidence in his voice? Whatever it was, the tension oozed out of me.

"Sure, Dad. What do we do?"

I was glad Abby asked that question, since it's exactly what I was thinking.

James looked around the table as he pulled out his cell phone. He pressed a speed dial number and spoke into the phone.

"Where are you, Cherry? Right. I need you back here ASAP. There was a report on tonight's news about a woman being dropped onto the Aston Expressway. Tell Rod to get the details. And have a word with Andy. Tell him we need reinforcements. Four guys; two to Heighley Grange Farm and two to the house. Be ready for trouble. I'll explain later."

He disconnected, folded the phone and slipped it into his jacket pocket. He might be tired, but he certainly knew how to lift a person's spirits. Smiling broadly, he stood up.

"Good to have something to do to take your mind off things, isn't it?"

Ten

Staffordshire Police Divisional HQ – 9.00pm

By 9.00pm the office presided over by Chief Inspector Paul Morrissey was still a scene of quiet but determined activity. That was how he liked it. The weekend was a minor nuisance, but he had no intention of allowing other people's days of rest to interfere with what could well be his last murder investigation. Twenty-eight years in the force, since leaving the army, had gradually sapped his energy. He was now constantly tired, physically and mentally, and he knew that he had little left to give to the job. Retirement beckoned, and he was ready to submit. He would not be coming back to perform new tricks for the likes of Amanda Redman.

His desk was positioned so that he could see everyone in the room, usually his sergeant and two or three constables, depending on the urgency and priority of their current investigations. This one was top priority. James Montrayne's involvement would have guaranteed that, even without that strange call from someone at the DTLO in London. What was their interest in Phil Simmons? Whatever it was, he couldn't guess and they weren't telling, but he was pretty sure it wouldn't turn out to have any bearing on the case. It was less than a day old, but his instinct, reliable more often than not, was leading him steadily towards a result. He was certain who'd done it. All he had to do was assemble enough evidence to prove it. It would be a highly successful conclusion to a moderately successful career, if he were at the centre of a press-fuelled blaze of glory.

Detective Sergeant Joanne Hayford sat at another desk, rather more utilitarian looking than the battered oak supporting DCI Morrissey's files and PC. She knew he had rescued the old desk from being thrown in the skip when they had moved from the old police station into their new divisional HQ about eighteen months earlier. She had wondered whether it had been a minor act of defiance after he had been passed over for promotion to Superintendent. Or maybe he just liked old wood.

Her back was to the outside window. It was dark now, but even in the daylight it wasn't much of a view. Just the police vehicle park, and a whole array of rooftops in various shades of grey. Across the room, on the wall facing her desk, was a large whiteboard. As she typed competently on her keyboard, images and text appeared on the whiteboard to summarise the findings of their day's enquiries.

Morrissey glanced at the board from time to time, but mostly he just gazed at the ceiling while chewing on the end of his pencil. He usually ignored his desktop computer, making copious notes in pencil, pretending a technological incompetence which was actually far from the truth. His pencils came boxed in dozens, and in a bad week he could chew his way through a couple of boxes.

At another desk, in the corner by the door, a uniformed constable was diligently searching files on the police database. Constable Mayblin loved his computer. For relaxation, a choice between a search engine and a paperback novel was no contest. The promise of the novel being read to him by someone with the attributes of Charlize Theron might just prize him away from Google, but no-one would bet money on it. Although he was sitting with his back to the wall so that he could see the whiteboard, he paid it little attention. He knew Morrissey might appear to be staring at the ceiling, but the DCI would land on him from a great height if he suspected the young constable was not giving his full attention to the task he'd been given. In any case, if he was audacious enough to allow himself to be distracted, it would not be the whiteboard he would be looking at, but the decidedly attractive profile of Detective Sergeant Hayford. In his book, she was definitely on a par with Charlize.

Morrissey wasn't much interested in Hayford's shape, size or colouring, but he was very much interested in what she thought. They had made a good team since she was promoted to sergeant two years ago, and he usually respected her judgement. Their occasional differences of opinion generally went in his favour, but he knew that her sharp mind and developing skills were hastening the time when the balance would change. But not quite yet; not if he could help it.

He stopped chewing his pencil and sat forward.

"Talk to me, Jo. Run through what we've got, and then you can get off to that smooth boyfriend of yours."

"The smooth boyfriend's in London. Went down on Friday would you believe. Claimed it was work"

She was actually rather glad he was away since, whatever justification he felt about his own working at the weekend, he would have made distinctly unpleasant noises about her working late on Saturday if he had been around to enjoy her company. Typical male double standards, she thought, but so far they'd been worth tolerating.

She tapped some keys and the whiteboard cleared. Some more taps and Phil Simmons name appeared in the top left corner. As more information appeared in a column below the name, she spoke her thoughts, knowing that Morrissey would rather listen to her voice than read off the wall.

"Montrayne's call came in at 6.23 this morning. Dr Culver examined Simmons at the scene and confirmed that he could have died exactly when Montrayne says he did, at around 6.20. However, since Simmons had been exercising and then fell in the lake saturating his clothes, body temperature is not going to give a very accurate time of death."

"So, he could have died a good bit earlier."

"Yes, sir. Or later, theoretically, but the first officers were on the scene by 6.40 so .. .. .."

"Quite." Morrissey seemed pleased enough with that. "Go on, Jo, what about the *how*."

"Dr Culver will do the full post-mortem tomorrow morning, but he's already sent blood samples off for analysis. The blow on Simmons' head was consistent with falling in the lake and banging his head on a rock. The rock was above water and SOCO identified a blood smear and sent that for matching. Dr Culver thinks the blow occurred before death but can't say yet whether it was the cause of death."

Morrissey grunted. "Always did like to hedge his bets, that fellow. Still, when he does get round to it, I'm willing to bet that he'll find something else actually killed Simmons. Come on, Jo. I'm still waiting for the *how*."

A tap on the keyboard and an enlarged photo of a patch of mud almost filled the whiteboard. In the centre was a small cylindrical object, silver where it wasn't streaked with grime. One end narrowed to a sharp point, and the other end sprouted a long green tuft of some kind of fibre, almost half as long again as the silver body.

"The dart is 0.177 calibre," said Hayford. "It could be responsible for the puncture wound which Dr Culver found on Simmons' neck. We should know for certain tomorrow."

She could hardly believe what she was saying. Death by poisoned dart? This wasn't an Agatha Christie mystery.

"I know for certain now," replied Morrissey. "The dart did it, and Montrayne fired the dart. Trouble is, we can't prove it yet."

Joanne Hayford wasn't sure they would ever prove it. Try as she might, she couldn't quite stop herself liking James Montrayne. He had been very co-operative, and remained even-tempered in spite of Morrissey's frequent provocation. His story hadn't changed in the slightest, no matter how many times they made him tell it, and she would bet her pension, well, maybe a week's wages, on the grief he showed for his dead friend being entirely genuine. But, she wasn't going to argue with Morrissey. That never worked. Just play the evidence; feed it to him, and let him work it out for himself. He usually got there in the end. She didn't mind that he still believed he was a better investigator than she was. In his day, he'd been pretty good, but that day was past. Still, he was retiring soon, so what was the point in upsetting the old fart.

"Montrayne's rifle was 0.25 calibre, and that was the only airgun we found at the scene. And we don't know yet whether the dart was contaminated with anything which could have killed Simmons."

Morrissey was not to be dissuaded.

"Suppose Simmons died around 5.20 not 6.20. Culver won't argue with that. Suppose Montrayne used the 0.177 Steyr that was found at his house. Suppose he shot Simmons at 5.20 and then took the Steyr home before returning to the wood and making the call."

Hayford knew there were two good reasons why this theory would not take flight.

"Natalie Simmons said Phil left the house at 6.00am. He usually began his morning runs at that time. He couldn't have been in the wood at 5.20."

"Natalie Simmons could have been mistaken. I don't know what being heavily pregnant does for you, but me, I'd be whacked out at 5 in the morning. She probably didn't even check the clock."

"She says she did, because she wasn't sleeping and wondered if she should get up. And Surjit Guram, Montrayne's handyman, confirmed that Montrayne drove off at about 5.45."

"That could have been after he'd been back to return the Steyr. Once ballistics have finished with it, I'm betting we'll have all the proof we need that that's what fired the dart."

Hayford sighed, but took care not to let Morrissey hear her. He was building a case on supposition and fresh air. She decided to push a bit to see how flexible he was prepared to be.

"If Simmons usually left for his run at 6.00, what would have made him leave earlier this morning? And how would Montrayne have known what time to expect him?"

"They were friends, Jo. Maybe Montrayne arranged to meet him. We're checking phone records to see whether there's been any recent contact between them?"

"Assuming you're right, sir, what would have been Montrayne's motive?"

"Come on, Jo. Apply the principle."

She knew exactly what he meant. Very early in her working relationship with Morrissey, she had discovered that he regularly applied what he called the *GAS* principle. In his view, the motivation in any crime could usually be boiled down to Greed, Anger or Sex. The trouble was, she couldn't see how any of these applied to Montrayne.

"Sorry, sir. You've lost me now. I just can't see it."

"Sex, girl, sex."

Constable Mayblin smiled. He'd been thinking the same thing, although in an entirely different context. Jo Hayford looked blank.

"We will discover," said Morrissey positively, "that James Montrayne was having an affair with Natalie Simmons." Her mouth opened and eyebrows disappeared into her fringe, but he appeared not to notice and ploughed on. "Her baby is probably his, not her husband's. And that is another reason why we can't trust her statement about the time Phil set off on his run. She's protecting Montrayne."

Humouring him was one thing, but this really did deserve a protest.

"Do you know something I don't, sir, because I've not found any evidence at all pointing that way."

"Montrayne is a friend of the family, but she also works for him. This won't be the first time a workplace romance has ended up with a murder."

She stared at him without speaking and Morrissey knew she was not convinced. That was a nuisance, since he could really do with her support. This case was going to be difficult enough to prove without having Hayford dragging her feet. He knew that Montrayne was on more than nodding terms with the Chief Constable, which meant he had to tread carefully. Surprisingly, Montrayne hadn't mentioned the Chief Constable once during his several interviews. Most people wouldn't have hesitated to trade on their influence with higher authority. And then there was Montrayne's father to be wary of. Suddenly the penny dropped.

"Mayblin, you checked that mobile number that called Phil Simmons' house this morning. Just tell me again who that cell phone belonged to."

"It wasn't an individual, sir. It was registered to the DTLO in London."

Of course. The DTLO. It wasn't Simmons they were interested in. It was Montrayne.

"Mayblin. Time to stop gazing into space and get those fingers working. Look up the DTLO. Who's the permanent secretary, or whatever they call the head lad down there?"

It didn't take long, but Morrissey managed to get through another inch of pencil adding to the pile of splinters overflowing from his ash tray. The crystal bowl was never used for its original purpose these days as the whole of the new building was a smoke-free zone.

"Got it, sir." Mayblin paused long enough to give a significant look to Sergeant Hayford before he continued, "The *head lad* is called the Director General and for the past four years that has been Alistair John Graham Montrayne."

"Thought so. James .. .. Alistair .. .. Montrayne's father." He drew out every word of the name. "You're a genius, Mayblin."

Constable Mayblin took that as his due, but Jo Hayford was still unhappy.

"I admit it's slightly intriguing, but I don't see that it proves anything. And what is this DTLO? What do they do exactly?"

Mayblin answered that, hoping to impress her with his newfound knowledge.

"Government department that seems to sit somewhere between the Department of Trade and Industry, Defence and the Foreign Office. They keep an eye on foreign contracts. Make sure we don't sell arms to the wrong people... ... bribe foreign officials... ... that sort of thing."

Hayford ignored the eager-to-please look he gave her, and turned back to face Morrissey.

"So there could have been a perfectly innocent reason for someone from there to be phoning the sales director of a company with substantial overseas customers."

Thus she demonstrated her own newfound knowledge of Lichfield Tube, and Philip Simmons' role within the company. She couldn't have Morrissey thinking she hadn't done her homework.

"I'd accept that, Jo." Morrissey knew he had to win her over. "Except that they were phoning on a Saturday morning. Early. Why would they do that? It only makes sense if Montrayne senior was trying to warn Mrs Simmons what to say or not to say. Trouble was... ...he, or someone acting for him, got me instead, and had to end the call quickly. I won't be surprised if the DTLO finds a reason for asking to be kept informed about this investigation. You mark my words. Montrayne senior's behind it. He wants to make sure he can keep Montrayne junior one step ahead of us."

It was all beginning to fit, but he'd have to be so careful. James Montrayne must have phoned his father as soon as he'd contacted the police. He'd have to remember to check the phone records. Clearly Montrayne had powerful people who'd be more than ready to fight his corner unless the evidence against him was absolutely conclusive. Yes, he really did need Hayford's support on this.

"Look, Jo. Montrayne claims someone else was in the wood this morning, and that person attacked Simmons, but there was only one set of footprints by the lake, apart from Simmons running shoes, and they matched Montrayne's boots."

Hayford nodded. She knew this was true. There had been one or two other prints on different sections of the path, but they were faded and washed out, definitely not made that day.

Morrissey continued, "Montrayne said he was there to deal with rats that have been pestering the hens on Heighley Grange farm. Rick Childers said that the last time Montrayne did this, he worked close in around the chicken sheds. So why did he decide this time to shoot in the woods?"

"He did tell us that," replied Hayford. "He said he'd found rats using a run which looped around the side of the lake and led into the field with the new shed and enclosure. And it suited him to shoot in the wood because he wanted to try out his new rifle." According to Montrayne, his father had bought him a Theoben Eliminator 0.25 calibre FAC rated gun for his birthday. The same gun they had found him with that morning. It had a night vision scope and he simply wanted to check it out.

"You were in the woods today, Jo. Did you see any rats?"

"Thankfully, no," she admitted.

"And neither did anyone else. Not one. All day."

She felt her confidence beginning to waver. There was no evidence that anyone else was involved. And if no-one else did it, then it had to be Montrayne. Trouble was, there was no proof that he did. Pity there were no early morning walkers to witness what happened. Or were there?

"What about that tampon and tissues found in the bushes behind Montrayne's hide?"

They had been found by constables using metal detectors to try and locate a 0.177 airgun which could have fired the dart. It had been an old penny coin that got them scavenging in the leaves and, though no-one had thought the finds would be any use, the tampon and tissues had been bagged and labelled anyway. No need to waste time on analysis until they came up with someone to match them to.

"What about them?" replied Morrissey. "We also found used condoms, sweet wrappers, a baby's dummy, an odd shoe .. .."

She sighed, "I know. I know"

He continued, "We don't know who left it, or when. Would you change your tampon at night in a wood?"

Constable Mayblin looked up, interested.

"I wouldn't even be in a wood at night."

Morrissey grinned, and pointed a finger at her like a gun.

"Quite."

There was a short silence, broken eventually by Mayblin who thought it time someone took a bit more notice of him.

"There is something else, sir."

"Something else, Mayblin? Has your needle-sharp mind detected something I've missed?"

The mock horror in the DCI's tone was not lost on the constable so he felt encouraged to go on.

"Not exactly, sir. It was just a thought. James Montrayne was in the Royal Marines. I happen to know that they regularly go over to Belize on training exercises."

"How in hell's name do you happen to know that?"

"I thought about joining for a while, before I went to police college."

"OK, but I still don't see the relevance."

"Well, Belize is one of those places where curare comes from."

Morrissey stared at him, and then looked thoughtfully at Hayford, noting the expression of sheer disbelief on her face. Mayblin looked doubtfully at the pair of them.

"I only thought .. .. .. that is .. .. .. well, it seemed best to mention it."

Slowly shaking her head, Hayford finally spoke.

"You have seriously got to be kidding. I mean .. .. .. Curare for heaven's sake!"

Morrissey still looked thoughtful.

"I know, Jo. I know. A dart poisoned with curare. Sounds like something out of *The Avengers* doesn't it. Though I suspect you'd make a better Emma Peel than I would John Steed." He smiled ruefully for a moment, but then became serious. "Think about it though. If it was that dart which killed Simmons, it had to be loaded with something."

Sergeant Hayford knew that, implausible at it sounded, Constable Mayblin's idea would have to be checked out. She stood up and stretched.

"OK, constable. Your idea. You check it out. Find out if Montrayne ever served in Belize, or in fact anywhere in that part of the world."

She turned to Morrissey.

"I think we're stuck now, until we get the results of the post-mortem. Anything else you can think of, sir, that can't wait 'til tomorrow."

"Can't think of anything, Jo. But I do wonder what our boy's doing with himself right now."

Sergeant Hayford shrugged, but her tone of voice as she replied suggested she was still not unsympathetic towards Montrayne.

"After the day we've given him, I reckon he'll be doing just what I intend to do. Going straight home for a decent night's sleep."

Morrissey grinned. "Good job the smooth boyfriend's in London then."

Mayblin sighed. At least he could dream.

Eleven

Heighley Lane –9.15 pm

After James had made his phone calls, there was nothing much else to do but wait. I didn't like it. That call from the bogus social worker had scared me. I don't know whether he'd believed Rachel or not, but either way it didn't matter. They were thorough. They'd send someone to check out the farm anyway, just in case. And we were just sitting here while whoever they sent was getting closer by the minute. Even from central Birmingham, at this time in the evening, they could be here in less than an hour.

I told James we had to hurry, but all he did was smile and tell me not to worry.

"Everything's in hand, Lizzie," he said, but it didn't seem to me that anything was in hand. He didn't seem to realise what sort of people he was going to have to deal with, and deal with soon.

Then Cherry reappeared, and that reassured me a little. He was a big man, though not as big as James, young and fit, the sort of man who looked as though he knew how to take care of himself. As his SUV pulled into the yard, James went out to meet him and to fill him in on what we thought was happening. Their conversation took place out of earshot, but it appeared to me, as I looked through the kitchen window, that it was James who was in charge and Cherry who was receiving instructions. I couldn't quite work out their relationship, but found that I was beginning to believe in their confidence. More importantly than that, at the moment, it seemed as though they really were on my side.

I couldn't bear waiting any longer in the kitchen on my own. Rachel had taken Debbie off to get her ready for bed and, I think, to reassure her that everything was going to be OK. Abby had gone with them. Since James was obviously going to be busy, it had been decided that Abby should stay over for another night, in spite of the possibility of intruders appearing on the scene. Apparently, everyone had seemed confident that Cherry and his mates could take care of anything in that line. Chick had gone over to the accommodation block to talk to the young people there and to tell them to be sure to stay indoors for the rest of the evening.

I'd had enough of waiting so I went out into the yard.

James watched me come but didn't say anything to me as he was back on his cell phone, listening as some one fed him information. Floodlights were on in the yard, so everything could be clearly seen, and I wondered whether that was a good idea with uninvited guests likely to arrive very soon. I didn't have time to mention my concern because as soon as James had finished on his phone, a big, black Mitsubishi Warrior eased into the yard. I expected to see two big guys emerge, guys with height and width and bulging muscles, and quickly discovered I was only half right. The one who climbed out from the passenger side fit the bill exactly, but the driver was barely more than my height, slender and, even in the combat fatigues and boots, definitely female.

The sound of the Warrior's arrival had brought Chick to the door of the accommodation block. His chuckle, as he took in the scene, was gently reassuring.

"I see Sonia's come dressed for war," he said as he wandered over, giving the woman a friendly wave.

James didn't introduce the newcomers but, with no explanation, he told me to get in his car, a dark blue Jaguar XJ which fairly glistened under the yard's floodlights. Apart from wondering how he could afford it on a teacher's pay, I gave the car and its ambiance of luxury no other thought. I was too concerned about being, once again, in the grip of circumstances beyond my control. I wanted to argue but James was engrossed with Chick and Cherry, and the two newcomers, and it suddenly dawned on me that I either trusted him or I didn't.

So I got in the car. As I sank into the soft leather, I was momentarily distracted by the heaviness of the door as I pulled it shut. In the past three years, I had occasionally travelled in prestigious, luxury cars but none had felt quite like this one. It wasn't just the weight of the door that surprised me, but the sound it made as it thudded shut.

Then I forgot about it as I watched the others talking together, planning, giving and receiving instructions, and I resented the fact that I'd been excluded from it all. I found myself wondering if I ever really would be free of the power of others, free to choose my own course and follow it without constantly being made to feel afraid. Then I thought about Angie and what choosing my own course had done to her. I'd never meant for her to get hurt. Of course, I knew what happened to girls who ran away and got caught, but it had never occurred to me that they would punish Angie just because they couldn't get at me.

And I remembered that she was still in danger and that we were supposed to be doing something about it. I started to open the door of the Jag to urge James to hurry, but there was no need. Before the door was fully open, the group broke up and James hurried round to the driver's side of the car.

As the Jag pulled slowly round the farm buildings to reach the main drive in front of the house, I asked James where we were going.

"To see someone who can tell us where Angie is," he replied, and then braked sharply to avoid crushing a rabbit which had become temporarily transfixed by the car's headlights.

"OK," I said, deciding not to press for a more exact location as I watched the rabbit regain the power of movement and hop away into the darkness. "So tell me who those people are that we left back there. Where did they come from?"

James began to accelerate down the drive. This was not a rutted cart track but a proper tarmac surface, about half as wide again as the car itself, with passing places at intervals.

"Friends of mine," he said.

"Must be good friends," I suggested, "to turn out in a hurry at this time in the evening."

He made no reply and I didn't push it because we were approaching the end of the drive and I was perfectly happy to wait for him to make the turn before resuming my grilling.

Except that I didn't get the chance.

Because so many vehicles used the drive, general public as well as trade and farm vehicles, the entrance had been widened out to make access easier. As James drew up to the broad, white stop line that marked the point at which the drive merged into the lane, the Jag was suddenly flooded with bright, white light.

A truck was parked in the lane to the right of the entrance, and its lights caught the Jag sideways on. I knew it was a truck because of the arrangement of the lights. The headlights were high off the ground, much higher than the Jag's, but what really gave it away were the extras. It was hard to tell with so much wattage blasting me full in the face, but there seemed to be four of them, high intensity spot lights, presumably mounted on a bar across the front of the cab roof. And all their power was directed into the Jag's interior.

My head was turned to look across James and out of the Jag's side window straight at the lights. It was instinctive. I couldn't help it and it was only for couple of seconds, but straight away I knew it was a mistake. If the occupants of the truck had adopted this crude but effective way of checking who was in the car leaving the farm, I had just given them a first rate view.

"It's them," I whispered, my voice hoarse with fear.

I'd been on the run for about twenty-four hours. Just one day of freedom, and now it was over. I desperately wished that it wasn't, but what could we do? The yard was at the back of the farmhouse. The lane was at the front. The others up at the farm wouldn't even see what was happening.

"Hang on," said James, and swung the Jag out into the lane intending to pull round the truck and leave it facing in the wrong direction.

But the driver of the truck was ready for him and, before we were even half-way into the turn, the truck lurched to the right effectively blocking the lane.

James slammed on the brakes, pulled the selector into reverse, and we shot back into the farm entry. I wondered for a moment if he was going to reverse all the way back up to the farm, but he braked to a stop about twenty yards in from the lane.

I turned to look at him. My heart was racing and I could actually hear it in my ears above the purring of the Jag's 4.2 litre engine. James was looking straight ahead while he kept the car in reverse, his foot firmly on the brake.

"What are we waiting for?" I asked urgently, with some satisfaction that, at least outwardly, I was as calm as he was.

He didn't look at me, but his composure showed he was fully in control of himself.

"For them to make a mistake," he said quietly, "so brace yourself."

I expected the truck to pull forward into the drive, facing us to continue blinding us with those spot lights.

It didn't.

It moved forward, but only to stop in the entry, sideways on. It was illuminated in the Jag's lights, but there was no light directed at us. There was space to front and rear of the truck but not enough for us to get through. The only way we could go was back.

But we didn't.

"And there's the mistake," said James as two figures appeared in the Jag's lights.

It didn't look like a mistake to me. The men, clearly illuminated against the side of the truck, looked everything I didn't want them to be. One was tall and well-built and threateningly confident. The other was shorter, of slighter build, but he was if anything even more menacing when I realised who it was. And they were carrying guns.

The one on the left was turned very slightly sideways, and I could see why. He was holding a long gun up to his shoulder. Whether it was a shotgun or a rifle, I had no idea, but it was pointed straight at the Jag's windscreen. It fact, it seemed pointed straight at my head, though whether he could actually see me I had no way of knowing. I just hoped not as I slumped down low in my seat.

"It's OK, Lizzie," said James. "They can't hurt you."

"Oh, yes, they can," I said, in what sounded to me almost like a squeal. Then I took a breath and carried on in a slightly less panicked tone. "In case you hadn't noticed, those are guns they're pointing at us. I don't know about the guy on the left. I've never seen him before. But I can tell you the one on the right will be carrying an HK45, and I know for a fact that he knows how to use it."

The guy on the right was indeed holding a pistol in front of him in a two-handed grip. In the glare of the Jag's lights his face looked sallow, not the usual olive tan, but I knew there was no mistake. This was Satish, the guy who I was sure had helped to toss Angie off the motorway bridge.

James kept his foot firmly on the brake and didn't take his eyes off Satish and his mate, but he reached out with his left hand and patted me lightly on the knee. It was oddly reassuring, but not nearly as much as his next words.

"You're quite safe, Lizzie. All the windows are laminated borosilicate, and if any of their bullets get through I'm going to be asking Jaguar for a refund."

I began to sit up again as the implication of his words sank in.

"You mean they're bulletproof?" I asked.

"The whole car is bulletproof. Bulletproof, bombproof, gasproof, and definitely half-witted thug proof. I bought it... ... ..." He stopped suddenly. "Here they come. Hang on!"

And on the words, he touched the accelerator, and the big car eased backward.

Satish and his mate began to fire as they walked steadily towards us.

James applied more power and the car surged back. Then, just as suddenly he slammed on the brakes, rammed the selector from reverse into drive, and floored the accelerator.

Outside was confusion. There were flashes and bangs, lots of them, bright even in the car lights, and in rapid succession. The long gun was obviously some sort of automatic rifle and we were approaching it fast. I couldn't help shrinking a little in my seat, but James wasn't going to be able to get his refund. Nothing penetrated the car's cabin.

And then we were on them and the rifle flashes abruptly swung high and then to the right as the big man tried to leap out of the way of 2780 Kg of growling metal. I don't know whether we hit him, and I couldn't see what happened to Satish but then we were stopped. The side of the truck gleamed black only inches in front of the Jag's radiator.

James looked at me. "Are you OK?"

I nodded. "Where are they?"

James looked in his side mirrors. There was a certain amount of light reflecting back off the shiny surface of the truck. Not much but apparently it was enough.

"Can't be sure," he said, "but I think they're both down. One your side, one mine."

He flicked the selector into reverse and we eased slowly back up the drive until eventually two figures appeared in our lights. The big man was on the grass to the left of the drive. He wasn't moving. Satish was off to the right, half on the tarmac, half on the grass. He too was still.

We sat and watched them, waiting for any sign of movement. We were still waiting when lights flashed into the car from behind. James glanced up in his rear view mirror while I swung round in my seat to look over my shoulder. Surely there couldn't be more of them behind us.

But, no, there weren't. It was the Warrior, silhouetted against the lights of the farm, presumably crammed with Cherry and the others, attracted by the sound of gunfire.

"Go and meet them," said James. "Tell them what happened."

"What will you do?" I asked as I opened my door.

"Make sure these two are harmless," he replied. "My friends are good, but they're all unarmed."

And I watched him march into the lights of the Jag, now made brighter by the addition of the array of lights on the front of the Warrior. I held up my hand to stop them, and found that James was right and wrong at the same time.

Three people got out leaving the driver, who later turned out to be Chick, behind the wheel. He was right because they were good. They didn't bunch but fanned out, two to one side, one to the other, away from the truck and out of its lights. He was wrong because they all seemed to be carrying shotguns.

I shouted that it was all over and we were OK, but they held their position until James told them it was safe to come in. At which point Chick, who had supplied the shotguns but was himself unarmed, climbed out of the Warrior and came to join us.

We gathered around the two bodies, first the big guy, then Satish. There was James and I, Cherry and the woman Chick called Sonia, the other guy whose name I didn't know, and finally Chick himself looking very pale in the flood of light.

The big guy had been carrying some sort of automatic rifle and it now lay several feet away where James had kicked it out of reach. Not that he needed to. The guy was dead. To stop visitors to the farm off-roading onto the field, the drive was lined with boulders at about five metre intervals. It was just the big guy's bad luck that when he jumped out of the way of the car, he chose to do it right on top of one of these boulders. As he'd landed heavily on his back, the rock had caught him behind his head and broken his neck. Satish was just as dead, his HK lying where James had kicked it, but neither car nor boulder was responsible. Two bright red spots on the front of his jacket, and another much larger one on his right cheek, showed where the last few shots from the rifle had found their mark.

By rights, neither guy should be dead. It was just their bad luck that things turned out the way they did, but none of us felt any sorrow for them, except maybe Chick whose compassion was greater than anything I'd ever come across before.

But as far as I was concerned, they had got what they deserved. Especially Satish, and not just for Angie, but for all those other girls he'd hurt in the few years I'd known him.

"So what do we do now, Boss?" asked Cherry.

"Turn all the lights off, now," he replied quickly, and in seconds the truck, the Warrior and the Jag were in darkness.

"Chick," he said, resting his hand on the farmer's shoulder. "We'll talk about this later, but right now I need your help."

Chick brushed a hand briefly across his eyes and sighed.

"What?" was all he said.

"Those fireworks we bought for the barn open-day, but never used because of the thunder-storms. Go and start setting them off now. If anyone heard those shots, we need them to think it was just fireworks. Can you do that?"

Chick nodded, and turned away. He obviously realised the need for speed.

James turned back to Cherry.

"Lizzie and I have still got to do what we can for Angie, so I need you to stay here with Abby."

"OK, Boss. Will do."

"Thanks," said James. "I appreciate it."

Then he turned around to look at the two bodies, and then the truck in the lane.

"Sonia," he said finally. "This is going above and beyond, and I've no right to ask it, but... ... ..."

"It's OK, Boss. They had it coming, so let's just see about getting the mess cleared up."

I was amazed at how readily they all went along with him. These were, I thought, law-abiding people. We had dead bodies on the ground and guns had been fired, but no-one seemed to have any notion that this was something the police might like to know about.

Not that I minded. I was just surprised.

"What about dumping them up in the Peak?" suggested the guy whose name I didn't know.

It seemed reasonable. I'd been brought up in Ashbourne, just south of Derbyshire's Peak District, so I knew there were some quite remote areas up there.

"I don't know, Sam," replied James. "It could work, but you get lots of walkers up there, and they don't always stay on the main tracks."

There was silence for a moment. We were all thinking of alternatives. I had one, but I didn't like to suggest it in front of people who seemed far more competent than I was. There was some shuffling of feet as they all looked around in the darkness trying to come up with an idea.

Still no-one spoke, so I decided to give my idea a try.

"James," I said quietly. "Are you really not going to call the police?"

I was shivering, and he saw it and put a hand on my shoulder.

"Not a good idea, I'm afraid. In this country, when a victim of crime defends himself he's often the one who ends up in jail while lawyers scream about the human rights of the villain. No, we'll keep this little bit of mayhem to ourselves."

His hand was reassuring and I moved in a little closer and spoke quietly. "In that case, I think I know of a place you can use."

I didn't really want the others to hear just in case my suggestion was a total non-starter, and for another reason as well, but of course as soon as I spoke they all drew closer to make sure they could hear.

"What is it?" asked James, when nervousness held me back from continuing.

"Well," I said, "they came from Birmingham, so why don't we send them back there? I know this old warehouse, you see... ..."

I paused, not sure whether they were taking me seriously.

"Go on, Lizzie," said James, encouragingly. "Where is it?"

I told him.

"Is it empty?"

"Completely," I said. "It's due to be pulled down, but there's been some sort of hold up in the planning committee, so I don't think it's going to happen for at least another couple of months."

"How do you know about it?"

This was the bit I didn't want the others to hear, but they were so close there was no way of avoiding it. James needed to know how I knew, so he could be sure that place was safe. I ignored them and spoke directly to him.

"There was a councillor, on the committee, and he liked to have... ... an escort... ... every now and then. That was usually me. Sometimes he'd take me to a restaurant, sometimes not, but it always ended the same way. Then after he'd done it, which usually took about two seconds... ... well, he'd just like to lie there and boast about plans he'd forced through committee, and others he'd blocked... ... He was a bit pathetic really. I think he knew he wasn't much use in bed, so he needed to be able to show off about other stuff. I didn't care. He always paid up front, and he was no trouble really. There was never any funny stuff... ... It was the last time I saw him that he told me all about this warehouse."

There was no sound from the others but, in the darkness, I could feel their eyes boring into me. I felt cheapened by my admission of the life I'd led, to these people I didn't know, and their condemnation weighed heavily on me. I was probably imagining it, but then it seemed as though James felt it too. I was standing very close to him and suddenly I felt his grip on my shoulder tighten as he drew me in those last few inches in a quick hug. His voice, quiet in my ear, said, "Well done, Lizzie. You're turning out to be something really special."

It was good to know that at least one of them didn't despise me, but it was more than that. It was safe and reassuring, like when my dad picked me up and cuddled me when some big girls at the Jamestown school had been bullying me.

My dad.

How different things would have been if he hadn't died.

My eyes began to well up, but then James took his arm away and asked, "I assume this warehouse is locked? And is there a fence?"

I drew back, and thought about what I'd been told.

"No," I said. "No fence, I'm sure. That was going to be a problem with demolition. It sides right up to the road so they're going to have to close the road to pull it down. The windows are boarded over with metal sheets and the doors... ... they're big ones for trucks to get in and out... ... they're padlocked. It's all to keep squatters out."

They all thought for a moment and then Sam said, "Sounds like it could do the trick, Boss."

And so, it was agreed. Cherry walked back up to the farm after Chick leaving the Warrior for Sonia. The bodies and their weapons were placed carefully in the truck, which turned out to be some sort of Dodge 4x4. It would have been easier to put them in the open bed at the rear, but it was decided that was a bit risky, even with them covered over, so they were eased into the rear seats of the cabin and held in place with the seat belts.

After getting a few more directions from me, and consulting a Birmingham A-Z which Sonia found in the glove box of the Dodge, she and Sam were ready to set off. James moved the Jag out of the way by pulling forward into the wide entry to the drive, and Sam drove the Warrior out to follow Sonia in the Dodge. Once the bodies in the truck had been discretely tucked away in the warehouse, and the bodies artistically arrayed to suggest some kind of falling out among villains, Sam would drive Sonia home. It didn't really seem necessary for them to come back to the farm.

As we leant against the Jag and watched their tail lights fade away into the dark, I asked James about something which had begun to puzzle me.

"These friends of yours," I said. "Why are they so willing to stick their necks out like this? I mean… … guns, dead bodies… … It's not your usual help-a-mate-out stuff."

"No, it isn't," he said. "But it's a long story, back when we were serving in the Balkans. Let's just say, they owe me."

Twelve

The Dower House – 9.15 pm

The darkness seemed intensified by the brilliant blue-white beams of the Jaguar's headlights as they searched out the course of the narrow country lane. Occasionally, the lights of an on-coming vehicle caused stars to shoot and sparkle and glisten on my side of the windscreen. No bullets had penetrated, but it didn't mean that they hadn't left their mark. Apart from some minor scratches, my side of the screen was clear, but on James's side there were three blossoming flowers up in the top corner. I shivered when I thought that in any other car, he would probably have been dead, but then I realised that in any other car James would not have just sat there waiting for them to come.

High hedges on both sides created a tunnel-like effect accentuated by the frequent overhanging trees. With the overcast sky eliminating moon and stars, I found I very quickly lost all sense of direction.

As I sat in the front passenger seat, trying to ignore the sparkles in front of me, and oblivious to the luxurious comfort of the soft leather, I worried like hell how all this was going to end.

The car braked sharply as James avoided flattening a fox that had inadvertently run out into the Jag's headlights. The jolt shook me out of my gloomy thoughts and I decided it was time I got some answers.

"Where exactly are we going?"

"To my house, to meet some more friends of mine. About another ten minutes."

"These friends of yours. I mean… … who are they? That lot back at the farm didn't look much like teachers."

He smiled, a little grimly I thought.

"They're not."

He seemed disinclined to offer any more so I tried to nudge things along a bit.

"So? Who are they? And how come you can just pick up the phone and they come running?"

There was another long pause, and I wondered whether he wasn't going to tell me because he didn't trust me. I couldn't blame him. He'd only known me a few hours. Then, after a long sigh and another avoidance manoeuvre, this time for a rabbit, he began talking.

"They work for a firm of security consultants. Cherry's ex Royal Marines, and the best close protection guy they have. Samson usually works .. .. .."

He broke off in response to my snort of stifled laughter.

"Yeah, I know. His name's Sam, but all the other squaddies called him Samson and it stuck. You can see why. Anyway, he usually works hostage rescue, but he's just back from a job in the Ukraine and he's taking a few days annual leave. Sonia runs the corporate security office, and when she's not doing that, she's a platoon commander in the Territorial Army."

In the gloom of the car's interior, I don't know whether he'd noticed the way my mouth hung open, but he glanced across and smiled.

"Sonia was giving a talk to the kids in the local Army Cadets when she got the call. Samson picked her up on the way... ... Now that's a thought... ... I hope she's got something to change into. It wouldn't do for her to go breaking into that warehouse while in uniform."

For about a mile, I could think of nothing to say. It was definitely comforting to have such competent people on my side. But then the incongruity of it all hit me again.

"But you're a teacher. What was that about serving in the Balkans? How come you know these people? And how can you afford them? Come to think of it, how can you afford this car? It must have cost a mint."

His fingers drummed lightly on the steering wheel, whether in exasperation or annoyance, I couldn't tell.

"Look, Lizzie. There's a lot I don't know about you, and there's a lot you don't know about me. If it's so important to you, we can sort all that out later but, for the moment, let's just focus on the job in hand. Two men died tonight, and your friend could be next, so let's just keep our minds on the important stuff. OK? ... ... Oh, and if the money bothers you so much, I inherited it from my godmother along with this house."

I shut up. His tone made it clear that he'd had enough of my questions. Then it suddenly dawned on me that he'd spent the whole day being grilled by the police over the death of his friend. Now, when he should be coming home to put his feet up, he was involving himself in something that was already turning out to be far nastier than he could have expected. So, yes, he could probably do without my stupid inquisition.

The car slowed and, amongst the trees, I saw an entrance coming up on the left. A wide entrance with massive stone pillars, set well back from the road. From either pillar a high brick wall curved away towards the road. The wall continued to edge the road for some distance to either side of the entrance, but I hadn't noticed it as we approached, probably because so many of the trees draped their branches over the top. As we swung in, I saw James press a button on the remote clipped to the visor, and an impressive pair of wrought iron gates parted to let us through. Gravel crunched under the tyres and I could see the drive ahead curving round to the right. A moment later, as we rounded the bend, the trees to the right peeled away to reveal an expanse of open lawn which glistened blue-green in the dipped headlights.

It wasn't a house. It was more like the sort of place you paid money to go and visit at the weekend. Don't get me wrong. It wasn't Chatsworth or Blenheim, but it was definitely a mansion, Georgian probably, built of brick. Not that I knew much about such things, but I seemed to associate those rectangular windows divided into smaller white-edged panes with being Georgian. Then there was the entrance. A pair of circular, white, fluted columns at either side of a large solid-looking white door which was flanked by more small white edged panes, and all topped by a triangular pediment, white again. This was all very easy to see, as the whole of the front of the house was lit by three flood lights set in the edge of the lawn. I'd no idea who his godmother had been, but she certainly hadn't lacked juice.

We drove past the front of the house following the drive round to the left, finally parking alongside a blue VW Passat, in front of what looked like stables, but were probably now garages. The rear of the house was almost as impressive as the front. More floodlights had come on activated, I assumed, by the car's approach. Or maybe they had been switched on by one of the two men who came out of the stable block to meet us.

James got out of the Jag and shook hands with the two new guys. He hadn't told me what I should do, but getting out seemed to be the thing, so I opened my door and stood hesitantly leaning on it, one arm on the top of the door, the other resting on the Jag's roof. James turned and beckoned me over to join them.

"Lizzie, meet John and Nat." The two men nodded but didn't reach out to shake hands. They were too busy taking in the state of the Jag's glass and paintwork.

"Hit a hail storm, did you, Boss," said John, the one who'd nodded first.

He was of medium height, bulky around the shoulders, and dressed in a dark suit and tie. Nat was taller, slimmer and more casually dressed in jeans and black leather jacket. He stared at the car and said nothing.

"Something like that," said James. "Just give me a minute and I'll fill you in."

He looked at me and smiled as he asked, "Would you like their biographies, or shall we get right down to it?"

I ignored him, and he turned away and led us through the still open door into the stable block. We were in a wide hallway with a door off to either side and a flight of stairs directly ahead. James led us straight up the stairs and into a large room which ran from front to back of the building and was furnished as a kind of sitting room come office, with the stairs coming up in the centre. To one side was a desk with a couple of office chairs, and to the other a settee, easy chairs and a coffee table. Behind the desk, mounted on the wall was a row of four large flat TV screens, each one giving different views of the house and gardens. As I looked at them, the view on all four changed, demonstrating that there were more than four cameras keeping watch over this property.

Seated at the desk, with his back to us, was yet another man I'd never seen before. He was working at a computer and I guessed he was responsible for the change on the TV screens because a few fast key strokes caused the views to change again. One of the views was replicated on his computer screen and he zoomed in to examine something more closely, before turning round to acknowledge our presence.

I stared at him. I couldn't help it. The right side of his face was badly scarred, the pink and puckered skin contrasting so strangely with the left side where a dark tan clearly showed Asian or Middle-Eastern genes. He would have been good looking once, and I wondered briefly how it must feel to have that confidence in your appearance savagely ripped away.

He appeared not to notice my stare, and looked at James who was settling into one of the easy chairs.

"Evening, Boss. Thought you'd have had enough excitement for one day. What's up then?"

"Tell you in a minute. Have the police been back again?"

"Nah. Not since that delectable sergeant carted you away earlier."

"OK, fine. Now just listen in, Surjit, and you'll soon know as much as we do."

As he spoke, James gestured for me to take the other easy chair as John and Nat settled on the settee. They both looked relaxed and comfortable, as though they were completely confident that whatever they were called upon to do that evening, they were more than capable of dealing with it. Wishing I felt the same, I sat, confident only of being totally out of place.

It took James only a few minutes to provide details of the situation as far as we understood it. He was clearly no stranger to briefing subordinates. Is that what being a teacher does for you? His narration was clear and succinct. The other three listened carefully, nodding a few times, occasionally raising an eyebrow, but never interrupting until James explained what Samson and Sonia were currently doing, and why.

"Cripes, Boss!" exclaimed John. "Andy's going to be shitting bricks when he knows we've been playing with corpses."

I'd no idea who Andy was, and no-one explained.

"I'll sort him out tomorrow," said James. "Don't worry about it."

"If you say so," replied John, in a tone which suggested that he wasn't going to stop worrying just yet.

James looked across to Surjit and asked, "Have we heard from Rod?"

"Just before you arrived. He rang a guy on the local paper who pretty much confirmed what you just told us. He said you'd probably want to know which hospital, and it cost him a bucket full of favours to find out. They took her to Heartlands. There's an eight-bed observation ward in A & E. Last he heard she was in one of those beds. She's stable, and there's a uniformed cop keeping an eye on her."

"Thanks," said James before turning to the rest of us. "OK. Suggestions anyone."

I sat quiet, hoping that no-one would ask the obvious. Inevitably, someone did. Nat sat forward on the edge of the settee and asked, "Look, if we know why that girl was tipped off the bridge, and we know who was responsible, and we think they might try again, why don't we just let the cops know and let them deal with it?"

James looked at me, and I thought he was waiting for me to answer but, before I could even begin to think of a sensible reason, he held up his right hand and started ticking off points with his fingers.

"One. I'm involved now. They've already made it personal by coming after Lizzie at the farm.

"Two. The police are already looking at me for Phil Simmons death – I'll tell you more about that later – so giving them another two dead bodies is not going to simplify things.

"Three. Apart from Lizzie, none of us have any personal knowledge of the people behind all this, or what they're involved in.

"Four. Lizzie is not going to talk to the police, or anyone else who would require her to give an address. Once she does that, there's a chance she could be found and next time she might not be as lucky as she was tonight.

"Five. We could phone in the information anonymously but there's no guarantee the police would take it seriously enough to act on it in time to protect Angie."

He stopped, thumb and all four fingers extended. We all waited to see if there was going to be a six. There was.

"Six. Angie is not a villain. She's a victim, so a continued police guard is highly unlikely. We know one of the guys who attacked her is probably one of our corpses but there's nothing to stop the ones who want Angie dead from sending someone else after her."

Nat nodded slowly. "So what you're really saying, Boss, is that whether we tell the police or not, Angie could still be dead by morning if we don't do something."

"You've got it," said James.

John seemed reluctant to speak, but he was looking at me intently, frowning hard. I stared back, wondering what he was thinking, and whether it even mattered. He didn't break off eye contact, but his words, when they came, were addressed to James.

"I don't like it, Boss."

Boss? Everyone kept calling him *Boss* as though he was some gangland chief. Then I remembered a movie I'd seen about a group of British soldiers on some kind of special mission. They kept referring to their commander as *Boss.* Were these two going to turn out to be former soldiers as well?

James didn't seem particularly worried by the comment. He just asked, "What don't you like, John?"

"Seems to me, we're getting dragged into something we don't fully understand, and all on the strength of an intuitive guess by someone of ... ..." He struggled for a moment, searching for the right words. Then he found them, not apparently caring what effect they might have on me. "Let's be clear about it, someone of rather dubious background, who's on the run from some even more dubious characters, who's already landed you in a load of shit, and who you've only known a few hours."

I wasn't sure whether he didn't like me, or just didn't trust me, or both. Not that it mattered. He was, after all, perfectly correct. Nat was looking at John and, from his expression, I guessed he pretty much agreed with what was said. And why not? They didn't know me, and I didn't exactly have a pillar-of-the-community reputation to back me up. I tried to think of some way of convincing them that Angie and I were worth helping, but couldn't come up with anything that didn't sound like begging. And what little bit of pride I had left wouldn't let me do that.

James stood and walked slowly over to the window which overlooked the yard between the stables and the house. It was still brightly lit. We all watched him. Nobody spoke. We all seemed to know he needed time to think. He was an impressive figure, standing there silhouetted against the light and I suddenly realised that, no matter what the others thought of me, I wanted him to trust me, just as I was beginning to trust him.

When he finally spoke, I knew it wasn't going to happen.

"You're absolutely right. None of us know Lizzie and it does seem unreasonable to put so much trust in her judgement. Whatever she was doing in Birmingham, and I know she hasn't been very clear about this, I don't think we're in any doubt it was pretty unsavoury."

I felt betrayed. He'd given me hope and now he was snatching it back. So much for all that praying! I just wanted to get up and leave, to go anywhere that would take me away from the judgement I imagined I saw in those dark eyes.

But as he spoke those last words, he looked directly at me and held my gaze as he continued, "But, you see, the trouble with me is that I have this tendency to be incredibly unreasonable. And, unlike any of you, I was there when Lizzie heard the news report. I saw the look on her face. I'm as sure as I can be that, true or not, Lizzie believes every word of the story she told me. So I'm willing to trust her on that."

He smiled as he saw the effect his words were having on me.

"And I think the fact that those two characters turned up at the farm shows that her fears are real... ... And there's something else you need to bear in mind. I knew Angie when she stayed at Heighley Grange Farm. She played with my Abby. She may have been a bit mixed up, but basically she was a good kid. If this girl in the hospital is her, and I'm not willing to take the chance that it isn't, then I'm certainly going to do what I can to help her."

I felt moisture welling up in my eyes, and my vision was becoming blurred. I blinked hard, not wanting to be seen wiping away tears. At the very moment when I knew exactly what I wanted to say, to thank him, I just couldn't get the words out. He didn't seem to mind, since he was no longer looking at me.

"OK, lads. You work for the company, for Andy, not directly for me. You're free to turn down any job you don't like. But I'm going to do this, and I have to say it's going to be a heck of a lot easier if you're with me. I'm going over to the house. You can have five minutes to talk it over. Lizzie, you come with me."

I was barely half out of my chair in response to this brusque command when I heard John speak again.

"No need for that, Boss. If Samson and Sonia are on board, then I guess we're in as well."

Thirteen

Sutton Coldfield – 10.00pm

It was after midnight by the time we had left the cars in the Heartlands Hospital car park in the Bordesley Green area of Birmingham, a few miles east of the city centre. Even though the Jaguar was driveable, and solid as a tank, James had decided that it would be safest to leave it tucked away out of sight at the Dower House.

"Best not to draw attention to ourselves," he'd said, so I had wondered what kind of unremarkable vehicle he planned to use. The VW maybe?

No. When it was time to leave, James drove the Jaguar forwards through the garage doors to the left of the stable entrance, minimising the possibility of curious eyes noticing the shot damage to the front. I wasn't sure what the vehicle was that he parked alongside. The interior lights of the garage were on so I could see clearly enough, but I just didn't recognise it. Even when he drove it out into the yard, I had no other impression than that it was big, and sleek, and fast. The badge on the front looked like some kind of trident but it meant nothing to me so, in making my way to the passenger door I went around the rear of the car looking for a name, make, or model. There it was in silver letters mounted on the dark, emerald-green gloss of the rear. Maserati.

So much for unremarkable.

In honour of our visit to the hospital, James had changed out of his camouflage fatigues, and was now wearing a dark-blue pinstripe suit which had to have been tailor-made. Even I could tell that those shoulders would never have fitted into a suit straight off the peg. I was still wearing the same clothes I'd put on after my midday shower. I felt I'd been wearing them for days.

Once we were on our way, I asked James in a part curious, part joking kind of way, if the Maserati was bulletproof as well.

He smiled as he replied, "Will it need to be, Lizzie?"

I shrugged, not knowing whether it was a serious question.

"Well, it isn't," he said. "The Jag and Cherry's Jeep both are since Abby always travels with one or other of us. This used to be my Godmother's car. Actually she was my great-aunt, and it came to me when she died… … It's a long story. I'll fill you in another time."

Now I was really curious, and not only about his rich old Godmother come great-aunt. Why did Abby need to be driven around in a bulletproof car? Sensing that James had told me as much as he wanted to for the time being, I reined in my curiosity.

On the way down to Birmingham we had made a detour to a small private hospital on the outskirts of Sutton Coldfield north of the city. A large floodlit sign at the turning off the main road welcomed us to the Aullton Foundation Hospital. We were obviously expected, even that late in the evening, since someone stepped out of the front entrance as we drew up, and climbed into the rear seat of the Maserati. I turned to look at him as we moved off immediately, and saw his face softly illuminated by the driveway lights. I put him in his early forties, though in that light I could easily have been wrong. But I was not wrong about the expression on his face. If I misread the tiredness in the eyes and the worry lines across his forehead, the downward turn of the mouth was a dead giveaway. Dangling from his neck on a long chain was some sort of photo ID, and lying on the seat beside his briefcase was a stethoscope. This was not a happy doctor.

James greeted him as we moved off. "I really appreciate you doing this, Barrie."

"I might feel better about it, if I knew what it was I was supposed to be doing."

As they were speaking, I was still looking towards the rear so I noticed John's Passat take up station behind us again. Just as I obeyed the twinge in my neck which told me it was time to turn round and face the front, a new pair of headlights was turned on somewhere ahead and to the left. As we cruised slowly past the side turn, a large, square-bodied yellow and white ambulance eased out behind us to become the filling in the Maserati-Passat sandwich. I glanced at James, but he was concentrating on making the right turn out of the hospital grounds onto the road which would lead us back over the M6 Toll to the A38. That accomplished, he put his foot down and the ambulance and Passat accelerated to keep pace. He spoke without taking his eyes from the road ahead.

"There's not much more I can tell you, Barrie. The girl's at Heartlands and, as far as we know, is conscious and stable. We don't know just how serious her injuries are but, if at all possible, we're going to have to move her tonight. We're going to need your judgement on that."

"James, this is crazy. I can't just waltz into Heartlands and start interfering with her treatment. She's not my patient."

"Yes, she is. As of just over an hour ago, when the full cost of 28 days residential care in her name was transferred to the Aullton Foundation's patients account."

My head jerked round and I'm sure my mouth fell open. I couldn't help it. This was the first I'd heard of any such payment. And then the penny dropped. Just over an hour ago, James had been tapping away on Surjit's computer for about ten minutes. I couldn't see what he was doing, and I hadn't really been interested, other than wishing he'd hurry up so that we could leave to find Angie. How much did 28 days residential care cost in a private hospital? And who was going to pay for it? No way could Angie or I come close to affording it. Before I could get my tongue in gear to voice these important questions, Barrie came back at James.

"So what is it I'm supposed to be treating her for?"

"Apart from having fallen off a bridge, I expect you'll find various STDs, possibly with complications. Drug abuse, and the trauma of prolonged sexual abuse. Is that enough to be going on with?"

James's diagnosis was right on the nail, though how he could have known that, I couldn't imagine. He hadn't asked me and I hadn't told him. I glanced over my shoulder to see how Barrie was taking it. In the gloom, I couldn't see much of his expression but I could tell that his face was now turned towards me and not the back of James's neck as it had been before. He was quiet, thinking, no doubt wondering whether I was suffering the same problems. I didn't turn away. I just waited for him to speak.

"STDs." He said it slowly, his face still turned towards me, with more than a hint of weary sadness in his tone. "What in particular?"

James glanced up to the rear-view mirror, but then looked ahead without speaking. I assumed this was a question for me to answer, but I hesitated. Somehow, I felt as though I was letting Angie down by talking about her medical problems. These weren't the injuries that had landed her in hospital. This was her life. What I said would cause Barrie to form an opinion of her as a person, an estimate of her character, a judgement of her worth.

"He needs to know, Lizzie."

James voice jolted me, but he was right. To get Angie to safety, Barrie had to know. And to hell with his opinion. I took a breath and got on with it.

"Gonorrhoea. She's had it before, and now she thinks it's back. But this time, it's worse. She's been getting some bad back pain. Oh, and a lot of stomach ache. She was thinking maybe it was all because she had Chlamydia at the same time. I told her to go back to the clinic, but I don't think she's been."

I saw slight movement as Barrie nodded.

"Hmm. Sounds like there could be pelvic inflammatory disease. Enforced prostitution?"

He said it as a question, but I sensed he didn't really need an answer. I was glad he said "enforced". Somehow, it seemed to absolve Angie from blame.

"And .. .. .. er .. .. .. HIV?"

His question hung in the air, heavy, loaded about equally with resignation and compassion. It was as though he was commenting on the inevitability of her condition; as though he had asked, "What else can you expect?"

"No!"

I flung it at him, violently, defiantly, staring him down. But he wasn't impressed, and in the end it was me who looked away.

"You're sure?"

His voice was quiet but firm. Persistent. I knew he wasn't going to let go. I assumed long experience had taught him how to cope with uppity clients. So I came clean.

"She was clear about two months ago. That's when she had her last test." I paused before adding, "I don't know what might have happened since."

"O..K.."

He drew out the syllables, letting me wonder if what I had said was somehow really important. It actually made me wish I could tell him more. And then I realised I could.

"Drugs?" His tone was soft; gently probing. I tried to think.

"Speed mostly."

"Mostly?"

"She tried Ice a couple of times that I know of. But mostly she used pills. No crack; no heroin. I know that for certain. I worked my ass off to keep her away from that stuff."

"You don't use it yourself?"

I hesitated. This wasn't supposed to be about me. I decided I'd had enough of answering questions.

"Honey," I said sweetly, "if you want me to give you a good time, it's so much better if I'm clean than if I'm wasted."

I felt the back of James's hand tap gently against my right thigh.

"Don't tease him, Lizzie. There's no point. You won't shock him."

It was the lightest of touches and I wasn't sure James even realised he'd done it. It was so natural to him. I remembered how he had been with Abby, and I could easily imagine him tapping her in that same kind of easy intimacy to draw attention to the words being spoken. It was the sort of thing my dad would have done. Father to daughter. I felt tears in my eyes as I considered what my dad would have thought if he knew all the things I'd been reduced to doing these last few years. Would he still have loved me? I clasped my hands tightly in my lap as I stared forward through the windscreen, holding the tears in check, seeing nothing. And then it hit me. James did know. Not all the details, but he knew the kind of life I'd been leading. And still that gentle tap, as if I was

Abby. As if I was his daughter. The tears flowed now and I reached up to brush them away with the back of my hand.

I remembered Barrie's question and was just about to turn to reply when I heard a grunt from the back, followed by, "Should I take that as a *No?*"

I nodded but said nothing and with that he seemed to have run out of questions. I continued to stare ahead watching the lights of oncoming traffic, and listening to the hum of the Maserati's powerful engine. I can't remember just what I thought about during the thirty minutes it took to reach Heartlands Hospital. My mind was racing, but the thoughts were all jumbled and confused. I suppose, underlying it all was fear, because I had absolutely no idea what was going to happen next. In the next few minutes? The next day? Next week? Next year?

On arrival, we headed for the car park with the Passat following, while the ambulance peeled off into the official waiting area. Once we had parked, I got out. I had sat still for long enough. There were lights on tall poles illuminating the car park, so everything was clear as I looked around trying to make out the way to the main entrance.

I saw it, and straight away I knew we were in trouble.

Fourteen

Birmingham Heartlands Hospital – 10.55 pm

The car was a Vauxhall Vectra, at that distance completely unremarkable since I couldn't see the badges that marked it as a VXR 2.8 V6 Turbo. But I could see the glint of bare metal in the vertical dent almost dead centre of the rear bumper and boot lid where a truck had reversed into Laddy's pride and joy only three days before. It had happened in the parking lot across the street from the massage parlour and I had seen every detail of the incident. His real name was Ladislav something or other, but we always called him Laddy, and he was so proud of his new toy. He had repeated it's name so many times, on every visit to the parlour, that it was etched on my brain; *VXR 2.8 V6 Turbo*. He boasted that the turbo was almost as powerful as his own supercharged organ, but I had thankfully never had opportunity to find out. The power of either, that is.

It had been early in the morning, just as the sun was coming up, and Laddy was sitting in the car waiting to come over to collect the night's takings. The truck was a plain white van, just making an early delivery to the run-down newsagents, one of several similarly dilapidated shops, which opened onto the parking lot. I was watching for Laddy since it was my job to count the money and have it ready for him with a full list of the night's transactions. I saw the driver get into the van and continued to watch as it swung round in reverse to get a good angle for driving out of the lot. I didn't hear a bang, but I did see the Vectra jolt slightly as the van hit, and I waited for the truck-driver to discover that this was to be the worst, and possibly last, day of his life.

Laddy had got out very slowly and walked to the rear of the Vectra, his right hand gliding along the roof as though stroking it reassuringly. He looked at the damage, and then turned to face the driver who had climbed out of the van instead of doing the sensible thing and driving off to the nearest police station as though all the demons in hell were after him. He spread his hands and shrugged his shoulders as though to apologise for his carelessness, which was exactly the wrong thing to do as his mid-section was left totally exposed to the vicious short-arm jab which Laddy landed right below the sternum. I almost thought I heard the whoosh of expelled air as the driver doubled over, and then the lesson began. I'd never seen Laddy in action before, but I'd heard people talking about him, and resolved long ago never to let myself get into the position of needing one of his lessons. He never lost his temper. Every kick, every punch, every jab and every chop was delivered with careful precision. No-one ever forgot one of his lessons, and only very, very rarely did anyone need to be taught twice.

When the lesson was over, Laddy bent down and grabbed the driver's hair, lifting his face inches off the concrete. Then he leaned close, and seemed to whisper in the driver's ear. Whether the poor guy was in any condition to understand or even hear what was said didn't seem to matter. This was the last part of Laddy's lesson. The warning. *Don't say a word to a soul, if you don't want this to happen again, because next time it won't be just you.*

Then Laddy came across to collect the takings, just as he always did, making no mention of what had happened only minutes before across the street. Needless to say, I hadn't mentioned it either. He just glanced at the figures on the sheet I gave him, and joked about the girls having had a busy night. I smiled. He said he must come and try me out sometime, and then he had left. I watched him cross the road, climb into his VXR 2.8 V6 Turbo and drive away. He never even glanced at the prone figure crumpled behind the van.

As soon as I saw that dent glinting in the hospital car park, I knew we were in trouble or, more accurately, Angie was in trouble. I reached out and grabbed James's arm, pointed to the Vectra and quickly explained what I thought its presence meant. As the others gathered round, I gave a quick but detailed description of Laddy focussing on the violence of his character as much as his appearance. While I was still speaking, Nat left us and strode over to the Vectra, looking all around as he did so, but giving most of his attention to the direction of the hospital entrance. We watched as he walked around to the front and laid the back of his hand on the bonnet. Then he came round to the rear and crouched down to feel the tailpipe. Straightening up, he ran back over to us.

"Still warm, Boss. Almost hot. Don't reckon he's been here long."

"OK," said James. "He's going to be cautious, and won't want to draw attention to himself. Also, he can't just go in and ask for her, not if he doesn't want to be remembered." He paused, calculating the odds of Laddy getting to Angela first. Then he turned to Barrie.

"You go straight ahead, Barrie, and find out what ward she's in. Full name, Angela Louise Lockhart. You know the story. She's your patient."

As Barrie left, walking as fast as he could without running, James turned to John and Nat.

"You two stick together. Lizzie's coming with me. Keep close, but not so close it looks like we're one group. I don't want us looking threatening."

Nat grinned. "Boss, you look threatening all on your own."

James just grunted, and John never said a word. He would do what needed to be done, but he still wasn't happy about it.

We set off after Barrie, in pairs about fifteen yards apart, following his example of walking as fast as we could without drawing attention to ourselves by running. As we came into main reception, Barrie was waiting for us.

"Ward 8, Surgical assessment. West wing, fourth floor."

He set off straight away and I immediately followed without checking to see if James was with me. When I did look, he was right beside me. John and Nat were following but still keeping their distance. The corridor was wide and well lit, but there was hardly anyone else about. A doctor turned out of a side corridor and came towards us. Tall, slim, early thirties. No white coat, but the stethoscope dangling round his neck was rather a giveaway. My heart pounded as he approached. I expected him to ask us, politely, what the hell we were doing there at that time of night. His sleepy eyes glanced at us in passing, but otherwise didn't seem to give us a thought. Perhaps we didn't look as suspicious as I felt, or maybe he just didn't care.

As we came to the west wing lifts, Barrie pressed the button, and James turned to signal to John and Nat that they should take the stairs. I could feel the tension building as we waited for the car to descend. My heart was still racing, and I wished it would calm down and start behaving itself. I was almost shaking with impatience by the time the lift arrived. Barrie kept looking nervously left and right. I wasn't sure whether he was anxious about being seen and recognised by a member of the hospital staff, or afraid of Laddy catching us unawares. I glanced at James and saw that he too was watching the corridors, but without any trace of nervousness. When the lift doors opened, it was empty, and the three of us stepped in. Again, it was Barrie who pressed the button, this time for the fourth floor.

I watched the lights of the floor indicator, almost holding my breath as we crawled slowly upwards. James stood at the back of the car, facing the doors his eyes, like mine, on the indicator lights. The car was supposed to hold six people, but I don't know where we could have put the others. Maybe on James's shoulders. In that confined space, standing so close to him, I felt tiny; not insignificant, just tiny. I felt like a child who had somehow got involved in grown-ups business, and I wished I was back in the wood and the whole wretched day could start over again. But I knew that couldn't happen, not because wishes don't ever come true, but because I had to be here, now, for Angie's sake. I was the only one who could reassure her that James and his friends were not there to finish what others had started. It was possible she might remember James, of course, from her time at the farm, but in her present fragile, possibly drugged state, I wouldn't want to bet her life on it.

When the doors finally opened, the first thing I saw was a trolley, the sort porters use to transport patients around the hospital. It had been pushed up to the far wall and left there. It was empty, apart from a small pile of folded sheets. Was it significant? I had no way of knowing but, at that moment, everything seemed significant. James stepped out first, looking quickly left and right. Barrie followed, and I emerged last stepping slowly and cautiously into the corridor. Glancing to my left, I saw John standing at the head of the stairs. A quick look to the right showed no sign of Nat. I watched James, waiting to follow his lead, but it was Barrie who spoke first.

"Wait here."

Then he took off, looking more purposeful than I think he felt, in the direction of the nurses' station half-way along the left-hand corridor. As I looked after him, I could see a number of doors, some open some closed, and there were open bays on both sides of the corridor both before and beyond the nurses' station. I could hear groans and snores and murmurs, but I could see no-one. Barrie's shoes made no sound on the polished floor. He stopped in front of the long counter and looked intently at the wall behind it, a wall I couldn't see. He didn't speak to anyone, so I assumed there was no-one at present manning the desk. He looked quickly around and then came straight back to us. Still no sign of Nat.

Before Barrie reached us, a figure stepped briskly into the corridor from a room on the left just beyond the nurses' station. She was tall and slender, dark-skinned, maybe Afro-Caribbean, and there was no doubt this was her ward. It wasn't her uniform of royal-blue tunic top and pants that breathed authority; it was the expression on her face as she bore down on us. She must have caught sight of Barrie as he stood at the nurses' station and cruised out to demand an explanation for his presence. She didn't seem in the least put out at finding herself confronting four intruders instead of one, and I wondered how James was going to handle her.

In the event, it was not James but Barrie who took charge of the encounter, surprising me by stepping directly in her path. She stopped, a little of the anger fading from her expression, as a touch of curiosity took its place. I assumed she had taken note of Barrie's stethoscope and the photo ID clipped to his breast pocket, but this was still her territory, and she wasn't about to give ground. Her voice was surprisingly soft, probably in deference to the sleeping patients, and her words were polite but there was more than a hint of steel in her eyes.

"Doctor. Is there something I can do for you?"

Meaning, "Get the hell off my ward and take your cronies with you."

"Actually, Sister Yuyun, there is," said Barrie reading her nameplate. His voice was also quiet, but equally authoritative. I supposed he couldn't have got to run his own hospital by being a sissy.

"I'm extremely worried about a patient of mine, Angela Lockhart. Are the police still guarding her?"

The sister looked past Barrie at the rest of us. She wanted to tell us to clear off, but she was also intrigued by our presence. Sensibly, we remained very quiet and still, allowing Barrie to handle it. A nurse appeared out of the same room the sister had been in, and she paused for a moment to take in the little tableau being enacted down the corridor. Then she moved off, out of sight, other duties no doubt taking precedence over curiosity. Sister Yuyun turned her gaze back to Barrie.

"The police never were guarding her," she said, with just a slight trace of accent. Not Caribbean, I thought. Maybe West Africa. "Two officers stayed until she was in a fit state to be able to give them a statement. That was all they wanted. After she had spoken to them, they left. That would have been about two hours ago."

"Sister, have you checked on her since the police left?"

"Of course. I'm sorry, doctor, but did you say she was your patient?"

"Yes, that's right."

"But I have her listed as Mr Fischer's patient. I don't remember you from his team, and I'm sure I don't have you listed as a locum."

Before Barrie could reply, James stepped forward and laid a hand on his shoulder. It kept Barrie quiet which was I presumed what was intended. Sister Yuyun's chin came up as her eyes lifted to James's face.

"Sister Yuyun." James's voice was calm and quiet, almost apologetic in tone. "I realise we are trespassing enormously upon your good nature, and I apologise for this intrusion."

As he was speaking, he reached inside his jacket and withdrew his wallet. He took out what looked like some sort of business card and handed it to her, replacing his wallet while she studied it.

"I recently arranged for Angela to be admitted to a private clinic. That is how she comes to be a patient of Doctor Harwood. I know her because a few years ago she used to play with my daughter when some tenants of mine were taking care of her."

Sister Yuyun was still looking at the card, her eyes clouded with confusion, but her expression was no longer hostile. I wondered what was inscribed on it, to bring about such a change in her.

"Sir, I understand your concern, but you still should not be here. Visiting hours ended at eight o'clock, and she is really not so seriously ill as to justify out of hours visiting."

"I am sure you are right, sister. Could I just ask you to check on her one more time before we leave?"

Leave? What on earth did he mean? There was no way we could leave her. Not with Laddy on the loose in the hospital. I reached out and took hold of his arm.

Sister Yuyun jumped at the chance of getting rid of us.

"Very well, sir. I can do that. Would you just wait here please?"

I pulled fiercely at his jacket and whispered, "We can't leave. Not now."

"Patience," Breathed James, without looking down. "Patience."

At that moment, there was a slight whirring sound, and the lift started to move. I looked up at the floor indicator and saw that it was travelling down. 3 ... 2 ... 1 ... It stopped on the ground floor. Before it began to rise again, we all heard the clatter of footsteps from the stairwell. Someone was coming up those stairs two at a time and at breakneck speed.

As the lift began to retrace its journey, John quickly took two steps backward so as to be out of sight of whoever was racing up the stairs. James looked at Barrie and pointed at the retreating back of Sister Yuyun, presumable to indicate that he should keep her out of the way. Then, he stepped directly in front of me so that all I could see was an excellent view of his broad back, and a very limited view of the corridor walls. I peered around him so I could see the lift and stairs. I was absolutely terrified, but I needed to see what was happening.

As the lift hit 2, John's leg began to swing in what would have been a vicious kick just as Ron emerged at full pelt from the head of the stairs. John retracted his foot just prior to connection with Ron's midriff, but he couldn't stop the swing and he turned full circle before dropping to a crouch as Ron collided with the corridor wall opposite the stairs, rolled to face us and hissed,

"It's him. In the lift. Alone."

As the doors opened, I was conscious of Barrie behind me speaking urgently to Sister Yuyun, but I wasn't listening to the words. My whole attention was focussed on the person emerging from that metal box.

Laddy was the same as always. Black boots; black leather trousers; black silk shirt; and the black Armani leather jacket which he boasted had cost him $2000 in New York last summer. Laddy's eyes gave no indication of his state of mind as he stepped into what he must have expected to be a virtually empty corridor. Three men, one huge, one big and one just average, stood watching him, obviously waiting for him. Nat to his front, John to his right and James to his left. But there was no confusion, no fear. Just the same empty bleakness as always.

And then he saw me and, just for a moment, his eyes widened.

"Holy shit... ... Little Di. Well, this is nice surprise, eh?"

His deep voice was calm and quiet, and heavily East European. And, even out-numbered three-to-one, infinitely threatening.

Standing behind James, and slightly to one side, I could see past his right arm, and I found myself looking directly into Laddy's eyes. For the first time ever, I found that I wasn't afraid of him. I held his gaze without flinching. With James between us, I knew that there was nothing he could do to me, and I was suddenly ashamed of all the times when the mere sound of his car drawing up was enough to start me trembling. I hated him for all the terrors he had made me feel, and I wanted to gouge those dark eyes right out of his face. My fingers were already curling into claws as I let him know the full force of my loathing and contempt.

"Go fuck yourself, you piece of shit."

James glanced round at me, eyebrows raised. I don't know whether it was the indelicate language that surprised him, or the fact that I'd spoken at all. I did mention my extensive gutter vocabulary, didn't I? Whatever he thought of my language, James more than made up for it in the courtesy of his own.

"My dear Ladislav. What a pleasure it is to find you."

James's voice was soft, conversational. He really did sound pleased. Then he caught me off guard by stepping forward and holding out his right hand. Laddy hesitated, saw that John had moved to cut off his escape back into the lift, and shrugged slightly. James continued speaking.

"I really have been wanting very much to meet you. Come, I think we need to talk."

Laddy still hesitated and then, to my amazement, reached out to shake James's hand. It was a mistake, and it took two or three seconds for Laddy to realise it. It was like one of those photo-ops where politicians stand there shaking hands for ever while news photographers get their pics. Nobody moved. Nobody spoke. Even Barrie and Sister Yuyun made no sound behind me.

Then Laddy started to twitch, and sweat broke out on his forehead. His mouth opened, and he began breathing hard. Still they held hands and, as I looked closely into Laddy's eyes only four or five feet away, I saw them blazing hate. He would kill us all if he could, lengthily and painfully. He would not forget this meeting, ever.

James continued, as though nothing unusual was happening.

"Such a shame our meeting has to be so short."

Just as he finished speaking, there was a faint crackling sound and Laddy's eyes began to roll back in his head. With a final crunch, James released his hand and Laddy tottered back moaning, his mangled hand dangling limply.

"I really think you ought to go to A & E," said James. "They'll soon get you patched up."

Nodding to Nat and John, he said, "Make sure he doesn't get lost."

They took an arm each and steered Laddy towards the lift doorway. He didn't struggle, but he turned his head just before entering the lift.

His teeth clenched against the pain of his hand, he said to James, "Who in hell are you?"

"Not someone you'll want to meet again, I assure you."

And then the lift doors closed and Laddy was gone. The whole incident had taken no more than a couple of minutes. In the ensuing quiet, I could hear Sister Yuyun speaking urgently to Barrie. I was amazed she hadn't already called for security, and I wasn't sure that Barrie would be able to control her for much longer. She was clearly puzzled, having not the slightest idea what was going on but, although her voice was still low and quiet, there was the definite weight of authority in her tone as she said to Barrie,

"If you don't explain immediately what is going on here, I'm going to call security."

Barrie looked to James, unsure now just how much to tell her. James obviously decided that the time for subtlety was over.

"Sister, perhaps you could explain to me, if we had not been here, just how you would have prevented that man from killing Angela Lockhart."

Glancing past James to the lift where Laddy had disappeared, Sister Yuyun was clearly startled, but she regrouped admirably.

"Sir, I've just about had enough. You have one minute to explain to me why I shouldn't call the police."

"Very well, sister. You already know that Angela was badly beaten before being thrown off that bridge. She should have died and, until the news broadcast this evening, the people who did it probably thought that she had. But then the journalists, subtle as ever, let the cat out of the bag. That man you just saw came to finish the job they started. As long as they know where she is, Angela will continue to be in danger. Even if the police believed in a continuing threat, they haven't the manpower for twenty-four hour protection, especially for .. .. er .. .. someone they don't regard very highly. That's why we're here, to take her to a private hospital. She'll be well looked after, safe and, most importantly, no-one will know where she is."

Sister Yuyun glanced down at the card which James had given her. Surprisingly, she was still holding it. She looked thoughtful.

"I suppose you really are .. .. ..?"

James smiled. "Indeed I am. Incredible isn't it?"

I was totally mystified. What was he exactly?

Sister Yuyun looked at Barrie.

"And I suppose he really is a doctor?"

"Every inch of him," confirmed James. "Dr. Barrie Harwood B.Med.Sci., MRCP, PhD and goodness knows what else besides."

Sister Yuyan shook her head. I was all set to plead with her, but then she spoke again.

"She's in a bad way. I saw what those people did to her. Some of her wounds I dressed myself." She took a deep breath and held it. I found I was holding mine.

"OK," she said. "This is way outside proper procedure, and Mr Fischer is going to want my hide but, if Angela is willing to discharge herself into your care, you can have her. On one condition."

We all waited to see what obstacle she was going to throw in our way.

"I'm going to call the duty SHO to check her out before she discharges herself."

A thought then struck her.

"How are you going to transport her?"

Barrie said, "We brought our own ambulance."

Sister Yuyun smiled for the first time.

"You did come prepared, didn't you?"

James smiled back, "Indeed we did, sister. Now if you'll just lead the way, I'm sure Angela would like to get this over with."

As she turned and started to walk away, I heard James whisper to Barrie, "Is this SHO likely to be a problem?"

I was relieved to see Barrie shake his head.

"No. He'll probably try to talk her out of a self-discharge, and he might want to refer it up the line to his registrar, but if she wants to leave with us he can't stop her."

And with that, following Sister Yuyun, he led James and me into Angela's room.

Sunday

1st May 2005

Aushra Paulauskaitė – Day Two

Vilnius, Lithuania – 6:00 am

Aushra lay still, staring intently through the gloom of her bedroom at the cracked and peeling ceiling above. It took a while for her to realise what day it was, but eventually her mental calendar sorted itself out and she smiled. Today, she and Jolanta were going to the Vilnius Akropolis, a huge shopping and entertainment centre which had the distinction of being the largest such facility in all the Baltic countries. She didn't shop there very often, but after she and Jolanta had gone there last year, just after the big expansion, both girls confessed to an unexpected sense of pride that such a place should exist in their city.

She rolled over, confident that there was plenty of time before she need think about getting up. She didn't feel so wide awake that further sleep was unlikely, but the movement made her suddenly aware of how much she needed to pee. She frowned, not because visiting the bathroom would certainly bring her to full wakefulness but because, for the first time since Mykolas had died, she had slept the night through.

It didn't seem right somehow that she could sleep peacefully so soon after he had died in such despair. Was she forgetting him already? Would it seem, in a few weeks' time, as though he had never been?

Here she was thinking about a shopping trip to buy clothes, toiletries and other essentials to start off her new job in England, while Mykolas, probably her oldest friend, was nothing more than a pile of ashes in the bottom of a cold urn. Oh, and she mustn't forget the suitcase. Jolanta was determined they should both have new cases to carry their new clothes into their new life.

She sat up, tears in her eyes. The Akropolis boasted an eight-screen multiplex cinema which they would not be able to visit today, for what could they do with all their shopping? But they had been there not so very long ago. She and Jolanta had treated Mykolas for his birthday.

Life was so unfair.

No point in lying down again. Her brain was now buzzing with thoughts that jumped from eager anticipation to miserable dejection. From joy to guilt and back again. She was confused, finding it hard to cope with these mixed up emotions.

No, there was no more chance of sleep this morning.

Better perhaps to spend the time working out what she might say to her new boss who was flying out from England tomorrow especially to meet her and, of course, all the other girls who would be leaving for England on Wednesday.

A new boss, new job, new clothes, new life.
Maybe life would turn out not to be so unfair after all.

Fifteen

Heartlands Hospital – 12.05 am

Sister Yuyun must have had reservations about the highly unusual activity on her ward that night, but her manner towards us surprisingly gave no indication of it. It was only when I looked closely at her face and noticed the lines of tension around her eyes and mouth that I guessed she was having a real struggle with the irregularity of what she was doing. A real stickler for procedure, I thought, our Sister Yuyun.

She opened one of the doors on the right of the corridor, the last one before the nurses' station, and looked in. Angie must have been awake because I heard Sister Yuyun say in a very gentle voice, "Hello, honey. Have we been disturbing your beauty sleep?"

There was no reply that I could hear, and Sister Yuyun carried on, "You've got some visitors, honey, and I think they're really keen to see you. You feel up to it?" There was still no audible reply but, apparently satisfied, she pushed the door wide and led us in.

I'm not sure I would have recognised Angie. Her once beautiful, creamy coffee complexion was ruined by swollen lips and livid bruising around her nose and eyes, and a row of stitches running vertically down her right temple. I don't remember exactly how it came about but, almost without thinking, I found myself, on my knees beside Angie's bed, clutching her right hand, which was free of drips and canulas, and weeping bitter tears of guilt and shame for what I had caused to happen to my best and only friend. Her bruised throat could only manage a faint whisper but it caused me to look up and begin to hope that she might not be as badly hurt as I first thought.

"Hey, Little Di. ... ... C'mon girl, ... we ain't dead yet."

Forty-five minutes later, it was all over. When the situation was explained, Angie was only too willing to come with us to a private hospital. It was perhaps a sign of her weakness that she never thought to ask who was paying. Of course, we had to wait for the young doctor on duty to turn up and to assure himself that Angie was, in fact, fit to be moved. And Barrie was right. The SHO did go off for a phone consultation with his senior colleague, which didn't surprise me. He didn't look much older than me and, although he tried to speak with calm authority, there was a weariness in his eyes from too many hours on duty.

Eventually, papers were signed discharging Angie into Barrie's care. A porter arrived with his trolley to transport her to the waiting ambulance, and Sister Yuyun lost her worry lines as she became more relaxed, at ease with herself over the rightness of her actions.

I wanted to go with Angie in the ambulance, but James told me to leave her to Barrie. He promised we'd see her later in the day, after Barrie had examined her and got her settled in and comfortable. Angie began to cry when she realised we were to be separated again so soon. I'd have been scared too, if I'd gone through what she had, and then found I was being whisked off to heaven knew where with people I didn't know. But when Barrie climbed in the back of the ambulance and sat beside her speaking quietly and holding her hand, she calmed down, and her tears stopped as the doors closed and the ambulance drove away.

James and I returned to the Maserati where we found John waiting for us, leaning against the driver's door. He told us Laddy was waiting to have his hand x-rayed and Nat was keeping an eye on him until we'd left. Apparently, Nat hadn't thought the damage to his hand sufficient deterrent and had been all in favour of breaking Laddy's arm or dislocating his shoulder while on the way down in the lift, but John seemed to think James wouldn't have been happy with that and held him in check. I would have been very happy for Nat to break anything he fancied, but I thought John was probably right. In the end it didn't matter. Just the threat had been sufficient to keep Laddy subdued. Or maybe it was the pain of shattered bones grinding in his hand.

Just for good measure, while we waited for Nat to respond to James's call to re-join us, John suggested walking over to the Vectra to put a knife through each of the front tyres. James looked around at the CCTV cameras, high on the poles at the corners of the car park, and shook his head.

"Apart from anything else, John, I'd actually like Laddy to be able to leave here as soon as he can. Once they pack him off home, I don't want anything holding him up."

Nat re-joined us shortly after with the news that Laddy was probably going to need an operation on his hand. None of us wept. He had also left Laddy in no doubt as to what would happen if he was ever found hanging around the hospital which, he had told him, would be a pretty pointless exercise as Angie was now long gone.

Since there wasn't much point in our hanging around any longer either, John and Nat left together in the Passat, presumably to go and grab an hour or two's sleep.

It's very quiet in a hospital car park at 3.00 in the morning. There was no sound and no movement; none of the bustle of people going about their ordinary, everyday business. After the stress of the last few hours, the dark shadows masked a multitude of threats for a lively imagination. I kept looking around, desperate to leave before Laddy appeared to reclaim his Vectra and the small arsenal he kept hidden in the boot. Peace and goodwill would not be uppermost in his mind, if he saw us within range of his customised Glock. I wasn't convinced he'd regard the cameras as much of a deterrent either.

James, however, seemed unconcerned. He did unlock the Maserati for me to get in, but he remained standing outside speaking on his mobile. From the little I could hear from the inside of the car, he was getting an update from Cherry at the farm. It was a short conversation so I assumed that there was not very much to report. Eventually, after a final look around the car park, he climbed into the car and we drove off, leaving Laddy to the hopefully not-so-tender mercies of A & E.

The drive back to the Dower House was fast and quiet. James concentrated on his driving and looking thoughtful. I wanted to ask what he was thinking, but I was too tired to persuade my mind to frame the questions. Street lights flashed past with hypnotic regularity, the pattern broken occasionally by the beams of an oncoming vehicle. I closed my eyes and allowed my mind to drift.

A picture of Angie's battered face kept reappearing amidst all the other thoughts and images of the past twenty-four hours. I could scarcely believe so little time had passed since I had tucked myself away safe and secure in that cocoon of holly. I thought of the potential problems piling up for James because I couldn't speak out about what I had seen in the wood. I thought of the possible danger to my new friends at the farm, because I had chosen them for my refuge. I thought of the immense pain I had caused Angie by running away and leaving her behind. I thought of all the things that had driven me to flight, the things I hated, and couldn't stand doing any longer. I thought of the person I used to be, still was really. I thought about leopards. I knew they were not supposed to be able to change their spots, but somehow I'd grown to hope that maybe they could. Well, maybe I could, at least.

So many thoughts. So many images. Except that it was all in the past. There was no future. Ahead was just a blank. I couldn't return to the farm, and I had no other plans. More street lights flashed by. I was sitting still, doing nothing, and travelling fast to nowhere.

After about forty-five minutes, the street lights died and the road became narrow and black, twisting and turning around hedges and walls briefly illuminated by the Maserati's powerful beams. I was pretty sure I knew where James was taking me, and I was suddenly surprised at myself for not having asked him earlier where we were going. First came the wall, overhung with tree branches, then the gates, the curving drive, and finally that grand old Georgian house.

As James drove slowly round to the rear, to the coach house garages, I sat very still and quiet in my seat. I wasn't sure why I was here. James had just done me a massive favour, taking care of Angie like that, and he might just want some recompense. I had no doubt he knew the sort of life I'd been living, and a bit of bedtime comfort might seem to him an appropriate reward. Then I thought of the prayers and stuff they'd done at the farm before we left, but wasn't much reassured. Religious people weren't immune from sexual urges, and those urges had brought more than one of them to my bed before now. What the hell. If that's what he wanted, he could have it. It wouldn't cost me anything.

But that was the trouble. It did cost; and, on the rare occasions when I'm being honest with myself, I acknowledge the fact that it always had. And when the cost eventually gets too high, and you can't pay it any longer, you go bankrupt; or commit suicide; or run away.

James got out of the car without speaking but, as he came round to open my door, I noticed him wave to the camera high on the gable of the coach house. Presumably Surjit was watching us on one of his many screens. As if to confirm this, the floodlights, which had come on as we'd driven round the house, flickered twice.

The car door opened and James waited while I wondered what to do. Get out. Don't get out. Daft really, since I'd long ago run out of options. I got out.

He gestured towards the rear door of the house so I turned and walked slowly towards the steps. I shivered slightly and put it down to the gentle breeze which felt quite cool after the luxurious warmth of the Maserati.

The doorway was lit by floodlights hidden in the shrubbery to either side so I was able to mount the three wide stone steps without stumbling. James used two keys to open the door, and then he went in before me to switch on the lights. I saw a large square hall painted in pale green pastel shades with many photographs hanging on the walls. The high ceiling was picked out with white plaster work, and a large chandelier hung in the centre.

James held the door open for me to come in, and I stepped forward uncertainly onto the polished wood floor. I heard the door close behind me. I gazed around at the photos while James locked the door before tossing the keys into a hideous blue and white Chinese looking bowl perched in solitary splendour on an ornately carved table in the centre of the hall.

"Welcome to the Dower House," he said, smiling slightly at my open-mouthed gaze.

"I'm sorry there's only me to take care of you but Mrs Siddons, my housekeeper, will have gone to bed hours ago. Would you like a drink, or something to eat before I take you upstairs?"

Upstairs! Maybe if I opted for a four course meal and a bottle of wine, it would give Mrs Siddons time to wake up. But before any of that, there was something I definitely did need.

"Could you point me to the bathroom?"

I was getting quite desperate for a pee, and there was also the old tampon problem again. Tampon! How on earth had I forgotten? Unless he was outright kinky, that should dampen any possible ardour.

"Of course," he said. "It's just through here."

Ignoring a staircase to our left, he opened the massive door in the wall opposite the entrance and I followed him through. We were in another hall, more rectangular than square and reaching right up to the roof of what I was fast coming to think of as an absolutely gorgeous house. The walls were covered with beautifully painted scenes which growing bladder pressure prevented me from fully appreciating. I did notice a balcony extending all around the hall at first floor level, but I couldn't see any way of reaching it. Navigating around the furniture, James led me to the further end of the hall, presumably near the front of the house. There were two doors at that end and, as we approached them, he seemed to hesitate.

Pointing to the door on the right, James said, "There is a cloakroom through there, but I think you'll be more comfortable if I take you straight upstairs."

I wasn't so sure and was about to correct him, but he was already opening the left-hand door which I saw led into the entrance hall at the front of the house. Following him through, I saw an elegantly carved staircase on my right, far more impressive than the one at the rear of the house, and James was already on his way up the stairs. I followed with a small sigh of resignation.

The upstairs hallway had doors leading off to left and right and James turned right to open the door which lead into a room at the front of the house. I peeped in. This was not a bathroom. This was a bedroom, and not the servant's quarters either, but I didn't think it was James's room. The massive brass bed against the left-hand wall could have been his. It was huge, ornate and highly polished, but somehow I couldn't imagine him sleeping under that flowery duvet. The wallpaper didn't seem quite his style either: pink with more small flowers. But the real give-away was the giant teddy perched amid the floral pillows.

I stepped passed James into the room, saying as I did so, "Don't tell me. It's *the flower room*."

"Almost," he smiled. "My aunt christened it *the pink floral room*. Until a couple of weeks ago, it was Suzanne's room."

Before I could ask, he pointed to a door at the far end of the room saying, "Your bathroom is through there. You should find everything you need. If you do want a drink or something to eat you'll find me in the kitchen for the next half-hour or so. That's back to where we first came in, and through the door to the left. Otherwise, have yourself a good sleep.

When you're ready for breakfast, press three on the phone by your bed and tell Mrs Siddons what you'd like. I'll tell her you're here before I go back to the farm."

I think he must have seen some alarm in my face, as he went on, "I'm going to pick up Abby for church." He smiled. "You're very welcome to join us if you want to, but I thought you'd probably prefer a lie-in."

I nodded agreement. "A lie-in sounds good."

He turned to leave, but added before closing the door, "I'll also ask Rachel to gather up all your stuff at the farm, and I'll bring it back here." He smiled again, but I thought his eyes looked tired. "It's been quite a day, hasn't it? Sleep well, and I'll see you about lunchtime. Oh, and in the afternoon, we'll go and see Angie."

The door closed and I was alone, wondering how I could have misread his motives so badly. So much for a passionate payback. He treated me more like his daughter; protective and considerate. Could that be useful? I retired to the bathroom to think about that.

Sixteen

Lichfield – 5.00 am

After only two hours sleep, Corrina Rigby awoke, scared and alone, on the soft leather settee in her modest but comfortable sitting room. On her salary at the *Lichfield Daily News* she should not have been able to afford the recently refurbished two-bedroom apartment in the large early Victorian mansion on the outskirts of Lichfield. She had only been able to rent it in the first place because her boyfriend had agreed to pay half the costs; everything, right down the middle. Which was very generous of him, considering he wasn't there for much of the time.

Andrew Spears was a newly promoted sergeant in the Staffordshire Regiment which, in spite of its name, was actually based at Tidworth, near Salisbury. He had met Corrina in the summer of 2003 shortly after the Staffords returned from their tour in Kosovo. By Christmas, they had decided they were sufficiently in love to risk sharing a home together. Corrina had offered to move down to Salisbury and try for a job with one of the local papers in the area, but both of them knew that scheme really wouldn't work. With Andy so often away on deployment, Corrina risked loneliness and isolation if she left her Staffordshire roots behind. Andy too had friends and family in the small town of Rugeley to the north-west of Lichfield, so that small cathedral city became their first joint home.

Andy, of course, could only stay there when he was on leave, but they managed to spend enough time together for their relationship to develop to the point where they began talking tentatively about the possibility of children, possibly even preceding them with a wedding.

And then the battalion had deployed to Iraq in the April of 2005. Not too big a deal, Andy had said, as they had begun to make provisional plans for a Christmas wedding. As his final leave came to an end, Andy had given Corrina his full share of the rent for the whole time he expected to be away. That was to be his last contribution to the life they planned together. Exactly a week later, at 10.30 in the morning, his Warrior armoured vehicle became the latest target for a roadside bomb on the main road out of Al Amarah heading south west towards Al Kahla. No-one inside the Warrior was injured, but its driving wheel was jammed by the blast, and it was clearly going no-where. Fearing further attack on their stationary, and thus even more vulnerable, vehicle, Sergeant Andrew Spears had emerged cautiously to scout for possible enemy activity. The sniper's bullet caught him as he turned, glancing off his body armour and starting a spin which exposed his right side and lifted his arm so that the second bullet entered cleanly under his right armpit, tearing through muscle, ribs and lung before finally ripping his heart to shreds. There would be no Christmas wedding.

Corrina was desolated, but tried desperately not to let it show. She hated to be the object of others' pity. Many of her friends and colleagues thought her hard, and even her mother began to wonder if she really had loved her soldier. But none of them saw her, evening after evening, staring at her blank TV screen. She hadn't turned it on since the day that BBC's Midlands Today had announced the death of an unnamed soldier in southern Iraq. They didn't see the tears, or hear the sobs, or feel her pain. They weren't there when, night after night, she lay on her damp pillow, struggling to find some sort of escape in a tablet induced sleep.

They saw only what she wanted them to see: a capable young woman, courageously getting on with her life, committed to building a career for herself in the exciting world of journalism.

Except that it wasn't always, or even usually, very exciting.

On that Saturday evening, Corrina had been driving back home after yet another dull day covering the annual Game Fair at Thurvaston Priory. For once, she had no music playing, while she tried hard to think of something new, or interesting, or exciting to say about what was, for her, one of the most boring events of the year. Obviously, many people didn't share her view, or the fair wouldn't be a regular sell-out year after year, but she couldn't see the attraction herself. She had tried.

She had shot at clay pigeons; tried her hand at fly-casting; watched horses, dogs and falcons at work; and, after visiting the airgun stand, had developed a reasonable understanding of what the sport of field target shooting was all about. But she couldn't wait to get home, until, that is, she was persuaded by a George Clooney look-alike in leather jacket and sunglasses to let him introduce her to the joys of 4x4 off-roading. The experience never quite achieved the promised exhilaration since the look-alike proved to have more show than substance, and accompanied it with roving hands and a superstar ego. After the Toyota Land Cruiser had broadsided inelegantly down a muddy slope to finish sideways on in a stream bed, Corrina had slapped the hopeful's face and told him that if he'd keep his hands on the wheel they might, with luck, just about finish the course.

He did, and they had, and Corrina left.

So her spirits, by now somewhat low, suddenly began to lift when she caught sight of the police vehicles pulled up on the grass verge near Heighley Woods. Forget the Game Fair; this could be a real story; a story to kick-start the career of the investigative reporter she longed to be. Maybe even a Woodward and Bernstein story. Her heart sank. Or maybe it would be one of those lost child, we all know she must be dead but we can't say so, stories. She hated those.

Ten minutes after stopping her car, she knew what type of story it would be: a murder mystery in which the police were confounded by the killer's ingenuity, until an intrepid reporter uncovers the sordid truth. Of course, she wasn't sure the police were confounded, or that the truth would be sordid, but she was determined to make it a good story. Her story. According to the police officer she spoke to, no-one from the Lichfield Daily News had visited the site that day.

She took as many photos as she could, from as close as the police would permit. Before packing up and driving off, she rang her editor to obtain a reluctant promise that she alone would represent the paper at the police press conference the following morning.

Once at home, she turned on her computer, shoved a portion of frozen pizza in the microwave, and settled down on the internet to find out everything she could about Philip Simmons, James Montrayne, Heighley Woods and Heighley Grange Farm.

By the time she had fallen asleep on her leather settee, the one she and Andy had chosen together, she had filled several A4 pages with scribbled notes.

Waking was still disorientating, the comfortable realisation of a new day dawning being quickly overshadowed by the knowledge that it was another day without Andy. She knew the Staffords would be coming home soon, and she dreaded that day as the final confirmation that Andy no longer existed in this or any other world. She was alone, and scared of being lonely, and unless she could lay her hands on some extra cash, she would soon be homeless. Maybe this story would do it.

She put on her face-the-world look, and began the new day.

Seventeen

Edgbaston - 6.30am

Ray Mellisse groaned. A phone call at 6.30 on a Sunday morning was bound to mean trouble. He rolled out of bed, taking care not to drag the duvet off Jennifer in the process, and grabbed his cell phone which vibrated quietly on his bedside cabinet. He pressed the answer button and said just one word.

"Wait."

He slid his feet into the suede moccasins which sat beside the bed, exactly positioned so that he could accomplish this in pitch darkness without fumbling, and then covered his naked body with the silk dressing gown which lay draped over the back of a Queen Anne chair. He didn't speak into the phone again until he had closed the door of his bedroom behind him.

As he made his way downstairs to his study at the rear of his 1960s neo-Georgian mansion, he listened to a report of the night's disaster. He didn't care about the damage to Laddy's hand. Why should he? He'd never met the man, just as he never met most of the people who worked his less legitimate enterprises. But he did care that Angie had disappeared and that Little Di had been on the spot to help her, with reinforcements apparently.

Sitting in his padded leather swivel chair, he slipped the cell phone into a cradle on his desk and immediately the caller's voice could be heard issuing from the speaker built into the cradle. He never used his landline for business, but he was quite phobic about holding his cell to his ear for any longer than absolutely necessary. He made sure, naturally, that there was no conceivable way that his cell phone could be traced back to him. He reached forward to adjust the volume, not wanting the conversation to be heard outside his study. Not that there was much chance of that as he'd had the room specially sound-proofed before he and his family had moved in. You never knew when someone might hear something they shouldn't, and Ray Mellisse was not a man to take chances.

Ray loved his two children. Graeme was fourteen, a lanky teenager, dealing reasonably well, so far, with the onset of adolescence. He attended a private college as a day student which suited him very well. His daily arrival and departure in a chauffeur-driven Bentley considerably enhanced his prestige in the eyes of his fellow students, particularly the female variety, or so he thought. He couldn't wait to have a car of his own. Nothing flash. A BMW Z4 would do. His young sister Sonia was six, blond, blue-eyed and very bright and she adored her father, just as little girls should. She attended St. Faith's, a private kindergarten in Edgbaston, and her talent for rapidly absorbing everything her teachers set before her, already marked her out from the crowd. The eight-year gap between her and Graeme was not intentional. Jenny had miscarried three times over that period, and she and Ray had almost given up hope of a second child when Sonia, contrary to all expectations, had stayed the full term in her mother's womb to finally emerge at a healthy seven and a half pounds.

Graeme and Sonia had no idea what paid for their big house, chauffeur-driven car and private schools, and Mellisse firmly intended that they should never find out. It wasn't that he was ashamed of what he did, but he knew that if anyone ever did to his Sonia what he had caused to happen to more girls than he could count, then he would personally chop that individual into small pieces and feed them through a mincer. That knowledge brought a vague awareness that Sonia, and Graeme too, would not be happy with the source of their father's earnings, and he couldn't bear the thought of losing their affection or respect, so they must never know.

And so he kept the volume low and the door to his study shut.

"Where is she now?"

Even through the electronic amplification, the caller's voice was apprehensive.

"We don't know, Mr Mellisse."

"That's not what I wanted to hear, Bruno."

"I know, Mr Mellisse, but she left her phone behind. We can't track her."

All the girls who worked the upmarket side of the business, the high-price call girls or escorts, were all given mobile phones which they were told to keep with them, and switched on, at all times. Ostensibly this was to allow their punters to get in touch to make appointments but it also served the very useful purpose of allowing Bruno to use the inbuilt GPS facility to track their movements while they were working.

"This is not good news, Bruno."

"I know, Mr Mellisse, but there's more. You said you wanted to be kept up to date so here it is. Do you remember that farm Angie talked about? Well, I looked them up on the net and rang yesterday evening pretending to be someone from Social Services. I asked about Diane Thomas. Never heard of her, they said. May be true; maybe not, but I sent Satish to check anyway. It wasn't far. Only about an hour or so. Anyway, he took a mate with him and.. .. .. well, there's not been a peep from either of them since. I've tried to raise them but both their cells are dead."

Ray Mellisse prided himself in never using the coarse swear words that so liberally littered the conversation of his associates, but he felt like using them now. He eased his head back against the soft leather and slowly breathed out.

"So where are they, Bruno? You'd better start finding out."

"I'm already on it, Mr Mellisse? I've sent Vince up to the farm. He's not a tough nut like Satish, but he's not stupid. If there's anything to find out up there, he's the guy to do it."

"I hope you're right Bruno. Don't make me start to lose faith in you."

"Sure thing, Mr Mellisse. But... ... well, I've been thinking. I mean... ... those two girls... ... they're just kids. Probably scared shitless. Chances are they'll just hunker down and keep quiet. Too scared of what will happen if they raise their heads."

"Maybe, Bruno. But one day, when they feel safe enough, their little consciences might get the better of them and one or other will decide to squawk. And there's something else. I need this thing sorted before the General Election. Little Di has some unfinished business with a video camera. That tape has to be finished before she gets taught her lesson. I don't care about the other one but I'm not about to have my plans derailed by a pair of worthless tarts. And don't you forget the rule. No girl ever escapes. For those without families, it's the one thing that stops them running. Knowing what will happen when they are caught and brought back. We can't allow these to be the first to get away, and we certainly can't allow Di to spill the beans on our honourable friend."

Bruno knew what he meant. For those girls who had families, the threat of what would happen to them if they didn't co-operate held them in check. For the others, it was the certain knowledge of a slow and agonising death if they ran, that ensured their co-operation. And there was, of course, the election.

"OK. OK. We've got to get them back. But... ...er... ... do you have any ideas?"

"What did Laddy say about these goons Di brought with her to the hospital?"

There was a pause as Bruno thought back to the frantic call he had received as soon as Laddy had been able to use his cell phone, ignoring all hospital signs to the contrary.

"Not sure goons is the right word, Mr Mellisse. The big guy that mashed his hand was dressed real smart. Not flash, just smart. And he spoke like... ... er... ... well, like that royal lot. Least, that's how Laddy put it."

"So where did Di find her *smart royal*? Ask around the clubs. Check the CCTV. And check the tapes from Di's massage parlour."

It wasn't just Mellisse's porn studios which sported high tech cameras. All his various clubs and massage parlours were littered with discretely placed cameras designed to catch all the exploits of employee and customer alike. You never knew when someone of significance might be caught doing something they would prefer their nearest and dearest never to know. Good tapes portrayed the customers in some most interesting and athletic exploits, and their sales had proved a very lucrative sideline over the years. For their own peace of mind, customers were usually able to convince themselves that the tapes they were given in exchange for large sums of money were genuine originals and that no other copies existed. Mellisse loved the gullibility of his customers.

"OK, Mr Mellisse, but what if he's not on them."

"Don't wait to find out. Put someone else on that and you take one of the girls down to the hospital. She can pretend to be Angie's sister come to visit. Somebody on that ward must know where she was taken. I don't know what time the shift changes but if you get onto it quick you might get there before the morning lot come on duty."

"OK, Mr Mellisse, I'm on my way."

There was one final point to make before hanging up.

"Bruno. You do whatever it takes to find them. Whatever! You understand?"

"You got it, Mr Mellisse. We'll get them."

Jennifer stirred as Mellisse eased himself gently back into bed. Awake but drowsy, she snuggled up close, and her long dark hair tickled his chin. Along with his children, she was the most precious thing in the world to him, and he wrapped his arms around her and held her tight.

Eighteen

The Dower House – 9.15 am

For the second time in two days, I awoke to bright daylight in a strange bed, this time in a room a little too much like a set from a Jane Austen drama for me to feel completely at ease. From the wall facing me, an elegant lady in a long dress with a couple of spaniels frolicking around her ankles stared down at me from her elevated position in a gilt frame. On the bottom edge of the frame, there was an inscription which I couldn't read from where I lay, so, having nothing better to do, I got up to see who she was.

Lady Alice Marchmont 1905

Not a Montrayne then. So how did she fit into things? I wandered round the room, surprised at how different it looked in daylight. The diffuse light of the brilliant mid-morning sunshine left no discernible shadows, and all the colours gleamed with a vibrant intensity. As I traced the floral pattern on the heavy drapes drawn back by the huge window, I thought how I rather envied Suzanne, waking up to this every morning. I wondered where she was now; in another gorgeous room, in a big house somewhere? What had taken her away?

I continued letting my thoughts drift as I straightened the bed and then wandered into the bathroom for a shower. I was regretting the fact that I had no clean clothes to dress in, when I suddenly realised that I had. Folded neatly on the chair beside the corner bath was a pair of beige jeans, a pale green, lamb's wool sweater accompanied by matching green bra and panties. Amazingly, apart from the bra being a cup size too small, everything was going to fit. So where had it come from?

It was at that moment that I remembered that I had drawn the drapes across the windows before getting into bed. They should not have been pulled back as they were now. Someone had been wandering about in my room pulling drapes and depositing clothes while I had slept on, stark naked, hopefully with the duvet still covering the essentials.

Still it wouldn't have been the first time I'd been on public display, and no harm was done, so I told myself it was hardly worth the effort of worrying about it. Except that I couldn't help being curious. For some strange reason, I hoped it hadn't been James.

I worked out how to make the shower come on - I'd been too tired to bother with it the night before – and waited for the water temperature to settle before stepping into the cubicle.

As I lathered myself all over, I thought of the damage done to Angie's body by Bruno and Satish. Rinsing the lather away, I wondered how long it would take for those injuries to heal. I also wondered if I would have taken such punishment for her if our situations were reversed. How long had she held out before telling them about the farm? Maybe she'd told them about Heighley Grange as a ruse to get them to stop hurting her, not really considering that I would actually have gone there.

However it was, last night's events proved that she had told them.

And now, Satish and his mate had gone missing, which meant that someone would almost certainly be watching the farm right now. I didn't know who they'd send but I did know how ruthlessly determined these men could be. I hoped, for Chick and Rachel's sake as well as the two girls, that at least some of James's soldier friends were still there.

I had never thought that running away would bring trouble for so many people. Perhaps, if I'd had some crystal ball to let me in on the future, I might have stayed with Angie and we would have gradually decayed together, self-sacrificing to the end. But I doubted it. I wasn't that noble.

Discarding the bra, which I tried on just to see the effect, I dressed and began to wonder what to do about breakfast. Completely forgetting James's instruction to use the bedside phone to call Mrs Siddons, I left my room and wandered off to try and find the kitchen.

What had James said? *Back where we came in, and through the door on the left.*

I took my time, staring at portraits, peering into rooms, looking at vases, ornaments and intricately carved furniture. I had been taken to posh country house hotels before, but they were nothing like this. They were just flash; dressing for the punters. This was the real thing; elegant and steeped in history, this was a home where real people lived, and I was fascinated.

I found the kitchen, just where it was supposed to be, but I wasn't prepared for its sole occupant and guardian. She was standing on the far side of an island work area beating something in a bowl. She had her back to the square wooden table which, with its four chairs, occupied the rest of the floor area. This room, like all the others, was very light, its large window looking out onto the rear courtyard and stable block.

The beating stopped as I walked in and I found myself being very carefully inspected by a pair of dark, unblinking eyes. I stared back, noting the wrinkles around the eyes and mouth; laughter lines, or bad temper? I was about to find out.

She must have been at least seventy-five, shorter than me, but still very erect. It had to be Mrs Siddons, and I'd half expected that when I met her I'd find her dressed in some sort of housekeeper uniform; not that I had any idea what that might be. In fact she was dressed in what appeared to be a plain white blouse – most of it was hidden behind the farmyard scene on her PVC apron – and a blue-grey patterned skirt which I could just see around the edge of the island. She finally laid down the whisk with which she'd been attacking the mixture in the bowl, and reached for a towel to wipe her hands.

"I see the bra didn't fit. Or perhaps you are one of those persons who just like to let everything hang loose?"

Her voice was quiet, without any accent that I could detect. Not exactly angry, or antagonistic, but definitely lacking in warmth. I felt like a student called in to see the principal for some misdemeanour.

I wasn't sure how to respond, and while I was still making up my mind, she beckoned me to come further into the kitchen.

"Come in, girl, come in. Don't just stand there wasting space."

I came in.

"There's coffee over there in the pot, or I suppose I could make you a cup of tea if you'd really prefer."

The heavy emphasis on *suppose* and *really* left me in no doubt what choice I was supposed to make.

Definitely not laughter lines!

"Coffee would be fine," I said, attempting a smile, but feeling so intimidated that I wasn't sure how far I succeeded.

"Good. Help yourself. Mugs are on the rack there."

While I did as instructed, she picked up the whisk and got back to her beating, before realising that introductions were still outstanding.

"I am Mrs Siddons, the housekeeper here. James did tell me your name, but I've forgotten."

I was surprised to hear her refer to James by his first name. If she had called him *The Master,* I wouldn't have been surprised, given the setting.

"It's Lizzie," I said, replacing the coffee pot and bringing my mug to the table. I really wanted milk in it, but didn't like to ask. Nor did I like to place my mug on the table's surface which was unmarked and obviously freshly polished.

"Coasters in the drawer."

There were, plus matching place mats. I took one out, rested my mug on it, and wondered if it would be OK to sit down without permission.

"You're standing around again. The chairs might look fancy, but they do work."

I sat and took my first sip of coffee. It was bitter and I must have pulled a face because I actually saw Mrs Siddons smile.

"Arabica, strength five," she said. "Lovely stuff. But for those of less discerning taste, there is milk and cream in the fridge to tone it down."

She pointed to a cupboard door under the work surface next to the window. Finding a fridge hiding behind the wooden door, I helped myself to cream, which had the desired effect, and resumed my seat at the table. I had no idea what to say next and the formidable Mrs Siddons wasn't helping. I watched in silence for several minutes while she continued beating the mixture in the bowl, occasionally adding herbs or spices from little bottles. She kept her back to me all the while.

Eventually, I began to find her silence more irritating than intimidating, and decided I could lose nothing by trying a simple question.

"Mrs Siddons, whose clothes am I wearing? Did you leave them in my room?"

The beating stopped and the housekeeper's shoulders seemed to slump a little. After a moment, she turned round to face me.

"Yes, I put them there. Sarah... ... Mrs Montrayne, that is... ... always left a few things here for when she came to visit. After she died, I didn't have the heart to throw them out, and they weren't doing any harm just sitting in the wardrobe."

I stared at her. I was wearing James's dead wife's clothes. I swallowed hard. Somehow this felt a little creepy. Maybe that explained the housekeeper's attitude.

"Is that what's annoying you," I asked, "because if it's the clothes, I didn't ask you for them. That was your idea."

She turned away to continue playing with her bowl and, for a moment, I thought she was just going to ignore me. Then, after a final loud and vigorous attack on her mixture, she laid down the bowl and reached for the towel. That last assault had caused tiny splashes to spatter onto her hands.

"No, it was James's idea. I didn't realise that he knew I'd kept those clothes of Sarah but... ... it seems he knew but chose not to say anything. And no, it's not the clothes that annoy me. You annoy me just by being here."

Her voice was quiet and steady but, it seemed to me, tightly controlled as though she was trying to hold some strong emotion in check. I was on the point of picking up my coffee and taking it back up to my room, when she turned to face me.

"No, *annoy* is the wrong word. You have caused me great concern by coming here."

She was still holding the towel and twisted it in her hands. I waited, but she said nothing more. My turn again.

"Mrs Siddons, I don't understand. I don't mean any harm to you, or to James, or anyone. And I won't be here long."

Those dark eyes fastened on mine and wouldn't let go, but I couldn't work out what was going on behind them. Then she came around the table to take the chair opposite to me. When she sat, resting her forearms on the table, she was still clutching the towel. It was her turn, so I just waited.

"James told me how he helped you last night."

The towel twisted, and then she seemed to realise what she was doing and began straightening it. It was one of those linen souvenir towels with a picture on, but she was going to have to work on it for a bit before I'd be able to tell what it was. Now she was looking at me again.

"If James finds someone in trouble, he gives them a hand. He can't help it. It must be in his genes because his mother's the same, poor dear, and everyone loves her for it."

She paused, but somehow I knew it wasn't my turn. She was just taking time to work out how to say the next bit. If it was this bad, I was beginning to doubt whether I really wanted to hear it.

"The last time James helped someone … … … well, someone in as bad a fix as you seemed to be, it was two years ago, and … … … it very nearly got Abby killed."

I was astounded and it must have showed, but I don't think Mrs Siddons noticed because she was now looking down at the towel spread almost flat on the table. I could have worked out the picture easily now, but I didn't even look. Who could ever have wanted to hurt Abby? Unless … … …

"Was there some sort of accident?" I asked.

"No, it wasn't that. Abby was kidnapped. It wasn't really for a ransom, although they did ask for money. It was to get James to back off from helping young Richard."

I looked the question, but she shook her head.

"No, you wouldn't know him. He's not around here anymore. Abby was snatched on her way home from a riding lesson. My poor Walter was driving, and when they tried to force him to stop in the lane he put his foot down and tried to get home. They shot his tyres and the car skidded off into a tree. He locked all the doors, but they simply smashed the windows and grabbed Abby."

She stopped, and there was obviously more to come, but I decided to let her take her time and not prompt her with more questions. Eventually it worked.

"The man who had Abby never intended to give her back, although we didn't know that at first. Well, to cut a long story short as they say, James got her back. It wasn't easy, and some people died, including a policeman, but Abby was safe."

It all made sense now. Cherry always hanging around, not letting Abby out of his sight. Even watching *Neighbours* with her. He was guarding her.

"What happened to the people who kidnapped her?"

"James never said, and it was better not to ask. But they were bad people… … with friends, so we can't help worrying about revenge. And that's all because Richard came to James for help."

She sighed.

"And now James is helping you. As if he didn't have enough to worry him with Mr Simmons dying like that, and the police getting all uppity."

I understood. In her shoes, I wouldn't have wanted me around either. All the more reason for moving on, as soon as Angie was well enough to come with me and we could look after each other.

"I really will be leaving just as soon as I can, Mrs Siddons."

She looked at me across a crumpled picture of Salisbury Cathedral and smiled. She actually smiled.

"No, my dear. You see, when James decides someone needs helping, they get helped whether they like it or not. James won't let you leave now until he's sure your troubles have been sorted. And there's your friend to think of too. It might take quite a while to see her fully right again. Quite a while."

She was clearly referring to Angie's need for drug rehab. James had told her more than he needed to, and I wondered why. She was only the housekeeper after all. I decided, now she seemed to be in a mood for conversation, to try a little gentle probing.

"I suppose you must have been with James a long time, Mrs Siddons."

I offered this as a statement, but it clearly invited a response. I wasn't disappointed.

"I have known him since he was in nappies, but I have only been with him, as you put it, since Lady Helena died and he inherited this house."

Was she the lady in my room, with the spaniels? No. Her name was Lady Alice Something-or-other. I wanted to ask if Lady Helena had been very rich, since James had mentioned inheriting money, but thought that Mrs Siddons might consider such a question a little vulgar. So, with an effort of memory, I tried another tack.

"Lady Helena must have been James's godmother."

Another statement-question.

"She was indeed. But, more importantly, she was also his great-aunt, and daughter of the tenth Marquess of Thurvaston. She married Sir Peter Marchmont, grandson of the Duke of Swaleburgh."

My lips pursed and I frowned slightly as I considered this.

"So … … is James a … … …" I struggled for the word. "I mean, is he a lord, or something?"

Her dark eyes watched me over the rim of her coffee cup. I guessed she was wondering whether to stop her revelations just there, or whether to give me the whole story. Eventually, maybe due to my winning smile, but more likely due to a natural talkativeness, she put down her cup and clasped her hands on the table in front of her.

"No, dear. He's not exactly a lord, or even a something. He's just a commoner, like you and me."

I didn't understand all this titles and nobility stuff, but I'd always thought that if you were related to a lord or lady you had to be more than just a commoner. So I asked her.

"Well, dear. It is confusing, I know. But if you are the holder of a title, duke, Marquess, whatever, then you are a member of the nobility. Your relatives may have courtesy titles, but that's all they are, a courtesy. In law, they are commoners and, unless they inherit a title, commoners they will always be."

I thought about that while taking a sip of coffee. I pulled a face as the remains were now barely lukewarm.

Mrs Siddons noticed, and smiled. At that moment there was a pinging sound.

"Get yourself some fruit juice out of the fridge, dear, and I'll rescue the croissants from the oven."

I hesitated, still wanting to talk, but now becoming aware of the delicious smell drifting across the kitchen. I wondered why I'd not noticed before.

"Go on, dear. Then I'll explain a bit more."

I did as I was told, helping myself to a glass of apple juice, and at the same time retrieving butter and apricot jam from the fridge. Mrs Siddons set a plate of crescent shapes, deliciously golden and flaky, in the middle of the table.

"Help yourself, dear. I put these in just before you came down."

Surprised by her thoughtfulness, I obeyed and, while the pastry melted in my mouth, listened as Mrs Siddons resumed her explanation.

"Lady Helena always had a soft spot for James, her being his godmother, you see. And she really took to young Sarah … …"

Her voice trailed off and a look of intense sadness came over her face. There was no wetness in her eyes or crumpling of her features. It was more a weariness of expression and far away bleakness in those dark pools beneath greying brows. I wanted her to carry on with the story, but felt I shouldn't prompt her.

"Sarah was a teacher when James met her. He was still in the Royal Marines. They married and two years later little Abby came along. Lady Helena was thrilled … … well, we all were. But a few months later, Sarah died. Some problem with her heart they said."

So that's what happened. No divorce, no accident, just the blind lottery we call health. Tragic.

"It was tragic, dear," said Mrs Siddons, echoing my thoughts, "Really tragic. She was such a lovely girl, full of energy, and such fun. Lady Helena was terribly upset when it happened. She told me they had offered Sarah a termination when they discovered the problem, but she wouldn't have it."

I hadn't touched my juice, and I noticed drops of condensation forming on the cold glass. Dusting flaky crumbs from my fingers, I reached for it, feeling its wetness against my fingertips. As I lifted it to sip at the apple juice, Mrs Siddons gave a deep sigh.

"James resigned his commission, he was a major by then, and decided to carry on where Sarah left off. He studied for a PGCE and became a teacher. He told Lady Helena he'd be better able to care for Abby as she grew up. He didn't want to be on the other side of the world fighting little wars while she grew up without him. Then Lady Helena died about a year, no … … nearer eighteen months it was … … after poor Sarah. James had just started his first teaching job, and she left him almost her entire estate. He needn't have worked at all then, but he seemed to feel he owed it to Sarah's memory to carry on doing what she had loved so much. That's when he came to live here, bringing little Abby with him, and Mrs Gormley of course."

There was a definite frostiness in those last words which I could not ignore.

"Mrs Gormley?"

"Aye. Gormley by name and gormless by nature. She was Abby's nurse. As good hearted as they come, but a real scatterbrain. Fair got on my nerves she did, and I was never so glad as when Lady Jessica – that's James's younger sister – gave birth to young Philip and she went off to look after him."

I was getting confused.

"So James's sister is a lady?"

"Courtesy, dear, remember? Just a courtesy."

She paused a moment, and a look of understanding came into her eyes.

"You're wondering why she should have such a courtesy title, aren't you?"

I nodded, and she pursed her lips, nodding back.

"Well that, I'm afraid, was the result of another tragedy. In 2003, James's uncle, the Marquess of Thurvaston, was flying his own plane up to his estates in Scotland. He loved flying. Even offered to take Lady Helena up, but she wouldn't go. Anyway, his wife and son were with him, and James's elder brother, Thomas. The cloud came down low and they just flew into a mountain. They all died."

Her eyes drifted away as she replayed that awful moment in her mind. I took up the story for her.

"So James's father became the Marquess of ... ... what was it ? ... ... Thurvaston. And his children could be called Lord or Lady."

Mrs Siddons returned to the present.

"That's right, dear. Although James should be known as the Earl of Aullton."

"So why isn't he?"

"Well, it's like this, dear. He started teaching as plain *Mister*. When his father became the Marquess, it was easier to just go on being *Mister Montrayne*. He didn't want to put people off by flaunting a title. He thought it might make it difficult for people to talk to him. Don't see why it should, myself. I talk to him."

She thought a moment.

"Money might put them off though. You see, when Lady Helena left him her estates, she thought he wouldn't have much else, being the younger son of a younger son. But now, when his father dies, James will end up being one of the richest men in England."

I was absolutely amazed.

"So why does he go on teaching?"

She smiled. "Like I said, dear. It's for Sarah."

I was startled by a loud buzzer somewhere behind me.

Mrs Siddons looked up quickly as I turned, startled, to see what it was. Some sort of alarm perhaps? Or maybe she was being summoned to another part of the house. Such things did happen in big houses, or so I supposed from certain movies I'd seen. Not the front door, because I'd seen enough last night to learn that no-one could just walk up to the house.

"It's the gate," she said, sounding rather surprised by the interruption.

The gate. Of course. Why didn't I think of that?

On the wall behind me, about head height, mine not James's, was a unit containing a small display screen, a speaker and some buttons. It buzzed again as I looked at it.

"Surjit would normally get that," Mrs Siddons explained, getting up as she did so. "But he's probably still asleep. James told him to lie in too, after last night."

She approached the unit and inspected the screen. Her head was now blocking my view, so I stood and came up beside her.

"Hmmm. Don't recognise the car," she muttered, and pressed a button just as the buzzer sounded for a third time.

"Yes, who is it?" she asked, abrupt and unwelcoming.

The voice which came out of the speaker was surprisingly clear and free of electronic distortion.

"Good morning. I was hoping to have a word with James Montrayne if possible."

The screen, I could now see, was split horizontally. The top section showed a wide view of the area in front of the gate, with a newish VW Beetle in the centre of the picture. The lower section was almost filled by the face of a young woman leaning out of the car's window towards the camera.

"Don't recognise her either." Still suspicious and unfriendly.

"I asked you a question, young lady. Who are you?"

The woman did not show any sign of being troubled by Mrs Siddons' frosty manner, and as soon as she spoke again I realised why. She was probably used to being treated with suspicion.

"My name is Corrina Rigby. I'm a reporter on the Lichfield Daily News. Can I see Mr Montrayne, or should I say … … "

"He's not at home," Mrs Siddons interrupted. The frost was now solid ice.

"Do you mean *not at home* to me, or really not at home?"

"I do not tell lies, young woman, even to reporters. I meant exactly what I said. Now show me some ID."

The face withdrew from the camera, and there was some rummaging in the car before eventually a small rectangular card was shoved up close to the camera. It was a Newspaper Society Press Card complete with photo of the woman in the car. I'd never seen one before, but I assumed it was OK. Not so, Mrs Siddons, suspicious to the end.

"OK, now your driving licence."

The Press Card withdrew and Corrina Rigby stared at the camera. For a moment I thought she was going to argue, but then she was back to rummaging. The driving licence was produced and flashed in front of the camera. Same girl in the photo. Same name.

"Satisfied now?" The reporter's voice held a weary exasperation.

"Not quite. Show me a credit card."

I couldn't help smiling. Mrs Siddons was obviously what they call a redoubtable character. Ignoring the protests issuing from the speaker, I glanced sideways at her, suddenly worried.

"Can she see us?" I asked.

Mrs Siddons shook her head.

The speaker was silent. Corrina Rigby was fuming.

"You're the one who wants to come in," reminded Mrs Siddons. "Now, let's see the card."

More rummaging and then an Amex card was waved at the camera.

"I didn't catch the name," said my redoubtable housekeeper. "Again please."

There it was: American Express, long number, same name.

"Thank you, Miss Rigby. I'm sorry you've had a wasted journey. It would probably be wise to call ahead next time. Good Morning."

She pressed a button and the speaker fell silent, cutting off the reporter's response. On the lower screen we could see her shouting at the camera, while the picture above showed her stabbing repeatedly at the call button.

"I turned her off," said Mrs Siddons turning to me with a perfectly straight face but with a definite twinkle in those dark eyes.

"You actually enjoyed that, didn't you?" I said, smiling the accusation.

"Most fun I've had all morning," she replied. "Now sit down and let's finish these croissants."

Nineteen

Queen's Hospital, Burton-on-Trent – 11:15 am

It had been a late night and Joanne Hayford had been looking forward to her lie-in this Sunday morning. There was no avoiding the fact that she would have to be back at the farm for 11:00 to visit the scene where the lad had been assaulted, and she'd have to get a statement from the guy who'd found him. She probably wouldn't have to bother the girls, although she did wonder about the shifty one, the one who didn't seem to want to catch her eye. Still, that might be nothing. From all she could gather, the farm was home to a few youngsters who had no reason to think well of the police.

   She was supposed to be back at the station after lunch, Morrissey had been absolutely clear about that, but at least she could be sure of having the morning to herself. It had been a muggy night and the day promised to be warm and dry, so she was pottering around her flat in a pale-blue, thigh-length nightie with a picture of a panda over each breast and an inscription below which read *The only thing rarer than these is a policeman on the beat!* The smooth boyfriend had given it to her for her birthday, and was almost offended that she actually liked it.

   Having crawled out of bed a little before nine, she had turned on the TV, more for company that for anything else. Although David Frost was doing his suave best to bring her up to date on current political events, her restless mind was elsewhere. Even while trying to decide what to eat for breakfast, her thoughts kept jumping back to Philip Simmons and James Montrayne, and that young woman with the scared eyes sitting in the kitchen at Heighley Grange farm.

   It ought to be muesli, but she just wasn't in the mood. She felt the morning deserved more than a bowl of rodent-fodder so she burrowed around in fridge and freezer to gather the ingredients for her favourite, though seldom indulged in, start-the-day snack. Fifteen minutes later, she settled down in front of Sir David, intending to give him her full attention. On her lap-tray was a plate containing a slice of wholemeal bread, toasted and buttered and coated with Marmite, and over this was piled a mound of scrambled eggs topped off with smoked salmon.

   There was a lot of stuff about the election, now only a few days away, but she quickly tired of the smart-mouthed politicians who lied through their teeth to get your votes making promises everyone knew perfectly well they would never keep. The smoked salmon tasted good, in spite of being one day past its sell-by date. She always assumed that suppliers allowed a good safety margin and managed her menus accordingly. It drove the smooth boyfriend crazy and, more than once, he had refused to eat with her because he'd caught a glance at the packaging which she had been too slow at consigning to the waste bin.

The TV regained her attention briefly when a familiar face flashed onto the screen and Sir Vernon Laycock gave a short interview outside his home at Hunter's Court. He played down the obsequious praise of the reporter, but he did confirm that he would accept a place in government should such a post be offered after the election. Assuming his party won, of course, which was by no means a sure thing.

Joanne wasn't sure exactly where Hunter's Court was, having never been invited to such a posh residence, but she had an idea that it wasn't very far from Heighley Grange, which brought her mind back to the point it was trying, temporarily, to escape from.

The girl with the scared eyes had been very uneasy about something, and Joanne had noticed how she hesitated before reluctantly giving her name. Given the background of many of the youngsters working on the farm, maybe shying away from the police was a natural reaction. And if it turned out she was hiding something, which seemed likely, the chances were it would have nothing at all to do with Philip Simmons or James Montrayne. Still, it wouldn't do any harm to run her through the computer and see what popped up.

She had just finished loading her dirty pots into the dishwasher when her mobile phone rang. She looked at the display, groaned and wondered whether to pretend she was still asleep and ignore it. She sighed. PC Mayblin was nothing if not persistent, and if she didn't answer now, he would keep on trying until she did.

"Morning, Charlie," she said, not even trying to hide her irritation. "Don't you ever sleep?"

"Hey, Sarge," answered Mayblin. "Why sleep when there's much more fun things to be doing?"

"Whatever fun you're involved in right now, Charlie, I'm not sure I want to know."

"You'll want to know this, Sarge. I've just had a call from the hospital. That lad who got knocked on the head in the field near Heighley Woods... ... Well, he's come round and the doc reckons he's fit enough to make a statement... ... Er... ... If you're busy, I could go if you like."

It was tempting, but she couldn't trust Mayblin to coax everything she needed out of a young man whose injuries would no doubt be compounded by suspicion and fear.

"No thanks, Charlie. Just leave it with me."

She took a few more details, and then told Mayblin he'd have to get someone out to the farm for the 11:00 appointment which she now would not be able to keep. She told him exactly what she wanted done and then tossed the phone onto the kitchen table and headed for the shower. She smiled as she went. From the delight in Mayblin's voice, she assumed that he was going to allocate the duty to himself.

It was just over an hour later when she strode along the entrance corridor to the Queen's Hospital on the outskirts of Burton-on-Trent. The direction signs were clear and well-placed and it didn't take her long to find the ward where Nathan Campion was being cared for. She was too early for normal visiting but, when she flashed her warrant card at the nurse who accosted her, she was shown to a side room off the main ward.

Joanne thought that the lad lying in the standard hospital bed seemed small for a seventeen-year-old, but with all the covers over him it was hard to tell. His eyes were closed when she entered but opened quickly when the nurse spoke.

"Hey, Nathan. Got a visitor for you."

She then surprised Joanne by moving to the foot of the bed, smiling down at the boy, clearly intending to hang around.

"I'd like to speak with him privately," said Joanne, pulling a chair up close to the side of the bed.

"Sorry," the nurse replied, still smiling. "Doctor Gates said you could have ten minutes, and Mrs Campion left word that if anyone from the police arrived before she got back, Nathan wasn't to be left alone with them."

Joanne smiled back at her to hide her own irritation. The boy was seventeen and was a victim not a suspect. She was perfectly entitled to talk to him without his mother, or some other responsible adult, present and, from everything she'd learned, his mother wasn't much protection against anything. Still, making a fuss about it would most likely cause him to clam up.

"OK," she said. "That's fine."

Sitting down, she showed her warrant card to Nathan and said, in a quiet, encouraging tone, "Hi, Nathan. My name's Jo Hayford. I'm from the police. We were a bit worried about you last night so when we heard you'd woken up I thought I'd come along and see if you can remember anything about what happened to you yesterday."

He reached out and took the warrant card from her hand. He stared at it for a long while.

"Nice picture," he said eventually. "Too nice. You're too pretty to be a cop."

"Thanks," she said, and tried to take back her card, but his fingers gripped it tightly while he continued to stare at the picture. After a moment, his hold relaxed and she removed the card from his hand.

"I don't like cops," he said, looking into her eyes for the first time.

"I know," she said, "and with good reason, I think."

His eyes narrowed at that as if he was surprised that, rather than being offended, she was agreeing with him.

She did feel that his antipathy was justified. His file showed him to be the only child of an alcoholic mother and an abusive father, from whom he had run away at the age of fifteen. The police had found him a few days later at the home of a lad believed to be in violation of his ASBO. He was immediately returned to his home to be swamped by the vodka-laden sobs of his mother and the surliness of his out-of-work father who, as soon as the police car was round the corner, had used his belt to beat the living daylights out of him. Two days after his sixteenth birthday, he had run away again to rejoin his ASBO mates. When the police caught him this time, he was running away from a fire set by his friends in a derelict house on the edge of town. He hadn't been responsible for starting it but, like them, he had stayed too long to enjoy their handiwork, and they had been spotted. This time it ended with a court order placing him in the care of the local authority until he was eighteen, which is how he came to be living and working on the farm. Joanne reckoned he had good reason to think of the police as the enemy.

"Yeah," he said. "Well... ..."

"Look," she tried coaxingly, "we both know you've been in trouble in the past, but this isn't about that. As far as I know, you've done nothing wrong this time, so why not just tell me what happened?"

He was silent for a while, and she gave him time to think it over. Pushing him wouldn't do any good. He would tell her if he wanted to, or not at all.

When the silence continued, she decided it wouldn't do any harm to try an indirect approach.

"Sometimes," she said, "I like to go for a run early in the morning. It's quiet and not too many people about... ... I like time to think, when nobody's telling me what to do. My favourite place is along by the canal... ... I guess you like to escape sometimes, too."

When he didn't respond, she thought she'd lost him, but then his head turned on the pillow so he could look at her again.

"Yeah," he said, nodding slightly. "I like the quiet... ... That's why I was there... ... the old shepherd's hut. It's nice in the morning... ... Peaceful."

His eyes were still on her, but it was as though his gaze was focussed on some distant point way behind her.

"Did you see anyone coming up from the woods?"

"Yeah, I saw him... ... well, someone coming up the path anyway. I couldn't say for sure he'd been in the woods. He was coming up quick like, but not running."

"Did you recognise him?"

"No way. He was all togged up in some dark gear... ... and he had something over his face."

"So you don't know whether it could have been James Montrayne?"

His amazement was both obvious and genuine.

"His lordship? You've gotta be kidding."

"Why's that?"

"Coz this guy wasn't big enough... ... Not tall enough. Not wide enough... ... It wasn't him... ... Why'd you think it was."

Joanne smiled. "I didn't. But I just needed to be sure."

"Yeah, well. It wasn't him."

She got him to explain how he'd first been spotted by his attacker, and everything else he could remember, which wasn't much. He hadn't noticed that the stranger was carrying anything as he came up from the woods, but he couldn't say for sure that he wasn't. In fact, it seemed as though he didn't have much to offer that was any use at all until she asked about the stranger's footwear.

"Boots," said Nathan. "When he knocked me down, they were right in front of my face. And then the bastard kicked me."

He rubbed the side of his forehead which was discoloured and swollen just into the hairline.

Remembering the footprints found at the lakeside, she asked, "Can you recall anything about them? Colour, style, anything at all?"

"They were just boots," he said, and then thought for a moment. "But they were new. There was dirt round the bottoms, but the tops and the... ... you know, those fancy bits the laces thread through... ... well they were all clean and shiny. They were sort of... ... browny colour."

"OK," said Joanne slowly, her mind suddenly racing with possibilities.

Nathan picked up on it. "That's important, isn't it?"

"It could be," she replied cautiously. "Thanks."

At which point the nurse decided that her time was up, and emphasised the point by telling Nathan that he should try to get a bit more sleep before lunch.

Joanne thanked him again, said goodbye, and was on her way to the door when his voice stopped her.

"Hey, miss," he said. "You can come visit again, you know... ... if you like."

She smiled. "Thanks, Nathan. I might just do that. You get well now."

Just under an hour later, she was sitting in the ruins of the old shepherd's hut above Heighley woods enjoying a meagre picnic of ham sandwich and diet Coke which she'd bought from the WRVS café at the hospital on her way out. It wasn't that she didn't trust Mayblin to do the job right. She just wanted to see the site for herself, especially after what she had learned from Nathan. All there was to show for Mayblin's visit was police tape marking out the area around the ruined hut.

She had approached the tumbled stones very carefully, understanding Nathan's appreciation of the peacefulness of the site. Making sure she placed her feet only on the stones, she had avoided contaminating the many impressions which could still be seen in the soft ground. From her vantage point up on the pile, she thought about what she could see. It was pretty much a jumble of prints around the stones, but she was sure there were four, maybe five, different sets of footprints, approaching from the direction of the farm, which would fit the facts as she knew them. One set would belong to Nathan, one to the girl with the scared eyes (she made another note to herself to run her through the computer as soon as she got the chance), two sets to the younger girls, and the last to his lordship's mate, Mr Cherville-Thomas.

So where were the prints of the guy who had attacked Nathan?

Having finished the sandwich and half the bottle of Coke, she climbed up on the field boundary wall and scanned the route of the path above and below the stones of the ruined hut. Even with her near perfect eyesight, it was hard to make out any detail on the ground at more than a few yards, so she began to edge along the top of the wall in the direction of the gate into the road about one hundred yards away. Once she was clear of the haphazard fall of stones around the ruins, there were clear patches of ground where the footsteps of walkers using the public footpath kept the grass at bay.

There were footprints all right, like a whole army had tramped down the path. Then she remembered that this was the direction from which the ambulance crew had approached the day before, and everyone had presumably exited this way to see Nathan safely en route to hospital. If there were boot prints to be found which matched those in the wood, they were going to be very hard to discover.

So she started to make her way back, still balancing on the top of the wall, past the stones of the hut and several yards beyond, in the direction of the woods.

And there they were. Several clear sets of boot prints heading in both directions up and down the path. Even without a picture to match them to, she was certain they were the same as the ones of which photos and casts had been taken the previous day down by the lake. Which meant… … what? If these were the prints of the guy who had attacked Nathan, then they didn't belong to James Montrayne. So two people, wearing the same style boots, had been in the woods yesterday morning. Coincidence, or something else entirely?

Lowering herself to sit on the wall, Joanne took out her phone and leant forward to take several pictures of the prints. That done, she used the phone for its primary purpose to call Mayblin and ask whether any photos or casts had been taken of the prints further down the slope. The constable didn't have the advantage of having spoken to Nathan so she knew it may not have occurred to him even to look. It hadn't, so she told him to send out a scene-of-crime team to secure a wider area and to see whether the prints could be tracked right back to the lake in the woods.

The sun was shining amidst cotton wool clouds in a blue sky, so Sergeant Joanne Hayford decided that sitting here in the countryside guarding a footpath was a much better use of her Sunday afternoon than sitting at her desk in the office. She sighed contentedly and made her way back to the rest of her Coke. Very occasionally, policing did have its benefits.

Twenty

Venice – 9.45 am

Nadera Husseini was sitting alone on a bench in the Biennale Gardens, about three hundred yards from her hotel on the Via Garibaldi. She liked the gardens. They were bright and colourful, and she hadn't expected to find them in this city of canals and faded palazzos.

Nadera was worried. She usually was, for she had never really learned how to enjoy her work, which made it a wonder that she had survived at it for so long. For ten years, she had worked for Abdullah bin Hamad Al-Mubarak, head of security for one of the more senior Saudi princes doing work that was usually more intellectually demanding than it was physically dangerous. She had wheedled the most astounding secrets from western businessmen and diplomats, while plying them with carefully crafted misinformation, and had never once had to resort to sleeping with any of them. It had been a close run thing on several occasions, and Al-Mubarak would certainly not have held her back from using her undeniable charms in such a way. No, it was her own conscience that prevented from employing the ultimate in her art of persuasion.

But in all those ten years she had never even had to think about killing anyone.

Until now.

John Salisbury was different from the others she had been sent after. He had dared to defraud the Saudi government. True, it was for a sum of money which most of the princes wouldn't even consider small change, but even Nadera understood the principle of revenge. Salisbury could not be allowed to profit from such audacity. She had known when Al-Mubarak had charged her with the task of finding him that the assignment was not one of the highest priority, and she had frequently been given other short-term missions, but always she had returned to the hunt for the missing Salisbury.

The intensity of her efforts had increased after several component failures at the desalination plant resulted in significant loss of production. This was a disaster for national pride as well as an economic setback as several neighbouring states were becoming dependent on the supply of fresh water from the Saline Water Conversion Corporation of Saudi Arabia. When further failures occurred at King Abdul Aziz Brigade Headquarters of the Saudi Arabian National Guard, Al-Mubarak had been ordered step up the hunt for Salisbury and the embezzled funds.

And now she had him, which is why she was worried.

The timing for this had suddenly become absolutely crucial. John Salisbury had to die that night and it was her responsibility to make it happen. She had been told that one of Al-Mubarak's private contractors, the current politically correct name for mercenaries, would fly in to Marco Polo later that day. He was a former sergeant in the British Paras name of Dave Talbot. If she had not been able to eliminate Salisbury by the time Talbot arrived in Venice, the termination process would be out of her hands, and she very much wanted to handle this one herself.

She had flown into Marco Polo Airport the previous day on an EasyJet flight from East Midlands Airport in the UK. That had been part one of her plan for the eradication of John Salisbury. In spite of the fact that arson was not one of her top-rated skills, the blaze she instigated in that dental surgery on the High Street of Burton-upon-Trent looked as though it should have done the trick. She hated working at night, even though she knew that her instructors were right when they taught her that darkness can cloak a multitude of clandestine activities. The trouble was, it also meant that you couldn't always see what you were doing, and that could be dangerous.

Like the time several years earlier when she had dodged the blade aimed for her heart only to step into an ornate but ancient chamber pot, unfortunately not empty. This had caused her to trip and fall straight into the arms of her would-be assassin. She had survived only because he had been as startled as she was, giving her a moment to regroup and grab the handle of the pot. His youthful resolve had melted once he had been smacked across the temple a couple of times with half a ceramic pot dripping with urine. Since the young man had once been dear to her, any temptation to seize his knife and plunge it into his chest had been easily resisted. She had simply dropped the broken pot and fled, never again feeling totally comfortable working in the dark.

As she thought about that incident, her gaze wandered around the gardens. There was colour everywhere, luscious and vibrant, but her eyes didn't really take it in. Nor did they notice the cats meandering through the plants or sunning themselves on the mown grass. When she'd first spotted them days before, she'd wondered briefly why there seemed to be so many cats in this part of the city. It was a question to which she hadn't yet found an answer.

She shook off the memory and forced her thoughts back to the present. She had come to the gardens to give herself time to review her plans before her appointed meeting with Salisbury. She knew he would be desperate to see her again. He had been captivated from that first moment, two weeks before, when he had caught sight of her as he strolled around the Naval Museum. She had been cautiously tailing him since early that morning, not even certain then that she had found the man she was after.

The name was wrong, Josh Barnett, and his appearance did not exactly match the old photo given to her by Al-Mubarak, but there was no doubt that she had at last tracked him down. He had even admitted it to her, eventually.

*   *   *   *   *

It was the gondola that was responsible. The asymmetric shape of these craft was not so apparent as they glided elegantly along the canals propelled with fluent ease by stripe-shirted gondoliers. But out of the water, the strange asymmetric lines of the black painted boat exhibited in the museum were plainly evident. It was an oddity that caught her attention, and she moved in closer to the gondola to read the information board. When she next glanced up to check the whereabouts of the man she was supposed to be observing, she was startled to find him standing only a metre away, observing her.

"Fascinating isn't it?" he said with a sidelong glance and a slight smile. "I never realised they built them like that until today."

"It is … … … intriguing," she replied cautiously, fixing her eyes back on the exhibit, not at all sure how to proceed. If she tried to continue following him, he was bound to notice. For a moment, neither could think what to say next. Her mind was working overtime wondering how to turn the situation to advantage; his was desperately trying to work out how to extricate himself from the embarrassment of being thought to be making advances to a decidedly attractive young woman.

"I'm sorry," he said finally, with unassumed diffidence. "I should not have interrupted your thoughts."

He began to move away and she realised she had two choices: lose him, or keep him close and make absolutely certain of his identity.

"No," she said quickly. "You are quite correct."

She saw him pause and turn back towards her. She baited her hook.

"This shape is most strange," she mused, sounding truly puzzled. "I thought the wood had bent with age, but perhaps this is not so?"

Her rising intonation left the question hanging. It was an invitation he could not resist and he began sharing the knowledge which he himself had gained only moments before.

"The gondolier stands at the stern." He lightly laid his hand on her arm to draw her to the rear of the boat, letting go as soon as she began to follow him. "Just here. But he stands on the right hand side, rowing with just a single oar."

"Yes, I see," she smiled in encouragement. "I suppose that the canals are too narrow for the boats to have oars on both sides. They would … … … tangle up."

"Exactly," he smiled back, suitably encouraged. "But the problem is, that if the boat was symmetrical, it would … … …"

A slight frown had creased her forehead. He thought again.

"If the boat was the same on both sides … … …"

She nodded. "Ah, yes."

"Well, that would upset the balance of the boat and cause it to pull to the left. So, to correct that, the gondola is built so that the left side is twenty-four centimetres wider than the right."

He looked down into the wide brown eyes smiling up at him and was utterly bewitched.

"I wonder … … have you had the opportunity yet … … I mean, I assume you don't live in Venice?"

"No," she assured him. "This is my first visit actually. I am truly fascinated."

"Well, in that case, have you had the chance yet to travel the canals in a gondola?"

"No," she said, leading him gently on. "But I think I must do so before I leave."

And so she hooked him, and then kept him dangling and squirming for two whole weeks while she tried to find the location of the money.

They had visited glass factories on the island of Murano, admired the lace and the brightly painted houses of Burano, visited the ancient cathedral on Torcello, toured the Doge's palace, drunk chocolate in the Piazza san Marco and, of course, inspected the Rialto Bridge from a gondola.

Over intimate dinners she had told him snippets of her past, before she had been drawn into her current occupation. Her childhood memories had held him enraptured, and he had contributed many of his own. Slowly she had built up this tit-for-tat exchange until, after almost a week, she reached the point of her most private memory, her first love affair.

He was young, only a few months older than she was herself, and worked on her father's farm outside Buraydah in the Qassim Province of Saudi Arabia. She explained how they had met in the orange groves when she had been taking food to her father. She had not been alone. When outside the mud-brick house that was her family home, she was hardly ever alone. Usually, she was accompanied by her older brother. That first brief meeting of eyes had passed unnoticed by her brother. Repeated on successive occasions, it had developed into a meeting of hearts.

She began to yearn for a more tangible meeting, when she could talk to him, hear his voice, and they could share their hopes and dreams. But such a thing was not permitted. To meet him, unaccompanied by any member of her family, was unthinkable and would bring great dishonour upon her. But still she longed for it.

Then one day it happened. Purely by chance, the young man was sent on an errand to her house. She was alone in the courtyard which he passed through on leaving. Again their eyes met, and lingered, and longing began to fill them. He came to her; he spoke to her; he sat with her; he held her hand.

And that was how her brother found them.

She never saw the young man again. She heard that he had been taken away to be severely whipped before being forced to sign an undertaking never to repeat the offence. She understood Islamic Law but could not prevent a smouldering anger from taking hold of her, to the extent that she refused point blank to marry the man her parents had chosen for her. Weeks of bitter recriminations followed as she stubbornly refused all attempts to make her change her mind. Her brother told her that she had dishonoured the family and must marry immediately. To continue in her refusal would only bring further dishonour.

The day before she sneaked out of the family home, her brother lost all control, and beat her relentlessly in a frenzy of garbled abuse. She could not understand his notions of honour. They seemed distorted and compassionless, and did not fit with what she'd been taught in school and by her mother. That prematurely frail lady seemed sympathetic, but was powerless under the male domination of her family.

On that last night, ostracised by the rest of her family, she lay alone in her room nursing her bruises and planning how to make her escape. It was then that her brother had come with his knife, determined to end the shame which he felt had been brought upon his household.

And so she had fled to lose herself in the darkness. Here Al-Mubarak had found her and, with a high-handed disregard for Saudi law, had befriended her, nurtured her, coached her and trained her until, he believed, she was entirely his.

This final morsel, of course, she not disclose as she brought her touching reminiscence to its end.

These details, both intimate and tragic, had all the merit of being absolutely true. Their hesitant disclosure invited John to produce an equally poignant recollection of his own. He had not disappointed her, and gradually the details of his inglorious business career and subsequent embezzlement had begun to emerge.

Skilfully extracted information had gradually built up a picture of a gentle, humorous, somewhat naïve man whose mind was a vast reservoir of irrelevant information with little practical use. A man with sufficient funds salted away to live very comfortably, but without extravagance. A man whose memory was so bad that everything he needed to remember was diligently filed away on his laptop, even his bank account details though these, she had learnt, were carefully encrypted. A man whose self-deprecating manner was surprisingly endearing, particularly in view of the fact that he made absolutely no effort to entice her into his bed, despite his all too obvious infatuation.

He was, in fact, a gentleman, albeit a slightly dishonest one. And after two weeks, she really didn't want to see him dead.

But Al-Mubarak had decreed it, so it had to be.

As long as the laptop was preserved.

If Talbot were allowed to do it his way, Salisbury's death would be neither swift nor painless. She couldn't let it end that way.

So her plan had to work, and in the next three hours.

Twenty-One

Edgbaston – 4.45 pm

The garden was deserted now, all the chairs around the pool abandoned, but for one. Jennifer Mellisse stretched and yawned. It had been a very satisfying day. Their guests for cocktails and Sunday lunch had included the local MP, a couple of City councillors, a doctor and his wife and a brace of foreign businessmen. The male – female balance of the guests had almost been maintained, but a well-known lady racehorse trainer had cried off at the last minute due to an outbreak of something nasty in the stables.

Her children seldom graced these functions. When it came to serious conversation, they had the same boredom threshold as most other young people, and they begged to be allowed to hang out with their friends instead. Jennifer usually gave permission, though she was very proud of Graeme and Sonia and loved to show them off, but she knew that compelling their attendance, even for only a short period, would only make them sulky and resentful.

Apart from their absence, she enjoyed these occasions. The conversation was usually entertaining, often interesting, as people influential in their own fields discussed a variety of topics under her very gentle manipulation. She was an excellent hostess, always ensuring that everyone had an opportunity to contribute to the discussion, and no-one hogged the limelight for too long.

Ray Mellisse felt very proud of his wife, with every justification, as he watched her slow movements from the window of his study. She belonged to the respectable strand of his life while having no notion that another strand even existed. Without the ability to clearly compartmentalise his life, Ray Mellisse would have gone under years ago. Without too much difficulty, he managed to maintain a clear level of separation between his legitimate enterprises, some quite highly regarded in the local business community, and his other less honest, but highly profitable activities wherein lay the principle source of his wealth.

Mellisse sighed. If only Angie had had the decency to fall under that truck instead of on top of it, half his current problems would be over. But it was Di's actions that really pissed him off. Di probably wasn't her real name of course. He'd no idea what it was, but that hadn't been an issue up to now. He'd picked her up off the street as a runaway and arranged for her to work in one of his clubs. From there she had been recruited by Bruno for other, more specialised work which involved servicing the needs of certain preferential clients. She had done well for herself, even being put in charge of the latest batch of unwary incomers from Lithuania. And all the time she had been waiting her chance to do a runner. Just when he needed her for a particularly important job.

The trouble was Mellisse couldn't be certain just how much she knew about his clients, or his operations or, most importantly, the degree of his own involvement in them. She certainly knew about the girls supplied to business conferences in remote country houses. She definitely knew the details of the traffic in young girls from the former Soviet Baltic states to service the clubs and brothels of Birmingham's growing sex industry. She probably knew most of the clubs and massage parlours which comprised his less respectable business portfolio.

But, worst of all, she knew his name. If only he hadn't taken a personal interest in her when he'd seen her for the first time out there on the street in front of his club. If only he'd kept his distance then, she would not now be able to make the connections, to join up the dots.

He was still fuming over his own stupidity when the phone rang. He pressed the button on the speaker.

"Evening, Mr Mellisse." Bruno's voice was cautious, subdued, and Ray knew that the news would not be good.

"Bruno."

There was silence. Definitely not good. Ray's simmering anger began to boil.

"Now, Bruno. All of it. Right now! Or so help me I'll come down there and fillet you with my own hands."

It might have been an empty threat, if Bruno hadn't seen him do exactly that several years ago when one of the pimps running a cluster of brothels in south-central Birmingham had started skimming an extra cut off the top of the proceeds. Not only was it stupid, it was carelessly done, and it was the insult of being taken for a fool that had so enraged Mellisse. When he had questioned Bruno about discrepancies occurring in the accounts, and learned about the pimp's sudden increase in expenditure, he had become incandescent at being scammed by such a sloppy incompetent. When Bruno offered to *permanently terminate his contract* Mellisse had almost agreed. He usually allowed Bruno to contract out the *terminations* thus distancing himself from the messier side of his business, but this time he was too angry and he had wanted to make a point.

So he had done the job himself. Bruno had set it up, and Ray had wielded the knife in as neat a job as any butcher filleting a side of beef. When the decaying remains had been discovered in several bin bags on a refuse tip, Bruno had gradually let slip to those who needed to know that The Boss had handled this one himself. The effect was salutary. No-one knew who The Boss was but, after this, no-one wanted to find out either.

"Sorry, Mr Mellisse," said Bruno, though his tone did not sound particularly contrite. "I wasn't trying to wind you up. Just sorting my thoughts out." Another pause, though only slight this time. "First, the hospital. I took Sally over there with me. You don't know her, but she's enough like Angie to pass for her sister. No good. Paperwork shows Angie left during the night but no-one knows where she went. Night staff had already gone off when we got there, so I tried Charlie."

By this, he meant Charlie Croker, a failed three-year medical student who had allowed a drug addiction to mess up what could probably have been a promising career. Charlie had also gambled and run up enough debt in a casino owned by Mellisse to give Bruno the stranglehold he needed when a particular type of job came up. "Charlie got the name of the ward sister, and tried the *urgently got to get a message to her* approach, but he couldn't get a number or address. He hung around for a while to see if he could get access to the computers, but no dice. He'll be back this evening when they come on again at six."

"Doesn't sound like he tried very hard, Bruno."

"He's just a kid, Mr Mellisse. I only used him 'coz he knows hospitals. I've sent Jock Williams along with him this evening. That should concentrate his efforts."

Ray knew Jock. A hard man from Glasgow who came south when the Scottish police made his home town too hot for him.

"OK, Bruno. Second?"

"Second is that farm. I sent Vince along there like I said. Now get this Mr Mellisse; that farm is crawling with cops and there's talk of a dead body."

He waited for a response but there was just silence. Ray was thinking hard.

"Would you know anything about that, Bruno?"

Bruno knew he was on delicate ground here, and there was a moment's silence before he replied.

"Why would you ask that, Mr Mellisse?"

The reply was immediate and hardening in tone.

"Don't mess me around, Bruno. You told me a while ago that our expediter could see a problem brewing and, if I remember right, this problem has a house somewhere near that farm. So, tell me straight. What do you know?"

Telling it straight was the only way with Ray Mellisse. Bruno knew that, so he unloaded the whole story as far as he knew it.

"Well, it seems some guy got himself topped yesterday in a wood not far from the farm. Cops are trampling all over in their big boots looking for clues, asking questions. You know the drill... ... Now our expediter told me that if he was right about that problem, then he might need to do a bit of tidying up. Makes me wonder if this is his idea of tidying."

"Keep going, Bruno."

"Seems the dead guy's one of the locals. Name of Philip Simmons."

"So?"

"So, he's one of the bosses at Lichfield Tube. He could have been the problem."

Mellisse felt the anger rise up in him. This was getting complicated and, while he contemplated the possible consequences, he let the silence go on for so long that eventually Bruno asked, "You still there, Mr Mellisse?"

"I'm here, Bruno. Do you have anything else?"

"Well, Vince was stopped once as he was walking along the lane. He had to give ID but they seemed to accept he was just a townie out for a country walk. He's clean so no worries if they check up on him. That farm usually lets Joe Public pay a quid to wander around with his family looking at the animals, but no go today. Police have put the farm off limits except for those who live there or work there. Couldn't try the farm shop either 'coz it's closed on Sunday."

Mellisse was thinking hard. He needed to be absolutely certain about what had happened.

"Are you sure of this, Bruno. The dead guy couldn't be Satish?"

"That's just it, Mr Mellisse. Vince wondered at first if it could be Satish or his mate, but there seems no doubt it was some guy called Simmons. One of the locals."

"Any way it could it be connected to Satish going missing? Or to those girls?"

"Can't see how, Mr Mellisse."

"No, OK. So the farm's a dead end for now?"

"Actually, maybe not."

Ray hadn't been aware of his head drooping a little at the lack of positive news, but this comment caused him to look up, attention focussed.

"I'm listening, Bruno."

"Well, Vince took a dog with him, for show really. Anyway, he took it for a walk up the lane. Nothing more harmless than a guy out walking his dog. He met another bloke doing the same thing, and they stopped for a chat. Dog people do that, apparently. ... ... Yesterday morning he was walking his dog, that's this other guy, and he saw this girl. He couldn't remember much about her, except that she was scruffy, dirty, probably drug-ridden, and looked like she'd been dragged through a hedge backwards. His words. He obviously didn't like her. In fact he didn't seem to like the farm much either from what Vince could make out. I can't say this girl really sounds like Di Thomas, but you never know."

Ray shook his head as he thought. It really didn't sound at all like Di. Men usually liked her a lot, and no-one ever described her as scruffy. And as for drugs, he knew well she had resisted every attempt to draw her down that route. But, like Bruno said, you never knew.

"Leave it for now, Bruno. But if the farm shop's open tomorrow, send someone up to ask around. Make sure it's someone she's never seen before, just in case she really is there. And Bruno, tell them to be discreet. We wouldn't want her doing another runner."

"You got it, Mr Mellisse. Discreet. I'll call you later about the hospital. Oh, and I'll keep trying to get hold of the expediter and see what he knows."

"Do that. Oh, and Bruno. Anything at all on Satish?"

"Sod it, I forgot. No, there's still no peep at all. Cell's still off. Vince couldn't find any sign of him. I did wonder if the police might have picked him up."

"Why would they do that?"

"Well, the pair of them did go tooled up. So, if they got stopped… … you know, near where there's been a killing… …"

"I don't think so, Bruno. If Satish was stupid enough to get himself arrested, you'd know by now. He knows the drill. He wouldn't waste his phone call."

Ray switched off the speakerphone. He stood and stretched and thought about the damage this stupid girl could cause. Hadn't he taken her off the street, arranged a job for her and a place to stay? He had even allowed Bruno to give her extra responsibility. And now the ungrateful bitch chose this moment to chuck it all in and do a runner. And with the election only four days away.

As far as the country was concerned, it probably wouldn't change anything. The Prime Minister would still be in power, albeit with an almost certain reduced majority in Parliament. The army would still be fighting in Iraq and Afghanistan. London would still be a target for Islamic terrorists. France and Germany would still be tussling to see who could be the dominant power in Europe, at the expense of the UK. And the power brokers in the City of London would continue to dominate world markets.

But one small thing, in a small town in the Midlands, definitely *would* change, and with it Mellisse's ability to control some of the country's most influential people.

If any other girl had run it would scarcely have mattered, apart from the principle of never letting any of them leave his service without permission which, of course, was never given. But this girl was different.

He had meticulously planned how to become one of the most powerful shapers of policy in the new government, and all without his ever having to stand as a candidate. Little Di was his key to making it happen. The irony was that the silly cow probably didn't even realise it. He had to get her back undamaged, at least until her part was over. After that... ...

Twenty-Two

Hunters Court – 5.00pm

Sir Vernon Laycock actually felt his cheek muscles relax as he closed the heavy oak door which usually kept out the riffraff from Hunters Court. The smile which he'd kept in place all afternoon, with increasing difficulty during the last hour, finally slipped quietly away. Today the riffraff had not been kept out and the smile had been their reward, along with a substantial buffet tea, for turning up to hear yet more campaign promises and to pledge in return their support in these last days before the election.

At forty-nine years old, physically fit and pleasing to the cameras, he was an ideal candidate. He had lived in the county for many years, most of them in this same former hunting lodge, built during the American Revolution and eventually inherited by his wife, Lady Charlotte. He was chairman of a successful international corporation, FerroTech Plc, with influential contacts in the City of London, so he definitely understood the needs of business and commerce. His prospective constituents may not be certain how much he really understood *their* needs, but they did know how various local schools and charities had benefited from his many generous donations over the years.

Staffordshire East was a safe constituency, and had been since the General Election of 1945 when Winston Churchill's Conservatives suffered their landslide defeat at the hands of Clement Atlee. The Government was expected to lose a number of seats in the upcoming election but no-one, except perhaps the current Conservative candidate, anticipated that Staffordshire East would be one of them. Sir Vernon's political agent was convinced he would romp home with a majority of at least 7,000 in spite of the fact that he had never stood for election before.

The current MP, Charles Wilberforce, had served his constituents for twenty-two years and, whatever they thought of his voting record in Parliament, assuming they ever checked, he had always been well respected for his passionate involvement in community affairs. Wilberforce had been suffering the early onset of Parkinson's disease when he had last been returned to Parliament in 2001, and for two or three years his vigour had seemed undiminished. Latterly, however, the symptoms of his illness had begun to be picked up by cameras in the House of Commons causing some of his constituents to begin asking, quite rightly, whether he could any longer tolerate the rigours of Parliamentary life.

When the constituency party announced early in the New Year that Wilberforce would not be standing at the next election, they assumed that a rigorous search would be needed to find a successor.

Not so!

A memo from Central Party Headquarters, soon after the announcement, recommended that the local committee consider approaching Sir Vernon Laycock, a figure prominent on the local scene and well known to members of the committee, not least for his generous donations to party funds. Many wondered, though none openly asked the question, whether the recommendation was based on his undoubted knowledge and expertise in domestic and international commerce and financial affairs, his equally unquestioned involvement in local issues, or his marriage to a distant cousin of the Prime Minister.

Even Sir Vernon himself was not absolutely sure what tipped the balance in his favour. He had a shrewd suspicion that his wife had been attempting to pull strings with her cousin, but he also had a very accurate perception of his own abilities and knew that he was more qualified than any of the candidates being put up by the other parties. His only question had been *did he really want the job?*

If all that was on offer was a term as constituency MP, then probably not. But a ministerial post was something else again, and he had been led to believe that, once elected, he would not have to wait long before such a position came his way.

And so, he had begun campaigning, and with every passing day it had been increasingly born in upon him just how much he wanted to win. He visited schools and care homes for the elderly; he spoke at meetings in churches and village halls; he even went door to door canvassing support, something he hated doing but which he was told by his agent was essential, if only because his opponents were doing it.

He still managed to keep up with his business affairs which, these days, meant working longer hours than he'd become used to. He trusted the boards of his various companies, with one possible exception, and although he held the reins of control fairly loosely he would never drop his hands completely. Having more money than he would ever be able to spend, he was ready for a shift in direction. Who knows, in time, he might even have a shot at governing the country.

He heard the phone ring and was reaching for the handset which sat on the Sheraton table in the hall when the ring was cut off. He heard his wife's voice in the drawing room speaking softly and then she called out.

"Vernon. It's for you. Gordon Russell."

Sir Vernon sighed. He'd been looking forward to a relaxing evening in the company of his favourite single malt which hadn't featured anywhere amongst the varied drinks on offer that afternoon. Neither Lady Charlotte nor the malt would require that he smile at them all evening, and neither would be particularly perturbed if he chose not to bother to engage them in conversation. He was surprised at the intrusion, not because it was in any way unusual for him to take business calls at the weekend, but there was nothing significant happening at Lichfield Tube that he was aware of, and Gordon Russell did not call him for social chit-chat. The relaxing evening looked as though it was all set to disappear rapidly down the pan.

Looking in through the open door to the drawing room he saw Lady Charlotte already at ease on the sofa with a drink in one hand and the phone held negligently in the other. He told her he'd take the call in his office and backed away, almost knocking over one of the girls sent by the caterers he'd engaged for the afternoon. The girl, smartly dressed in white blouse and black skirt, stayed upright but the tray she had been carrying from the dining room back to the kitchen flipped over depositing on the hall carpet at least a score of plastic plates, one serving tray, and rat's feast of assorted titbits left over from the buffet.

Turning, Sir Vernon found himself looking into a pair of terrified blue eyes in a face that seemed scarcely a day over sixteen, and probably wasn't. Cheap labour! When the child spoke, her voice quivered.

"I'm sorry, Sir Vernon... ... I'm really sorry... ... I ... ..."

As her voice trailed off Sir Vernon bent to dust some crumbs from the lower legs of his trousers. First Russell, and he still didn't know what that was about, and now this. He could feel the anger rising in him.

"Please, Sir Vernon... ... I'll clear it up... ... If you complain, they won't pay me."

He saw the sheen in her eyes as she held her tears in check, and he decided to do the same with his anger. He'd love to let rip but he knew it wouldn't be fair and he prided himself on his fairness to those who worked for him and with him. People certainly didn't like it when his fury was unleashed, but they could never complain that it was undeserved. Many liked him, many didn't, and Sir Vernon found he didn't really care so long as they got the job done.

Glancing down again at the mess, he asked, "What's your name?"

"Anita... ... sir... ..."

"Hmm... ... Well, Anita, do you see that button on the wall?"

Lines appeared on the flawless skin of her forehead as she struggled to work out what was happening. She turned to see where he was looking and noticed the bell push set in the wall above the telephone table. She nodded.

"Good. Well, if you press that button a young man called William will appear and you can tell him that I need this cleared up. If you smile at him, I'm sure he'll be delighted to help. He's not very bright, but he is susceptible to a pretty smile."

Ignoring her confused stare, he retreated down the hall to his study at the back of the house. He faintly heard the bell ring as he closed his study door.

Wondering what disaster was looming, he sat in his ancient, but extremely comfortable armchair whose cracked leather seemed oddly out place beside the highly polished walnut top of his equally ancient desk. He reached for the phone, pressed a button to pick up the call, and answered in his customary manner.

"Laycock."

There was a slight pause before he heard the caller speak.

"Sir Vernon. I'm terribly sorry to bother you at home, and on a Sunday, but something's happened and I thought I ought to let you know before it hits the papers tomorrow."

Visions of a factory in flames or, worse, another scandal concerning a Middle East contract quickly subsided as Russell told his story. Sir Vernon didn't really know Philip Simmons, although he had met him on several occasions and the news of his death didn't really affect him greatly. He was, however, worried about the company.

"How is this going to affect the Rosyth deal?"

The Royal Naval dockyard at Rosyth on the Firth of Forth in Scotland had recently done very well in securing contracts for refitting a number of the Royal Navy's surface ships including the largest of the Type 42 destroyers, HMS Edinburgh. Since Lichfield Tube had developed the ability to supply Test Certification to the Naval Engineering Specification, they had been able to bid for the contract to supply a range of tubes, fittings and pipework that would be required in some of the refits. It was Phil Simmons who had bypassed the major metal stockists who normally obtained such contracts and who then subsequently sourced their materials from companies like his own Lichfield Tube. He had made a direct approach to the dockyard appropriations office with apparent success. The deal was almost done. Price, availability, quality, certification had all been agreed. Simmons had just been waiting for the first order.

"We're OK, Sir Vernon. Phil's already done all the work, and Harry's right up to speed on everything."

Harry Wilson was Lichfield Tube's sales manager, working directly under Phil Simmons. He was a good plodder and, having been inherited by Phil when the latter had taken over as Sales Director, had actually done quite well since Phil had the knack of making up for Harry's deficiencies with his own drive and initiative.

"He'd better be, Gordon. This first order may only net fifty grand or so, but if this goes right there'll be a shipload more to come. You can rewrite your brochures and update your website and Lichfield Tube will be firmly on the international map. You can't afford to mess it up."

There was silence on the line as Russell absorbed the barely disguised threat.

"As I said, Sir Vernon, everything's in hand."

"It had better be. I've got bigger and better companies than yours in the FerroTech group and any one of them could have gone after this business and beaten you hands down."

"I realise that, Sir Vernon," said Russell, although he had often wondered why all the competition had come from outside the group. Not one FerroTech company had put in a tender to the dockyard.

"Well, if that's true, Gordon, you will also realise that I have deliberately held them back. They sent realistic quotations to any of the big stockists who approached them, but none of them tendered the dockyard directly. They're not bleeding like you are. They're not desperate for the business."

"Sir Vernon," Russell interrupted. "Things at Lichfield are not… …"

"Yes, they are, Gordon. You need this. You've done well to stop the rot as quickly as you have but you need to get your turnover up and you need to increase your profit margins. You've got your new testing division, and you need it to be known that you can supply a quality product to the highest spec. You need the prestige this will bring when you can claim to supply a Royal Naval dockyard, and your products can once again be found on HM ships."

There was silence again as Russell wondered whether to protest against a verdict which he knew in his heart to be right on the nail.

"Look, Gordon. I'm sorry Phil Simmons is dead. I really am. But the man has a heart attack or whatever it was, and we have to move on. You've got too much at stake. If you think Harry can't handle this, tell me now and I'll send you one of my best closers. I don't want to do that because it'll look like we don't trust you, but if that's what's needed… … …"

He let that hang for a moment.

"Harry can handle it, Sir Vernon. I'll be watching him."

"See that you are, Gordon, because I'm going to be watching you."

"Yes, sir. I was supposed to be going over to Lithuania tomorrow to check out a new supplier in Vilnius, but Mitch Portess has volunteered to go instead. He knows what we need."

"A new supplier? What was wrong with the old one?"

"Quality, sir. Goods not up to standard."

"Hmm. You know what I think about quality, Gordon. I won't put up with rubbish for myself, and I don't want to hear about rubbish being passed off onto our customers. Make sure Portess knows what he's looking for."

"I will, sir," said Russell, thinking that his chief field officer needed no advice from him when it came to knowing what was needed to please their customers.

Twenty-Three

The Dower House – 7.45 pm

The visit to Angie in the afternoon had not gone as I'd hoped, simply because she'd been too exhausted to concentrate for very long, and Barrie had ruthlessly shooed us away after about twenty minutes. There was so much I'd wanted to tell her, plans I'd wanted us to make, but all I'd been able to do was tell her how sorry I was for nearly getting her killed, and sit sniffling by her bed holding her hand while she told me it didn't matter. Promising to come back soon, I had reluctantly left her, and James had brought me back to the Dower House. I might have resented the officious way that Barrie had ushered us out of Angie's room, but I had no doubt, from what I overheard of his subsequent conversation with James in the corridor, that he was taking really good care of her.

The rest of the day had been fairly uneventful, and for that I'd been grateful. Abby had given me a grand tour of the house before dinner which we had eaten, not in the rather grand dining room as I'd expected, but in the much smaller breakfast room adjoining the kitchen. Mrs Siddons had prepared traditional roast beef with Yorkshire puddings, and she and Abby obviously had some sort of competition going to see how high the puddings could be encouraged to rise. In spite of high expectations as Abby had peered through the glass door of the oven, they had eventually failed to come up to scratch, as Abby's school ruler ultimately proved. Although short in stature, they were nevertheless deliciously light, and we forgave them their shortcomings.

After dinner, James had excused himself saying he had things to sort out, and Abby had persuaded me to join her in watching a DVD called *Parent Trap* which I had never seen but was prepared to at least appear to enjoy for her sake. In fact I'd been able to enter into the spirit of the thing with very little effort, and I readily joined Abby in laughing at the plight of Dennis Quaid's deliciously evil, prospective wife, as her pursuit of him was terminally undermined by his two scheming daughters.

Once that was over and Abby had taken herself off to get ready for bed, James had come to join me in the drawing room. It was strange how much more at ease I felt in his presence compared with the night before, and I was aware that somehow this was tied up with having had the opportunity to observe him with Abby. Their relationship had reminded me so much of myself with my father, and I remembered how much I had loved my father, trusting him absolutely. Somehow, I found myself wishing that I could trust James as Abby did, and the realisation had scared me since I hadn't trusted any man for over half my life. It also brought back feelings of guilt because I still hadn't told him that I had been in the wood that morning, and could clear him of any suspicion in Phil Simmons' death. Maybe the police would clear him anyway, and I wouldn't have to bring myself to their notice, with all the consequences that would from once again coming under their scrutiny.

James had taken one of the easy chairs while I had remained on the sofa where I had sat through the movie with Abby snuggled up next to me. For what seemed like ages, he just sat watching me as though he was trying to make up his mind about something. I wasn't nervous; just curious, wondering if this had anything to do with the sorting out he'd mentioned earlier.

Eventually, he breathed deeply and nodded. Mind made up.

"Lizzie," he began, more tentatively than I'd been expecting. "We both know what sort of life you've been living these past few years."

I tensed, aware of the shutters coming down to resist his probing. He was aware of it too.

"It's OK," he said. "I don't need to know any of the details, and I won't ask you any questions, except for this... ... Have you any family, anyone, anywhere, who ought to be reassured that you are safe and well?"

I wasn't sure where this was leading, but it wasn't really a question I had any problem answering.

"No. No-one."

He just continued looking at me. I knew he was waiting to see if I was going to add anything more. I decided it couldn't do any harm to humour him.

"My parents both died when I was eight... ... Car crash."

It was a long time since I'd spoken about them and, hard and tough though I'd become, I could feel my eyes moistening at the memory of what I'd lost. I wasn't sure if James had noticed, but I blinked hard and hoped the tears would stay put and not start running down my cheek.

"I'm sorry to hear that," he said, but he made no move to come nearer to me. "Who took care of you after that?"

Took care of me! That was a joke.

"I lived with my aunt and uncle 'til I was sixteen. They're both dead now."

He thought about that for a moment.

"So you have no-one you can go to? No-one who'll take you in?"

I shook my head.

James stood up smiling. "Would you like a drink, Lizzie."

Suspicion and disappointment gripped me simultaneously. Did he think he'd got to get me drunk or slip me a roofie to get me into bed? Immediately, I felt guilty for being so suspicious, but I couldn't help it. In my experience, men were driven far more by the urges in their pants than they were by impulses in their brains. Fact of life.

It must have shown in my face because the smile faded and he looked slightly puzzled.

"Mrs Siddons usually makes a drinking chocolate about now, but you could have tea or coffee if you prefer."

I breathed out, long and slow, ending on a quiet chuckle. I would go on being suspicious because that's what kept me safe, but it's nice to be wrong every now and then.

"Drinking chocolate would be good. Thanks."

I half expected him to press a button or pull a bell-rope, but he just left the room for a moment, presumably to tell Mrs Siddons to make one extra.

When he returned he sat down in the same chair and resumed watching me. I waited patiently, knowing something was coming, but just not sure what. Eventually he said, "Lizzie, I want to ask you a favour."

What favour could I possibly do for him?

"You know the girl whose room you're using? Suzanne?"

I nodded. I didn't know her of course, but I knew who he meant.

"Well, she's been a kind of au-pair, looking after Abby while she's working on her thesis for her Masters at Derby University. Like most students, she needed the money."

I nodded again. Her presence in the house was beginning to make some kind of sense now.

"A couple of weeks ago, her father was taken ill and she moved back home to Duffield to help her mother take care of him... ... ... I've just spoken to her this evening and she's not going to be able to come back. Her father has to make frequent visits to hospital, and her mother doesn't drive... ... ... Things aren't looking very good I'm afraid. Suzanne seems to be coping OK at the moment, but her mother's taking it very hard."

I thought I could see where this was leading, although I could scarcely believe it was possible.

"So, what does this have to do with me?" I asked.

"I need someone to take Suzanne's place, or rather Abby does, so I wondered if you'd mind sticking around for a while."

I shook my head slowly, not because I didn't want to stay, but because I just couldn't figure out his angle. There had to be more to it but, apart from the obvious, I couldn't work out what it was, and the obvious was beginning to seem less and less likely.

"What would that involve?" I asked.

"The main thing is keeping Abby company. Mrs Siddons is a treasure, but Abby needs someone a couple of generations younger... ...

We never had any other children and Suzanne became something of a big sister to her. We didn't have any formal arrangement other than that I paid her £200 per week with board and lodging thrown in. She did most of her studying during the day when Abby was at school, although there were times when she came into school herself to help out if we were a bit short of teaching assistants or parent helpers."

He looked at me obviously expecting some sort of response, but I was so amazed at his proposition that I could think of nothing to say. In so many ways it was the answer to everything; a safe place to stay, an income, a real chance to start again with people who actually seemed to care what happened to me.

I almost told him then, about the wood, but all the reasons why I shouldn't surged up from where I'd buried them, so I just sat still gazing at the carpet saying nothing.

James pursed his lips presumably trying to make sense of my silence. Eventually he said, "On the other hand, if that doesn't appeal, we could probably help you find a job." He smiled a little crookedly. "Maybe in a different field from what you're used to. And I'm sure we could find you a place to stay… … … But Abby would certainly be disappointed."

I looked up then. "You've asked her?"

"Certainly I asked her. I wouldn't dream of saddling her with someone she didn't like. And she really seems to have taken a liking to you. But you must make up your own mind and do what's right for you."

The trouble was I didn't know what was right for me. All my attention had been so focussed on escaping the past that I had scarce given a thought to the future.

At that moment, the door opened and Mrs Siddons came in followed by Abby who was now dressed in pale grey pyjamas with the word *SLEEPY* on her top curving in a half-moon above the figure of a sleeping dwarf. She was carrying a small tray on which were three steaming mugs and a plate of biscuits. Mrs Siddons adjusted the position of the coffee table saying, "She got it all ready herself so you'd better make sure you enjoy it."

Abby put the tray down on the table and looked from James to me, and back.

"Did you ask her? What did she say?"

Mrs Siddons left the room slowly, patting cushions and adjusting ornaments as she went. I rather thought she was just as interested as Abby herself in the answer to those questions.

"We were just talking about it when you came in," said James, "and Lizzie is still thinking what to do."

Abby had come and plonked herself down beside me as her father was talking and, as he paused, she looked up at me frowning.

"What's to think about? It'll be cool, Lizzie. Really. And you can have time off when you want. Suzanne liked it here and she didn't have much time off 'coz she doesn't have a boyfriend. She said she wanted to get her studying done first. But you can have time off if you've got a boyfriend. I won't mind."

It all came out in an excited rush that was hard to resist.

"I don't have a boyfriend."

"Hey, that's great, 'coz when I said I wouldn't mind if you went off to meet him, I was just being polite."

She snuggled up, linking her arm through mine. "So you will stay, won't you?"

I looked at James, but he simply raised his eyebrows in silent echo of her question. So I turned my head slowly and let my eyes travel down to Abby's trusting, pleading face. In the end it wasn't a hard choice at all.

"I'll stay."

* * * * *

My first duty, it seemed, was seeing Abby up to bed, which I did as soon as she had finished her drink. Not that she wasn't perfectly capable of going to bed on her own, but I discovered she liked to get into bed and just chat for a few minutes until she felt sleepy. No hardship at all.

When I came downstairs again, James was still sitting in the drawing room where we'd left him. Although he looked up and smiled when I entered the room, I thought his expression seemed troubled so I asked straight out, "Are you regretting asking me to stay?"

He shook his head. "Not at all. Just the reverse actually. It's quite a relief to have you here. But there is something I should have explained to you before pressing you to a decision."

As I crossed to the sofa to resume my place, I told him, "I do know about the kidnapping, if that's it. Mrs Siddons told me about it this morning."

He looked both surprised and relieved. "Yes, that was it. I really ought to have told you myself."

"That's OK," I said, deciding I might as well get as full a picture as possible. "Did Cherry start guarding her after that?"

"Pretty well straight away. He's always with her when she's not with me. He's a good lad, and he's very patient with her, but it's female company that Abby needs"

"Is that why Suzanne came to live here?"

"Yes, but… … er… … let me just go back a bit. You might find Abby occasionally gets upset for what seems to be no apparent reason. It's not like it was, during the months after the kidnapping, but sometimes it still happens. Abby was traumatized for weeks after she was rescued. We had a young psychiatric nurse living here for the best part of a year, but then she felt she had done all she needed to and ought to leave and get on with her career. But Abby missed her company. That's when Suzanne came. A friend of mine knows her mother and Suzanne was looking for some kind of part-time work to see her through her degree. It worked out well all round."

"How long was she here," I asked.

"A year, just about. Her Masters is a two-year course, part-time. She has a bit under a year to go. I hope this thing with her father doesn't … … … Well, you know what I mean."

I did indeed. Unless she was a pretty tough character, caring for her father and supporting her mother could sabotage her chances of getting a good degree, or even of gaining her masters at all. And that could affect the rest of her life.

"Anyway," he went on, "that's why I decided to ask you to stay. Abby gets on really well with Cherry, and he takes amazingly good care of her, but she still needs female company."

"I'm surprised you decided she needs the company of a female like me. I'm not exactly finishing school quality."

"You're not *a female like you*, Lizzie," he replied firmly. "You are just you. So let's just leave it like that for the moment and see how things work out."

That suited me fine but I was still amazed that he would be trusting me with the care of his nine-year old daughter.

Another thought struck me.

"Do you still need Cherry? I mean … … It was two years ago. It's not likely to happen again, surely."

James stretched out his long, powerful legs, and relaxed back into his chair.

"Probably not," he said, "but Abby likes Cherry and he's always taken good care of her. The person who took her before might be off the scene but … …" he must have seen my expression since he said, "Don't ask… … Anyway he had … … associates… … They might still see Abby as a soft target. So we took precautions and I bought the Jag. We used to have a Vauxhall Omega. Nice motor; big enough to fit me, and perfectly suitable for our needs. But it wasn't up to resisting an armed attack."

"And the Jag is," I said, thinking back to last night.

He smiled. "You wouldn't think it just to look at it, would you? But if anyone tries to shoot the tyres on it, the car just keeps going. You can fire a machine gun at it, throw grenades at it, set off a bomb under it, and it just keeps going. Fully armoured, you see. And so is Cherry's Jeep."

"Isn't that a bit excessive?" I wondered.

"Now? Yes you're probably right. But back then, we didn't know what might happen. As I said, the kidnapper had some pretty nasty associates, many of whom are still out there. And there was someone else involved… … An extremely unpleasant character, but he came from a wealthy family who had very powerful friends. We just didn't know what to expect, you see… … … And there was something else to worry about as well. Abby refused to get in a car. Something to do with what had happened. Her psychiatric nurse said that in Abby's mind, the car was a trap and, therefore, a dangerous place to be. So, we set out to show her that our car was actually a very safe place to be and, eventually, after a visit to the Jaguar factory, she was finally convinced. The car cost me £200,000, but fortunately I know someone in the USA who is ready to take it off my hands for exactly that amount as soon as I'm ready to part with it."

My mouth dropped open as I took in the cost of the car, but he didn't seem to notice as he took a deep breath and let it out slowly.

"But I'm not sure I'm ready yet to take that security away from her."

I drew my legs up under me and settled into the corner of the sofa while I thought about what he had said. It seemed that he was more concerned with Abby's peace of mind than he was about the serious possibility of another kidnapping. So there was probably no real danger, unless … …

"James, have you thought that Mr Simmons getting killed might be tied up with the guy who kidnapped Abby?"

"I've wondered about that but … … well, I just can't see the connection."

"He could be trying to frame you."

"Yes, but if it's revenge he wants, and he – or someone paid by him – was in the wood, why murder Phil? Why not just kill me?"

"Hmmmm." I didn't know the answer to that. I decided I wasn't really very good at the detective stuff, so I gave up.

James stood up. "You can still change your mind about staying, if you want."

I smiled up at him.

"No-one else is offering to drive me around in an armoured limo. I think I'll stay."

Monday

2nd May 2005

Aushra Paulauskaitė – Day Three

Vilnius, Lithuania –6:00 am

Aushra lay still, staring uneasily through the gloom of her bedroom at the cracked and peeling ceiling above. This was probably the most important day of her life so far, and she could not help feeling a little nervous. Today would be her final test. The two previous interviews had secured her a position with the English company, but today she would learn just what that position would be. When she'd first heard about this job in the English Midlands and thought about applying, she had told herself that, for the money they were offering, she didn't mind what sort of work she did. But she knew now that she did mind, and that was why she was nervous.

Later that morning she would meet her new boss for the first time, and he would decide what type of work she would be given to do.

She knew she would not be a lowly cleaner. She had asked about that at her first interview. She didn't have to go to England to be a cleaner. She could do that sort of work in Vilnius if she wanted to. But she didn't want to. She had a brain, and her school grades showed she had the ability to use it. So she wanted a job with prospects.

She turned onto her side, wriggled a little, and pulled her pillow into her shoulder to get comfortable. Her bed was old, but she felt warm and cosy, and definitely didn't want to get up yet, even though she was sure that further sleep would be impossible. There was nothing more she could do to prepare for the meeting, but as long as it was ahead of her, she was not going to be able to put it out of her mind.

What would he be like, this Mitchell Portess? She knew that he must hold quite a senior position in the company, since she was an observant girl, and she knew anxiety when she saw it. On her last visit to that small office near the Holiday Inn on the north side of the river, she had not missed the apprehension that came into the faces of the staff when Portess's visit was mentioned. At the time, she thought that's all it was, nervousness about the boss from Head Office turning up on your turf. But now, lying here with nothing else to think about, and her meeting with him imminent, Aushra wondered if it was only his position and power that caused people to fear Mr Portess.

It was a stupid thought, and she had no real reason to think it, but nevertheless it nagged away at her until eventually she sat up in bed hugging her knees. In an effort to ease her mind, she began to go over all the things she had been promised about her new life in England.

The main thing that mattered was that she would be with Jolanta. They would be sharing the same lodgings, arranged for them by the company, and would be working in the same premises, if not necessarily in the same office. They would probably start off as administrative assistants, whatever they were, to someone in middle management, always assuming that they made a good impression on Mr Portess later that morning.

She tried to imagine herself walking into his office, shaking his hand, being invited to sit down. What kind of first impression would she make? Perhaps she should address him in English, just to show him what an asset she would be. Answering the telephone would have no fears for her. And clothes. What should she wear? She suddenly realised that the few new clothes she'd bought to take to England came into the smart-casual category. OK to tide her over until she knew the company dress code, and had a pay check to help her abide by it, but were they the style and cut to impress a boss?

Too late to worry now. She swung her legs out of bed and stood, almost tripping over the duvet that seemed to follow her feet of its own accord. Kicking it aside, she began to rummage through her meagre wardrobe. Smart-casual wasn't a bad look and, done right, would have Mr Portess's eyes leaping out on stalks.

Twenty-Four

Lowfields Primary School - 7.55 am

We left just before eight o'clock that Monday morning. I had woken at seven and drawn the heavy curtains to reveal a dull, overcast day. A quick shower, and another foray into what was left of Sarah Montrayne's wardrobe and I was ready for breakfast by seven thirty. Abby took little notice, other than a quick hello, as I came into the kitchen. The Breakfast programme on TV was showing an interview with Robbie Williams, something I couldn't compete with at that time in the morning. James, however, became very still, his teacup frozen in midair, as his eyes took in the pale lilac blouse hanging loose over the grey trousers which I had selected for my day in school. After a long moment, he returned my *Good Morning* and allowed the cup to resume its journey.

It hadn't occurred to me before then to wonder what might be the effect on him of seeing me walking around in his dead wife's clothes. Yesterday, he hadn't seemed to notice, or care, what I was wearing. I wondered if today's outfit brought back a particular, possibly painful, memory and, if he hadn't beckoned me over to the table, I would probably have thought about going back upstairs to see if I could find something else to wear.

As it was, breakfast proceeded to the accompaniment of the TV, with little conversation, and we left promptly as soon as it was over. James was driving the Maserati with Abby up there in the front beside him. We were on our way to school. Just another day in the life of the Monteith family.

Abby had asked why we were taking the Maserati and not the Jag and James told her that he'd noticed that the car needed some work doing on it so Cherry was taking it to get it fixed. That seemed to satisfy her. It made me wonder whether all that armoured stuff wasn't such a big deal for her any more.

James had asked me the previous evening what I wanted to do for the day, but it hadn't really been much of a choice. The farm was definitely off-limits for me since we knew that Angie had told Bruno about it, and it was more than likely that someone would be watching it. I had wondered if Cherry could give me a lift to the hospital to visit Angie, but that was a non-starter. The private army James had called up on Saturday night had all now left the farm and gone back to their normal work, so it was left to Cherry to keep an eye out for trouble over there. I didn't fancy spending the whole day mooching around the Dower House, even though Mrs Siddons seemed to be getting acclimatised to my presence there. So, school it was.

I relaxed in the back and listened to the father-daughter chatter in the front. It was light, inconsequential stuff, and I suspected James kept it that way on purpose.

As we approached Lichfield, the spires of the cathedral rose up in the distance to tower over the city. I knew nothing of Lichfield's historic past but just the sight of those slender stone needles pointing to the heavens was evocative of some bygone age of mystery and ceremonial power. It was a beautiful monument to a past rooted in beliefs and customs which I had never understood. At school they had taught me many things including both history and religion, but while the former had fascinated me, accounting for my *A* grade at GCSE, the latter had been, at least for me, boring and irrelevant.

I suppose it was the thoughts prompted by those spires that caused me to remember that strange experience on Saturday evening when I had sat with a group of apparently normal, sane people and listened to them talking to some being I couldn't see, couldn't hear, couldn't touch and had never believed in. They had been fully involved, and I had been left sitting on the edge, watching, listening, wondering. If that was praying, it was weird. And another weird thing was, it hadn't happened again, and I had been with one or other of them almost continuously since. Perhaps it was just something they did in dire need, but not at other times. Maybe I would ask one of them, if the opportunity should arise. Or maybe not.

The school was on the outskirts of Lichfield in what seemed like a relatively new housing development. I suppose, judging by the size of the trees and shrubs in the beautifully kept gardens, the houses must have been there for at least ten years. According to James, Lowfields Primary School had been built in the mid-nineties, and he had come there as Deputy Headteacher just two years ago. For several months he had been Acting Headteacher due to the extended sick leave of his current boss, Owen Williams, who had been Head since the school first opened. James didn't tell me what was wrong with Mr Williams, but it was clear that he was not expected to be returning to work anytime soon.

I had no idea what James had planned for me to do since Abby was obviously going to be in class all day. Wondering how boring the day was going to be, I followed the pair of them from the school parking lot through a keypad controlled security gate and a similarly secured entry door. At first, I was surprised that it was necessary, in such an apparently quiet and pleasant neighbourhood, but then I remembered that I of all people should know that children are prime targets for a particular sort of perverted mind. I also knew that apparent respectability is no guarantee of anything.

I wondered whether James had deliberately placed himself between my eyes and the keypads, or whether he was just so big that it happened by chance. In the end, I decided it didn't matter. The entry code was probably a closely guarded secret anyway.

Once inside, James turned to Abby saying, "Why don't you give Lizzie a tour of the school. If any of the staff are about, you can introduce her and explain how she has come to take Suzanne's place."

To the left of the spacious entry hall was a glassed in reception area and, presumably, secretary's office. Ahead were staff toilets, and to the right another office. Corridors went off to left and right. I was interested to see that the door to this other office, clearly marked *Headteacher* to avoid any misunderstanding, had no keypad and James unlocked it with a key on a bunch he extracted from his briefcase. As he opened the door, he turned back to Abby.

"As soon as the other children start coming into school, make sure you bring Lizzie straight back to me."

Maybe I was being over-sensitive, but his words cut deep, showing me that for all his friendliness he did not regard me as a fit person to associate with the nice children in his middle-class school.

"Maybe I should just stay here," I said, with a bitter edge to my voice. "Can't have a person like me polluting your sweet little kids, can we? You never know, I might start showing them how to... ..."

My voice trailed away, partly because I didn't really want to finish what I'd begun to say, but mostly because of the expression on James's face. He looked stricken, his mouth falling open, his eyes troubled.

"Lizzie, I'm so sorry. I should have explained. Everyone who has contact with the children, volunteers as well as staff, has to have a CRB check these days. There hasn't been time to do that for you, so that's why I can't let you loose with the children... ... That's the only reason I said what I did, I promise you."

I felt utterly stupid. I'd never heard of CRB checks. I didn't know what to say to redeem the misunderstanding, and I very much wanted to because Abby was starting to look upset.

James rescued me.

"It's still quite a new thing, Lizzie. The Criminal Records Bureau was set up a few years ago to make sure that... ..." He took a breath as though picking his words carefully. "... ... people who might hurt children don't get jobs working with them."

I thought he might ask me what a CRB check on me might throw up, and I was very relieved that he didn't. The truth was, I had really no idea.

"I didn't know about this CRB thing," I said. "Sorry."

He smiled. "That's OK. Now why don't you trot off with Abby, and when you come back I'll show you what I'd like you to do today."

I nodded OK and trailed off in Abby's wake, listening to her assurances that her classroom was the absolute best, and that we'd start there.

* * * * *

We spent so much time in Abby's classroom, while I admired every contribution of hers to the bright and colourful displays on the walls, that I had met only one other teacher, a young woman who seemed barely older than me, before children began to drift into school. It seems these were the ones with special responsibilities for helping teachers get various materials ready for the first lessons of the day. Abby remembered her instructions and delivered me back at James's office.

James's desk was large and modern with a light teak finish, and he had it set away from the wall so that he could sit behind it facing the door. There were the usual in and out trays, a desk tidy with assorted pens pencils and other paraphernalia, and a variety of papers which he seemed to be working on, but there was no computer. That was on another desk which was pushed into the corner to the right of the door as I went in. Since it was also against the one wall with a window, this meant that the screen would not be affected by sunlight shining on it. In the large area in front of James's desk was a coffee table and a couple of wooden-framed easy chairs with covers of some kind of tweedy fabric. Presumably for visitors.

James indicated one of the chairs saying, "Well, Lizzie, how do you like being back in school?"

"Feels strange," I replied. "Makes me think of when I was in junior school. It's weird being here. Seems almost like the bit in between never happened."

Then I thought of all that *had* happened and I went quiet. A messed up life was what had happened as I'd progressed from grief through betrayal to plain exploitation. My eyes were far away and I barely noticed as James came round from behind his desk to stand by the other chair. He held some forms which he laid down on the table. He bent down slightly to try and catch my eye.

"Do you feel like a drink, Lizzie?" he asked. "Someone's usually got the urn heated up by now."

"Sure," I said, dragging my mind back to the present. "Coffee, if that's OK."

"Coffee, it is. Shan't be a moment."

And he wasn't. The someone hadn't let him down.

He was back quickly, but not before I'd had a chance to glance briefly at the forms. As soon as I saw the heading at the top, my mouth went dry and I knew I was going to need that coffee.

He kicked the door shut behind him and put two steaming mugs down on the small slate coasters which sat on the table. Sitting down, he reached for the forms.

"I'm supposed to get you to fill in one of these," he said. "School policy. Everyone working here has to do it, even volunteers."

"What exactly is it?" I asked, trying to sound as though I didn't care.

"It's a request to the Criminal Records Bureau to check whether you have a police record."

My mouth opened but I said nothing. I knew my eyes were staring, but I could think of nothing to say. He obviously picked up on my imitation of a scared rabbit because he smiled reassuringly. At least, I'm sure he meant it to be reassuring, but it didn't really help at all.

"I don't think we're going to want to do that for you, are we?" he said, more of a statement than a question.

I shook my head slowly, wondering how far this was going to go.

"That's why I asked Abby to bring you back here as soon as the other kids began to arrive. If you don't spend time with them, don't talk to them, no-one's going to think twice about you."

I was relieved. I had wondered if he was using this as an excuse to go digging into my past, but it seemed he was still content not to know. Although … … he clearly suspected enough to know I wouldn't want a CRB check done.

But what the heck was I going to do all day if I wasn't going to be allowed to talk to anyone? I'd enjoyed being with Abby and Debbie at the weekend, and I had actually been looking forward to spending time with these kids today, maybe even helping them with their work.

"So … … do I just hide in here all day, 'coz if that's the plan I'd rather have stayed back at the house?"

"Well, I wouldn't … … …"

His words faded and he looked up surprised and, I thought, a little angry, as the office door opened and a rather large lady came stomping into the room preceded by her impressive bosom. I judged her to be in her early forties, a touch under medium height and clearly with no ambitions to be a size double zero. She had curly red hair - possibly natural I thought, checking her roots - cut fairly short and a face that had probably looked angry from the day she had bullied her first victim in nursery school. It was clear from her entrance that she was not one of those delicate flowers in need of assertiveness training.

She looked down her nose at her boss and said, "James, I need a word."

Just like that; no *excuse me;* no *am I interrupting?*

I looked from her to James, wondering how he'd respond.

"Morning, Louisa. On the warpath again?"

She didn't reply; just turned her nose to me, glaring as though expecting me to make myself scarce.

James stood, towering over the invader. I guessed he did it just to force her to look up. It's hard to look down your nose at someone at least a foot taller than you are.

"Louisa, did I ever tell you about the rules for coming into my office?"

"It's not … …"

Was she about to say it wasn't his office?

"I really did think I had made it clear." His interruption was perfectly calm and polite, but his words easily drowned out hers. "If the door is open, just knock and walk in. If the door is closed, knock and wait. Simple really."

She was seething.

"I need to see you before registration. Those budget figures need to be reviewed."

"I'm perfectly happy with the figures, Louisa, as I told you last week. I'm happy. The Governors are happy. Now if you really need to discuss it, I'll talk to you at lunchtime, but at the moment I'm busy."

As he spoke, he reached past her for the handle of the still open door and held it while at the same time stepping closer to her gradually easing her, spluttering and protesting, out of the office.

With the door finally shut again, he turned back to me.

"She's confused. Part of her thinks that, in spite of my money and privilege – those are her words, by the way – I should earn my living like everyone else. Another part of her thinks I've got so much money I should leave this job to someone who really needs it. She wanted the deputy's job and I beat her to it. She's had it in for me ever since, even though she got the acting post when I was bumped up to Acting Head."

I was intrigued. Her dislike of him seemed way over the top.

"But why? Surely people get beaten for jobs all the time."

He sat down again and sipped at his mug of tea.

"Well, I think part of it is professional jealousy, but a big chunk of her problem is that she hates privilege. Anyone with family money is an undeserving layabout; if you have a title you're a thieving brigand who stole from the peasant classes; and if you have the misfortune to be royalty you're a leech sponging off the wealth of the nation. Ardent socialist, you see. Trotsky would have been proud."

He was smiling, so I smiled back. "Wow! And you're not exactly short of cash. And you have to work with her every day."

"I try to bring a little sunshine into her life, but her thunderstorm always seems to block it out."

"So what's this budget she's bothered about?"

"Ah. She manages the staff development budget and she wants more money. It's for courses, training, stuff like that. We increased it over last year's budget, but not enough to suit her. She's the area rep for her union so she needs time off for union duties and the cost of the supply teachers to cover her absence also comes out of that budget. She does seem to have an awful lot of duties."

"Was there really no spare money for it?"

He chuckled, a deep throaty rumble, strangely attractive and reassuring. "No Headteacher will ever admit to having spare money. School budgets are an absolute nightmare." He paused and looked around as though wondering whether to say any more.

"We could have done it, but only by saving money elsewhere. And the saving Louisa had in mind was Jane Sutton. She came to us in January on a two-term contract so we could have three reception classes instead of two for the Spring and Summer terms. For some reason we had a big intake in January this year. It happens sometimes. Now we're in a new financial year, Louisa wants to let Jane go after this term since we won't have so many children in reception in September. Then we could bring in another temporary contract after Christmas when we get the second intake. That would probably have saved about £7000."

I was puzzled. "Isn't that actually quite a good idea?"

"Maybe, except that Jane's an NQT, and she's going to be a first rate teacher."

I gave the puzzled look again. "NQT?"

"Newly qualified teacher. She has to do three terms to get her final qualification. I don't want to mess that up for her. And I actually do want to keep her. She's too good to lose. But on top of that, Louisa shouldn't be in favour of using temporary contracts in that way. The unions don't like it and she's a union rep. She ought to have been looking out for Jane, not trying to dump her just to fund her own activities."

"Hmm, she sounds a right bitch."

James frowned.

"Well, she does," I said, a little on the defensive.

"I know," he said quietly, still frowning. He sighed. "I shouldn't have told you all that. Can't think why I did. If anyone else had done it, I would have said it was unprofessional."

"Don't worry," I reassured him. "My memory's quite flexible. Forgotten already."

"Really?"

"Actually, no. But I can pretend."

Somewhere close by an electric bell sounded.

James stood up. "We'd better get a move on. The kids are coming in and I'm going to have to take assembly soon."

Drawing me over to the computer, he explained how Suzanne had been going to start entering all the books in the school library onto a database which the children could access. Nobody, it seems had the time to do it or, at least, that's what they said. James thought it had more to do with the fact that it was a fairly boring chore which no-one had the slightest inclination for. So now it was my job, at least for that day.

James called up the database and, soon after he went off to assembly, the secretary wheeled in a trolley-load of books. I was set for the morning.

* * * *

James was in and out of the office all morning, but we didn't converse much. He was often on the phone, but even when he wasn't I didn't like to interrupt him. He just went from one task to the next, non-stop. Anyway, I had my own work to focus on and I was fairly confident I would clear that trolley by lunchtime, until disaster struck.

He was a little above medium height, slender, and well dressed in a dark blue business suit with faint pinstripes. A blue and white striped shirt, white collar and plain red tie completed his wardrobe. He strode into the office without waiting to be invited. True, the door was ajar and he had knocked, but this guy was authority with a capital A. He knew it and I knew it. I just wished James was there to deal with him.

Fortunately, courtesy with a capital C was also part of his alphabet. As I swivelled my chair to face him, he switched his gaze from James's empty desk over to my corner. He was probably in his mid-forties, handsome, with a full head of slightly greying dark hair. He held a newspaper in his left hand.

"Good morning," he said, "assuming it still is." He glanced up at the clock on the wall to check.

"Now, you're not Suzanne. I've met her. So who can you be, I wonder?"

His voice was pleasant, a little posh maybe, but friendly.

I stood up. It seemed the right thing to do.

"My name's Lizzie. Suzanne couldn't come anymore. Her dad's ill. So I'm helping out for a while."

He held out his hand.

"Lizzie, is it? We don't hear that name quite so much these days. Are your parents fans of *Pride and Prejudice*, do you know?"

They'd never mentioned it that I could remember, but then it would have been a long time ago. I had seen the TV adaptation, and remembered rather admiring Lizzie Bennett, so I knew what he was getting at but I didn't see that it was any of his business. Still, it seemed like a good idea to humour him.

"I'm sorry," I said, giving his hand a firm shake to demonstrate a confidence I didn't actually feel. "I really don't know, and since they're both dead there's no way to find out."

He held on to my hand for a fraction longer than he should have, while staring at me with an oddly puzzled expression. When he finally let go, he seemed slightly embarrassed. Some nice men go like that when they find themselves alone with a pretty girl.

"I'm truly sorry to hear that, Lizzie. I hope James is taking good care of you."

"Yes, he is," I replied, still wondering who this gentleman was, and wishing he would go away.

"I'm awfully sorry, Lizzie," he said, as if reading my thoughts. "I'm Gordon Russell, Chair of Governors. I need to have a word with James. Do you happen to know where he's hiding?"

"I'm sorry, Mr Russell, but I really don't know."

"Not to worry. Er… … Do you mind my asking, Lizzie? What is your last name?"

I suppose if he was really the Chairman of the school Governors he had every right to ask, but the question still seemed a little odd.

"It's Burleigh," I said, after hesitating a moment.

Every muscle of his face, every crease, line and furrow, froze instantly in place as he stared into my eyes. I stared back, wondering what was the matter with him. I was as sure as I could be that he'd never made use of my services, which was the only reason I could think of for his giving me such a strange look. His mouth opened as though he was about to speak but then, from the doorway, I heard the voice of the school secretary.

"Good morning, Mr Russell. I've sent a message to James. He should be with you in a moment."

Slowly, he turned round to face her. He cleared his throat, twice, before addressing her in a tone almost resembling the easy familiarity of his first entrance.

"My dear Mrs Waterson. On the watch for me were you? I don't suppose you could possibly rustle up a cup of tea, could you?"

"Of course, Mr Russell… … and… can I say how sorry I was to hear about poor Mr Simmons?"

"Ah… … yes. Thank you, Mrs Waterson. It's a tragic business. We're certainly going to miss him."

As she left, he turned to me. The silence was weird. He couldn't hold my gaze now. His eyes flicked over to the window, to James's desk, to me and, finally, to the floor. He cleared his throat again and, just as I thought he was about to say something, we both heard heavy footsteps coming along the corridor. Now he did speak.

"Er… … I'm sorry to sound rude but do you think you could possibly take a break for a few minutes? I have something confidential to discuss with James."

"Of course," I said, looking uncertainly at the door. I didn't mind leaving them alone but, in the light of what James had explained earlier, I wasn't sure where to go. Russell must have sensed my hesitation because he suggested, "Why not keep Mrs Waterson company? Ask her about her daughter in Australia. She'll keep you entertained for hours." He smiled. "I know from experience."

Half an hour later, I could have taken an exam on Australia; climate, the property market, employment prospects, beaches, deserts, spiders, snakes. I'd had it all, including photos of Mrs Waterson's new grandson. All the time I kept watching James's office door through the reception window. When it finally opened and he emerged briefcase in hand, I was so amazed that I stood, cutting her off in full flow.

In the short time I had known him, I had never seen him look so blazingly angry as he did then.

Coming across to Mrs Waterson's door, he said, far more calmly than I expected, "Gather up your things, Lizzie. We're leaving."

"But … …" I wanted to ask what was going on.

"Not now, Lizzie. I'll explain as we go."

As I picked up my jacket and handbag, he said to Mrs Waterson, "I'll be back to collect Abby at the end of the day." He paused, thinking. "Probably best if it's a bit after, actually. Could you let her know, and ask Katie to look after her for ten minutes or so?"

"Er … … Of course … … Yes." She was obviously desperate to ask what had happened but, equally obviously, didn't dare.

As we left, Gordon Russell stood in James's office doorway sadly shaking his head. There was no sign of his newspaper.

Twenty-five

A38 Staffordshire – 11.55 am

As we drove away from the school parking lot, James was very quiet. He hadn't spoken all the way out to the car. Although he'd opened it up for me to get in, he hadn't immediately followed suit. I had just sat there with absolutely no idea what was going on, while James had stood close to the driver's door, apparently resting his forearms on the roof of the car. I guessed he was probably looking across it and over to the school. He was very still, and I didn't like to interrupt as it seemed he had some pretty heavy stuff to deal with.

Just how heavy, I could never have imagined.

As I waited for him to get in the car, I wondered why he had dragged me away from the presumably necessary job he'd given me to do. Not that I minded. By the time Russell had arrived, I had begun to realise why no-one on the school staff had been willing to take it on. Talk about mind-numbingly boring. But I could see the point of it and had been willing to stick it out. So, whatever it was that had caused James to leave in such a hurry, I couldn't see why he needed to take me with him. I could have carried on with the books until Cherry came to collect Abby, and then come home with them.

Eventually we left. James mumbled something in the way of a brief apology as he started the Maserati and we were about five minutes into the drive before he spoke again.

Without taking his eyes from the road he asked, "Can you reach my briefcase?"

He had tossed it onto the back seat before we drove off and it wasn't easy to reach but, by undoing my seatbelt and squirming around, I was able to grab hold of the handle. As I refastened my seatbelt, he told me to look inside. There were combination locks, but he hadn't set them and the case opened easily. The first thing I saw was a newspaper, the same one I'd last seen in the hand of Gordon Russell. The Lichfield Daily News, early edition.

"Take a look at the front page, Lizzie."

I took out the paper and lowered the lid of the case, leaving it balanced on my lap, and spread out the tabloid sheets on the top.

There were only two stories on the front page, both of them accompanied by photographs of people I recognised. As I took in the headlines, I actually gasped, feeling my stomach contract as I breathed in sharply. I knew now why James had taken me with him. Sister Yuyun, smart and efficient looking in her hospital uniform, stared up at me with her dark unsmiling eyes.

"Are you OK?" James glanced at me this time, if only briefly.

I nodded slowly, unable to speak for the moment, as my eyes rapidly scanned the article.

Sister Yuyun had failed to turn up for her shift on Sunday evening but, when her car was spotted in its usual place in the hospital staff parking lot, security had been alerted to watch out for her. It seemed as though her colleagues had been more curious than alarmed, until her body was discovered an hour later rolled under a Japanese SUV not far from her own Honda Civic. She had been stabbed once, below the ribcage, with a thrust that had gone deep, up into the heart. All her personal belongings had been taken and police were treating it as a mugging turned nasty.

"Sister Yuyun," I croaked, barely recognising my own voice. "You don't think it was a mugging, do you?"

"No, Lizzie. I think we can safely bet the farm on the fact that she died because of our visit on Saturday night."

"Could it have been Laddy, do you think?"

"Probably not. His hand was pretty well mangled. My guess is that it was someone sent by whoever Laddy works for."

I breathed deeply, and swallowed the lump in my throat.

"They're not just going to let us go, are they?"

"I'm afraid it doesn't look like it, Lizzie."

He looked at me again, a little longer this time.

"They want you and Angie badly, and you've given me nothing about why that is, or who they are. I need the whole story now, Lizzie. Not just the short, cleaned-up version. I need to know what I'm dealing with here. I need to know who's behind this, and why he's doing it, and I think you know."

I nodded, eyes closed, lips tight. I didn't like it, but I knew he was right.

Stalling for a moment, I asked, "What do you think she told them?" Then I realised as soon as I'd spoken how stupid the question was.

James glanced my way without speaking. His expression was so grim that I felt a slight shiver inside. I wasn't frightened of him. He just seemed so distant, and angry. His eyes returned to the road ahead as we cruised south along the A38 dual-carriageway at a steady seventy miles per hour. His grip on the steering wheel relaxed as he flexed his fingers, straight then curled, straight then curled, and he took a couple of deep breaths which seemed to reduce his anger since, when he spoke again, his voice was as calm and steady as usual.

"If she put the card I gave her into her purse, we can assume the killer has it. So, whether or not Sister Yuyun told him anything, he will know there's a connection between her and me. If she left it in the hospital somewhere, and she didn't tell him anything, then we could be in the clear, at least from them."

"What do you mean?" I asked nervously. "Who else is there to worry about?"

"The police. So whatever Sister Yuyun said or didn't say, one way or another, we're in trouble. When they start talking to staff on the ward, someone's going to tell them about our visit on Saturday night. There was at least one other nurse who saw us with Sister Yuyun. It won't take long for them to find us on CCTV somewhere, and then they're going to want to ask me some more questions. I'm in big enough trouble with them as it is. Next time they take me in, they may not be so quick to let me go."

In the midst of everything else, I'd forgotten all about Phil Simmons. I wanted to reassure him.

"But you didn't kill Mr Simmons. They won't be able to prove you had anything to do with it."

"I'm not so sure, Lizzie. I reckon they're going to have a jolly good try. Read the other story."

I'd been so wrapped up in the news about Sister Yuyun that I hadn't looked any further at the second story on the front page, the story accompanying the photo of James with his school just evident in the background. There were a few children in the picture, too small and fuzzy to be recognised but, from the way they were dressed, I guessed the photo had been taken at the school sports day.

Lichfield Daily News

Suspicious Death in Heighley Woods
by
Corrina Rigby

    Chief Inspector Paul Morrissey confirmed today that the body of the man found dead in Heighley Woods early on Saturday morning was that of Philip Simmons, sales director of Lichfield Tubes Ltd. Confirming that the police were treating the death as suspicious, Chief Inspector Morrissey played down reports that Mr Simmons had been shot with a poisoned dart fired from a high powered air rifle.

    The only other person known to have been in the woods that morning was local millionaire Headteacher, James Montrayne, eldest son of the Marquess of Thurvaston, a senior civil servant in the Department of Trade and Industry. Montrayne, who called the police claiming to have seen Mr Simmons collapse near the lake, told them that he had been hunting for rats, known to nest near to the lake in the woods, and to be a nuisance to the nearby free-range chicken farm. Montrayne is known to have had at least one rifle in his possession at the scene, but police refused to comment on speculation that this may have been the murder weapon.

    Montrayne spent all of Saturday helping the police with their enquiries, but was eventually released without charge.

    Enquiries at Heighley Grange Farm revealed that Montrayne was indeed expected to be hunting in the woods on Saturday morning and that, as a keen member of the local Rifle Club, he has a number of rifles which he keeps at his Georgian mansion in Abbots Newton. The secretary of the club, Ruth Farquhar, revealed that Montrayne has won several competitions in recent years. Mrs Farquhar also expressed some surprise that Montrayne should have been hunting rats in the woods, rather than on the farm itself, if protecting the hens was actually what he was aiming to achieve.

    Mr Simmons' wife Natalie, who is expecting her first child, is a supply teacher at Lowfields Primary School where Montrayne is Acting Headteacher. She is also a Sunday School teacher at the Valley Road Baptist Church where Montrayne is the church treasurer. According to the pastor of the church, Rev John Middlehurst, James Montrayne and Natalie Simmons took a party of young people from the church on an adventure holiday to Ross-on-Wye during the recent school holidays. Mrs Simmons has often been seen travelling to and from the school in Montrayne's luxury Jaguar XJ. Montrayne was described by a neighbour as being a frequent visitor to the Simmons' family home.

Mrs Simmons has so far been unavailable to comment on the nature of her relationship with Montrayne. Attempts to talk to the elusive Montrayne at his home were unproductive as our reporter was refused access to the grounds.

Police are continuing their enquiries but refuse to speculate on when they will have enough evidence to make an arrest.

I laid the paper down flat on the briefcase and looked at James. I was astounded by the way the article was obviously constructed to imply his guilt. If I had not known with absolute certainty that James hadn't killed Phil Simmons, this story would have really made me wonder. It was clear that the reporter had gone to great lengths to obtain and manipulate her facts to create an impression of guilt, but I had no idea why. I wondered whether we ought to have let her in when she called at the Dower House yesterday morning, and whether it would have made any difference if we had.

I said again, "James, you didn't do it."

"At the moment, that's not the point. It's what people choose to believe that matters. That article was enough to make Gordon Russell wonder about me, and he appointed me to this job. Before he turned up to see me, he'd had several calls from parents, including one of the parent governors, insisting that I was suspended until this is cleared up. Apparently one of the parents works for the Lichfield Daily News and saw the article as it was being printed. He saw it as his parental duty to put the word out. I bet he really enjoyed doing that."

"Why would he?" I asked, surprised.

"Because I had to exclude his little monster for a day last term for hitting a teacher with a rounders bat. He kicked up a stink then. This will have given him a right thrill."

"So what happened with Mr Russell?"

"I think he enjoyed our meeting even less than I did. He said he didn't want to suspend me but, with parents getting fired up by the article, my position was becoming untenable, at least for a while. He offered me the option of compassionate leave without pay, making it my choice not his. It will look better that way if this Rigby woman gets to know of it, which she probably will. So I took it."

I noticed we'd passed the junction for the M6 Toll Road, and the green fields were coming to an end as we approached the northern outskirts of Birmingham.

"James, where exactly are we going?"

"To see some friends of mine."

I wondered whether these were the same friends who had turned out on Saturday night. I didn't have time to think any more about them as James immediately spoke again, his tone of voice a definite command.

"You need to start talking, Lizzie. Who exactly are these people, and why are you and Angie so important to them?"

I was amazed how awkward and embarrassed I felt as I quickly reviewed the facts which I would have to reveal. For the past three years, I hadn't been troubled by concerns about what other people thought of me, apart from Angie who was the only person I cared about and had dared to trust. The girls I worked with, the customers in the clubs and massage parlours, the clients in secluded back rooms, the special clientele who required my services in discrete hotels and country houses, all cared as little about me as I did about them. Perhaps it was because, for the most part, I despised them that their opinion of me was of such little importance.

But this was different. For some reason, I did care what James thought of me. I also cared about the opinion of Abby and Debbie, Chick and Rachel, all of them church-going people whose condemnation I would do a great deal to avoid. This time it wouldn't be me doing the despising but them, as soon as they discovered what I'd been doing for the past three years. I couldn't do anything about that, but I could try to stop anyone else getting hurt. James was right. He needed the truth, so I took a deep breath and began.

"I ran away from home when I was sixteen, got as far as Birmingham and ran out of money. I was hungry and dirty and homeless and scared. Eventually, I was picked up off the streets by a guy who offered me a job and a place to stay. I lived in a flat with two other girls and worked in a club run by a friend of his."

I hesitated. This was the difficult bit and I actually felt myself colouring up as I tried to explain the work I'd been doing. I stared at the road ahead, not looking at James.

"After a bit, the work changed. They wanted me to do … … other stuff. … … You know … … By then I'd learnt enough to know it wasn't a choice. It was … … do it, or else. So I did, and men seemed to like me, so I was in demand."

I risked a quick glance to see how he was taking it. He was doing that steering wheel grip again, so I assumed he wasn't too pleased.

"What you're saying is, you were picked up off the street as a runaway, and coerced into prostitution."

"Yeah."

I heard the little touch of defiance in my drawn-out reply, and decided I didn't care. After all, how could he possibly know what it had been like for me back then?

"So who were you running away from, Lizzie? Your aunt and uncle?"

I didn't have to answer immediately since we were slowing for a large roundabout with a huge eighteen wheeler lumbering along on our nearside. There was a hiss of breaks as the truck slowed before the driver hit the accelerator and rocketed onto the roundabout. James hung back, somehow sensing that the truck-driver would cut the lanes as he tore round the tree-covered island. Sure enough, he did. James eased round after him and, as the truck shot off down the A38 towards Birmingham, James took the next exit and headed into the parking lot of a massive Asda-Walmart.

Once we had parked in a secluded corner of the lot, he asked me again, "Who were you running away from, Lizzie?"

I shrugged. "It doesn't matter."

He turned in his seat and looked at me for a long time. Eventually, without taking his eyes from mine, he said, "An instructor in the Royal Marines once told me, it doesn't matter how many times you fall down, it's how many times you get up again that counts. So let's just say you've taken a pretty heavy dive, and now you're trying to get up again. I'm not here to judge you. Only to help you. But to do that, I need to know what you know. Is that OK?"

I swallowed, and then nodded slowly.

"Good," he said, and held out his right hand for me to take. I lifted my hand from where it was still resting on the newspaper, and slid it into his. He didn't shake it, as I expected, but just held it gently. My hand was completely buried in his, just like when my Dad had held it. It felt safe.

"Then that's a deal, Lizzie. You be straight with me and I'll get you out of this."

He released my hand, although at that moment I would have let him go on holding it forever. Stupid. He wasn't my Dad and never would be even though, at a pinch, he could just about be old enough.

"I think," I began tentatively, "there are probably three reasons they want to get us."

He looked surprised. "Three?"

"Yes. The first is simple. Girls aren't allowed to run away. They get brought back. Always. And then they're punished."

I paused. I'd never been punished, but I'd seen it happen once. Just the memory of what had been done made me feel sick. James waited quietly for me to continue.

"They try to stop anyone running away by threatening their families. If we run, and they can't hurt us, they'll hurt our families instead. Most girls believe them and are too scared to run."

I looked out of the window at all the ordinary people - dragging kids, pushing shopping trolleys, hurrying about their ordinary business - never knowing what it's like to have someone threaten to break your bones, or rape your sister, or your mother, or your child. Ordinary people. Ordinary lives.

"The second thing," I said, "is that Angie and I know about the incomers."

"Incomers? Who are they exactly?"

I wasn't used to feeling ashamed. Exploited maybe, humiliated, even sometimes degraded and pretty worthless, but seldom ashamed. Until now. But then, in the last few days, I'd been feeling a lot of things I wasn't used to. I looked straight ahead.

"They're girls from Eastern Europe, Lithuania mostly. The last lot, five of them, came through some kind of agency in Vilnius. They thought they were signing up for office jobs; secretaries, typists, admin. That sort of thing. Then the agency guy who met them at the airport took their passports and carted them off to a big, old house in Sparkhill. He told them they were going there for training before starting work."

Out of the corner of my eye I saw James shift in his seat and I knew he was watching me.

"I can guess the rest," he said. "They were told they owed money and wouldn't get their passports back until they paid off the debt. And they're only offered one way of earning enough to buy back their passports. Do any of them ever manage to do that?"

I shook my head. "Never. More likely they're sold on to someone else as a … … a sex slave. They fetch maybe three, four, even five thousand pounds. I know of one girl who was sold for ten."

James was angry now. I could sense it in the way he looked and moved and breathed. But I knew he wasn't angry at me.

"But they never sold you, Lizzie.

"No, they didn't. I think I was valuable enough to them as I was. I had some important clients, rich men, business men, politicians, even one religious bloke, a minister of some sort. In the end, they made me responsible for training some of the other girls. That's how I met Angie. Not long ago, I was put in charge of showing the ropes to the latest batch of incomers. Keep them calm; keep them hoping; but make sure they understood what would happen if they didn't cooperate. At first they were scared and angry, but later they were just scared. They all had families back in Lithuania, and I was told to show the girls pictures of them, and explain what would happen to their mothers or fathers, brothers or sisters, even boyfriends, if they didn't behave."

"And did they … … behave?"

"Usually. There was one girl who swore she'd never do what they wanted. But after she'd been drugged up, raped a few times, and tapped around with a baseball bat, she calmed down. I'd … … … had things done to me since I was eight years old. I ran away from it, and ended up running right back into it. What I mean is … … I was used to it. These girls weren't. It was hard. … … … What I'm trying to say is … … I know the system. How it works. And a lot of the men involved. … … So they don't want me telling what I know to the police."

My hands were clasped over the newspaper on top of the briefcase. James reached out with his left hand and gently placed it over mine.

"Lizzie," he said, his voice low and deep with emotion, "I'm a Christian, I truly am, but if anyone ever did to my Abby what these men have done to you, I'm very much afraid I'd deal with them first and worry about forgiveness later."

I looked at him and I was crying. My Dad would have said that.

Through my tears, I blurted out, "I never could understand that forgiveness thing. How can anyone be a Christian and *not* want to stop evil people doing terrible things?"

"That's a tough question, Lizzie, and maybe when this is all over, we can wrestle with it a bit. But you said there were three things?"

I pulled my left hand away from under his, and wiped at my face.

"The third thing is the one that probably matters most of all. I know the man at the top. There's hardly anyone knows who he is … … but I do."

My nose felt damp and I sniffed. I couldn't reach the tissues in my bag because of the briefcase still resting on my lap.

"He's the guy who picked me off the street when I came to Birmingham, and got me the job. Nothing wrong in that. Nothing illegal. But I've seen him again a few times. Even been in his car once when he wanted me to be good to an important friend of his."

I sniffed again, and James reached across and opened the glove compartment and pulled out a wad of tissues. He handed me one, and left the rest lying on the newspaper. His expression encouraged me to go on with increasing confidence.

"The thing is … … I kept my ears open … … and my eyes. I wasn't trying to find out anything special. I just … … always had this feeling that … … well, you never know when a bit of information might come in useful."

I've read of people smiling ruefully, and I guess that's what I did now.

"I know who he is … … I know where he lives … … I know what car he drives … … I know some of his important friends … … and I know some of the villains he deals with ... ... but I've got no real proof that he has ever personally done anything wrong. The trouble is ... ... he doesn't know how much I know, and that's probably why he wants me back so badly. He doesn't know whether I've got information that could put him away for good. So he can't risk having me on the loose."

I stopped, and there was a long pause. James was waiting for me to tell him the name of this person who was so desperate to silence Angie and me, and I didn't realise I still hadn't told him.

"Are you going to keep it a secret, Lizzie?"

I suppose I must have looked puzzled.

"You haven't told me his name."

"Ooooh. Sorry. He's called Ray Mellisse ... ... But it won't be him chasing us. I'll bet anything it's Bruno organising the hunt. ... ... He'll be reporting back to Ray, though. He always does. And he'll do whatever Ray tells him."

James reached over again and laid his hand lightly over mine. I was clutching a rather damp tissue, but he didn't seem to mind.

"Thanks, Lizzie. I imagine it wasn't easy telling me all that."

I looked across at him and smiled.

"Actually ... ... I feel a whole lot better now I have done."

"Good... ... Now, I think, it's time to make plans."

He started the Maserati and eased out of the parking space, carefully avoiding a young mum pushing a loaded trolley with a small child in the baby seat.

"Where are we going," I asked, surprised that I wasn't hearing more about these plans.

"Oh, I thought I told you? That's why we've come down here. To visit some friends at RRISC. You met some of them the other night. I rather think we're going to need their help."

Twenty-Six

Pan European Solutions – 12.25 pm

Paul Agnew rode the elevator to the fourth floor of Grasojen House, a relatively new five-storey office block, purpose-built in glass and brick to house the headquarters of a fast-growing and amazingly successful company called Pan European Solutions. Agnew didn't know what the name meant, but then hardly anyone else did either. Most people were similarly uninformed about what the company actually did, but there Agnew was at an advantage. He worked for its boss, a pillar of Birmingham's commercial community, called Raymond Charles Mellisse.

He enjoyed the rare occasions when he had to come out to GH, as the offices had come to be known, since it brought him up close to the whining, growling, howling, screaming visitors to Birmingham International Airport. He loved to watch aircraft landing and taking off, but it was the sounds of their engines far more than the sight of their sleek, streamlined bodies that really thrilled him. He could stand under the flight path of an aircraft on approach and, with his eyes closed, judge the exact moment the landing gear came down just from the sounds coming from the plane. He didn't know why he was so fascinated. He simply knew that he always had been.

Today was different. As he had skirted the airport complex in his dark blue BMW 525, he scarcely even noticed the Emirates Boeing 777 which came in almost directly over his head. Climbing out of the car in the secure parking adjacent to the GH building, he glanced automatically in the direction of the terminals and runways but his mind was far too preoccupied to register any of the sights his eyes passed over.

A pleasant female voice, with only a faintly robotic timbre, informed him that he had arrived at the fourth floor and that the doors were about to open. He took her at her word and eased himself off the rear wall of the elevator. He was about to step forward into Ray Mellisse's outer office when his cell phone vibrated against his chest. When he removed the phone from an inside jacket pocket, the device seemed tiny in his huge hand. It had become normal for him as cell-phones had shrunk in size to use his thumb nail to depress the keys because when he used the pads of his fingers he always ended up pressing several at once. Checking the display, he paused inside the elevator and used his thumb nail to answer. When the doors tried to close again he stuck out his foot to block them. After listening for a few seconds he smiled, removed his foot and instructed the elevator to drop him down a floor.

In just under fifteen minutes, he found himself once again on the fourth floor being warned that the doors were about to open. This time he stepped through. He was aware that Mellisse would know exactly when he had entered the building and would not be pleased at being kept waiting. But he didn't mind. The last fifteen minutes had changed everything.

As Agnew emerged from the elevator, a rather large young man in a dark, well-fitting suit, looked up for a second time in his direction. With a good honours degree from the LSE, Roger North had been looking forward to making his pile in the City and then retiring in his mid-thirties. Others had done it so why not he? Unfortunately, where others had usually managed to avoid the temptation to enhance their personal investment at the expense of clients' funds, Roger had not. It was also unfortunate that some of the funds subjected to his temporary, but unofficial, borrowing were actually in the portfolio of one Raymond Mellisse. The deficit should only have been visible for just over twenty-four hours, assuming anyone was looking. Someone was. Concerned about fluctuations in the markets, Mellisse chose that very day to conduct an in-depth analysis of his holdings. Extremely angry but, at the same time, attracted to North's albeit misused financial acumen, Mellisse, in the person of Bruno, had offered him a choice: the North Sea wearing a concrete overcoat, or a position in his company doing whatever Mellisse required. It was a no-brainer.

"Hi, Rog," said Agnew as he emerged from the lift.

"So, you're staying this time, are you Bruno?" replied North looking over at the huge bear of a man. He was a lot younger than Paul "Bruno" Agnew, and he worked out three or four times a week, and he was sure that, if push came to shove, he could take Bruno with no problem. Probably! But he didn't want push to come to shove because Bruno's intimidating stare always reminded him that, so far as anyone knew, no-one ever yet had taken Bruno in any kind of confrontation, fair or otherwise. The only person he ever deferred to was Ray Mellisse.

"Sure, Rog. Is he in?"

"Of course he's in. And pissed at you for taking your time. What's going on that I don't know?"

"I'm sure there a whole heap of things, Rog. But, if he thinks you need to know, he'll tell you."

As he spoke, Bruno crossed to a door in the centre of the wall that ran at right angles to the elevator shaft, and waited. He stood sideways to the door, all the time holding North's gaze until the younger man leaned forward and pressed one of the many buttons arrayed on his desk.

"Bruno's here, Mr. Mellisse."

In response to something he heard through his earpiece, North nodded to Bruno who opened the door and walked through.

"You'd better be bringing me something good, Bruno," growled Mellisse, making no attempt to hide his anger and impatience.

"I think you're going to like it, Mr Mellisse," replied Bruno, flourishing the file folder which he'd been given on his quick detour to the floor below.

Mellisse had for the moment forsaken his substantial, though vulgarly modern, executive desk and was sitting comfortably at one end of a large leather settee which had its back to a huge window overlooking the airport complex. Bruno loved the window, except for the fact that highly efficient sound proofing almost eliminated the noise of aircraft engines. The rest of the office with its plain walls, plush carpet and modern paintings, all of which were original, were of no interest to him. Papers had been strewn on the seat beside Mellisse, but he gathered these together as he said, "OK, Bruno. Let's hope you're right. Sit. Tell me what you've got."

Bruno eased himself into one of the two matching leather chairs that faced the settee and therefore the window, but he took great care not to let his gaze linger on the fascinating scenes outside.

"Remember the card that Jock found in that nurse's handbag? Montrayne?"

Mellisse nodded.

"Well I set Barney onto tracking him down."

Barney Peters, christened Bernard by elderly and old-fashioned parents, was the resident IT specialist at Pan European. More imaginative and sympathetic school friends had changed his name to Barney and so it had been ever since.

"You didn't tell him why?" queried Mellisse.

"No, Mr. Mellisse. I'm not stupid. He just thought he was doing a background check on a possible client."

"OK. Good. So what did he find?"

Bruno opened his folder.

"He found James Alistair Christopher Montrayne, Earl of Aullton and son of the thirteenth Marquess of Thurvaston who runs some department in the MOD."

Mellisse stared, and let out a long slow breath. Before he could speak, Bruno continued.

"Yeah. One of the nobs. But there's more." He looked down at the papers in the folder.

"His great-aunt was married to Sir Peter Marchmont. You know … …"

"Yes, I do know," Mellisse interrupted, surprise giving a sharp edge to his words. "He practically ruled the City in the Thatcher years. There wasn't much he didn't have his hand in."

"Well, seems like most of what was in his hands ended up in Montrayne's when he and the old lady copped it. No kids you see."

Mellisse frowned. "No, I don't see. If this Montrayne is one of the top nobs, what's he doing getting involved with those two tarts?"

Bruno turned over a page. "According to Barney, that was the tricky bit. But it seems it goes something like this." He sat forward, studying the notes in the folder.

"In April 2003 there was a plane crash up in Scotland. Small, private, twin-engine job. Montrayne's uncle, the twelfth Marquess was aboard with his wife and son, and his nephew who was the elder brother of Montrayne. Dived into a mountain and blew up. No survivors. Up to then, Montrayne was just plain Mister, but after that, everyone moved up a notch, and his dad became Marquess which rather pissed him off because he was perfectly happy being an ordinary bloke doing an ordinary job."

"Well he must have been a son of a Marquess, so he was hardly ordinary," interrupted Mellisse. "And running a department of the MOD is not on everyone's CV."

Bruno nodded slowly. "Maybe not. Anyway, when Sir Peter died everything went to the widow, and when she died in ninety-nine she left the whole lot to Montrayne. His old man, who wasn't a Marquess then, doesn't seem to have been too fussed about it, which seems a bit odd. Anyway, Barney can check it out if it's important, but he hasn't had time yet, and he was up most of the night working on this."

Mellisse shook his head. "Probably doesn't matter. What else?"

"Barney couldn't work out what he's worth, but this Montrayne owns a chunk of London, with other estates all over the place, including Scotland. He's got major holdings, sometimes majority holdings, in a range of companies even I've heard of. But here's the thing … …"

He paused to find his place in his notes.

"He was in the Royal Marines when he got married in '95. Left in '98 as a major after his kid was born. Probably didn't feel like retiring early with a bullet in the head. Anyway, seems like the wife had a heart problem, and she snuffed it not long after the kid was born. She was a teacher, and loved it, so Montrayne decided to give it a go and signed up for a year's PGCE. After the wife died, it was just him and the kid, Abigail. Don't know why he carried on with the teaching when he had all that money, but… … I suppose Barney could find out, if its important."

"How did Barney get all this?" Mellisse asked, speaking slowly and in a tone that anyone other than Bruno would have taken as threatening. "You've not had him breaking into medical records and such like?"

Mellisse had no moral objection to hacking into anyone's database, personal, corporate or government, but Barney believed, along with most other Pan European employees, that he was working for a legitimate company and Mellisse wanted to keep it that way.

"No, course not, Mr Mellisse," replied Bruno, not in the least affronted. "Obituaries. The Times and Country Life. Stuff like that. Very informative according to Barney."

"OK," said Mellisse, satisfied. "And Montrayne is still teaching." He began to smile. "A millionaire school-teacher. Can't be many of those about."

Now Bruno also began to smile. The punch line was coming.

"Probably the only one, Mr Mellisse. But not for much longer."

Mellisse cocked his head slightly and raised his eyebrows. Normally he reacted badly to being played, but he had known Bruno for long enough to realise that something good was coming. He would allow Bruno his teasing moment.

"Really? And why is that?"

Bruno took a paper from his file folder and held it out to Mellisse. It was Corrina Rigby's article printed off from the Lichfield News website. Bruno carefully watched Mellisse's expression during the few moments it took to read and reread the article. It was clear to him that the words were not generating the expected level of satisfaction. In fact, if anything, Mellisse appeared puzzled, even slightly annoyed.

"Why haven't I heard about this before?"

"Because this means it's nothing to do with us, Mr Mellisse," Bruno sounded put out, defensive. "And I only just got it myself."

"Is it true?" asked Mellisse, wondering if Simmons's death really could be just a fortunate coincidence.

"Who knows?" shrugged Bruno. "And who cares? Look … … this is good for us. This guy Simmons gets himself topped, so he's no more bother, and Montrayne goes down for it."

"From everything you've given me so far, he won't go down easily. This story sounds like crap to me. Are you certain we had nothing to do with it?"

Bruno tried to appear affronted, but there was a wariness in his expression.

"Straight up, Mr Mellisse. None of our guys was at that farm until after it happened. I checked."

"OK. But this says that guy Simmons was something big at Lichfield Tube. I assume it's the same Lichfield Tube that's been a nice little earner for us these past few years?"

"Same one, Mr Mellisse."

Mellisse sat back, the fingers of his right hand gently massaging his chin as he thought. He looked fairly relaxed but his eyes were as cold, as hard and as sharp as an ice-pick.

"Then what's going on, Bruno?"

Big as he was, and tough as he was, Bruno experienced a touch of fear. It was only the faintest of twinges but it was, for him, a novel experience. He had been Mellisse's minder, chief fixer, even confidant, for the best part of ten years, but he knew that the security of his position rested on his never slipping up. He hadn't seen this coming, but he saw himself now on the lip of a bottomless chasm from which he needed to draw back with the utmost haste and no little finesse.

He took a deep breath and thought carefully about his next words.

"It's like this, Mr Mellisse," he began slowly. "I told you there was some bother brewing at Lichfield Tube. Nothing much. Just some guy snooping into things he shouldn't. I told our... ...er... ...expediter that you wouldn't want to be bothered. He should sort it himself."

"You mentioned my name." Mellisse's voice rose as he slowly uttered the words.

"No, Mr Mellisse. No. You know me. I know the rules. I just said the boss doesn't bother himself with stuff like that. I just said you'd want it sorting... ... quiet like."

Mellisse banged his fist down on the article lying on his desk.

"You call this quiet?"

"Wasn't what I had in mind, Mr Mellisse, but in any case it's looking like it was this Montrayne that did it. Just think about it for a minute. This could work for us. The snooper's out of the picture and Montrayne, who's started being a right pain in the arse, is in the frame for doing it. Should put a stop to him interfering."

Mellisse sat back and allowed his eyes to wander over to the window while he thought.

"Have you asked your... ... expediter about this? Made sure it wasn't him?"

"Not yet. He's out of the country. He always refuses to talk about this kind of stuff on the phone. Bit paranoid if you ask me. Whatever... ... this can still work for us."

Bruno had a point. Guilty or not, Montrayne just needed neutralising a bit, in a non-lethal sense.

"OK," he said, bringing his gaze back to Bruno. "Maybe we can help this story along a bit. Give it some substance. Doesn't matter whether Montrayne actually goes down for it or not. We just need him ... ... preoccupied for a while. Give us time to get our business done and get clear."

"What do you have in mind, Mr Mellissse?"

Mellisse ignored the question. "What else have you got?"

The change of direction caught Bruno by surprise, and then he beamed as he remembered the snippet he'd been saving; a name in a list which had meant nothing to Barney but everything to Bruno.

"Montrayne's businesses," he said still smiling. "Seems like his lordship owns a private hospital."

This time he got the reaction he expected.

"That's right, Mr Mellisse. The Aullton Foundation Hospital. Now what do you want to bet he's got Angie wrapped up all right and tight in one of those private rooms?"

From that moment, it didn't take long to put a plan together. It would have to be done in the evening when there would be sure to be plenty of visitors about and a couple of extra strangers could go unnoticed. A quick injection of something nasty, maybe uncut heroin, would see the job done. And as long as they used the right contractors, Mellisse liked that word as it sounded so much more professional than assassin, there would be nothing to trace the deed back to him.

He leant back, stretching with quiet satisfaction.

"You've done well, Bruno."

"Credit where it's due, Mr Mellisse," replied Bruno in scrupulous fairness. "I wouldn't have got this without Barney. He's a good lad."

"Indeed he is, Bruno. A good lad. Maybe I'll give him a bonus." He paused and thought for a moment. "But then again, maybe not. I don't want him thinking this was anything more than a routine background check... ... OK, that's Angie sorted. Now what about Di?"

"Should be easy enough, Mr Mellisse. We know she's with Montrayne. We just need to find out where they are, and distract him long enough to get her. Pity we can't just dispose of him, but I guess that would raise too much of a stink with the police already sniffing around him. Still, we know where he lives now and we also know he spends a lot of time at that farm."

"Do we?" asked Mellisse.

"Sure. The guys went back this morning and did the farm tour. All legit. No strong-arm stuff. They found some young wench packing eggs who'd have done anything for a bit of ready cash. She lives on the farm, dumped there by Social Services and a Court Order that'll keep her in care til she's eighteen. She keeps her eyes open and she said Montrayne and his kid go there a lot. Not so surprising when you realise he owns the place. The folk who run it are just tenants. She doesn't know anyone called Di, but there was a new girl being shown around by the two kids on Saturday afternoon. They called her Lizzie, but that's got to be her."

"Lizzie," said Mellisse slowly, savouring the name. "I like that. I wonder why she changed it?"

"Lots of girls do, Mr Mellisse. Doesn't have to be a reason."

"Whatever," replied Mellisse. "I don't suppose it matters now. She'll be back in our hands by morning."

And then the second plan was born.

Twenty-Seven

RRISC Birmingham – 12.50 pm

About ten minutes after leaving the Walmart parking lot we turned off into some kind of industrial estate. Just inside the entrance, near a lay-by at the edge of a neatly-mown grassy mound, was a huge sign-board listing all the businesses on the estate and locating all of them on a colour-coded map. We drove on without stopping so I assumed James knew where he was going. All the units looked relatively new. Some were large and impressive like the corporate HQ of multinational businesses, with others ranging down in size to small individual warehouse units of no more than five thousand square feet. All the roads had grass verges and more green spaces separated the various units. The planners had also been very generous with their trees which dotted the open spaces in irregular clusters, one of which, rather larger than the rest, skirted a small lake. Not a bad place to work, if you had to get stuck in an office or warehouse.

After a couple of turns, we pulled into the parking lot of a two-story brick-built unit. There were spaces for about a dozen vehicles out front, but a drive leading off round the side of the building presumably led to more parking at the rear. There were several cars scattered about the lot, all of them fairly recent models except for an immaculate dark green E-type Jaguar parked in the slot next to the entrance which I presumed was reserved for the CEO of RRISC, whoever that was. As we pulled into the vacant slot next to the E-type, I glanced to my left at a gleaming blue-black Mercedes SUV. I had no idea what model it was but it looked as though it had only just left the showroom. The driver glanced in my direction and just for a second his eyes looked directly into mine before they returned to his paperback book. He was dark, and slightly foreign looking, maybe eastern European. Probably somebody's chauffeur, waiting for his boss.

The pillared pediment of the reception entrance was dead centre in the front of the building giving the premises a kind of symmetrical neo-Georgian look. The sign above the pediment said *RRISC* in large capitals, and in smaller letters underneath *Rapid Response International Security Consultants*. The glass doors in the shadow of the entrance denied any attempt at classical Georgian authenticity. They were heavy, and modern, and had a strangely greenish tint to them. As we walked towards them, I saw some kind of intercom system set into the wall to the left of the doors. It was flush with the brickwork, silvery looking, matt not shiny, with a circle of small holes in the upper half, presumably for the speaker and microphone. Below the holes was a small screen, maybe two inches square, like on my cell phone, except that this was grey and blank. Below that was a numbered key pad, four rows of three going one to nine with the bottom row being *0, Enter & Call.* A small sign below the key pad read *Visitors – Press Call to speak to Reception.*

I think I expected James to press the *Call* button, but he didn't. He positioned himself so that I couldn't see the key pad and started pressing. I didn't mind. What's the point in a security system if you're going to let any old Tom, Dick or Jane see your key codes? From the way his arm moved, I guessed he pressed some buttons on the key pad, then put a finger or thumb on the little screen before pressing some more numbers and then *Enter.* I did glance at the glass door to check his reflection and see if I could make out what he was doing and was surprised to see that the glass showed no reflections at all. Strange. Again, I didn't mind as I wasn't really interested in knowing his codes. I was just curious as to how the system worked.

Pressing the *Enter* button was all he let me see, and immediately one of the glass panels slid sideways to allow us to pass through into Reception. This was a large pleasant space with dark green carpet and pale green walls decorated with large unframed colour photographs of various far-flung parts of the world. A curved reception counter occupied the far left-hand corner of the floor space, while over to the right was a coffee table and four comfortable-looking easy chairs, presumably for visitors. Tucked into the corner behind the table and chairs was a coffee machine and a water cooler, also presumably for the use of visitors.

Were we visitors? I assumed not, since James had his own entry code. But why did he? What was his connection with this place? The more I was getting to know him, the more I was realising that I didn't actually know him at all.

As I looked around, James turned towards the reception counter. The woman sitting there had looked up briefly as we entered, smiled at James, and then returned to whatever she was doing. I could hear the tapping of computer keys but couldn't see the screen or keyboard as they were below the level of the counter top. Presumably her phone system was down there as well since the polished wood of the counter top was completely clear, apart from a visitors' book and a tray containing some kind of plastic badges.

I looked at her more closely as James approached the counter. I guessed she was in her late thirties, though she could have been older. Her brown hair was thick and wavy, framing her face with dark curls. Her mouth was a little too wide to be beautiful and her face a little too long, but I could see that most men would find her attractive. She stopped typing and looked up again.

"Hello, James." Her tone was cheerful and her smile welcoming. Probably everybody got that, but the warm glow in her eyes as she looked up at him was definitely not for sharing around.

She gabbled on before he had a chance to reply.

"Sorry about that. I was in the middle of a complicated sentence and I knew if I stopped I'd forget what I was going to say. Were we expecting to see you today?"

"No, you weren't, Mel, but something's come up."

He turned back to me then, as though sensing my hovering indecision, and gestured towards the facilities in the corner.

"I dragged you away so quickly, Lizzie, you must be dying of thirst by now. Why don't you help yourself to a coffee, and take a seat for a minute?"

I did, and also made a tea for James since I'd already learnt that this was what he preferred. I sat down placing one mug on the table and sipping tentatively from the other. The coffee was surprisingly good and the mugs were a fine bone china. These guys certainly didn't do things on the cheap.

While I was busy with the drinks I kept listening, hoping to find out exactly why we were there. James asked for someone called Andy and was told he had a client with him, apparently a new and potentially lucrative client, and would probably not be free for another half an hour. That didn't seem to matter.

"That's OK, Mel. How about Rod? What's he up to?"

"Playing with his computers as usual. Probably hacking into the Pentagon or the MOD… … Maybe even your bank account. He's got to pay for that new boat of his somehow."

I glanced across and saw she was still smiling at James. I definitely knew that look and wondered whether she had any rings on her left hand. This was a total certainty, no-question, come-on. Nothing I'd have picked up on just by listening, but it was definitely there in her eyes. I'd heard of people having very speaking eyes, and hers were talking volumes. I wondered which she fancied most, him or his money. Unfair of me, I suppose, but in my limited experience most things came down to sex or money, often both.

Was it reciprocal? Did he fancy her? Nothing in his voice, and no way of reading his expression as he still had his back to me, but somehow I didn't think so. There had been nothing in his manner as we came in to suggest anything more than polite friendliness which, I was beginning to learn, was his normal manner with most people.

"Maybe I'd better go and see him before he cleans me out," James replied and then looked over to me.

"Come and meet a friend of mine and … …"

Mel's voice was a touch less friendly as she interrupted.

"I don't think your young lady has signed in yet."

James didn't seem to notice the change in tone.

"Quite right, Mel. Just keeping you on your toes."

He lifted the Visitors Book from the counter and brought it over to the coffee table. Sitting opposite me, he nodded at the mug of tea.

"Is that for me? ... ... Thanks."

He completed the next entry line in the book while he tackled his drink, and then returned it to Mel. A few moments later, rather reluctantly I thought, Mel handed over a Visitor's pass on a cord so I could hang it round my neck. I was surprised to see it had my photo on it, just head and shoulders, but it had obviously been taken as I'd walked in to Reception. My name was there too. No surprise in that, but I was amazed to discover that I worked for a company called Aullton Estates. I wanted to ask James what that was all about, but decided that it was probably best to wait for a more suitable moment.

Telling me to bring my drink with me, he then led me through another keypad controlled door at the rear of the Reception area and into a short corridor. To the right were blue carpeted stairs doubling back in two flights to lead to the next floor. Apparently, Rod's office was up there and, two more secure doors later, we were in a room that looked as though it could have doubled for NASA control. At one of the terminals sat a wiry looking guy with long, brown hair drawn back in a ponytail. He swivelled his chair round as we entered. I put him somewhere in his mid-thirties with a beard that was either finely trimmed, or was designer stubble in need of attention. His hooded brown eyes focussed immediately on me and, although his words were clearly addressed to James, his gaze didn't waver.

"So what brings you here, O Lord and master?"

"According to Mel, I'm here to stop you draining my bank account."

The brown eyes crinkled at the corners, but still didn't shift their focus. There was something in his eyes I didn't like. Something I'd seen before. Many times.

"Too late, Boss. I did that yesterday. Donated it all to a home for wayward girls in Acapulco."

"Well, I'm glad it went to a good cause."

"As good as they come, Boss. You never know when you might be in need of a wayward girl."

His last comment was said slowly, almost wistfully and, throughout the banter, Rod's eyes remained fixed on me: they roved over my hair, my eyes, my breasts, my waist, and right the way down my legs to my toes, and once they arrived at the floor they started all the way back up again. I was used to men looking at me and I knew exactly what he was seeing. I can't help the genes that gave me the hair, eyes, skin, teeth, body shape that make men's heads turn and stare. But there are different ways of staring.

I've come to think that men look at a beautiful woman as they might an oil painting. Some note colour, texture, shape and form and they wonder at the way these different elements combine to produce the effect that has them enthralled. It doesn't matter who it belongs to, or whether they'll ever see it again. For a moment, or maybe two, or three, they marvel at this awesome creation, simply appreciating it for what it is. And then they move on.

Others are so stirred by what they see, they cannot be happy unless they have the chance to possess it. They fantasize about how to make possession a reality. Some want to hold it for ever, but others find that temporary custody is a far more satisfying arrangement. I had been many a man's temporary possession, so I know how to recognise when the fantasy of ownership runs riot and true appreciation starts to shrivel up into barely concealed lust.

I was seeing that right now, and his next words confirmed the direction of his thoughts.

"And ah... ... speaking of wayward girls, Boss, is this that chick from Saturday night?"

After James's scrupulous politeness in the face of everything I'd told him, the unveiled scorn in Rod's voice sliced through the flimsy veneer of respectability that I had put on with Sarah Montrayne's clothes that morning. I felt the rage start in my stomach, tensing the muscles, then rising up my back and into my shoulders. I tried to swallow but my mouth was dry and my throat constricted. I tried to control the surge of anger as I heard James reply in a tone that would have scared me rigid if he'd been speaking to me.

"Just explain to me, Rod, exactly what makes you think you can speak in that way about a friend of mine."

Rod seemed not to take the hint.

"What can I say, Boss? Sonia told me when she came in this morning. Something about a hooker," he glanced at me, totally unaware of the trouble about to descend on his head, "in trouble with her pimp and you charging in like a white knight to the rescue."

His eyes began their roving act again, but didn't stray far from the centre of my chest.

"Still, I can't say I blame you, Boss. Very tasty. I wouldn't have minded a bit of her myself, if I'd got there first. Gonna keep her, are you?"

I felt James's hand on my shoulder, whether to comfort or restrain I wasn't sure, and I didn't care. He started to speak but his words didn't register. I didn't care what he was saying, and I didn't care what he thought. The only thing I cared about at that moment was wiping that lecherous smirk off Rod's face. I moved fast.

One of the girls at the massage parlour had found herself from time to time in an awkward or threatening situation. She'd learnt how to take care of herself. *If you can't crush his balls, then smash his nose,* she used to say. *Don't slap, that just makes him mad; and don't punch because you'll damage your fingers.* And she'd shown me how to strike with the heel of my hand, fingers curled to protect them. It was a short-arm jab with all the weight of my body behind it, driving his nose upward towards his eyebrows. Rod yelled, toppling backwards, hands clutching his face, restrained only
by the desktop behind him. His eyes were streaming with tears, and blood seeped from between his fingers.

If this had been out on the streets, I'd have been twenty yards away by now and sprinting fast, but as it was, I stood and watched breathing hard as red drips made patterns on his shirt. I expected yells and cursing, maybe even an attempt at retaliation, but Rod seemed to shrink into his chair, no trace of the macho posturing of just a few seconds earlier.

James hand was there again, gentle but definitely restraining. His voice was far from gentle.

"You asked for that, Rod. Positively begged for it. Now go and get cleaned up and then get back in here. I've got a job for you."

Rod staggered up out of his chair, hands still shielding his face. His voice was slurred and whining.

"Why'd you let her do that, Boss. She's damn near broke it again."

James was not sympathetic.

"Well it can't look any worse than it did already."

He opened the door.

"Now, go and get yourself sorted."

Rod stumbled out of the room muttering to himself. James closed the door.

"I'm sorry about that, Lizzie."

I shook my head. I was still trembling from the rush of adrenalin. I wasn't ashamed of what I'd just done, and I didn't regret it, except that somewhere deep inside, so deep I was scarcely even aware of what it was, there was a dawning hint of disappointment that I hadn't been able to be a bigger or better person. I wasn't about to apologise or explain, but it turned out that wasn't what James wanted. He wanted to give me some sort of excuse or explanation for Rod's behaviour but, at that moment, I found I just didn't want to talk about it. I had thought my skin had toughened over the years but something in Rod's eyes as much as what he'd said had really got to me.

"He's not a bad bloke really. Just a bit messed up. Which is why we now keep him tied to his computers. And with those, he's a total genius."

I shrugged. It didn't matter. But James went on.

"About two years ago, he and Surjit were working a hostage extraction in Somalia. At first, everything went as planned, but right at the end it blew up in their faces. Literally. They'd made the deal, recovered the hostage but then their vehicle was hit by an RPG."

I frowned. I'd heard the term, but wasn't sure what it was.

"A rocket propelled grenade. Their Jeep was armoured, but not heavily enough. It flipped over and burst into flames. Rod was flung clear, without a scratch. Surjit crawled out, but then realised the hostage was still trapped in the back. He went back calling for Rod to help. Rod stayed clear and kept yelling for him to come away because he could see the flames were getting too close to the fuel tank. Surjit ignored him and got the hostage out just seconds before the tank blew. That's when the fire got him. At that point, he was between the hostage and the car. Rod knows that logically he did the right thing, but he can't forgive himself for freezing while Surjit got the job done. He was no good for work in the field after that, hence the computers. Something he's always had a flair for. Surjit was in hospital for several months, and then came to work security for me... ...This was just after Abby was kidnapped and I decided to beef up security at the Dower House."

I looked up at him, wondering why he was bothering to tell me all this. But I didn't wonder too hard as I didn't really care that much. And anyway, something else struck me.

"What happened to the hostage?"

"Currently CEO of one of the more successful NHS Trusts here in the Midlands. She actually seems able to deliver an efficient service as well as making sure the Trust balances its books. A rare achievement."

She! Strange how I'd assumed that the hostage was a man.

"Does Surjit think his sacrifice was worth it?"

"I'm not sure he thinks of it like that. For him, it was a matter of honour. He took the job, and was then committed to getting the hostage out. Simple as that. And he succeeded. His body may have taken a hit, but his personal pride is totally undented."

He paused and looked around the room, Rod's domain.

"With Rod it was the other way round. Body intact, head messed up. The hostage was a woman, and he let her down. He let his mate down.

He was very hard on himself. He's had counselling, still does, I think. But he can't allow himself to get close to a woman any more. He looks, he talks, but it seems as though it's all intended to keep the woman at a distance rather than draw her in. He lets his behaviour build a wall, and that way he'll never find himself in a position where he might let her down. I could be totally wrong, of course, but that's my attempt at amateur psychology."

I shrugged again and that disappointment I felt about myself was no longer buried quite so deep. I couldn't help it, but my eyes began to well up, and I looked away so he wouldn't notice. He was distracted then as the door was flung open and a young man I'd never seen before charged into the room.

"What the hell's happened to Rod? He's in the gents crying his eyes out and filling the sink with blood."

James reached for a phone as he spoke.

"Hello, Jimmy. Just settle down. Rod had an accident, that's all."

He pressed some buttons and spoke into the phone.

"Mel? Rod needs some first aid. Nosebleed... ... He's in the gents... ... Yes, I know. Just find someone to sort him out, will you?"

He put down the phone and looked at me. While his attention was distracted, I had managed to dry my eyes on my sleeve.

"Lizzie, this is Jimmy. Technically, he's Rod's assistant, but it's a bit of a moot point which of them is the greatest hacker."

Jimmy smiled as he looked at me, all concern for Rod evaporating. He was tall and skinny with a bush of red hair and rimless glasses. His fair skin was lightly freckled and he looked about twelve years old. Well, maybe fifteen. He stepped towards me.

"Hi," he said, and then brushed his right hand against his trouser leg before holding it out tentatively towards me. He withdrew his hand almost as soon as I touched it, and shoved both hands deep in his pockets. His bashfulness helped to restore some sense of balance after what had just occurred.

"Jimmy, something's come up," I heard James say. "I was going to ask Rod, but now it will have to be you. I need this fast. Everything you can get."

There was a rustling as James handed over the crumpled newspaper which he'd brought with him from the car. A few moments silence, and then, "Hells teeth!"

"Quite."

James's response was perfectly calm, and I watched the expression on his face as Jimmy sat down and gave careful attention to Corrina Rigby's article. After a few moments, he looked up.

"How much of this is true, Boss?"

"Pretty much all of it."

"Hmmm. You didn't do it, did you, Boss."

No reply.

"No. Course you didn't. Daft question."

Silence.

"So why's she got it in for you? ... ... This is deliberate stuff. Carefully contrived. Not actionable ... ... or, at least, I wouldn't think so... ... She hates your guts. Why? What have you done?"

"I have no idea, Jimmy. Absolutely none. Which is why I need you. Who is she? What's her motive? Is she being paid? Coerced? Anything you can find out that will tell us what she's up to."

"You got it, Boss. But it'll take time. Who shall I bill it to?"

"Me. Assuming my bank account is still intact, of course."

Jimmy looked like a schoolboy, asked a question he couldn't understand.

"Why wouldn't it be?"

"Never mind, Jimmy. Quick as you can... ... And there's something else I need you to do."

There was a slight pause before I heard Jimmy's reply.

"OK, Boss. Whatever you want, you know that. But Andy's on my back about ... ... well, we're just starting another job. And, according to him, that's bloody urgent too. You know what he's like. Always wants everything yesterday."

James response was immediate and decisive. I had no doubt he was going to get what he wanted, regardless of what Andy required.

"I'll talk to Andy and get you some backup. Now ... ... that reporter. Everything you can find. Same for Phil Simmons, even if you think I might already know it. Family, friends, colleagues, finances. You know the sort of stuff to look for. And dig around his company too. See if Lichfield Tube has anything going on that could have got him in trouble. Somebody killed him for a reason. I want to know who, and why."

"You don't think the police'll find that out, Boss?"

"Not while they're looking at me they won't."

"I guess not." Jimmy looked over at me. "And what about... ... er... ... Lizzie, was it? How does she fit into this?"

I turned at this, wondering what James would reply. Sonia obviously hadn't spoken to Jimmy.

"She doesn't. She's not involved. I'm helping her with something else."

Jimmy's dark eyes flicked over to me and then back to him.

"Well, if ... ... er ... ... well if she needs any computer help ... ... I mean ... ... computer stuff ... ... I ... ... well, I'd like to help too."

James's eyebrows twitched.

"Aren't you going to be too busy, Jimmy?"

"Yeah, well… … I mean, I'd do it on my own time, Boss."

He looked at me and smiled. He was a nice boy, behaving as nice boys do. I couldn't help smiling back.

James reached for the telephone to the right of Jimmy's keyboard.

"OK, Jimmy. Everything you get, as soon as you get it. Let me know."

Jimmy twisted round to see him.

"Sure thing, Boss. Where will you be?"

"Can't be sure, but Surjit will know. Send anything you dig up to him. He'll know what to do with it."

Something in Jimmy's tone changed as he replied. I couldn't say exactly what it was except that he seemed almost reflective.

"OK, Boss. Er… … How's he doing?"

I watched him carefully, but he didn't look at me. In fact, I couldn't be sure just where he was looking. James was holding the cordless phone in the palm of his hand, looking at the buttons.

"Doing well, I think. The medics have done all they can for his face, so no more hospitals. I don't reckon they've done a bad job, considering."

Jimmy nodded and turned back to his keyboard.

"Good. I'll be in touch then, Boss."

He started typing and the screen lit up.

James pressed a button on the phone and asked Mel if Rod was OK. It seemed she wasn't sure but someone was looking after him. It also seemed that Andy was now free so we went to find him. Jimmy was hammering away on his keyboard as we left, but I saw him sneak a quick look over his shoulder as I pulled the door closed.

Out in the corridor, James walked a few paces and then stopped. He turned and looked down at me.

I thought he was going to say something but he didn't have a chance because some way down the corridor behind him a door opened and a tall well-built figure stepped out. His business suit was well tailored to fit muscular bulges in all the right places. Short-cropped fair hair topped a smiling, freckled face that was not exactly handsome, but was probably good-looking in a craggy sort of way.

"What're you doing skulking out here, James? Mel said you wanted to see me."

There was just a touch of Scottish lilt in his voice.

James held my eyes for moment longer before he turned round.

"Hello, Andy. I need a favour."

"Thought as much. If you ever turn up when it's not a board meeting, it's because you want something."

Turning back into his office, he said, "Come on in you old sod and tell me what trouble you're in this time."

I followed James and his friend into the office and stopped dead. Seeing the person who had been waiting there, I realised straight away that we were in deeper trouble than either of us had appreciated.

Twenty-Eight

Old Park Rifle Club – 1.05 pm

Joanne Hayford sat in her black Focus ST2 taking care not to drop the tiniest crumb on the immaculate ebony upholstery. That wasn't easy to do when you're alternately chewing a multigrain baguette filled with crispy bacon, and a giant sausage roll. The newspaper on her lap was doing a magnificent job of retaining the debris which tumbled with every mouthful, but she knew she would have to be very careful how she moved once her impromptu picnic was complete.

Sergeant Hayford was immensely proud of her sporty motor in spite of the gaping hole that the finance payments made in her monthly paycheck. She kept it immaculate and normally made it a rule never to eat while sitting in the vehicle but, when the rain is coming down like a monsoon flood, a dry skin takes precedence over a crumb-free carpet. Anyway, she could always vacuum the car at the filling station on her way home.

She had originally intended to skip lunch since her bathroom scales had been particularly unkind to her recently. She had made a note to replace them, now that it was obvious they were becoming worn and unreliable. Maybe her washing machine needed replacing too, as it seemed to be shrinking those skirts which always used to fit so well. Still, just to be on the safe side, skipping the odd lunch couldn't do any harm. Not that her mum would agree. In her view, Joanne had always been too thin. She couldn't abide these skimpy little flibbertigibbets prancing around in their size zero fashion wear. In vain had Joanne assured her that she was nowhere near size zero, and had no intention of coming even close to such a ludicrous standard. But Mum always knew best, and Joanne loved her for it.

Unfortunately, on the opposite side of the road from the police parking lot, a sandwich bar loomed temptingly, enticing all and sundry with the promise of the widest range of fillings in the world. As far as she was aware, no-one had yet contested this claim, and once you set foot over the threshold you could see why. Cooked meats of every sort; vegetarian concoctions that looked and smelt so good that many an avid carnivore had fallen for their charms; fish, minus scales and shells, smoked, dried, mousse or paste; salads, dressed and undressed, English, Mediterranean, Thai, and anywhere else in the world you care to think of. White bread, wholemeal bread, soft baps, crusty rolls, paninis, baguettes, it was a sandwich gourmet's paradise, and the police loved it.

So, Joanne had succumbed and was now enjoying the crummy consequences.

It had been her idea to come to the Old Park Rifle Club, once she had learned that James Montrayne claimed to be a member. If those airgun darts really were his, and she was beginning to have serious doubts about that, it was possible he could have bought them here, though maybe that would be too much of a long shot. She smiled a little at the mental pun, and took another bite of her baguette causing a large piece of crispy bacon to slip from the bread and drop onto the newspaper next to the remains of her sausage roll. She picked it up and slipped it into her mouth, finally licking her finger and thumb to enjoy every vestige of the bacon's salty tang.

She was making her lunch last since, when it was over, she would no longer have any excuse for lingering in her car. She would have to cross that almost deserted parking lot with raindrops the size of marbles shattering on the slick tarmac. She would be totally drenched. No she wouldn't! She would drive as close as she could to the club house entrance and then sprint the last few yards. Soaked maybe, but not drenched.

She took a sip of diet Pepsi and slipped in the last of the sausage roll as she watched raindrops bouncing off the roof of a nearly new Land Rover Defender parked near to the clubhouse entrance. What was DCI Morrissey up to? He hadn't really wanted her to come here, had he? It wasn't that he'd actually ordered her not to, but he'd made it obvious that, in his opinion, it would be a complete waste of time. These club members would all stick together, and no-one would admit to knowing anything that would help to make a case against Montrayne. Still, it was a stone that should be turned, and she was going to peer under and see what she could find. If nothing crawled out, then so be it. At least she would have tried.

Amazingly, as she chewed thoughtfully on the last piece of her baguette, the rain seemed to be easing off, and as the last satisfying morsel slipped down her throat, it reduced to little more than a moderate drizzle. No need to move the car. *Now*, she thought, opening the door and sprinkling the crumbs from her newspaper onto the damp tarmac. Grabbing her slimline leather briefcase – a present from her mother when she'd made detective sergeant – from the passenger seat, she slipped out, slammed the door and pressed the remote. It was all an illusion. As she released the button on the remote, the heavens opened and the whole of Niagara began to dump on her head. Cursing, she sprinted past the Land Rover and into the building.

Once inside she paused for a moment both to get her bearings and to shake off as much of the rain as hadn't already soaked into her hair and her jacket, which wasn't much. She wondered whether she looked as frightful as she felt, and then decided not to worry as there wasn't a lot she could do about it anyway. Except that there was. Directly facing her, opposite the entrance door, was the ladies room. A few minutes in front of the mirror with paper towels and a comb and she felt at least marginally respectable again.

Just as she was reaching to open the door, it swung towards her with such force that it almost crushed her hand against the wall. The woman following in its wake pulled up just in time to avoid barging full tilt into Joanne.

"Terribly sorry. I thought I was the only one here."

She was about Joanne's height, a little heavier maybe, but not so much as to detract from an undeniably well-proportioned figure well set off by a fluffy lilac sweater above black well-cut trousers. She was probably in her late thirties and wore just enough make-up to enhance the natural beauty of a woman in her prime.

"That's OK," replied Joanne, backing away to allow her to pass. "No harm done."

The woman looked at her thoughtfully.

"Are you a member?"

"No, but I do need to talk to someone who is."

"I see. Any old someone, or a particular someone?"

"Any."

"Well, in that case, you can have me. But you'll have to wait a moment. I have some urgent business to attend to. Have a seat out there in the lounge and I'll come through in a minute."

Joanne left to find the lounge while the newcomer retired into the ladies room to attend to her business.

The lounge was just an open area off the entrance hall, large enough to accommodate about twenty five plastic covered easy chairs arranged in groups around small, low tables. The plastic seemed a bit tacky until Joanne thought about marksmen lying about on the ground and then coming inside for a coffee. She couldn't see mud or grass on any of the chairs, or in fact on the floor, so the members obviously took steps to keep everywhere clean. Reassured, she sat and prepared to wait.

She had barely had time to open her briefcase before she heard footsteps crossing the entrance hall.

"Sorry, again. I'm the only one here at the moment and I'd been hanging on for ages waiting for a call from the council planning office. We want to put in a new range, you see. People never ring when you're waiting for them, do they? As soon as I'd finished on the phone, I really had to dash."

She offered her hand to Joanne.

"My, how I do talk. My name's Ruth Farquhar. Can I interest you in coffee? I think I dare have another cup now."

Joanne half rose to shake Ruth's hand, and confirmed that coffee would be good, milk, no sugar. A few moments at the coffee machine in the corner of the lounge and Ruth was back with two steaming polystyrene cups. Joanne noticed the rings on her left hand as she placed the cups on the table.

"Thanks, Mrs Farquhar."

"Oh, Ruth, please."

Taking a chair on the opposite side of the table to Joanne, Ruth settled herself comfortably, eying her visitor with interest.

"How can I help you? Do you want to join the club?"

Joanne reached inside her jacket for her warrant card folder which she laid on the table near enough for Ruth to pick it up. Puzzled, Ruth put down her coffee and picked up the folder, opening it to view the badge and then turning it sideways to read the information on the card. She closed it, laid it back on the table and retrieved her coffee.

"I suppose this means you don't want to join the club, Sergeant Hayford."

Reaching for the folder, Joanne smiled.

"Actually, under other circumstances, I might have considered it. But no. I need to ask you some questions."

Ruth was no longer looking, or sounding, quite so friendly.

"About James Montrayne?"

Joanne's eyebrows lifted slightly.

"News travels fast."

"I read the paper like everyone else. And some reporter was pestering me yesterday. She completely bollocks up what I told her, of course, and ended up printing total tripe. If you believe a word of that story I shall have to seriously revise my opinion about the intelligence of the average police officer."

Was there a compliment buried somewhere in there? Joanne wasn't sure. She drew a copy of the story out of her briefcase; just a single sheet, not the whole paper.

"If you've read that story, Mrs Farquhar," she decided a bit of formality wouldn't hurt, "you will realise that, as it stands, it probably is perfectly true. It's what's implied but not actually said that I'm having a little trouble with."

"Are you saying you don't believe James did it?"

Joanne sighed.

"I'm saying that all I'm interested in at the moment is gathering evidence and, in the end, I shall believe whatever that evidence tells me."

Ruth sat forward in her chair.

"Well, it won't tell you that James Montrayne killed anyone."

Joanne sighed again. She was getting good at it. Maybe Morrissey was right and this was a total waste of time. She tried to speak politely, but she knew the irritation showed.

"So, now that we've drawn up the battle lines, are you ready to answer a few questions?"

Ruth held Joanne's gaze for a moment or two, and then she settled back in her chair without losing eye contact. She seemed at ease, as though knowing that she was in charge of the situation, but her smile was completely without warmth.

"Of course. Ask away."

Joanne drew a large ten by eight photograph from her briefcase and laid it beside the newspaper article.

"Do you know what that is?"

Ruth leaned forward and picked it up. The photo was a blow-up of the dart found near Phil Simmons' body.

"Is this what's supposed to have killed that man in the wood?"

Joanne ignored the question.

"What can you tell me about that dart?"

Ruth turned the photo and looked at it more closely trying to read the numbers on the ruler that had been placed next to the dart to give scale. She pursed her lips.

"Can't be sure of the calibre, but it's probably 0.177. You can get 0.22, but they're less common, and I think they used to be available in 0.25 but I've not seen or heard of any of them in years."

She laid the photo back on the table and asked again, slowly and firmly, "Is that what you think killed him?"

Joanne gave in, hoping that a little give on her side might draw out something useful.

"We're not absolutely sure... ... but it is possible."

Ruth smiled.

"Fair enough. Well, what you've got there is a typical airgun dart; feathered tail, sharp point and that waisted hard alloy barrel. A company called Marksman in the US used to make them...... maybe still do. This could be one of theirs. Used to be very popular a few years ago. Short-range indoor stuff. Mostly used by kids."

Joanne was surprised at how much Ruth knew. She didn't look the type. But then, what was the type? A butch middle-aged woman in tweeds? She really had no idea.

"OK, thanks," she said. "Can you say what type of rifle would fire these things?"

Ruth chuckled.

"You're kidding, right?"

Joanne's eyes drifted before settling on the photo. What had she said? Ruth was making fun of her and enjoying it.

"I'm sorry," she replied, rather stiffly. "I don't understand."

Ruth took pity on her. "You asked about a rifle."

"Yes. To fire the dart."

"No way. Not unless you're a moron. Or an amateur who doesn't give a toss about taking care of his guns."

Joanne was genuinely puzzled.

"I'm sorry. You've lost me."

Ruth sat forward on her chair, realising that the information she had to give would probably do James Montrayne a lot more good than harm.

"You don't use a dart in a rifled barrel. They're for smooth bore guns. Put one of those darts in a rifle and you'll knacker up the barrel. It won't be accurate. A smooth bore pistol, that's what fired this. A Gat, maybe, or a Marksman BB gun."

Joanne sipped her coffee and thought about that one.

"Do you use pistols here at the club?"

Ruth smiled.

"Sure, but nothing that fires darts. They're banned here. So are BBs and copper pellets. Too hard, you see. Ricochets can be dangerous. Lead only. It's a safety thing."

"So you don't know anyone who uses darts like this? Maybe for fun, outside the club."

Ruth shook her head.

"Are you seriously telling me that you've never seen or heard of any of your members using these sort of darts?"

"Absolutely. These guys are all serious shooters. And that includes James. They don't mess with toys."

Joanne sipped at the remains of her coffee, grimaced, and then put the cup down. It was almost cold. She quickly assessed what she'd been told, assuming for the moment that it was true. Montrayne would probably not have wanted to ruin his rifles by firing darts, and he would have to have done it more than once to be sure of range and accuracy. And if he had done it, the rifling in the barrel would show signs of damage caused by the darts. The lab was working on that one, carefully testing each one of the rifles Montrayne had surrendered. If he'd used a different gun, smooth bore long gun or pistol, or even a rifle he didn't care about damaging, then where was it? They'd searched the woods, and this very morning divers had scoured the lake. Nothing.

"Did you check out the boots?"

Ruth's question jerked Joanne's mind back to the interview, but the change of subject flummoxed her.

"I'm sorry. What boots?"

Ruth was frowning as though she was trying to remember something that hadn't quite surfaced in her mind.

"The boots that match the footprints that you found in the wood."

It was Joanne's turn to frown, though she tried hard not to. What did this woman know about the footprints? There were plenty of them and they were starting to become a bit of a puzzle. Mostly they showed the tread pattern of a size twelve hiking boot. The only other fresh prints to be found by the lake were those which matched the running shoes worn by Phil Simmons. It was a puzzle because there had been other prints of various sizes and tread patterns on the path leading to the clearing, and more on the path leading away from it, but in the clearing itself only those two sets. It was almost as though the ground in that area by the lake had been smoothed over while the dirt was damp. Almost as though it had been prepared to take clear prints.

"Well?" Ruth prompted.

Joanne ignored her, still trying to think this through. There were also the prints leading up to where Nathan had been attacked. Same size, same tread pattern. But, for some reason, they were completely absent from the actual site of the assault. They reappeared beyond the ruined hut, but only sporadically, where they were not obscured by the prints of the paramedics coming down from the road.

"Look," said Ruth. "I watch CSI. I know the kind of stuff you guys do. And I know you'll have found prints all over the place where this happened. So, have you matched them?"

Joanne found her attention grabbed by the insistence in Ruth's voice. They had matched the prints, of course. And with no difficulty at all. James Montrayne had willingly surrendered his boots, even though he knew they were a perfect match for the only boot prints found in the clearing. She couldn't tell Ruth that, of course.

"If we had, I couldn't tell you. But why does it matter so much?"

Ruth was no longer frowning. Her memory was clear now.

"Last Sunday – that's a week ago, not yesterday – a visitor came into the shop." She pointed over to the corner of the lounge where Joanne could see an opening leading to some kind of display area. The space was not lit at the moment so she couldn't clearly make out the contents, but there were various types of clothing and other items on racks or on the shelves lining the walls.

"A visitor?" she asked. "Not a member?"

"No. He said he was the guest of someone, and was thinking of applying for membership."

"Did you get his name?"

"No, but someone must have, because he'd have had to sign in. Do you want me to check the book?"

"Yes, please." Then she changed her mind, still not sure where this was going.

"Actually, no. We'll do that in a minute. What did this visitor want?"

"Well, that's the odd thing, although it didn't seem so at the time. He was asking about James Montrayne's boots. He said he'd spoken to James and had been admiring them. He claimed he needed a large wide fitting, and those boots would probably suit him fine. He wondered whether James had bought them in our shop and meant to ask him, but James had left before he got round to it."

"Claimed?" interrupted Joanne. "You said he claimed he needed large boots."

"Yes... ... It's just that the boots he was wearing didn't seem that big. I know I only got a brief look as he walked away but... ... well, that was my impression."

Forget the dart, thought Joanne. This was seriously interesting.

"So, could you tell him where James bought his boots? Was it in your shop?"

"No, we don't stock them. James bought them on a trip to Canada last year. Yukon All-weather Trailblazers. They're a really good boot. Expensive too. You can probably buy them over here, but I didn't know where to tell him to look. In the end, I suggested he try the internet to find a local stockist."

"Did you see him talk to anyone else?"

"No. He thanked me for my time, left the shop and I didn't see him again."

Joanne looked around, particularly up in the corners of the lounge and out in the entrance hall.

"Do you have CCTV?"

Ruth sat forward, alert, wanting to help.

"Not in here, but around the outside, yes. And on the exterior ranges."

"How long do you keep the tapes?"

Ruth smiled.

"Not tapes. We're fairly hi-tec here. Digital images. Do you want to look?"

Joanne did, and about half an hour later she was able to leave with two video files copied onto one of the two flash drives which she permanently carried in her briefcase. Ruth had no trouble in identifying the stranger, even though his face seemed always to be at least partially obscured. It was his clothes that made it easy. Ruth was certain he had been the only man in the club that day wearing blue-green camo smock and trousers. It was strange that no camera had picked up his face. Everyone else could be seen at different times, either full face or in profile, but not this guy. And there was no record of him in the visitor book. No member had signed him in. Joanne wondered about that as she made her way slowly back to her car. The rain had stopped.

Her phone rang just as she reached for the door. It was DCI Morrissey.

"Get yourself down to Birmingham Heartlands Hospital. Our friend Montrayne has been busy again. I want him found. I want him arrested. I want him in jail. And I want you to tell me what the hell he's been up to."

Twenty-Nine

Police HQ, Lichfield – 1.20 pm

Detective Chief Superintendent Peter Hilton crashed through the door so violently that it slammed back against the wall causing the door handle to chip yet another sliver of pale green paint from the growing dent in the plaster. As it rebounded, he grabbed the edge of the door and flung it closed behind him. He tossed the papers he was holding down on his desktop and looked around his office as if hoping to find someone to lash out at. Of course, apart from himself, the room was empty, just as it should be.

That was a pity really.

When he'd had a bollocking himself, he always felt better if he could release all the pent up anger, resentment and frustration by letting fly at someone junior to himself. As it happened, it wasn't just any old someone he needed this time. One particular, fairly senior officer, who in Hilton's opinion was well past his sell-by date, was about to receive both barrels of DCS verbal buckshot.

Still breathing hard, he eased himself down into his oversized swivel chair and reached for his phone.

"Morrissey. Up here. Now!"

He was sure he wouldn't have to wait long. He was wrong. It normally took any reasonably fit officer well under a minute to reach his office from anywhere in the building. It was three minutes and twenty-five seconds before a knock sounded on his door. He was actually reaching for his phone to demand, with threats, Morrissey's immediate presence, when the door opened.

Chief Inspector Morrissey hadn't run up a flight of stairs in years – he had underlings to do that when occasion demanded it – and he hadn't been in any hurry to leave his desk just because the DCS was blowing a gasket. Nevertheless, once he'd sorted his notes from the phone call that had immediately preceded Superintendent Hilton's summons, he hadn't dawdled. So, when he pushed open the door to DCS Hilton's office with only the briefest knock, he was a little redder in the face than usual. The tone of his greeting which pre-empted Hilton's expected rebuke suggested that perhaps his colour owed as much to his rising temper as to exertion.

"OK, so which stiff-shirted tight-arse has been breathing down your neck this time?"

"Shut the door, Morrissey."

Hilton struggled to rein in his anger as he waited for Morrissey to obey. He was after all a senior police officer with significant responsibilities. Bawling out an underling was one thing, but verbal brawling with an officer who usually gave as good as he got was quite another. Unfortunately, the DCI didn't seem at all concerned about who, in the adjoining corridor and offices, might hear the vocal scuffle as he stood his ground glaring at his boss.

"Shut the bloody door."

Morrissey, taking the rising volume as a dangerous sign, decided to cooperate, albeit with bad grace, and he kicked the door to before leaning his back against it with his hands in his pockets.

"You really are a dammed idiot, Morrissey. Do you know that?"

"If you say so, sir."

"I do say so. And so does the Chief Constable and the Lord Lieutenant."

Morrissey's eyebrows rose in genuine surprise.

"The Lord Lieutenant?" he asked incredulously, removing his back from the office door. "What's he got to do with anything?"

"Apparently, he has a lot to do with many things, and one of them at the moment is James Montrayne."

"Aaaah."

Hilton took note of this single drawn-out syllable with a fair degree of satisfaction. This was going to be easier than he thought. Without raising his voice, he began turning the screw.

"Colonel Sir Rupert Chadbourne, baronet and newly-appointed Lord Lieutenant of this dear county was, until he recently retired due to injury, an officer in Her Majesty's Royal Marines."

"Bloody hell!"

Morrissey shoved his hands deeper in his pockets and his shoulders slumped.

"Quite," snapped Hilton with satisfaction. "Not only did he serve with Montrayne, they even bloody-well trained together, and on top of that … … …"

"No, no, no," interrupted Morissey. "Don't tell me. He plays golf with the Chief Constable."

"My, my," said Hilton sarcastically. "We might make a half-way useful detective out of you yet."

Morrissey's anger began to reassert itself. He didn't mind the insults. He could be equally offensive himself when the mood took him, which was going to be pretty soon if he wasn't careful. Straightening his back and squaring his shoulders, he looked across the desk at his superior, making no attempt at all to hide the contempt in his eyes.

"The Lord Lieutenant has no right to interfere in an active police investigation, and the Chief Constable, with all due respect," a quality which his tone and demeanour showed to be altogether lacking, "has no right to order me to cover up evidence."

"Get off your high horse and stop talking bollocks," said Hilton.

"What the hell do you mean?"

"I mean, neither Sir Rupert nor the Chief Constable are trying to sabotage your enquiries. They both want a thorough, by-the-book investigation and not a trial-by-media fuelled by your incompetence."

He turned over one of the papers lying on his desk and shoved it towards Morrissey.

"Especially," he continued, "if James Montrayne turns out to be completely innocent."

"He isn't," responded Morrissey automatically, as he picked up the article cut out of the Lichfield Daily News. It was the first time he'd seen it and, as he read it slowly pausing to reread certain sections, a warmth began to spread through the whole of his upper body as excitement bumped up his heart rate.

"Innocent, my arse," he said. "Motive, means and opportunity. We've got the lot."

"You've got nothing," replied Hilton, and this time it was his turn to fail to hide contempt, "and a copper with your years in the force shouldn't need me to point it out to you. Have you been speaking to that reporter?"

"Like hell, I have!"

Morrissey tossed the paper back on the desk.

"Is that what this is about? Is that what's got the Chief's knickers in a twist?"

DCS Hilton looked thoughtful, ignoring Morrissey's questions. The article looked like a farrago of vicious nonsense, and he would be glad to believe that Morrissey had no part in it. The trouble was that it wouldn't be the first time that the Chief Inspector had used the press to shake the tree to see what came loose when he was a little short on evidence. But not usually this early in an investigation.

"This article has nothing of any substance," he said, "Opportunity you've got, certainly. As to means, the labs are still working on that. But motive? You're plucking at straws."

"Straws!" yelled Morrissey, pointing at the paper. "What the hell do you call that if it's not motive?"

"I'd call it wild speculation, bordering on libel."

Morrissey was furious, and was about to give free rein to his emotions when Hilton cut him off.

"Shut up and sit down."

Sensing a stubborn refusal was imminent, he repeated the command.

"Sit, Chief Inspector, and you might learn something."

As Morrissey pulled a chair close to the desk and slumped into it, Detective Chief Superintendent Hilton watched him with something very close to pity in his hazel eyes. Morrissey had, for many years, been a thoroughly competent officer. His clear-up rate, if not outstanding, had certainly been way above average. Younger officers, sergeants and inspectors alike, had found their career prospects enhanced as a result of what they learned from working with him, as long as they managed to avoid assimilating any of that maverick independence that had prevented him from rising to any rank higher than Detective Chief Inspector. Although that independence remained, and was if anything even more pronounced, competence had sadly diminished over the past year or so. Younger inspectors worked their own cases, answering directly to Hilton, while Morrissey plodded on with a sergeant who was probably brighter than he had ever been. A down-beat and rather sad ending to what had, for the most part, been a quietly illustrious career.

It was no surprise that Morrissey should want to go out on the sort of high which this murder case could give him. No surprise that he should want a result before retirement should hand the glory over to someone else.

It just needed to be the right result.

Hilton's voice was calmer now, quieter, less confrontational. This was not due in any sense to a change of mood, but was a deliberate strategy to try and ensure Morrissey's cooperation.

"The Lord Lieutenant has known James Montrayne far longer than you or I. There is just no possibility, in his view, that Montrayne would kill someone over a woman."

Morrissey smiled, his own voice much more moderate as he replied.

"And how often have we found close friends and family members completely astounded at what their loved ones have been up to? The Lord Lieutenant's view is no different from theirs. It's opinion, nothing more."

Hilton noted the smile and wondered whether he was being patronised. The thought almost overturned his strategy and a slight edge came into his voice.

"There is a little more to it, I think. What you and I did not know, and the Lord Lieutenant does, is just how devoted Montrayne was to his wife Sarah. Her death almost destroyed him, and certainly brought his career in the Marines to an abrupt end."

"I know," responded Morrissey. "I read about that. But it was years ago."

"Seven years," said Hilton. "And he was totally devastated. The Lord Lieutenant has assured the Chief Constable that there is no shortage of people willing to testify that he hasn't looked at another woman since."

Morrissey took a moment to consider that.

"These people... ... All women who fancied their chances, I suppose?"

"Many of them, possibly," replied Hilton. "But not all, unless you'd like to include the Lord Lieutenant's wife in that category."

"Hmmm." Morrissey considered the implications of all this and, after a moment, thought he could see the flaw.

"Are you saying that Montrayne will now be celibate for the rest of his life, because of his love for a woman who died seven years ago?"

"Well, as to that, who can say?" replied Hilton. "I'm sure the Lord Lieutenant wouldn't deny that maybe, eventually, he might meet someone ... ..."

"Exactly," interrupted Morrissey, slapping the desk top to make his point. "And who is to say that Natalie Simmons was not that someone."

If he expected Hilton to be dismayed by his logic, he was to be disappointed.

"Apparently everyone except the writer of that article." He gestured towards the paper lying on his desk. "You've got to look into it. Of course, you have. In fact, the Chief Constable insists that you do. But you're going to find this Rigby woman is a lone voice, and you might want to ask yourself why she's doing it."

Morrissey leaned back in his chair and took a deep breath. Both hands came up to the sides of his head and he stroked his greying hair with short forward motions. Hilton had seen him do this on many occasions when he was thinking hard. He waited quietly and let the process run its course. Eventually, Morrissey's hands dropped.

"If Montrayne is so clean, why is he bringing out the big guns in his defence?"

"He isn't."

"Oh, come on. Are you telling me he didn't phone Sir Rupert to get him to twist the arm of the Chief Constable?"

"It's true Sir Rupert did receive a phone call, but it wasn't from James Montrayne."

"Then who ... ...?"

"I don't know. Nor does Sir Rupert. The caller, a man he thought, asked him if he'd seen the paper and, when he said no, just told him to get hold of a copy ASAP and act as he thought fit."

"Montrayne could have got someone to do it for him."

"No need. He and Sir Rupert are close friends. If he wanted him to know about the article, he'd just pick up the phone himself."

"Maybe."

Hilton looked at him, eyebrows raised.

"OK," said Morrissey. "I guess so. Probably."

"Right," said Hilton. "You're going to carry on with what you're doing, and get this sorted. The only thing the Chief Constable insists on is that this investigation is led by you and not by some reporter with a grudge. Whatever this Rigby woman is up to, don't let her cloud your judgement."

Morrissey frowned, and Hilton knew he was stung by the implication that he might be losing his grip. Nevertheless, the point needed to be made. Perhaps a rare use of Morrissey's first name might drive it home.

"Paul, you know how to run a case. You've done it well too many times. Just don't let this one run you."

Sensing the interview was at an end, Morrissey stood up smiling grimly.

"Montrayne did it, you know. And maybe it wasn't because of Mrs. Simmons, or any other woman. But I'll find out what made him do it, and nail this case down tight."

He turned and was making for the door when a final thought struck him.

"Before I came up here, I was talking to an Inspector Gupta from the West Midlands force. They have a dead nurse at Heartlands Hospital and a security video of Montrayne at the hospital the day before she died. A nurse on the same ward as the dead girl saw Montrayne on her ward on Saturday night, and she identified him from the video. So maybe you're right. Maybe we're looking at a different motive entirely."

Hilton thought about that.

"Why did Gupta contact you?"

"I asked neighbouring forces to let me know about anything that cropped up with Montrayne's name in it. Gupta was in the process of writing up his report when he saw my request. He rang straight away. I've not had chance to follow it up yet, but Sergeant Hayford's on her way down to Birmingham now.."

"Interesting," said Hilton, and meant it. This was a turn he hadn't expected, and for the life of him he couldn't see any connection between the nurse in Birmingham and Philip Simmons. There was clearly a great deal he still did not know.

"Keep digging, Chief Inspector," he said, and then grudgingly, "Well done."

Morrissey nodded and turned to leave, delivering his parting shot as he opened the door.

"You know, sir, if the Lord Lieutenant wants to be involved, he can always turn out as a character witness at Montrayne's trial because, one way or another, his lordship's going down."

Thirty

RRISC – 1.35 pm

I followed James through a substantial outer office, presumably where Andy's personal assistant usually sat in residence. She, or he, was not there and the computer workstation was for the present unoccupied. The soft, dark-blue carpet continued through to Andy's own inner office, the décor of which was just what you'd expect of an upmarket security consultant wanting to impress potential clients. I saw trees through the large window in the end wall. I saw comfortable, leather-covered chairs. I saw a large modern desk and the edge of a computer monitor. And standing in front of the desk, sorting papers in a leather briefcase, I saw the most dangerous man I have ever met.

He was not tall. Maybe five foot eight or nine, and stocky. Which meant that his dark suit was clearly tailor-made, since it fit him perfectly. His black hair was slicked back with gel, which seemed to accentuate the wide cheekbones and slightly flattened nose. And then there were his eyes. Even when he smiled, and he could do so quite charmingly, those black eyes were completely without expression. I saw him now in profile, his face turned slightly away from me, but in my mind I could see the image of his face so close above mine that my skin broke out in a sweat and I almost vomited right there on that expensive blue carpet. Before he could close his case and turn around, I stopped in the outer office, swallowed the bile, turned and headed straight back out into the corridor.

Behind me, I heard the chirp of a mobile phone, and then that deep, slightly accented, almost jovial voice that I had so easily come to hate.

"Why, Raymond, my friend. What can I do for you?"

I looked left and right but didn't know which way to go. I had no idea what lay behind any of the doors which I could see. The only room I knew was the one where we had left Jimmy interrogating his computers, so I headed there at a fast trot thankfully meeting no people or security doors on the way. As I turned the handle to Jimmy's door, I hoped fervently that Rod was still fully occupied with bleeding into his sink somewhere.

Whatever was the case with Rod, Jimmy turned out to be alone. He was so engrossed in what he was doing that he didn't immediately turn around. I tried to shut the door quietly behind me but, before it could close, I felt pressure from the other side which I had no chance of resisting. I backed into the room watching as James entered quickly, his face showing a mixture of anxiety and bewilderment.

As the door finally closed, Jimmy seemed to take note of the invasion and half turned in his chair. James spoke first.

"What was that about, Lizzie? What's going on?"

I was angry and scared. I had so wanted to trust him, and he very nearly got me killed.

"You lied to me," I hissed at him. "You told me I was going to be safe."

James was frowning now, more puzzled than ever.

"Lizzie, I promise you. As long as you're with me, you will be safe."

I shook my head. "I don't believe you."

I felt a hand lightly touch my arm from behind, and I spun round hand raised and ready to lash out. Then I saw Jimmy's face. It was full of such concern and embarrassment that I stood frozen, my mind whirring, desperately trying to make sense of what was happening. Jimmy's hand had lost contact as I whirled round, but it was still held out towards me.

"The Boss won't hurt you, Lizzie. He wouldn't." Then, seeing I was not convinced, he added, "The Boss will help you any way he can, Lizzie. But he'll never hurt you. He just doesn't do that."

His hand dropped, and he looked even more embarrassed.

He shrugged and his eyes dropped. "He really doesn't."

James was right behind me now and his hands were very gentle on my shoulders as he turned me round.

"It wasn't Andy, was it? You didn't run when you first saw him."

I looked up at him and suddenly I wasn't angry any more, and not so scared either.

"So," he continued, "It had to be that guy in Andy's office."

I nodded.

"Do you know him?" he asked.

I nodded again.

"Well, you're one up on me," he smiled, presumably trying to encourage me, though his frown didn't entirely go away, "because I've never seen him before."

I nodded again, this time to let him know that I did believe him.

I heard a movement behind me and, a moment later, a hand again touched my arm. Lightly. Tentatively. It was Jimmy. He had placed his chair ready for me.

"Why don't you sit down, Lizzie?"

Then, clearly feeling his part was done, he took a chair in front of another bank of screens and keyboards several feet away, and sat watching James and me.

James had stepped back so that he now leaned against the door. He glanced at Jimmy.

"Can you lock it?"

"Sure." Jimmy pressed some keys at his workstation and I heard a slight clunk from behind James.

"Override," said Jimmy. "Like when I don't want to be disturbed."

James didn't move. "OK, Lizzie. Tell us about him."

I didn't look, but I could sense Jimmy's eyes on me; those huge, dark, innocent, admiring eyes, staring at me through rimless glasses. Well, they wouldn't be admiring for much longer, and maybe not so innocent either.

My hands were bunched up tight. Not clasped, just curled so my nails were digging into my palms. I looked down at them and began.

"His name is Alexei Borisov, and he's Russian mafia. He's working on a deal to take over the supply of girls coming into Birmingham. He thinks it's a growth market." I actually managed a smile, or maybe it was a sneer. I couldn't make my mind up. "And it looks like you guys are going to help him."

"No way!" Jimmy was up out of his chair. "You must have made a mistake, Lizzie."

My hands uncurled, and I rubbed my palms along the top of my thighs.

"No mistake, Jimmy. I know him."

He wasn't convinced. "Well, how would you know someone like that?"

"Easy," I said. "I was paid to… … spend time with him… … and … … I overheard him talking with someone else I knew … … He didn't know I was listening. Still doesn't, or I'd be dead by now."

I was watching James, so I couldn't see Jimmy's reaction, but his voice was laden with incredulity.

"So, what were you … … were you spying."

"If only."

Jimmy couldn't let it go. "I don't understand. Who were you working for? What … …"

James cut off his probing, and I was grateful. I liked Jimmy, not in any boy-girl way, but he seemed a really pleasant kid and I didn't want him to think badly of me.

"That's enough for now, Jimmy. If Lizzie says he's Russian mafia, I'm prepared to believe it. But what's he doing here? What does he want from RRISC?"

I had learnt a lot during the paintballing and other activities in that country mansion, but I couldn't remember ever having heard a mention of RRISC. I was shaking my head when the door handle rattled. The door stayed closed. There was a loud knocking and then Andy's voice.

"Are you in there, James? What the hell are you playing at? Rod? Jimmy? Open this door, now!"

The fear was back. I wondered whether Andy still had the Russian with him. James didn't seem worried, but I had no idea what he was thinking. He stepped to the side of the door so that he would be behind it when it opened. He motioned me to go and stand close to Jimmy over towards the side of the room. I did, and was surprised to find Jimmy moving to stand in front of me. As I said, he seemed a nice kid but I hadn't put him down as being well-endowed in the guts department. My mistake.

Then I heard James ask, in a perfectly normal, conversational tone, "Are you on your own, Andy."

"Of course I'm on my own, you daft sod. What the hell's going on?"

Then, still in the same calm tone, James said something that both chilled and encouraged me.

"Andy… … If you're not alone, come back when you are, or you and your friend will find this is not going to turn out well."

There was total stillness on both sides of the door. I was standing behind and slightly to the side of Jimmy who chose that moment to glance back at me. His eyes were huge and full of uncertainty, but all he did was to move slightly to ensure I was completely hidden behind him. Then we heard Andy speak again.

"James… … I'm on my own, damn it. The corridor's empty. Now let me in."

James nodded at Jimmy and a moment later there was a click as the lock was released. I expected the door to be flung open and Andy to come charging in, but I was wrong. He came in slowly, nudging the door with his foot, and with his hands clasped behind his head. Both moves were, I assumed, intended to avoid giving any provocation. I was peering around Jimmy's shoulder and, for those few paces, his eyes never left mine, presumably because I was the unknown in that situation. When he was clear of the door, Andy spoke again .

"Should I put them down now?"

It seemed as though he was talking to me, so I nodded, just as James pushed the door closed and said, "You needn't have put them up in the first place."

"Hmmm." Andy lowered his arms and glanced behind him. "Well, you seemed just a little bit touchy, so I thought it safest."

James came round to face him and was close enough that Andy had to tilt his head back to look him in the eye, not something he was much used to doing, I fancied. Jimmy and I didn't move, and I wondered how this was going to play out. There was a harshness in James's voice as he replied.

"If I thought you knew that you were making deals with the Russian mafia, I'd be more than a little touchy, because that would mean you've deliberately broken our agreement."

Since I didn't know Andy, I found it hard to read the expression on his face. There was definitely something there, but I didn't know what to make of it. James seemed to be satisfied though because he nodded and stepped back.

"You didn't know, did you?" he said, much more a statement than a question.

It turned out that Alexei Borisov, in the form of Alex Borsberry, had approached RRISC to buy into their SAP and CP programs. These two courses, Security Anti-Penetration and Close Protection, conducted with others on a suitably adapted country estate on the Welsh borders, were apparently sufficiently well-respected to have come to Mr Borsberry's notice at a time when he was expanding his commercial interests in Eastern European markets. Effective security was apparently essential to his somewhat nebulously expressed business development, so he wanted his personnel trained to the highest standards. Andy Graham had just signed a contract to provide that training.

I could tell he didn't like it. Or, at least, he was making a good show of not liking it.

"I'll kill the little … …"

"Probably best not to," interrupted James. "I think it's quite possible that someone else may just do that for us."

Everyone was quiet at that. I wondered if he would elaborate but he didn't. His eyes were distant as though he was focussed on something totally outside that room. He was the only one of us still standing. Jimmy was back in his chair which he had pushed a little way from his workstation and swivelled so he was sideways on. I was perched on the edge of the workstation, to the side of him. Andy had taken the only other chair in which he now sat reversed so that his forearms lay across the top of the chair-back, his chin resting on them. He looked up at James.

"We can't let it rest. I'm going to have Jimmy … …"

His voice trailed off as his eyes turned to Jimmy.

"Didn't you say you needed the afternoon off? Dentist or something?"

"Yeah, that's right," Jimmy nodded. "Then I got a call this morning saying not to come. Seems the dental surgery burned down sometime over the weekend."

"You're kidding." Andy sat up in surprise. "What happened? Do they know?"

"Not sure yet, but after the call I checked with a guy I know on the local radio news. First reports are that it was arson."

"So," said James, "Someone doesn't like your dentist."

"Yeah, well I'm with them on that," replied Jimmy. "But I wouldn't burn his place down."

"Hmmm." Andy dropped his chin again and rubbed it gently against the back of his wrist. "What I was going to say was, Jimmy can dump whatever else he's working on and start digging up everything he can find on this guy Borisov."

Jimmy looked across at James and said slowly, "Well, actually … …"

He was interrupted.

"Jimmy's working on something for me, at the moment, Andy, but I'm sure he can pull in Borisov as well."

Jimmy nodded vigorously. "Sure can, James."

Andy looked from one to the other, and then his gaze settled on me.

"I suppose this is a good time to tell me why you decided to pay us a visit today. I assume it wasn't because of Borisov?"

It took a while to tell the story, mainly because Andy kept interrupting with questions, some of which we could answer and some we couldn't. At first, he thought that the threats to Angie and me and the killing of Sister Yuyun were somehow linked to James and the killing of Phil Simmons, but James soon set him straight on that.

"OK," he said at last. "I'll pull in Tony Bridges to give Rod a hand with the other stuff. His next course doesn't start 'til Friday evening, so he's got a few slack days, and he's pretty good with the IT. And that will give me the chance to fill him in on Borisov."

Tony, I learnt later, was in charge of the SAP courses which Borisov had just signed up for.

All the while we were bringing Andy up to speed on what had been happening, Jimmy had been playing with his computers. In the momentary silence as Andy stopped speaking, we all heard Jimmy's exclamation of surprise.

"Woooow!"

I slipped off the workstation where I'd been perched and stood behind Jimmy so I could see the screen that had got him so excited. James joined me and Andy trundled his chair across saying, "What've you got, Jimmy?"

"After James told me what he wanted, I started some searches running. One of them is looking for any reference to people Philip Simmons has worked with. The program then looks for patterns in the results and … …"

"Spare us, Jimmy," Andy interrupted. "What have you got?"

"Phil Simmons used to work for Salisbury Marine Components, run by a guy called John Salisbury. The thing went belly-up when Salisbury emptied the coffers and scarpered a couple of years ago. That was when Simmons went to work for Lichfield Tube. Well … …" He wagged his right index finger at the screen. "According to this, John Salisbury was dredged out of a canal in Venice late last night with most of his face and half his hands missing."

I was trying hard not to visualise a mutilated, water-logged corpse when James and Andy both spoke at once.

Andy asked, "Coincidence do you think?"

James asked, "If he was that badly damaged, how do they know it's him?"

"Personal effects apparently," replied Jimmy, answering James's less speculative question. "Including his passport. Police there have asked the UK for dental records to make a positive ID."

"I wonder where he lived," mused James quietly, more to himself than the rest of us. Nevertheless, Jimmy took it as a serious request, and tapped away at his keyboard. A moment later, he had the answer.

"A village called Walton, not far from Burton-on-Trent."

"Well, well, well. Now wouldn't that be a coincidence?"

We all looked at James who was smiling down at Jimmy.

"What?" asked Jimmy, confused.

"If you and he had the same dentist."

At that moment, James's cell phone began ringing, and we all waited as he reached into the inside pocket of his suit jacket. The smile still lingered as he answered, but quickly drained away to be replaced by an anger more fierce than anything I could ever remember seeing. And I wondered, as I watched him closely, whether there was more than a little fear in those blazing eyes.

Thirty-One

A38 Staffordshire – 1.50 pm

The driver of the Mercedes SUV was still engrossed in his paperback long after the two occupants of the Maserati entered the building. He had watched them approach the entrance but, apart from noting the man's unusual size, he hadn't given him a thought. It was the girl who interested him, particularly her rear end, whose every movement beneath the grey trousers was observed with relish. He was just beginning to imagine what that excellent rear would look like without the mask of grey fabric when it disappeared through the doors. Sighing he had returned to his book, not a classic of any description, but one selected at random from the top shelf in the shop at a motorway services. He had hoped it would help to improve his English but progress was slow and, if it were not for the appeal of its decidedly lurid content, he would have given up long ago.

He wasn't aware of his employer's return until he heard the opening of the rear nearside door. Closing his book, he slipped it into his jacket pocket and glanced in the rear-view mirror.

Alexei Borisov relaxed contentedly, half turned in his seat so that he had an excellent view of his driver's left ear. Not that he had any interest in any of his driver's bits and pieces except as parts that could be removed, without anaesthetic, should it be necessary as punishment or perhaps *pour encourager les autres*. In spite of the fear and awe which he inspired in his employees, such harsh measures were occasionally required.

Borisov looked between the front-seat head-restraints towards the entrance to the RRISC building and smiled in satisfaction. It had been a good meeting. Five of his most trusted lieutenants were going to receive state-of-the-art training in Security Anti-Penetration and Close Protection, something which he hoped would help to keep him alive longer than a good number of his fellows. Russians in his line of business, unless they were very clever, very careful, and very lucky, tended to have a rather limited life expectancy. When he'd asked around about what security outfits could cause him trouble, RRISC had been high on the list of those to be extremely wary of. So it had seemed a logical step to find out all he could about their systems, techniques and procedures while at the same time pushing his own men's competence to a previously unheard of level.

Of course, as soon as he heard the name of the company's chief executive, there really could have been no other choice.

Yes, it had been a very good meeting. And not as expensive as it could have been. Definitely a worthwhile investment in what he hoped was going to turn out to be a highly lucrative enterprise. Which reminded him; better see what trouble Ray Mellisse had got himself into. He had taken Ray's call in Andy Graham's office but, when he had realised what Ray was asking, he had quickly cut it short telling him he'd call back in a few minutes. He had been so focussed on the call that he never noticed the large man and the very pretty young woman who had come briefly into Andy's outer office. If he heard their voices, it was only as an annoyance which caused him to concentrate all the more on what Ray was trying to tell him. By the time he had ended the call, they had gone.

Ray Mellisse had done well over the years. Borisov didn't mind admitting it. He could admire a tight, well-run organisation particularly when the annual profits ran into seven figures. But there was no doubt that there was substantial room for growth. He wasn't sure who had told him that Birmingham was well on the way to being the sex capital of the UK, but this was a notion that had taken control of his mind. He saw the potential and knew that he could make it work. It all hinged on a steady supply of girls; young women, teens and children. The contacts were already in place, and supply routes established from several of the former Soviet republics, including Lithuania, Borisov's country of birth.

His parents were Russian, his father being a major in the KGB, posted to Vilnius in 1975. Since his loyalty to the Motherland was at no time in question, and Lithuania was within the communist bloc, his pregnant wife had been allowed to accompany him. So it was that Alexei, born five months later in Lithuania to Russian parents, acquired a very handy duel nationality the full usefulness of which could not have been imagined in the years before independence was attained in 1991. With Gorbachev in power in Moscow from 1985, the concepts of *perestroika* and *glasnost* began to gain ground. Borisov senior started to see the writing on the wall. He had always been an astute political economist and, although a full colonel in the KGB, was still on station in Vilnius.

As the eighties neared their end, there was a growing move among the people of Lithuania for a return to the independence which they had briefly enjoyed between the two World Wars. The KGB was not prospering so well under Mikhail Gorbachev as it had under his predecessor, Yuri Andropov, and there was growing pressure from the democratic reformers for its scale of operations to be reduced. Colonel Borisov, anticipating a recall to Moscow, began to make his arrangements. The fate of the KGB was sealed when its head, Vladimir Kryuchkov, tried and failed to oust Gorbachev from power in the coup of August 1991.

Restructuring and force reduction were inevitable but, for those who had made the necessary arrangements, civilian life in the new Russia held almost limitless opportunities. With a growing number of Russians living below the poverty line in the early nineties, Nikita Borisov and his family grew fat on the proceeds of illegal imports of western goods into the former Soviet Union. Young Alexei learnt the business from an early age, and found that he had a natural aptitude for protecting his father's business interests from the effects of free-market competition. Members of what was coming to be known as the Russian Mafia had disappeared at irregular intervals until about two years ago. That was when the Borisov's competitors grew tired of having their numbers reduced and decided in turn to eliminate Nikita Borisov. He had turned up, without his head, sunbathing naked on the beach at the Black Sea resort of Gelendzhik.

Alexei had been given a simple choice. Leave Russia alive or stay and be buried. Lithuania had never seemed so inviting as it did at that point. It hurt both his pride and his pocket to have to terminate abruptly his father's businesses, but there was an up-side in that much of their accumulated wealth lay in secret accounts in either Switzerland or the Caymans. So, even after leaving his mother well provided for in Moscow, it wasn't exactly a poverty stricken refugee who flew into Vilnius in the autumn of 2003. Nor had he been alone. Of the nine men who had been on the plane with him, five were now booked to take the RRISC course. All had been convinced by recent events that their future was probably more secure outside Russia than within. Borisov liked to think of these men as his *business managers.*

And the business he was currently most interested in was that of Ray Mellisse. More particularly the select clubs and low-class strip bars, the high-class call-girls and the street prostitutes, the brothels and massage parlours, in short, everything that related in some way to the selling, lending or hiring of female flesh. Ray had his sights set on higher things and was ready to leave his rather inglorious past behind him, for a price. His valuation was, of course, considerably higher than Borisov was prepared to pay, but the Russian was confident that compromise would be reached. He didn't like parting with money but he felt that the opportunity to buy a well-run organisation was preferable to starting from scratch in a country he didn't know, or taking it by force and creating a bunch of enemies he didn't know.

Unfortunately, it appeared from Ray's brief phone call that the handover was not going to be quite as trouble-free as he had hoped.

Telling the driver to get the SUV moving, Borisov reached into the inside pocket of his new tailor-made cashmere suit and withdrew his cell phone.

"Raymond. You say you have problem."

He listened without interruption for several minutes. He had come to admire the precise way in which Ray delivered information. He even wondered whether he ought to emulate it himself. Say what you have to say coldly, calmly, clearly and concisely – he could remember four *cs* – no idle threats, no histrionics, no excuses. Just the facts. It was amazing how powerful such a delivery could be.

He understood also why Ray wanted the job done by his, Borisov's, people. He wanted men who could never be traced back to him because they didn't even know the job originated with him. Men who could be out of the country within hours of the task's completion. Men who could easily be replaced. Borisov's men. Except that Borisov had no intention of sending his people away once the job was done. They were in very little danger, being completely unknown in the UK, and they were too valuable where they were. Still, what Ray didn't know, he couldn't grieve over.

"OK, Ray, I got it. Hospital we do later, like you say. Other girl … …"

He paused, frowning. "You say I know her." He shook his head. "I not remember. But, you right. Must do her first. You have men at farm. They wait … … watch … … my men get there … … hmmmm … … forty minutes. I send men to house. Give post code for GPS. I go to school and watch."

He broke off to tell his driver to get back on the A38 and head for Lichfield. He then returned to his cell phone and asked, "This Montrayne, why not we kill him too?"

He listened while Ray outlined the likely consequences of killing James Montrayne. Setting aside the police investigation, too many important people, he said, powerful people, wealthy people, would ask questions, apply pressure, toss money around until the truth was uncovered. Much better just to entangle Montrayne even more deeply in the snare of his own troubles and leave the police to deal with him.

He could see how this would make sense to Ray, but Borisov didn't like it. Killing one girl, and kidnapping the other, would make Montrayne angry, and an angry man with money and powerful friends could make an awful lot of trouble. Without letting it be known to Ray, Borisov decided that a simple road accident could deal with Montrayne and give him the chance to snatch the girl and, done right, no-one would need to ask awkward questions. All he needed to do was find them and, with men watching at all the most likely locations, he was confident that he would.

"Tell me, Ray. This Montrayne. What car he drive?"

He stored the details of two cars away in his memory without repeating them aloud. That was a shame, because if he had, his driver could have told him exactly where to find a Maserati with a personalised number plate.

As it was, the Merc was half-way to Lichfield before the driver, overhearing Borisov directing his men to various locations, realised which girl and what car his boss was talking about. For about half a second honesty fought with discretion over the issue of whether to tell Borisov what he had seen in the car park at RRISC. Since he placed great value on all his appendages, discretion won and his attention returned to the road ahead and the voice from his GPS. If his boss hadn't noticed the Maserati, why should he be expected to do so?

Thirty-two

DTLO London – 2.10 pm

George Holborn was not happy. Lunch for him was usually a satisfying experience whose elastic duration was tolerated by the head of his department only because, when he was not eating or drinking, George had actually been remarkably good at his job. Over a number of years, he had represented the British Government in negotiations involving BAE Systems and Saudi Arabia, the consequences of which had been highly beneficial to the British economy. It was unfortunate, and by no means George's fault, that recent disclosures in the media suggested that the successful negotiations had also been highly beneficial for the personal economy of certain Saudi princes. In reverse mode, he had also been involved in blocking the sale of BAE's Hawk jets to Indonesia in 1999 when it was feared that they would be used, not as trainers, but as combat aircraft against the indigenous people of that country. Yes, George at his best had been very good. Even George at his not-so-good was better than many people's best. And so he stayed, rewarded for past service, as his retirement crept ever closer, and his lunch breaks ever longer.

Sadly, lunch today had not been satisfying. His guest had been amenable, cooperative even, and the information George had acquired almost worth the effort. But George had made a mistake. One he promised himself he would not repeat. He had instructed his assistant to allow his guest to choose the restaurant. Only when it was too late did he realise his error. When checking his diary for the appointment made by the delectable Miss Shauna Watson – all his assistants had been delectable – when she had arranged the meeting, he had seen the dreaded word **Sushi** in the name of the establishment. He had almost decided not to go.

Who in their right mind could enjoy chewing raw fish in the middle of the day, or indeed at any other time of day? George certainly couldn't, with or without that disgustingly vinegary cold rice. Having picked and prodded his way through the meal for politeness sake, garnering in the process enough information to identify the end-user in a rather dubious arms sale, George had returned to his office with pangs of hunger gnawing away in the pit of his rather generous stomach. Hunger was an unusual experience for George and he couldn't make up his mind what to do about it. Miss Watson would happily send out for something, if only he could decide what he fancied. Apart from the delectable Miss Watson. Still undecided, he pressed the button on his intercom to signal that indispensable lady to come through to his office.

Contrary to the imaginings of his junior colleagues, George had not appointed her on the basis of her looks. Well, not entirely. Miss Watson was the proud possessor of a very good PPE from Oxford, with energy and shrewdness to match. Her official title was Personal Assistant, but she had the good sense not to be offended that George always called her his secretary. In fact she had her own secretary, and several other assorted underlings to do her bidding. She rather liked her job and had, surprisingly even to herself, actually grown to like George.

With a light tap on the door, she entered his office. With her dark blue suit (M & S not Armani), dark blue tights and dark blue shoes, her face, framed by long dark hair just short of shoulder length, shone brightly by contrast. Except for special occasions, she used little makeup, relying mostly on skin tone and bone structure to work their wonders. She smiled at the sight of George lolling back in his chair, feet up on his desk.

"You called, O Master."

"Yes, I ruddy well did."

George liked that word, *ruddy*. If anyone ever accused him of swearing, he told them it was the name of a duck adding that he was very partial to duck.

"You didn't enjoy lunch then?"

"No, I ruddy well didn't."

"I thought it might be educational for you. Expand your gastronomic horizons a bit."

"My gastronomic horizons have expanded as far as they need to. And so has this." He patted his rounded paunch with some affection. "But it's rumbling away like a boiler-makers' reunion. What do you suggest?

"Alka-Seltzer?"

"Witch! You know what I mean"

Miss Watson relented, and put an end to his suffering.

"How about a plate of smoked salmon sandwiches, a light granary bread spread with cream cheese, and a baby-leaf salad garnish?"

George grinned.

"Shauna, I take it back. You're an angel. But tell them to go easy on the salad. Can't go overdoing it."

She stepped up to his desk, lifted the phone and rang through the order to a small but fashionable restaurant just down the street. She then rang one of her own secretaries and asked him to wait five minutes before setting off to the restaurant to collect it. These manoeuvres were well rehearsed and their outcome, for George at least, always extremely satisfying.

Miss Watson looked down at him,

"Now we've dealt with the trivialities, how about the important stuff?"

George grunted and was about to take issue with her notion of trivialities when his phone chirped. He stretched out a hand for the cordless handset but Miss Watson beat him to it.

"Deputy Director's office," she announced in her usual brisk telephone voice. "How can … … Oh, it's you Paul. Where are you? … … … How long do you think? … … … Can you give me some idea what it's about? … … … I see. OK, I'll tell him. Just get here as soon as you can… … … OK. Goodbye."

She replaced the handset and pursed her lips in silent thought as she looked down at George. He looked back in growing impatience.

"I suppose you realise," he said, "that if you'd let me take that call, I would now know whatever it is that you're wondering how to tell me."

"Hmmmm." As always, she was completely unfazed by his tone of voice. "Paul seems to be a little excited. He doesn't want you to leave the office until he's had a chance to speak to you."

"Cheeky blighter. What's he up to?"

"He wouldn't say, but he's got himself stuck in traffic at Hendon. Looks like an accident at the bottom of the M1. Could be one hour, could be five. You know what these things are like."

George did, all too well. There was nothing he hated more than to be sitting still on a stretch of road along which he had been expecting to be cruising at eighty miles an hour in his treasured Ferrari 360. He sighed. He hadn't thought about Paul Riddings or Phil Simmons all day, but now he was intrigued and found he was impatient to hear what Riddings had discovered on his trip to the Midlands. Still, even George didn't have the power to clear a blocked motorway, so it was back to more immediate matters.

"Sit down, Shauna. Let me fill you in about what happened at lunch. It rather looks as though TW Systems may have to rethink this contract."

It was just over two hours later that Riddings finally arrived at the DTLO building. Miss Watson, now back in her own office, saw him first and took him immediately through to George.

"Paul's here, George."

Closing the door behind her, she moved to sit in an easy chair by the coffee table in the corner of the office furthest from George's desk. She placed a note pad and a small digital recorder on the table pressing the **On** button as she set it down. Riddings looked about uncertainly, until George pointed at the upright chair immediately in front of his desk.

"Sit down lad, and catch your breath, and then tell me what's so ruddy important that I've got to sit here like a stuffed fart waiting for you to show up."

He really did look as though he needed to catch his breath. He must have run up all four flights of stairs, thought George. Must be something wrong with the elevator. Unless he's one of these fitness freaks. Don't sit when you can stand; don't stand when you can walk; don't walk when you can run; don't use the elevator when you can kill yourself running upstairs.

"Sorry, Mr Holborn."

Definitely out of breath. Probably not as fit as he thought he was.

"All right. All right. That's enough rest. What's this all about?"

Riddings placed his briefcase on George's desk and flipped the catches. He had actually come up in the elevator, and had been very relieved to find it working. He had hit another jam coming through central London caused by a bomb scare in Trafalgar Square. Everyone was so cautious now after those terrorist bombings back in 2000 and 2001. They had been IRA, but there were now Islamist extremists to worry about. Leaving his car on a meter, which would probably run out before he could get back to it, he had run the best part of two miles, dodging traffic and carrying his briefcase, to get to the DTLO. He definitely wasn't as fit as he thought he was.

"You wanted me to keep a check on the police investigation into Phil Simmons' death."

"Yes, and ruddy well praying it's not connected to our own investigation."

"Quite, sir. Well, so far … … it doesn't look as though it is."

George slapped his palms down on his desk top.

"Excellent, Riddings. Well done."

"Nothing to do with me at all, sir… … fortunately."

Miss Watson, who had been watching him carefully, noticed a strain in his voice which had nothing to do with his breathless arrival. She spoke up quietly from her seat in the corner.

"Paul, whatever it is you don't want to tell us, it will be much better if you just get it over with."

Riddings turned in his seat slightly so that he could see both her and George.

"Right, Ma'am."

He recognised Miss Watson's rank even if George didn't.

"I decided to take the straight forward approach with the police so I just rang up, told them it was me who'd called the Simmons' house on Saturday morning, and asked if anyone could tell me what had happened to Phil."

"And could they?" she asked.

"At first … … no. The policeman I spoke to was very cagey. Said they couldn't give out information to the public. But when I pressed a bit, he put me through to some female officer who sounded as though she was really pleased I'd called. She wasn't in the station at the time but she asked if I'd be willing to come along later to talk to her. I thought I might learn something so I agreed."

"When was this exactly?" interrupted George.

"Sometime after lunch yesterday."

George wasn't happy with that.

"Why did you wait so long? We sent you off before lunch on Saturday."

"Yes, I know, sir. But if I was going to learn anything at all, I thought I'd better wait long enough to allow the police investigation to begin to take some sort of shape. And it has."

"Well as long as that shape doesn't include us, I shall be well content."

"Actually, sir, I don't think you will."

Miss Watson cleared her throat and Riddings glanced across at her. In an attempt to get his report back on track, she prompted him before George could once again draw him off at a tangent.

"Tell us what happened at the police station, Paul."

George looked at her, half-inclined to insist that Riddings first explain his last comment, but his more reasonable self told him that they would have a much clearer report if he could stop himself interrupting. Miss Watson knew what she was doing. She knew it and George knew it. So he kept quiet.

Riddings looked once at George, and then focussed his attention on Miss Watson. She was much easier on the eye.

"I was interviewed by a DS Hayford. She asked me what I was doing up from London and what was my connection to Phil. How well did I know his family … … friends … … that sort of thing? I gave her the stamp collector story, and said we were due to attend a stamp auction in Derby on the Saturday afternoon. We weren't, as you know, but there actually was an auction that afternoon so it all made sense if they decide to check."

He glanced at George, just to show he hadn't forgotten who was the boss here, and then continued.

"It then began to get complicated… … She asked me whether I knew the person who had found Phil's body."

He paused before delivering what he expected to be a substantial shock.

"It was James Montrayne."

"Yes, we know that," said George, casually defusing Riddings' bombshell. "James phoned his father yesterday afternoon and put him in the picture."

Then he caught Miss Watson's eye and hastily added, "But get back to what you were saying to the police."

"Not much more to add, sir. I said I knew James because I work for the government department run by his father. I hadn't seen him recently, and I knew nothing about rat hunting, on Saturday or at any other time... ... ... I know we agreed that I'd say James was a friend, but it seemed better not to do that because this police woman seemed just that bit too interested in him... ... I thought ... ... Well, if they start looking at James very closely, as they well might since he was there when Simmons died, they'll see I've had no correspondence with him, made only one phone call to him that I can think of, and have met him only a few times."

"You stuck to the truth, in fact," commented Miss Watson.

"It seemed best."

"OK. Now, what did you learn?"

Riddings looked from her to George, absolutely certain that his next bombshell would not be so easily defused. He reached into his briefcase and took out a copy of the Lichfield Daily News. He dithered, not quite sure to whom he should give it. Miss Watson gestured to George and, as Riddings placed the paper on the desk and removed his briefcase, she came across the room to stand beside George's chair. The explosion was not long coming.

"Hell's teeth!"

Riddings had expected surprise and shock, but in George's shout and in the rising colour of his face he was aware of sudden and violent anger. Miss Watson was also aware of it and she laid her left hand gently on his shoulder as she slowly reread the newspaper story. Ready as she was to step into George's shoes, she had no wish to do so as a result of a heart attack over which she had presided.

"OK, George. This isn't as bad as it sounds."

"Bad? ... ... Bad ? ... ... Course it's ruddy well bad!"

"No, George, it really isn't."

She looked up from the paper and saw Riddings watching her carefully. His eyes flicked to George and then back to her. He smiled and nodded very slightly. She smiled back. Riddings had picked up on her train of thought.

"It's like this, George," she said, her voice quiet and persuasive. "We didn't want the police looking too closely at Lichfield Tube in case it compromises our own investigation. This ... ..." she picked up the newspaper, "will make sure that they keep looking elsewhere, at least for a while."

"But James didn't do it, damn it! And that woman is saying he did."

"No she isn't. Read it carefully and you can see that all she's done is put down a load of facts, which I assume can be proved to be true, which together invite the reader to draw a particular conclusion. It's a smokescreen; all innuendo and assumption. No substance. If she had proof of anything, she'd have used it."

She looked at Riddings for support which he was only too happy to give. If she were to become his boss on George's retirement, which rumour suggested was highly likely, then her good opinion was a prize earnestly to be desired.

"Sir, she has nothing solid to link James to Phil Simmons' murder and, although this … …" he pointed to the newspaper, "this may start the police looking more closely, they can't dig up what isn't there to be found. They'll need a lot more than she's given them to be able to charge him with anything, and all the time they're looking for it, they won't be nosing around Lichfield Tube."

George wasn't happy. A most unwelcome thought was trying to ease its way to the forefront of his mind.

"But … …" He didn't know how to finish.

Miss Watson did it for him. "But … … what if James actually did it?"

There was a silence which dragged on for longer than any of the three were comfortable with, but no-one seemed inclined to break it. There was no eye contact as each mentally reviewed everything they knew about James Montrayne and the present situation. Eventually, it was George who delivered his conclusion first.

"He didn't do it." His voice was calm now, and his verdict delivered with absolute certainty, his words carefully chosen. "I've known James for many years… … There might be circumstances when his actions result in someone getting killed, and I'm not just talking about his military service. We all have our suspicions about what happened when Abby was kidnapped… … But there's no way he would ever kill anyone for personal gain. Revenge … … money … … lust … … call it what you will. He simply wouldn't do it."

Realising her hand was still resting on his shoulder, Miss Watson patted him reassuringly a couple of times and moved away.

"I don't know James as you do, of course, but … … I think you're right."

Riddings nodded, his gaze still fixed somewhere in the middle of George's desk. He didn't really know James Montrayne at all, certainly not enough to state with certainty what he may or may not be capable of doing in any given circumstances, but his instinct was screaming at him that this was a setup. Who was behind it and why they were doing it, he had no way of knowing, at least, not yet. And that was what worried him.

Because if James did not kill Phil Simmons, and someone wanted to make it appear that he did, the most likely suspects were those most at risk from Phil's unauthorised rummaging through the computer files at Lichfield Tube.

He looked up, first at Miss Watson then at George.

"We could let the police go their own way for two or three days, but we can't wait too much longer before telling them what Simmons was involved in. For one thing, if someone is seriously trying to set James up for this, they might throw in some evidence which can't easily be refuted. For another, they'll probably wipe all the files so there's nothing to show they had any reason to dispose of Simmons. Oh ... ... and when she does find out, Sergeant Hayford is going to be seriously pissed that I didn't give her the whole story when I saw her yesterday."

Miss Watson had been watching George, knowing his affection for James, and worried how he might respond, but he seemed calm now, almost relaxed as he addressed Riddings.

"Well, young Paul. Doesn't look as though you've any time to waste, does it."

Thirty-Three

Lowfields Primary School – 2.15 pm

The children were excited. A shower of rain earlier in the day had cut short their lunchtime break, and they were glad now to be back outside again, albeit for only fifteen minutes. Some ran hither and thither, shouting, full of exuberant energy; some played with balls or ropes or other inexpensive toys which had escaped being banned on grounds of safety, or value, or practicality; some sat on the many newly installed seats which bordered the play area, talking, reading or playing. And a few who, for the moment, couldn't find anyone to talk to them, or play with them, or maybe even like them, clustered around the teachers and teaching assistants whose unfortunate lot it was to supervise the afternoon break.

Katie Cooper always seemed to attract the largest group. Small, athletic and dark-haired, she was one of the latest additions to the staff at Lowfields Primary School. In spite of being only in her second year of teaching, she was highly competent, full of initiative and enthusiasm, and well-liked by both her children and her TA.

She was also highly observant, which was probably just as well for a certain member of her class who was about to find herself, and those she cared about, in serious trouble.

As she rose from a crouch after soothing her second set of tears that playtime, Katie glanced across to the school car park. About twenty-five yards away, close to the fence, in what had become its usual spot, sat a gleaming, black Peugeot 206cc. She had only taken possession of it about a month ago after several weeks of frustration and inconvenience following the abrupt, but overdue, demise of the old banger she had previously driven. Flashing along on a bright sunny day – Katie was never one for hanging about – with the roof down and her hair contained by the strangest hat ever seen above such a pretty face, was still a sufficiently new experience to make her heart soar. Just looking at the car now, across the grass that separated the car park from the play area, gave her a thrill.

And then her eyes lifted to the road beyond the car park. Because it was at a slightly higher level, she could see the vehicles passing along it unobscured by the parked cars of the staff. One vehicle didn't pass. A dark-blue Mercedes 320 CDI slowed and pulled up about fifty yards short of the school's main entrance. It was strange because parents would not normally start arriving to pick up their children for another forty-five minutes or so. Even stranger, she didn't know of any of them who would spend over £40,000 on a luxury SUV. She'd read about this model in her dad's Auto magazine when she had been looking for the review of the

Mercedes CLK cabriolet. That was the car she had promised herself just as soon as she became Chief Education Officer for Birmingham, or pigs sprouted wings, whichever came first. She hadn't realised the SUV had made it onto the road in the UK yet.

Ignoring the child who took hold of her hand and began wiping his nose on the sleeve of her jumper, she watched as a man in a dark suit got out of the rear passenger seat of the Mercedes. He walked forward to where he could see down into the whole of the school parking lot and stood for a moment as though scanning the cars for a particular vehicle. He was not tall, maybe five foot nine, but even at that distance he seemed powerfully built. His dark hair, slicked back with gel, gave him the look of a sinister Andy Garcia, though maybe not quite so good-looking. He moved a few paces to his right, stood and looked again, and then returned to the SUV.

Katie took a quick look around the playground, but saw nothing untoward happening. The TA who helped with her Year Four class was over the other side dealing with a girl who had slipped and hurt her knee. Katie liked Sarah, her Teaching Assistant, mainly because Sarah, in spite of the ten years' experience behind her, never behaved or spoke in a way that made her feel inadequate. Others in the school were not so supportive, although that didn't apply to the Year One teacher who shared the yard duty this afternoon. Jane Sutton was on the brink of successfully completing her NQT year although, unlike Katie, she was at present on a temporary contract. Being just as conscientious, she was walking slowly around the playground, accompanied by the usual small group of acolytes, keeping a watchful eye out for misbehaviour or accident.

Katie's eyes flicked back to the Mercedes.

It was just sitting there, and she began to experience a very uncomfortable sense that all was not as it should be. She had known something was wrong at lunchtime when James left so abruptly with the young woman who was apparently Abby's new companion. Rumours had begun to fly around the staffroom fuelled by the production of the Lichfield Daily News by one of the parents who came in regularly to help as a volunteer in the afternoon. Katie didn't believe the rumours, any of them, even though she didn't know James very well. But she did know Abby, having taught her for over eight months, and she knew how that little girl talked about her dad. Katie might be young but she was experienced enough to recognise the harm that ill-informed and ill-intentioned gossip can do to an innocent person's character. All she knew for sure was that James had left at lunchtime on indefinite compassionate leave. The Chair of Governors had made that clear in a brief announcement to the staff before they had their lunch. But that was about the only thing that *was* clear.

And now this. Her first thought had been that the occupants of the Mercedes might be police, but she quickly dismissed that idea. She was sure police officers were not given luxury SUVs to play with, and they certainly didn't earn enough to buy their own. Not unless they were bent, which was rare though not totally unheard of. Anyway, police officers would surely have come straight into school to make whatever enquiries they wanted to. They didn't need to lurk outside.

Strange men loitering around school gates was always a worry, and she had been told during her induction to report anything of that nature to the school office immediately. But from all she had heard, problems of that kind nearly always involved single men acting alone as they tried to lure unsuspecting children into their cars. She couldn't imagine someone like that using such a conspicuous vehicle when the last thing they would want was to be noticed. And if men with that inclination stood outside a school watching anything, it would be the children, not their teachers' cars.

These men were after something else.

While Katie attended to the various children demanding her attention, her eyes kept drifting over to the Mercedes. As she gradually moved over in Sarah's direction, she decided to ask her Teaching Assistant whether she knew who the Mercedes belonged to, or whether she remembered seeing it before. Sarah, a quietly-spoken but very sympathetic and encouraging colleague in her mid-thirties, was unable to help but, as a mother of two young daughters, she urged Katie to report the vehicle to the office as soon as playtime ended.

Three minutes later, the children were lining up to process back into school. Once in their classroom, with the youngsters settled down to work, Katie asked Sarah to watch them while she went over to the office. As she left the classroom, she paused in the doorway to look back. Her eyes found Abby sitting at her usual table, talking quietly with Jamie Thompson about the mapping project they were involved in. At least, Katie assumed it was work they were talking about, although you could never be absolutely sure. To see the animation in her smiling face, you would never believe she had suffered such a traumatic experience only a couple of years ago.

With the door half closed, Katie froze.

Surely it couldn't be happening again. James had told her last summer, when it was decided she would be teaching Abby's class, about the kidnap and the terrors his daughter had experienced, just in case there were any signs of anxiety or withdrawal when Abby was in class. But there had been nothing. Just a happy little girl making the best of growing up without her mum. She was amazing.

Katie came to a decision. James might not, for the present, be running the school, but Abby was still his daughter and it was right that she share with him her growing suspicions. She slipped her hand into the pocket of her trousers for her new ultra-slim, ultra-compact, ultra-everything cell phone. Most teachers left them in their lockers but she liked to keep hers on her. It had too many useful applications to sit ignored for most of the day. She checked her phonebook for James's cell number. All the teachers had it, in case there was an urgent need to contact him when he was out of school. She took a deep breath, hoping that she wasn't about to make a complete idiot of herself. Then she pressed the call button and waited.

"James, it's Katie… … from school."

It didn't take long to outline her suspicions and, as soon as she gave him a description of the vehicle and its passenger, his reaction told her she had done the right thing to call him. She listened carefully to his instructions, scarcely able to believe what he was telling her, and wondering whether she would have the nerve to do what he was asking of her. But, she knew she had to, for Abby's sake.

"I won't let you down, James," she said. "I promise."

And she rang off.

Katie stared at her phone. For a moment, she thought a message was coming through. It seemed to be vibrating in her hand. Then she realised that it was her hand that was shaking. She took a deep breath, shoved the phone back in her pocket and, ignoring school rules, set off at a run for the school office.

The secretary's office door was open, and Mrs Waterson sat behind her desk working her way through a pile of letters that she thought needed answering. James would probably have told her to toss them in the bin, and not waste time replying to people he had not wanted to hear from in the first place. But James wasn't here, and she was still suffering from the shock of all the rumours and accusations. She didn't believe them, which made them all the more upsetting. So she tried to take her mind off them by writing letters.

She heard Katie approaching and looked up in time to see her come charging full pelt through the half-open door.

She listened, her dry lips parted in amazement, as Katie rattled off her story. She tried to take it in, and genuinely thought she had, but she was still too distressed by everything that had happened to concentrate properly. Perhaps if she had, Katie's sacrifice would not have been necessary.

Leaving Mrs Waterson to call the police, as James had instructed, Katie set off at a slightly slower pace towards the classroom of Louisa Coppello, Acting Deputy Head and Ardent Socialist. Whatever her other faults, Louisa was competent and professional. In spite of herself, she too had been having trouble believing the rumours about James, but she had set them aside for the present while she concentrated on trying to interest her Year 6 class in the technology of the Industrial Revolution in readiness for a visit to the Black Country Museum.

It said a lot for her control over her class that when she stepped outside to speak to Katie there was no sudden outburst of chatter or movement. A few heads turned curiously towards the door but her TA, working with a small group of special needs children in one corner, had no need to intervene to keep order. Perhaps it was the fact the Mrs Coppello could still be seen through the glass panel in the door that caused the exercise of such remarkable restraint, or maybe it was the fact that the children were genuinely enjoying, and were therefore engrossed in, the varied tasks she had set them to do.

Katie spoke rapidly, almost breathless in her excitement. Mrs Coppello nodded approvingly during the first part of her narrative, but then she frowned as she realised that Katie had spoken to James before coming to see her. Katie ignored the all too obvious warning signs and blundered on to explain what it was that James had asked her to do.

"No, Katie," was the response. "I can't allow you to do something so stupidly dangerous. James should never have asked it of you."

"But Mrs Coppello … …"

Katie had not been teaching at the school long enough to feel comfortable calling this strong-minded lady Louisa, and after this she probably never would.

"No, Katie," even more forcefully this time. "We shall wait for the police and allow them to deal with it. If they are not here before it's time for the children to go home, I shall go and stand at the school gate and watch this Mercedes of yours myself. If the people in it do mean any harm, they're not going to do anything stupid when they know they've been seen and can be identified."

Though it actually sounded quite reasonable, Katie didn't like it but, before she could get a word in, Mrs Coppello continued.

"You, Katie, will go back to your class and stay with them until the bell goes. If James is not here then, keep Abby with you until he comes. Do not let her out of your sight. Do you understand me?"

Katie nodded. She knew she would get nowhere by arguing. You never did with people like Louisa Coppello. Opposition just made them dig they heels in further.

"Good, and on your way back to class tell Mrs Waterson I want to know the moment the police arrive."

Her green eyes were still fixed on Katie's when she opened the door of her classroom and a subdued murmur of discussion and activity drifted out. With a slight raising of her carefully plucked eyebrows, she nodded dismissal and Katie turned away.

Leaving the secretary's office after delivering the message, Katie made her decision. It was risky. She would probably lose her job and maybe a good deal more besides. She thought she had been scared before, but it had been nothing like this. Her heart was racing in time with a growing pounding in her head; her mouth was dry and breathing was becoming difficult. Stupid asthma, always there to add to her problems whenever she was under stress. She was having difficulty swallowing, and she felt sick. As she stood in the corridor, she leant forward resting her hands on her knees and took several slow, deep breaths.

When she straightened again, she felt a little better. She remembered someone saying to her once, or maybe she'd read it somewhere, that being brave isn't the same as not being scared. A truly brave person is one who is scared, but goes ahead and does what needs to be done in spite of it. Well, now was the time to find out just how brave she really was.

She strode back to her classroom to collect Abby. There were twenty minutes to home-time.

Thirty-Four

RRISC – 2.20 pm

James finished speaking and slipped his phone back into his pocket. He looked at me, and I realised that it wasn't as easy as I'd thought to read what was in his eyes. Now they just seemed blank, as though he was pushing his emotions deep inside where they could be controlled and wouldn't show.

"Borisov is sitting outside the school," he said. "Mellisse must have brought him in to try and get this settled quickly. Either he thinks we're in school and he's waiting to pick us up when we leave, or he knows we're not and he's looking for a chance to grab Abby and force a trade."

I thought quickly. Andy was about to speak but I got in first.

"No, he won't do that."

James frowned. "Then why is he there?"

Everyone was watching me and I could sense the mood of impatience, the need to be doing something, and quickly.

"I mean... ... he's like Mellisse. He won't do it himself. He's watching, sure, but as soon as his guys get there, he'll be gone. He'd never get his hands dirty when there's a chance of witnesses. He and Ray use others to do that."

I could tell from their faces that they saw the sense in what I was saying, but that raised another problem which James immediately picked up on,

"We know what Borisov looks like and we know what he's driving, but if other men take over we shan't know who to look for. And nor would the police, assuming they respond in time."

He checked his watch and moved towards the door. "We'll keep to the plan I gave Katie, and pray she can keep her end together."

I walked over to follow him into the corridor, but he put his hand on my arm to stop me.

"No, Lizzie. It's you he wants. You'd best stay here out of the way."

Jimmy was right behind me, hands on my shoulders, trying to draw me back into the room. His voice was gentle, pleading in my ear.

"Stay here with us, Lizzie. You're safe here."

For years I hadn't felt safe anywhere. My sense of security had exploded when I was eight and the shattered pieces had never come back together again. Until two days ago, when this gentle giant had walked into my life and told me that everything was going to be OK. I had believed him, just as I'd always believed my dad, and I now knew with illogical, but absolute, certainty that as long as I was with him I'd be safe. I was absolutely not going to let him leave me.

Jimmy wasn't holding me tightly and I easily shook free of his restraining hands.

"I'm coming with you," I said, looking up into James's face. "I know where I'm safe, and it isn't here."

There were protests of course, but I wasn't listening and James was in too much of a hurry to argue. He strode off, and I ran to keep up.

James didn't speak as I opened the door of the Maserati, and he didn't try to stop me getting in. I stared through the windscreen as he reversed quickly out of the parking space. Just as he swung the wheel over, I caught a glimpse of Andy striding rapidly out of the building with, believe it or not, Rod hard on his heels. I felt the thrust in my back as the Maserati leapt out of the parking lot, but I snatched a quick look over my shoulder in time to see Andy and Rod climbing into the E-type. Reinforcements, it seemed, were close behind. I wondered about that. Maybe I had misjudged Rod; or maybe he was just doing what he was told.

I sat back and tried not to flinch as James pushed the Maserati through the mid-afternoon traffic. Parents, mums mostly, were on the roads now, making their way to their children's schools in the twice-daily carbon-generating taxi run. I stayed quiet as James seized every opportunity to move up through the press of traffic, using both lanes of the dual carriageway. There was nothing dangerous about his driving that I could see although, not yet having learnt to drive myself, I'm perhaps not the best judge. He seemed to be using the power of the car for acceleration rather than speed, as he slipped into gaps created by less urgent travellers. I glanced over at him once or twice and noticed his lips moving, but I couldn't hear any words. I wondered briefly if he was silently cursing the other drivers, but that didn't really seem likely. Maybe he was praying.

I jumped at the sound of a horn, vigorously applied, right behind us. I looked back to see a Range Rover only yards to the rear, so close I had no doubt as to the meaning of the gesture made by its woman driver. She seemed incensed at James for slipping the Maserati into the space she had allowed to develop in front of her. As I watched, she slowly dropped back allowing a gap to build up between us. I almost laughed when I saw the green sheen of the E-type glide into the newly created space. She sounded her horn again, and Andy raised his hand in an ironic thank-you.

Any mild sense of amusement had completely faded by the time I had turned around again in my seat. People were getting hurt and it was all because of me. I knew in some kind of abstract way that it wasn't really my fault, but the facts seemed to dispute that. If I had not run away,

Angie would not have been beaten up, Sister Yuyun would still be alive, and Abby would not now be in danger. Fault was not the issue; I felt responsible.

As we pulled away from the roundabout near the Asda-Walmart superstore, and the industrial estates and retail parks were replaced with open countryside and green fields, the vehicles on the A38 began to thin out and we picked up speed. Up to that point, I hadn't spoken since I didn't want to interfere with James's concentration in the heavy traffic but, with the car now racing north unimpeded by slower vehicles, I turned slowly in my seat so that I could see him when I explained how sorry I was for having brought all this trouble into his life. I didn't get further than opening my mouth.

"This isn't your fault, Lizzie, whatever you might think."

I was so weighed down by the sense of responsibility for having brought all this trouble into lives that didn't deserve it that my voice was quite unsteady as I began to argue.

"Yes," I said. "Whatever you may say, it is my fault. If I had stayed in Birmingham and... ..."

I wasn't surprised when he interrupted me. I think I had almost been hoping he would. I wanted to be convinced that I wasn't to blame. It weighed so heavily on me that it was almost unbearable.

I waited to see what was coming. I didn't want to argue any more. I was still sitting sideways in my seat, right leg curled under me, my left foot on the floor.

James checked his mirrors, and then glanced across at me. The Maserati was doing about seventy miles an hour so he didn't hold my gaze for long. Just before he turned his eyes back to the road, I was surprised to see him smile. For a moment, I wondered how he could smile when Abby may well be in so much trouble, and then I realised that the smile had nothing to do with himself or Abby, but it was for me. Reassurance.

"I left the Royal Marines in 98. Sarah was very ill when Abby was born, and... ... well, she died. I knew I couldn't face all the overseas postings when I was going to be needed so much at home. A guy called Peter Greenhalgh was promoted to fill my place. I knew him, though not well. Within two years, he was in Kosovo with 45 Commando as part of KFOR, where I would have been had I not resigned. One day he was flying out of Pristina in an American Apache helicopter, and the thing crashed somewhere near the Albanian border. It wasn't even shot down. Just some bit of metal decided it had done enough, and it sheared apart. Everyone on board was killed."

His eyes were staring straight ahead, his lips slightly pursed. I hoped he was concentrating on the road, since we were still doing seventy with a white van closing rapidly from behind in the outside lane, and a tractor some distance ahead moving very slowly in our lane. I needn't have worried. James clearly had no problem multitasking. The Maserati kicked me up the rear as he floored the pedal and shot past the tractor well ahead of the white van. He then settled back to a steady seventy again, allowing the van the privilege of overtaking us.

"It was tragic really." He was back to his story. "They were the only casualties in the whole of that deployment."

He turned towards me again. Still only a brief glance.

"Now, it was my resignation that began the train of events that led to Peter being killed in Kosovo. So, you tell me, Lizzie. Was it my fault that he died?"

It wasn't, of course. I could see that. At most, one could say that it was a consequence of his resignation. But, fault?

I said, "You know it wasn't, James. And I can see what you're trying to tell me."

Without looking at me, he reached across and lightly patted my knee. I had noticed him do it to Abby, a comforting, encouraging, reassuring gesture. It was all of that for me, just as it had been when my dad used to do it. Often it had been an attempt to reassure me when I was worried that I'd done something wrong. I'd grab hold of his hand, just as I gripped James's hand now, and he would smile, and I knew everything was OK. It was such a strong memory that it was like my dad was reaching out to me, and I think I would have held on to James's hand if he hadn't so quickly removed it and placed it back on the wheel.

"Good," he said. "There are already too many people walking around carrying guilt they were never intended to bear. You don't need to be one of them."

The Maserati cruised past the Young Offenders Institution at Swinfen Hall, nearing Lichfield but still at least ten minutes away from the town centre. With all the extra traffic at that time of day as parents drove a mile or two to school to pick up their children, it could take twice as long to reach Lowfields. But James wasn't actually going to the school, as Katie could have explained to Louisa Coppello if only she'd been prepared to listen.

Thirty-Five

Lowfields Primary School 2.55 pm

Katie Cooper entered her classroom with a show of confidence that she didn't feel. She crossed over to where Sarah, her TA, was working with a group of children, and touched her lightly on the arm to draw her away from the group. Standing beside one of the room's large windows, she explained in a quiet voice that she had to leave early and Sarah would have to continue managing the class for the last part of the afternoon. This wasn't a problem. The work was already set, and the children well underway with their activities. Sarah was a senior level TA, qualified to manage the class during the teacher's absence. She accepted Katie's explanation that she was taking Abby to meet her father without the slightest twitch of her delicate eyebrows.

Katie knew she had to take care not to say anything that would worry Abby, so she just told her that her dad needed her to leave early. While Abby tidied away, packed her bag and collected her coat, Katie went quickly to the staffroom to retrieve her shoulder bag from her locker. Although they were a nuisance because they took up valuable floor space, the new lockers had been installed after a teacher's handbag had been looted when left under a chair in the staffroom. Even Katie thought it safest to cram her multi-purpose holdall into the small compartment provided for her use.

When she got back she found Abby waiting for her by her desk. Grabbing her coat off its hanger, Katie waved goodbye to Sarah and led Abby from the room. Once outside, she told her simply that her dad couldn't get back in time to meet her, so instead they were going to meet him.

"Can't Cherry meet me?" asked Abby. "That's what usually happens when Dad's away and can't get back in time."

"I think he gave Cherry a job to do today, and he can't get here any quicker than your dad."

"OK."

Abby wasn't a placid child, just sensible and cooperative, and Katie thanked God for it. If only all her class were the same, teaching would be a breeze.

"We're not going to use the front door," Katie told her. "So I want you to wait here by the side door while I go and fetch the car round."

Abby didn't understand. "But I can walk round to the car with you."

"I know you can." Katie was thinking quickly. She knew she had to try not to say anything that might frighten the child. "I need to take my laptop and the box of National Curriculum folders. Could you get them and bring them to the door while I fetch the car?"

Abby looked as though she was about to ask why they hadn't brought these items from the classroom when they first left but, in the end, she just gave her usual OK and went to get them.

Katie hurried round to the staff car park. She knew that no staff were supposed to bring their cars down this side of the building, access being restricted to vans making deliveries to the school kitchen. Still, by the time this was over she was probably going to lose her job anyway, so what did one more broken rule matter?

She stopped dead as she turned the corner of the building, and drew back quickly.

The Mercedes SUV was still there, but drawn up tight behind it was a blue Toyota Rav4. Two men were standing beside the Mercedes talking to the occupant of the rear seat through the open window. As she watched, they stepped back and the Mercedes pulled away. They turned and stood for a moment looking down at the school and Katie could see they were big men, tough-looking, who filled out their black tee-shirts with impressive bulk. She didn't think they could see her as she peered around the corner, half hidden by a drainpipe. For a moment, she didn't know what to do, but then she decided that different watchers in a different car didn't really change anything. James's plan was still the best option.

She waited until the men turned to climb into the Toyota, and then she came quickly round the corner, walking fast but not running towards her 206. She opened the door and eased herself onto the leather seat, resisting a very strong urge to look up towards the Toyota to see if she had been observed. James had told her that they would not be looking for her or her car, so what she was about to do ought to pass near enough unnoticed. That didn't stop her hand shaking slightly as she turned the key to fire up the engine. Still without looking up to the road, she pulled out of her space.

One minute later, she was turning her car around on the wide tarmac area down near the kitchen entrance. Abby pushed open the door, holding Katie's laptop case in her right hand and nudging forward a grey plastic box with her feet. Another minute, both box and laptop were safely in the boot and Abby was strapping herself into the passenger seat. Katie looked across at her.

"All set?"

"Sure," said Abby, perfectly calm and unconcerned.

Katie eased forward slowly. It was still a little early for parents to be arriving, but you could never be sure just when they'd start turning up to gossip, or moan, or generally enjoy a good natter.

Past the school building now, and in full view of the Rav4, Katie drove slowly up to the school gates. The Toyota was parked along the road to the right of the entrance, which was the direction Katie really wanted to go but she decided it would probably be safest to turn left.

She pulled into the road and accelerated gently, still hoping not to attract any attention from gentlemen in black tee-shirts.

She checked her mirror.

The Toyota remained stationary.

She checked the road ahead and looked again in her mirror.

The Toyota hadn't moved, but a white Vectra with a light bar on the roof was easing up to the curb in front of it.

Two police officers got out, put on their caps and adjusted their utility belts. Katie looked ahead just in time to see traffic lights twenty yards ahead of her turning red. She stopped and watched events in her mirror.

The police officers looked up and down the road, conferred, glanced at the Toyota and then entered the school grounds through the pedestrian gate.

The Toyota slowly moved off, pulling around the police car, and beginning to close the distance to Katie's 206.

What did it mean? Maybe nothing. Probably the black tee-shirts realised that little good could come of hanging around now the police had arrived, and just wanted to put some distance between themselves and the school. Katie wondered whether she should now turn round and head back to the school. Had she been wrong to leave in the first place? She was still trying to make her mind up when Abby nudged her.

"Miss Cooper. The lights are green."

And so they were. As Katie let in the clutch the horn of the Toyota sounded its impatience only yards behind them. She pulled away, accelerating quickly up to the thirty mile an hour speed limit.

And then she noticed Abby looking back over her shoulder at the Toyota, her attention drawn by the sound of the horn.

"Abby, turn round. Don't look at them."

"What's the matter, Miss Cooper?" asked Abby obeying, but puzzled by the sharp tone in her teacher's voice.

"Nothing," said Katie. "It's fine."

It wasn't convincing, so Abby tried her own attempt at reassurance.

"They're only rude people who think they own the road just because they drive a 4x4."

"Let's hope so," replied Katie, wondering whose view Abby was expressing. She also hoped that the black tee-shirts hadn't recognised the child, assuming they knew what she looked like, which was quite likely considering the ease and sophistication of today's electronic communication.

She made a right turn and the Toyota turned with her, but now seemed to be dropping back. Maybe they were simply heading out of town, as she was. At the next traffic lights, she went through on green but the Toyota was caught by the red, making no attempt to jump the lights. A small car and a Tesco home delivery van turned in behind her at the lights. The Toyota was well behind now and seemingly untroubled by the fact. Katie sighed heavily with relief.

She would stick to the plan, and take Abby to meet her father.

With the cathedral spires behind her, she pointed the 206 north in the direction of Curborough and began to relax. This was not one of the main routes out of Lichfield, but it was the most direct way to the place where James had arranged to meet them. The country road would take them past the site of the former RAF Lichfield where old aircraft hangars could still be seen amid the newer structures of the developing industrial estate.

Abby chattered on in her friendly unassuming way, pointing out unsteady calves and late lambs, tumble-down barns and picturesque farm houses. Katie mumbled in response but couldn't tear her eyes away to look since the twists and turns of the road demanded her full attention. They had lost the Tesco delivery van before they crossed the railway line on the outskirts of town and the road was clear behind them.

A jangling sound interrupted Abby's chatter. On getting into the car, Katie had tossed her bag as she usually did down into the passenger foot-well where it normally sat in the empty space. Today it nestled against Abby's right ankle where she felt the gently vibration of a mobile phone. She stopped in mid-sentence and glanced at Katie.

"See who it is, Abby."

Not used to being invited to delve into the recesses of a teacher's handbag, Abby seized this rare opportunity. Retrieving the phone without too much unnecessary rummaging, she studied the display.

"It says *SCHOOL*, Miss Cooper."

That meant someone was calling from the phone in the school office, not a personal mobile. Probably Louisa Coppello. Probably with the police at her elbow and ready to accuse her of God only knew what.

The jangling continued, insistent, threatening.

"Ignore it, Abby."

Frowning slightly, Abby looked as though she was about to argue, but then the ringing stopped as the phone switched to voicemail.

Katie checked her mirror but the road behind remained empty. Not that she could see very far back as her view was restricted by the frequent twists in the road. About a mile or so from the railway line, they entered a reasonably straight stretch. Abby was chatting again, keeping up her running commentary on the countryside rushing past, but Katie could feel tension building inside her again as her eyes continually flicked up to the mirror. If that Toyota was still behind them, this was her best chance of spotting it. And if it was there, it could be for no other purpose than to follow the 206 all the way to wherever James was waiting for Abby. She checked again.

Nothing.

She looked ahead to the approaching bend, and then back to the mirror.

Still nothing.

She began to turn into the bend and glanced up for a last check.

The Rav4 came into view for no more than a second at the end of the straight and then was lost behind the curve of the hedge.

"Ah man!"

Katie hit the steering wheel hard startling Abby who stopped talking in mid-sentence and looked at her with a frown of worry creasing her young forehead.

"Are you OK, Miss Cooper?"

Katie came to a decision.

"I'm fine, Abby, but there's something I need to tell you."

She paused, wondering how to explain without frightening Abby too much.

"Your dad couldn't come back to school because some people are looking for him, and for that girl who came with you this morning."

"You mean Lizzie?"

"Yeah. Lizzie." She checked her mirror, but didn't expect to see the Toyota because of the curving road.

"Those men who hooted at us back at the traffic lights… … well, I think they saw you when you turned round. I think they realised who you are and decided to follow us to find your dad."

Abby swung round to look back.

"Are they there… … behind us?"

"Yes."

"I can't see them."

"They're there… … Probably trying to keep far enough back not to scare us, but on these roads… … with so little traffic… … they can tail us all the way to your dad. Easy."

"Are you scared, Miss Cooper?"

It was a small, soft voice; the voice of a child who was scared and trying hard not to show it.

"No," lied Katie, "because we're going to ditch them before we get anywhere close to your dad."

"Cool," said Abby, her fear slightly diminishing. "What are we going to do?"

Katie marvelled for a moment at the amount of trust Abby placed in her. She knew that even today, in spite of many media reports to the contrary, many children still had a high regard for their teachers, bestowing on them a surprisingly high level of trust, even affection. She wanted to be the sort of teacher who could foster that in her pupils. It hadn't occurred to her before that maybe she already did.

"Miss Cooper," Abby prompted again. "How are you going to do it?"

Katie was feeling pressured. She did have an idea, but she hadn't properly thought it through. Her first instinct had been to phone James and tell him they were being followed, but she knew where he was travelling from, and he wouldn't yet be close enough to be any help. In any event, the last thing she wanted to do was to end up leading the Toyota straight to him. So, there had to be another way.

As calmly as she could, she said, "Just wait a minute, Abby, and I'll tell you what's going to happen."

James hadn't told her who the men at the school were, only that they were dangerous and probably armed. He hadn't known whether the police would respond quickly enough, or even at all, to a call about an emergency that hadn't happened and about which the information was mostly supposition. Although they might take seriously a warning about a potential paedophile loitering outside the premises, James couldn't guess what priority an overstretched police force would give it if an actual and more immediate emergency should happen. So he had asked her to bring Abby out of school, and get her safely away, leaving the watchers with nothing to find. He hadn't tried to pressure her in any way, but she had found she couldn't resist the worry in his voice.

And it was actually quite exciting even though, if all went according to plan, there would actually be remarkably little danger. She'd been sure she could make a good story out of it to tell her mates, perhaps boosting the adrenalin quotient by enhancing her role a bit.

No need now. There was enough adrenalin flowing for half-a-dozen stories, and the only plan that she had come up with involved a manoeuvre that even thinking about scared her half to death.

She was fairly sure that, in a straight race from a standing start, her 206 could easily outdistance the Toyota. But this was not a straight race and, on these country roads, speed could very well get her and Abby killed. Not an outcome James Montrayne would be happy with. So, in spite of her fears, she decided to go for the alternative.

She had already picked out a stretch of road in her mind, but she wasn't certain it was wide enough. She had used that road many times and knew that, on the rare occasion that she encountered a vehicle travelling in opposite direction, they always passed each other with ease. It would have to do because there was no more likely spot between here and Fradley Junction where James would be waiting. She just hoped that no other vehicle would need to use that particular road in the next five minutes.

"OK, Abby," she said, in as confident a voice as she could manage. "Here's what we're going to do."

Abby listened, mouth open, brow furrowed, as Katie outlined her plan. There was no doubt that this was going to be dangerous, though clearly not for Abby herself. Miss Cooper was going to make sure of that. Still she felt sick, and her right leg was beginning to tremble. She remembered the last time someone had chased her. She remembered the car crash, and the blood, the gunfire and the shouting. She didn't want Miss Cooper to die, but she couldn't do anything to help. She was scared also for her dad and for Lizzie. She was a powerless victim, just like before, and she felt crushed by emotions she couldn't clearly identify. She turned to look behind, tears trickling slow and quiet from sparkling eyes.

Katie caught the movement and glanced across at her. As she took in that stricken look on the child's face, she felt suddenly overwhelmed by an anger fiercer than anything she remembered feeling before. She hadn't asked for this, and if there was any other way she would take it but, in the rush of her adrenalin high, she told herself these guys had made a serious mistake in trying to mess with one of her kids. Bravado or bravery? She didn't care. She was going to get this done.

"We're nearly there, Abby... ... You remember what to do?"

Abby nodded slowly, and tiny drips of salty water fell onto the front of her coat.

This was it. The road ran straight ahead for at least half a mile. There was a farm entrance on the right hand side towards the end. There were no vehicles approaching.

"When I swing into that entrance, leap out and hide by the hedge. If you don't see me coming back to pick you up, run to the farmhouse and use my phone to call your dad."

She checked her mirror.

No Toyota.

Maybe she was wrong. Maybe this was all a mistake. Maybe she had scared Abby for nothing. Maybe she was a total idiot.

She checked again.

Nothing.

They were nearing the farm entrance. She began to brake, and checked her mirror for the last time.

And there it was. Sinister. Threatening.

Well, maybe not for much longer.

Katie swung the wheel hard over and braked hard. The 206 slid to a stop half-way through the entrance, and Abby leapt out clutching Katie's cell phone in her left hand.

Reverse gear. Quick look in both directions. Nothing but the Toyota.

Katie was back on the road, heading straight for the black tee-shirts.

She had practised this manoeuvre on the old airfield near to her home in the Black Country where the runways had not yet been developed into access roads for industrial units. A private flying school was based there and a friend, who had a miniscule share in a Cessna Skycatcher, had offered her a bit of fun on a slow flying day, not in the air but in her new 206.

She accelerated hard, and the distance closed rapidly. She knew exactly what she had to do, and how, but could she get the timing right. Too soon, and they'd run her off the road. Too late, and … … well, too late was too late, and she'd be past caring.

Unless they simply stopped and blocked the road!

Why hadn't she thought of that? She clenched her teeth in exasperation. Stupid! Stupid! Stupid! If they just did that simplest of manoeuvres, she was finished. And so was Abby.

Still, she hadn't thought of it, so maybe they wouldn't either.

Closer. Closer. They weren't stopping.

Closer. She swung across the wrong side of the road.

She was heading straight for the Toyota.

She could even make out white faces above the black tee-shirts.

This was the ultimate game of chicken. Katie knew she wouldn't flinch, but she couldn't be certain that they would. And for this to work, they had to. Was this what it felt like to have five seconds to live?

She turned on her lights and blasted her horn. Anything to unnerve them.

She started to brake. She was going too fast.

With thirty yards to go, the Toyota began to move out of her path.

Yes! Yes! Yes!

Katie screamed her exultation.

Her right hand was holding the underside of the steering wheel at eleven o'clock. Her left hand grasped the handbrake lever.

With the vehicles still twenty yards apart, she hauled hard on the steering wheel to pull the 206 into the path of the Toyota. As she began swinging to the left, she hauled on the handbrake and her right foot jabbed sharply at the brake pedal. The rear wheels locked and the back end of the 206 swung around on the level grass verge to the right of the road.

As her car pirouetted, the rear wheels slid back onto the tarmac surface of the road just as the Toyota drew level. The rear offside of the 206 smashed into the front nearside of the Rav4 swinging the SUV over towards the hedge. The black-shirted driver tried to correct, but his instinct was to turn away from Katie's 206 which took him over the verge and into the hedge. Not so bad; probably survivable, except that he hadn't taken account of the tree, of which there were many lining the road.

The old oak had stood there for over two hundred years, and wasn't going to be deterred from another two hundred by any mobile tin box which couldn't stay where it belonged.

For a moment, having swung a full one hundred and eighty degrees, the 206 was stationary, at a slight angle across the road due to the collision.

As Katie let in the clutch and pulled away, she risked a glance at the Toyota. To her disappointment, it didn't seem badly damaged by its encounter with the oak, but she could see that the airbags had deployed, and there was no sign of movement inside the car.

And still, there was no other vehicle in sight.

She slapped the steering wheel in delight and relief, and immediately grimaced at the sharp pain in her right shoulder, the result of being slammed against the door by the force of the collision. Ignoring the clunking rattle from the rear of her precious, but no longer pristine, 206cc, she settled herself cautiously in her seat and, breathing deeply to calm herself down, she drove sedately back to retrieve her charge.

Job done.

Thirty-Six

The campaign trail – 3.00 pm

Newton-by-Grangewood was a bustling village community right on the edge of the largely rural constituency. Whilst not ignoring the town at the heart of the constituency, Sir Vernon Laycock knew that most of the votes lay in the suburbs and surrounding villages. His election agent, Christopher Spillane, had made sure during the last two weeks that Sir Vernon was seen and heard at least once in every section of the community. Each household was visited by someone from campaign headquarters, and any voter who expressed a wish to speak to Sir Vernon in person was granted their request. It made for a gruelling campaign, but Chris repeatedly assured his candidate that the result would make it all worthwhile.

Sir Vernon would have come to Newton even without Chris's urging. He had attended the secondary school back in the days when it had been King James's Grammar School, before the comprehensive bug had begun to erode its standards. His father had been the chairman of a family-run brewery some distance away, but the beauty and tranquillity of the village amply justified the daily commute. The young Vernon, an avid reader of Richmal Crompton's *William* stories, had revelled in the freedom of village life. While he never intentionally emulated the exploits of his young hero, he found himself inwardly propelled by the same boundless ingenuity and soaring optimism. That which would have driven William to be a pirate captain or an Indian chief, eventually took Vernon to Nottingham University and thence to a career in engineering which would eventually lead to his knighthood.

It was through one of his larger engineering companies that Sir Vernon had been able to provide the funds, just three years ago, for the Newton-by-Grangewood Leisure Centre. Replacing an older and somewhat dilapidated gymnasium on the site of the King James's Community College, the leisure centre provided a swimming pool, sports hall and gymnasium for the villagers, doubling as state-of-the-art indoor sport facilities for the college. Needless to say, this ensured that Sir Vernon was a popular and well-known figure in the village long before he ever announced his intention of running for Parliament.

Still, as Chris continually reminded him, every vote counted and none should be taken for granted which is why Sir Vernon was spending the afternoon at Newton Village Hall. Every Monday and Thursday, afternoon tea was laid on in the hall for the more senior members of the community for the princely sum of one pound per head. Although many members of the Village Hall Committee were themselves past retiring age, the Seniors Tea was run as an independent club, hiring the hall like any other club and, unlike some of the others, paying its own way. It never seemed to occur to any of the regulars to wonder whether one pound per head was sufficient to cover the cost of all the drinks, sandwiches, cakes and other elegant trifles which found their way onto the tables week after week.

It did occur to Sir Vernon to wonder, and he decided to put the question to the club's treasurer, a formidable lady of eighty-three years called Mrs Lydia Winterton – she laid great emphasis on the *Mrs* - who looked as though she might still give the SAS a run for their money through the Brecon Beacons. She assured him that they never had any trouble funding the events, and even had a sufficient surplus to enable the group to go on a number of coach outings every year. Convinced the sums did not add up, Sir Vernon pressed her and was surprised to discover that the group received a generous donation every month from something called the Aullton Trust. Curious, he tried to draw out a few more details but her response curtailed any further enquiries.

"My dear Sir Vernon," she chided, as though he were some impertinent schoolboy, "the Trust does not seek to advertise its generosity. I respect that… … and so should you."

"Indeed, Mrs Winterton, you are perfectly right," replied Sir Vernon, conscious that his primary task that afternoon was courting votes.

He made a mental note to get someone to look into the Aullton Trust. If another body had influence in this village, he wanted to know who, why and how much.

"I'm ninety-five," warbled a thin voice, interrupting his reflections with an accompanying tug on his right sleeve.

Looking down he saw a weather-beaten face etched with so many wrinkles it could have been one hundred and ninety-five. The lady's eyes were sunk deep in their sockets and her lips were thin and grey. The hand gripping his sleeve was just a claw of skin and bone. In almost ludicrous contrast, her head was crowned with a luxuriant perm of white locks which curled round her ears and into the nape of her neck. He found himself staring, almost dazzled, wondering whether it might be a wig.

"Ninety-five," she said again, apparently aware that she didn't quite have his full attention. She punctuated her statement with another tug on his sleeve.

"Really," he replied, lowering his eyes a fraction and looking into those sockets. "And you look so much younger."

"No I don't," she said. "I look as though I've died and they dug me up for the tea."

Since she followed this with a wide grin, he dared to try a reply in kind.

"Well then, I have to say you are the most entertaining corpse I've met all afternoon."

There was a definite twinkle down in the depths of those sockets.

"And here I am thinking *you* came here to entertain *me*," she said, releasing his sleeve and patting the seat of the vacant chair next to her at the table.

Realising that there was for the moment no escape, he turned the chair slightly to face her and sat.

"So," warbled his new companion, "I listened to your talk and I still don't know why I should vote for you."

Sir Vernon quickly reviewed the speech he had given once the more important business of eating and drinking was well underway. He also tried to weigh up his interrogator. Was she looking for the bigger picture, or was she only concerned with policies that would directly benefit her own personal circumstances? He was still formulating his reply when the claw jabbed him in the chest, not something he'd been used to since his schooldays.

"You'll need to be quicker than this when that lovely Bill Turnbull gets you on the BBC Breakfast show… … if you're elected, that is."

Sir Vernon smiled, acknowledging the hit. He decided on a compromise approach.

"I could chatter on about all manner of things that may not be of any concern to you," he said. "So why don't you ask me a question and I'll do my best to give you a straight answer."

"A straight answer?" she snorted. "And here I was thinking you wanted to be a politician."

"If getting a straight answer to your questions, Mrs… … er… …"

Those dark sockets twinkled again.

"Shufflebottom," she replied. "Edith Louisa Shufflebottom. And if I'd had *my* way seventy years ago, it would have been *him* taking *my* name not me being saddled with his."

"Well, Mrs… … er… … Edith. May I call you Edith?"

"It's better than the alternative."

"Well, Edith. If it's straight answers that you want, that in itself is a good reason to vote for me. Obfuscation is not something I have any patience with."

"Ob… … what?"

"Obfuscation. Er… … it means… …"

"I know what it means," she grinned. "I was just yanking your chain."

Wondering what American TV programme she had culled that expression from, he returned her grin with genuine warmth. They talked for about twenty minutes covering a range of topics from the invasion of Iraq to the winter heating allowance for pensioners. She actually seemed to like his answers, not necessarily because they were what she wanted to hear, but because of his clarity and obvious sincerity. It occurred to him during their conversation that this was definitely not time wasted. Whenever he glanced around, he noticed elderly eyes looking in Edith's direction. Her judgement of his performance would be relayed to everyone present by the end of the afternoon.

Then, just when he thought he was home and dry, she hit him with the one question that he hoped no-one would ask.

"Once you are elected, Sir Vernon, and I rather think you will be, I don't think you'll be happy just sitting on the back benches." He was about to give some modest disclaimer but she didn't give him the chance. "So when you move up, and the press start digging into your past, what skeletons are they going to find to embarrass all of us who vote for you?"

Skeletons?

This was exactly the question that Chris Spillane had asked at the outset of the campaign. Late one evening, in the small room hired to be their campaign headquarters, Chris had been brutally direct.

"Whatever you've done or said, even stuff that other people might think you've done or said, that can be dug up and used against you, I need to know now. If I know up front, I can prepare for it and deal with it... ... Whatever it is, I need to know."

Sir Vernon had tried to protest that there was nothing, but Chris would have none of it.

"Don't tell me nothing. Everyone has something... ... Think... ... Take your time... ... But don't you tell me *nothing.*"

So Sir Vernon had thought about it, and Chris had been right. Eventually, he had revealed everything, from unpopular business decisions, through speeding offences, to minor peccadilloes dating from his student days at Nottingham. Everything, that is, but one.

He never mentioned Diane Thomas and his frequent overnight visits to a certain country hotel on the outskirts of Worcester. It was just far enough from home to justify an overnight stay if he'd been working late at FerroTech's thermo-technology plant on the southern outskirts of the city. His assignations were usually in quiet, out of the way places, although he had on several daring occasions dined with Diane at the Carlton Grand Hotel in Birmingham. He soon realised that this was foolish vanity, but he had enjoyed the looks his young guest had received from other male diners.

What was it Chris had said? *Stuff that can be dug up?* No-one could dig this up because no-one even knew there was anything to look for. And if anyone did look, they would find nothing… … because Diane was a will o' the wisp. She was always available and highly tangible when he needed her, but she evaporated into obscurity once his needs were met. Perhaps, with a political career in the offing, his movements would come under much greater scrutiny. Well, there was no perhaps about it. So maybe, with infinite regret, he would have to let Diane go.

No maybe about it, he thought, with Edith's piercing gaze upon him. That episode would have to come to an end.

But how should he answer Edith's question? He knew that he should not be seen as trying to put together a diplomatic non-answer to a sensitive enquiry.

"Nothing I have ever done makes me unfit to represent you in Parliament. There is nothing in my past which can hinder me in any way from working for the best interests of you and the other voters in this constituency."

She smiled, but he thought he could detect a hint of disappointment in the curve of those thin lips.

"Was that supposed to be a straight answer, Sir Vernon? Are you telling me you have no skeletons?"

"Any skeletons I *may* have in my cupboard are personal and private as, I'm sure, are yours. If they have any bearing on my public life, it is only to make me more understanding, more tolerant, more compassionate and more aware of the human frailty that characterises us all… … I will not embarrass you, or anyone else who votes for me. That is my straight answer."

She stared at him for several long moments, and then she seemed to slump in her chair as tiredness overcame her.

"Good. Then I'll try to stay above ground long enough to make sure you don't," she said, more quietly than before. "I like you. Don't let us down."

He wrapped her thin hand in both of his and smiled. "I won't," he said.

He had stood up and just turned away when her tired voice drew him back.

"By the way," said Edith Louisa Shufflebottom. "You were quite right."

He looked down at her smiling face, puzzlement on his own.

"The hair," she said. "It is a wig… … but don't tell anyone."

Thirty-Seven

Fradley Junction – 3.15 pm

We were getting close, moving more slowly now that we were on a side road and no longer racing up the A38. Just a few minutes, James said, so I started watching out for the canal bridge which he had told me marked the entrance to the parking area at Fradley Junction.

I didn't see it, but instead, at an intersection up ahead, I noticed a blue Police Diversion sign, one of those temporary fold-up things that they use where there has been an accident. Apparently the road going off to the left was obstructed and all traffic was directed to continue straight ahead. As we passed the junction, I tried to look down the blocked road, but all I could make out were blue flashing lights and some white vehicles way off in the distance and then the hedge intruded to hide them from view.

There was no reason to suppose that they had anything at all to do with Abby and her teacher, but my stomach felt tense and chilled and I turned to James to ask what he thought was happening. It would have been a daft question so, in the end, I didn't ask it. He could have no more idea what was happening than me. But I saw him check his rear-view mirror a couple of times while I watched him so I turned around to look behind.

Andy's green E-Type had slowed and pulled onto the grass verge just past the junction. Andy and Rod climbed out of the car and walked around the police signs and disappeared. I turned back to James.

"They've stopped."

"I know."

"But… … aren't you going to wait for them… … find out what's happening?"

"Don't worry, Lizzie," he said, his voice showing none of the tension which I knew he must be feeling. "If that's anything to do with us, Andy will let us know. Meanwhile, we press on to meet Abby."

I was puzzled.

"How did he know you wanted him to stop… … to check that out?"

"We served together for a good while, Lizzie," he replied somewhat enigmatically. "He just knew."

A few minutes more and I saw the hump of a bridge in the road ahead with a narrow entry on the left immediately before it. James slowed and swung the big car through the entrance onto a narrow tarmac track leading to some brick buildings a couple of hundred yards away, adjacent to an almost empty parking area. On our right was a strip of grass separating the track from the dark waters of the canal. A number of boats rested, still and quiet, at their moorings. There were cabin cruisers mixed in with the traditional narrow-boats more commonly associated with British canals.

At the end of the track a gate barred access to the courtyard, maybe a wharf in days gone by, in front of the old brick buildings. Just before the gate, James swung left again and headed for one of the three lonely vehicles occupying the parking lot.

As we neared the black Peugeot 206cc, both doors opened and I heard a yell of excitement from Abby. She was alongside his window before he'd finished parking the Maserati in a slot two spaces away from the 206. She moved back so he could open his door, and as soon as he climbed out she leapt into his arms. I came out of the Maserati more slowly, and walked around the rear to stand close by without intruding into their space. Clasping him tightly round the neck, with her legs dangling, Abby was talking so fast I could barely make out what she was saying. And then she started crying.

"It's OK, sweetheart," said James. "It's OK. You're safe. No-one's going to hurt you."

For a moment, there was no response, and then she gradually stopped sobbing into his collar and lifted her head.

"Dad, you didn't see them. They were following us. I thought they were going to get me."

James kissed her cheek and hitched her up so she was sitting on his right forearm. I guessed he'd carried her like that so many times when she was small. Most people would not find it so easy with a child her age, but James handled her as though she was nothing but feathers. She still clung fast round his neck and laid her head on his shoulder. The sun sparkled on the faint streaks of moisture on her cheeks, but there were no more tears now. The sobbing had stopped. The arms supporting her told her she was safe, and the anxiety ebbed away.

I wondered for one stupid moment if he'd hold me like that if I was afraid and distressed. Of course he wouldn't. I wasn't his child. I wasn't anybody's child. Not any more. I looked away from them; away from a relationship so special I ached for one just like it, but I knew it would never happen.

Then I wondered what had happened to Miss Cooper. I turned towards the 206. She hadn't moved. She was standing very still on the other side of her car watching us. I had first met her for only a few minutes that morning. I didn't know her at all, but I could tell from the blankness of her stare that something was seriously wrong.

James attention still seemed to be focussed on Abby, so I walked around the back of the 206 and stopped dead.

The rear lights were gone and the boot lid was crumpled so much that I was amazed it was still closed. The rear off-side quarter panel was smashed in and the driver's door was scratched and dented. I couldn't understand how all the glass had remained intact. Miss Cooper watched me coming and, as my eyes took in the extent of the damage, she too stepped back from the car to assess the injury done to her pride and joy.

I ran my hand along the unmarked roof and came to stand next to her.

"I think I might have killed someone," she said in subdued tone, quite different from the bubbly effervescence of the morning, "but I don't seem to feel anything."

I was startled. I looked again at the car. This wasn't front end damage.

"But surely they must have hit you," I protested, "not the other way round."

I heard James approach and saw her eyes flick away to somewhere over my shoulder.

"No," she said. "I did it."

James and I said nothing. Abby sniffed.

"To be fair, it seemed the only thing to do," Katie went on. "Only... ... I didn't think... ... I didn't realise what might happen to them... ... I just wanted to stop them."

At that moment, James phone started ringing. He reached awkwardly into his jacket pocket to pull it out left-handed. He glanced at the display and then put it to his ear.

"What did you find?"

He listened, spoke, listened some more, glanced at Katie, and then finished the conversation with, "In the café, Fradley Junction. Meet us there."

Replacing his phone, he smiled at Katie. "Rav4?" he asked. "Blue? In a hedge?"

She nodded, clearly worried in spite of his smile.

"Then you haven't killed anyone."

She sighed and her shoulders slumped as the relief flooded through her. Then she straightened up and asked, "Are you sure?"

"Very. Now come on. I think it's time we all had a drink. And you, young lady," he smiled again at Katie, "have a story to tell."

The café was housed in one of the brick buildings which bounded three sides of the courtyard, the canal itself making the fourth side. It was warm, bright and cheerful and, while Katie and I seated ourselves at a table in the back corner, James and Abby ordered coffees and cakes. They were just coming over with the trays when I heard a deep-throated rumble from outside. Katie and I both turned to look out of the window where we saw the beautiful curves of the E-Type pull into the car park.

Unloading the trays onto the table, James winked at Katie and said, "Looks like your audience just got a bit bigger."

He had obviously prepared for that, since there were four coffees, a pot of tea for Katie, and one diet Coke along with a plate of assorted cakes and biscuits. He pulled over two more chairs and Katie and I adjusted ours so we could all fit round the table. He was just returning the trays to the counter when Andy and Rod came through the door.

There were greetings, and introductions for Katie, as we all made ourselves comfortable round the table. Abby was the first one to grab a cake, a calorie-loaded slab of chocolate caramel shortbread, but Katie and I weren't far behind, blueberry muffins for us. It must be a girl thing because the three men seemed to take no notice of the remaining goodies on the plate. Then I realised it was actually a man thing. None of them wanted to be the first to succumb.

Abby would have none of it. "Go on, Dad. They're really scrummy."

Smiling at her with great tenderness, he also took a piece of chocolate caramel, and the others followed suit, taking a Kit-Kat and a jam tart.

We all listened with the greatest attention as Katie told her story, with not more than a million interruptions from Abby. When the two of them had finished, Andy told us what he'd discovered from his quick foray down the blocked-off road. Suggesting that he was acting for the farmer who owned the hedge and the tree which had been assaulted by the Toyota, he had learnt that, while the vehicle was probably a write-off, its occupants weren't. The driver claimed he couldn't remember what happened. There were no witnesses.

Finishing his brief account, Andy looked across the table at Katie. "If you do lose your job for today's work, come to me. You did well. I'll find a place for you."

Abby immediately looked concerned. "Is that true, Miss Cooper? Could you really lose your job?"

James intervened. "She could, but she won't. I'll make sure of that."

And that finished it. No-one doubted he could do just what he said.

There then began a debate about whether the two in the Toyota were actually trying to make a grab for Abby, or whether they were only following in the hope of being led to James and me.

Since Abby was sitting next to James, he couldn't see her face, but I could tell she was becoming anxious again, so I intervened to cut that short.

"No, It wasn't Abby they wanted. Look... ... It's clear those guys were Borisov's men, and we know he is connected somehow to Mellisse. We know Mellisse is desperate enough to try anything to get his hands on me, so I don't think there's any doubt... ... I'm the target."

I'd hoped that would make Abby feel better; that this was my nightmare, not hers. But, from look in her eyes, I'm not sure it helped.

The others were nodding.

"So where does that leave us?" asked Andy. "You want to bring in the police?"

He looked from me to James and waited. Rod just kept quiet, staring into his coffee. He looked like a guy with a lot on his mind. I couldn't make him out.

James seemed to be waiting for me to speak, but I didn't know what to tell him. I didn't want the police involved now any more than I had on Saturday, but this was no longer just about me. Other people were getting hurt and I didn't know how we could stop it.

"Excuse me."

We all turned towards Katie.

I was glad of the interruption. Maybe someone else had a good idea.

"I know you all have a lot to sort out, but... ... well, I need to get home. My car's a bit bent and... ... er... ... since I can't drive it, I'm stuck."

She watched James hopefully, but before he could respond another thought struck her.

"And what am I going to tell the insurance people? Will they tell the police? Should I?"

She put her hands up to her head, fingertips just touching in her hair, and we heard her mumble, "Ah man! What a mess!"

James stood up.

"Don't worry about it, Katie. I'll take care of it."

Taking out his mobile phone, he wandered over to the window. He needn't have bothered because we were all eves-dropping on his end of the conversation anyway. After a few minutes he came back to the table.

"All done," he said. "No insurers. No police."

"Who d'you get?" asked Andy.

"Billy," replied James, sitting down. Andy nodded.

"Friend of mine," said James to Katie. "Runs a used car place over near Burton. He'll be out here with a tow-truck in half an hour or so. Pick up your 206 and get it back to you in a few days. Good as new."

"Yeah," said Katie, "but… …"

"I know," interrupted James. "Don't worry about the cost. I owe you. Oh… … and he's bringing you a spare to be going on with. All his courtesy cars are booked out, but he's got something he took a couple of days ago in part exchange. It's not been spruced up, but I told him you wouldn't mind that."

"OK," she said. "Cheers. Appreciate."

I could tell she was wondering what sort of clunker she was being saddled with, but didn't like to argue if James was picking up the tab for her repairs.

"Now," said James, "let's see what we can come up with while we wait for Billy."

Not a lot. We talked a great deal. Even Rod joined in, but we couldn't come up with a plan to neutralise Mellisse and Borisov that didn't stray across the lines of legality by quite a hefty margin. James was in enough trouble with the police over Phil Simmons' death without exposing himself to more scrutiny. And, as Andy vigorously pointed out, RRISC was a legitimate and highly respected business, so much so that certain police authorities even paid for the use of their training facilities. He was not going to jeopardise that. Against all my instincts, I even suggested tentatively that the best course might be to tell the police everything. I hated the thought of doing it, and was very afraid of what the consequences might be for me.

I needn't have worried. None of the men had any confidence that the police would be able to pursue the case objectively, fixated as they were already on James as the likely killer of Phil Simmons. I could have spoken up then and confessed to having been in the wood, but I didn't see the point. A person with my background was hardly likely to be accepted as a reliable witness. More likely, the police would just assume James and I were in collusion.

We were still debating when we heard the sound of a heavy diesel coming down the track by the canal. Katie was facing the window so she saw it first and I noticed a shadow of disappointment cross her face. I turned round so I could see outside and realised immediately the reason for her lack of enthusiasm. Preceding the gleaming, bright orange tow-truck down the track was a small far-from-gleaming Mini of the old 1960s vintage. Dark green under its coating of dust and grime, it was not an object to send anyone, let alone Katie, into transports of delight.

I caught her eye and gave her a rueful smile. She shrugged and, after a moment, smiled back. It was a beggars-can't-be-choosers thing.

I didn't think James had caught the exchange between Katie and me but, when he stood to go outside to greet the newcomers, he winked at Katie and said, "It can't be as bad as all that."

In the end, we all went out to watch the poor old 206 being hauled up onto the flat bed of the tow-truck. The Mini sat there forlornly, between Andy's gleaming E-Type and an equally beautiful Mercedes CLK 320. According to the plate, the soft-top Merc was about a year old but, sitting there with the top down, it looked immaculate.

Billy was a tall guy, wiry and tough-looking, with a strong west-country accent. In his smart grey suit, he wasn't my image of a typical used-car salesman. I wondered how he'd managed to squeeze his legs into the Mini. I assumed he must have been its driver as I'd seen a different man in overalls manoeuvring the tow-truck into position. James and Billy shook hands and, after quick introductions all round, drew apart from the rest of us to stand at the rear of the mini. The mechanic with the truck asked Katie for her keys, and checked whether there was anything in the car that she wanted to remove before he took it away.

There was all the stuff from school, plus her shoulder bag, a road atlas, and the highly colourful hat which she liked to wear when driving with the top down. There were other bits and pieces as well, and initially she said she wouldn't be needing them, but the mechanic persuaded her that it would be best to clear out the car completely. Abby and I helped her but, once we were loaded, we weren't sure where to put everything. James, who had obviously been watching us, realised the problem and beckoned us over.

As we approached, Billy called out, "It's OK. You can put it straight in. The car's open."

We started to ease round them to get to the Mini, but Billy lifted a hand to stop us, saying nothing, but giving James an oddly questioning look.

Something was up. I could tell from James's expression, absolutely straight-faced but with a very slight crinkling around the eyes. It didn't occur to me to wonder how I could come to read him so well in just a couple of days. But I was right.

"I'm sorry, Katie," he said. "I should have explained. This really was the best Billy could do at such short notice."

He took her arm and turned her slightly so that she was facing not the Mini but the Mercedes.

"I told Billy you'd like one with a folding top, and he just happened to have this handy."

Katie's jaw dropped at the same time as the box she was carrying. Fortunately, it was Abby who was holding the laptop.

"If it's not to your liking," drawled Billy, smiling as he realised what was going on, "I could probably find you something else in a day or two."

We all looked at Katie, and we knew he wouldn't have to.

"It's going to take a while to get yours fixed up," said James. "So have some fun with the Merc in the meantime."

We never did see the owner of the Mini.

Thirty-Eight

Rome – 3.20 pm

Nadera Husseini lay back on the double bed and gazed at the ceiling of her hotel room. It wasn't much to look at, just a neutral shade of pale cream merging with walls of the same colour, square corners with no fancy cornice. In fact, it was just what you might expect of a small, clean, two-star, family-run establishment within walking distance of Rome's Termini Station. The plainness of the ceiling, or indeed the walls, or the furnishings, was of little consequence to Nadera. She wasn't seeing any of them.

The stare of her unfocussed eyes was completely disconnected from the turbulent images playing in her mind. She couldn't get rid of them. She tried to block them out by thinking how different her future would now be. She told herself that what she had done was necessary, as indeed it was, that it had to be done that way, which it did, and that her victim had deserved his fate, which may have been true. But no amount of rationalisation could neutralise the emotional trauma of brutal, cold-blooded murder.

In all her years of working for Al-Mubarak, she had never even come close to carrying out an act of such brutality as that which she had committed the previous evening on a quiet canal in Santa Croce. Although she had been able to summon up all the resolution needed for that moment of execution, the hours which followed were filled with an almost unbearable mix of shame and disgust. It was true that it was pressure from Al-Mubarak which had forced her into it but, even under pressure, you always have a choice. She just hoped she could live with hers.

The body would probably have been discovered by now, and might already have been identified as the fugitive John Salisbury. The identification was important, so she had made sure that the passport in his pocket was not the one in the name of Josh Barnett, but was in fact the original which Salisbury had obtained before the idea of plotting to defraud had ever crossed his mind. While it was true that John no longer looked much like the photo in the passport, taken some nine years previously, that was not going to be an issue.

In the quiet water of an old boathouse beneath a decaying palazzo, a middle-aged Englishman had taken in his last breath of air before, acquiescent in alcohol-induced torpor, he was dragged under the surface to be introduced to the spinning propeller of a water-taxi, temporarily and unofficially borrowed for the purpose. Blood, bone and brains from disintegrating face and fingers had briefly discoloured the murky water before Nadera had hauled the mutilated body from the vicious blades. Less than twenty minutes later, the corpse lay bobbing gently in a canal not far from the Doge's Palace in the San Marco district of Venice. In a narrow street adjacent to the canal was a small hotel in the Best Western group which had, earlier that day, accepted a telephone reservation from an English gentleman claiming to be John Salisbury.

It would not be difficult for the police to piece together the events of that evening. Arriving in Venice, probably by train since there was no record of his flying into Marco Polo, Salisbury had phoned around to find a hotel which could accommodate him. Having made the reservation, he had eaten in a restaurant off the Piazza San Marco, consuming two bottles of wine in the process. Witnesses, when questioned later by the police, would testify to having seen him, or at least someone answering to his description, in the restaurant and also later in the evening weaving his way along the Calle Larga San Marco, carrying a small holdall. No-one had actually seen him fall in the canal, but it was obvious what must have happened. A drunken lurch, and in he went, to be hit almost immediately by a passing water-taxi whose driver didn't realise, or didn't care, that something had been chopped to pieces by his propeller.

No witnesses to anything untoward, no evidence of foul play, no evidence of anything other than a tragic accident. Even the holdall, left at the side of the canal, contributed to this conclusion. Containing both cash, in the form of Euros, and American Express travellers cheques, along with a couple of changes of clothes, the leather bag had been left undisturbed. Unfortunately for those who would be interested, neither the holdall nor his clothing contained any information which could be used to locate the missing Saudi money. That was destined to remain a permanent mystery, even to Al-Mubarak.

Returning the borrowed water-taxi to its mooring where, apparently, its absence had not been noticed, Nadera and her accomplice had made their way on foot across the city to the Santa Lucia railway station. They had some time to wait before they could board the 6:43 train to Rome, but neither of them felt much like talking. So they had sat on the platform, each occupied with their own thoughts, in less than companionable silence. A nondescript pair of travellers, she looked nothing like a Saudi intelligence agent, and no-one would ever take her companion to be a former member of the British Paras.

Arriving in Rome soon after 11.00, it had not taken many calls from a station pay phone to find a small hotel with rooms to spare for one night. They needed the sleep before moving on to whatever was next in store. Neither could know what that would be until contact had been made with Al-Mubarak.

Nadera's mobile phone lay beside her on the pale yellow bedspread, just out of reach of her right hand. It didn't appear to be anything special, but its advanced American technology allowed her to speak to Al-Mubarak without either of them needing to worry about who was monitoring the airwaves. It was time to make the call. She had been rehearsing what to say for the past half hour, the words to use, the tone of voice, but she still wasn't sure whether she could pull it off. She listened for sounds of her companion in the room next door, but heard nothing. Maybe he was lying down as well. No, more likely he had gone down to the hotel's small bar come lounge to make use of its free internet terminal. She remembered him saying that there was something he wanted to check on but, in her distressed state of mind, she hadn't given it much thought.

She sat up, swinging her legs over the edge of the bed and, after taking a deep breath, reached for her phone. Pressing the speed-dial for Al-Mubarak, she listened and waited. She had no idea where he might be; Riyadh, Paris, London, even New York. She didn't care where her call was routed to, just as long as it wasn't Rome.

The well-known voice answered with customary brusqueness, demanding to know where she was.

"Hiding," she replied evasively, and allowed Al-Mubarak's explosive response to die down before she resumed her script. She had told herself before making the call that she would have to sound scared and confused but, now that she was actually speaking to the man who had shaped her life, the fear in her voice was no pretence.

"The job is finished, just as you wanted."

"Good, Nadera. Good. I knew I could count on you. When did you complete the … … business?"

"Last night, just as you said… … After Talbot arrived. Since he was coming anyway, I waited for him. But that was my mistake wasn't it?"

"What mistake? You have got the documents, haven't you?"

"Talbot has them. He cleared out Salisbury's hotel room. He has all the papers… … No, he isn't here! Do you think I'd be speaking to you now if he was?"

She knew Al-Mubarak would be confused by her response, and she had to keep him off balance, which was not an easy thing to accomplish when dealing with a man as single-minded and ruthless as he was.

"Why did you send Talbot to kill me?"

This wasn't easy. She had never lied to Al-Mubarak before. He had been both friend and mentor, albeit a very demanding one, and she had always tried her very best to attain the high standards he set for her. As she listened to the silence her question had generated, she reminded herself that he didn't own her, that she had a right to choose her own life. It was a right that many women in her country had no understanding of, but it was a right she was now prepared to fight for, even kill for.

"Nadera, I don't understand you. Talbot went to help you. Even do the job for you. But he certainly had no instructions to harm you. Not in any way. You must be mistaken."

It was her turn to stretch out the silence, to gather herself for the big lie.

"I was not mistaken. Talbot tried to stick a knife in me and drop me in the canal, so how does that fit with someone who is not here to harm me? Tell me that!"

"Nadera, believe me, he had no instructions to do that."

More silence, as both thought carefully what to say next.

"I want to believe you," said Nadera finally. "But if you did not tell him to get rid of me, then who did, and why?"

"I'll find out," replied Al-Mubarak, "but it's just possible that he is acting on his own. Did you say he has Salisbury's papers?"

"Yes."

"All of them?"

"Everything. I tried to stop him, but that was when he turned on me and tried to dispose of me in the canal."

"You should not have allowed him to do that. Those papers were your responsibility... ... But I think we know what it is that he is after, don't we?"

Nadera managed to turn her sigh of relief that she had Al-Mubarak hooked, into a gasp of disbelief that Talbot could be so stupid.

"Surely he must know that you will find him. Even with Salisbury's money, he can't hide forever."

"I suspect he believes he is a more capable man than Salisbury, and indeed he is. But you are right, Nadera, I will find him. Have you any idea where is he now?"

"None. It's over twelve hours since I lost him, and I've been keeping out of sight ever since."

"Nadera, Nadera. Didn't I teach you better than that? Why did you not call me immediately?"

She had been waiting for this question and everything now hinged on whether he accepted her answer. She had rehearsed the words already, but she still hesitated before speaking, as though reluctant to tell him what she feared.

"After Talbot attacked me, I thought you might have decided that I had become too involved with John Salisbury, and was no longer to be trusted. I thought you had ordered Talbot to dispose of me. I was scared, so I made my way to the Ospedale Civile and hid in the ladies' room."

Al-Mubarak's voice was soft, thoughtful, as he replied. "If that is what you believed, Nadera, why are you calling me now?"

"Because I've had time to think. Talbot's attack was too clumsy and, on past experience, your plans for disposal have been rather more subtle than a knife in the ribs. And I still have something Talbot wants… … something you also want… … the numbers to Salisbury's accounts. The papers alone will not be enough."

"So you need to get out of Venice."

"Yes. Talbot will know by now that he doesn't have the account numbers, and he will be looking for me. I've booked a seat on the KLM flight from Marco Polo to Zurich this afternoon."

"If he's looking for you, there's a good chance he'll be watching the airport."

"I know, but he can't be everywhere. I'll have to take the chance."

"Wait a minute, Nadera. I have a contact in Mestre. He doesn't work for me, but he is a good Muslim and has helped us in the past. Tell me where you are, and I'll have him come and find you. He'll be able to get you safely out of Venice."

She hadn't expected this but a moment's reflection convinced her that Al-Mubarak's suggestion could work to her advantage. After all, since she wasn't in Venice, there was no possibility of anyone actually finding her. If she arranged a meeting and failed to show, Al-Mubarak would be forced to at least consider whether Talbot had got to her first.

He obviously misinterpreted her hesitation, as he continued, "I have absolutely no reason to harm you, Nadera. In fact, after what you have said, I have every reason to keep you safe. On my father's grave, I promise you will not be hurt. Forget your flight and just tell me where you are. We'll get you out of there."

"Give me a moment," she replied, as though thinking of a rendezvous. It didn't really matter where she chose, although it had to sound authentic.

"I'll be at the Holocaust memorial in the Jewish ghetto at 3.00."

Al-Mubarak chuckled. "A good choice, Nadera. Talbot is not likely to look for a Saudi girl amongst the Jews. I'll email Fahd your official photo. He will show you this, so you know to trust him. He has a visa to work in a tourist bureau in Mestre. He will show you this also. Do as he tells you and I will see you here in Riyadh tomorrow."

"Thank you. I will do as you say."

She cut the connection and, with a huge sigh, collapsed back onto the bed.

It was done, and Al-Mubarak had actually believed her. She closed her eyes and breathed deeply. It was odd, but the tension of her conversation with Al-Mubarak seemed to have cleared her mind of the horrors of yesterday evening. It was not that she didn't remember, but the recollection was no longer quite so vivid.

Time to bring her accomplice up to date, and also to discover what his own research had thrown up.

She gave herself a few moments more to allow the tension to bleed away before she sat up. She was looking around for her shoes when she heard the sound of a door closing. Someone had entered the room next door from the corridor. Glancing over at the adjoining door, she was not surprised when, a moment later, it was jerked open to reveal her rather dishevelled and out-of-breath accomplice.

"Change of plan," he said. "You'd better come and look at this."

"What is it, John?" asked Nadera, looking fondly at the intruder.

John Salisbury, alive and well, though somewhat breathless, reached for her hand to pull her up off the bed.

"We need to go to England," he said.

Thirty-Nine

Fradley Junction – 5.30 pm

The orange tow-truck was first to leave Fradley Junction. The mechanic drove, with Billy up front beside him, and the 206 securely strapped down behind. As they pulled away, Billy lowered his window and gave a cheerful wave while shouting to Katie, "Mind you don't bend it." I did wonder whether Katie might be so awed at the prospect of driving the CLK that she wouldn't really enjoy it, but I needn't have worried. As she prepared to follow the tow-truck down the drive, I think we all sensed her suppressed excitement. She was trying to hide it, as she looked over the unfamiliar controls trying to remember Billy's instructions, but her apparent nonchalance didn't really convince us. I was glad. I felt she needed something to take her mind off the stresses of the afternoon.

We were debating whether to adjourn to the café for another drink when James's phone rang. It was Surjit calling from the Dower House. James had brought him up to date earlier and asked him to check security around the premises. There was a dark blue Rav4, another one, parked on the grass verge about one hundred yards from the pillared entrance to the drive up to the Dower House. I wondered whether Borisov had done a deal with Toyota for a job lot. It was on the opposite side of the road just at the point where it bent around to the right so, helped by the branches of overhanging trees, the vehicle was not readily visible from any distance. The entrance to the driveway, however, would certainly be visible to the two occupants of the Toyota.

That was bad enough but Surjit had also contacted the farm. Knowing about the tail from the school, and the stakeout at the Dower House, it had occurred to him that, if they were covering all possibilities, it was likely that the farm was also being watched. He was right.

There had been no reply from the farmhouse, which was not entirely surprising. Chick was probably out working and Rachel would have been collecting Debbie from school. Not having Chick's mobile number, Surjit had rung the farm shop and spoken to the girl in charge. At first she had been a little nervous, never having met him or spoken to him before, but she became more talkative after he'd explained that he worked for James Montrayne and was ringing from the Dower House. Not wanting to alarm her, he told her that some friends of James were expecting to meet him there and he asked if she'd noticed anyone hanging around, probably two of them, probably in some type of 4x4.

"I can see them now," she had said, and offered to go and give them a message.

Thanking her, but saying that wouldn't be necessary, Surjit had just asked her if she could see the number plate so he could be sure it was the right people. No problem, she'd said, as the 4x4 was parked facing the shop, not sideways on. He then let her chatter away for a few minutes as she explained that she'd wondered who they were as they'd been there about half an hour, obviously weren't interested in the farm tour, hadn't come into the shop to buy anything, and only seemed to be interested in comings and goings in the car park.

Telling her not to worry and someone would be over to meet them soon, Surjit had rung off, and immediately called James.

The 4x4 was still there twenty-seven minutes later when two armed response vehicles of Staffordshire's Tactical Support Team cruised into the car park, sirens off, but with headlights and light-bars flashing. Chick was in the farm shop at the time, helping the girls cash-up the day's takings, and he was later able to give us a blow-by-blow account of the mayhem my phone call had stirred up.

It had been James's idea to bring the police in, despite Rod's fears that, if these were indeed Borisov's men, they would undoubtedly be armed. There would be visitors at the farm, he said, women and kids mostly, and someone could easily get hurt if the police miscalculated. James had argued that his reservations about police competence did not extend to the armed response team, and so the call was made. By me, since a female voice was needed to give credibility.

999 got me a fast response. I was a scared mum with two young kids come to let them have some fun on the farm after school. Two men in dark clothes had arrived in a dark blue 4x4 and had been acting very strangely. They didn't do the tour, didn't go in the shop. They just watched the kids in the playground. I was worried for the kids so I'd written down the number of their car, and had approached it on the side away from where they were standing. On looking inside, I had seen a gun, half-covered by a blanket lying on the back seat. I was scared. I didn't know what to do. I was desperate. I needed help. I was brilliant.

It helped that the guys were back in their car when the police surged in, but Chick said they were superb. And scary as hell in their dark clothes, body armour, helmets, and all with webbing belts hung with Glock 7 automatic pistols. In less than five seconds, according to Chick, the black 4x4 was surrounded by officers pointing their Heckler and Koch MP5s into the vehicle, but in such a way that no officer was directly in the line of fire of any other. All civilians, children and adults, magically found themselves way outside the police perimeter.

Half a minute later, both of Borisov's men were flat on the ground beside their vehicle, hands cuffed behind their backs. They had given up without protest. Fast.

Both had been armed, one with a pistol in a shoulder holster, the other carrying one stuffed in his belt. Chick and the girls had watched open-mouthed from the farm shop as police recovered a rifle and a shotgun from the rear of the 4x4.

Rod had been right about the weapons and I grinned at him in relief. I was finding my attitude towards him changing. At first, he'd been careful not to catch my eye so, on the first occasion that he had done, I had offered a brief smile in what I hoped he would take as an apology for what had happened earlier. Being here with him, and remembering what James had told me, I found I was feeling increasingly sorry for my violent outburst. I had remembered something which I once said to a Street Pastor who offered me coffee and doughnut late one night in the centre of Birmingham. He was a big guy, tall and well-built, probably a prop-forward on the University rugby team. In spite of his size he'd been quietly spoken, obviously well-meaning, but clearly hadn't a clue what caused girls like me to be living as we were. I'd finished our brief conversation by saying, "You can't understand me, because you don't live my life." I had judged Rod, without understanding his life. And it was beginning to look as though I might have been totally wrong.

We all listened as Chick phoned the action through, in real time, to James on his mobile. He'd held it out on speakerphone for us all to hear. We never did discover whether the police eventually realised that the scared young mum had not made her phone call from anywhere in the vicinity of Heighley Grange farm. But we were totally sure they were never going to find the phone. It was a cheap, untraceable, pay-as-you-go model, which was now lying, dismembered and half-buried by black mud, at the bottom of the Trent and Mersey canal.

Which only left the two at the Dower House.

James and Andy seemed surprised that Borisov should have left his men so exposed, but this was a gift horse they weren't going to examine too closely.

James reckoned the police could be used again for the pair at the Dower House. Time wasn't critical; no-one was in immediate danger. The previous tactic just needed a few variations. The model and colour of the vehicle was a huge plus. Had they been anything else, we'd have had to come up with a completely different plan.

James made the call this time, and it wasn't 999. He dialled the direct line of the Assistant Chief Constable. He even had it on speed-dial in his mobile phone.

"You never know," he said as he dialled, "when these things might be useful."

We waited as it rang, wondering whether it was burping out its tone to an empty office, and then it was picked up.

"Ah, David. This is James Montrayne… … … No, this has nothing to do with Phil Simmons… … … I know you can't. I wouldn't expect you to interfere. Listen, David, you remember when Abby was kidnapped two years ago?"

ACC David Fletcher, then Chief Superintendent Fletcher, had overseen the police investigation following Abby's kidnap. A skilled and efficient officer, he and James had got on well together, surprising perhaps, given the circumstances, and they had met several times since at different functions. James had told us this as he explained why he was dialling direct rather than using 999.

"Yes, thanks, David. She's fine. In fact she's with me now. But the thing is, I think someone's trying to snatch her again… … … No, no danger at the moment. Perfectly safe… … … Have you seen a report yet of a dark-blue Toyota Rav4 lurking outside my school this afternoon?"

After that, it didn't take much to bait the hook. A dark blue Toyota, probably the same one, now parked on the verge, half hidden by trees, just short of the entrance to the Dower House. And then to give that little tug, just to lodge the hook securely, James said, almost as an after thought, "If they're serious about this, they may just have someone watching Heighley Grange farm. If they've done their homework, they'll know that Abby often goes there after school."

By the grin on James's face, and the way he lifted his phone slightly from his ear, we could all tell that ACC Fletcher was very much aware of recent events at the farm. He had probably been keeping a close eye on things, as this was not everyday fare for the Staffordshire police.

A few more exchanges and the conversation was over.

"The boys in blue have their uses," said Andy, as James returned his phone to his jacket pocket.

"Occasionally," snorted Rod, "when they're not too busy harassing motorists, or locking up blokes who are just trying to protect their own property."

We'd all heard the story on the morning news of a former soldier accused of assault because he tried to stop a gang of teenage thugs from terrorising his street. He was arrested; the gang went free. The British justice system at its most ludicrous.

"Well," said James. "This time they *are* being useful. Fletcher is sending the same two teams to the Dower House with helicopter surveillance."

We waited.

Andy suggested we have another drink but the café owner said he was getting ready to close. Nobody tried to persuade him otherwise.

We hovered around the courtyard waiting for news from Surjit. He had called briefly before James had rung the ACC, to say he had repositioned one of the remote cameras to look directly down into the Rav4, but there had been nothing since.

These guys were not used to waiting while others leapt into the heat of the action. Rod paced up and down the wharf, while Andy got out his mobile. I didn't know who he was calling, since he was walking away from us down the tow-path before he was connected. I watched as he stood still by a beautifully painted narrow-boat and wondered with mild curiosity why the call seemed to be getting so heated. I could hear no words, but the body language was plain to see. Jerky movements, turning on the spot, looking up at the sky one moment and then down at the ground, finally looking at his phone in exasperation and terminating the call.

When he saw me watching, he shrugged his shoulders, and started walking back, dialling another number. This time he called his office and began what turned out to be quite a lengthy conversation with Mel. James sat on a wooden seat and watched a narrow-boat cruising slowly towards the next lock. Abby kept looking at her dad and then at me, and several times seemed on the point of saying something which never quite made it past her lips. I could sense her edginess so I reached for her hand and told James we were going to watch the boat go through the lock.

I was on edge too, because this wasn't about Abby, or James. This was about me. Ray's determination to find me, and to do whatever it was he had in mind for me. It all made me wonder whether there was any real chance of ever being free of him. And how was Borisov going to react to losing six men in one day?

We stood on the narrow hump-backed bridge and looked down at the lock gates. We listened to the water roaring below us as the level behind the gates dropped to the level on our side. Soon the level would be the same on both sides of the gates and they would be able to open and allow the narrow-boat to enter the lock.

Abby was explaining all this to me with the confidence of a regular visitor to the canal, but I wasn't really listening. I pretended, for her sake, and I think I got away with it, but it wasn't easy.

The tension had caused my mind to drift back to another time of waiting. The room had been small and quiet, smelling slightly of disinfectant and aniseed. The disinfectant made sense but I never understood about the aniseed. I remembered sitting in that room, trying not to cry or scream or hit someone, waiting for the result of my latest HIV test. I knew I should have insisted the guy used protection, but he always gave me a good tip on top of the normal rate, so I had just let him get on with it. I needed every pound I could find for my escape plan. Afterwards, I had watched him carefully as he'd opened the same brown, slightly scuffed, leather briefcase, to take out the same white envelope, with the same number of crisp £20 notes. The thing that was not the same, the thing that sent my heart racing, caught my breath in my throat and scared me rigid, was what lay under the white envelope. It was an A5 size leaflet, coloured patterns and printing, but the only thing I noticed before he shut the case was the title, which said in big letters Fuzeon and, in slightly smaller letters underneath, Enfuvirtide T-20.

Why was my latest client carrying a leaflet on the most recent drug to be approved in the UK for the treatment of HIV/AIDS?

Closing the case, he had looked at me, and obviously noticed the stricken look on my face. He had smiled, a little sadly I thought, and said as he walked to the door, "Don't look so surprised, Di. Where else do you think I got it, if not from you?"

It hadn't been me. I was sure. But not so sure that I didn't rush to the clinic as soon as I could to get myself tested. Not so sure that I didn't sit there with a block of ice in my stomach as I waited for the result.

That block of ice weighed heavy once again as we waited there on that narrow bridge confronted by a scene of postcard tranquillity. The bow of the narrow-boat emerged from under the bridge to enter the lock through gates which had opened in front of my eyes, and which I had no memory of seeing happen.

We had a good view and Abby was enthralled. She chattered on and didn't seem to mind that she wasn't getting much in the way of answers.

Back then, at the clinic, the news had been good. Reassuring. But it had prompted me to think seriously about getting out of that life, before the day came when the news would not be good, and I was sentenced to a shortened life with no parole.

Now, I waited again. Hopefully for good news. But even if it was, and all the bad guys were taken away and locked up for as long as possible, at the very least on a range of firearms offences, this would not be the end of it.

Even if Mellisse decided it should be, that I wasn't worth the effort, Borisov would not.

Borisov would want his revenge.

He would want it slow, and lingering, and exquisitely excruciating and, from what I knew of him, he was not one to worry much over collateral damage.

Forty

Stazione Termini, Rome – 6.25 pm

John Salisbury peered out at the station platform from the window of his three-berth sleeper. He had pulled down the blind immediately on entering the compartment thirteen minutes previously and now had to squint around the edges. He knew that the possibility of being seen and recognised was about as remote as the chance of being mistaken for George Clooney, but even so it was a risk not worth taking. He was dead, thoroughly and completely, at least officially, and he needed to stay that way.

  He was also alone, and that was what worried him. Nadera had been right to insist that they travel to the station separately. A couple is both more noticeable and more memorable than a single nondescript man or woman, especially if it is a couple that certain people may be looking for. Not that Al-Mubarak's men really would be looking for a couple in Rome, at least not yet, but Nadera wanted to be sure of leaving no trail particularly on CCTV. Now, as he waited in the compartment, Salisbury found his anxiety growing with every minute that they had to be apart. He had bought the tickets for the sleeper with his Josh Barnett credit card issued over a year ago by a small bank in Liechtenstein. He didn't need the three berths but, at the last minute, this was all that was available. He had sent a text to Nadera's phone telling her the number of the compartment, and then he waited.

  The numbers of people on the platform had swelled briefly and then thinned down as it began to near departure time. She had left the hotel before him, but there was still no sign of her.

  A slight scuffling on the other side of the compartment door caused him to twist round sharply, but the trundling sound of little wheels on the bottom of suitcases told him it was just a couple of passengers passing in the corridor outside.

  Back to the window, easing the blind away, first one side then the other. Nothing.

  Or was there?

  A young blond girl, early twenties maybe, strolled leisurely onto the platform. She wore a Michigan University tee-shirt which did nothing to hide the contours of her upper body and the briefest of shorts which showed as much tanned leg as possible without offending any decency laws or, at least, the official ones. As she looked up and down the platform, wisps of straw-coloured hair drifted around her face, half-hidden by huge round sunglasses.

As she turned, he caught sight of a well-stuffed backpack with a rolled jacket held fast under two of its elasticated loops. A brown suede jacket which he had last seen across the back of a chair in Nadera's hotel room.

He took a deep breath and let it out slowly as he watched her set her gaze on a particular section of the train some way down the platform from him, and walk slowly but purposefully towards it. As she drew close to the selected carriage, she passed out of his line of sight.

He sat on the edge of his narrow bed and waited, expecting to hear at any moment a light tap on the compartment door.

Nothing.

Three minutes passed, and then it was 6:36, departure time.

He was looking at his watch when he felt the slight jerk. He jumped up and pulled the blind clear of the window. No doubt. They were moving.

He reached for his jacket which lay on the bed and extracted his phone from the inside pocket. He had just finished typing in the message *Where are you?* and was about to press send when he heard a scraping in the corridor followed by a firm knock on the door. Why had he expected a light tap? Nadera wasn't a scared mouse by anyone's standard.

He opened the door and she grinned at him as she brushed past dragging her backpack behind her. Slamming the door, he caught her free arm and turned her towards him. Given a moment, anger would have swelled to replace the swiftly departing anxiety, anger fuelled rather than quenched by her obvious safety. But she didn't allow him that moment. Before he could demand where she had been, and why she hadn't told him of her plans, she had dropped her backpack to the floor and flung both her arms around his neck. He felt the softness of her lips brushing against his own and, since his mouth was opening to rebuke her, she began teasing him with her tongue. Against such treatment, his anger stood no chance.

A while later, the blond wig discarded, Nadera sat at the end of the lower bunk, her legs tucked under her, and her back against the carriage wall adjacent to the window. She was content. Despite the strength of their rapidly developing affection for each other, John had been unusually restrained in the area of physical intimacy. She had begun to wonder whether he thought himself too old for her, in spite of the obvious pleasure her company gave him. For herself, she had no doubts. She loved him, pure and simple, and not just because he offered a chance to escape from a life she hated, and from the control of a man she despised.

The tenderness and passion in his recent embrace had both surprised and electrified her, and if he had tried to remove her clothes and draw her down onto the bed, she would not have resisted, in spite of the constraints of her faith and her culture. But he hadn't and, in a strange way, she was glad. She had never met a man who showed her so much respect, and now she was sure love was returned, she was content to wait for the consummation of that love until he had put this mad scheme behind him.

She gazed at him, sitting awkwardly at the other end of the bunk, and smiled.

"We did it, John. I think we actually did it."

Salisbury nodded, but didn't look happy.

"It shouldn't have been you that had to kill him."

She knew this had been troubling him, but there really hadn't been any other way.

"John, we talked about this. You might have taken that money, but you never killed anyone in your life."

"Neither had you before yesterday."

"No, but at least I had been trained for it. Al-Mubarak took care of that."

She smiled, a little sadly. "It was training I never thought I'd need, but when I learnt Dave Talbot had been sent to kill you, I knew then we had no choice."

He nodded and gave a little shrug.

"I expect you're right." He thought for a moment. "I'd probably have ended up letting him drown me, or if I'd done that bit right and drowned him, I'd have got my own face and fingers chopped up in the propeller."

Nadera thought he was probably right, but decided it was best not to agree too readily.

"Killing him, I didn't really mind," she said. "He was an enemy, a killer himself, possibly many times over if he has worked long for Al-Mubarak... ... ... I did not enjoy the butchering of his hands and face, but it was necessary."

Salisbury looked at her, knowing that she had done skilfully and professionally what he had not been qualified to do. It unsettled him. He somehow felt less manly because of it, and he couldn't quite work out why this didn't seem to be a consideration with her.

"Do you think it will work?" he asked. "I mean, will the police, or coroner, or whoever, actually believe that body is me and not Dave Talbot?"

"Yes," said Nadera firmly. "They will believe it because they have no reason not to. And we are safe, my love. Safe from him; safe from the police; safe from Al-Mubarak; safe from everyone."

She paused, deciding a little revision was necessary.

"At least, we were safe until you got this ... ... this ... ... stupid idea, to go back to England."

Salisbury swung his legs off the bunk and slid along to her end. He reached out and took her left hand in his right. He knew she didn't like the way he kept logging on to the *Lichfield Daily News* website, thinking it best if he could completely cut himself off from his past. But he couldn't help himself. He was driven by a curiosity, seated in his longing for the home he had loved. He had always thought it couldn't do any harm, just keeping up to date with what was happening in the old town. Until today.

When using the internet in that small hotel lounge at lunchtime, Salisbury had learnt of Phil Simmons' death. He had also read Corrina Rigby's article. That was when he decided.

"I have to go, my love. I can't help it, and maybe it is stupid, but it's something I have to do."

"But why, John. Just after we have finally got you dead, so no-one will be looking for you, ever again. Why risk it all over something you can't change?"

Salisbury turned slightly, still holding onto her hand, but enough to be able to look into her face.

"I liked Phil Simmons. Always did. And I could never quite get rid of the feeling that, in doing what I did, I let him down. Maybe I can't change what's past ... ... well, of course I can't change it, but I may be able to change what's going to happen next."

"But how can you?" she asked, exasperated but trying to sound patient.

She wished they'd had more time to talk this through before having to book the train tickets, but that would probably have killed any chance they had of obtaining an overnight sleeper to Paris. In fact, they only had this compartment because of a last minute cancellation. In the end, after she had seen the *Lichfield News* articles for herself, she had reluctantly agreed to his rash scheme knowing there would be time to talk on the train. She had all night to talk him out of it since they were not due to arrive at the Gare de Bercy in Paris until 09:10 Tuesday morning. From Paris she would go with him to any place in the world, except maybe Saudi Arabia.

They were sitting, a little awkwardly, side by side on the narrow bed. She snuggled close and laid her head on his shoulder.

"Surely," she said, "You must realise that the people you will want to see, are the very people you must not see."

"Of course, I do," he replied, giving her hand a squeeze. "Which is why I can't do this without you. I want to stay dead, believe me. So, if there's any face to face stuff to be done, I'm afraid you'll have to do it."

She lifted her head and wriggled round to look him fully in the face.

"You're really serious about this, aren't you?"

He returned her gaze steadily.

"I am," he said quietly. "Phil Simmons was a good lad. Whatever it is that happened to him, he deserved better."

He paused, took a deep breath, and licked his lips, still keeping eye contact.

"I don't know this fellow, Montrayne. But I do know Natalie. She was devoted to Phil, just as he was to her. I suppose it's possible Montrayne was infatuated with her, even if she didn't care for him, and who knows what a bloke might do in those circumstances?"

"Bloke?" said Nadera, frowning as she savoured the new word. "What is this... ... bloke?"

"Oh, er... ... a chap," replied John adding, when he saw she still hadn't quite grasped it, "I mean a man."

"Ah. You think this, this bloke, killed from passion for Mr Simmons' wife?"

"Maybe," said John. "It's possible... ... I don't know. But if he did, I'm going to make sure he pays for it."

Nadera looked worried. "What do you mean to do to him?"

"I've not decided yet," he answered and, seeing the anxiety on her face, he added, "I may not have to do anything."

She was now looking very confused, so he tried to explain.

"If those reports in the paper are right, the police may already be looking in the right place. I just don't want to take the chance that they might make a botch of it. If I'd cared enough, I could have warned Phil not to take a job at Lichfield. I always thought there was something not quite right there." He smiled grimly. "Look who's talking... ... Anyway I told myself he'd be OK. He was a straight-up guy. He didn't go looking for trouble. I could have warned him... ... But I didn't. So, I owe him."

He was still holding onto her left hand, so Nadera raised her right to his cheek and rubbed it gently. She saw the inevitability and, because she loved him, she resigned herself to it.

"You'd better tell me," she said. "All of it."

So he did.

Forty-One

The Dower House – 6.30 pm

Abby and I had been at the bridge for about ten minutes before James called for us to come back. Although Abby produced a slight moan of disappointment at not seeing the complete navigation of the lock by the narrow-boat, her shoulders were drooping as we walked slowly back to the others, and she admitted that she would be glad to get home. I knew just how she felt.

I wanted to know what was happening, but James said he would explain as we drove back to the Dower House. With brief goodbyes, we climbed into our cars and Andy and Rod led the way in the E-type, back down the track beside the canal to the road where they turned right, and tore away with the subdued roar of its throaty twin exhausts. Rather more sedately, we turned left and cruised almost inaudibly in the direction of the Dower House.

I was sitting up front with James while Abby was strapped securely in the back. I half turned in my seat ready to prompt him to give us the news, when he forestalled me with a finger raised to his lips. At the same time, he glanced in his rear-view mirror to check on Abby. The mirror didn't work for me, so I turned further round to see if she was OK. She was lying back, looking very small against the plush, dove-grey leather, her eyes closed, breathing gently.

I turned back to James, wondering if he didn't want to wake her, or whether he was just trying to give her time to fall fully asleep. It turned out to be the latter since, after a couple of minutes and several glances in the mirror, he began to explain.

Surjit had been keeping an eye on the Toyota with his CCTV, waiting for the police to show up, when suddenly the two watchers were spooked by a helicopter which swept in without warning low over the trees. Even as the chopper came into view, the Toyota was already screaming away past the entrance to the Dower House, leaving twin streaks of churned earth on the grass verge. The helicopter had turned, hovered briefly and then set off in pursuit. Surjit had already picked up the phone to relay this development when an unmarked, dark-coloured, Range Rover flashed across his screen heading in the same direction as the Toyota. It had no light-bar on the roof but Surjit saw headlights and blue grill lights flashing. That was as much as he'd been able to pass on, other than his opinion that the occupants of the Toyota would have to be very fortunate indeed to escape this multiple pursuit.

As we approached the house, there was no mistaking the spot where the Toyota had been waiting. James slowed as we passed but there was nothing to see but the twin trenches dug by the spinning tyres of the four-wheel drive.

James pressed the remote to open the gates as we turned into the Dower House entrance. Gravel crunched under the tyres, almost masking the melody which told James he had an incoming text message. He glanced down at the display on the phone, now perched in its cradle, and then ignored it. The Maserati swept gently round the curve of the drive, hemmed in by trees on either side. Escaping the shade, we emerged into the golden glow of a beautiful spring evening but I had no time to appreciate it since James hit the brakes so fiercely that my seatbelt locked bruising my left shoulder as it was flung violently against the unyielding strap. Behind me, I heard Abby murmur sleepily, and then she was quiet.

Looking up, I expected to see black Toyotas and men with guns but instead, in the centre of the enormous expense of lawn, I saw a huge silver helicopter, its upper surfaces tinted gold by the descending sun. No men, no guns, no Toyotas, just this beautifully elegant machine perched low on the freshly trimmed grass. I could understand why it must have been a surprise to see it there, but I couldn't see what had made James brake so sharply. Sideways on, the machine looked far from threatening.

Two blue stripes, one narrow, one broad, swept along from its pointed nose, below the three side windows, curving up to taper away to nothing just before the tail fin. Painted on the fuselage above the two rearmost windows in some kind of italic script was the word *Grand*. The machine probably wasn't as huge as I first thought, but it must still have been over forty feet long from rotor-tip to tail fin, the top of which had to have stood at least twelve feet off the ground.

It took only seconds to absorb the scene and, when I turned to look, James was sitting frowning at the machine, lips pursed, fingers lightly tapping the steering wheel. He seemed more annoyed than worried.

"Who is it?" I asked. "The police?"

He smiled at that, although I wasn't sure there was any humour in it.

"Hardly," he said. "I don't think the local police budget can stretch to an AgustaWestland Grand."

This could be worrying if he meant that villains had rather more elastic budgets than their pursuers, but I soon discovered that it was a different sort of adversary that had dropped into our scene.

"I'm sorry, Lizzie, but I'm rather afraid that you're about to make the acquaintance of my father."

He released the brake and the Maserati crawled round to the rear of the house while I kept my eyes on the helicopter wondering how many millions it must have cost, and why James was worried about my meeting his father.

I was soon to find out.

Hurrying in through the back entrance, leaving James to wake up Abby, I went straight upstairs to my room. Once there, I slowed the pace considerably and took a leisurely shower, eventually dressing in more of Sarah's left-behind clothes. All the time I listened for the sound of the helicopter taking off. It wasn't that I was afraid of meeting a real live Marquess. I just didn't want to meet this particular one if I didn't really have to.

But there was no avoiding it.

With nothing much else to do, I spent about ten minutes staring down at the silver bird on the lawn. It seemed smaller from this angle, a gleaming jewel on green velvet.

And then the phone rang. I jumped. No-one had called my room before. James wanted me to come down to the library.

There was a free-standing, full-length mirror in one corner of the room, to the left of the door. I stopped and stared at myself before reaching for the handle. I didn't need to see myself. I knew I looked good. Long, brown hair, washed and brushed; bright eyes, long lashes, clear skin; a long-sleeved cream blouse, pleated under the breasts, but not too tightly; a chocolate-brown, calf-length skirt with embroidered patterns; beautiful, hand-crafted (it said so on a label inside) brown, suede boots. By anyone's standard, I was a knock-out. I didn't glory in it. It was just the way it was.

The trouble was that I feared the Marquess's standard might not be quite the same as anyone's.

I took a breath, reached for the door-handle, turned it, and headed for the stairs.

I passed many pairs of eyes as I walked slowly along the upstairs corridor. Some smiling, others mocking; some encouraging, others accusing; some sharply piercing, others hidden beneath ages of dirt. Family portraits presumably. I wondered just what sort of family this had been in days gone by, and why the latest head of this noble brood needed to see me in the library.

I had discovered that there were two ways of reaching that room which was situated on the ground floor in the front left-hand corner of the house. Reaching the foot of the main staircase, I could turn left and go through a very tranquil kind of sitting room whose blue damask wallpaper was, according to Mrs Siddons, over one hundred and fifty years old. Or I could double back to the rear of the entrance hall and pass, via the mural hall, into the main dining room.

I chose the latter route, for no other reason than it would take me longer to reach the library. I was in no hurry to meet this Marquess, which was why I then diverted to the kitchen to check on Abby whose voice I could hear from the mural hall chatting to Mrs Siddons. I found her sitting at the table beside a man whom I had never seen before. I guessed he was in his early thirties, smartly dressed in a dark-blue, double-breasted suit. He looked at me across the table and a quick smile lit up his rather craggy features.

In front of both him and Abby was a large bowl of thick, golden-coloured soup and between the bowls a basket of warm, crusty bread. Abby looked up and smiled as the combined aroma of bread and soup drifted into my nostrils. As if aware of the reaction of my taste-buds, Mrs Siddons immediately grabbed a fresh bowl and offered to fill it with the delicious smelling concoction.

"It's home-made," she assured me.

"And full of lumps," said Abby. "Just how I like it."

"It really is good," added the man in the suit, still smiling. "Far superior to the packets and cans I'm used to."

It was tempting, and not just the food. There was a strange warmth and security to that kitchen, in spite of the presence of the smiling stranger. But I had already delayed long enough.

"Sorry, Abby," I said. "I think your dad wants me."

"Hmmm." She pulled a face, wrinkling her nose. "He probably wants you to meet Granddad. Watch out. He's in a real grump. Much better to stay here and talk to Mike. He's Granddad's pilot. He used to fly helicopters in the army. He tells really funny stories."

Funny stories or a grumpy Marquess? I knew which I'd prefer, but also knew I didn't have a choice. I tried a smile, but it didn't really work.

"I'd better go," I said. "But thanks for the warning."

I retreated with Abby's not very encouraging advice echoing in my ears.

I went through the door leading into the main dining room which was large enough, again according to Mrs Siddons, to seat upwards of twenty guests in comfort. It was a room designed to impress and certainly didn't have the comfortable feel of the family dining room at the back of the house. From here, another door in the far corner of the room led to the library. Having crossed the huge room, I hesitated in the corner with the door ajar. It was one of those double doors that you find in the better class of stately home where the door to one room may be separated by two feet or more from the door to the other, depending on the thickness of the wall. As I stood in the gap between the doors, I could hear raised voices coming from the library.

I glanced back into the dining room, to make sure no-one was watching my odd behaviour, and then I pulled the dining room door almost closed behind me. Listening at keyholes may not be advice listed in a book of country-house etiquette, but it had often stood me in good stead in the past. On this occasion, I wished I had stayed in my room.

I didn't recognise the voice of the person speaking, but I assumed that the rather deep, unfamiliar tones belonged to James's father, the umpteenth Marquess of Thurvaston.

"I've already told you, James, Riddings was not up here spying on you. In fact, when I sent him I had no idea you were involved in any way in the death of this Simmons person."

"I am not involved," replied James emphatically. "I just happened to be there when it happened."

"Yes, I understand that," said his father. "And so does Riddings, which is why he took it upon himself to phone Rupert Chadbourne."

"Rupert," exclaimed James in surprise. "What's he got to do with this?"

"Leverage," replied the Marquess. "Enough perhaps to stop the local police from chasing their tails and disappearing up their own backsides."

There was a slight pause and then he continued, "I wouldn't have known anything about all this if I hadn't caught Riddings sneaking out of the building late this afternoon. Not his fault, of course. George was trying to protect me, silly fool, which reminds me. I must have words with George tomorrow. No time before I left today."

I began to wonder how much longer I could stand there before having to enter the room, or before someone looked into the dining room and caught me eavesdropping. Supposing it couldn't be long, I was just lifting my hand to knock on the library door when James began speaking again.

"That newspaper article. I've had somebody checking up on that reporter... ... Corrina Rigby. That was the call that interrupted your rant earlier... ... Rigby, sad to say, has a definite axe to grind. Her step-father was Peter Greenhalgh. I knew him slightly. Royal Marines major, like me. When I came out, he took my slot, which is how he ended up with the peace-keeping mob in Kosovo in 2000. You probably don't remember, but there was an American Apache helicopter... ... It crashed near the border with Albania. It wasn't fired on. Some bit of the mechanics failed and that was it. Everyone on board was killed, and Peter was one of them... ... Oddly enough, I was speaking about him only a little while ago."

I recognised the story and believed I understood what James was thinking.

"So what does this have to do with what's going on now?" his father asked impatiently. Clearly, he didn't underttand.

"If I hadn't resigned, I'd have been there, not Peter."

"You can't think she blames you for her father's death?"

"Step-father... ... and yes, I think she might. Especially if she thinks I chickened out."

"Don't be so foolish. Nobody could think that."

"She might, if she's not thinking straight. And that might just be the case. I wasn't in Kosovo, and I'm not in Iraq... ..."

"What does that have to do with it?" the Marquess snapped.

"Her boyfriend was a sergeant in the Staffords," said James, with more patience than I thought his father deserved. "Deployed to Iraq last month. Just over a week ago, his Warrior ran over an IED... ... ripped open the underside and four guys died. Rigby's boyfriend was one of them."

"Aaaah," said his father, in a more moderate tone. "That could do it."

"It certainly could," agreed James. "And then my name crops up in a story, so all that pent-up emotion takes control of her, and she really goes to town on it. There really isn't any truth in that article, you know."

"Oh, I'm sure there isn't. I already told you that. I know how you felt about Sarah, and I know you'd never wreck someone else's marriage. But... ... there are some things I don't know, and it's time you put me in the picture."

I wondered what he meant, and it seemed as though James wasn't too sure either.

"I don't know what you're getting at," he said, after a slight pause.

"What I'm getting at," said the Marquess, his words slow and emphatic, "is a black 4x4, parked near this house, which tore away as soon as my chopper appeared. A black 4x4 which was pursued and detained not far from here by armed police. That doesn't seem to fit anywhere in the Phil Simmons scenario, unless there's something about that which you haven't told me."

He hadn't raised his voice but the quiet calmness of his tone seemed, even through the door, almost threatening.

"I've told you all you need to know," replied James, more steadily than I would have done.

"I think not," said his father sharply. "This girl you have here... ... and where is she? She can't have got lost and it doesn't take half-an-hour to walk downstairs."

"This girl, as you put it, is called Lizzie," replied James. "And I expect she heard you ranting on and decided Abby would be better company. She'll probably do best to stay out of here until you've gone."

"Exactly my point," replied his father. "Abby may well be better company for her, but can you honestly tell me that you think she is the right sort of company for Abby? It doesn't matter how you dress it up, that girl's a prostitute plain and simple. I could scarce believe what Surjit was telling me. What on earth were you thinking of to allow her into your house?"

"Yes, well, I might ask what you were thinking of to begin interrogating my staff while I'm away."

"James, I'm your father. I have every right to be here and to know what you are involved in. If that requires me to speak to your staff, that's exactly what I shall do."

"Well, just in case you've forgotten, Father, this is my house and not yours. And my staff, including Surjit, are paid by me and not by you."

The kitchen, with its hot soup and warm bread, with the comfortable Mrs Siddons and the trusting Abby, began to beckon very strongly. I didn't want any part of the conversation I was overhearing and I was actually turning to retreat to friendlier climes when I heard words that froze me rigid.

"I haven't forgotten. And nor have I forgotten that you nearly got Abby killed once," said the Marquess. "I'm not going to let you do it again. If helping that girl… … and, yes, I know that's what you're trying to do… … but, if helping her is going to put Abby in danger, or anyone else for that matter, then I must persuade you to think again."

There was a short silence before James replied and, from the tightness in his measured words, I thought he must be working hard to restrain his inclination for a more forceful response.

"If you think, after all that happened, that I would willingly put Abby in danger again, then you really don't know me as well as you should."

I wanted to be anywhere else but in that room but, as James finished speaking, I gripped the handle of the door, turned it slowly, and walked into the room.

James and his father were sitting directly ahead of me in green leather armchairs, either side of the fireplace. James was facing me at a slight angle, but the Marquess had his back to me and had to turn to see who had entered the room. Both men stood, James rather more quickly than his father, as I waited a little nervously with my hand still on the doorknob.

James had removed his jacket and it lay draped over the back of the chair by the far window. He looked comfortably at ease with the knot of his tie loosened and his shirt cuffs turned back, but his father presented a very formal appearance. He looked every inch the senior civil servant. His dark pin-stripe suit, accompanied by well-shined black oxfords and striped tie over a plain white-collared, pale-blue shirt, would have pointed me in that direction even if I hadn't already known his profession. But there was more to it than that. The way he stood, one hand resting lightly on the back of his chair, his head tilted slightly up so that he seemed to be looking down his nose at me from some superior height, all proclaimed him to be what I assumed he was. A man of power and authority who was accustomed to getting his own way.

His face was totally unreadable, but I didn't like the way he was looking at me. I wondered what he saw. I knew how I looked. After all, I'd checked before I came downstairs, but I suspected that those dark eyes were seeing far beyond the visual image. Was he seeing the real me? And then I smiled slightly as I realised that even I wasn't sure who the real me was any longer.

"Is something amusing you, young lady?" asked the Marquess in a voice heavy with disapproval.

I don't know whether it was his tone of voice or his brooding dark eyes or his haughty manner, but I suddenly felt as cold as ice. Something had triggered my memory, and in that moment I knew that this was not the first time that we had met.

I found that I was holding my breath as I turned and walked straight back into the dining room. Behind me, a phone began to ring.

Forty-Two

Lichfield Daily News – 6.40 pm

Corrina Rigby stared into the dregs of her eighth, or was it ninth, or tenth, coffee of the day. Her china mug was chipped and stained from constant use. She held it in both hands, resting on her desktop, rocking it gently. The cold, brown sludge oozed lethargically around the bottom.

Strands of light brown hair drifted round her face as she sat, hunched forward, ignoring the hum of activity which surrounded her tiny cubicle. In less than an hour, deadlines closed and the paper would be put to bed. Tomorrow's edition would be printed without her story. It lay shredded in her editor's waste bin.

No corroboration, he'd said.

A personal vendetta, he'd said.

A legal minefield, he'd said.

"Get some verification," he'd said, "and you can have your story. Otherwise, drop it."

She'd tried, of course, but no-one who might be able to help would talk to her, and those who would talk to her knew nothing useful.

She knew for a fact that James Montrayne was a man who didn't care about hurting people as long as he got what he wanted. She was convinced he had killed Phil Simmons in that wood because he was having an affair with Simmons' wife. And she was now certain there was a massive cover-up underway.

It was all so clear to her, but her chicken-hearted editor would not allow her to go to print without solid witnesses and hard facts.

They had to be out there, and she would find them, but not in time for tonight's deadline.

So she drooped dispiritedly while others polished their stories for that night's print run.

And then her phone rang.

Slowly she raised herself upright, pushing her mug away from her. She gazed at the phone. The sense of urgency with which she had begun the day had completely evaporated. She wasn't sure she could be bothered to answer it.

But, as heads began to turn towards her, eyebrows raised at her obvious lethargy, she shrugged and reached for the handset.

"Corrina Rigby," she said, half-heartedly stifling a sigh.

Silence. She wasn't altogether surprised since people did occasionally dial her number before they'd worked out how to say what they had been plucking up courage to tell her.

Still, tonight she wasn't in the mood for nurturing a shy source, so she was on the point of replacing the handset when she heard a man's voice.

"Miss Rigby?"

She sighed again. She was not going to be let off so easily.

"Yes, this is Corrina Rigby. Who are you?"

The caller ignored her question.

"I read your article today… … About James Montrayne."

She sat up straight and flung out a hand for her notebook, knocking over her mug and tipping a trickle of brown sludge onto her desktop.

She just caught herself from swearing into the phone and instead prompted her caller.

"And… … …?"

After a brief hesitation, the man's voice continued.

"You suggest… … … That is… … you seem to be implying some sort of relationship between James and Natalie Simmons."

James! she thought. *This guy knows Montrayne quite well.*

"Do you know James Montrayne."

Another pause. Then, "Yes."

"Do you know Natalie Simmons?"

"Yes."

Right on! she thought. *This is going to be good.*

"Do you know anything about the nature of their relationship?"

"I do."

There was something in the caller's voice that sounded familiar. Maybe they'd spoken before. She tried hard to remember.

I need this guy's name, she thought. *But don't rush him. I don't want to lose him.*

"So… … what can you tell me?"

This time, the pause went on so long that she began expecting to hear the click of the receiver being replaced at the other end. She didn't dare speak in case she provoked the very thing she feared.

He didn't hang up.

"I've heard that journalists protect their sources… … Keep them confidential."

"That's right."

"Frankly, I don't like journalists. I'm not sure I can trust you."

"You can, Mr er… … …"

He didn't take the bait, but he seemed to make up his mind about trusting her.

"James came to see me a few weeks ago. He told me he had begun an inappropriate relationship with Natalie."

"Inappropriate?" she queried.

"Don't be coy, Miss Rigby. You know what I mean. *Inappropriate* was the word he used... ... I wasn't surprised... ... I'd begun to notice the way they looked at each other... ... And then I began to wonder about the baby."

Here it comes, she thought, trying not to salivate over the handset.

"You mean Mrs Simmons' baby?" she asked.

"That's right... ... I asked him straight out if it was his baby."

"And what did he say?"

"He didn't answer directly. He told me Phil Simmons believed the baby was his and Natalie also believed that."

"But... ... what about Montrayne? Did he think the baby could be his?"

"I can't answer that."

"Can't... ... or won't?" asked Corrina exasperated at the sudden prevarication.

"Can't," Miss Rigby. "James wouldn't say any more about the baby, which I suppose you might construe as... ... suspicious, if you choose."

"Not exactly hard evidence, is it?"

"Not exactly, Miss Rigby... ... But you may take it from me that James was very worried about his relationship with Natalie... ... and about what Phil might do if he found out about it."

There was a slight pause and Corrina thought he'd finished, but then he began again as though just remembering something.

"He also told me that he would do anything to make Natalie happy. *Anything,* that's what he said."

Corrina looked down at her notes. It might be enough, but only if she could establish the identity of her informant. She wouldn't publish his name of course, but her editor would not accept this as adequate corroboration without knowing from whom she had obtained the information. Who was it? Why was his voice familiar?

And was it all true?

Of course it was. It tallied exactly with what she had believed all along. And it fit the facts, as far as she knew them.

She had to get her caller's name.

"You asked a little earlier whether you could trust me. How do I know whether I can trust you? Can I believe what you're telling me?"

"That's up to you, Miss Rigby. But... ... there is one more thing."

Brilliant she thought. *More is definitely good.*

"What would that be?" she asked.

"You might like to know that James has recently installed some sort of call girl in his house at King's Newton."

Corrina was so startled that she nearly dropped the handset. Whatever she had been expecting, this was definitely not it. And, if it was true, how did that fit into the scenario that her caller had been presenting?

"I don't understand," she said. "Why would he do that?"

"James's problem, Miss Rigby, as he explained to me, was that his... ... natural passions... ... were rather kept in check in the years after his wife died. His relationship with Natalie allowed him the release of those pent up passions. Unfortunately... ... well, after what has happened, he will need to stay away from Natalie for some considerable time. To avoid suspicion, you see. But I suspect that now his passions are aroused, he cannot restrain them as he once did. Hence the young woman now residing at the Dower House."

It made sense.

"And... ... er... ... there's one other thing, Miss Rigby."

He sounded hesitant, as though he felt he had already said too much. Corrina had a strange feeling that he didn't really want to be speaking to her at all.

So why had he called?

Since *the other thing* was not forthcoming, she decided to prompt him again and try and extract a name from him.

"And what is the other thing, Mr ... ..."

It took a few moments of patient waiting, something Corrina was not terribly good at, but then she had it.

"If you get the chance to see this young woman, you will note a strong resemblance to James Montrayne's late wife. That, you may suppose, is why he chose her. And... ... it's not Mr... ... It's Reverend. James is a member of my church."

Of course. Of course. No wonder the voice had sounded familiar. She'd interviewed the minister for her first article. She had already begun to thank him for this latest information when she realised that the line was dead.

She looked at the clock on her desk, and excitement coursed through her.

There was still time.

Forty-Three

The Dower House – 7.00 pm

He had never been a client of mine. I was sure of that. But whether James's father had ever made use of the services offered by Ray Mellisse's other girls, I had no idea, and I wasn't sure I wanted to find out.

I considered this as I sat on my bed. I had come straight back to my room after leaving the library so abruptly. I had thought I was safe in this gorgeous, old, Georgian relic of a house, but I now wondered if I'd made a terrible mistake.

It could only have been a few weeks ago that I had found myself sitting in the lobby of the Carlton Grand hotel in central Birmingham. I was waiting for my favourite client whom I usually met there and whom I had always known only as Michael. Occasionally, when he needed a companion for dinner, the theatre, and overnight entertainment, I was his preferred choice. On this particular evening, I had dressed in a slightly shimmery, dark-blue, cocktail dress, which Michael seemed to like, and had been dropped off at the hotel by Bruno around six o'clock. The plan was to have an early dinner in the hotel restaurant before Michael and I would stroll round to the Alexandra Theatre for a performance of some play I'd never heard of. And after that… … whatever he wanted.

The hotel lobby was comfortable, modern and bright, with a scattering of easy chairs clustered around low tables. The contrastingly high, and elegantly curved, reception desk was immediately opposite the automatic entrance doors. Not surprisingly, Michael was always waiting for me on his own, usually seated at one of the tables.

Except that, on this occasion, he wasn't. He was standing by one of the chairs where presumably he had been sitting, resting his right hand on the top of the chair-back, and listening with apparent interest to the gentleman facing him. I could see Michael clearly, and his eyes flicked to mine as soon as I entered. I took his hurried glance to indicate that I should not join him until he was alone. I wouldn't have done anyway, so I walked over to another group of chairs and sat down, half-turned towards Michael and his friend, creating the impression, I hoped, that I was waiting for someone.

Unfortunately, the exchange of looks between Michael and me, brief though it was, had not gone unnoticed by his friend. Their conversation quickly finished, and the friend turned to leave. He was not as tall as Michael, but was just as well dressed. An elegant business suit, hand-made – I had learned to recognise these things – was carried well on his spare frame. As he turned, he let his eyes rest on me for a moment. I couldn't help glancing up at him, but then immediately looked away, although he was still clearly there at the edge of my vision. I had this sense of brooding haughtiness, almost disdain, before he turned away and, with a smile I definitely didn't like, James's father had wished Michael a pleasant evening.

The trouble was, as I sat there on my bed reliving that scene, I couldn't work out what it meant.

And I wasn't going to work it out. Not that evening anyway. Within a few minutes, James was banging on my door.

"Lizzie. Open up, quickly!"

I wondered what was the matter with him. My sudden exit from the dining-room came nowhere close to justifying the urgency of those four words.

He was already trying to open the door before I could get to it to turn the key. In my agitation after the encounter in the library, I had turned the beautifully enamelled key and locked my door. I wasn't sure I wanted to unlock it.

The door rattled.

"Lizzie, please. It's Angie."

That did it. I still had my hand on the key as the door began to open. I stepped back in time to avoid having my nose rearranged by the door, and the rest of me trampled on by James's size twelves.

He had obviously run up from the library since he was slightly out of breath. I suddenly realised how frightening he could be, not just because of his sheer bulk, but because of the tremendous power and energy radiating from him. He grabbed my jacket which was draped rather inelegantly over the back of the Queen Anne chair, seized me by the hand and dragged me from the room, talking all the while.

"That was ACC Fletcher on the phone... ... just as you skipped out... ... When this is finished you must tell me why you did that... ... At first the cops thought all the guys they picked up were Russian... ... the two in the crash; the two outside here; the two at the farm... ... until one of them cracked open."

I was hurtling down the stairs now, trying hard to listen whilst at the same time avoiding pitching headlong to the bottom.

"He was in the car outside here. Shouldn't have been there, he said. The Russian mafia don't approve of the local help, but they were a man short and he'd done little jobs for them, so he was press-ganged."

In the hall now, heading for the front door. It stood open and I could see the helicopter glistening, almost iridescent, in the glare of the floodlights which lit up the whole of the front of the house.

"Thing is, according to him, there weren't six. There were eight. That's why David rang. There are two more out there somewhere... ...

And the only other place where they'll expect we might turn up is the hospital."

I had a brief glimpse of James's father in a doorway to my left, and then we were out of the house, down the steps, and running across the lawn to the helicopter.

I wanted to ask James why he was so sure that these remaining two, who he was so worried about, knew which hospital we had left Angie in. But I was gasping for breath and, even if I could have spoken, I would have been drowned out now as Mike fired up the Grand's twin turbines.

Only minutes later, I was sitting down, strapped in, and feeling the thrust beneath me as we lifted from the ground. Trying to catch my breath, and allow my mind to catch up with the rest of me, I looked around the cabin. There were six seats, three facing forward and three aft. James was in the middle seat facing forward, and I was opposite him. He seemed calmer now, more relaxed, perhaps because this stage of whatever we were doing was not under his control. He just had to let it happen until it was again his turn to seize hold of events and drive them along.

He was watching me, eyebrows slightly raised, questioning, as though he was waiting for me to launch a thousand questions at him. So I made a start.

"Just the two of us?"

I tried to make it sound light, almost flippant, as though I was quite used to being dragged from stately homes and flung into helicopters. But it didn't quite come out like that. Still, James did give me an appreciative smile.

"Three actually. There's Mike up front there, though he did make it clear that transport is all we're getting from him. Nothing extra-curricular was how he put it."

This was sounding ominous.

"I think I should warn you," I said, "that I don't do extra-curricular either. I'm not terribly good at crawling round in the dark shooting people."

"Not necessary," replied James. "Reinforcements are on the way."

"Andy?" I asked.

"No, not this time. I called him, but he's already back home, which is top side of Derby. Too far away. Rod's nearest, so Andy's going to send him."

"What about Surjit and Cherry," I interrupted. "Couldn't they come?"

James shook his head. "No. Surjit looks after security at the Dower House, and I need Cherry to stay with Abby. That's his job when I'm not there. She still needs that reassurance. So, we're getting Rod and hopefully John and Nat, since they all live south of Lichfield, and aren't scheduled for anything else this evening." He smiled. "Except maybe Sky Sport and a few cans of lager."

The smile faded as his eyes focussed on mine. He held my gaze for a moment, serious, thoughtful. I blinked but didn't look away.

"Lizzie. What made you rush out of the library like that?"

This didn't seem like the best time to start explaining, but then... ... when would be a good time.

"Your father," I began, and then stopped. Now was not the time. "You father doesn't mind you borrowing his new toy?"

"Oh, yes," said James, "he minded. But he saw he didn't have much choice."

"Too long by car," I suggested.

"Thirty minutes, plus. Much quicker in this."

"When will we be there?"

He glanced down at his watch."

"Three, maybe four minutes."

My mouth dropped open. I couldn't help it. It was all too fast. I had no idea what was likely to happen, or what I was supposed to do, or even whether I would be able to do whatever was needed of me. I needed more information. Fast.

But James was ahead of me.

"Barrie will already have moved Angie to another room. No change to the admission records, so it won't be easy to find her. He's having hospital security check the CCTV tapes, and current images, for anything that doesn't look right. If anyone's skulking in the bushes we don't want to scare them into action before we're ready, so Mike will put us down on the Air Ambulance spot, and Barrie will have an ambulance waiting for us."

He smiled and shrugged. "I'm not of a size and shape that's easy to miss, so I'll be the patient. You're my doctor. As soon as we land, a couple of Barrie's paramedics, or nurses, or whoever he has available, will shove in a stretcher for me and a set of scrubs for you. The lights will be off in the cabin, so get into them quick, over your clothes but with your jacket on top. Understood?"

As I nodded, I felt a drop in forward speed, and the helicopter began to descend. When did he work all this out? Still, I thought, you can't get to be a major in the Royal Marines without being able to think on your feet.

"Once in the hospital, we'll go straight to Angie. Your job is to reassure her and keep her calm. If Barrie's security guys spot anything, we'll try and hold on until Rod and the others arrive, but if things kick off before they get here, you stick with Angie and I'll deal with it. OK?"

"OK."

Mike was good, no doubt about it. I scarcely felt the chopper touch the ground. I knew we were down when the cabin door opened and I could just make out two men in hospital uniforms silhouetted against the interior lights of the ambulance which had reversed up to the helicopter and now had its rear doors open. The stretcher appeared, scrubs were put on, and two minutes later I was walking along a hospital corridor beside James still being wheeled along on his gurney.

The elevator was half-way down the corridor. We stopped at the doors, and one of the paramedics pressed the **UP** button. When the doors opened, they both glanced up and down the corridor before pushing the gurney into the elevator. There was no-one else in sight. Stepping back into the corridor, they watched me standing beside the gurney. They both had a slightly puzzled look on their faces. It was a look that said they had carried out their instructions to the letter, but they hadn't the faintest idea what was going on.

As soon as the doors were closed, James threw back the blanket covering him and climbed off the gurney. I started to strip off my scrubs, but James said to keep them on until we were in Angie's room. Hardly had he said that than the elevator doors opened and we were able to step out into the upper corridor. Several doors down on the left land side, Barrie was waiting outside a closed door. It had a number, as did all the doors, but nothing to indicate what or who was inside. Once we were all in the room, I remembered my instructions and pulled up a chair to the edge of Angie's bed.

I heard James talking to Barrie but I didn't take much notice. I was looking at Angie. Yesterday afternoon she had been tired and listless, remote and unable to concentrate. Drugs were dealing with her pain, and probably helped to make her dozy. But in all that she had seemed peaceful, and safe, and cared for. Now the bruising down the left side of her honey-coloured face was a livid explosion of colour, and around it her dark hair curled and knotted in greasy strands. There was a sheen of sweat on her forehead and upper lip and a slight tremor to the fingers of her right hand which I lifted gently and held in both of mine. Something or other was being pumped into the back of her left hand from a drip on the other side of her bed. She looked utterly pitiful, and there were people waiting outside to come in and take from her the only thing of value she still possessed. Her life. Bruised and battered and drugged-up she may be, but inside was a beautiful person who had almost given up the struggle of trying to get out. She deserved one last chance of breaking free from all that had made her into the person she hated being. We both did.

My attention was drawn away from Angie by the opening of the door. The man who came in was medium in every way; height, weight, colouring. The sort of guy you'd never pick out in a line-up. For the moment he was distinguished by his uniform, but when that came off he'd be lost in the crowd. He wore a white pilot shirt with dark epaulettes on the shoulders, each announcing *Security* in gold lettering. On the right breast of his shirt was a complicated coat-of-arms surrounded by the words *Aullton Foundation Hospital* in a ring of blue letters. His navy-blue tie also had what appeared to be the same coat-of-arms. On his left breast was a name badge which announced him as Peter Kingston. He looked smart and efficient, which was more than you could say about most rent-a-cops; in my admittedly limited experience, you usually got one characteristic or the other, seldom both. He closed the door quietly behind him, and didn't speak until it was secure.

"Nothing," he said, looking at Barrie. "There's no-one out there now, and I've got lads watching the monitors for all the outside CCTV, front, back and sides."

"What about inside?" asked James.

"Well, hang on a minute. You've got to realise those cameras don't cover every square inch. This is a hospital, not a top-security prison. One of the lads and I did a visual check, from inside the building, of those areas not covered by the cameras."

"And you saw nothing?"

"Nothing. But there are lots of places someone could hide out there, and we wouldn't spot them until they moved."

"OK," said James. "So what about inside?"

"That's covered too," replied Kingston. "But again, we don't have cameras everywhere. If I use the lads I've got to watch the monitors, I've got no-one patrolling inside apart from me. It's a toss-up. The cameras give us better all-round coverage, but to do that, with any degree of certainty that we'll spot anything, needs four men. You know, switching cameras, interior/exterior, adjusting angles and zoom etc. But if they're all in the Security room, they can't be out in the building."

James frowned. "I do all that at the Dower House with only one man."

I thought of Surjit, competent and reliable, surrounded by all his computers and display screens, and it suddenly occurred to me how lonely his job must be sometimes.

Kingston wasn't happy at the implied rebuke.

"I'm sure you do, sir," he said. "But I bet you have alarm systems, infra-red, heat sensors, motion-detectors, night-vision… …"

"OK, OK," interrupted James. "I take your point."

He thought for a moment. Kingston kept quiet, and Barrie looked from one to the other.

"So," said James, "we're sure there's no-one out there now?"

Kingston nodded, then decided to add a note of caution. "As sure as we can be."

"And no-one could have come into the building without being seen, with your boys monitoring all the screens in the Security room?"

"Right again. All the entrances are covered. And the only people who've come in are staff or bona-fide visitors."

James thought about that, looking from Kingston to Barrie, over to me, and back to Kingston again.

"OK. Well, I think your boys can stop watching the outside now, apart from one maybe to keep an eye on the drive and look out for my people arriving."

Kingston didn't like that, and neither did Barrie.

"Are you sure, James?" he asked. "If they turn up now, they could walk right in, or maybe sneak round the back, and we wouldn't know."

They all looked towards the bed, as if the thought raised their awareness of Angie's vulnerability. James's eyes passed over Angie and locked on mine, while Kingston and Barrie both stared at the scared, battered and dishevelled girl gazing at them wide-eyed from the bed.

Still with his eyes on me, James said, "All the other pairs were in place hours ago; the school, the farm, the Dower House."

I nodded. I could see the point he was making, and all of a sudden I was very scared. But I didn't want to let it show, so I made the point for him in a voice remarkably firm and steady considering the chill I felt inside.

With my eyes fixed on his, I said, "They're not outside. They're already here, inside the hospital. They weren't just coming after Angie. They were waiting for us"

Forty-Four

The Dower House – 7.25 pm

Alistair John Graham Montrayne, thirteenth Marquess of Thurvaston, Lord of umpteen other places, and Director General of the DTLO, found himself strangely at a loss. It was not a sensation he was accustomed to, and he therefore found it slightly worrying. Here was James pinching his helicopter to dash off with that young woman, who vaguely disappointed him by not looking at all like the image his mind had created of her. When she had appeared briefly in the library, she had looked so young, fresh and, yes, apprehensive. On hearing from Surjit that she was a working girl from Birmingham, he had pictured someone older, more worldly-wise, confident perhaps, even brash. Not this fresh-faced child with the big brown eyes, who vaguely reminded him of someone else.

He stood at the front door, watching as James and Lizzie boarded his helicopter. *Lizzie Burleigh,* he thought. *Elizabeth Burleigh.* But the name struck no chord in the recesses of his mind. The girl had a vague resemblance to James's deceased wife Sarah, but he recognised that and was therefore fairly sure that this was not the similarity which tugged at his memory. It was starting to annoy him that he couldn't remember when a small hand slipped into his and gripped it tight.

He looked down at Abby and saw her attention fixed on the now rising helicopter. They watched in silence as the Grand gained height before its lights began to swing around and it headed off south towards Birmingham. Still they watched, holding hands, unspeaking. The shape of the Grand, a shadowy silhouette against a darkening sky, faded quickly, leaving only the lights to mark its position. Soon they too disappeared leaving only the unmistakable throb of its motors to fade gradually into the night.

"Why couldn't I go with him?"

It sounded like a straightforward question, but Montrayne knew her too well and loved her too much for his ear to miss the plaintiveness underlying the simple words.

"Well, since I couldn't go either, perhaps your father thought I might like the pleasure of your company," he tried, smiling down at her.

She didn't look up. Her eyes were still gazing off into the blackness which had swallowed up her father and Lizzie.

"And," he said, remembering an interminable evening during the Easter holidays, "Cherry absolutely hates Disney Trivial Pursuit, so if you had gone I would have no-one to play with."

At this, she did turn and reward him with a brief smile. More a prize for effort, he thought, rather than any real enthusiasm. Still, it was something. He turned, still holding her hand, and drew her back into the house. Cherry was waiting just inside the door, and he moved to close it quickly behind them. He had arrived while James was on the phone to ACC Fletcher, and had been quickly briefed before James had gone in search of Abby to say goodbye. At a nod from the Marquess, Cherry disappeared in the direction of the kitchen, keen to make the acquaintance of a bowl of Mrs Siddons's home-made soup and fresh-baked bread.

Montrayne wondered how he could possibly keep Abby entertained until bedtime, when his mind and hers were both fixed on an unknown situation developing many miles away. He wished Suzanne were still here. She always seemed to have the knack of lifting Abby's spirits and giving her thoughts a new direction when she was a little down. Suspecting, with some relief, that the Disney game was not going to do the trick this time, he led Abby through to the mural hall in the centre of the house. This room rose all the way up through both stories and the attics above to three massive skylights in the centre of the roof, designed to flood the interior of the house with light.

The original mural, occupying all four walls from floor to skylight, had been full of mythological beasts, heroic well-endowed gods, and bare-breasted nymphs attending seductive goddesses. Sadly, according to some, and mercifully according to others, it had been damaged by fire in the May of 1945.

* * * * * * * * * *

Airmen from RAF Lichfield, billeted there for the last two years of the war, under the combined influence of euphoria at the German surrender, and a remarkable quantity of French brandy unearthed from the cellar, had erected a celebratory bonfire in the centre of the hall. Diary accounts, newspaper reports, and one rather fuzzy photograph all confirm that the resulting pyre had been most impressive.

Pilot Officer Robert Murdoch had chosen an outlet other than the bonfire for his exuberance, assisted enthusiastically by a young WAAF officer of undeniable talent. Trouserless, he was on the point of entering with inflamed vigour into the spirit of the moment, when the tang of smoke caught the back of his throat. Always a gentleman of immense presence of mind, Murdoch knew instinctively what was required of him in such a situation. He ignored the smoke and applied himself to his moment of celebration. That done, to the intense satisfaction of his WAAF accomplice, he retired still trouserless to the balcony which circled the mural hall on the first floor.

At the base of the smoke which was beginning to billow rather threateningly around all three stories of the hall, he could see flickers of red, yellow and gold. The brandy he had consumed may not have impaired his performance in the bedroom, but it had certainly disrupted logical thought. The fire must be put out, and what better way than urinating on it from a great height. The resulting stream curved gracefully from between the balustrade but, while impressive by most standards, it was inadequate to the task. In fact it made absolutely no impression whatsoever on flames which Murdoch could now hear crackling through the smoke which was beginning to sting his eyes and make him cough.

Surprisingly, the retching seemed to clear his head and at the same moment he realised that he was not alone on the balcony. His half-naked WAAF was coughing at his side and rubbing her eyes. Pushing her in the direction of the nearest bathroom to turn the taps of the tub full on, he ran to all four corners of the balcony to grab the red buckets of sand placed there against an eventuality which no-one expected to happen. But now it had, he threw the contents of each bucket in turn into the centre of the flames. That done he dashed with the four empty buckets into the bathroom. The water in the bath was not yet deep enough to cover a bucket so he filled each as quickly as the tap pressure could manage. He and his WAAF then carried two each back to the balcony and tossed the water in unison into the smoke. Murdoch assumed that four buckets at once would have more effect than one at a time.

The pair lost count of the number of time they did this; back to the now decently full bath, fill the buckets, back to the balcony together, toss the contents over, back to the bath... ... ...

At first it was touch and go whether it would work, but eventually their persistence paid off before their stamina gave out. No-one else assisted their efforts. Those on the ground floor who had not been overcome by the smoke or the brandy had fled outside to escape the throat-clogging, eye-stinging, lung-burning atmosphere of the hall.

The house had been saved, and even the hall itself was remarkably unscathed except for a substantial hole surrounded by scorched timber in the centre of what had once been a beautifully laid lime and oak timber floor. Lady Helena, whose husband, Sir Peter Marchmont, had inherited the Dower House following the death of his mother in 1942, was not at all sorry when she finally came to view the damage to the hall in the summer of 1945.

In places, the heat had damaged already friable plaster which was now crumbling from the lathes which held it to the wall. Huge chunks of the mural were missing and where the heat had failed to reach, smoke and soot had left their mark, indelibly. So, at Lady Helena's command and to her great delight, the walls had been entirely stripped of their plaster and the mural, which she disliked so much, disappeared into the family's archives. She commissioned a new mural from a rising local artist who was making his mark by working in the style of the recently, and tragically, deceased Rex Whistler. Unlike Whistler, Simon Brooke had been unable to fight due to lameness from birth which surgery had been unable to correct. So, when he wasn't drawing maps for the War Office, he spent time developing his art.

The Dower House at Kings Newton was by far his biggest project to date but, by the time he had finished, his reputation was assured. The estates of the Marchmont and Montrayne families adorned the walls of the new mural hall. From castles in Scotland, to farmsteads in Derbyshire, forests and rivers, pastures and mountains scaled the heights of the hall. Thurvaston Priory rose above the stone and marble fireplace in the centre of one long wall, and everywhere animal life abounded. Badgers and pine martens lay hidden in the shadows of the forests; foxes and rabbits scurried amongst heathers while Jacob sheep and black-eyed Jersey cows grazed the open pastures. Owls swooped and eagles soared, and Lady Helena loved them all.

And so, sixty years later, did Abby.

* * * * * * * * *

Montrayne had been going to lead her into the drawing room to find a DVD that would enthral her without boring the pants off him but, as they entered the hall, he was seized by inspiration.

"How would you like to play hide-and-seek?" he asked hopefully.

She stopped walking and turned to look up at him, her forehead creased slightly in puzzlement.

"Grandad," she said, "you don't do hide-and-seek."

"I used to," he replied with a smile of pleasure at the memory. "And I seem to remember that I was pretty good at it too."

She thought about that and decided to concede the point.

"As good as Suzanne anyway," she said. "But you haven't played in ages. Not since... ..."

Not since the kidnap, he thought, knowing that was what she was thinking. But what he actually said was, "Not since Suzanne came to stay."

"No," she said. "Not since then."

She twirled around taking in all the scenes depicted on the walls. Ending up facing him, she said, "But if you really want to play you'd better watch out coz I've got loads better."

It was a game she had played ever since she had been old enough to talk. Whoever was hiding had to choose a place somewhere in the mural; a castle turret, a rabbit hole, a copse, a cow-byre or an anthill. They were all there, plus hundreds more locations all waiting to offer sanctuary to a little girl whose short life had provided too many things to hide away from. Whoever was searching was allowed a set number of questions to try and pinpoint the hiding place. Montrayne knew he had no chance of winning. He didn't know the details of the mural well enough. But winning wasn't the object tonight.

"How many questions, Grandad?" asked Abby. "Will five be enough, or do you think you'll need ten?"

"Probably a hundred if I'm to have any chance of finding you," replied Montrayne, content now that her mind seemed focussed on the game.

"Hmm," said Abby. "That's too many. You can have fifteen, no more. OK?"

"OK."

And so they played. The game lasted almost an hour, as they took it in turns to hide and be sought. And Montrayne lost every time, until his keen eye picked out some stonework on a small island in the middle of a lake high on the wall somewhere to the north-east of Thurvaston Priory. Deciding arbitrarily that this must be a shepherd's hut, he survived Abby's fifteen questions and delighted her with the ingenuity of his hiding place.

"I must get my camera," she said. "Don't go away."

She danced off to the drawing room and emerged a moment later holding the Canon Sureshot that Montrayne had bought her for her last birthday.

"Is that to take my picture because I'm so clever?" he asked.

"No, silly," she said, smiling. "I've started taking photos of all the good hiding places. I've got loads."

Skipping off in the direction of the kitchen and the rear staircase, she called out, "Just wait here a minute."

A moment later she appeared on the balcony opposite the Priory wall. She aimed her camera at the lake, adjusted the zoom, and took her picture. She took a couple more just to be sure, waved to Montrayne, and disappeared.

When she returned to the ground floor of the hall, Montrayne patted the space on the chaise longue beside him saying, "Come over here and let me see."

Adjusting the camera setting so they could view the pictures she had taken, she snuggled up close so they could easily see the small screen. Montrayne smiled to himself. Entertaining Abby was not why he had come up from London in such a hurry this afternoon, but just at that moment, as he felt her warm, fragile body curled up trustingly beside him, he realised that there was nothing he'd rather be doing.

"So, what have we got?" he said.

They looked at the three of the shepherd's hut, now convinced that this was what the stones must be, and then Abby began showing him some others that she had taken when she was teaching Lizzie how to play the game.

And then he saw it, and it hit him like a thunder clap.

Abby had taken several of Lizzie sitting on the chaise longue, looking at different areas of the mural, but one of them had caught her sideways on, facing straight ahead, but with her eyes glancing up and off to the side in the direction of the camera. There was no doubt. He now knew exactly where he had seen her, dressed differently, but in just that same pose. The question was, what to do about it.

Forty-Five

Aullton Foundation Hospital – 7.45 pm

It didn't make any sense for them to be coming after Angie like this. There was no point to it. She was no threat to anyone. She never had been. And if it *was* her they were after, why hadn't they made their move already, before we arrived? What were they waiting for? Us. It had to be us.

Kingston looked at me steadily for a moment, weighing what I'd just said. He obviously didn't like the idea that the guys he was looking out for might already have slipped past his net and could be somewhere in the building. He turned back to James, which was probably natural considering the way his size dominated the room, but it still struck me as slightly odd since it was Barrie who was actually Kingston's boss.

"So, what do you suggest?" he asked.

I didn't like the way he now ignored me, so I answered before James could speak.

"You could get your men to review the CCTV from mid-afternoon... ... say..."

I thought for a moment and noticed James watching me, one eyebrow raised as though encouraging me to go on.

"The first pair appeared at the school about 2.30," I said, and then decided we needed to allow a margin for error. "So why don't you go back half-an-hour from that and check the tapes from 2.00?"

James nodded at me and smiled before turning to face Kingston.

"OK?"

"Sure," he replied. "Except that they aren't tapes. The recordings are all digital which means we can specify search parameters."

"Then you'd better get searching," said Barrie, clearly feeling that he needed to contribute to the decision making. "Two men, arriving together in a 4x4, somewhere after 2.00 this afternoon."

Kingston frowned, but James intervened before he could question Barrie's instruction.

"You know what to look for?" he asked the security man.

"Sure," Kingston replied. "No assumptions. Check everything."

Barrie looked puzzled and, as Kingston left the room, James explained.

"They may not have come in a 4x4. They may not have arrived together. They could be pretending to be visitors, patients, er... ... service staff. In fact anyone who might be thought to have a reason for being here. Now... ... can you go and check your visitors book? I presume everyone has to check in?"

"Everyone," said Barrie.

"Right. Check who arrived this afternoon, visitors, service people, everyone. Quick as you can, but no fuss. Then call me... ..."

He took out his mobile phone and adjusted the settings, before slipping it into the breast pocket of his shirt.

"OK, it's on silent vibrate. Now... ... call me about anyone you don't know or can't explain. I'm going along to Angie's old room in case they show up there, but I'm guessing they'll already have checked it."

I felt Angie's hand clutch tightly at mine. I hadn't been sure how much of this she was following, but she was fully with it now. And the sharp squeeze of her hand seemed to jolt my brain.

"James. Get Kingston to check... ..."

"Already on it," he said, lifting his phone to his ear. "Kingston? ... ... Check the camera for... ..."

He turned to Barrie. "What's the corridor for Angie's old room?"

"T3," replied Barrie immediately.

"Corridor T3," said James into his phone. "Print off stills of anyone who went into that room, and send copies to this phone. ASAP. And... ... What?... ... You're kidding... ... OK. OK... ... Look... ... Don't try tackling these men on your own. They're almost certainly armed, and more dangerous than you can imagine. And keep a look out for my guys. They should be here soon."

Barrie looked sheepish. "Sorry, I should've thought. There's no camera in that corridor. I guess Kingston told you that?"

James pursed his lips in obvious frustration and nodded.

Barrie muttered, "I'll go check the visitors and log-in books," and left, and I expected James to follow, so I got up to make sure the door was locked after him. I needn't have bothered, for two reasons. First, there was no key or bolt. It was one of those electronic locks that opens with a card, like you get in hotels these days. Second, James didn't leave. He stood over by the door watching us. I didn't want him to go, and I think he sensed it.

"I'll stay with you until Rod or the others get here," he said.

I couldn't deny that I was relieved, but didn't have time to say so because he was moving quickly past me to get to Angie. She was trying to push herself upright, but didn't seem to have the strength. He picked up a remote from the table beside her bed and pressed the button to adjust the angle of the backrest. In a moment, she was sitting up as comfortably as she could be given her condition. Her voice was so faint I could barely hear the words.

"What's... ... going... ... on?"

Between us, James and I gave her a quick summary, trying hard to reassure her that, whatever was going on, she was safe and need not worry. We were still working on the reassurance when James's phone began to vibrate. He answered it, listened, then slipped it back in his shirt pocket.

"There's trouble. Barrie says there's no answer from the nurses station on T3."

A moment later there was a knock on the door and Barrie slipped into the room. He was rather pale and breathing quickly.

"Two visitors, both men, came in together just after six thirty."

We all looked up at the clock on the wall opposite the bed. Seven twenty-five.

"The last pair were picked up not far from the Dower House soon after five," said James. "So, if these two here got word of that, and I'm betting that they did, why did they wait over an hour before coming in? And where were they waiting all that time?"

It was obvious. Or, at least, to me it was, but then I'd been thinking about it.

"They were waiting for us," I said. "Outside at first because they wouldn't want to draw attention to themselves. So they waited until visitors started to arrive after tea. Then they could tag along and come in with them. And now they're in the building, waiting to get their hands on Angie and me. Only, moving Angie made it more difficult for them. So now they're working out what to do."

"OK," said James. "Makes sense. And waiting probably wouldn't a bad thing for them. Gave them a chance to see whether the police were going to show up here."

"Yes," said Barrie. "But where were they all that time?"

"I'd guess they were tucked into the entrance to that new business estate just over the road," replied James, having had time to think it out. "Not directly opposite the entrance to here, but close enough to see folk arriving. OK, so they signed in. Have we got pictures?"

"Kingston's printing them off now."

Exactly on cue, there was a knock at the door, and a loud whisper. "It's Kingston."

He slipped quickly into the room as James opened the door. In his hand were some eight by ten colour photos.

"My money says these are your guys," he said, handing the pictures to James. "They both gave what looked like Russian names, and they were talking Russian. Or, it sounded like Russian to the guy on duty. Could have been something else though, but probably from that part of the world."

"That fits," said Barrie. "They both signed in to visit Pytor Rutskoy. Russian dissident. You've probably seen him in the papers, speaking out against Putin. He does quite a lot of that apparently.

Anyway, Rutskoy was served his dinner at six thirty, just before these men arrived. His tray should have been cleared away by now, but I can't check as I can't get any reply from the nurses' station on T3."

"What corridor is Rutskoy on?"

Barrie hesitated, his face growing ashen. "T3."

James's eyes closed briefly, and his right hand brushed through his hair, back to front, just as I'd seen him do before when he was thinking hard. When he opened his eyes they were looking straight at me, narrowed and thoughtful.

"Rod should have been here by now. And the others. They don't live that far away."

His voice was quiet and I didn't think he was speaking to me; rather just thinking out loud. Then it was decision time.

"Barrie," he said. "I can't leave the girls here on their own. You stay, and I'll go and take a look down T3."

Barrie nodded, but I wasn't sure who was more scared; him or me. Not sure how much use he would be as a protector, I was looking round for something that would do as a weapon when I heard James leave the room.

* * * * *

James stepped quietly into the corridor, looking quickly to left and right. To the right, towards the elevator, nothing. To the left, a woman walking towards him holding a little boy by the hand. Mid-thirties, well-dressed without being flashy, she wore her long beige coat open and it flapped as she walked. She kept glancing down to her little boy, maybe five years old, reassuring him that Daddy would be coming home soon. Ignoring the elevator, mother and son took the adjacent stairs to the ground floor.

James watched them out of sight before setting off in the direction from which they had come. This corridor was T5, paralleling T3 which was across the open quadrangle around which the hospital had been built. T2 and T4 ran along the other two sides of the quad. There was no T1. There were two nurses' stations on the upper floor: one on the outer corner of T3 and T4, and another similarly placed at the junction of T5 and T2. It was this second one that James was heading towards.

He could hear conversation and the light tapping of fingers on a keyboard before he reached the corner. Two nurses, both female: one standing, sorting through medications on a trolley, one sitting, entering data on her computer. The one standing, tall, dark-haired, thirty-something, quite attractive, was wondering why Doctor Harwood had missed his evening round. Apparently, she looked forward to his usual tour of all the nurses' stations just after the evening shift change and before he himself left for home.

"Wouldn't mind going home with him myself given half a chance."

"Why hasn't he given you the chance? He's not seeing anyone, is he?"

"When?" Several more pills went into tiny plastic cups. "He seems to spend all his waking time here."

"Hmmm." More tapping on the keyboard. "He's not gay, is he?"

"Absolutely not."

They both looked up sharply as James deep voice broke into their reverie. They both knew who he was. James Montrayne, Earl of Aullton, the man whose foundation funded their hospital. The tall girl smiled slightly, quite unabashed, but the nurse at the computer had the grace to blush slightly.

James gave them no time to respond to his interruption.

"Can you call the other nurses' station on T3?"

They both looked at him curiously before the tall one with the medicines reached for the phone on the wall behind her. She pushed three buttons and waited. Her eyes drifted to James as she listened to the ringing in her ear. James returned her gaze but his mind was focussed on an unanswered phone over one hundred yards away on the other side of the building. The keyboard was silent now, as they all waited for a response, even though James alone knew the significance of the protracted silence.

The tall nurse shook her head and raised an eyebrow as if to ask whether she should continue to let it ring. James let his eyes drift down to the name badge pinned above her left breast.

"Thanks, Amanda," he said, turning away.

"It's Mandy to my friends," she said to his back, as she replaced the phone. "That's if you ever feel like getting friendly."

When he stopped a few yards down the corridor, her heart jumped as she wondered if she'd gone too far. The frown on his face as he turned back towards her convinced her that she'd not just stepped over the mark, but cleared it by miles.

James had heard her comment but it wasn't that which troubled him. Seeing them, light-heartedly going about their everyday business, it had suddenly dawned on him just how many people's lives were now at risk, here in this building, because a Russian mobster had to prove a point. If Rod and the others had arrived in time and the Russians could have been dealt with outside the building, it made sense to keep the police out of it. It would have been a long stretch to persuade them that this could have anything to do with an attempted kidnap of his daughter. It might also have caused the police to review their assumptions regarding the other Russians they had arrested. It would all have become very messy, with Lizzie and Angie both coming under scrutiny, and the police trying desperately to join all the dots between the girls, the Russians, James and the death of Phil Simmons.

They have their uses, these boys in blue, but they have an unfortunate habit of fixating on the obvious. In James's experience, suspicion always won out over imagination.

Yes, keeping the police out of it had certainly been the right decision at the time. But now? Even as he turned back to Amanda, his mind was racing. Maybe there was a way to satisfy police curiosity without confusing their simple minds with too many facts. How fortunate that Rutskoy should have booked in when he did.

"Mandy," he said as he approached the counter of the nurses' station. "I need a favour."

"Of course," she smiled back. "Anything at all."

"First, can I have your passkey?"

She was startled. She was perfectly ready to give him her phone number, but her passkey was something else. Still, he did own the place, so what the hell. She slipped the card from the breast pocket of her dress and handed it over.

"Thanks, Mandy," he said, taking the card and tapping it lightly on the surface of the counter. "Now, I want you to call 999 and tell the police that two Russians have entered the building, and you have reason to believe they have come to kill or kidnap Pytor Rutskoy. Emphasise that this is the guy who regularly speaks out against Putin and is a friend of Alexander Litvinenko."

Amanda's mouth opened, the smile completely gone. Her forehead wrinkled as her eyes narrowed, startled by his words but not sure whether to believe them.

"Have you got that?" James continued. "Write it down if you're not sure."

After many years of dealing with overworked, stressed, sometimes eccentric doctors who often flung information at her expecting her to catch it on the run, Amanda's ability to grasp and filter stray bits of data was highly tuned.

"Er... ... it's OK. I've got it. Rutskoy... ... Putin... ... Litvinenko."

She turned to reach for the phone but then hesitated.

"This is for real? You're not... ...?"

"And tell them," James cut her off, "that you can't raise the nurses' station next to Rutskoy's room. No-one has answered the phones there since the Russians came in."

She stared at him, eyes wide and round. This was for real. No question.

"And, Mandy," he said, looking directly into those huge, brown eyes. "Keep my name out of it. If the police should ask, tell them you're speaking for Dr. Harwood. I just left him. He knows about the Russians. Security just told him."

The nurse sitting at the computer had listened to this exchange at first with amusement but then in total astonishment. As James turned away, she reached for her own desk phone, pressed 9 three times and handed it up to Amanda.

* * * * *

James heard Amanda's first words to the police, but his long legs carried him quickly down T2 to its junction with T3, and her voice rapidly faded away. At the corner, he stopped and looked back to where the nurse was still speaking on the phone. She gave a little wave with her free hand, and what looked like a thumbs-up sign. James waved back, and then stepped around the corner and stopped.

Corridor T3 stretched away, wide and empty, all the way to the abandoned nurses' station at the far corner some fifty yards from where he stood. There were doors down both sides of the corridor, some open, some closed. Adorning the plain sky-blue walls between the doors were a variety of landscapes, large photo-prints down the left-hand side, watercolours to the right. He could hear the sound of a television, a game show which he didn't recognise, through the slightly open door to his left. Along on his right, a door stood wide open, and a child's laughter drifted out in response to teasing from "Grandad." James wondered whether child or Grandad was the patient, and hoped they would both stay safely in their room.

He walked softly down the centre of the corridor, his eyes flicking left and right, passing over the pictures and reading the doors. Patients' rooms had the name of their occupants printed on cards inserted into brass holders. Some of the other rooms were also named with etched brass plates, *kitchen, lounge, bathroom* etc. and some just had numbers. Most of the patients' rooms had their doors at least slightly open, but James knew that the door he was looking for would almost certainly be shut tight.

It was.

The second door from the end on his left. A flat-surfaced, royal-blue door, just like all the others he'd passed, except for the name on the card, *Pytor Rutskoy*. The door on the opposite side of the corridor stood wide open. The bed was unoccupied, the bed-clothes rumpled. The name on the door said *Angela Lockhart*. James stepped lightly across the corridor and listened. No voices. No sound of movement. He looked through the crack between door and door-frame. No-one.

He could just see about one-third of the entrance to the en-suite bathroom. The door was wide open. No sound. No Russians. He trod lightly into the room, the dark-blue carpet cushioning his steps. Best to be sure. He'd always taught his men, *If there's no-one else to watch your back, do it yourself.* He wasn't going to tackle Rutskoy's room without knowing the one behind him was empty.

And then, as he peered into the bathroom, he heard it. Behind him. Not a cry. Not a moan. Just a slight whimper. The sort of sound you might hear in a hospital and not think it unusual.

As James swung round, he felt the heat of anger mounting in him. So far, in what had become a very full day, he had accepted each challenge as a problem to be solved by a bit of clear, logical thinking. But that pathetic, strangled whimper triggered a different response. Someone, very close by, was being hurt, and for no reason but being in the wrong place at the wrong time. James was aware of the anger, and he made no effort to control it. Although it may sometimes conflict with what some saw as the Christian ethic, James never allowed his anger to override his judgement. He always believed that there were some things it was right to be angry about, and the ruthless infliction of pain on someone who neither deserved it nor could resist it was right at the top of his list.

He was moving so quickly as he crossed the room that he almost fell over the bedding-laden trolley that appeared suddenly in the doorway. The young woman pushing the trolley stepped back into the corridor looking startled, but unafraid. James recognised her as a nursing auxiliary from her short-sleeved, grey dress with burgundy piping to sleeves and collar. He knew there had recently been some new appointments. Young women from Poland, or some other East European country. He hoped her English wasn't going to be a problem.

Pulling the trolley into the room, he beckoned for her to follow. She did, but only as far as the door. Her face was narrow with high cheekbones, and its most attractive feature was a pair of sparkling green eyes which told him quite clearly that she had no intention of joining him in that empty room.

He had to gain her trust, and quickly, as she had given him a plan.

"My name is Montrayne," he said. "Lord Aullton."

She frowned, as though the words ought to mean something, but she couldn't think what.

He pointed to the logo embroidered on right breast of her dress.

"Aullton," he said, and reached into his jacket for his wallet. He handed her his driving licence and a business card.

"Aullton," he said again and pointed at himself.

She examined the business card, then the photo on the driving licence, and suddenly, the penny dropped. A new anxiety came into her eyes which James interpreted to mean that she was now afraid of a reprimand for some unknown fault. She pointed into the room.

"I … … make … … bed," she said. "Sister … … she tell."

"Yes," replied James. "That's fine. You are not in trouble."

He spoke slowly, saying each word clearly.

"I just need you to help me. OK?"

She frowned, and he wondered if she understood. *Don't we check their English when we give them these jobs,* he thought. Then she brightened.

"You … … help … … make … … bed?"

"No, Jacinta," he said, reading off her name badge. "We are going to change the bed in Room 236, Mr Rutskoy."

"No," she shook her head. "He OK. This … … bed … … change."

Nice wasn't working, and James was running out of time.

"Jacinta," he said, moving the trolley aside to step close so he was towering over her. He thought momentarily of gripping her shoulders, but he didn't want to actually frighten her or, in today's climate of *sue-anyone-you-can-anytime-you-can,* end up accused of assaulting her. "Just do exactly what I tell you. Do you understand?"

She looked up. He was standing so close that the smooth skin of her throat was stretched tight as her head tilted back. She swallowed nervously, intimidated but not giving ground.

"Understand," she said. "Not… … stupid."

"Good. Now listen carefully."

He manoeuvred her trolley across the corridor so that it was in front of the door to room 236. It wasn't the girl herself he needed so much as her voice.

He had no idea what he was going to find on the other side of the door, but he didn't dare wait for the police to arrive. They would not appear quietly; sirens and blue lights for sure, ruining any possibility of a surprise assault. Once they turned up, the thing would turn into a siege, a very unhealthy mix of armed and determined police versus armed and ruthless villains with an unknown number of innocent and defenceless hostages caught in between.

Of course, there was no guarantee that his way would be any better, but he did, at least for the moment, have that most crucial advantage. Surprise.

Forty-Six

The Dower House – 8.30 pm

Abby was in bed. She wasn't asleep, but her eyes were definitely starting to droop before Charles Ingalls had even begun to sort out his family's troubles in their Little House on the Prairie. Her eyes were still fixed on the flat screen TV perched on the chest at the end of her bed, but she was beginning to lose the thread of the story. It would all come right in the end, she thought dreamily. If Charles didn't sort it out, then Laura probably would.

When she had first asked her dad, about a year after the abduction, she had discovered that he was not at all keen on her having any sort of TV in her bedroom, let alone the huge, wall-mounted, flat screen that she'd been asking for. In the end, they had both compromised, and Abby soon found she was perfectly happy with this 19" LCD TV with its built-in DVD player.

It was the TV that had made it so easy for Montrayne to persuade Abby to think about bed once their game of hide-and-seek was over. The excitement of the afternoon had wearied her more than she had realised so that, when Mrs Siddons had supported the Marquess with an offer of hot chocolate and freshly baked cookies, Abby had easily succumbed.

She smiled sleepily now as her grandfather lifted the empty plate off the Winnie-the-Pooh duvet, and dusted a few stray crumbs off Tigger's head. She lifted her arms to give him a hug as he bent down to drop a kiss on her forehead and, as he began to straighten, whispered, "Is Daddy home yet?"

There was only the tiniest pause before his reply.

"Not yet, sweetheart," he said, and then with a confidence he didn't feel, "But I'm sure he won't be long now."

"Will you tell him to come and see me when he gets back?"

"I don't expect he'll need any telling," replied her grandfather, "but I'll do it anyway."

"Thanks."

Her eyes flicked to the TV screen and then back to Montrayne as a thought flew into her mind.

"Are you going to see Grandma tonight?"

He noticed the worry lines on her normally flawless forehead, and lowered himself gently to sit on the edge of her bed.

"I don't think so, sweetheart. Not this time. I'll stay here until your father gets back and then I think I'll get some sleep. Just as you need to do, young lady. We both have to be up early in the morning. You have school, and I need to be back in London."

"Daddy said I might not be going to school tomorrow."

"Did he?"

James had not yet mentioned this to his father, and it strengthened the belief of the Marquess that there was more going on than he'd been told. Still, there was no good cause to be served by worrying the child.

"Well," he said. "We'll see what your Daddy says in the morning. No need to worry about that now. And as for Grandma, I'll be back at the Priory for the weekend, for the usual Trust meeting, so you can come over and visit us then. How do you like that?"

"Cool," she replied, and then as an afterthought, "I like Grandma."

"I know you do, sweetheart. I'm quite taken with her myself."

She smiled and closed her eyes as she snuggled down into the pillow.

Almost in a whisper, he heard her say, "I love you, Grandad. Can you turn the TV off, please?"

"Love you too, sweetheart. Goodnight."

He picked up the remote from the duvet, and stood slowly so as not to disturb her. Having silenced the TV, he looked back at her, perfectly composed, no worry lines now. As he watched her breathing gently, he knew that there was nothing that he would not do to keep her safe. He hoped fervently that James knew what he was doing getting involved with this girl, Lizzie, and all the problems she seemed to carry along with her.

Lizzie! It was time to get something straightened out about that young woman.

He left Abby's room quietly, no great feat considering the long, soft pile of her carpet, but he didn't close her door. He knew she liked it slightly open, so soft light from the corridor could filter through the narrow aperture. Another hangover from the abduction.

He sighed and made his way straight back downstairs to the library. Only when he'd got there did he remember to call Cherry's mobile and let him know that Abby was safely tucked up in bed for the night.

With the curtains drawn across the windows, and soft light radiating from the Murano crystal wall sconces, the library usually seemed a warm and cosy room. Montrayne remembered some very agreeable conversations taking place under the weighty authority of the thousand or so volumes that lined the walls.

There was, however, nothing agreeable about the conversation he was now contemplating as he sat in the same chair he had occupied earlier. His Blackberry was in his hand and his thumb gently caressed the screen while he played through in his mind different opening gambits, considering how each might develop to gain him the advantage he wanted. Of course, this strategy only really worked when you knew what pieces your opponent had on the board. Everything could suddenly be thrown into turmoil if the piece you had thought was a pawn unexpectedly turned out to be a queen.

What was Lizzie, a pawn or a queen? He really had no idea.

Having no reason to delay any longer, he searched his phonebook for a number and pressed the call button.

"Hello, Vernon. It's Alistair Montrayne. Sorry to be disturbing you at home."

"Alistair. Always a pleasure to speak to you, my dear chap."

"There won't be much pleasure in this, I'm afraid."

The first of many pauses.

"Is that so? Then you'd better tell me what this is about."

"I rather think you can shed some light on a little problem that has surfaced in my neighbourhood."

"A little problem? Well, fire away. I'll do what I can."

"Do you remember that evening we met for drinks at the Grand Carlton? Maybe three, four, weeks ago?"

A pause. *"Not sure I do."*

"We were just going over the fine print for that Bahrain Defence Forces contract."

"Ah, yes. My side of things was pretty well tied up, as I remember. Just a few minor wrinkles to iron out. It was your agreement with the Bahrain Police over their rather lax attitude to people trafficking that was holding things up. And... ... er... ... how are you progressing with that, might I ask?"

"We're... ... progressing." Noncommittal. Save the leverage for when it might be needed.

"Glad to hear it, my dear fellow. Delighted... ... but I'm sure that wasn't what you rang to tell me?"

"Quite right."

"You mentioned a problem, I think."

"Indeed. Our discussion went on a little longer than expected, if you remember. And before I left, a young woman arrived. She had, I think, come to meet you."

Another pause, rather longer this time. *"A young woman, you say. I don't think so. You must be mistaken."*

The Marquess knew he was on delicate ground, but he wanted the truth, and was in no mood to be messed around.

"No mistake, Vernon. I saw her waiting for you."

Silence.

"She was about twenty. Very pretty. Long chestnut hair. She was, I seem to remember, wearing a blue dress. Dark blue."

"Ah, yes… … I'm sorry, Alistair. I'd forgotten. If you hadn't been in such a hurry, I'd have introduced you. It was… … my niece. She's… … er… … studying at Birmingham University."

"Vernon. I think you and I both know that your niece went to Oxford, is now pushing thirty and works for an advertising company based in New York."

Silence.

"Vernon. I'm not trying to embarrass you or create a problem for you. Quite the opposite. I need your help."

He waited, and was beginning to wonder whether more direct pressure might be needed when he heard a sigh drift heavily from the phone.

"You're right, of course, Alistair. I should have known you'd catch on. Another sigh. *"What do you want to know?"*

"I need to know what that girl is involved in. I don't mean… … the services she may have provided for you. That's not my concern. There's something more serious going on… … dangerous even… … and I need to know what it is."

"You're right again, Alistair. This is not your concern. Whatever is going on, as you put it, has nothing to do with you. I advise you to stay out of it."

"I can't stay out of it. That girl has turned up here."

"Here! .. … You don't mean your London house."

"No, no. I'm at the Dower House with James. Flew up this afternoon only to find this girl's been living here since Saturday."

"I don't understand… … You really must be mistaken?… … What's her name?"

"She's calling herself Lizzie. Elizabeth Burleigh."

"No, that's not right. Must be a different girl. The one you saw at the Carlton was called Diane Thomas."

There was genuine surprise in his tone, and a hint of something else as well. Anger? Fear perhaps? Or was it just the shame of being found out? Hard to tell.

"No mistake, Vernon. She probably has half-a dozen different names. And, according to James, she has made no secret of her… … profession."

"But… … what's she doing there?"

"That, Vernon, is exactly what I'm trying to find out."

"Surely James hasn't… … hasn't taken her up."

"I can't be sure. I'm inclined to think not, but… …"

"Alistair, you had better hope to God that James hasn't taken up with her, because if he has then you have no idea what kind of trouble you could be in."

"It seems we're in trouble already, and I have no idea why... ... But I think you do, Vernon. So it's time to start talking."

"I can't help you, Alistair. I'm sorry."

"Vernon, did you ever wonder what would happen to your chances in the election if it were to become known that you regularly consort with a prostitute?"

"Alistair!! You wouldn't."

"Absolutely not. But the fact that *I* would not tell anyone doesn't mean that *she* would not. Especially if she had something to gain by it."

"I'm aware of that possibility. In fact, I have recently paid a substantial sum of money to make sure the girl is taken care of. Now I know where she may be found, you may take it from me that she will shortly cease to be a trouble to you, to me, to anyone."

"Vernon, are you saying what I think you're saying?"

"I'm saying the matter is being taken care of. So you can stop worrying and get back to making sure my Bahrain contract can be signed on time. There's a lot of money at stake and I don't want the Americans muscling in on it."

Time to apply the leverage.

"I don't think I can give my full attention to Bahrain, Vernon, while my mind is so occupied by the intrusion of this tiresome wench into my family."

"Just do what you're paid to do, Alistair, and leave the rest to me... ... Now, if you'll excuse me, I have a phone call to make. Goodnight."

Montrayne stared at the screen of his Blackberry, as though he should be able to read there all the things that had not been said in this very unsatisfactory conversation. It was not in his nature to sit back and do nothing, but he could think of no action which he could take that did not run the risk of making matters worse for James, and all because he found himself in the very unfamiliar position of not having a clue what was going on.

Forty-Seven

Aullton Foundation Hospital – 8.35 pm

Pytor Rutskoy was terrified. He had given some TV interviews, and been published several times in the Guardian, but he would never have believed that he had angered the government of his mother country so much that he could become a target of assassination. But when those two thugs had burst into his room, what else was he to think?

He couldn't know that they'd never heard of him until they were told, in a call from their boss at five twenty-three, to use visiting him as a ploy to gain them access to Angie. Nor could he know that they had no intention of harming him, as long as he kept quiet and did as he was told. He didn't understand why they hadn't killed him straight away instead of hiding in his bathroom. Nor did he understand how they could expect him to eat the meal which had been brought to him exactly on time, and only minutes before they had burst into his room. It had sat there, roast beef and Yorkshire pudding, congealing on the tray the nurse had pulled across the bed for him. He had no appetite as long as those two Russians – he thought they were Russian, although he had some difficulty placing their accent – glared at him from the safety of his bathroom. He could just about stand the glare. It was the silenced automatic pistols that really took away his appetite.

And now there was another problem.

His gall stones successfully removed, he was expecting to be discharged the following day. He was now perfectly capable of taking himself to the bathroom whenever necessary. No more indignity with bottles and bedpans. Sadly, he was now in danger of suffering the even greater indignity of wetting his bed. Fear was exacerbating his need for the bathroom, but he knew he couldn't possibly bring himself to perform the necessary function with those two supervising every step of the process. Perhaps he should just give in and let his bladder empty itself. It would anyway the moment they killed him, so what did it really matter.

A short while ago, the taller of the two had left his room to reappear moments later pushing two nurses in front of him. The older, slightly taller of the pair was Ruth Turner, the sister in charge of that wing. She might be well into her forties, but she was still a very attractive woman. At least, Rutskoy thought so. He appreciated her wide smile, her white teeth and the way her brown almond eyes crinkled with amusement at his frequent attempts at gallantry.

There was no amusement there now. Her eyes were wide and moist as she struggled to keep her fear under control. She was kneeling on the floor at the foot of Rutskoy's bed with a silenced Glock just a couple of inches from her forehead. She had an arm around the shoulders of Satnam something-or-other, the nurse with the unpronounceable surname. Rutskoy watched the two women as the older of the two Russians spoke to them in heavily accented English.

"Where is Angela Lockhart?"

It was the man holding the Glock to her face who had spoken. The other, younger and stockier, stood watching Rutskoy, his Glock hanging loosely by his side. Rutskoy couldn't take his eyes from it.

The voice was harsh and guttural, drawing out every syllable. Sister Turner shook her head, unable to speak.

"One more time, I ask nice. After that, my friend here stop being nice. You understand?"

Sister Turner didn't move, but tears began to trickle from her eyes, as the harsh voice continued.

"My friend here, he enjoys young women... ... He likes them to hurt... ... He likes them to moan... ... You understand? Hmmm?"

Rutskoy heard the low moan that trickled from the lips of the young nurse as she leaned into Sister Turner.

"Ah, she understands. Good. Now unless you tell me what I want, my friend will start to do things to your young... ... colleague... ... that's right, colleague? She will moan many times before he finish. You don't talk, she moan. You understand?"

Satnam flinched as the Russian's hand stroked her hair, and Rutskoy wished with all his heart that he could have that Glock in his own hand for just a second. He knew how to use it and knew that's all it would take. One second. To put a bullet in the head of each of these monsters.

But, covered in blankets, with a tray across his legs, there was just no way he could grab one of those Glocks.

"You understand?" the Russian asked again, this time placing the tip of the silencer under Sister Turner's chin and forcing her to look up at him.

She tried to nod, but the gun prevented her from moving her head. The Russian, watching her closely, knew he had her cooperation.

"So, I ask again." He lowered the gun a fraction. "Where is Angela Lockhart?"

Rutskoy looked at her, fascinated. Was he about to see her brains come gushing out of the side of her head? Were they about to treat him to a foretaste of what he was sure his own fate would be before the night was out. Sister Turner swallowed and tried to work some saliva into her mouth. It didn't seem to help. Her voice was just a croak. And Satnam moaned again.

And then they heard it, and froze. All five of them. Rutskoy, the two Russians, the two nurses, still as any tableau.

The knock came again, and a woman's voice, young and foreign, could be heard saying, "I change bed, Mr Rutskoy. I come in now."

There was a click as the passkey overrode the lock, and a bump as a trolley pushed the door slightly open.

Through the widening crack Rutskoy saw the front of a trolley piled with sheets. Behind it, well back in the corridor, a young woman in a grey dress whom he vaguely recognised stared in at him. Then her head jerked slightly and her eyes flicked to the left. He hadn't made his money by being slow on the uptake. He understood her silent message. As the door continued to drift open, he saw a large man, a very large man, pressing himself tightly against the hinged side of the doorframe.

For one moment Rutskoy was the only person in the room who could see all the players in the unfolding drama. He knew what was coming, and he was ready.

James watched the door ease slowly open as Jacinta pushed against it with her trolley. At first, he could see little of the room, but then a grey and white bedside unit came into view against the back wall. Then the edge of the bed and, finally, its occupant. It was hard to judge Rutskoy's age or build as he sat slumped against his pillows, but James caught that sudden awareness in his eyes when Jacinta jerked her head before moving away from the door as he'd told her.

The door stopped moving and through the crack between door and frame James saw two men. They were standing, both looking towards the door, and both carrying guns. He also saw two women kneeling huddled together at the foot of the bed. Then there was a flash of movement as the shorter of the two men dashed to stand behind the door ready, presumably, to grab the girl with the trolley as she came into the room.

James moved back slightly. If he could see through the crack, so presumably could the Russian. He took a deep breath, held it for a moment, then released it slowly. He didn't want to do this. Not for his own sake, but for Abby's. She'd already lost her mother. What would it do to her to lose him as well? Two men, widely separated, both armed. He had faced worse odds, but one of them could still get lucky. And then the thought was gone, vanished like smoke blown on the wind.

A final glance at Jacinta to check she had moved far enough back to be out of the line of sight of both Russians, and James leapt through the doorway.

His right foot shoved the trolley forward with enough force to crash into the side of Rutskoy's bed. Neatly folded sheets tumbled from it onto the floor.

His left shoulder crashed the door back on its hinges, crushing the Russian behind it into the wall. As James rolled his body into the door, his right hand flew forward and up, releasing the handle at the rear of the bedpan which he had removed from the trolley. It might only be polypropylene, and not the old enamelled pan of the early NHS, but at something over a kilo it was still twice as heavy as the fragmentation grenades he used to toss around. The distance was only ten feet, and he hadn't lost his touch. The blunt nose of the pan crunched into the upper lip of the second Russian as his gun hand began to swing back from the trolley to James. The Russian had scarcely registered the impact when his left ear caught the full force of a viciously hurled plate of congealed roast beef in gravy. He never noticed Rutskoy's yell of satisfaction, since a sledgehammer seemed to have swung up into his crotch. James kicked out again, this time into the Russian's left knee causing him to slump sideways.

His gun hand swung wildly as he battled with the agony in groin and knee and tried to regain his balance. Then his hand was gripped by a power-driven vice which crunched his fingers into the metal of the Glock and fire blazed through his shoulder as the ball-joint was twisted free of its socket. He seemed to rise from the floor and, propelled by an irresistible force, hurtled towards the door which was starting to swing closed as his compatriot pushed himself away from the wall, shaking his head and blinking rapidly.

The younger Russian was dazed. Blood was running freely from his nose and lips where they had most fortuitously been smashed by the coat hooks on the back of the door. The back of his head throbbed from its violent connection with the wall, not plaster-board as many were, but a strong supporting wall. His gun had dropped from his hand as the double impact fogged his brain, and scarcely had he decided that he should try and pick it up, than his face was once more crushed as the head of his compatriot careened into it.

James watched the two Russians crumple into the corner behind the door. *It shouldn't have been that easy,* he thought. *Thank God they weren't the highly trained ex-Spetsnaz which some Russian mobs had managed to recruit.*

The Glock which he'd wrenched away from the first Russian sat comfortably in his right hand covering the figures writhing in the corner. The older guy was moaning from the fiery pain of his dislocated shoulder, made worse by the efforts of the younger man underneath him to try and heave him off.

"Keep still," said James in a voice loud enough to cut through the groans.

When the writhing continued, he moved just close enough to kick the leg of the younger man, repeating his command more loudly.

"Keep still, you fool. It's finished."

This time the heaving stopped, but it wasn't over. Not quite.

Somewhere underneath one or other of the Russians was another Glock. James couldn't see it now, but he knew it was there. Maybe one of them already had his hand on it.

"It's there," said a voice to his left.

He risked a quick glance at the man in the bed. Rutskoy was looking over at the door, his left arm extended, pointing.

"Down there." His voice was urgent now

And there it was. Black, compact and deadly. A Glock 19, pushed up against the door, only inches away from the younger Russian's right hand. And his fingers were already moving towards it. The rest of his body was covered by the older Russian who was still now, although continuing his low moaning.

"Don't do it, you fool."

James's voice was harsh and menacing, as he'd intended it to be. The fingers stopped their gentle slide towards the gun and a bloodied face peered at him over the older Russian's left shoulder.

To emphasise his command, James shifted his aim slightly so that his Glock was pointed directly in the centre of the young man's forehead. Locking his gaze on the man's tear-filled eyes, James shook his head.

"If you fancy being dead, then go ahead," he said, in a more conversational tone. "Otherwise, let's just call it a day."

The Russian nodded, and slowly began to withdraw his hand from the gun.

Then his eyes widened and with a tremendous effort he flung the older Russian to his left while at the same time leaning to his right to make a grab for the gun. James caught that flash in his eyes and was already moving as the older Russian screamed in agony as he fell on his damaged shoulder.

James really didn't want to shoot anyone. With the trouble he was in already, another dead body in his vicinity was probably more than the police could cope with. And there were other reasons why he was reluctant to put a bullet where it so clearly belonged.

So he lunged forward and swung his right foot with all the force and precision of a Beckham penalty. The Russian's hand closed over the grip of the gun, but as he lifted it James's foot came up and the beautifully polished, round toe of Mr Taylor's bespoke Oxford broke his jaw in two places. He was unconscious before he could pull the trigger.

Now it was over.

Tuesday

3rd May 2005

Aushra Paulauskaitė – Day Four

Vilnius, Lithuania – 6:00 am

Aushra lay still, staring dreamily through the gloom of her bedroom at the cracked and peeling ceiling above. Rain was pattering against her window and beyond it, down in the courtyard, muffled sounds disturbed the peace of the dawn. Nothing threatening. It was just the usual scuffs and mumbles of neighbours setting off for work, trying not to be too noisy, but never quite succeeding. Knowing what she was listening for, Aushra eventually heard a bicycle rattle over the cobbles.

It was moving slowly, its ancient mudguards tinkling with every bump in the uneven surface. She could imagine its owner, a man barely into his forties but now looking twenty years older, bowed down with a burden no man should have to bear. Every morning, he would push his bicycle out of the courtyard before mounting to cycle off to begin his shift as a driver of the number nine trolley-bus. Until a few days ago, he would have left with a smile and a cheerful wave to the wife who always saw him off at the door. But that was before Mykolas threw himself from the Zaliasis Bridge. No man should have to arrange a funeral for his son, but too many were having to do so in these difficult times.

Aushra stared at the ceiling, her eyes dry, her cheeks free of tears. She was surprised that she could think of her friend now without crying. Was that a good thing? Or did it mean she no longer cared as much as she had done such a short while ago? Was she beginning to forget Mykolas in the excitement and anticipation of the new life opening up ahead of her?

No, she thought. *He was my friend. I'll not forget him. Wherever I go, I'll not forget him. Ever.*

She hoped that her determination would stand fast against the eroding effect of time.

She turned over onto her side to face the window, remembering how yesterday the number nine bus had taken her along the Konstitucijos prospektas for her appointment with Mr Portess. It had been a strange meeting, not at all what she had expected. The other girls had been there as well, at the same time, so he had met all five of them together. Aushra had been expecting an individual interview to discuss the nature of her work, to finalise terms and conditions, and to go over the practical arrangements for setting up home and starting work in a new country. Of course, this had all been referred to by local company representatives at earlier meetings, but so far she had received nothing in writing. None of the girls had.

And after the meeting, they still had nothing in writing.

Being inexperienced in these matters, they were not worried. Mr Portess had spoken about their induction into the company and painted a glowing prospect for each of them, with just the right combination of job satisfaction and financial reward. He hadn't been able to tell them the name of the company they would be working for since, as he had explained, there were a number of businesses in the group and they would be given a position appropriate to their ability and aptitude following induction. He would be flying with them on Wednesday's Lufthansa flight from Vilnius to Birmingham. On landing, he would hand them over to his personal assistant who would give each of them a briefing pack containing, amongst other useful information, copies of their contracts which would be finalised once they had completed their induction. They would then be taken to their temporary accommodation. As soon as they felt settled, he had said, they would be free to look around for more permanent accommodation of their own choosing.

He had tried very hard to be pleasant, smiling a lot as he spoke to them in heavily accented Lithuanian. He was not fluent, but they had been impressed by the fact that he tried at all. Most English people couldn't be bothered to make the effort to learn their language. He had asked about their families, and said he expected they would be sorry to be leaving home. Aushra had not before realised that she was not the only one amongst the girls who had no father living at home. Hers had walked out on the family when Aushra was only six, and two of the other girls had similar experiences. The fathers of the other two had died, one in a car accident and the other from cancer. Oddly enough, none of the five had brothers either.

What a strange coincidence, thought Aushra. *It seems almost to bind us together somehow.*

Mr Portess did not have much else to say to them, and had eventually ushered them out, still smiling.

But his smiles had held no warmth, and his piercing blue eyes had seemed to Aushra to be hard and cold. She wondered, as she lay there thinking over the meeting, just how tough and ruthless you had to be to achieve success in business. Her trouble was that she liked people too much to be prepared to trample over them in a desperate scramble to climb the corporate ladder. She told herself it didn't matter. To do the job well and enjoy it, and to earn promotion on her merits, was all she really wanted.

And she would do it well, she was sure of that. She was determined to give all her attention to the six weeks of induction, and to learn everything she could.

She sat up hurriedly. That's what she'd forgotten to tell her Mum yesterday evening. Mr Portess had asked them to warn their families that there would be no contact during that induction period. He said it was quite an intensive time and they would need to stay completely focussed on their work. It wasn't a rule, he had assured them, when a couple of them had started to look worried. There was no prohibition or anything of that sort, but experience had shown that homesickness had been worse in the early stages of their employment when young people had constantly been phoning home, and this of course distracted them from their training. *Use the phone to let your family know you have arrived safely,* he had said, *but at least warn your mothers not to worry if they don't hear from you for some weeks after that.*

Aushra got out of bed and decided to make herself a drink. Her Mum would be awake soon and she would tell her what Mr Portess had said, before she went off to work at the Duona bakery. She knew her Mum wouldn't like it, but she would understand. She had been amazingly supportive of her daughter's dream of a new life, but Aushra would reassure her again that she would certainly not follow the example of the daughter of her mother's friend at the bakery.

Veslava Legatiene had gone to England five months ago, hired by the same agency that had recruited Aushra. After that first phone call to say she had arrived safely, she had never been heard from again. She had clearly taken very much to heart the advice not to call home, and Aushra had promised her mother that she would find Veslava and persuade her that it was now time to get in touch with her family.

She had no idea it was a promise that would prove so hard to keep.

Forty-Eight

Aullton Foundation Hospital – 12:15am

The room was quiet and Angie was sleeping peacefully. She had been fretful earlier wnen Barrie had her moved to yet another room, but I had stayed with her, reassuring her that there was nothing to worry about. I didn't mention the men with guns or the armed police prowling the grounds. There was no point, and it would only have made her even more nervous and agitated. She was already struggling enough with the treatment she was receiving for her drug use and the battering her body had received. I wanted to protect her from any more damage, physical or emotional. So I had tried to settle her mind by getting her to think about what lay ahead, a future without strip clubs, lap dancers, massage parlours and brutal or pathetic punters. I worked hard at it and found I was making it sound so attractive, even achievable, that the longing in my own mind became almost unbearable.

Eventually she drifted off to sleep and, for the first time, I was able to ask James what had happened after he left us earlier in the evening. Even with Barrie to watch over us, I'd been scared, but for Angie's sake I had tried to hide it. I suppose it was all the worse because we had no idea what was going on.

In real time it hadn't actually been very long, maybe half-an-hour after James had left us, before a young nursing auxiliary with a strong eastern European accent had knocked on the door asking for Doctor Harwood. She had seemed flushed and excited, but she informed Barrie that Mr James had told her to say that everything was OK and the police would soon be here to sort things out.

I heard the sirens almost immediately afterwards and worried that they might frighten Angie, but she was lying back with her eyes closed, breathing gently, looking more peaceful than I had seen her in a long time. Then I had remembered that Barrie had given her an injection soon after James had left.

Shortly after the sirens, Barrie's phone rang. It was Kingston, and the conversation was brief. As he slipped his phone back into his pocket, Barrie beckoned me to join him by the door. Then, whispering so as not to disturb Angie, he told me that he'd learnt from Kingston that the police were here and everything seemed to under control.

"I need to go and see what's happening," he said. "Will you be OK?"

He glanced over at Angie as he spoke and I was surprised at the look of tenderness in his eyes. Compassion in a doctor such as Barrie was not remarkable, but this was something more.

Whether I was frowning, I'm not sure, but Barrie seemed to interpret my expression as one of uncertainty.

"I can get Kingston to send someone to stay with you, if you want," he said, but I shook my head and assured him that we would be perfectly OK.

After he left, I went back to sit by Angie, still wondering about James but no longer quite so anxious. She stirred and became restless and I took her hand wishing I could calm the dreams that were troubling her. She was actually a year older than me, but she seemed so small and vulnerable that I found myself becoming quite determined that I would do everything I could to bring some hope into her future. She wasn't trained for anything. She'd passed no exams, having run away from home at fifteen, but she was a bright girl, or had been before the drugs had begun to wear her down. Maybe I could ask James for some money to get her started. For some reason, I knew I couldn't ask him for money for myself, but I wouldn't mind asking for Angie. Then perhaps she could take a course and train to be... ... I didn't know what... ... but something.

I was still thinking about this when Barrie came back, and he had company. Rod and John followed him into the room and I was so glad to see them that I completely forgot that first meeting with Rod at the RRISC offices. I checked Angie was still asleep before I let them explain what was happening because I didn't want her to hear anything that might upset her. She seemed more settled, the agitation of her dreams fading, but still well out of it.

We stood in a huddle by the door, speaking in low voices, as Rod explained what had held them up.

When they had first arrived, several minutes after the police, Rod and John had not been allowed out of their car. When asked, they said that they were just visiting a patient, but the police officer, a young fresh-faced lad who was definitely not one of the armed-response team, told them they'd best go home and come back tomorrow. He then had to go and deal with someone else who'd just driven into the car park so they had decided to just sit tight for a bit and see what happened. Rod passed the time by trying to get in touch with James who didn't answer immediately but, after about fifteen minutes, he called back and filled them in on what was happening. Several minutes after that, Barrie had gone out and told the police that Rod and his colleague were needed as they were each a possible tissue match for one of his patients who was seriously ill. He assured them that it was important for the well-being of his patient that they be allowed in and that he would personally vouch for them. The police had dithered, but when Barrie had insisted on taking their numbers so that the hospital's lawyers would know who to sue if the patient suffered as a result of this delay, Rod and John had at last been allowed in.

Then I told them the little I knew, which didn't add much to what they had already learned from James, on the phone, and Barrie, as he'd led them to Angie's room. After that, we none of us seemed to know quite what to do.

Barrie made several calls, checking in with various members of his senior night staff, and then excused himself to go and talk to the police to find out how seriously the working of the hospital was going to be hindered by their continuing presence.

James and I had gone back to the helicopter, having checked with the police that we were free to leave. Rod and John were last seen tossing a coin to see who was going to stay in the room and who got to keep the night nurses company at the end of the corridor. Nat, according to John, was out with his on-off girlfriend, and probably had his phone switched off. James thought that the two of them should be enough, especially since there were still a number of police about, gathering whatever evidence they could about the attack on Rutskoy.

When James had first seen them, in the corridor outside Angie's room, his voice and expression had been surprisingly grim.

"What took you so long?"

"Sorry, Boss," Rod had said, a little put out by James's tone. "We had to wait for the boys in blue to let us in."

"I don't mean that," James replied. "You should have been here well before the police. So what kept you?"

I was looking at Rod and thinking about what James had told me. I wondered just how reliable he would be if things turned nasty again. I didn't know him at all but, as I watched his expression, even I could tell that he was genuinely puzzled by James's reaction.

"I don't get you, Boss. We got here as soon as we could."

James wasn't convinced and Rod knew it.

"Look," he said. "I didn't even finish my can after Andy called. I phoned John here to tell him I'd be along to pick him up, then I jumped in the car and left. John was on his doorstep when I pulled in, so no holdup there. No traffic, no delays... ... Straight up, Boss, we got here as quick as we could."

James looked at him steadily for a moment and then nodded.

"OK," he said, and that was it.

In the few minutes it took to travel back to the Dower House in the helicopter, I asked James why he had seemed so put out with Rod. I wasn't suggesting he had been wrong or unfair and I definitely wasn't trying to stick up for Rod. I was just curious. Whether it was James's military background, I don't know, but apparently it was all to do with timing. He knew exactly when he had spoken to Andy and asked for backup. If things had happened exactly as Rod had described, James calculated he should have reached the hospital at least twenty minutes sooner than he did. So what had delayed him? James wondered whether the thought of having people depending on him in a physical, maybe violent, confrontation had brought Rod's fears back to the surface. Maybe he had delayed because he couldn't face the thought of what he might have to do. Or maybe he had thought that if he waited long enough the situation might be resolved before he arrived on the scene. If it had not been for the continuing police presence at the hospital, James would not have been happy at leaving Rod to take care of Angie, even with John in support.

If I had known what was going to happen next, I would not have been willing to leave her either. But none of us knew, and could never have known, so we were caught totally unprepared.

Forty-Nine

Paris Gare de Bercy – 9:15am

After fourteen mostly sleepless hours, they had arrived at Paris Gare de Bercy at nine fifteen that Tuesday morning. Although their berths on the *Palatino* had turned out to be surprisingly comfortable, it was well into the early hours before either of them had felt inclined to settle down to sleep. In any other couple similarly situated, their wakefulness might have been attributed to an enthusiasm for passionate physical activity. In John and Nadera, however, it was their minds that pulsated with energy rather than their bodies.

This had been no surprise to Nadera. In fact she had expected nothing else. She thought she was beginning to understand John's natural reticence, and was content to wait as he progressed along his own journey towards physical intimacy. As long as he didn't keep her waiting too long.

What she was not content with, however, was the way they were embarking on this mad scheme with virtually nothing in the way of forward planning. Now she had finally found, in this gentle, considerate, fraudster, a man she could love without reserve, and having then successfully killed him off, she was determined not to lose him in an adventure of chivalrous stupidity.

Immediately after they had eaten the set menu in the Palatino's functional dining car, they had returned with great relief to their compartment. At their table for four, they had been joined by two large French ladies who were returning to Paris after a long weekend in Rome. Throughout the meal they had insisted on relating, in a mixture of French and very bad Italian, every aspect of their recent itinerary, even producing a digital camera and waving the small viewing screen in front of John or Nadera to illustrate the beauty or sheer wonder of the places they had visited.

John had heard it said that enthusiasm was infectious but, after close on an hour of it, both he and Nadera had decided that unadulterated, and in close proximity, it was utterly repelling. Entering their compartment, they discovered that it had shrunk substantially. In their absence the conductor had made up their beds ready for sleep, all three of them, not just the two that were actually needed.

It took several minutes to work out how to reverse the conductor's well-intentioned mistake, so they could sit in reasonable comfort on the lower bunk without risking decapitation from the one above. Nadera was determined that she would not allow either of them to begin thinking about sleep until they had at least the outline of a viable plan.

"Why are we doing this?"

She asked the question not with any intention of trying to dissuade him, but simply to get him to clarify exactly what their objective was.

John thought about the question for a while, and then he thought about his answer. With Nadera, he decided, honesty was always going to be best. She waited patiently, half-turned towards him, at the opposite end of the bunk. Her head was tilted slightly to one side, eyebrows raised, encouraging him without speaking.

"Guilt, I suppose," he said finally, without looking up to catch her eye. "Phil Simmons was a good lad. A good engineer too, and a good manager."

He sighed, head still down. "Thinking back, I reckon I should have let him run the company. He'd have made a darn sight better job of it than I did. We'd both have made a decent living … … and," he smiled wryly, "we'd both still *be* living."

She stretched out and touched his knee which was just within reach.

"Yes, my love," she responded. "You must not think I do not understand this. But tell me please, what is it that you… … we… … can do, that the police cannot do?"

John gently rested his hand on hers, softly caressing it. The touch seemed to change his mood, and he began to speak with rather more determination.

"I'm going to make sure the police get it right."

"My love, you are not a… … a detective. You do not understand how to do these things."

"True," he admitted, thinking that he'd had trouble lately detecting what day it was. "But *you* understand how to do them. You've been trained in these things. You can be Sherlock Holmes and I'll just be Dr Watson."

Since her knowledge of English Literature was even more sketchy than most A-level students, she failed to grasp the allusion, but she did catch the drift of what he was saying.

"If I am to be your detective," she said, "I cannot do anything without some facts. Where are those papers you printed from the hotel computer?"

John dragged his holdall up onto the bunk and searched around in it, eventually pulling out a sheaf of rather crumpled sheets of white A4 paper. Some were just covered in black type while others had pictures intermingled with the text. Two sheets had nothing more than a somewhat faded blow-up of a photograph. The hotel would not allow patrons to print in best quality mode as it used up too much ink. It didn't matter. The faces of the figures portrayed were clear enough.

He laid one of the photographs on the bunk, turned so Nadera could see it more easily.

"James Montrayne," he said

Nadera adjusted the paper slightly and found herself looking at a head and shoulders shot of a man in his late thirties, dark-haired, brown eyed and, she had to admit to herself, not at all hard on the eyes. Still, good-looking or not, he was the enemy until proven otherwise. She noticed from the reference at the bottom of the sheet that the picture had been lifted from the website of some organisation called The Aullton Foundation.

"What is this?" she asked, tapping the paper.

"Apparently it's some kind of charitable trust which sponsors several private hospitals in the UK and a lot more in Africa."

Nadera's eyes narrowed as she picked up on the word *sponsors*. "Africa... ... Yes I see they need sponsors, but do private hospitals in England not earn money?"

"Well, yes. I guess so," John replied. "But I noticed that at least half the beds in each hospital are reserved for non-fee-paying patients referred by churches and charities all over the UK. I don't know why. I didn't bother to check for any more information on that."

"Hmmm," she thought about this. "Does this... ... foundation... do anything else?"

John picked up another sheet and glanced down it before replying.

"It says here that they have a scheme called **Moving On** which offers grants to young people from disadvantaged backgrounds who are struggling to make a start in life."

He read a bit more, and began shaking his head slowly.

"What?" asked Nadera.

"Well, it gives an example, a case study. A girl they call Sonia – obviously not her real name – was sexually abused by her father, ran away from home, started selling herself on the streets before she was sixteen, and ended up taking to drugs."

He looked up at Nadera. "I'm not a father, but I don't understand how anyone could do that to his own child."

"No," she said, her voice unusually quiet as she thought of her flight from her own family. "I do not understand this either."

John stared at her, remembering what she had told him about her own family's treatment of her and wondered whether he should mention it or just move on. He decided to move on.

"Anyway," he said resuming the story. "Somehow she got involved with a church group helping girls on the streets in Bradford and they referred her to an Aullton Foundation hospital to get clean of the drugs and the STDs. Ah... ... that makes sense of the reserved beds now. Anyway, after that the Foundation gave her a grant to go to college and study catering, and it says she's now graduated and has just started her own events catering business with a loan from the Foundation."

Nadera picked up the photograph from the bunk and examined the face more closely.

"So what is it that this James Montrayne does for the Foundation?"

John smiled. "Not a lot probably, except that it's his money that keeps it going."

"He is a rich man then?"

John's smile widened. "I'm not sure rich is superlative enough."

He picked up another sheet from the pile on the bunk. "This is an article from the archives of *The Guardian*. The obituary of Sir Peter Marchmont. When he died in 1990, he left an obscene fortune to his wife Lady Helena. £2.3 billion! I mean, how can anyone be worth £2.3 billion?"

"I don't know," replied Nadera. "But it happens in my country so why not in yours?"

"Yes, well, your country's stuffed full of oil. What's mine got these days?"

Nadera just shrugged.

"Don't worry," she said. "I am sure your government took a large amount in... ... er... ... what do you call it?"

"Inheritance tax. Yes, I'm sure you're right. Not much consolation though."

"Perhaps not," she replied. "So what does this Lady Helena do with her millions?"

"She leaves them to James Montrayne, that's what she does," he responded. "She was his great aunt, and she and Sir Peter had no children of their own."

"So this James Montrayne," she said, waving the photograph at John, "he is a ... ... what is the word?"

"Philanthropist?"

"Yes, exactly. Philanthropist. So is he the man to kill your Mr Simmons?"

"Why not? People with money often seem to think they can do whatever they like."

"Is James Montrayne such a person?"

"That, my sweet, is just what we are going to find out. And if he is, then we shall make sure that even his millions will not stop him getting what he deserves."

"And you know how we are going to do that?"
"I have an idea, yes."
"And if we learn that he did not kill Mr Simmons?"
"Then I think I might have an alternative theory."
"You mean you know who else might have done it?"
"Exactly."
"Then tell me, please."
So he did and, after that, they made their plans.

Fifty

The Dower House – 9.15 am

The sky was untarnished azure. The sea was a flat calm but, for some reason, my boat was rocking none too gently from side to side. I lay stretched out in the bottom, luxuriating in the strange, downy softness of its solid timbers, and basking in the warmth of the sun I could not see. The rocking became more vigorous and I began to roll with the motion of the boat.

I reached out my hand to its wooden sides to try and steady the movement, and then leapt up in horror as some unidentified monster surged from the deep to seize my hand in its gaping mouth.

And then it giggled.

I opened my eyes to stare at the monster which had rocked my boat and chewed my fingers, and I saw Abby, sitting on the edge of my bed, bouncing up and down as she held on to my hand.

She giggled again.

"Wake up, sleepyhead. It's past nine o'clock and I'm not at school."

"Abby," I groaned. "You horrible creature. Tell you what. I'll wake up, if you stop bouncing."

"Hmmm. OK."

And she did. But as the motion ebbed away, so too did her childish glee, and her expression became both serious and slightly anxious.

I was still trying to keep my part of the bargain, by remaining sitting up with both eyes open, when Abby asked the question I think she had woken me up for.

"Lizzie, where did you and Daddy go last night? And why has he had to go and talk to the police again this morning?"

I knew I was on difficult ground as I had no idea what James had already told her. Before I could gather enough thoughts together to give her an answer that might satisfy her, she tossed out another question.

"And why can't I go to school today? Daddy just said he'd tell me when he comes back from the police station… … I don't mind staying home," she added reassuringly. "It's cool. Honest. But… … I just wondered why."

I decided to begin with a question of my own.

"Is your grandfather still here?"

She looked surprised. "No. Mike flew him back to London before I got dressed. Didn't you hear them take off?"

I understood her astonishment. After all, the machine must have lifted off right outside my window. To sleep through that racket I must have been totally zonked out. I shook my head slowly.

"I thought you noticed," I said, "how fast asleep I was."

"Well, I did," she replied. "But now you're awake, you can tell me what's going on."

I still hesitated, and immediately saw the frustration building up behind her narrowing eyes and pursed lips.

"I'm not a child, Lizzie," announced this grown-up eight year old. "You can tell me the truth... ... Is Daddy in trouble again?"

So that was it. I felt better. At least I could reassure her that her father was not in trouble. Well, no more than he had been on Saturday, anyway.

I squeezed her hand, rather surprised to find that I was still holding it.

"No, Abby," I said. "Your dad's not in any more trouble with the police. I knew he was going to have to go and see them this morning, but it's only to help them. That's all."

She wasn't reassured. "I know about helping the police with their enquiries. I told you. Remember?"

She had, as well. That first time we'd met, back at the farm.

"No, no, Abby. It's not like that. He really is helping them."

I felt the pressure of her fingers relax a little.

"Honest? Just helping? Like, telling them things they need to know?"

"Just like that," I said.

"Hmmm."

I looked at her pretty young face, and saw the question in those wide innocent eyes. I wanted to respond to her trust, but I didn't want to take away her innocence, or as much as remained to her after her experience two years ago.

"Abby," I said, in a masterstroke of playing for time. "Why don't you go down and ask Mrs Siddons to sort us out some breakfast? Then I can get dressed, and when I come down I'll tell you what you want to know."

She looked at me with just a hint of suspicion. "You will?"

"I will. Now, off you go and let me get up."

As soon as the door closed behind her, I made another raid on the wardrobe of Sarah Montrayne. I assumed that it had been Mrs Siddons who had been busy while we were out yesterday, stocking the closet with dresses, trousers and skirts, and filling the chest of drawers with blouses and underclothes. Where the clothes had been stored previously, I had no idea, and didn't like to ask. Nor did I understand why James had not disposed of them when he came to live at the Dower House.

As I sorted through them, pulling out the garments I would wear that day, it suddenly dawned on me that Sarah Montrayne had a remarkably narrow taste in clothes. According to the labels, everything – skirts, jumpers, bras, pants, even shoes – all came from either M & S or Next. No other store was represented.

I sat on the bed, looking at the jumper and skirt I'd laid out to wear. I picked the jumper up and felt its woolly softness. I rubbed it against my cheek and smelled it. And then I understood. It was Mrs Siddons, all right. But she hadn't been resurrecting the hoarded clothes of a dead wife. She had been shopping, and probably some place where Next and M & S are fairly close together.

And then I checked the bras. No longer the wrong cup size as it had been on Sunday. That clinched it. I felt a little foolish as I should have noticed yesterday, but then I blamed my lapse on having to get dressed in a hurry to set off in time for school.

But why pretend that I was still wearing clothes that had belonged to the former Mrs Montrayne? I shook my head and smiled. It was almost certainly James. He probably didn't want me to feel embarrassed at having him pay for all my clothes. As if I'd have cared.

Still, it showed a tactfulness and courtesy that I'd not had much experience of. I found I rather liked it. And the style wasn't half bad for M & S. I was quite surprised.

After that, I did my best to be quick, but Abby was still working up quite a steam of impatience by the time I made it to the kitchen.

"Come on, Lizzie," she said, touching the back of her hand to a mug on the table in front of her. "Your coffee's nearly gone cold now. I could have had ten showers in the time you've taken."

"Well," I replied. "When I take a shower, I think it adds to the experience if I actually get wet. So then, of course, I have to dry off."

"I get wet," said Abby, both her tone and expression brim full of indignation. "And soapy. And I dry off properly too."

"Of course you do, dearie," said Mrs Siddons, smiling as she slipped a basket of hot croissants onto the table. "Lizzie was just teasing you, that's all."

"Oh," responded Abby. "Well in that case, she can make up for it by sitting down and telling me everything that happened last night."

With that settled, she helped herself to a croissant and a spoonful of apricot jam and looked at me expectantly as she began to make inroads into her breakfast.

Mrs Siddons, however, didn't seem at all sure that it *was* settled. "I don't think it will do any harm to wait until your father gets home. Will it Lizzie?"

I wasn't sure whether she was asking my opinion, or advising me, in her role of Abby's protector, not to say anything until I had James's approval. Still, since I'd already made up my mind, it didn't really matter.

"It's OK, Mrs Siddons," I said. "I don't mind explaining what happened."

Seeing her stiffen as she prepared to argue, I added, "Why don't you sit down and join us. Then you can be on hand to help me edit the story if necessary."

"Edit," said Abby, as Mrs Siddons plonked her mug of coffee heavily on the table and pulled up a chair. "What's that?"

"It's like a reporter, dearie," said the housekeeper, with a very meaning look at me. "Deciding how to tell a story."

"Oh," said Abby, after a moment's thought. "Well get editing, 'coz I want a really good story."

"Right," I said. "Well here goes."

I had decided to tell her the truth. I hated being lied to, and I never wanted Abby to feel that she couldn't trust me. Maybe my edited version wouldn't be the whole truth, but that was only because I didn't want to frighten her. Surprisingly, Mrs Siddons didn't interrupt once.

I told her how we'd gone to visit my friend, Angie, at the hospital and we'd used her grandfather's helicopter so we could get there quickly. I told her about a Russian gentleman who was also a patient at the hospital in the room opposite Angie's. I told her about two bad people who had broken into his room to make trouble. I told her that her father had sent for the police who had come and taken the men away. And this morning her father had gone to the police station to explain what had happened so that they could write it all down.

Simple, straight-forward and, to judge by the relief on Mrs Siddons' face, a much tamer version than the one James must have given her before he left. Needless to say, Abby didn't let me tell the story without interruption, but at least she accepted my carefully crafted answers without further interrogation.

The story over, and the last of the flaky crumbs licked from our fingers, something which Mrs Siddons reminded us was most unladylike, I wondered how we were to spend the rest of the morning while we waited for James to return. I should have known by now that his redoubtable housekeeper would have the answer.

"Abby, dear," she said, while clearing the dishes from the table. "Why don't you take Lizzie down to the trout stream and see if you can spot the otters?"

Judging by the way she leapt from her chair, this scheme clearly met with Abby's approval. I rather liked the idea myself as I had never seen a real live otter in the wild, or anywhere else for that matter.

"Come on, Lizzie. Let's go out to the stables and find you some wellies. I don't suppose you've got any."

I cast a quick glance at Mrs Siddons and noted the pursed lips and the faintest hint of a blush in her cheeks. Wellington boots had not been on her shopping list.

Finally equipped with wellies and waterproof jackets, and accompanied by Cherry, we set off for the trout stream which ran through the woodland skirting the rear gardens. I had forgotten the necessity for Cherry's presence, but Abby just seemed to take it for granted that if her father wasn't present, everywhere she went, Cherry went.

Over the next couple of hours or so, I found our bodyguard to be a very agreeable companion. I discovered very quickly that he was fully prepared to enter into the spirit of our expedition, and in his free and easy conversation he didn't talk down to either of us. I was surprised by this as I had more than half expected that he would; to Abby because she was a child, and to me because... ... well, because.

Encouraged by this, I dared to ask him a question that had been hovering in my mind ever since we found Nathan on Saturday afternoon. While Abby was crouched down on the river bank trying to spot the otters, I nudged his arm to get his attention.

"When we found Nathan, on Saturday, you... ..."

I paused, trying to find the right words to frame my question. I needn't have worried. He was well ahead of me.

"You're wondering why I scuffed out all those footprints... ... which reminds me. I forgot to thank you for not mentioning it to that police lady when she came up to the farm."

"I didn't want to cause any trouble."

"You didn't want to draw any attention to yourself, you mean," he said, softening the accusation with a grin.

I smiled and nodded, acknowledging the truth of what he'd said.

"OK. Well I think you deserve a favour in return... ... I thought some of those prints looked as if they could have been made by James's boots. I've been with him loads of times when he's been wearing them. I thought he'd got enough bother going on without these prints messing things up so... ... I smudged up the ground and tried to get Nathan to hospital without any fuss. Whether it helped things at all... ... I don't know."

"Maybe it did help," I said. "It doesn't seem to have made things worse anyway."

He nodded and seemed about to say more when we were both distracted by a squeak from Abby.

We eventually returned to the house around twelve thirty, having made the acquaintance, albeit at a distance, of a pair of European otters, proud parents of two small pups. We expected to see James's Maserati parked in its normal place by the back door of the house. It wasn't there.

Abby sprinted off down the side of the house to see if her dad had left it round at the front. Cherry strode after her while I followed more slowly, hoping desperately that nothing had gone wrong during this morning's visit to the police. I hadn't gone far before it became obvious that the car was not there. The slump of Abby's shoulders as she turned back to face Cherry and I said it all.

James had left before nine. Last night, the police said that taking down his statement should take no more than an hour at most. How long to get there and back? Another hour? He had been away too long.

I knew we were in trouble.

Fifty-One

Pan European Solutions – 10:15 am

The argument had been going on for several minutes, one voice loud and angry, the other cold and restrained. To Bruno, sitting quietly at ease facing the huge picture window, it was all very predictable. Raymond Mellisse sat behind his massive desk, his measured words delivered with an icy calm, while Alexei Borisov was on his feet, loud and vocal, punctuating every sentence with a waving fist or stabbing finger.

Bruno knew that Mellisse had liked the idea of dealing with the two runaways at a distance, using Borisov as his tool because it not only served the purpose of sorting his problem, but also gave him a chance to observe the Russian in action. If this transfer of business assets was to proceed smoothly, Mellisse needed to know what sort of man he was dealing with. It wasn't a case of discovering whether the Russian could be trusted. It was taken as read that he couldn't. Mellisse was much more interested in learning whether Borisov actually had the capability to deliver on his promises. Now this too seemed in doubt.

Bruno remembered how angry Mellisse had been on hearing, yesterday evening, how botched the job had been. So badly botched, in fact, that several of Borisov's men had ended up in police custody while the two girls remained on the loose. Not that the news had precipitated any ranting, yelling, or throwing of objects. That wasn't Mellisse's style. Not any more. It was the icy bleakness in his eyes and his tightly clipped words that warned Bruno of the fire raging beneath the cold exterior.

So Bruno continued to listen with interest to recrimination and accusations on the one hand; justification and counter-accusations on the other. Borisov had promised to deal with the two girls and, so far, he had failed, to Mellisse's clearly enunciated disgust. The lack of success, according to Borisov, was down to bad information supplied by Mellisse. Neither was willing to accept responsibility for what Mellisse described as a farcical sideshow by a comic-opera mafia.

Bruno sat back and let them get on with it, though his right hand never strayed far from the Beretta M9 pistol which sat comfortably in a specially designed and reinforced pocket inside his jacket. He didn't expect trouble from Borisov, but that didn't mean he wasn't ready for it. If required, he was perfectly willing to slap him around the head with the M9 to calm him down a bit, but there was no suggestion yet that Mellisse was thinking along those lines.

As always, Bruno found the picture window in Mellisse's airport office enticing but not today wholly engrossing. Borisov's fierce gestures and loud accusations were a little distracting, which was a shame as he was fairly sure that it was a new Embraer E175 trundling along the taxiway towards him. He didn't know anyone had started flying 175s out of Birmingham, and he would have liked to get a good look at the livery before the aircraft disappeared from view below the level of the window.

There was a flurry of movement at the edge of his vision as Borisov stomped around the colossal desk, reaching out as if he might grab hold of Mellisse by the throat. With very little movement, the Beretta was in Bruno's hand, and the oiled metallic sound as he cocked it reached through Borisov's fury to stop him as suddenly as a two-by-four across the chin.

There was complete silence for several seconds, and nobody moved. Finally, before anyone could speak, the tableau was disturbed by the ringing of the phone on Mellisse's desk.

"Come and sit down, Mr Borisov," said Bruno, as the phone continued to ring. "Let the guvnor get on with his business."

His deep, throaty voice was quiet and steady, just as he'd learnt from Mellisse himself, but its very calmness seemed to make it all the more intimidating.

Borisov turned slowly, keeping his hands well away from his sides. As he did so, the ringing stopped when Mellisse picked up the phone. Borisov shrugged and breathed out heavily through his nose. When he spoke it was as though the words had to be forced out through his lips.

"It OK," he said. "All OK. You not need gun."

"I hope not, Mr Borisov," replied Bruno. "The guvnor only just got through decorating this office. Shame to spoil it so soon. Now why don't you be a good little Russian and come and sit down over here."

Borisov's indignation at being called a *good little Russian,* or indeed a *little* anything, never found its way into words. He was seething, but not to the point of stupidity. The M9 was not a small gun, and Bruno's hand was too steady, his expression too determined, to allow Borisov to do anything other than comply with the request to sit meekly on the settee. Except that his pride did not sit comfortably with meekness. Stalemate.

Before his stillness could be taken by Bruno as a refusal to obey, Borisov was let off the hook. His mobile phone rang. Since a bullet in the head was not his preferred way of ending the meeting, Borisov did not rush to grab his phone. He brought his hands slowly together across his stomach and gently eased his jacket wide open to expose the butt of a heavy automatic sitting holstered under his left armpit. As his mobile continued ringing, he looked enquiringly at Bruno.

For a moment Bruno stared at the partially concealed automatic. He was surprised to find Borisov carrying a gun when he appeared to have plenty of goons working for him who were more than willing to take the risk of carrying an illegal weapon. He knew Mellisse didn't carry a gun on the premise that it was not an appropriate adjunct to a successful businessman's attire. There was also the fact the risk just wasn't worth it, especially when you have a supply of disposable personnel willing to take that risk for you, at very reasonable cost.

"Which pocket, Mr Borisov?" he asked, not wanting Borisov's hands straying anywhere near that automatic.

Borisov wiggled his right hand and pulled that side of his jacket wider to reveal the opening to an inside pocket.

"OK, Mr Borisov," said Bruno. "Just do it slow."

At that moment, the phone stopped ringing as it switched over to voicemail. Borisov reached for it anyway, extracted it and looked at the display. Letting his jacket fall, he pressed some keys and put the phone to his ear. He did not speak but what he heard obviously pleased him as his lips began to stretch into something resembling a smile.

Glancing back to Mellisse who was still in conversation on the phone, Borisov replaced his own in the same pocket as before, and came to sit on the settee opposite Bruno. His movements were confident and relaxed as though it was entirely his own idea to sit down and not a response to Bruno's demand.

"You not need gun," he said again. "See? All quiet. All relax. We talk like... ... er... ... like good businessman."

Bruno's expression didn't change and nor did the position of his M9, so Borisov, slowly and deliberately, fastened the middle button of his suit jacket.

"See," he said. "We businessman. Not need gun."

Bruno nodded and thought for a moment before saying, "Fair enough."

He replaced the M9 in its special pocket but kept his own jacket open and made sure that his hand didn't stray far from that readily available butt. Borisov gave no indication of having noticed this lack of trust on Bruno's part and leant back against the comfortable leather spreading his arms expansively across the back of the settee. He turned his head slightly to look past Bruno at a large picture hanging on the wall behind him. Bruno knew the picture well. A grey road winding downhill towards a colourful patchwork of fields which, in his view, a child in primary school could have painted just as well and for a fraction of the price Mellisse was reputed to have paid.

With Borisov settled down, he lifted his eyes to let his gaze stray back to the window. The Embraer was now out of sight which made Borisov's little tantrum all the more irritating. Maybe he'd get a chance to shoot the stupid jerk before too long.

The movement was only slight, barely noticeable out of the corner of his eye, but it was enough to drag his eyes away from the window. He froze and cursed inwardly as he realised that for once his supreme self-confidence had over-reached itself.

The pistol in Borisov's right hand had not come from his shoulder holster. This Smith and Wesson Shield with its polymer frame was smaller and lighter than the cannon still concealed under his jacket. Bruno watched it warily, not daring to move. He had no idea where the gun had come from. A pocket? An ankle holster? What did it matter? He'd miscalculated big-time.

Behind Borisov and to his right, Mellisse ended his conversation and replaced the phone thoughtfully on his desk. He was smiling, until his eyes took in the tableau in front of him.

"Alexei... ... ..."

Borisov didn't give him a chance to finish.

"Ray... ... my friend... ... would you please tell this person that if he ever point gun at me again he is dead man?"

Mellisse knew enough about the Russian to realise that this was no idle threat.

"I think he's got the message, Alexei, so why don't we all just settle down and put the toys away. We've got business to sort, and that doesn't include fighting amongst ourselves."

Borisov raised the pistol and aimed it at Bruno's forehead.

"In the body, this 9mm might not kill you. So I shoot you in the head... ... if ever you disrespect me again."

Bruno licked his lips.

"Ah," said Borisov. "Now I think he has the message. Yes?"

Bruno nodded, and Borisov lowered the gun although he kept it deliberately in view.

"Ever done any business with the Chinese, Alexei?" Mellisse asked, a complete non-sequitur intended to turn matters in a new direction. He stood up and came over to stand behind Bruno's settee, where he could look down on Borisov. The Russian stared up at him, a look of puzzled enquiry on his face.

"No? Well, perhaps you should think about it. That sweet little deal on the phone is going to net me one point five million over two years."

His eyes flicked to the pistol resting on Borisov's thigh, but he decided to ignore it.

"And there's more to come... ... and every quid legit. Can't be bad, can it?"

Borisov was intrigued and thought of asking for more details but hesitated when he thought of the pleasure it would undoubtedly give

Mellisse to refuse further explanation. In any case, restoring his own reputation was more important at the moment. He smiled up at Mellisse, self-satisfaction oozing from his lips.

"You do not judge me well, my dear Ray. I better than you think. A little while and one of your problems will be gone. Pooof. No more."

Mellisse's smile disappeared and there was a hint of unease in his sharp reply.

"Which one?"

"The one you throw from bridge, but not kill," replied Borisov, thrilled at being able to point out that Mellisse also had employees who were less than competent.

"Ah. Angie," said Mellisse. "Good. How are you going to do it?"

"I have… … er… … colleague. He go hospital now."

"What sort of colleague?"

Borisov just smiled.

"What I mean," said Mellisse, wishing he could get Bruno to smack the smile off Borisov's face, "is can he do the job?"

"Of course, my friend," said Borisov. "He very skilled. More than your man here, I think."

Mellisse patted Bruno's shoulder, restraining any inclination for a violent retort, and walked around the settee to sit down at the other end from Bruno.

"If you don't want to say who it is, that's fine. Just make sure he does it right. No foul-ups this time."

"Trust me, my friend. Everything just like you want."

"Well remember this," said Mellisse. "I want Di, or Lizzie, or whatever she's calling herself, undamaged. You take her as soon as you can, but you keep her alive until she's recorded that video I need. Get me that and afterwards you can do what you like with her."

Borisov's smile become something of an unpleasant smirk.

"Thank you, my dear Ray. There is much I think I like to do with her. Perhaps she will not die so very quickly. Eh? Maybe I make my own video."

For a moment, Mellisse did not respond. He did not like Borisov and, although he was aware that friendship was not necessarily a prime requisite in a business partnership, he was beginning to realise that he didn't altogether trust him either. And Mellisse liked to deal with people he could trust.

Once this was all over, and Lizzie's scripted interview safely recorded, he was strongly tempted to let Bruno put an end to their temporary business relationship.

Permanently.

Except that Borisov was almost certainly connected to some seriously heavy people who could make Mellisse's life very miserable if provoked.

He sighed.

"Whatever you like, Alexei. She'll be all yours."

Fifty-Two

The Dower House – Lunchtime

Cherry sent Abby and me into the house to find Mrs Siddons and to ask whether there had been any word from James. He watched us all the way to the back door and then he went into the stable garage to ask Surjit the same question.

As usual, we found Mrs Siddons in the kitchen but we had scarcely begun to speak before our words were drowned out by a loud buzzing noise. This time I knew what it was without being told. Someone was at the gate.

We all gathered round the little screen on the wall, but none of us pressed the microphone button to enquire who was at the gate. Abby peered closely at the screen but then drew back with a downcast look when she realised it wasn't her father's car waiting to be let in. Not surprising, really. James would just have used his remote to open the gates.

Without our touching anything, the picture zoomed in and we could now see that there were two people in the car. Then Surjit's voice came over the speaker, asking the occupants of the car to identify themselves. The passenger door opened and a man got out. He stood by the car for a moment looking up at the camera mounted on top of the gatepost. It was one of several that covered the entrance, and not the one whose image we were looking at, but we could see him clearly enough.

He was medium height and build and wore a dark business suit. Using both hands, he grasped the front of his suit jacket and opened it wide to expose a blue and white striped shirt. He held the jacket open for a few seconds before releasing it and walking around the front of the car to the box set on the post by the driver's door. He bent forward to speak into the microphone.

"Why did he do that?" asked Abby.

I knew. I'd seen the right movies. "He wants us to think he's harmless."

Then we heard his voice coming through the speaker.

"My name is Paul Riddings. I work for Lord Thurvaston. If you wish to verify that, call the DTLO in London. I'll wait."

He straightened up and looked back at the camera.

"He doesn't mind having his picture taken, does he?" I said. "I wonder what he wants."

We had to wait several minutes to find out. Mr Riddings was beginning to fidget before we heard Surjit's voice again.

"Who do you report to at the DTLO?"

We saw Mr Riddings give a little start, and then he bent once again to the microphone.

"George Holborn, usually."

"And why can he not vouch for you today?"

"He'll be with Lord Thurvaston. They were due to appear before a Parliamentary Select Committee this morning."

"Who is Mr Holborn's personal assistant?"

"That would be the delectable Miss Watson."

"First name?"

"Shauna."

"OK. She says you're a rising star."

We heard Riddings' laugh.

"And she's a heavenly body."

This time Surjit chuckled. "Probably best you don't let her hear you say that. Now hold your ID up to the camera."

Riddings took out a small wallet, opened it and held it up to the camera he'd been staring at.

"Not that one," said Surjit. "The camera by the microphone."

We saw a DTLO photo ID waver on the screen. I assumed it was OK. I'd never seen one before. Surjit seemed to think it was OK too.

"Who's the other guy in the car?"

"Taxi driver."

"Pay him off."

More waiting and then we saw the taxi reverse enough to be able to swing around back onto the road. As it disappeared, Surjit spoke again.

"Take off your jacket and drape it over your arm. When the gates open, walk slowly up to the house. Someone will meet you. Oh… … and just so you know… … You see that red dot on your shirt? … … At the other end of that is a .30 calibre rifle. Just in case… …"

As the gates began to open, I wondered if it was Cherry holding the rifle. I asked Mrs Siddons what she thought.

"Probably, dear," she said, with no more concern than if we'd been talking about a walking stick. "We'll find out soon enough. And while we're waiting, who'd like a ham sandwich?"

We were so curious about the arrival of Mr Riddings that both Abby and I forgot to ask if there had been any word from James.

The phone rang. Mrs Siddons picked it up.

"Yes. We're all in the kitchen… … Very well."

And she hung up.

"Surjit asks us to stay in the kitchen while they meet Mr Riddings and find out what he wants. So, my dears, how about that sandwich?"

I was amazed at how calm she was, when I was desperate to know what was going on. James should have been back by now, and I wanted to know whether Riddings had any news of him. Abby's brooding anxiety had returned and, although she sat down, she didn't touch the sandwich that Mrs Siddons placed on the table in front of her. I nibbled at the delicious home-baked ham and tried to encourage Abby, but it wasn't easy with my own sense of unease growing by the minute.

The hands of the kitchen clock crawled, and even Mrs Siddons ran out of heartening conversation before the door finally opened and Cherry came in. If he'd ever had a rifle, there was no sign of it now.

He looked down at Abby and smiled. I'd heard that US Secret Service agents were supposed to be willing to take a bullet for the President, and I wondered if Cherry was willing to take one for Abby. Seeing that smile, I thought he probably was.

"Mr Riddings has seen your dad," he said to her. "Things are taking a bit longer than expected so he won't be back until later. Now why don't you stop worrying and eat your sandwich. I bet that bread was fresh baked this morning."

"I'm not hungry," she said.

"OK," he replied. "Not to worry. Mrs Siddons can save it for later. Shame you can't keep your strength up for when your dad gets home though."

They just looked at each other for several seconds, one smiling, the other sullen. Then Abby gave in.

"OK, you win."

She picked up the sandwich and started to eat.

Cherry then turned to me.

"Lizzie, there's a paper I think you ought to take a look at. How about I show you while Abby finishes her lunch."

I looked at him, puzzled.

"It's in the library," he said. "Come and take a look."

The paper *was* in the library, and Paul Riddings was holding it. He was once again wearing his suit jacket, and was lounging casually in the chair James had been occupying the previous evening. He looked up from the paper as I came in, and seemed to debate whether I was worth the polite gesture of standing up. Judging by the time it took before he stirred, it was a close run thing, but eventually he came to his feet.

Cherry introduced us and I wondered if I was expected to shake hands, but Riddings seemed to think that was one step of politeness too far. He just nodded and sat down again. He held out the paper in my direction and said, "You'd better look at this."

Ignoring his deliberate brusqueness, I stepped forward to take the paper from his outstretched hand, and looked at the front page. It was, as I'd expected, the Lichfield Daily News and it was red hot.

I had been wondering where he'd hidden it as he walked up to the house with his jacket over his arm, but that thought quickly flew from my mind as I began to read the front page. By the end of the first paragraph, I could feel the anger expanding through my chest. It seemed as though I was actually quivering with rage, but when I looked at my hands holding the paper they were rock steady. The heat that began at the back of my neck, continued to spread as I carried on reading.

It was Corrina Rigby again. This time I too was brought into the firing line, and she had no reservations about revealing to the world my past profession. It wasn't being referred to as the prostitute which got me riled up, though I certainly didn't like the word, and I knew why I didn't like it. I'd been thinking about it a lot since coming to this house. The word was a label which conveyed so much more than just the way I had earned my living. It was as though it defined my whole being; everything about me from personality, through belief system to lifestyle. It confined me within a particular mould, denying any possibility of change. It established my place within the social order, and sought to ensure that I stay there.

No, it wasn't that word which caused the sudden flare of rage. It was the barely veiled suggestion that James killed Phil Simmons because of an overwhelming passion for Natalie Simmons whose baby, the article insinuated, he had probably fathered. It was an unforgiveable pack of vicious lies, and oddly inexplicable too. Why was this country bumpkin reporter waging such a vendetta? And who could possibly be the mysterious source referred to in the article. A close personal friend, it said. Who?

Cherry was standing very close, perhaps waiting to steady me if it should seem that I needed it. I didn't. Not now. I crumpled the paper and flung it down.

"This isn't true," I said, my voice surprisingly firm.

Riddings looked up at me curiously.

"How do you know?" he asked.

I looked from one to the other. Cherry and I were still standing. Now was the time. I couldn't hide the truth any longer and was relieved to find that I didn't actually want to.

"Cherry," I said, "why don't you sit down. It will probably help to save you from falling down when I tell you how I know."

They both looked surprised, but Cherry did as I suggested pulling over a fancy straight backed chair from by the desk. I was near to one of the leather chairs, so I sat there, opposite Riddings and Cherry.

Sitting forward slightly, back straight, hands in my lap, I told my story. Not all of it, and not in detail, but enough for them to understand how I was absolutely certain James had not killed Phil Simmons. Whether they were just too amazed to speak, or whether they sensed the awkwardness I felt in having to reveal so much, I couldn't tell, but neither made the slightest attempt to interrupt, and their silence continued for several seconds after I had finished.

I wished I knew what Cherry was thinking as he was the one I felt I was getting to know, the one I expected to react first, but it was actually the stranger, Riddings, who broke the silence.

"Why... ..." he began, frustration and probably more than a little anger in his voice. "You stupid little cow. Why didn't you tell this to the police on Saturday?"

I couldn't give him the real reason and, stung by his rudeness, I couldn't be bothered to think of an alternative. It was then that Cherry supplied one for me.

"Scared, I guess. Eh, Lizzie?"

I nodded.

"I told myself that I could always come forward later. You know... ... if the police really started to think James had done it... ... But then all this other stuff started happening... ... and now... ...after that... ..."

I pointed to the newspaper which lay crumpled on the carpet where I'd flung it in disgust.

"After that, who's going to believe a single word I say? I might come in a shade higher than OJ on the credibility scale, but I wouldn't count on it."

Riddings stared at me, hard, and I didn't like what I thought was going on in his mind. It made me all the more certain that I'd let James down, badly. Riddings shook his head without taking his eyes from mine. I refused to drop my gaze, and then Cherry rescued me from this staring contest.

"Maybe with the police," he said, in a quiet voice, almost thinking aloud.

"I'm sorry," I said, tearing my eyes from Riddings cold stare.

"Your credibility," he replied. "Maybe the police wouldn't believe you... ... Well, let's be fair. They almost certainly wouldn't believe you. But the Boss has believed in you right from the beginning. And, I have to say, his judgement has always been spot on."

There had never been any spark between Cherry and me, no real chemistry, and he offered this in his blunt, matter-of-fact way. Nevertheless, I felt some odd emotion misting up my eyes. There was nothing Mills-and-Boon about it, just the gratitude of unexpected friendship, but it gave me a new determination.

I looked back at Riddings. Had his expression softened a little? It really was too hard to say.

"Where do you fit in to this?" I asked him. "James hasn't mentioned you, not even once, these past few days, so how come you've turned up now, right when he's not here to vouch for you?"

Cherry fielded that before Riddings could reply.

"Let's not get sidetracked, Lizzie. He is who he says he is, and he's here with Lord Thurvaston's blessing... ... I checked."

"OK," I said. "But that still doesn't tell me what he's doing here."

This time Cherry stayed quiet, and we both waited for Riddings to reply. It took a few minutes while he organised his thoughts, probably deciding what he should or should not tell us. It seemed that the longer we waited, the more uncomfortable he became. The fingers of his right hand which had been gently massaging his chin began tapping against his lower lip. I wondered what it was that he was trying to hide.

And then, suddenly, his lips twitched but I could see no humour in that faintest of smiles.

"I never tell people what I don't think they need to know," he said. "Combination of instinct and training, I suppose. But... ..."

He extended his hand, fingers upright palm towards us, forestalling the interruption that was already tripping off my tongue.

"I guess, we're now at the point where you need to know. So here goes."

He sat back in his chair and, without swearing us to secrecy or anything stupid like that, began his story.

"I came up here on Friday to meet with Phil Simmons. He's... ... hmm... ... been helping the DTLO with an investigation into some of Lichfield Tube's overseas contracts. I... ..."

I couldn't help interrupting.

"Do you mean Phil Simmons was killed because of some investigation of yours, and you knew about it? And all the time James is taking the blame."

The question began with indignation, but ended in anger.

"No," he said. "And if you'll just keep your pretty little mouth shut for a bit, I'll tell you what I do mean."

His tone was argumentative, confrontational. He didn't like me and didn't mind it showing.

"No," he said again, this time looking at Cherry. "It was nothing like that. I'm sure of it... ... Well... ... pretty sure, anyway. The investigation... ... it was just trade stuff. It's possible there could be charges of fraud... ... maybe other things besides, but nothing businessmen commit murder for. At least... ..." He looked suddenly doubtful. "... ...none that I've come across so far."

"OK, let's accept that for now," said Cherry. "So where does James fit in?"

"He doesn't," Riddings answered. "He wasn't involved in the enquiries into Lichfield Tube, and he's certainly not involved in Phil Simmons' murder... ... And if I wasn't sure about that before, I'm damn sure now after what you've just told us."

"So why are you here," I pressed, still not clear what was going on.

"Yes," said Cherry. "I'm still wondering about that."

"Two reasons," replied Riddings. "First, I need to find another way of carrying on our enquiries into Lichfield Tube. I need to find out, if I can, what it was that Phil wanted to tell me on Saturday. Maybe the police will come up with something. I'm sort of liaising with a detective sergeant called Hayford. Nothing official, but she seems willing to keep the channels open."

"We've met her," said Cherry. "Seems nice enough, for a copper. But just watch what you give her. It's not always a two-way street."

The sudden narrowing of Riddings eyes suggested that he didn't appreciate this bit of advice.

"This is what I do for a living," he said, a little huffily.

"Yes," replied Cherry, with no apparent concern for Riddings' feelings. "And it's what she does for a living too."

There was a moment's silence while Riddings decided whether to develop his prima-donna role, or just get on with the story. Impatient, I prompted him before he'd made up his mind.

"That was first," I said. "So what's second?"

From his look, it was obvious he resented my questions. Maybe he thought he should be directing the conversation, and not me. Then he seemed to relax, apparently deciding not to be any more of a prat than necessary, and continued.

"Second... ... I'd actually like to make sure that James Montrayne doesn't get stitched up for something he didn't do."

"Why," I asked, not sure I believed him. "Why would you be so concerned?"

He pursed his lips and actually allowed himself a smile. Not much of one, but it was a definite improvement.

"Actually, I'm not," he said. "Now there's honesty for you... ... But I do work for someone who is very much concerned... ... James's father. He told me, last night, to get my arse back up here and see what I could do, since he wasn't in a position to get involved. When he told me he was coming up himself, I hitched a ride in his chopper. Now I wish I hadn't since it meant leaving the car in London."

I glanced across at Cherry who was watching Riddings with a very thoughtful look on his face.

"I thought you said you came up here on Friday," he said.

"That's right," said Riddings. "But then I've been going to and fro trying to keep the office up to date on what's happening."

He paused and licked his lips.

"Look, do you think we could get some coffee?" he asked. "I'm parched."

There was a phone handset on the coffee table between our two chairs, so I reached for it and pressed the number for the kitchen. After I'd told Mrs Siddons what we needed, I sat holding the phone, remembering when James had explained how to dial the room numbers and how to get an outside line. It suddenly dawned on me that I still had no idea why James was so late coming home from the police station.

"Coffee's on its way," I said. "Now, what do you know about James? Why is he so late?"

At this, his frowned and worry oozed from his slightly hooded eyes.

"Ahh," he said. "Well, he is, as they say, helping the police with their enquiries. No... ..."

He held up his hand to stop me butting in again.

"Just listen for a minute and stop interrupting... ... I knew from Lord Thurvaston that James was going to be at the police station this morning, so I decided to meet him there and also see if I could get anything more from Sergeant Hayford. When I got there, he was in an interview room giving his statement about last night. Should be with me soon, according to the desk sergeant. And then... ..."

He broke off as Mrs Siddons entered with a tray laden with coffee cups, milk and sugar. She looked around, noting our sudden stillness and, as she placed the tray on the coffee table, she said to me, "Abby keeps asking for you. She's worried about her father, and nothing I say seems to help. Have you ... ...?"

She clearly wanted to know if I had any news, but didn't like to ask outright.

"Tell Abby," I said, "that I'll come and find her in a few minutes."

She looked at me steadily for a moment, then nodded and left the room. I wondered if she resented the fact that I, a relative stranger, was being given information that was denied to her. Still, no good worrying about that now so I pushed the thought aside.

As we each took our cups from the tray, Riddings continued.

"I'd only been waiting a couple of minutes when some older gent came strutting through, grinning like he'd just won the lottery and waving a newspaper at the desk sergeant. Next... ... I'm not sure just how long after... ... DS Hayford came stomping down the corridor like a valkyrie looking for a candidate for Valhalla."

He paused briefly, as though daring me to query the allusion which we both knew I didn't understand. I decided not to rise to his petty challenge so, after a moment, he continued.

"She looked so furious I expected her to ignore me, but then she stopped and ended up carting me off to a small office tucked away out of sight of anyone... ... I don't think she planned what happened next, she's seems too professional... ... but she was just so mad she had to unburden to someone... ... I just happened to be handy, involved a little, but not part of the system."

The story was dragging on a bit but I didn't like to interrupt the flow. Cherry, on the other hand, was getting impatient.

"Great story, old lad, but do you think we can just get to the facts?"

Riddings didn't exactly pout, but his lips definitely twitched.

"I've just got there, *old lad,*" he said, barely hiding his indignation, "so just shut up and listen."

We did, so he began to rattle them off.

"One: the old gent was DCI Morrissey. He'd read that article in the paper and saw his chance to close the case. Two: he interrupted DS Hayford's interview, confronted James with it, and told him it was time to confess. Three: James's solicitor, who'd been with him from the start, told Morrissey it wasn't evidence of anything, and told James not to comment. Four: Morrissey said he also had evidence linking James to the murder of a nurse in Birmingham. Five: Hayford tried to stop him and suspend the interview, but Morrissey wasn't having any of it, and told her to advise James of his rights so the questioning could go on. Six: she was furious, firstly because she hadn't even completed taking his statement about last night, and secondly because Morrissey was way out of line with the so-called evidence, so she cautioned James, told him to take his lawyer's advice and stormed out of the interview room... ... In that little room, flashing fire like she was, phew... ... was she hot!"

He waved his hand up and down as if fanning the flames.

Cherry and I stared at him, and Cherry just beat me to the next, and most important question.

"So, is the Boss under arrest?"

Riddings' hand stopped flapping, paused for a moment, and then dropped to rest on the arm of his chair.

"I don't know for sure," he said, "but I left Sergeant Hayford looking for a way to pull the rug from under Morrissey without blighting her own career at the same time. Not easy, I imagine."

I was puzzled.

"Why is she so keen on sticking her neck out?" I asked. "What's in it for her?"

Riddings looked me in the eye, and smiled in a way I really didn't like.

"I think our lady sergeant has the hots for his lordship," he said. "And I also think that she doesn't want to go down with Morrissey's ship when the mess he's creating comes unravelled."

I couldn't think what else to ask. I was too caught up with the idea of Sergeant Hayford developing some sort of emotional attachment to James. I found it oddly disturbing, though I couldn't have explained why.

Cherry took up the questions again.

"So what happens now?"

"We wait," replied Riddings. "Don't see what else we can do. I did try getting the Lord Lieutenant to take an interest... ... Rupert Chadbourne, you know, James's old CO... ... but I don't think I can play that card again. The Chief Constable won't like interference at that level."

I suddenly remembered something, and looked across at Cherry.

"Who was that person James phoned yesterday... ... from Fradley?"

"That would be ACC Fletcher," he said, looking thoughtful. "Now I'd definitely be surprised if he's not taking an interest... ... especially if Sergeant Hayford manages to whisper in his ear."

"So you think there's a chance they might let James go," I asked, with rather more heat and urgency than I'd intended.

I was asking Cherry, but he passed the question over to Riddings.

"What do you think?" he said. "You were there."

"From what Hayford said," replied Riddings, "I rather got the impression that Morrissey was banking everything on overwhelming James with that... ..." He pointed to the paper still lying crumpled on the floor. "... ... and pressuring a confession out of him. James, of course, won't oblige. The other evidence just doesn't stand up, so my best guess is that Morrissey will have to back off and James will be released on police bail. If Hayford does get to Fletcher and he sticks his oar in, I'd make that a certainty."

I didn't hear the door open but I guessed from Riddings' quick glance over my shoulder that someone had entered the room. As I turned to see who it was, I wondered whether Mrs Siddons had left the door slightly ajar on purpose, curiosity having overcome her sense of propriety. In the space between the double doors, where I myself had stood only yesterday evening, was Abby. She was stiff and straight-backed, trying hard to be grown-up, which only made her look all the more like the vulnerable child that she was. Her eyes glistened with tears that threatened to cascade down her cheeks, and her voice, as she asked the question on which her whole world depended, was not quite steady.

"When are they going to let daddy come home again?"

Fifty-Three

Aullton Foundation Hospital – Lunchtime

Sometime during the morning, Angie had fallen asleep. The damage she had sustained in her fall was sufficient to require a high measure of pain relief which, together with the medication she was being given to deal with her other infections, and the withdrawal from her illegal drugs, was placing quite heavy demands on her sadly damaged system. Barrie Harwood was happy for her to sleep as much as possible. His only concern was the dreams that seemed inevitably to come with it.

Towards lunchtime, Angie began to drift slowly back to wakefulness. In that sleepy haze, she had no idea where she was, or how she'd come to be there, but her heart began to race as her confused mind pictured the man who must have brought her there.

Bruno.

She was scared to open her eyes in case he saw she was awake and pulled out his pliers to place them around her fingers, bending, twisting, tearing, breaking them one by one to make her tell him... ...

Tell him what?

She couldn't remember. But her mind had not forgotten a previous occasion when she'd seen those pliers used on a girl from Lithuania whose twin sister had escaped the house and fled. Bruno wanted to know how she'd done it and where she had gone and it hadn't taken many fingers before the girl was begging him through her screams to be allowed to betray her twin.

Angie lay still, breathing shallowly, hoping no-one would notice she was awake. Then she became aware of a faint smell; not unpleasant, just strangely out of place.

Unless... ...

And then she had it, and with the realisation her fear bled away as quickly as it had come. Disinfectant. She remembered now. She was in hospital, safe from Bruno, safe from Mellisse, safe from everyone who wanted to do bad things to her. For the first time in a long time she was being looked after by someone who really seemed to care about what happened to her. She opened her eyes hoping to see Dr Harwood.

She liked him. Actually, she liked him a lot. He might not be the most handsome man she'd ever... ... Well, what did that matter? Some of the most good-looking creeps had also been the most brutal.

No, she liked the gentleness of his voice and the compassion in his eyes as he spoke to her. She liked the way he took time to explain what was wrong with her, and what he was doing about it. She liked the way he held her hand when she was frightened and hurting. And she liked the way he smiled every time he came into her room, as though she was the most important person in his schedule that day.

But when she turned her head to see who was sitting beside her bed, it wasn't Dr Harwood. A stranger lounged in the chair, one leg crossed over the other, and with his attention fully engrossed in the motoring magazine open in his lap.

This was someone completely new. Mid-thirties, blue denim jacket and jeans, and with thick brown hair drawn back in a ponytail. Brown eyes flicked towards her, drawn by the movement of her head, and she noticed bruising around the bridge of his nose and his left eye. With dark stubble on his face, he didn't look a very encouraging sight, but his voice held no trace of threat so she allowed herself to be slightly reassured.

"Well, well. Awake now, are we, Miss? ... ... And how are you feeling today?"

His tone was perfectly neutral, neither friendly nor hostile, but there was a strange coolness to those brown eyes. She stared at him, trying to remember whether she was supposed to know him. He hadn't been here earlier when she'd had her breakfast. Dr Harwood had been here then, and there had been another man with him, about the same age as this one but looking smarter in a dark blue blazer and fawn slacks. And he'd said his name was... ... ... John. Yes, that was it. So, who was this?

"Who are you?" she asked as she tried to push herself into more of a sitting position. "And... ... what are you doing here?"

"Name's Rod, Miss," he replied, eventually stirring himself to ease her a little higher on her pillows. "I'm here coz James couldn't stay."

He saw her frowning and added, "That's my boss, in a manner of speaking, James Montrayne, and he had Lizzie with him. She couldn't stay either, but they'll be back later."

At Lizzie's name, Angie's frown deepened. Who was Lizzie? Her mind tried to rerun the strange events of the past few days searching for the name, and after a moment or two it came back to her. Her friend Di was calling herself Lizzie, and James was that huge friend of hers who'd helped Dr Harwood get her moved to this hospital. He'd been here last night for a little while, and Lizzie had stayed with her when her bed had been moved in the middle of the night. And then she remembered her fears on waking.

"Are you here to protect me?" she asked. "From Bruno?"

"Well, Miss. I won't pretend to know this Bruno. So let's just say I'm here to keep you company and to make sure no-one bothers you."

She thought about that for a moment and then nodded, although she wasn't sure what a wiry fellow like this could do if confronted with a bear of a man like Bruno.

"Doctor's around somewhere. Do you want me to get him?"

"Yes... ... No... ... er... ..."

She did want Dr Harwood, but not for anything specific and she didn't want him to think she was pestering him, when he was being so good to her. She lay back, quiet for a while, and eventually Rod's eyes dropped back to his magazine. If this was what keeping her company meant, she wasn't impressed. Maybe he's just shy, she thought. Some men are, especially when they're alone with a girl.

Now John had been completely different. He had kept up a flow of friendly conversation while she ate her breakfast, and even cut into fingers for her the toast which had accompanied her scrambled eggs. Not that she'd actually eaten much of it, but he hadn't seemed to mind.

"Where's John?" she asked, turning again to look at Rod.

"Gone to grab some lunch," he said, his eyes lingering on his magazine for just long enough to let her know what he thought of his babysitting duties.

She couldn't think why he didn't like her, since he didn't know her at all. She hoped it wouldn't be long before John or, even better, Dr Harwood came back.

And then the door opened and she looked eagerly towards it, but it wasn't John, or the doctor. Another stranger stood there. Her life seemed full of them today. This one was quite tall, she thought, and had an air of respectability in his dark blue business suit. He was clean shaven with close-cropped fair hair. Although he was big and well-proportioned, he was nothing like the size of James. Rod had looked up just as quickly as she had, but then relaxed when he saw who it was.

"Hi, Rod," said the stranger, pushing the door closed behind him. "Everything OK?"

"Sure, Boss. No problems."

"John?"

"Lunch."

"OK. Well, look. Why don't you go and join him, and I'll spell you for a bit."

Rod stood up. "Sure, Boss, if that's OK. Thanks."

It seemed to Angie as though he couldn't leave quickly enough but, although she hadn't especially liked him, she felt faintly uneasy at being left in the company of yet another person of whom she knew absolutely nothing. Her only reassurance was that Rod had called him Boss, so presumably he too worked for James Montrayne.

Rod was almost out of the room when he turned back to the newcomer as a thought struck him.

"When you called me last night, Boss... ... to pick up John and Nat and come here... ... can you remember what time it was?"

"I'm not sure I can, offhand," said the stranger. "Why? Does it matter?"

Rod stood in the doorway, looking thoughtful.

"Not sure really. It's just that... ... Well... ... James seemed to think we took our time getting here yesterday, and I know I left straight after you called."

"Were you held up getting here?"

"No. No problems at all. Straight run through, just like I told him, but he didn't seem convinced."

The stranger smiled and shook his head slightly.

"I shouldn't worry about it, Rod. James has got a lot of things on his plate at the moment. He was probably just a bit wired up, that's all. I'll have a word with him."

"OK. Thanks, Boss."

And with that he turned and pulled the door closed behind him.

The stranger watched him go, and then turned to stand at the foot of her bed looking at her. She saw he was handsome, in a craggy sort of way, but there were lines of worry etched on his face. He smiled down at her, but there was something not quite right about the curve of his lips, and she saw a strange sadness in his blue eyes.

"So, you're Angie," he said.

Still with that strange smile on his lips, he moved across to the window and looked out. She watched him. It was more of an inspection than a casual glance as his eyes searched left and right, then up and down. She wondered if he was making sure no-one could get in, but that wasn't likely. She knew the room was on the first floor as Dr Harwood had told her that morning and, from her bed, she could see no sign of trees close to the window.

When he turned slowly away from the window, her eyes widened as she watched his right hand appear from inside his jacket. Her pulse began to race and when she tried to lick her lips she found her mouth was as dry as desert sand.

His smile had gone and the lines of worry seemed, if anything, deeper. The sadness she had noticed in his eyes was now echoed in his voice as he raised his silenced automatic pistol towards her face.

"I need you to keep quiet, Angie. Do you understand?"

She managed to nod her head very slightly, just once. She knew that if she cried out he would shoot her, and she also knew that, with the silencer on his gun, no-one would hear it happen. She didn't know that the sound of a silenced automatic was actually a lot louder than the gentle *phutt* that she'd heard in the movies. That bulbous tube pointing directly between her eyes might suppress the crack of the expanding gases that followed the bullet out of the barrel, but nothing could quieten the mechanical sounds of the hammer strike and the slide recycling to load the next bullet from the magazine. Not that it mattered. Even if someone heard the sound, they would never realise what it was.

He backed slowly towards the door, his gun never swerving from her face, and then he reached out with his left hand and turned the lock.

"Good girl," he said. "That's good. Believe me... ... I don't want this to be any worse than it has to be."

She was terrified. It was odd. Her mouth was still dry but sweat was now running down her face. And she was puzzled. If he'd come to kill her, why didn't he just get on with it and leave?

"If you make a sound, Angie, I won't just shoot you, I'll shoot the doctor, and I don't think you'd want me to do that. Actually, I don't want to do it, but if you make me, then I will. Do you understand that?"

Again that slight nod, and he was about to speak again when he saw her lips move. Too scared to speak, she just mouthed the word at him, and he understood.

WHY?

He was standing at the end of her bed now, stooping slightly, his right hand still holding the gun on her, but his left hand was reaching for something in an inside pocket of his jacket.

That single word, unspoken but intensely powerful, rocketed through his brain unlocking a long-dead memory and freezing all movement.

In 1995, Captain Andrew Graham had been a captain in the Royal Marines when he was posted to the Rapid Reaction Force as the war in Bosnia was coming to its end. One afternoon in September, he and his men had found themselves in a small village on the outskirts of Sarajevo from which the Serbs had recently withdrawn. In a ruined house with half a roof and three walls, he had his first view of Serb brutality. The bodies of six women, naked and horribly abused, were found strewn around the least damaged room. A seventh, a teenage girl, also naked and showing vivid signs of a severe beating, was still breathing. Before she died, she gasped out her tale of terror and pain, of torture and rape.

Confronted with this, Andrew Graham has asked one question. *WHY?*

There had been no answer, of course, except the trite but true one that war brings out both the best and worst in men. It just seemed so unfair that Bosnia seemed to be putting all its emphasis on the latter.

The girl's face, as she'd related her horrific tale to their Bosnian interpreter, had stayed with him for months, troubling his days and disturbing his nights, until he had finally managed to lock it away deep in his subconscious.

But now the key had been turned, the vision released, and the face of a fifteen year old Bosnian girl lay next to Angie's on the pillow.

Andy blinked rapidly, and the face faded until only Angie's remained. The terror and pain were still there and, if what James had told him was true, there was also sexual abuse and physical injury. And he was here to make it worse.

He took a deep breath and forced himself to look into her eyes.

"I'm just like you, Angie. I don't want to be doing this, any more than you wanted the life you're running away from... ... We're people trapped by circumstances, and we're both trying desperately to get out."

He paused, but there was no acknowledgement in those widely staring eyes.

He was suddenly aware that this was his chance to choose between being the best or the worst, and it genuinely grieved him that he knew what his choice would be.

"I need to take you away from here, Angie."

At that, there was a flash of understanding in her eyes.

"Yes," he continued. "And to do that, I need to put you to sleep... ... You see, I need to be sure you won't cry out."

With his left hand, he withdrew a plastic bag from an inside pocket and tipped it to allow a loaded syringe to fall out onto the bed.

"A small prick, Angie," he said. "That's all. Just a small prick... ... Now turn your head to look to your left."

At first, he thought she might refuse, preferring to be shot than to endure whatever else might be in store for her.

"Remember, Angie. If I have to shoot you, then I'll shoot Dr Harwood as well."

Slowly, she turned her head away from him. He came round to the other side of her bed and turned her arm to expose the vein in her elbow.

"Good girl," he said. "Now just keep still."

Transferring the gun to his left hand, he reached for the syringe with his right. Flicking the plastic sheath off the needle, he gently inserted it into the vein. She didn't move, although he probably caused her more discomfort doing it one-handed than a trained professional would using both hands.

He hesitated. If he depressed the plunger there was no turning back, and he couldn't rid himself of the feeling that he would then be no better than those Serbian animals at Sarajevo. But he would at least be alive, with money and a job and a future.

He pressed the plunger and withdrew the needle.

"It's over, Angie."

Her head rolled on the pillow and, as he once again looked into the eyes of a Bosnian child, he hated himself more than at any time in his life.

"I'm not going anywhere am I?" asked Angie. "That wasn't to send me to sleep?"

Slowly, he shook his head.

"I'm sorry, Angie."

And then it hit her. In a sudden rush of rapturous euphoria such as she'd never experienced before, the heroin overdose infiltrated her defences. The last thing she noticed before she slipped into unconsciousness was a knocking which grew to a pounding in her ears as her heart rate peaked before beginning its final descent into permanent stillness.

Fifty-Four

Lichfield Police Station – Lunchtime

ACC David Fletcher was wishing he'd stayed in Stafford. It wasn't as if he hadn't got enough work up there to keep him occupied, and there were four or five weeks before this review of the staffing establishment in Trent Valley became anything like urgent. It had been a foolish impulse which prompted him to use the review as an excuse for being in Lichfield that morning, and he had not reached the rank of Assistant Chief Constable by submitting to foolish impulses.

To make matters worse, the office available for his use at the Lichfield Police Station was both cramped and ill-equipped, with insufficient staff to run around at his beck and call, and it didn't even give him a decent view of the cathedral. And it was coming up to lunchtime. The staff canteen here wasn't a patch on that select little bistro just a minute or two from the Cannock Road HQ in Stafford. Pierre could always find him a table, no matter how busy they were, and if Fletcher didn't have time to leave his desk, Pierre was more than happy to send round something mouth-watering, but easily manageable.

Fletcher was well aware that his discomfort had nothing to do with these minor irritations. He was frustrated by the fact that he was too senior to do what he really wanted to do. It was not his job to get involved in the nuts and bolts of an on-going investigation, and it was definitely not his job to influence the direction of an investigation. That was Chief Superintendent Hilton's job, but Fletcher wasn't entirely convinced that the DCS was pushing in the right direction, or even knew what the right direction was.

So, he had come here to do himself the very thing he knew he shouldn't.

He liked James Montrayne. At first it had simply been respect for the way James had conducted himself during the time of Abby's abduction, evolving quickly into grudging admiration for his ability to get her back unharmed using methods that were never fully explained. The liking had come later, as they had continued to meet from time to time at mostly official, and occasionally private, functions in the county and elsewhere. He wasn't a fool, and he knew it was possible to misread a person's character or motives. But his gut instinct would not allow him to believe that James had killed Philip Simmons, in spite of the garbage that now lay staring at him from the surface of his undersized desk.

He knew he was going to have to tread carefully. Hilton was already making noises about pressure from on high, so any line he took must not have the least appearance of personal interest. But there was another, rather more political, dimension to this case, which he should probably be able to exploit quite successfully. It also had the quite legitimate benefit of falling within his jurisdiction.

James Montrayne was the son of a very senior and highly influential civil servant, who happened to be a peer of the realm who owned a substantial part of the county which Fletcher's police force strove to protect. The Lichfield Daily News, with its miniscule circulation, was not going to create much of a stir, but the local TV news was bound to have picked up the story by this evening, which meant that the heavyweight newspapers and the BBC would soon start sniffing around. The characters involved were just too high-profile for the story to slip by unnoticed. If DCI Morrissey was barking up the wrong tree, the Staffordshire police were going to end up with a considerable amount of dog mess smeared all over their boots. And, with all the money at the disposal of the Montrayne family, there would be lawsuits which wouldn't even have to be successful to ensure that any shortcomings in the investigation, or the officers involved, would be gleefully picked over by the media and broadcast on the hour in full-colour sound-bites. The Home Office would definitely not be pleased.

He picked up his phone and dialled an internal number. He waited, and then heard some clicks as the call was rerouted. A woman's voice answered.

"Where is Superintendent Hilton?" he asked brusquely, in response to her not very polite enquiry as to how she could help him. It further irritated him that she didn't recognise his voice and he had to identify himself.

"Oh, I'm sorry, sir," the female voice replied, without sounding it. "Superintendent Hilton has gone up to Burton."

"Burton?" echoed Fletcher. "I thought he was down here this morning, working with MID."

It was the Lichfield office of Staffordshire's Major Investigations Department, headed by DCI Morrissey, that was handling the investigation into Phil Simmons' death.

"He was here, sir, certainly. But after his... ... er... ...meeting with Chief Inspector Morrissey he returned to Burton."

It was not unreasonable. Hilton was the head of the Trent Valley Division, and its HQ was in Burton, but why so suddenly, and without a word.

"He was aware of my visit today?" Fletcher asked.

"I believe so, sir. But I understand that he thought you were working on the establishment review, and his presence was not required."

"I see," said Fletcher. "And who are you?"

"Detective Sergeant Hayford, sir."

"Hayford," he said. "Aren't you with MID."

"Yes, sir."

"Good. In that case, you can brief me on the … … the Philip Simmons case."

He had almost said the James Montrayne case, but caught himself just in time.

"I'm in my office, such as it is. Come on up."

While he waited, he contemplated Hilton's return to Burton. It was fairly clear, he thought, what was going on. The Superintendent had a disagreement with Morrissey about the course of the investigation, gave his instructions, and left quickly before he could be leant on by the ACC. Fletcher smiled briefly. It would be interesting to hear what Sergeant Hayford had to say.

When she entered his office a few moments later, he pointed to one of the two chairs across from his desk and invited her to sit down. He was surprised to see that she had come empty-handed. So much paperwork had to be completed these days that there must be a cartload already on this case. So why hadn't she brought some, at least to reassure him that she knew what she was talking about? He had met her a few times, and had read reports about previous cases, but he realised that he actually had no clear idea of her level of competence. Time to find out.

"You're working the Simmons case under DCI Morrissey?"

"Yes, sir."

Only two words, but Fletcher had the distinct impression of… … surliness? No, that wasn't it. Suppressed anger, that's what was flashing in her eyes, exuded from her posture, and dripped from her tongue. Fletcher was intrigued.

"Then perhaps you'd like to bring me up to date."

"Sir, I don't know what you've already been told."

"Assume nothing, and talk me through it."

So she did. From her first call to Heighley Woods on Saturday morning, she took him through the investigation up to the point when DCI Morrissey instructed her to caution James earlier that morning. When he wanted more information, or clarification on some point, he asked for it, and she did her best to oblige. As she did so, she felt her anger bleeding away. She was being asked for her opinion by someone who listened and was prepared to take her seriously.

When she finished, Fletcher nodded. She was good. Everything from memory, clear, concise and without hesitation. He didn't like what he'd heard, so he decided to try and dissect it a little more.

"Sergeant Hayford, that must be one of the clearest briefings I can remember being given. But let's just make sure I've got this right."

He glanced down at the notes he'd been taking as Joanne was speaking.

"Philip Simmons appears to have been shot with an airgun dart, found at the scene?"

"Yes, sir. 0.177 calibre."

"But the only rifle found at the scene was 0.25 calibre, which James Montrayne admits is his."

It wasn't really a question, but Joanne decided to answer anyway.

"Yes, sir. The woods, and the surrounding fields and hedgerows were searched thoroughly with metal detectors and no other rifle was found... ... Mr Montrayne, or should I call him Lord Aullton? I'm not quite sure."

"We've been calling him Montrayne up to now, so let's just carry on with that, shall we?"

"Very good, sir. Well, Mr Montrayne had several other rifles and a shotgun at his home, and one of those was a 0.22 calibre Air Arms S410 Xtra which is FAC rated. And an S410 carbine in 0.177 calibre."

"FAC eh? I assume he had all the right paperwork?"

"Yes, sir. Everything in order and bang up to date."

"And, if what you told me a few moments ago is correct, that .177 carbine could not have been the rifle that fired the dart."

"That's right, sir. Even assuming that Montrayne had the time to swap the rifles, or even get someone else to do it for him, that S410 was in pristine condition. The mechanism was cleaned and oiled, the woodwork highly polished, and the air tank was completely empty. It also has a ten-shot magazine which is not adapted for use with darts."

Fletcher made several ticks against his notes and said, "That seems to rule out Montrayne as the shooter of the dart. Hmmm. But you said that DCI Morrissey was not convinced."

"No, sir. He believes Montrayne could've had an accomplice who cleaned up the rifle and returned it to Montrayne's house."

"Possible, do you think?"

"No, sir. Setting aside the problem with the magazine, the security man at the Dower House is adamant that no-one came into the grounds between the time that Montrayne left and my arrival later that morning."

"And he would know? With certainty?"

She allowed herself to smile.

"I think so, sir. Security there is state of the art. They had it installed after the child's kidnapping a couple of years ago."

"OK. Let's leave the rifle... ... Now, what about the dart. You're sure that it was this that killed Simmons?"

"No, sir. It was the drug, and the subsequent blow on the head which killed him."

"OK, well let me put it this way. Are you sure that this dart couldn't have been lying around in the mud for months before we found it on Saturday?"

"Let me put it this way, sir" she said, taking the liberty of echoing his words. "There were traces on the dart of the drug later found in Simmons' blood."

"So this dart administered a fatal dose of... ... what was the drug again?"

"Succinylcholine, sir. And no, it didn't. The drug would have to have been smeared on the surface of the dart, and it's most unlikely that enough could have entered the bloodstream."

"So, what does DCI Morrissey think?"

"He believes that Simmons was pulled to the ground and the drug was injected by hypodermic. The dart, tainted with the drug, was then thrust into the puncture. Simmons then struggled to his feet... ... the drug takes up to a minute to take effect... ... so, he's on his feet, begins to lose control of his muscles, stumbles and falls into the water cracking his head on a rock close to the edge."

"And the dart?"

"Simmons managed to pull it out before he collapsed, or it was knocked out as he fell."

Fletcher made some more ticks.

"And DCI Morrissey believes Montrayne did this?"

"He does, sir."

"So how does this square with what you've told me about his belief that Montrayne fired the dart from this ... ... what was it... ... S410?"

"I'm really not sure, sir."

"Take a guess."

"Then I would say that DCI Morrissey is probably hedging his bets."

"And what do you think? Could Montrayne have used the hypodermic?"

"No, sir. That is to say, he could, but why on earth would he? Why create such an elaborate scheme whose sole purpose seems to be to point the finger at him? It doesn't make any sense."

Fletcher agreed, though he didn't say so. To him, it was Morrissey's conclusions that didn't make any sense.

"What... ... er... ... leads Mr Morrissey to hold to these conclusions?" he asked.

Joanne hesitated. This was getting onto dangerous ground. Reviewing the case was one thing, but telling a superior officer, in this case a very superior officer, that another superior officer was barking mad was not the best way of advancing your career. Fletcher watched her, sensing the reason for her hesitation.

"Don't worry, Sergeant. This is an informal meeting. Whatever you tell me today will not harm your career."

Joanne was not so sure but, on the other hand, refusing to answer wouldn't do her a lot of good either.

"DCI Morrissey believes Montrayne was supplied with the succinylcholine by that nurse who was killed in Birmingham a couple of days ago. He believes Montrayne had her killed to stop her talking."

Fletcher was astounded. Joanne hadn't referred to this in her initial briefing.

"Is there any evidence of that?... ... I mean, has any of the drug gone missing?... ... Did the nurse herself have access to it?"

"Mr Morrissey seems to think anything's possible, sir. But the hospital records don't show any of the drug to have gone missing. And, no, that nurse would have no direct access to it."

"Would it show? I mean... ... if any of the drug was missing, would it show up in the hospital records?"

"I really couldn't say, sir. But Mr Morrissey says that the NHS is such a shambles that anyone could walk off with anything and no-one would know."

"But, you said that nurse had no access to the drug."

"Yes, sir. That is, no, sir. Not in the normal course of her work."

"So, what do you think happened to her?"

"I think it was a simple mugging that went wrong. And that is the line being taken by the West Midlands force... ... in spite of Mr Morrissey's insistence on linking it to Montrayne."

"Does Montrayne have any connection with this nurse?"

"Only that he met her briefly on Saturday night when he arranged for the transfer of a patient from her ward to a hospital which he owns in Sutton Coldfield."

"Oh, yes, I know that one," said Fletcher. "PC Williams, you remember, he was shot in that house siege in Cannock last year... ... well, he was treated at the Aullton Foundation, at no cost, as I recall."

Joanne smiled.

"I don't remember it, sir, but what you say doesn't surprise me. From what I can gather, a lot of patients get free treatment at that hospital, including the girl who was transferred from Birmingham."

"How does she fit into the Simmons' case?"

"She doesn't, sir. I'm sure of that. And even Mr Morrissey isn't trying to make that one fly."

She saw ACC Fletcher's eyebrows rise and realised that her tone of voice had come very close to the border of disrespect.

"Sorry, sir," she apologised.

Fletcher said nothing for a moment, but held her gaze for long enough to let her know that, informal as this meeting may be, there were still boundaries that were not to be crossed. His fingers tapped lightly on the surface of his desk and he glanced out of his window at the uninspiring view as he thought back over what he'd been told. Joanne waited patiently for his next question, and idly counted the various notices pinned to the board on the wall behind Fletcher's desk. Then the tapping stopped as he remembered something she had told him earlier, something that needed teasing out a little bit.

"You mentioned earlier," he said, pulling his gaze without difficulty from the window, "that footprints were found at the scene in the wood."

"Yes, sir."

"Just one set?"

"Two sets, sir. A pair of heavy-soled boots, and the running shoes worn by the victim."

"Oh, yes. Of course. But apart from the victim's, there was only one set of prints."

"Apparently, sir."

"And they matched the boots Montrayne was wearing that morning."

She hesitated, because she had not yet had confirmation of her suspicions.

"Come on, sergeant. Did they match or didn't they?"

"It…would…seem…so…"she said slowly.

He looked at her thoughtfully, and she gazed straight back, unsure whether her stare would be construed as disrespect. She hoped not, as she actually had a lot of time for the ACC. She was relieved to see him smile.

"You don't seem entirely convinced, sergeant."

"No, sir."

"Well, go on. Don't keep me in suspense."

She thought of the photos taken of the footprints, both at the scene and on the footpath going up past the old shepherd's hut. She also thought about the dental-stone casts that she had asked the Scene of Crime Officers to produce for her. They had seemed a little miffed that she had asked, as though she didn't trust them to do their jobs properly, but her sharp eyes had noticed something which could be significant and she hadn't wanted to risk losing it.

"Some of the prints definitely matched the boots Montrayne was wearing. There were some nicks on the right sole and the general pattern of wear made the match conclusive. And, in any case, Montrayne made no secret of the fact that he was there."

"You said *some* of the prints. Does that mean that there were others?"

"*I* believe so, sir. Yes."

He caught her emphasis on the word *I*.

"But DCI Morrissey doesn't agree with you."

"Actually, sir, he refuses to discuss it with me. And I can't press it because I'm still waiting for the report from forensics."

"What do you expect the report to say?"

Without the report, she only had her gut instinct and the evidence she believed she could see in the photographs. Now she had to commit herself before ACC Fletcher, she hoped very much she was right.

"I believe there were two people at the scene, apart from the victim. I think the second person, not Montrayne, was wearing the same style boots as Montrayne but they were newer. The photos seem to show the tread in some of the prints to be more sharply defined... ... clearer, if you like... ... without the nicks or wear patterns. I can be more positive when I get the report from forensics on the casts."

She watched as Fletcher pursed his lips and gently massaged his chin with the fingers of his left hand. Than he reached for his phone.

"Let's give them a nudge, shall we?"

She listened while he *nudged* forensics into action. She knew it wasn't their fault that they were snowed under with work, but she also knew that they would probably have completed the report more quickly if Morrissey had been banging on their door every five minutes. The call went on for several minutes, with Fletcher alternately bullying and listening. Finally he put the phone down.

"They eventually got one of the techs to examine the casts under a microscope while I waited," he explained. "You were right. The prints definitely came from more than one pair of boots. Which makes me wonder how a third person, intent on committing villainy, could know in advance what boots Montrayne would be wearing... ... Or could it just have been coincidence?"

He saw the gleam in Joanne's eye and smiled.

"You've got something more to tell me haven't you, sergeant?"

"Yes, sir."

She told him about her visit to the Old Park Rifle Club the previous day, about Ruth Farquhar, and about the unidentified stranger who had been asking how to get hold of a pair of boots like the ones Montrayne wore when he was shooting.

"Thank you, sergeant," Fletcher said when she'd finished. "That's good work... ...But there's just one last thing... ... What about this?"

He held up the paper with the latest edition of Corrina Rigby's scurrilous tales.

"Is there *any* substance to this, or is it just the trashy rubbish it seems?"

This wasn't quite so easy. Joanne knew exactly what she thought, but it was based more on absence of evidence rather than anything conclusive. She was reluctant to commit herself to a statement which might later come back to chew her behind.

"I don't know who the reliable source is in today's piece, this supposed friend of Montrayne, but I'm not convinced. The source doesn't sound like much of a friend, which means it could be someone with a grudge, maybe even the person wearing the other boots. And so far, we haven't found anyone to substantiate the rumours of any kind of affair between Montrayne and Natalie Simmons. And, yes, we have tried."

She looked at the paper, now lying crumpled under his left hand, and then back up to the blue eyes of the ACC. She liked those eyes, she thought. Pity he's married. Then she took her thoughts in hand, and decided to commit herself.

"I was the one who broke the news to Mrs Simmons. She was totally devastated. Genuine, sincere, unadulterated grief. No question… … She wasn't having an affair with James Montrayne, and if ever a DNA test were to be done, then that baby will be 100% Philip and Natalie Simmons… … That paper is trash."

There, it was done, and she felt the better for it. She hadn't sought this interview with the ACC, and would never have gone behind Morrissey's back in spite of her misgivings about his line of enquiry. Being asked for her opinion was a different matter, and she didn't think she had done herself any harm by the frankness of her replies. She was just curious as to what would happen next, but didn't like to ask.

As it happened, she didn't need to. The ACC could just have thanked her and sent her away, but he seemed to think a little reward was in order, even if only in the form of verbal encouragement.

"You've done well, sergeant. Very well. I think a word with DCI Morrissey would be in order now, don't you think?"

She had a sudden vision of Morrissey sitting in the other chair being interrogated by the ACC while she sat by and watched. The DCI would kill her. Well, if not her, then her career. Loyalty, that was what was always being drummed into her. And she had just been extremely disloyal, even though she had only spoken the truth. Fletcher seemed to read her thoughts.

"Don't worry, sergeant. I shall not refer to our conversation. I'm just grateful to you that I now know the right questions to ask the Chief Inspector… … You had better go and release Mr Montrayne, with our apologies for having detained him unnecessarily… … And don't worry about Morrissey. He will be otherwise engaged."

Fifty-Five

The Dower House – Early afternoon

As I looked into those beautiful eyes, brim-full with tears, I felt my heart aching. Abby was trying so hard to be brave but no-one knew better than I the terrors of that scared little girl. I got up quickly and went over to her. I reached out to pull her close and felt her arms grip tightly round my waist. Her hair tickled my chin and I felt the wetness of her tears through my shirt.

Her voice was muffled, but the words were clear enough.

"Tell me, Lizzie. Please. What's going on?"

I was trying to decide whether I dare reassure that her daddy would be home soon, in spite of not knowing for sure that it was true, when I suddenly realised that there was no need.

We all heard it at the same time.

The crunch of tires on gravel.

Abby's head came up with a jerk that banged my teeth together, and we all looked out of the library windows in time to see the Maserati glide round to the back of the house. With a little shriek, Abby was out of my arms and racing back through the dining room to the rear of the house. I sensed rather than saw Cherry standing up and when I turned to look at him and Riddings I saw that they were both grinning.

Together, with me slightly in the lead, we set off to find James.

We discovered him in the kitchen, hugging Abby tightly, but looking over her head at the display screen for the front gate. Coming into the house to find her, he had been distracted almost immediately by the buzzer. Mrs Siddons was nowhere to be seen and it later turned out that she had gone over to the laundry room behind the stable garage where her daughter-in-law was attending to the bed linen. James looked over as we entered and our eyes met. Oddly, he held my gaze, smiling, for what seemed like ages, and only broke eye contact when Riddings brushed past me.

"Well, well," said James. "The troops are out in force. Where did you spring from, Paul?"

Riddings' reply was interrupted by another loud and very long blast from the buzzer. Since James was still a little hampered by Abby, Cherry pushed by me to stare at the screen.

"That's Andy's Jag, Boss," he said. "Shall I let him through?"

James nodded. "Yes, I saw it. You'd better open the gate before he deafens us all. And… … er," he jerked his head towards the rear of the house, "go and let him in."

When Andy came in through the back door, escorted by Cherry, we all knew straight away that something was definitely wrong. Even Abby sensed it, and she looked anxiously from Andy to her dad clearly wondering, as we all were, what new disaster had been dropped on us. I was beginning to worry about her. From what I'd picked up over the last few days, it wasn't long since she'd returned to something like normality after the trauma of her kidnapping. So far, she had coped amazingly well with the worry of recent events, but I didn't think it would take much more to send her tumbling back into that dark place from which it had taken so long to draw her out.

And maybe next time it would take far longer to restore her. I didn't understand much about child psychology, but I did wonder whether next time, the damage could even be permanent.

"Hey, Abby," I said. "I bet Andy and your dad could do with a cup of coffee. How about we leave them to it for a few minutes while we go and change our grubby clothes."

We were still wearing the same gear we'd had on for our otter hunt earlier in the day. Seeing Abby hesitate, I ploughed on.

"I still haven't seen you in that new sweater and jeans you were telling me about."

She wasn't hugging her dad any longer, but she still held him tightly by the hand. When she looked up at him she saw he was smiling. Watching his eyes, I saw the tension behind that cheerful expression, and I wondered whether there was any significance in the fact that Abby, who had known him far longer and far more intimately than I, apparently did not.

James gave her a gentle nudge in my direction saying, "Go on, sweetie, or you'll be dropping mud all over Mrs Siddons' nice clean floor."

It was a bit of an exaggeration, but Abby looked down at her grimy jeans, soiled by crawling through the undergrowth down by the river, and took his point.

"OK, but you'll stay here?"

"In the conservatory," he said. "Come and find us in there."

"OK."

When she came towards me, I caught James's eye as he mouthed the words *Thank you* over her head. I smiled briefly before taking Abby's hand and leading her upstairs to change.

It was just over half an hour later when we made our way down, via the mural hall and the drawing room, to the conservatory on the south side of the house. By asking Abby to come to my room as soon as she was ready, and by dithering over my choice of clothes, and asking Abby's advice, I had stretched out the time as long as I could. Then, in a flash of inspiration, I had phoned from my room to ask Mrs Siddons, who was now back in the kitchen, to take two glasses of her freshly made lemonade to the conservatory, thus alerting James and the others that we would soon be invading their meeting.

They were ready, all smiles and forced cheerfulness, as we made our entrance. I still had no idea why Andy had come, but if he had brought bad news, they were all hiding it well. James was seated on a cane-work settee, of which there were two in the conservatory, along with four matching armchairs. I would not have expected the delicate pattern of interwoven canes to be substantial enough to support his large frame, but it seemed to be coping quite adequately. He patted the small space remaining beside him for Abby to go and sit down.

"My word," he said as she went towards him. "Aren't you the smart one?"

Cherry echoed this with practised comments of his own which showed not just the familiarity of his relationship with Abby, but also his genuine affection for his child protectee. Andy added his own admiration, as one who'd known Abby from a baby, but it seemed to me that there was something a little odd in the way he spoke. I couldn't put my finger on it, but his tone struck me as rather off-key. Riddings, the stranger, just nodded quietly.

Before sitting down, Abby unselfconsciously gave a quick twirl, spreading out the hem of her jumper to show off the intricate pattern of Disney characters running round it. James applauded and then gave her a hug as she sat and snuggled up to him.

Since the other three men were all occupying armchairs, I took the fourth one just as Mrs Siddons returned with a rather sheepish enquiry.

"I'm sorry, sir. I forgot to ask before. Will you, or any of the gentlemen, be wanting any lunch?" She looked around before adding, "You must be a mite peckish by now."

"Thank you, Mrs Siddons," he replied. "Perhaps some of your ham on the bone with crusty rolls. For… … er… …" He looked at the others with raised eyebrows receiving a nod from Riddings and a shake of the head from everyone else. "For two then, please, Mrs Siddons."

When she had left, James looked across at me and said, with an offhand casualness that did not for a moment deceive me, "I was wondering, Lizzie, whether you've ever been up to Scotland."

Abby looked up in surprise. "Do you mean Aullton?"

"Well now, how did you guess?" he asked teasingly. "I thought Lizzie might like to go and stay for a few days. Don't you think she looks as though she needs a holiday?"

Before she could answer, he turned his eyes towards me and explained, "I have a place up in the Lammermuir Hills. It's a bit off the beaten track, and most of it's open to the public this time of year, but the private apartments are secluded and fairly comfortable. It can seem a bit eerie when the wind whistles round the turrets but... ..."

Abby was on the edge of her seat. "Don't listen to him, Lizzie. It's the coolest place ever, I mean, really EVER. It's like Disney's fairy-tale castle, and the turrets have those funny pointy roofs... ... and you can go riding and boating... ... and the deer will just be having their babies and... ... Oh, Lizzie, we've got llamas, a whole flock of them. Is it flock? When do the llamas have their babies?"

This last question was directed to James, who was smiling at her sudden excitement.

"I'm not sure when they're born," he said. "And it's a herd not a flock. At least, I think it is... ... So, do you think Lizzie would like it."

"Don't be silly, Daddy," she said, nudging him with her shoulder. "Course she'll like it, won't you, Lizzie?"

I looked at the pair of them, her eyes sparkling with excitement, while his were no longer smiling but focussed on mine in a very meaningful way.

"I think it sounds... ... wonderful," I answered, assuming that this was the right response. Apparently it was, since James nodded slowly, once.

"I'm glad about that," he said, "since I've arranged for Mike Coleman to fly you up there first thing tomorrow morning."

My surprise must have been obvious since he went on to explain that, after taking the Marquess back to London that morning, Mike had flown a couple of minor dignitaries up to Edinburgh for a two-day conference on industrial regeneration. James had phoned him to check where he was and how many flying hours he had left that day. It seemed he had enough to fly down but not enough to make the return trip back up to Scotland. Anyway, Mike had agreed to do it as long as he could stay overnight and make the trip back up in the morning. After a good lunch at Aullton House, he would then be ideally placed to collect his two passengers once the conference ended and deliver them back to London. James didn't mention who was paying for the trip.

"So he should be here in time for tea," he concluded.

Abby was gently bouncing up and down on the edge of her seat.

"Dad, don't you think Lizzie will need some company?"

"Well, she'll have Mike, and Andy here has offered to go and keep her company. And then there's Mrs Elliott and all the other staff up there so... ..."

"Yes, I know, but... ... Dad, can't I go with her? You won't let me go to school, and it's going to be boring if Lizzie's not here."

"You could always go and see Debbie."

"No, I can't. She's at school all day. Please, Dad... ... Please."

Then another thought struck her which she delivered as though this was the clincher that settled the discussion.

"And I still haven't had a ride in Grandad's helicopter, and you promised I could and now Lizzie will have had two rides."

James turned to lift her onto her feet as though she had no more weight than a doll and said, "How good are you at packing?"

Abby gave a squeal of delight, wriggled free and scampered from the room.

"Brilliant," she shouted over her shoulder.

I got up to follow but James called me back. Cherry went to make sure that Abby had indeed gone upstairs and to supervise what would otherwise have been very haphazard packing.

With the closing of the door behind him, a heaviness settled on the room. It was now that I learnt why James was so keen to send me away. I slumped down, stunned, as he explained that someone as yet unknown had got into Angie's room at the hospital and injected her with an overdose of heroin that was almost certainly lethal. I just couldn't understand how it had happened, with so much care being taken to guard her.

"It was my fault," Andy said, and there was no mistaking the anguish in his voice. "I sent Rod off to get his lunch and watched Angie while he and John were away. A medic came in, and he really looked the part, stethoscope, ID badge, everything. He said it was time for Angie's next injection and... ... I stood and watched him while he gave it to her. Then he left, and almost straight away Rod was banging on the door because he'd forgotten his magazine. I must have accidently turned the lock when I closed the door after the phony doctor left and Rod couldn't get in."

He paused, as if giving me the chance to ask questions, but I was too shocked to think of anything to say. After a moment, he continued.

"It was Rod that noticed how still Angie was, so he called Doctor Harwood. By the time he arrived, Angie had stopped breathing and Rod was giving her mouth to mouth. After that it was chaos, so I went to see if hospital security had anything on the guy with the needle. They had nothing on camera and since it was pretty obvious he had totally buggered off, I thought I'd better come and tell James, and you of course, what had happened."

I picked up on the ray of hope he'd left flickering.

"So Angie might not be dead. They might have saved her."

James sighed. "They might, but I have to say it doesn't seem very likely. Andy phoned Rod just before you and Abby joined us, and it really wasn't looking good."

Tears began to tumble down my cheeks and I dropped my head into my hands. James came over and knelt down by my chair. I felt his hands on my shoulders as he drew me towards him. Instead of being comforted, I began to shake as the sobs increased in intensity, driven both by grief for Angie and guilt for what I had inadvertently brought upon her.

"I… must… go… to… her," I gasped, between sobs, into James's shoulder.

"No."

I heard his voice, soft, close to my ear.

"You're going up to Aullton, as we agreed. There's nothing you can do for Angie and if, by some miracle, she comes through this, I'll fly her up to join you."

I started to protest but he pushed me gently back into the chair so he could look into my eyes. Pulling back, he let his hands drop so that they were resting lightly over mine which I now clasped in my lap.

"I need to get Abby away from here," he said, almost pleading with me. "As long as she's here, she's at risk. I can't take the chance of her being hurt. Not again."

His eyes were reaching deep into mine, searching for some indication that I understood his fears. I think we had both forgotten there were others in the room.

"If I suggested she leave me and go up to Scotland, she'd refuse. I could insist and send her kicking and screaming, but that wouldn't really do much for her peace of mind. So I schemed a little."

I was too upset to think about whether I was offended or not, but I said, "So you're just using me to get Abby away from here."

"No, Lizzie. I want you safe too. I have to admit I underestimated your Mr Mellisse. I never realised how determined he would turn out to be, or how dangerous. With you and Abby safely away and out of reach, and Angie too if she pulls through, I shall be free to do what's necessary to deal with him."

I eased my hands away from his and brushed the tears from my cheeks.

"What are you going to do?"

Still kneeling in front of me, he said, "I'm not sure, in detail, but if I can get the evidence to link him to that nurse or to the attack on Angie, then I'll let the police deal with him."

"And if you can't get the evidence?"

He stood up and reached out a hand to draw me to my feet. Holding me at arm's length, he said, "Then I'll deal with him some other way. That I promise you. Now, will you go to Scotland?"

"I'll go."

"Good girl. Now, go and pack."

He looked around, remembering we had an audience.

"Andy here is going home to collect his stuff and then he's going back to take turns watching Angie overnight. He'll be back here in the morning to go with you to Scotland. He can catch up on his sleep during the flight."

I was hardly through the door when I thought I heard the distant thump of a helicopter's rotor blades. I really didn't want to leave James, but I understood why he believed it was for the best. Maybe I'd even get to see Angie before I left for Scotland with Abby. If only she could survive the night.

Fifty-Six

Old Park Rifle Club – 3:30pm

Sergeant Hayford saw to the release of James Montrayne, and offered him the appropriate apology suggested by ACC Fletcher. From her previous experience of the great and the good – which she usually interpreted to mean the wealthy and powerful or, alternatively, the ruthless and the amoral - Sergeant Hayford half expected to take some flak from his Lordship, along with threats of a lawsuit for wrongful arrest. So she was more than a little surprised when he listened to her brief explanation and apology with a slight smile and without once interrupting her. On being told he was free to go, he stood and looked down at her for a moment before nodding and holding out his hand. After a brief hesitation, in which she envisioned strong fingers crushing her own relatively delicate hand, she took it and they shook briefly.

She stood aside for him to leave the interview room ahead of her, but he surprised her again.

"I want the person who killed Phil Simmons just as much as you do," he said. "Maybe even more. So if you need any help, just ask. There's no need to arrest me and drag me in here. Oh, and… … if you can manage to keep your DCI well out of my sight I think we'd probably all be better off."

She didn't reply. She just nodded her head slowly and then watched as he left the room. After that, she decided that perhaps Lichfield Police Station would not be the safest place for her to be when DCI Morrissey emerged from his interview with the ACC. Her boss would be all set to explode, even if Fletcher had been able to hide from Morrissey where he had got his information. She had seen the DCI erupt before and the fallout was loud, vehement and indiscriminate. And this would be even worse since Morrissey, with retirement just around the corner, had nothing to lose.

She managed to leave the building prior to detonation having left word with Constable Mayblin that she was following up on the forensics report on the footprints in the wood. She deliberately left it very vague as to where she was going and who she was planning to see. And if Morrissey tried to get her on her mobile, well… … it wouldn't be the first time she'd had a dead battery.

She had very little hope of learning anything new at the Old Park Rifle Club, but it beat hanging around waiting to be buried under a heap of verbal manure.

The weather was better than it had been the day before, a bit of light cloud and definitely no rain, so she wasn't surprised to see several cars parked outside the clubhouse. Getting out of her Focus ST500 she stood for a moment, forearms resting along the top of the door, and listened. Nothing for several seconds, and then she heard it, muffled by the buildings but unmistakeable nevertheless. The ranges she now knew were on the far side of the clubhouse, and somebody was obviously practising. She wasn't familiar enough with firearms to recognise the calibre, but the shots were definitely not coming from an air rifle. She wondered briefly what satisfaction there was in punching holes in a piece of card covered in concentric circles. Then she told herself there wasn't much difference between this and chucking darts into a circular board down the pub; or rolling large, black balls across a manicured green; or hitting small white ones around a golf course. And rifle shooting, of course, *was* an Olympic sport.

Anyway, it wasn't the shooter she was after. She was looking for Ruth Farquhar. She found the club secretary in her small office, dressed just as smartly as she had been the previous afternoon. The trousers were still black but the sweater today was a creamy white. She looked up from the papers on her desk when Joanne tapped lightly on the glass panel of her open door.

"Ah. Sergeant Hayford. Back again so soon?"

Ruth's voice was pleasant but with sufficient undertone to suggest that she could have done without the interruption.

"Afraid so, Mrs Farquhar. Could you spare a few minutes?"

Picking up what appeared to be an official letter from the pile on her desk, Ruth held it up shaking her head slightly.

"You know, sergeant, I really don't understand these council planners. Do you think they're specially selected because they have an Honours Degree in Stupidity? In that phone call yesterday – you were here, remember? – I answered every question about our planning application, and every bit of that was just confirmation of what we'd already submitted in writing. Every bit! Can you believe it? And now I've had this letter this morning from some sixteen year old clerk querying our measurements. So now I've got to go out there with a tape measure, just so as to be able to say I've done it, and then write back confirming that every detail in the drawing is spot-on accurate. You'd think they have something better to do with their time than write useless letters."

She dropped the paper, looking thoughtful.

"Do you think Parkinson was studying council workers when he wrote his Law?"

Joanne had lost her drift and, being used to entirely different laws, looked thoroughly puzzled.

"You know, sergeant. Parkinson's Law. *Work expands to fill the time available for its completion.*"

Now that *did* ring a bell but, feeling she was in some way a council worker herself, Joanne replied, "Possibly, though with me it's more a case of *Work contracts to allow as much as possible to be fitted into the not-enough-time available.*"

Ruth smiled. "Touché, sergeant. I like it."

Then, with a sigh, "I tell you what. You come and hold the end of the tape measure for me and we can talk as we go. How's that?"

It sounded fine to Joanne so, after a brief pause to search for a clipboard on which to fix a photocopy of the plans for the proposed new range, and a slightly longer pause to find the fifty metre surveyors tape measure which Ruth was sure was in the cupboard somewhere, the two ladies set off for the ranges.

It didn't take Joanne long to discover that her visit to the club was going to turn out just about as fruitless as she'd expected. Ruth had spoken to every member who had visited the club since her visit the day before, but none of them remembered seeing the stranger who asked about James's boots.

"I even printed off a photo from the camera files," said Ruth. "I thought maybe his clothes might trip someone's memory but … … nothing. I might have better luck at the weekend, specially Sunday. That's when most of the members turn out. There's not many can make it during the week, because of work and so on."

They were outside the main building now and walking down a kind of open gallery rather like one side of a cloister except that the green space it looked out on was rectangular rather than square. The open side of the gallery was divided into bays, each one looking down the length of the rectangle to a high earth bank backed by an even taller concrete wall some one hundred metres away. Joanne stopped when she saw that one of the bays was occupied.

"Don't worry about it," she said. "It was a bit of a long shot anyway. Just see what happens at the weekend and, if anything comes up, give me a call."

"Ok," replied Ruth, stopping beside Joanne and smiling to herself when she noticed how intently the police sergeant was observing the young woman sitting on the tartan blanket which almost filled the bay.

A bolt-action rifle, barrel resting on a padded bipod, poked out down the range, but the girl was temporarily ignoring it as she sat cross-legged engrossed in refilling a small magazine with what seemed to Joanne like miniature bullets. When five had been loaded to her satisfaction, she laid down the magazine and reached for an empty one to begin the process again.

"This is Jane," said Ruth, and the girl looked up, nodded without any particular friendliness, and returned to her task. She appeared to Joanne to be in her early twenties, good-looking in an unremarkable way, and obviously irritated. Probably because she picked her spot in the hope of being undisturbed.

"Her dad has a farm over Grangewood way," Ruth went on, "which is where Jane does her hunting."

"Hunting?" echoed Joanne, with no clue as to what Ruth was referring to.

"Vermin," said a new, slightly contemptuous, voice. Jane did not look up as she spoke. "You know the things. Rats, squirrels, rabbits, even the odd pigeon if it sits still long enough."

"Ah," said Joanne, pointing to the rifle. "And you … … er … shoot them with that."

"Well I don't beat them to death with a club."

Ruth came to Joanne's rescue.

"That's a sporting rifle, designed for the purpose. It's an Anschutz XIV carbine. That means it's got a shorter barrel so it's easier to handle in the woods. It's a .22 rimfire, so it's nothing like the guns you've been looking at in connection with James. You can use it with a ten shot magazine but Jane prefers a five because it doesn't stick out so much. Jane comes here to practise at least once a week."

The unfriendly voice came again. "If you can't kill it with one shot, you've no business to be out there hunting it."

"Quite right," acknowledged Ruth. "Now we'd better move on. Jane doesn't like to be watched when she's practising."

As they moved away, Joanne whispered, "I'd never have guessed."

"I heard that," said Jane from behind them. "Now why don't you run down that range and pretend to be a squirrel?"

As they walked to the end of the gallery, Ruth explained that behind the high grass bank to the side of the range there was about a fifty metre strip of open ground which belonged to the club. The plan was to push the bank back and extend the gallery to create two more ranges which would ease the pressure on match days when so many ranges had to be dedicated to competitors.

"Trouble is," said Ruth, handing the end of the tape to Joanne, "there are a couple of anti-gun nuts on the council who can't seem to bear the thought that so many of us actually enjoy shooting for sport. If they had their way, they'd close us down rather than let us expand. It's not as if we're even killing anything down here, for crying out loud."

"And they're on the planning committee?" asked Joanne.

"One is, and he knows there are no real grounds for refusing the planning application. The mean-spirited sod's just being bolshie for the sake of it... ... Anyway, let's just get the measuring done and we then can forget about him."

As Joanne obeyed instructions and held the end of the tape to the brick column which marked the end of the gallery, something caught her attention. Attached to the column, on the side facing down range, was a wooden block secured in place with black strapping tape. It was positioned about waist height and, as she looked down curiously, Joanne noticed that it was not rectangular in cross-section as she'd first thought but triangular. Fixed to the longest face of the block, so that it was angled across rather than down the range, was a small box maybe seven inches by five and three inches deep. It was coloured in shades of green, a camouflage design.

"What's this?" she asked Ruth, tapping the block with the back of her hand.

"Oh, that's just... ..." Ruth's voice tailed off, her eyes became unfocussed, and her mouth hung open. For several moments she was still, then her face glowed with excitement as she moved to Joanne's side whispering, "Holy cow!"

She stood in front of the camouflaged box, staring down at it.

"Jane, come here... ... ... I wonder... ... I wonder... ..."

There was no sound of movement from along the gallery, so she called again, louder this time.

"Jane, we need you. Over here. Now."

There was another pause before the girl replied, sounding tired and irritated.

"OK, OK. Be there in a minute."

Joanne was completely at a loss to understand what had provoked this sudden burst of excitement.

"What is it?" she asked.

Ruth eyes sparkled. "That, my dear sergeant, might just make your day." Then, a little louder, "Jane, where are you?"

"I've got to tidy my stuff. Keep your knickers on."

"Is this hers?" asked Joanne, her hand resting on the top of the block.

"It's her latest toy, "replied Ruth. "A twelve meg, wide-angle, infra-red camera. She put it here just to try it out. We thought it might be fun to see what wildlife strolls across the range when we're not here. She'll be using it for finding the most likely places for targeting vermin on the farm, and it might just... ..."

She stopped as Jane appeared carrying her gun case.

"Jane, when did you set this up?"

"Couple of weeks ago. Why?"

"Hmm. So the batteries are probably dead now?"

"I guess. Does it matter?"

"It bloody well does matter," replied Ruth, irritated by Jane's off-handedness.

"All right. All right. No need to get narky. What's this all about anyway?"

"Sorry." Ruth took a breath. "Do you know when the batteries gave out?"

"No," said Jane abruptly, and then surprised both ladies by grinning. "But I can check, if it means so much to you. The date and time on the last picture will show when they died. That's what I was trying to find out, you see. How long they last. And how good the infra-red quality is."

"Would they still have been good on the Sunday after you put it up?"

"Sure. I checked them when I was here last Tuesday and they were fine then."

Joanne suddenly grasped what Ruth was getting at.

"You don't think… …?"

"I certainly do think… … Jane, can we have a look at the SD card and see what's on there?"

Jane stared at the two women, her head slightly cocked to one side. There was an intensity in their gaze that made her frown in growing realisation that there was more to this request than mere curiosity about her camera.

"Well, yes. I guess so. Er… … there's a small viewing screen in the camera, or would you rather… …"

Ruth interrupted. "Could you just take the card out so we can look at it on my laptop?"

"Look, Ruth," said Jane, her own curiosity roused. "What's going on? Come on, it's obvious something's got in your knickers. What is it?"

It still took some coaxing, and a sight of Joanne's warrant card, but eventually Jane agreed to extract the SD card on condition that she be allowed to come and see for herself what all the fuss was about.

On their way back to the office, Joanne said quietly to Ruth, "Do you really think it's possible that this guy could be on here?"

"Actually, I do," Ruth replied in an equally soft voice. "I'm sure it was that afternoon that James was trying out his new S410 Xtra. It's a .22, FAC rated, and good out to 100 yards. That's why he was on this range. He'd already got smaller than half-inch groups at fifty yards so he was seeing what he could manage at a hundred. If our guy was watching him, there's a good chance he could have wandered into the edge of the frame. That camera's got a wide angle, remember."

Hey, you two," called Jane from the rear. "I'm still here, you know. So just stop with your cops and robber secrets."

When they reached Ruth's office, Jane handed over the camera card and set off to find herself a cup of coffee. The other two waited impatiently for the laptop to boot up, Ruth at her desk drumming her finger tips on the surface, Joanne standing behind her tapping her toes soundlessly on the rough carpet.

Jane appeared with her coffee, just the one Joanne noted, as the images began to appear on the screen. They were in groups, colour by day and black and white by night. It was obvious immediately that the grass of the range took up most of the shot. The gallery was only just in view, and someone would have had to walk right to the end to come within range of the movement sensor of the camera and trigger the shot. Jane explained that she had set it up that way so the camera would not be taking a picture every time someone moved in the gallery. Joanne's hopes dwindled. What had been a long shot at best now faded to become a miniscule dot on the horizon of possibility.

She raised her eyes from the screen to gaze through the window at a much nearer horizon and wondered how much longer she could put off returning to the police station and the bollocking that was waiting for her.

Suddenly she was aware that there had been no movement for several seconds. Ruth's hand on the mouse – she preferred it to the laptop's touch-pad – was still and the screen was frozen. The date showing in the bottom corner was Sunday just over a week ago, and the time was 14:23. Down the left-hand edge of the picture was a man who had obviously been making his way to the very end of the gallery. It was a clear, full-frontal image, and Joanne held her breath as Ruth zoomed in on the man's face. It was slightly fuzzy with that degree of enlargement but clear enough for all that.

"Yes," whispered Ruth, and then growing louder with each word, "Yes. Yes! Yes!!"

"Is he what all the fuss is about?" asked Jane, peering in for a closer look.

"Do you know him?" asked Joanne. "Did you see him that day?"

"No, never seen him before. Well, he's a villainous looking sod, isn't he? You wouldn't forget those eyes in a hurry."

She was right, thought Joanne. Even in the washed-out colour of the enlargement, the man's eyes were a startling blue. Perhaps because she'd seen *Layer Cake* only the week before, she was reminded forcefully of Daniel Craig. You didn't easily forget his eyes either, although the actor's sexy charm was a far cry from the cold menace in this guy's stare.

His hair was lighter than Craig's too, and cropped short, while his face was rounder with a haze of fair stubble.

"This is him, isn't it?" she asked Ruth, hardly daring to believe in such a breakthrough. "This is the boots guy. You're sure."

"One hundred per cent," replied Ruth, turning to smile up at her. "Now I suppose you want some copies of this."

Fifty-Seven

The Thurvaston Arms – 5:00pm

The small country inn was all that they could have hoped for. It was tucked away down a narrow lane, way off the beaten track, and overlooking the water-meadows in a wide loop of the River Trent. A hurried search, using the only free computer in a crowded internet café near to London St. Pancras railway station, had offered several promising choices for somewhere to stay. When the Eurostar from Paris had pulled into the station three minutes early at one twenty-five that afternoon, they had at least the outline of a workable plan, but they needed the internet to make a start.

First, identify a small, mid-range country hotel somewhere north of Birmingham which John had never frequented before, and which he and Nadera could use as a base for the next stage of their operation. Second, hire a car using John's Josh Barnett credit card and driving licence which was still the old paper version, not the newer photo ID. Third, take the M1 or M40 north to the midlands and check in to their chosen hotel. Fourth, having settled on Corrina Rigby as their most promising source, find her and encourage her, by whatever means, to reveal where she was getting her information from. Five … … well, there wasn't a five just yet, since this depended very much on what they prised out of Miss Rigby.

When John had phoned ahead to check whether the Thurvaston Arms could accommodate them, he had given way to Nadera's logic. After sharing the sleeper on the train, she could see no reason why they should incur extra expense by reverting to separate rooms. It didn't occur to him, when confirming the reservation with his Josh Barnett card, that he could ask for a twin rather than a double bedded room, so he was a little perturbed when the first thing he saw on entering the room was a four-poster king-size bed. Nadera on the other hand just gave it a momentary and rather thoughtful glance and passed on into the room, a twinkle in her eye and a slight smile lifting the corners of her mouth.

John was all for phoning down to reception to see if there were any other rooms available, but Nadera overrode him.

"We do not want to bring attention to ourselves," she said firmly, adding with an even more pronounced twinkle, "and if you do not want to sleep with me, you can always take the chair. It looks comfortable enough."

The chair, one of a pair facing a wall-mounted TV across a low coffee table, did indeed look comfortable, so John simply nodded, completely unable to confess to her that in all his twenty-odd years since puberty he had never slept with anyone, never seen a woman naked, except in pictures or a movie, and certainly never touched one. How could he admit to anyone that, if he should find a naked woman in his bed, he was horribly afraid he might not know what to do with her. No, that wasn't right. He knew what he would like to do, especially with Nadera, indeed *only* with Nadera, but he had no confidence that it would be what *she* wanted, or if it would be enough to please her.

She loved him. There was no doubt of that after these last few days. And he loved her, no doubt about that either, so this lack of confidence of his would have to be confronted sooner or later.

"Look," he said. "If it all goes well this evening and we find ourselves back here, I think… … maybe, I won't take the chair."

"Well, that is a relief," she replied with a grin that caused his heart to flip. "I was beginning to think that you didn't like me."

"No you weren't," he said, grinning back, relieved the decision had at last been taken.

"Hmmm," muttered Nadera, hoisting a holdall up onto the bed. "Well now that is decided, let us put all this stuff away."

All this stuff were the contents of a suitcase and two holdalls all of which had been bought for cash from different stores at Fosse Park, a large shopping complex just off the M1 on the outskirts of Leicester. Leaving Italy in such a hurry, and wishing to leave no trail behind them, they had arrived in England with very little in the way of clothes and other essential personal items. At PC World, Josh Barnett had paid cash for a laptop which had both Bluetooth and Wi-Fi capability. Not wanting to risk signing up for a contract, they would use whatever Wi-Fi connections they found available. While Nadera was in the shower, he booted up the laptop went online using the hotel's password conveniently listed in the guests' handbook. Before she had emerged, robed in white towelling and with hair dripping, he had created an icon image, essential for their plan, and found an address for Corrina Rigby.

Just under an hour later they had left the hotel, clean and in new clothes, ostensibly to dine with friends in the village nearby. Twenty-three minutes after that, they were sitting in their hired Toyota Avensis on a quiet suburban road about twenty yards short of the large Victorian mansion in which Corrina Rigby had her apartment. There were still a couple of hours of daylight left, but the afternoon sun shone on the rear of the house so the front, with its cobbled horseshoe in-and-out driveway, was in shadow.

Nadera took a quick look around inside of the car. She didn't really need to because she had already checked for identifiable marks and had removed the rental firm's sticker from the rear window. Over-cautious perhaps, but where her safety and freedom were at stake, she was disinclined to take chances. She had also smeared mud over the number plates, just in case.

"Remember, John," she reminded him, "you must not let her see your face. My face is not on file anywhere in this country, but yours may be. And do not speak unless I ask you something. You are just my driver, and my minder, nothing else. You understand?"

"It's not rocket science, love."

"Maybe not but, like a rocket, it could easily blow up if something goes wrong. So please, do it just like we agreed."

A couple of minutes later, she made a call on her new pay-as-you-go mobile as John eased the car forward past the drive entrance, then past the exit, stopping just before the door of the house disappeared from view. Then they waited. It wasn't long before they saw, through the rear window, a slight figure in a short coat and jeans emerging from the house to trot lightly down the front steps.

Nadera got out of the Toyota and waited by the rear door for Corrina Rigby to join her. The reporter's steps clattered on the cobbles and then slowed as she approached the car. Pausing about six feet away, she looked up and down the street before focussing on Nadera.

"You said on the phone that you have information about James Montrayne."

There was uncertainty in her voice, as though she was beginning to wonder if this was really a good idea.

"That is right," said Nadera. "Your stories have been good. You are right about Montrayne but, unless you have more than you have printed so far, your information is not conclusive. I can change that."

Rigby had printed everything she knew, thought she knew, or could guess at. She had nothing more, so the offer of additional evidence to clinch her story was all too tantalising. But still she hesitated.

"Why would you do that?"

Nadera watched her without speaking. Rigby looked again up and down the road. The only person in sight was an elderly man walking his dog across the street from her. She watched him for a moment, then switched her gaze back to Nadera.

"OK," she said. "What do you have?"

"Pictures... ... and a tape. Oh, and a short piece of video, if you're interested."

Rigby's mouth dropped and her eyes widened. John and Nadera had debated what evidence they should dangle in front of her. Too little and she might not bite; too much and they might scare her off. Perhaps they *had* overdone it a little, but as Nadera watched the change come over Rigby's face, she knew they had her.

"Can I see them?"

"Sure," said Nadera. "They are in the car. See."

She opened the rear door for Rigby to look in and as the reporter approached, ducking slightly, a laptop carry-case was revealed in the far corner of the rear seat.

"The tape is in the front pocket of the laptop case, and the rest is on the hard drive. You can look at it in the car and, if it's what you want, then you can download it onto your flash drive. You did bring it with you?"

"Sure," replied Rigby, a little more confidently now. "It's in here." She patted the black leather bag hanging from her shoulder.

"Good," said Nadera, flashing a bright, friendly smile, as she gestured for Rigby to get into the car. "Then let us do this, and we can be on our way."

Rigby got in and then, when it was obvious Nadera intended to follow her into the rear of the car, she slid across the seat and pulled the laptop case onto her knees. Immediately, John started the engine and the car began to move.

"Where are we going?"

Rigby sounded surprised, but not particularly anxious.

"Just somewhere where you can look and listen without fear of anyone peering in at us," reassured Nadera. "Please leave the case closed until we stop."

Five minutes later, they were in a country lane bounded by wide grass verges and ragged hedges. Whatever was growing in the fields on either side, none of the car's occupants either knew or cared. Some way along, the lane turned to the right beside a tall spreading oak tree. On the bend, right next to the tree, was a field entrance protected by a wooden gate set well back from the road and almost hidden by the overgrown hedge. John had spotted it as they had driven over from the hotel, and marked it down as suitable for what they had in mind. A quick inspection of the gate had shown that it was well rotted and clearly hadn't been opened in years. Whoever farmed the land obviously had an alternative means of access.

Backing up as close to the gate as possible, ignoring the rear parking sensors which screeched at every waving blade of grass, John was in a position to view the lane quite easily in both directions. The ladies in the rear were completely hidden from any passing vehicle by the oak on one side and the curving hedge on the other. John left the engine running.

Rigby hefted the case on her lap.

"Can I look now?"

Nadera nodded.

Rigby tugged at the zip on the case, opened it and lifted the lid of the computer. She pressed the power button and waited. She licked her lips and tapped her fingers lightly on the front edge of the keyboard. The screen lit up as Windows loaded and then, in the centre of the screen, a single icon appeared. Rigby stared at it. It looked impressive, like some sort of government seal, but she knew she didn't recognise it. She moved the cursor and clicked on the icon and was immediately faced with what she assumed was a password request. She assumed because the characters were not English. They looked more like Arabic, or … … Hebrew. She glanced curiously at Nadera, and the blood drained from her face as she froze in icy horror.

In her left hand, Nadera held something which even Miss Rigby, for all her inexperience, recognised immediately. Boxy, black and compact, its magazine protruding from the bottom of the pistol-grip, the micro-Uzi was rock steady.

Nadera was sitting half-turned on the seat with her gun hand resting on her left thigh. The muzzle was pointed, completely unwavering, at the left side of Rigby's belly.

"Yes, it is a little frightening, isn't it," said Nadera. I should warn you that it is loaded with nine millimetre parabellum rounds which, if you force me to pull the trigger, will tear through your guts and rip them to shreds before punching a massive hole in your right side. It would be better, I think, for both of us if you do not make me pull the trigger."

Rigby seemed to think so too because she sat absolutely still, mouth open, eyes wide and staring at the black pistol which seemed huge in Nadera's delicate hand. As it happened, the reporter was a total novice when it came to firearms, which is exactly what John and Nadera had hoped for when they had made a slight detour into Burton-on-Trent as they came across from the M1 to the Thurvaston Arms. The object of their detour had been a fascinating shop which John had visited in his younger days when staying with a school friend in Burton. In addition to locks, keys, security devices and sundry other hardware, the shop sold airguns, rifles and pistols, of various makes and types.

The Uzi now threatening Rigby's gut was in fact a very good, full metal, replica. It was not a spring gun, but one which used CO_2 as its propellant for 0.177 lead pellets. Far from ripping through her guts, the little pellet would be lucky even to penetrate her clothing. Nadera knew that, but she hoped very much that Corrina Rigby did not.

"What… … what… …"

Assuming Rigby was trying to ask what they wanted, Nadera was about to explain when a faint tang reached her nostrils, and she smiled. This was going to be even easier than they had hoped. Miss Rigby had just wet her pants.

"You are in no danger from me, Miss Rigby," said Nadera in a voice that throbbed with controlled menace despite the reassuring words. "As long as you tell me the truth, of course. The last person I had to kill only died because he insisted on lying to me. This is what you might call a fact-finding mission. If I get the facts, the mission is over, and no-one is hurt. But I must make it clear, Miss Rigby, one way or another I will get the facts. I hope you understand."

The tang was stronger now, and Nadera hoped profoundly that Miss Rigby had greater control over her bowel than she did her bladder.

"You can nod, Miss Rigby, if you understand."

There was a faint twitch which Nadera chose to interpret as a nod.

"Good," she said. "Now listen to me carefully. The seal on the screen in front of you… … ah, I see it has disappeared… … just press a key, if you will… … good. Now look carefully. That is the seal of my country's secret service… … this seal, in fact."

With her left hand she flipped open her old Saudi ID, snapping it closed before Rigby had a chance for anything more than a quick glance at it. The seal icon on the screen had been cobbled together quickly in their hotel room, on the assumption that Rigby would not know one government seal from another. It seemed she didn't.

"My name is Eliana Weintraub. You see, I trust you. I tell you that as a gesture of good faith. Woman to woman. Now I am going to tell you something about my government… … another gesture of goodwill. Unfortunately, if any word of this ever appears in your newspaper, or is ever repeated to another person, goodwill is then terminated, and so will you be, probably painlessly but I cannot guarantee that. I hope you understand. A nod is sufficient."

Again the twitch, though this time a little more positive. Nadera saw that Rigby's eyes were no longer quite so wide with terror. The slight narrowing showed that her reporter's brain was working again, wondering perhaps where all this was leading and what, if anything, she might gain from the encounter. Nadera hoped that Rigby was noting her middle-eastern complexion which, together with her assumed name and her rather straight nose which could so easily be mistaken for Jewish, would lead Rigby to some completely false conclusions. So she began to weave her tale.

Philip Simmons worked for a company which had a contract with the Israeli government. The contract was extremely sensitive. She and John had not felt they needed to go into detail on that. Simmons death had caused the Israelis to wonder whether someone was working to subvert the contract. Since there was a great deal at stake, again no details, it was essential to know whether Simmons' death was linked to the contract or whether he really had died for the reasons Rigby had been hinting at in her newspaper articles. Why had she been targeting Montrayne? Were her stories trustworthy, or merely spiteful fabrications? In effect, where had her information come from, and how reliable was it?

Corrina Rigby's reporting career had not so far taken her any nearer to international espionage than a stroll past Thames House on her way to view the work of a local artist on temporary display at Tate Britain. But she had heard of the Israeli Secret Service and she was sure she knew an agent of the dreaded Mossad when she saw one. So she gave up her sources, confused and terrified and, as she did so, it dimly occurred to her that what she surrendered in the face of physical danger, she would never have given up in a court of law, even under the threat of jail. It saddened her to realise that her courage had its limitations. Perhaps investigative journalism was not to be her forte after all.

Ten minutes and several more threats later, John and Nadera drove away from the Victorian mansion having watched Miss Rigby make her way, somewhat unsteadily, inside.

Next stop, with the aid of their laptop and the AA Routefinder, since their Toyota did not come equipped with satnav, was Newton-by-Grangewood and the home of the Reverend John Middlehurst.

Fifty-Eight

The Dower House – 5:30pm

"She's stable, James. She still can't remember anything about what happened, and it's possible she never will. She was injected with a massive dose of heroin but I'm sure it was polluted with something else. I shan't know what until I get the tox report back, and that will take a while. She's very drowsy, barely awake most of the time but I think, only think mind, she's going to be OK. But if you're really set on moving her, tomorrow would be better than today. And if you are going to whisk her off to Scotland, I'd better go with her."

James took the call just after five thirty while I was still upstairs with Abby. Seeing I was there to supervise, Cherry had left us to it. I think he was glad to escape the ordeal of trying to persuade Abby that it wasn't really practical, or necessary, to take her whole wardrobe. It became easier when I hit on the idea of explaining that a helicopter can only carry so much weight and, since we would probably be back here before long, taking all her winter coats, woollies and fleecy boots would probably be straining its engines more than necessary.

"But it gets cold in Scotland, Lizzie."

"Of course it does," I agreed. "In winter. It'll be warm enough up there now, and getting warmer."

"Hmm, OK," she said, trying hard to be convinced, but then her eyes widened. "Crumbs, Lizzie. Midges. We'd better take the midge cream and the… … er… … well, you know. Those allergy pills."

I didn't know, but took her word for it that midges might be a nuisance, so we were searching for the repellent wrist-bands, the antihistamine cream and the Piriton tablets when the phone rang. I had no reason to suppose that the call had anything to do with Angie, but I was so desperate for news that I left Abby rummaging through the cabinets in her bathroom and went downstairs to find James.

He was still in the conservatory. I could hear voices and my heart sank when I realised that Paul Riddings was still with him. I'd come to understand men like him who both despised me and desired me at the same time. Unable to handle their own conflicting emotions, they'd take it out on the girl. We'd try to cope with the abuse by despising them in return, but it didn't really work. How could it?

James was relaying the gist of his phone call to Riddings but, in spite of my need for information, I didn't like to just barge in on them. James had told me to treat the house like my home, but it wasn't, and I couldn't. I hovered in the drawing room, near the door but out of their line of sight, and listened. I was getting good at that.

James was clearly relieved and I understood why. He'd been feeling guilty ever since the attack. He had promised Angie protection and felt he had let her down. It didn't seem in the least odd to him that, even though he barely knew this girl who was my friend, he should be feeling such a strong sense of responsibility for her safety. It was this, I was sure, that had decided him to move her far away from Mellisse and his Russian friends.

I didn't want to get caught eavesdropping, so I started to move quietly away when Riddings voice stopped me. After Andy had left to pack his bags for the morning and return to the hospital, Riddings had stayed to enjoy the ham sandwich prepared for him by Mrs Siddons, and to bring James up to date on the DTLO investigation into Lichfield Tube and the help he'd been receiving from Phil Simmons. Some of it, it was clear, James knew already.

It seemed he had insisted on being briefed by his father before he agreed to vouch for Riddings when that obnoxious young man had first appeared in the neighbourhood. As he listened carefully to Riddings account, it became apparent that his original brief had been far less detailed than he had realised. When Riddings told him that the company's products could end up in armoured fighting vehicles or high security installations belonging to a foreign government, the questions James asked showed that this was something which he had never considered. And it had most definitely never occurred to him that the company's Managing Director, his own Chair of Governors, might connive at falsifying certification for these products. Even now, he couldn't understand why he should do such a thing, unless it was somehow connected with safeguarding the company's financial viability by enabling them to tender for contracts at substantially below the opposition. But even so, it was a risky business, and hardly something Sir Vernon Laycock and Ferro-Tech would want to be associated with.

Apparently Phil Simmons had some experience of this kind of deception at a previous company he had worked for, and it hadn't taken him long to spot similar irregularities at Lichfield Tube. The trouble was that he wasn't sure which contracts were involved or how high up the chain of management the knowledge went. It was this that he was trying to find out when he had died.

"And you don't think that provides a better motive for murder than all the stupid rumours that have been circulating about me?" James asked angrily when Riddings came to the end of his account.

"Only if it's true," replied Riddings, his casual tone showing he was unaffected by James's anger. "Simmons had found out something which seemed to worry him, and he would have filled me in on Saturday if he hadn't gone and got himself killed."

I could hear the lack of concern in his voice, as though Phil Simmons had been nothing more than a pawn in someone else's game. Of little value and easy to sacrifice. James heard it too.

"Just show a bit of respect, can't you? The man's dead."

"Yes, I know. And a nice looking widow he's left behind as well."

There was silence from the conservatory, and I wished I could see what was happening, but didn't dare take a look. I expected to hear James's voice but it was Riddings who spoke.

"I don't suppose there's any truth in what the papers say about you and the delectable Mrs Simmons? I'm sure I couldn't blame you. She's a right little hottie in spite of the bump."

I half-expected to hear the sound of a massive fist crunching the bones of Riddings' nose, but I was beginning to realise that wasn't James's normal way of dealing with people who annoyed him.

"You must be good at what you do, Paul," I heard him say. "Otherwise I don't suppose my father would employ you. So I'm trying to work out whether your offensiveness is deliberate, or whether you're simply a crass idiot who can't help it."

"Hang on, hang on," Riddings replied rather hurriedly. "I'm not saying you could have had anything to do with Simmons getting killed like that, it's just… …"

"I know exactly what you were saying, Paul. And I think, for now, I've heard enough."

After a moment's silence, I heard slight scuffing sounds and knew the men were getting to their feet. I backed further away from the doorway. But Riddings still had a final shot to fire.

"While we're being blunt, James, why did you let yourself get mixed up with that little whore? I mean… … it's all over the papers. And I know it's true about what she does for a living because your father told me. He can't understand why you let his granddaughter make friends with a tramp like that. I'd have thought you'd got more important things to worry about just now than her trim little arse. She's a looker, I'll give you that, but she's just a worthless bit of trash who's only going to bring you… …"

I never found out what he thought I was going to bring.

"That's enough! If you'd spoken to me like that ten years ago, I'd have put you in hospital. You're lucky I'm a bit more restrained now. You're a nasty little worm, but I'll let you walk out under your own steam as long as you do it now."

There was a moment's quiet before Riddings emerged from the conservatory, his face flushed I was sure with anger rather than shame. I've no idea what colour my own cheeks were but, if the pounding in my chest was any guide, they must have seemed on fire. I made it look as though I was just crossing the drawing room from the mural hall. I tried to keep my voice calm, as though I'd heard nothing.

"I just wondered whether there was news of Angie," I said to James who followed hard on Riddings' heels.

"In a moment, Lizzie. Riddings here is just leaving."

Taking out his mobile, he co-opted his head gardener, Ethan Finch, to chauffeur Riddings over to Lichfield where he could either find himself a hotel or book himself on the next train to London. James didn't really care which, and neither did I. We were both glad to see the back of him.

While James escorted him to the door to hand him over to Finch, I slowly folded myself onto one of the settees in the drawing room. I hated Riddings for what he had said, but there was no denying the truth of it. I was a whore. It didn't matter that I hadn't chosen to be. That had been my life for the best part of three years, which meant that in the eyes of most people I really was a worthless bit of trash, just like he'd said. I was as confused as Riddings about why James had interested himself in me, though I was pretty sure it wasn't the obvious. He'd passed up too many opportunities for me to think it was my body he was after. It didn't matter. Whatever his motives, I knew I couldn't stay with him, living in his house, starting to feel part of his family. I'd do what he wanted for as long as it took to get safely away from Mellisse and then... ... Well, maybe James would buy me a passage back to St Helena.

The trouble was that I was by no means sure any more that returning to my remote childhood home was really what I wanted. I loved the scenery, or at least the pictures etched in my mind of hillsides covered with lush vegetation and stark rocky outcrops. I had loved the slow pace of life among warm and friendly people, but who would remember me after ten years? I'd always ignored it before when people said **never go back,** but now I was beginning to think they may have been right.

I was sitting with my elbows on my knees and my hands cupping my cheeks when James came back into the room. I didn't look up. For some reason I didn't want to make eye contact. Then I heard him speaking, but his voice was quiet and directed to someone out in the hall.

"I'm going to be busy for a few minutes... ... Yes, and Lizzie too... ... No, we're not going anywhere. I promise. Why don't you go and tell Mrs Siddons what to put in your picnic for tomorrow. You'll want something to nibble on as you fly up to Aullton House... ... That's it. Good girl. We'll come and find you in a few minutes."

Abby must have finished packing. She was a great kid. She just took me as I was and didn't worry about what I'd been. Already I loved her dearly, and the thought of leaving made me ache inside.

I heard the door close quietly and then James was sitting beside me on the settee. He didn't touch me but I sensed him watching me.

"You were listening weren't you, Lizzie? You heard what he said."

I nodded. "Yes… … and he's right. I am what I am."

I felt him move and I wondered if he was going to put his arm around me. He didn't. I wouldn't have minded. I needed someone to cuddle up to, someone who didn't care about what I was or what I'd been, but just cared about me. But he didn't reach out and I didn't move.

"He's not right, Lizzie."

I still didn't move.

"He's not right and I'll tell you why."

I still didn't move, but this time he did and I felt the back of his hand brush lightly against my forearm.

"Wouldn't you like to know why he's wrong, Lizzie?"

It was the touch that did it. I lifted my face from my cupped hands and turned towards him. His expression was serious, thoughtful, but I saw in his eyes the same sparkle which had shone out of them that evening in the farmhouse kitchen when he'd first agreed to help me.

"OK," I said. "Tell me."

"I know what it feels like, Lizzie. No, don't shake your head. I mean it. I know. I was a marine for eleven years and… … well, there were times when we just had to let off steam. It was before I met Sarah… … and I did things which I'm really not proud of. Like most of my friends back then, I was young, foolish, and randy as hell. Don't get me wrong. We never hurt anyone, but we definitely knew how to have a good time… … What I'm saying is this. Down through the years since then, I've learnt a few things. The most important as far as you're concerned is this. The things you've done… … the things you've been forced to do… … they are not who you are. They're just a tiny part of your life. No… … I know. At the moment, they seem huge. But they're just a tiny part of the whole of your life and – get this, Lizzie – they do not define who you are. They absolutely do not define who you are."

I wanted to believe him, but right then it felt as though they absolutely did define who I was, and there really was no way of escaping that.

He took my hand then and it quivered under his. My whole body trembled as I tried to hold back the tears, tears that needed to be shed, tears that would wash away my past and set me free. I could feel them dampening the corners of my eyes as I looked into his, and I saw there the kindest face I'd ever seen, except perhaps my dad's.

"Lizzie, you're a bright young girl, with wonderful opportunities ahead of you. Your future isn't built on your past, you know... ... but on who you are inside. You're a beautiful girl, with a beautiful heart, and I'm proud to have you as a friend for my little girl. She loves you already, I think."

He smiled, and I couldn't hold the tears back any longer. They flowed in torrents, dampening the front of my shirt. My nose began to run, and my shoulders shook. And then I really began to cry, heaving great gulping sobs, weeping like I hadn't done since they told me my mum and dad were gone.

His arms drew me towards him and I buried my face in his massive chest. He didn't seem to mind at all that his shirt was getting covered in snot. I don't know how long we stayed like that, probably not long, but it felt so good I didn't want him to let me go.

"Daddy, what's the matter with Lizzie?"

I don't think either of us had heard the door open, but at the sound of Abby's voice I pulled away from James, brushing at my cheeks.

"Don't worry, sweetheart," he said. "I think she's just happy. Tell you what though... ... You could go and find her a box of tissues."

Abby screwed her face up in puzzlement before spinning around and skipping away muttering, "I'm glad I don't get happy like that."

I watched her go and, with my eyes still fixed on the door, I whispered, "I can't stay here, James."

I sniffed and tried to dry my eyes on my sleeve.

"You know I can't stay... ... Everyone's read that paper. They don't know it's not true so every time they see me... ... well, they'll think... ..."

"I know, Lizzie," he said. "Why else do you think I'm sending you up to Scotland?"

I frowned. "To keep Abby safe, and to get me away from Mellisse."

He smiled. "Yes, well, that too. But up there, they don't read our local rag. Probably never even heard of it. So they'll just accept you for who you are, not for what anyone else says about you. Your new life has begun, Lizzie. Get used to it."

I had no idea what to say. My head was spinning with the possibilities those words conjured up, and my emotions were strangely complicated. Fortunately, Abby returned just then with a roll of kitchen towel in her hand.

"You looked as if you needed something soft, strong and super absorbent," she said, with a hint of pride in her achievement. "So I brought you this."

Fifty-Nine

Tollhouse Hotel Lichfield – 7:00pm

Joanne Hayford was angry. In fact she was more than angry. She had passed through the blazing heat of rage and frustration and was now coldly seething.

Armed with her copies of the boot-man's photo, she had returned to the station hoping that her breakthrough would at least be enough to dim her DCI's ire, and maybe – remote chance, but worth a try – actually snuff it out entirely. She hadn't even been given the chance. Released from the ACC's office, Morrissey's fury had been fuelled by the discovery that not only was James Montrayne at liberty, but Sergeant Hayford was nowhere on the premises. Nor was she responding to her mobile phone which Constable Mayblin tried to contact on several occasions under the Chief Inspector's menacing glare.

Morrissey contained himself rather like the boiler of a steam engine whose safety valve has jammed shut. Every passing moment saw the pressure building until the needle on his gauge went into the red and every welded seam and rivet was straining from forces desperate for release.

And then she returned. Seams split, rivets popped, steam escaped and shrapnel flew in all directions. The exploding fury of DCI Morrissey was heard the full length of the corridor. Officers ducked for cover and kept their heads down. Sergeant Joanne Hayford stood before the blast, her eyes fixed on a spot somewhat above her boss's head, trying her best to ignore the rolling thunder of sound and fury. She wasn't quite sure Macbeth was on the mark about it signifying nothing, but then maybe she didn't have the context just right. She didn't try to argue with Morrissey, or to placate him. She had never been one to waste energy in futile effort. She stood immobile, blotting out the accusations, threats and recriminations, until eventually he began to run out of steam. His final words were to inform her that, since she had some leave owing, she was to take it immediately. He did not want to see her again.

He had shredded her career and character beyond anything which normal protocol allowed. But in spite of that, she didn't retaliate. He was a sad figure, coming to the end of his usefulness, and he was digging a very substantial hole in which to bury himself. He would soon be gone. In the meantime, on leave or not, she was determined to keep digging on her own account.

It was on her own account that she had kept quiet. If she once opened her mouth to respond, she knew that there was no chance at all that she would be able to restrain or moderate the violence of her language. So she reached into her briefcase and removed a copy of the boot-man's photo. On the back she wrote *Old Park Rifle Club* and *Boots?* She placed the picture in the centre of his desk, looked him once in the eye, turned her back and walked out.

What next? Taking a holiday, much though she felt in need of one, was out of the question. On the other hand, carrying on with her enquiries while officially on leave could get her into trouble. She sat in her car outside the station and thought about her options.

She decided that Morrissey's obsession with James Montrayne was so illogical there was no point in trying to understand it. Which made her realise that she had an obsession of her own. It was not so much to do with clearing Montrayne as it was to get to the truth of what had happened in the woods last Saturday morning. His Lordship was attractive, no doubt, but she currently had her own boyfriend with whom she was well content. Or she would be if only he could drag himself back up from London. If Montrayne was innocent then the truth would clear him, but it was the truth that counted above all else.

Thinking about that very large and self-assured peer suddenly put her in mind of his friend – or was he just an associate? –Paul Riddings. She frowned as she remembered talking to Riddings just after she had stormed out of the interview room, leaving Montrayne and his lawyer confronting a smugly overconfident Morrissey. She knew she had behaved badly, unprofessionally even, and she rebuked herself for having let her temper get the better of her. She didn't think she had given away much that hadn't already appeared in the media, but there was still no excuse for her behaviour. She knew it and, looking back on it now, she felt very uneasy about how close she had come to losing her self-control.

Maybe she hadn't given much away but Riddings hadn't given much either. He had asked questions which her flayed emotions had driven her to answer all too easily, but he had told her very little in return. Maybe it was time to see if there was anything worth dredging out of him. She reached for her mobile and dialled the number he'd given her.

She was surprised to find that he was actually in Lichfield, in the process of booking into a small hotel in the heart of the city within a stone's throw – almost – of the cathedral. He sounded irritated, but perked up when he realised who was calling, and agreed to see her as soon as she could pop round. Normally she would have walked; the distance could only have been a quarter of a mile at most. On this occasion, she took her car not wanting to have to return to the police station later to pick it up and risk bumping into Morrissey again.

It took a moment or two, speaking to Riddings from the lobby on the hotel phone, to convince him that the small lounge-bar, though public, might be a better place for their discussion than his room but, in the end, he agreed to come down. She tried to decline his offer of a drink but he was persistent – in an overconfident, pushy, God's-gift-to-women sort of way – so she accepted a lime and tonic, hoping that her crossed legs combined with his own good humour might just prise loose something useful.

This time it was Riddings' emotions that steered the conversation. He was peeved at the way Montrayne had dismissed him, packing him off and dumping him in this hotel without taking him any further into his confidence. If this delectable police woman really did have the hots for Montrayne, she should be made to realise that there was far more serious game available, well-hung and ready for serving.

So, under the influence of his third glass of Scotch – the first had been from the mini-bar in his room before coming down – it seemed perfectly natural to him to impress her with his importance to Montrayne's father. It seemed best to him to play down the title, so he placed his emphasis on the Marquess's position as head of the DTLO in London. He wanted to impress her with his own significance in the civil service hierarchy and his prowess as an investigating officer but in the process, without actually intending to, he gradually laid out for her all the details of Phil Simmons' concerns about Lichfield Tube.

She didn't ask many questions. She didn't need to. She simply re-crossed her legs once or twice and allowed the drinks and his own self-importance to do the rest. She found it a struggle to rein in her anger as she learnt just how much Riddings had kept back from her, but she managed to keep her smile in place and encouraged him by running the tip of her tongue over her lips a few times. While nodding in appreciation of his shrewdness, she was itching to slap the self-satisfied smile off his face. She didn't discourage him by trying to take notes. This had nothing to do with having a good memory, which she did, but had everything to do with the presence of the digital voice recorder sitting in her open bag in the middle of the low table between their chairs.

When his story reached the point where he had phoned the Simmons home on Saturday morning – one of the few things he had already mentioned when questioned earlier – Riddings stopped, looked at his empty glass and ordered another drink. Joanne's glass was still half-full.

"So," she said, leaning forward and speaking slowly, "you were actually working with Philip Simmons to try and expose some sort of corruption in Lichfield Tube's overseas contracts."

"You've got it," replied Riddings, his oily smile still in place. "And we... ..."

He stopped as a young waitress appeared with a glass on a small tray.

"Thanks," he said, eyes fixed on her blouse as she leant forward to place the new glass on the table and retrieve the empty one. As the girl straightened and turned away, Joanne saw her roll her eyes in complete disdain. Probably not of men in general, Joanne thought, as she pretended not to notice. Just this one in particular.

"So," she said again. "You were saying… …"

Drawing his gaze away from the girl's retreating behind, Riddings thought for a moment.

"Yes… … right. Well, we almost had it nailed when poor old Phil had to go and get himself killed. That's it. End of story. He was our only way in."

"Your only way in," Joanne repeated. "Your only way in… … So did it never occur to you that this provides someone at Lichfield Tube with a damn good motive for taking Philip Simmons off the scene, permanently?"

He frowned, looking slightly affronted at her questioning of his judgement.

"No," he replied. "Not really."

"You've got to be kidding," said Joanne, allowing her scorn to show, and abandoning completely her previously alluring pose. "How could it not?"

"Easy. Simmons was careful. The security on their computer network is lousy. It was due to be updated when they were taken over by Ferro-Tech but, so far, the lazy sods haven't got round to it. Bad for them, good for us. There was simply no way for anyone to track what he was looking at. Believe me. The guy was paranoid. Not even his wife knew what he was up to."

Joanne was disappointed, but not yet ready to give up.

"Are you familiar with all of the staff at Lichfield Tube?"

He looked at her suspiciously.

"Some," he said. "Not all. Why?"

She reached into her bag, careful not to knock the recorder, and extracted one of the photos which Ruth Farquhar had printed off for her.

"Do you know who this is?"

"Does he work for Lichfield Tube?"

"You tell me."

He didn't touch the picture. Just looked at it lying on the table. She gave him credit for actually studying it before giving an answer. He shook his head.

"Can't say whether he does or not. Can't say for certain I've never seen him before, but I don't recognise him." He leaned forward seeming to stare at the eyes of the man in the picture. "I think I'd remember if we ever met."

He sat back in his chair.

"So, who is he?"

Joanne didn't reply. She scooped up the photo and slid it back into her bag. Riddings watched her, ever hopeful.

"What do you say to discussing this some more over dinner?" he asked.

"I'd say, I'm more inclined to arrest you for withholding evidence, obstructing justice and wasting police time," she told him.

He relaxed back in his chair clearly unimpressed by the implied threat.

"If that's what turns you on, Sergeant. But I'm sure, if we work at it, we can probably find a more interesting way of getting better acquainted."

"We may well get better acquainted, Mr Riddings, but not I assure you in any way that you would find the least bit interesting."

She had kept her voice calm and quiet enough not to attract any attention, but her deliberately measured tone began to penetrate his suave veneer. She was sure he'd been drinking in his room before joining her because what he'd downed while in the lounge could hardly account for the distant look in his eyes. He stared, a slight frown creasing his forehead, as though what she had just said couldn't possibly make sense. She decided to press on while she had him unsettled.

"In fact, Mr Riddings, I have every intention of arresting you unless you can give me a good, and I mean very good, reason not to."

He actually began to look sullen, which gave her hope. She normally made it a habit not to issue empty threats, and this was one that she most certainly wouldn't be able to follow through on. She hoped his drinks had dulled him enough not to call her bluff. She wasn't sure what had made her do it, unless it was the need to be absolutely certain that he wasn't holding anything back.

She waited.

He waited, resentfully now. What did the silly cow want? This was turning into an absolute pig of a day. Montrayne had shown no appreciation for all his efforts, and now this jumped-up provincial hick, instead of putting-out in appreciation of his candour, was threatening to ruin his evening.

"Mr Riddings?"

How could she make his name sound so threatening? His career path had seemed so smooth, but getting arrested would do more than put a bit of a pothole in the way. More like a massive landslip. He dredged around in the sludge of his memory for something to give her.

"There's something," he said cautiously, not sure if it would satisfy her, but it was the only thing he could think of. "It could be nothing at all. I don't know. Just a coincidence maybe."

She waited.

"The MD of Lichfield Tube is Gordon Russell."

He said it as though it meant something. She didn't see the significance.

She raised an eyebrow and waited.

"Gordon Russell," he said again. "He's also Montrayne's boss at the school. Chair of Governors. He gave Montrayne the push yesterday. Indefinite leave until this is sorted out."

He shouldn't have had the drinks. He knew that, but he was still sharp enough to see that she wasn't getting it.

"What if Russell suspended Montrayne to help build up suspicion against him? What if Russell is behind the smears in the press? Somebody has to be. Worth a look, don't you think?"

It wasn't much more than guesswork and coincidence, but Joanne was convinced by now that he'd given her all he could. Anyway, she'd had her fill of his smug self-assurance and just wanted to be rid of him. Still, as he said, worth a look.

"Where can I find him?" she asked, without any hint of enthusiasm.

He shrugged his shoulders. "Home probably. Somewhere in Elmford Cross."

She knew the village. Maybe twenty minutes' drive. She reached for her bag and stood.

"Thank you, Mr Riddings. Enjoy your evening."

He began to rise.

"Are you sure you won't… … …"

He slumped down. She was already half-way to the door.

Sixty

Newton-by-Grangewood – 7:30pm

We were still eating dinner in the family dining room when the phone rang. There was only James, Abby and me. To the disgust of Mrs Siddons, Cherry had sent for a massive take-out pizza to share with Surjit in his garage quarters. She had just begun gathering up the dinner plates when her husband Bill put his head round the door to say that a Reverend Middlehurst was asking to speak with James urgently.

"Can't it wait?" asked James.

"He says not, sir. He really was most insistent."

Mrs Siddons said she'd hold off on the puddings for a few minutes, and James left to take the call. When he came back to us he was frowning as though the phone call had dumped on him news he could well have done without. As Abby turned towards him, his expression lightened and he managed a smile that only partially masked the worry in his eyes.

"Is Mr Middlehurst OK, Daddy?" she asked.

"He's fine, sweetheart. He just wants to talk to me about something so I told him we'd call in on our way over to see Angie."

It had already been arranged that James would take me to visit Angie after dinner, which hadn't pleased Abby very much. She had rather hoped to have us both to herself for the evening. Mrs Siddons had saved the day by offering to show Abby how to bake the sweet-chilli sausage rolls that she wanted for her picnic in the morning. And if she was really good, she'd be allowed to have one for her supper later on. It was second best, but she seemed happy enough as we said goodbye.

It was a twenty minute drive to the manse, a modern detached house on the outskirts of Newton-by-Grangewood. The land on which the housing estate was situated had been farmland prior to the 1960s, and the villagers had objected most strongly to its development. As always, however, the project had gone ahead anyway, allowing the deacons of the Baptist church to snap up a bargain before the rise in house prices had turned their modest investment into a modest goldmine.

The drive had parking for three vehicles, but was completely empty as James pulled the Maserati to a stop in front of the double garage. The front door of the house was opened before we reached it, and a man whom I presumed to be the minister stood on the threshold staring out at us.

I expected him to invite us in but he just continued to stare at us. Or rather at me.

"Who's this?" he said eventually.

"I think you know very well who it is, John," replied James firmly. "So let's not play games, eh?"

"Yes, OK... ... But why did you have to bring her with you?"

He seemed sullen and resentful but, from the little James had been able to tell me on the way over, I couldn't see any reason for it.

James moved closer so that he seemed to tower over the minister, even though he was standing on a lower step.

"You told me," he said slowly and quietly, "that you know where Corrina Rigby got her information for that story in the paper today. Lizzie here was mentioned in that story and it didn't exactly flatter her so I think she has a right to hear what you have to say, don't you? ... ... Now, are you going to let us in?"

Some more staring and a long drawn-out sigh, and then he stood back to let us through the door.

His study was not large but, with sunset still an hour away, it was surprisingly light thanks to the wide, south-facing window in the end wall. It was obviously a room designed for work, but it felt comfortable. Shelves of books lined two walls, while the third, the window wall, was almost completely taken up by a large desk positioned so that the minister would have his back to the room when sitting in the well-worn swivel chair. It was a good arrangement as he wouldn't have to keep coming around the desk to retrieve whatever books he needed to help in preparing his sermons, and if he needed inspiration from nature, he could look directly out through the window behind the desk across the garden and out into the fields and distant woods. It would also keep the sunlight off the computer screen which sat towards the back of the desk slightly to the left of centre.

Most of the floor space was taken up by three undersized and ill-matched easy chairs which turned out to be unexpectedly comfortable as we obeyed John's automatic instruction to make ourselves at home. It seemed a strange thing for him to say, incongruous, bearing in mind his obvious uneasiness over our visit.

John Middlehurst looked far from comfortable as he remained standing, not looking directly at either of us, his left hand running through his short black hair, occasionally scratching at his scalp but mostly just stroking the hair forward. His breathing was just a little too rapid, and his eyes darted around the room fixing on nothing and probably seeing nothing. Later I would understand how his mind was totally absorbed by the realisation that the day he had been dreading for several months had finally arrived.

He clearly had no idea how to begin.

I could see pain too in James's eyes, as he realised that it wasn't just information that John had to share. There was something very much more personal involved here. John was his friend, his minister, someone he had liked and trusted. I think we both wondered whether that trust was about to be betrayed.

Maybe it already had been.

James wasn't used to being hurt by betrayal so, if that was the case, this interview wasn't going to be easy for either of them. I didn't understand yet what was going on, so I was content to watch things unfold. Eventually James shook his head slightly, understanding that he would have to take the initiative. He took a deep breath and looked up at John.

"Sit down, John, there's a good fellow. We're going to get stiff necks if we have to stare up at you for the next half hour."

John stopped rubbing his head and dropped into the third easy chair. He looked from James to the floor and then back again. He brought his hands up, palms together, fingertips touching his lips, as if he was about to start praying. But he was just gathering his thoughts, trying to compose his mind for what he undoubtedly saw as the ordeal ahead. Once he started, it all came out in a rush.

"It was me who gave that reporter the background for her last story," he said. "Did you know that?"

We stared at him. That last article had mentioned someone close to James, but we had just taken that to be reporter's licence. When John had told James that he had information about who was feeding Rigby her stories, he had never expected this.

"No, John. And if anyone but you had told me, I'd never have believed it."

John's fingers curled over as he clasped his hands under his chin. His eyes flickered around once more, and then he nodded as though some inner conclusion had been reached. His hands dropped to the arms of his chair, and he looked directly at me. I tried to feel angry, but he seemed so miserably pathetic.

"I didn't want to," he began. "I really need you to believe that. I just had no choice … … … at least … … that's how it seemed. Of course, I realise now … … I did have a choice. We all do, and I made the wrong one for all the wrong reasons."

"I haven't a clue what you're talking about," James interrupted. "Just settle down and tell us what happened. I mean, why did you think you had no choice."

John pursed his lips, and nodded.

"Yes, you're right. OK." He closed his eyes and sighed. "It's just that I never thought I'd have to tell this to anyone."

James frowned. "Doesn't Susan know?"

He looked around, listening. "And where is she? And the kids?"

John's head was lowered, his eyes fixed on some spot on the carpet, and he spoke without looking up.

"They're out. It's band practice night… … and Susan's selling tickets for the summer concert. That's why I asked you to come round now."

James stirred and started to reach out, but then let his hand drop.

"Well now you've got us here, you'd better start explaining just what it is you've been up to."

There was a long pause, and I wondered if John was going to need a heavier prompt to get him going. Then, without looking up, he began.

"It started with an email. A piece of spam that slipped through the filter. It sounded as though it had come from some mission group working in Birmingham and it had a link to a website. I clicked on the link and found myself on some sort of porn site. I didn't realise at first. I thought it must have something to do with helping girls to get out of that sort of life. It was stupid, I know, but I'd just never seen that sort of thing before. There were menus to select photos or movies. You could sign up or just take a guest tour."

I knew exactly what he was talking about. I had seen sites like that and could only be thankful that Mellisse had found me too useful to him in other ways to have me performing in so-called adult movies. I knew how it worked. Dangle the bait, sink the hook and haul the punters in. I wasn't really surprised he'd been caught. He might be a Baptist minister, but he was still a guy.

John sucked in his lower lip, chewing on it. As his silence continued, James leant forward to prompt him again, but after a moment he carried on.

"I don't know what made me do it. Curiosity, maybe. But I clicked the button and took the tour. I'd never seen anything like it. Part of me felt excited, but another part of me felt sick and guilty as hell. I closed it down."

He looked around, taking in the photos of Susan and his boys hanging on the wall. He smiled, a wry, cynical curl of the lips, totally without humour.

"Sounds daft, I know, but I felt so dirty I went straight upstairs and took a shower."

I was amazed at his reaction. I'd come across many men who despised the girls who provided the sexual services they demanded, but none who despised themselves for needing those services. Or at least, none who had allowed their self-revulsion to surface. Certainly, I'd never met a man who judged himself so harshly because he'd looked at a few naughty photos, or explicit movies. I glanced at James wondering if he felt the same. From what he'd said about his time in the Marines, this wasn't exactly unknown territory for him. His eyes met mine and we both realised that the minister was judging himself by a higher standard than anyone either of us had ever met before.

He looked back to John, trying to make eye contact, and actually smiled at him then, only slightly, but with just a touch of understanding.

"Not as daft as you think," he said. "Happens all the time. Trouble is, you can scrub off your skin, but you can't clean out what's in your mind." He looked back at me. "Not so easy that, is it?"

I slowly shook my head, understanding that he knew me far better than I would have thought possible. John answered as though the question had been addressed to him.

"No," he said. "You can't. Certainly I couldn't. As soon as I'd dressed, I came down and deleted all the temporary files and cleared out the browser history. I wanted no trace left of any of that stuff. But I couldn't get it out of my mind. I felt so guilty for giving in to that moment's temptation. I felt I'd let God down, my family, the church, everyone who trusted me. Eventually, after a lot of prayer, I felt God's forgiveness and I was able to put it behind me. Or so I thought."

There was more silence, and James became restless, aware of how the time was racing on.

"Look, John," he said. "If we're going to get this over before Susan and the children come home, we need to hurry it along."

John nodded slowly, and it was obvious that, hard as it was to make his first confession, this next part was even more difficult. We waited, willing him to start talking, and not wanting to push him so hard that he just clammed up and refused to tell any more.

"Back in January, I had to go to Birmingham."

As soon as he said that, I had a flash of total comprehension. I knew what was coming. Not all the details, of course, but the general idea. A vulnerable minister on the loose in the sex capital of Britain.

"There was a conference on at a church in the city. It lasted until well into the evening. I was on my way back to the car-park when I passed this club. I knew what sort of club it was and suddenly all the stuff I'd seen on my computer, on that screen there .. .."

He half turned, and jerked his thumb over his shoulder in the direction of his computer.

"It all came back into my mind. I thought I'd forgotten it. I thought it was all behind me, but there it was. It was like being invaded, taken over. I tried to walk on, past the club. I did walk on, about fifty yards or so, but then I was drawn back. It was as though my mind blanked off every response that might have stopped me. Susan, the kids, God, church; all blanked out. I had never, ever in my life, experienced such overwhelming temptation, and I couldn't handle it. If I'd been wearing something that marked me as a minister, the collar perhaps, maybe that would have stopped me going in. But I haven't worn the collar in years. I was just a normal guy in a suit, so before I really knew what was happening, I was through the doors, signing up. I didn't have enough cash, so I used my credit card."

James let out a deep sigh.

"Ooooh, John. I suppose you still had your briefcase with you."

"Yes, I'd not been back to the car."

"Did you keep it with you, or did you check it at the desk."

"I was going to keep it with me, but the girl on the desk said it would be safest if I checked it in, so I did."

"And it has a combination lock, right?"

"Y.e.e.s"

"Was the combination set, or had you just pressed the catches shut?"

"I guess I just pressed them shut. I don't usually bother with the combination."

"So anyone who .. .. .. "

"Look, I know. I know. And you're right. It was stupid. I just didn't think, and I've regretted it bitterly ever since, more than you can ever imagine."

As we watched, he put both his hands up to the top of his head and pressed down as though his skull was about to explode. He was rocking slightly back and forth in his chair, his emotions barely under control. I sensed James felt he needed to do something before he saw his friend topple right over the edge.

He sat forward, reached out, and very lightly touched John's knee.

"Something else happened, didn't it?" he asked. "Later on, perhaps."

John stopped rocking and his hands slowly dropped into his lap.

"You're right," he said. "Yesterday, an envelope was delivered by hand. It was some teenage kid I'd not seen before. You know the sort: spiky hair and skate board."

He sighed and shook his head slowly.

"I had no idea what was in it. I don't know whether the kid was told to give it only to me, or whether he'd have shoved it through the letter box if he'd not seen me in the garden. I can't bear to think what would have happened if Susan had opened it. She does sometimes, with stuff that looks like bills or business letters."

He paused, clearly doing the very thing he couldn't bear to do, so James moved him quickly on.

"What was in the envelope, John?"

"Photos. Lots of them. Big, and in colour, and very detailed. And I'm in every one."

"The club, that night?"

"Yes, the club. The girls were pretty near naked. There was pole dancing, and … … er … … Well, there was lap dancing, too."

"And you were … … involved?"

There was no answer. Just silence, which told its own story.

James frowned. There had to have been more than just the photos.

"What else was in the envelope, John?"

There was no response at first, and then John looked up. His eyes glistened with tears of shame and humiliation, and the raw misery was plain to see.

"A letter. Unsigned, of course. It told me what I should say to that reporter. Make it seem as though you had a reason for killing Phil. Which you didn't, of course. We all know that. It was very clear about what I had to say … … even mentioned a girl you have staying with you… …"

He looked at me. "This girl… … You were in one of the pictures, you know. There was a circle round your face. I'd never met you, so I wouldn't know, but the letter said it was you. It made me feel… … well, as though what I told the reporter wasn't a total pack of lies. And… …"

He tailed off into more silence.

"And if you didn't do what you were told, more pictures would be sent to Susan," James finished for him.

"Yes, and to the neighbours and folk at church."

"Do you still have them?"

"No. I shredded them. Couldn't risk Susan or the kids finding them."

"The letter as well?"

John nodded, burying his face once more in his hands. "Shredded."

James stood up, unable to sit still any longer. As he did so, I thought I saw a shadow flicker at the bottom corner of the window, but when I turned to look more closely there was nothing. Only the gathering gloom of evening as the sun slid down behind the trees at the back of the house. Probably a bird, I thought, turning back to look at James, so badly let down by someone he'd trusted.

But he wasn't looking hurt at all. I could tell his mind was working overtime, weighing the implications and considering options. There wasn't much room to pace about but I think he would have done had it been possible.

John's hands slid down over his face until his fingertips again rested against his lips. It looked as though he was going to pray but his eyes were bleak and without hope.

"I can't escape. They know who I am. They have pictures of me and the girl. The lap-dance. If I don't keep on doing whatever they tell me, I'm finished… … I'm finished anyway. James … … if Susan and the children find out about this, I don't think I could live with the shame of it… … and I'll never be able to face my friends in the church. They'd think I'm a hypocrite, and I am. There's nothing I can do. I've nowhere to go… … I'm finished."

His pathetically weak voice was that of a man completely swallowed up by the consequences of his human frailty. Another man might have found the scenario acutely embarrassing, but for a minister of religion, a shepherd adored by his flock, it was soul-destroying. I found my earlier anger had entirely slipped away. I found myself feeling sorry for this man, so broken up by what he'd done. I understood, too. He was just as much a victim of Mellisse as I was.

"No, you're not finished," said James emphatically, then adding with characteristic understatement, "I grant you, Mr Mellisse is turning out to be a real nuisance, so I think it's time that somebody sorted him out. If the police can't do it, then I think someone else is going to have to do it for them."

John looked up, amazement for the moment overcoming the shame.

"Do you mean you know who it was?" he asked. "You know who sent those pictures?"

James moved slowly in the small space, stretching his arms, arching his back, as he gathered his thoughts. After a moment, he looked down at me.

"John's been honest with us, Lizzie. We need to tell him our side. OK?"

I nodded.

"This is for you, John, and no-one else. No-one. You understand?"

John looked from James to me, puzzled. He nodded.

"The man behind all this is called Raymond Mellisse. He's a Birmingham… … businessman… … entrepreneur… … whatever. He does legitimate stuff, but he also runs the sex clubs, and brings in girls from overseas for prostitution. He's a rich thug in a smart suit and he's sleazy as hell. This young lady, Lizzie, is staying with me to keep her safe from Mellisse. She and another girl have run away from him, and he wants them back… … or dead. He's tried for both. According to Lizzie, he has some sort of pipeline into Lithuania which he uses to entice girls into the UK with offers of jobs. It's not until they get here, that they find the job is not what they were expecting. So far, I've just been trying to keep Lizzie and her friend safe and out of his reach. I intend to go on doing that."

I noticed he didn't say where he planned to keep us safe, and thought it was probably best that he didn't.

"Once they're all safely tucked away, I'll come back and deal with Mellisse."

"Can you do that?" asked John with subdued hope.

"Oh yes," replied James. "But the police are going to have to sort out what happened to Phil, because I haven't a clue about that. Except… …"

"Except what?"

"Well… … my father, or at least his department, seems to think that Phil had uncovered something dodgy at Lichfield Tube. There's a guy called Riddings poking around which probably means they've been breaking the rules in some overseas defence contracts. Whether they're dirty enough to justify murder, no-one seems to know. I hate to say it, because I've always got on well with him, but the police are going to have to talk to Gordon Russell."

A certain harshness came into his voice as he added, "And they will too, as soon as Father's department comes clean about their own investigations."

It was as though he hadn't realised until just then how much resentment had been building up in him. Paul Riddings and the DTLO, including his own father, had left him hanging out to dry while the police went off in completely the wrong direction after Phil Simmons' murder. At some point in the not too distant future he and the Marquess were going to have a serious chat about family loyalty.

James stood still for a moment, looking down at the man who had been his friend for so many years. The man who had married him to Sarah, who had led the dedication service for Abby, who had helped to bear his grief through the tragic loss which followed soon after, and who had supported him through the trauma of Abby's kidnapping. He reached down and placed his hand on the shoulder of the man who was still his friend, as he decided it was time for a little reciprocity.

"John," he said quietly, "It seems to me you've got two choices here. Crumple under it, or get over it. It's up to you, but I'd rather see you get over it."

There was no response at first. Then John raised his head.

"Yeaah. Me Too. Trouble is… … I don't know what to do."

James was in a hurry to get on his way. We still had to visit Angie at the hospital, but a few more minutes wouldn't make much difference.

"OK," he said. "First off, let me tell you what you don't do. You don't tell Susan, you definitely don't tell the kids, you don't tell the church... ... in fact, you don't tell a living soul."

John stirred and started to shake his head, but James bulldozered on.

"I know. You want to confess, get it off your chest. Well, let me ask you. How many people are going to be hurt as soon as you start baring your soul? Just think about that for a minute."

He paused to let him do it.

"Now tell me what benefit there is in hurting so many people. No, don't. I'll tell you. Absolutely none. Susan and the kids need you, and so do the folk at church. You've helped them more times probably than they can remember, and they're going to need you to help them again. So don't mess it up now. You've done your confessing. You've confessed it to us and, if you haven't done it already, pretty soon you're going to be on your knees confessing it to God. And that's it. Done."

"I don't know, James. I... ..."

"Yes, you do know... ... OK, you feel a hypocrite. You say one thing and do the other. So join the club. We're all frail human beings, and we mess up sometimes, and when we do, we say we're sorry and move on. How many times have you told us God wants to forgive us, to change us and help us grow, not load us down with guilt? Well if you don't live that out now, you will be a hypocrite. So, accept the forgiveness and get on with life. Oh... ... and the next time you're tempted by anything like this again, call me. Anywhere, anytime, day or night, ring me. Got that?"

I wasn't sure about all the God stuff but, as I listened to the compassion he was showing to his friend, I felt a slight coldness inside as I realised how desperately I wanted never to let him down. I felt there was nothing I wouldn't do to ensure I never hurt him or betrayed his friendship.

There wasn't a great deal left to say, so it wasn't long before we left the manse. James told John not to worry, something of a forlorn hope, and reminded him again not to tell anyone else about Mellisse or the photos, pretty much a sure thing, and to get in touch immediately if any more photos or messages arrived.

As we climbed into the Maserati, and James reversed out of the driveway, I noticed a Toyota Avensis parked about fifty yards ahead, on the other side of the road.

Pulling quickly away from the kerb, we accelerated past it, heading for the A38, and Angie.

Neither of us gave the vehicle or its sole male occupant a single thought.

Sixty-one

The Dower House – Late evening

We didn't stay long with Angie.

I'd have been willing to sit up all night with her, but Barrie said there was little point as there was nothing I could do, apart from hold her hand. There was some doubt that she would even be aware I was there, she was so out of it. Then James said that I'd be far more use in the morning if I had a good night's sleep, but I still wasn't convinced until he added the clincher.

"As soon as Angie's well enough, and Barrie says it's OK, we'll find some way of getting her up to Scotland to join you."

"Tomorrow?" I asked.

James looked at Barrie who gave a shrug and said, "Maybe."

I looked at him, wondering just what he meant. Maybe she'll be OK? Maybe she'll be dead? Maybe she'll be a cabbage for the rest of her life, her brain fried by whatever chemicals had been pumped into her.

I didn't want to leave but, if I'm honest, I wasn't sure I wanted to sit still and watch Angie die either. In the end, I let James take me away.

It was quite late by the time we got back to the Dower House, but James asked whether a hot drink might help to relax me before I tried going to sleep.

Worth a try, I thought, knowing how screwed up I felt.

We retired to the kitchen, and James brewed a pot of Russian Caravan tea for himself and made a hot chocolate for me in the microwave. I had found I was acquiring a taste for the stuff. We were sitting on opposite sides of the kitchen table, waiting for our drinks to cool a little, when Mrs Siddons poked her head round the door. She wanted to say that Abby had enjoyed her baking, and had insisted on sampling the results before going off to bed only a little later than usual.

She wished us a rather prim goodnight, as though she wasn't quite sure whether she approved of the two of us sitting up late together. James smiled as he turned back from watching the door close behind her.

"She's a good soul," he said. "I don't know what I'd do without her."

There was something in his expression and tone of voice which took my thoughts back to the minister's house earlier that evening.

"You really care for her, don't you?" I said.

"I really do."

"And you really cared about that Middlehurst guy, didn't you? Even though he'd done his best to screw us both."

"Not his fault, Lizzie. And he did come clean and tell us, which he needn't have done."

I thought about that, and the way James had handled his wayward minister.

"It's all this God stuff, isn't it? Being a Christian and all that?"

James inclined his head with a faint smile, and gave a little shrug.

"Something like that," he said.

Which brought me to something I was curious about, but wasn't sure whether it was too personal a question to ask. I decided to give it a go anyway.

"So… …er… … what happened?" I asked. "Did you get converted or something?"

James smiled more widely, and the smile developed into a deep chuckle.

"More like *or something,* I'd say."

He didn't add any more, but there was a definite twinkle in his eyes as he watched me over the rim of his mug which he was holding with both hands. He didn't appear the least bit embarrassed or offended by my question, so I decided to plough ahead.

Returning his smile, I said, "Well go on then. There must be more to it than that."

"Oh, there was," he replied. "But I don't usually broadcast it unless someone particularly wants to know."

"OK… … Well I want to know."

I was surprised to find that I really was interested, and it was more than just idle curiosity, but I wasn't going to press him any more so I simply sat and waited. Setting his mug down, he nodded and pursed his lips, wondering perhaps where to begin. In the end, he began where I thought he would… … with his wife.

"Sarah was a Christian when I met her. Always had been, as far as I know… … Church, that sort of thing, right from an early age. I knew right off that her beliefs were important to her, and I wasn't going to change them. Not that I wanted to. She was a beautiful young lady… … and I don't just mean her looks… … though to me she was the most beautiful person I've ever known… … It was her character as well. Everybody liked her… … even those who thought she was nuts for believing in God."

"I think you must have loved her very much."

"I did… … and in a way I still do."

He paused, and his eyes turned away, focused on nothing, or perhaps on something only he could see.

"Yes," he said eventually. "I never wanted to change a single thing about her. That's what I'm trying to say. She had her beliefs, and all the stuff that went with that, like church and different charities and things... ... and she knew I wasn't going to try and interfere with any of that. If she'd been afraid I'd try to change her, we'd never have married. It worked the other way, too. She didn't keep preaching at me, trying to get me to believe in God, that sort of thing. She didn't even ask me to go to church with her, though I did go from time to time."

His smile was back again.

"That had more to do with wanting to be with her, than wanting to find God. Eventually, I plucked up courage and proposed. Some of her friends advised her against marrying me. I hadn't given my life to Jesus, as they put it, so in their eyes I was untouchable in the Christian marriage stakes. Sarah was worried about that for a while, but she was always a girl to make up her own mind. The more they tried to impose their own rules on her, the more she rebelled... ... even when her best friend flat out refused to come to the wedding... ... I really don't understand how some Christians love rules more than they love people... ... Anyway, that's another story. Sarah said yes so we got married and had our honeymoon over in America, visiting some of the sites that neither of us had ever seen before. We were in Colorado taking in the Rocky Mountains National Park – horseback riding, I might add... ..."

I couldn't help interrupting.

"How did they find a horse big enough for you?"

"No problem," replied James, rubbing his chin a little ruefully. "In fact they took great pride in telling me I was far from being the biggest feller they'd had to mount... ... Anyway, come Sunday, Sarah wanted to go to church so we drifted down to Fort Collins. We found this church somewhere on Timberline Road – actually one of the folk we'd been riding with recommended it – so we gave it a try."

His eyes drifted again as he took time to remember the occasion.

"We were strangers... ... I mean, we were welcomed and all that, so they knew we were British visitors, but that was it. They didn't know anything else about us. But when that pastor got up to speak, it was as though he was pitching his talk straight at me. It was weird, and the odd thing was... ...Sarah didn't seem to notice. There were no bright lights... ... It wasn't one of those Damascus Road things... ... and I didn't go out to be prayed for or anything like that... ... But... ... It was as though a lot of the stuff Sarah had been telling me, about God and such, suddenly seemed to start making sense. Like I say, it was weird, all the more so because I hadn't been expecting it."

It sounded weird to me too, but then I assumed it was one of those things that happened in churches. Singing, hyped up emotion, charismatic speaker, all working together, can bring about some strange reactions in people.

"So, what happened next," I asked. "Did you tell Sarah?"

"Not straight away. We stayed in town, had a look around, and eventually found a place to eat. Sarah was wondering why I'd been so quiet since church, but she didn't push it. She knew me well enough to know I'd tell her when I was ready, and … … eventually, some way into the meal I explained what I was thinking. Not that I was sure exactly what I was thinking, but she seemed to understand."

He smiled and gave a slight shrug.

"There you have it. Not the most exciting of conversion stories, is it?"

"I wouldn't really know," I said, and I really didn't, which left me feeling curious about one thing at least. "Did this experience, or whatever, actually change anything?"

"Hmmm," he said. "Not at first. It's probably more true to say it was the start of change… … Sarah told me how some people have a bolt of lightning, single point in time, kind of experience, a bit like Paul's Damascus Road thing… … But other people, maybe most folk according to Sarah, find it's more like starting out on a journey which takes you places you wouldn't previously have thought of going. On the way, you learn things you didn't know before, and somehow… … in the light of that… … your attitudes, your priorities, they begin to change."

He took a sip of his tea and then set it down to lean forward, resting his forearms on the table.

"Look, I could go on about this forever, but I'm probably boring you silly."

I tried to reassure him that he wasn't, and it was true. I really wanted to know; to understand why he thought the way that he did. He seemed to think I was just being polite.

"OK, Lizzie. Well, let me just say this. I've learnt a bit about God, about following Jesus' teachings, about the way God works in the world – and the way he doesn't, which is probably just as important – but there's a load of stuff I don't know, and there's a load of stuff I don't understand. So don't get me started on why Sarah died, and how I can still believe in God after that… … I don't know."

Strange, I thought. That was the very thing I did want to ask, but he was safe enough. I probably wouldn't anyway have had the courage, or impertinence, to put it into words.

We were both tired, so we just finished our drinks and lazily left the remains for Mrs Siddons to tidy away in the morning.

I went to sleep thinking of Angie.

I wondered if a quick prayer might help.

Couldn't do any harm, I thought.

I gave it a try, stumbling over the words, and was almost asleep as I finished.

Wednesday
4th May 2005

Aushra Paulauskaitė – Day Five

Vilnius, Lithuania – 6:00 am

Aushra lay still, staring excitedly through the gloom of her bedroom at the cracked and peeling ceiling above. Today was the day. It was hard to lie there motionless when her soul was crying out to be free of the bedclothes, to bounce to the window, fling it open and sing out to greet the lazy dawn. But her Mum would probably not be stirring for another half an hour at least, and Aushra knew she needed to let her sleep. They had stayed up late into the small hours talking softly over mugs of hot chocolate, reliving memories of their good times together. And there had been good times, perhaps not as many as they would have liked, but happy nonetheless. They had talked about Aushra's job and her future, and they had made plans. They looked forward to the time when they could be reunited, not here but in England, when Aushra had become settled in her work. Then Aushra would have a place of her own, and her mother would be able to give up her job at the bakery and go to join her and find work for herself in England. Mother and daughter moving on in a new life together.

But today Aushra's mum had to work. She couldn't afford to take a day off, and the bakery took a seriously dim view of employees pretending to be sick when they weren't, so in something less than two hours' time the two of them would say goodbye and part.

Some of Aushra's excitement faded at the thought of being parted from her mum. Nineteen years separated them, but their relationship in recent years had been more like that of sisters who, unusually perhaps, had grown to be the best of friends. At the end of today, her mum would come home to an empty house with no-one any longer to listen, or laugh or sympathise as she poured out her accumulated frustrations of the day. Aushra would have her fellow trainees and, of course, Jolanta to share the excitement and anxieties, the novelty and uncertainty that came with the joy of starting a new job. Much as she hated the thought of leaving her mum alone, Aushra knew she would not have passed up this opportunity for anything.

She had to be at the office near the Holiday Inn by ten o'clock that morning. A minibus would take the girls and their luggage to the airport where they would be met by Mr Portess who would have their tickets all ready for them. That was the only part of the day she was not looking forward to.

She couldn't explain it, but there was something about Mitch Portess that she didn't like. She hadn't told her mum for the very reason that she couldn't put her uneasiness into words, and she certainly didn't want to give her anything to worry about. She was upset enough that her daughter was leaving home. Aushra was also a mature girl for her eighteen years, and she was well aware that people sometimes didn't gel for no more sinister reason than a simple difference in personality.

But Mr Portess had been trying just a little too hard to be nice, and Aushra was suspicious of men who obviously worked so hard to be charmingly pleasant. It made her wonder what they were trying to hide.

Still, she thought, as she imagined her first ever flight in an aeroplane, he wasn't going to be sitting with them. He had said it was because he regarded them all as responsible adults and he didn't want to give the impression of shepherding them like school children, but the girls believed it was because he would be travelling business class and the company wasn't going to pay for mere trainees to do the same.

It didn't matter. Once in England, he would hand them over to his personal assistant and probably never give them another thought.

If our paths cross again, thought Aushra, *he will probably not even recognise me.*

Sixty-Two

The Dower House – 8.25 am

We had planned to leave straight after breakfast on Wednesday morning. As soon as I was dressed I went down to the kitchen, but I had absolutely no appetite. I was desperate to find out how Angie was doing, but terrified to ask. I think James must have seen the anxiety in my face since he told me as soon as I came through the door that he'd already phoned the hospital, and it looked like Angie was over the worst and likely to pull through.

    I flopped down into the nearest chair, holding back my tears of relief since Abby was already seated at the table, listening curiously to her dad's reassuring words.

"Is she still poorly then, this friend of yours?"

"Getting better," I said, with a rather shaky smile.

"Good," said Abby, and returned her attention to her cereal.

    James was also making the trip to Scotland, but in the Maserati. He didn't plan to with come with us because he had arranged to stop off and visit an old friend in Newcastle on the way up. I felt a really odd sensation, something completely new to me, when he told us that the old friend was a lady called Zena Walcott. It didn't help that Abby referred to this friend as **Aunt Zena** which made me wonder just how close she and James were. Why did it matter so much? It disturbed me that I was even thinking like this. James was helping me, but I wasn't sure I'd known him long enough to call myself his friend. And yet I felt strangely resentful of this lady who most definitely was.

    It was an uncomfortable conversation as we sat at the breakfast table and I tried to persuade James to let Abby and me go with him in the car.

"Why can't we?" I asked. "We don't mind going in the car."

"I do," said Abby immediately, through a mouthful of cereal. "You said I could have a ride in Granddad's helicopter."

"There'll be lots of chances for you to do that," I said, already sensing I was on a loser.

"That's OK for you to say. You've already had a ride in it."

"I know but… …"

I got no further. James had made his mind up and there was no changing it.

"It has to be this way, Lizzie. Use the helicopter and no-one knows where you're going, and no-one can track you. That's why I arranged an air ambulance for Angie as soon as Barrie said she should be

OK to travel later today. He won't let her be moved unless she's got full support facilities, and I can't have her going by road. An ambulance would be too easy to follow. A chopper is the only way. I'd cram you in with her, but there just isn't space enough."

There was a sudden silence. Abby had stopped eating. Her face was very still, her eyes wide.

"Daddy, who's going to try and follow us?"

I felt guilty at having let my selfishness provoke James into speaking so ill-advisedly in front of Abby. He immediately tried to retrieve the slip.

"No-one you need to worry about, love. It's just some nosey people who like to know what we're doing."

She frowned but seemed a little reassured.

"You mean like those… … er… … those papper whotsits?"

I was confused but James smiled.

"Paparazzi. That's right, sweetheart. Something like that."

After that, I just kept quiet and did as I was told. I had been going to ask why James was so keen on travelling by car if there was a real danger of being followed – he could easily have travelled in the helicopter with us, especially as Newcastle has an airport – but then it occurred to me that he might not mind being followed if it gave him the chance to deal with some more of the opposition. Then I began to worry and knew that I'd go on worrying until he re-joined us at Aullton House.

Abbey loved the flight up to Scotland or, at least, the first hour or so.

She had bounced around on the seats after climbing into the cabin of the Grand, enjoying the soft, creamy leather and, when I eventually suggested she settle down, she had opted for a forward facing window seat. The helicopter could take six passengers on two banks of seats, three facing forward and three to the rear. There was also an additional seat up front for the co-pilot, if one should be employed, which was rare on the relatively short journeys James's father had so far attempted. With a range of around five hundred miles, even the journey to Scotland came nowhere near to stretching the helicopter's, or the pilot's, capabilities.

Since there was space for Andy in the main cabin with us, I was surprised when he opted to sit up front with the pilot. Other than a brief hello, we hadn't spoken since he arrived at the Dower House as we were finishing breakfast. I thought he was looking strained and tired, which was surprising since he'd not had to sit up with Angie all night as he'd planned. Dr Harwood had decided to watch over Angie himself through the night, and a nurse had been paid overtime to give non-stop attention to the monitoring machines and the patient hooked up to them.

The flight took just over two hours, but seemed to last forever. I was getting more and more desperate to find out if Angie was actually going to be able join us today, but Abby's excitement helped to keep my mind off what was happening back on the ground. Mike took us up over Derbyshire's Peak District, and then skirted the western end of the Yorkshire Dales, following a course that took us between the busy airports of Manchester and Leeds on either side of the Pennines.

For the first hour or so, Abby lapped it up. Cherry was knowledgeable enough to be able to answer most of her questions about what was passing beneath us and, as I sat in my corner and listened to them, I realised how little I knew about this country where I had lived for the past ten years. I vaguely remembered something about Roman lead mines in the Peaks, but I knew nothing of hill forts or stone circles, sheep farming or eighteenth century enclosures. I certainly didn't know that Huddersfield once boasted more Rolls-Royces per head of population than anywhere else in the country. I wasn't sure why anyone would want to know that, but Cherry did, and I came to realise during that journey that there were depths to him which I hadn't previously imagined.

Our flight did not take us over the Lake District which we passed well to the east, but we were able to make out what Cherry assured us was Scafell Pike way off to our left. By this time, Abby was growing rather tired of the geography lesson, and the novelty of being waved at by walkers on the trails way below was wearing thin. A brief mid-morning snack went some way to relieving her boredom, albeit temporarily. We all agreed that the sweet-chilli sausage rolls had turned out fine, and Cherry congratulated Abby on her baking skills.

Eating over, she took her Nintendo DS out of her backpack, plugged in her earpieces, and allowed the game to shut us out. I couldn't tell which one it was, but her favourite of the moment seemed to involve some kind of mutant insects.

The cabin was so well soundproofed that none of us had bothered with the noise reduction headsets, but for some time my attention had been drawn to the phone which could be used not only to communicate with the pilot but also, and more importantly to me, with the ground. Once Abby had tuned us out and was well and truly focussed on her game, I picked up the handset and tried to work out which buttons to press. I sat staring at it in frustration, having absolutely no idea what to do. Eventually, Cherry reached across and took it from me.

"James?" he asked, starting to dial.

I nodded and he pressed several more buttons and held the handset to his ear. Finally, without speaking, he offered it back to me.

There was a ringing tone for a couple of seconds, and then I heard James's voice. All he said was *Hello,* but the sudden pounding in my chest made me realise how much I missed being with him. Since it wasn't much more than an hour since he'd waved us off, it wasn't so much the lapse of time that was the problem as the growing distance between us. In just a few days, I found I had grown used to his rock-solid dependability, and his constant cheerfulness even when disasters seemed to erupt out of nowhere. I could understand the loyalty of the men who had served with him in the Marines. Men like Cherry, who right now was committed to keeping his daughter safe, and me too, from anyone or anything that might pose a threat.

When I started speaking to James, Abby glanced up from her game.

"Is that Daddy?" she asked. "Can I talk to him?"

I told her she could speak to him in a few minutes and she seemed satisfied and turned her attention back to the small screen.

James was driving north on the M1 as we spoke, but he wasn't breaking the new law as I knew that the Maserati was fitted with a very fancy hands-free phone that played through the car's built-in speakers. I was careful what I said since it was clear that Abby's sharp ears were not entirely tuned out, but mostly I just listened as James told me what he knew about Angie.

"I managed to have a good chat with Barrie after you'd gone. Doctor Pritchard – that's his deputy – was already there, and he'll be running things for a day or two to give Barrie a break. From what he told me, it was a good job Barrie got to Angie as quickly as he did yesterday. It seems her symptoms were pretty classic for an overdose of heroin or some such. Then Andy told him about someone giving her an injection which Barrie knew he hadn't authorised, so he took a chance put her on something called naloxone, which is cracking stuff apparently, as long as it's given straight away. Too much of a delay and she'd be dead very soon, or at least very severely brain damaged."

Angie... ... a vegetable. I couldn't imagine it. It was all too horrible. I turned my face towards the window so Abby wouldn't be able to see my expression.

"But she's OK now?" I whispered and, in spite of the softness of my voice, he heard me, even picking up on the desperation I was feeling.

"Look, Lizzie. She's alive, and in a short while she'll be in the air ambulance and on her way to join you. She got through the night OK and she's still hanging on. Barrie sat up with her all through the night, and he wouldn't be letting her travel if he wasn't feeling optimistic. I'm not a medic so I don't really know what I'm talking about here... ... Barrie says she did seem to come round for a while soon after he started the naloxone, but she was very confused. She couldn't remember a thing about what had happened. Then she went unconscious again. Like I told you earlier, she was awake this morning but still very confused so I think, for now, we just have to wait and see."

I thought about that. It seemed to me that a lot of what we had been doing in the past few days had been of the wait-and-see variety, and I wished that there was some way we could hit first instead of just reacting all the time.

"Lizzie."

James's voice broke into my chain of thought.

"Lizzie. Are you still there?"

"Yes," I said. "Still here."

Having got my attention, there was a brief pause before he continued.

"Lizzie... ... Paul Riddings phoned this morning, just after you left. He sounded rather hung-over, but he told me you were in the wood on Saturday morning. That you saw what happened."

I immediately consigned Paul Riddings to an extended visit in a very hot place and wished very much that he'd kept his mouth shut. I was sure it was just a burst of spite aimed at driving a wedge between James and me. I knew someone had to tell him that bit of news, but I wanted James to hear it from me and Cherry had seemed to understand that. Obviously this busybody from London hadn't. A vague suspicion that I was being unfair to Riddings nagged at me briefly, but not enough to temper my sudden flash of anger. But when I replied, it was not anger but guilt tinged with more than a little shame that inflected my voice.

"Yes," I said, almost whispering again. "I was there. I meant to tell you last night but... ... well, I was so worried about Angie that I... ... I just forgot."

And I had. Anxiety about Angie had driven everything else from my mind.

"That's OK, Lizzie. I understand. But ... ... did you see who killed Phil Simmons?"

Unlike mine, his tone was neutral, but I knew he must be wondering whether I had been holding back some vital information which might have prevented all that unwelcome interest from the police and the press over the past few days. I realised that I was horribly afraid that he wasn't going to believe me whatever I said. I hadn't really lied to him, but he now knew that I hadn't been completely open either. I'm not sure at what point in the past three days I had realised that he was someone I could trust, absolutely and without reservation, but I knew I had come to believe that I could tell him anything .

Well, almost anything.

The trouble was that other more violently pressing events had pushed Phil Simmons' death to the back of my mind. I had no longer been deliberately withholding the truth. I just hadn't found the right opportunity to tell James the whole story.

"James," I said quietly, holding the phone very close to my mouth. "I'm sorry… …I should have told you before, except… … well, there's really so little to tell. I saw a vague shape, that's all… …I couldn't describe it… … couldn't even say if it was a man or a woman… … I didn't see what happened… … or how it happened… …or where this figure went afterwards. I didn't, James. I really, truly didn't."

My desperation hung there in the silence as I waited for him to reply. He was taking too long.

"James? I should have told you… … I'm sorry… … I know I should… … I don't know now why I didn't. I…think…it was just… …"

"You were scared, Lizzie. You didn't know me and you had no reason to trust me."

His voice was no longer neutral. It was gentle and reassuring, and immensely comforting.

"But," I said, hesitating, and scared of revealing too much, "I did have reason to trust you. I should have… … I do trust you."

"Well, I'm glad about that," he said. "But then, don't forget, we got caught up in all that stuff with Angie, and you didn't have much of a chance to tell me anything. So don't let it worry you. We can talk about it later."

I didn't realise that I'd been holding my breath until I let it out in a long sigh. I was still turned towards the window. A panorama of picturesque villages, rolling hills and winding rivers was unfolding down below with remarkable clarity, but my mind took in none of it. I risked a quick glance towards Abby, but it must have been a good game since she seemed totally uninterested in my conversation. Cherry, however, was lounging back in his corner opposite Abby with his eyes fixed on me and his ears tuned, I was sure, to catch every word.

I must have been quiet for too long, since James's voice came once again in my ear.

"Did you hear me, Lizzie?"

"Yes, I heard… … But I still feel bad I didn't tell you."

"No need. Believe me, there's no need. You're doing OK, and all I need for you to do now is look after Abby for me. This will all be over soon, I promise."

After a brief pause, I said, "OK." I couldn't think of anything else. But clearly James could.

"Can you pass me over to Cherry? I need a quick word."

"OK," I said again, "but then Abby wants to talk to you."

I surrendered the phone to Cherry who seemed to have been waiting for it, and that seemed to grab Abby's attention. She looked up from her game.

"Hey, Lizzie. You said I could talk to him."

"Yes, I know, sweetie. And you can. He just wanted to tell Cherry something."

She pouted and looked about to argue, but she settled for a sigh and, "Always last. That's me, always last."

"Maybe," I said, "that's because your dad likes to keep the best 'til last."

She smiled at that, but wasn't going to totally relinquish the point.

"Yes, well, don't you go and forget."

Her attempt at a frown was shared equally between Cherry and me, before she returned once more to her game and I returned to gazing out of the window.

I wondered whether the landscape slipping by below was England or Scotland, and what was this place we were going to? A fairy-tale castle, Abby had said but, much as I might hope for it, I couldn't see my story having a fairy-tale ending. I hoped James was right and it would be over soon, but my mind was leaping ahead now to what would happen afterwards. I still had no home, no money and no job, and absolutely no way at all of achieving my dream and getting back to that small island in the middle of the South Atlantic Ocean where I had once been so happy.

The truly scary thing was that I wasn't really sure any more that returning to St Helena was what I actually wanted. In my dream, nothing about the island had changed from the moment that my uncle had pushed me aboard the RMS St Helena with tears streaming down my cheeks. Yet however much time may stand still in dreams, I knew the reality would be quite different. The pathetic little girl whose parents had died so tragically would have long since passed from the memories of those cheerful islanders. Their lives would have marched on, television and the internet enlarging their horizons, new people coming and going, and I'd heard there were even plans for an airport at some time not too far ahead.

No, if I went back, I would be sure to find I did not belong.

But I didn't belong anywhere else either.

And somewhere, dormant in the bowels of the police computer system, were my name, my DNA, and probably my picture, all linked to a killing which I was most definitely responsible for some three years previously.

I was still struggling not to feel sorry for myself when I became aware that Cherry had moved along to sit opposite to me. I glanced quickly at Abby to make sure he had not forgotten to give her the phone, but I need not have worried. Her Nintendo was on the seat beside her, and she was curled up in the corner chattering away.

Cherry leaned forward hands clasped, forearms resting on his knees. He had obviously come to talk to me and it suddenly flashed across my mind that he was going to start coming on to me. As far as I could recall, he hadn't mentioned a wife or girlfriend at any time over the past few days, but there was no doubt at all that most women would agree he was a good-looking guy. His wavy brown hair was long without quite getting down to his collar, and it flopped forward now so he had to sweep it back with his left hand. It was a good strong hand with long tapering fingers and, as I carefully observed, not a ring in sight. As his green eyes watched me warily, I shifted uneasily and became aware of the palms of my hands starting to feel clammy.

I really didn't want this. It was all so strange. In my former environment, I was used to men making advances, and I always knew exactly how to handle them. Now, in this new world, I felt oddly insecure and vulnerable, and I wasn't quite sure why. I did know that I valued his natural friendliness, and I could appreciate his good looks with a kind of detached objectivity, but that was as far as it went. Indeed, I was certain that was as far as it would ever go.

In some weird way, I almost wanted to be a little girl again. I wanted to be loved just for being me, by someone big and dependable and absolutely trustworthy, who would wrap me in his arms when things went wrong, and comfort me and tell me everything would be OK. Someone who didn't want anything from me. Someone who just wanted to take care of me.

I was embarrassed at even thinking how awkward it might be to turn down Cherry's advances, so I was afraid that my cheeks must be flushed with the warmth I undoubtedly felt. If he noticed any heightened colour, he gave no sign of it, and when he began to speak I felt the warmth in my cheeks increasing, not from embarrassment this time, but relief. My stupid fears could hardly have been further off the mark.

"Looks like Angie might be coming out of it," he said. "Rod called James while I was on the phone so I had to go on hold for a bit but it turns out the silly beggar's not as daft as I thought he was. While the doc's been working on Angie, he's gone through all the security tapes – or whatever they call 'em now – and come up with a big flat zero. In the half hour either side of when Angie was attacked, there's no-one showing up on those recordings who shouldn't be there."

I stared at him, trying to work through the implications of this news. The flush faded from my cheeks as he gave me time to take it in. He glanced once at Abby who was still jabbering away to her dad, and he smiled at her excited chatter.

I could see only one explanation for Rod's discovery.

"You think one of the hospital staff has been got at, pressured in some way?"

He nodded. "Well we're not dealing with the invisible man, that's for sure."

"I don't suppose there was a camera near Angie's room?"

"No. Apparently they don't have them on the upstairs corridors. Only downstairs, and in reception, and at various places in the grounds."

"So what happens now?"

"Rod's going through the personnel files of all the male staff." He smiled. "The woman in charge of their HR department wasn't very thrilled, because Rod wouldn't tell her what he was after. But when he told her it was either him or the police, she opted for him."

"Do the police know what happened to Angie?"

"Don't think so. James didn't want to confuse their little minds once they'd got fixed on what they thought had happened with that Russian."

"So what's Rod looking for?"

"Anyone who fits the general description Andy gave. John's checking where everyone was around that time, and if they find anyone who seems a bit dodgy for the time when Angie was attacked they'll send their pictures to my Blackberry, and we'll see if Andy can pick out the villain."

"Are all these people still on duty? I mean... ... nobody's disappeared or anything."

"All still there. And the weird bit, so John says, is nobody seems to give a toss about being asked questions about where they were."

My hands still felt clammy, but it was anxiety now, not embarrassment, that was tying my stomach in knots.

"Is Angie safe? I mean... ... she's still at the hospital isn't she?"

Cherry nodded, and gave me a quick glimpse of his even, white teeth.

"Not for much longer. She'll be taking off very soon and in the meantime, James is paying Sonia overtime to babysit."

Sonia? Who the... ...? And then I remembered the girl in battle dress from Saturday night.

Cherry leaned back.

"So that's about it. You know what I know."

Not quite, I thought. I still had one question.

"Why didn't you tell James about me being in the wood on Saturday morning?"

He looked surprised, perhaps wondering how I knew he hadn't.

"Riddings told him this morning," I said. "So... ... why him but not you?"

He smiled. "Not my place. And I guess I thought you'd get round to it sooner or later."

At which point, with perfect timing, we were interrupted by an excited shout from Abby.

"Dad... ... Hey, Dad. We're nearly there. I can see our mountain. Gotta go now. Talk to you later. Love you."

She turned to me, and tossed the phone onto the seat opposite her.

"Look, Lizzie. Over there. Sort of... ... straight up the river."

I moved over to sit next to her so I could see out of the same window. Abby was pointing.

"See where the river bends? That mountain with the trees up one side looks down to our house. I can see it from my bedroom. Did I tell you I live in a turret, Lizzie? It's got a pointy roof, and it's the coolest thing."

We were following the course of the river as it wound to the right of Abby's mountain.

"Look... ... Look, Lizzie. It's coming now... ... Wait. Here it comes... ... Now, isn't that just... ... fairy-tale?"

I couldn't argue.

Aullton House was situated towards the eastern side of a wide valley whose western slope formed the foothills of Abby's mountain. The river meandered down the valley through open parkland dotted with trees, and passing perhaps half a mile from the house. There was much to see but I couldn't take my eyes from the fairy-tale.

The white walls shone in the late morning sunshine. There was no kind of symmetrical pattern to the buildings or, at least, none that I could see. It was a huge rambling house that had probably started with the square, central block and then extended outwards as successive owners had added extra wings, towers and turrets. Each of the rounded towers was capped by a tall, conical roof. Some of the towers grew up from ground level while others just sprouted out of the walls part way up.

If ever there was a place where Rapunzel let down her hair, or the handsome prince awoke the sleeping princess with a kiss, then this had to be it. It seemed as far away from the murky world I had left as it was possible to get. I couldn't tear my eyes away, even when Abby tugged at my sleeve.

"What do you think, Lizzie?"

I smiled as I searched for the right word.

"Perfect," I said at last, in response to another tug.

But I had forgotten that lurking in the heart of every fairy-tale there is a villain, and my story wasn't over yet.

Sixty-Three

Thurvaston Arms – 9.25 am

The sun was already creating brightly dappled patterns on the front lawn of the Thurvaston Arms Hotel when John Salisbury stumbled lazily from the four-poster bed and drew back the heavy curtains. A light breeze was teasing the branches of the horse-chestnut trees which bordered the lawn on the south-east side, causing the leaf patterns to dance and flicker on the shimmering grass. He stretched languidly and then ducked suddenly back out of sight as a young couple came into view from the front entrance of the hotel. Holding hands, they strolled leisurely across the grass in the direction of the river, pausing to look at a stone statue set in small pond in the middle of the lawn.

He smiled to himself. From that angle, even had they bothered to turn around and look up at his window, the couple would have seen nothing more than his face and upper chest. Nothing there really to get anyone excited. Nadera, on the other hand, was a far different proposition in the excitement stakes and, lying on her side propped on one elbow, she had an excellent view of the body which she had explored so thoroughly the night before. She laughed at the way John skulked behind the curtain, peering around it at something down in the garden.

"Come back to bed, John," she said in that low sultry voice which had so pleased him during the night. "We are, I think, most late for breakfast, so no need to hurry about getting dressed."

After an initial, and thankfully brief, period of inexpert fumbling, the night had developed most satisfactorily for both parties, which explained how they had both managed to sleep so late into the morning.

John turned to face her, the curtain twisting around him in graceful folds so that he looked rather like a decorously attired Roman statue. He was actually feeling rather pleased with himself, since he had every reason for believing that Nadera had not been the least bit disappointed with his overnight performance. However, when he spoke his voice took on a rather sheepish tone.

"Did I… … during the night… …" He rubbed his head with his free right hand. "I mean, I think… … during the night… … I might have… …?"

She pushed herself into a sitting position, drawing up her duvet-covered legs to hug her knees. Huddled in the middle of the bed she tilted her head to face him. Her raven-black hair fell forward and she raised her left hand to brush it back behind her ear. Resuming her knee-hugging, she looked quite serious as she thought about the moment he was referring to.

"If you mean... ... did you tell me, just before you so romantically fell asleep, that you wanted to marry me, then... ... yes you did."

She hadn't quite been sure whether he meant it and maybe now, in the cold light of day, he was regretting it. For her part, she had no difficulty recalling what her answer had been, but it seemed his memory wasn't quite so clear.

"Hmm. Rather thought I did." He grinned then and his eyebrows lifted in a question. "So... ... what did you say?"

She decided his lapse of memory needed a little punishment.

"Can't you remember?"

He squirmed inside his curtain.

"Well... ... no... ...Come on, Nadera. Don't keep me in suspense. What did you say?"

"I said that, after what you'd just done to me, if you did not marry me I would cut your bits off and throw them in the river."

He winced and peered down inside the curtain.

"Don't worry," she said. "Everything's still where it should be. So come on back to bed and make sure it's still working."

He did as he was told with appropriate enthusiasm after checking that the **Do not Disturb** sign was on the outside of their door. Some while later, though still a little breathless, he proposed again, this time with a little more finesse. This time, he remembered her answer.

Once they were showered and dressed, they left their room – now with a **Ready for Service** sign hanging on the door – and made their way to the bar. They were far too late for breakfast and still too early for lunch, but morning coffee was being served so they made do with almond croissants, scones and several cups of a rather good Fairtrade coffee. Once they felt sufficiently refreshed, they retired to their room to begin work.

The maids must have been watching earlier on for them to leave the room because the sign was now off the door, the bed was made and everywhere looked clean and tidy. The complimentary toiletries in the bathroom had been replaced which was a nice touch that they hadn't expected in such a small establishment. Rather than collecting the laptop and retiring to a secluded corner of the lounge, they would now be able to work in their room undisturbed.

From their surveillance and eavesdropping at the manse yesterday evening, they had two new names to work with, Raymond Mellisse and Gordon Russell. Their first job was to identify who these guys were and how they might be connected to Phil Simmons. Using the hotel's Wi-fi speeded things up enormously.

They quickly discovered that there was a Raymond Mellisse who had legitimate business interests in Birmingham, but the previous night's eavesdropping strongly suggested someone with an involvement – they weren't quite sure what – in other, less savoury activities.

"Who the hell is this guy?" asked John. "Is he a businessman or a pimp?"

"Could he not be both?" asked Nadera in reply.

John shook his head slowly. "Maybe," he said. "I really don't know."

So they set about trying to track him down. Assuming that he would choose to live within easy travelling distance of his businesses, they began with the electoral roll. Information contained on the Full Electoral Roll is not available via the internet, but an Edited Roll is commercially available for purposes like marketing and – more importantly to John and Nadera – search engines. Any individual on the Electoral Roll can opt to have their details excluded from the edited version but it seemed that Mr Mellisse had been so obliging as to forget to exercise this option. Assuming, of course, that the Raymond Mellisse that they discovered to be living in Edgbaston was the one they wanted.

Another search took them to the Birmingham Post and a brief article on the opening of new offices for a company called Pan European Solutions, chairman and managing director, Raymond Mellisse. Armed with this information, and a small fee paid to Companies House via their website, they confirmed that the two were one and the same. Another web-search provided them with a list of all companies of which Raymond Mellisse was a director. More searches came up with information on those businesses, but none of them threw up the slightest sniff of anything illegal.

"Maybe we're chasing the wrong guy," said John.

"Maybe," replied Nadera. "But if there is another, he doesn't exist on the internet."

More doubt was thrown on their search when another result from the Birmingham Post revealed a photograph of Mellisse at a charity dinner. Although he was named in the caption, he was clearly incidental to the main character in the picture, Sir Vernon Laycock, prospective Parliamentary candidate. Laycock was on his feet delivering a speech, and Mellisse was seated only two places away, next to Lady Laycock.

"This can't be him," said John, pushing back his chair from the long counter which served as dressing table, desk and bar. "I know Laycock. He was CEO of the company that bought out my father. He could be a ruthless sod, but I never thought of him as dodgy. He wouldn't be involved with the Mellisse we're looking for. I think we're wasting time here."

Nadera laid a hand on his knee before he could stand up.

"Wait one moment," she said. "We're going to try something else."

"What, like hack into his bank accounts?"

"No, you idiot. For one thing, we must not set off any alarms, and for another… … I doubt I could even do it."

He looked at her questioningly. In the relatively short time he had known her, he hadn't discovered much that she couldn't do. Her previous master had trained her well, but it was obviously too much to expect her to be proficient at everything.

"No," she said again. "I would like to hack into his personal computer but… …"

He smiled, and hauled his chair back to the desk.

"Now you're talking!"

"But," she repeated, "I can't be sure I could get out without leaving a trail."

He looked disappointed.

"So… … what are you saying? Are you going to hack him or not?"

"Not. Or at least, not yet. We're going to get off our bottoms and sniff around one of these companies. The question is, which one?"

While John made them both a cup of coffee from the replenished supplies, Nadera opened up the websites of each of Mellisse's companies that they had traced so far. She overlapped the explorer windows on her screen so she could jump easily from one to the other. On each site she brought up the **Contact Us** webpage. After moving from one to the other for a few moments, she sighed and turned round.

"John, where did you put the road atlas?"

"It's in my holdall," he said, putting down the kettle and reaching into the bag.

Taking the book, she laid it next to the laptop and opened it at the page showing the area around Birmingham. She looked back to her screen and sighed again.

"I don't know this place. Come and help me, John."

"Just a minute, love."

Dropping the tiny UHT milk containers into the waste bin, he picked up the two cups, minus their saucers, and brought them across to resume his seat beside her. Once settled, he squared the atlas on the desk in front of him and drew a pen from his shirt pocket.

"OK. You tell me where it is and I'll mark it on here."

As Nadera brought up each contact page and read out the location of the company, John made a circle on the atlas.

"Are we just aiming for the nearest?" he asked.

"Not exactly," replied Nadera, peering very closely at one of the webpages. "We want it close, yes, but it also needs to be a company that we could have a good reason for visiting, and maybe finding someone who will talk to us."

John waited for the next location but, when all he got was silence, he turned to see what was holding Nadera's attention. She was moving slowly from one webpage to the other, enlarging each one to full screen and frowning in concentration.

"Look at this, John."

She pointed to the bottom right-hand corner of the laptop screen. Just above the bar at the bottom which gave details of the website designer and other links to do with privacy and terms of business, there was a tiny bluish rectangle. She zoomed the page to enlarge it and the minute icon grew to reveal a strange gold pattern in the top half of the rectangle. It was almost triangular in shape but very fuzzy along the edges. Beneath the pattern, in block letters also in gold, were the words THE WIND IN THE WILLOWS.

They stared at it.

"That's odd," said John. "What site is this?"

"It's… …" and then she paused, her eyes narrowed as she took in what she was seeing. "It's Lichfield Tube Ltd."

"Bloody hell! Are you sure?"

Nadera pointed to the company logo at the top of the screen.

"Yeah, I see it," said John. "Last night, didn't Montrayne say there was a connection between Mellisse and Lichfield Tube?"

"It's strange," she said. "I don't remember that he did. In fact, he seemed to think they were not connected. But he definitely thought that there was something bad at Lichfield Tube. And he thought that was probably the reason for your friend being killed."

"Well, according to this, there obviously is a connection," said John, leaning forward to peer at the screen. "Does this site have a people page? You know… … personnel… … who's who, who does what."

Nadera clicked on a link and the page changed to show several head and shoulder photos. Beside each was a name, position in the company and brief bio. As she took in the details attached to the picture at the top of the page, Nadera sucked in her breath through pursed lips. Gordon Russell, managing director, smiled out from the screen.

"Well, well, well," said John. "So we know something Montrayne doesn't know. Russell and Mellisse, both on the board of the same company."

Nadera pointed at the screen.

"What does this mean? It says Mellisse is non-executive director."

John looked at the text beside Mellisse's picture.

"It means he's a kind of… … independent director. Not actually employed by the company. He's like a… … a watchdog."

Suddenly, he sat back, eyes still staring at the screen.

"That's it. I bet Mellisse got in there on the strength of his friendship… … or association, or whatever, with Sir Vernon Laycock. They're all tied together somehow. Can you print off those pictures?"

Nadera nodded, and a few clicks later the printer slowly churned out full colour pictures of Mellisse and Russell.

While they waited for the printer to finish, John thought some more about that strange logo Nadera had found. *Wind in the Willows.* On a bookseller's website it might have made some sort of sense, but what did it have to do with Raymond Mellisse? Nadera turned to look at him.

"What are you thinking?" she asked.

"It's that logo," he replied. "I can't work out what it's doing here."

"Do you know what it is?"

"Yes. That, my love, is the easy bit. It's the cover of *The Wind in the Willows.* Written about a hundred years ago by Kenneth Grahame who was, I believe, secretary of the Bank of England."

She stared at him.

"I went to the Bank of England Museum," he explained. "Years ago, before I had to… … you know."

Nadera smiled.

"I know," she said. "Well, see what your criminal mind makes of this."

She opened the contact page of each of the companies in turn, scrolled to the bottom right-hand corner, and zoomed each page. It wasn't present on every one but, on four of them, there it was, *The Wind in the Willows* in blue and gold.

"I missed it at first," she said, "because each window was reduced. I only needed the address. But when you look at the whole window for these four, there it is down in the corner. What does it mean?"

"Have you tried clicking on it?"

She moved the curser to hover over the tiny picture, but it didn't change to a hand like it usually did if a hyperlink was present. She clicked anyway and they both waited, but nothing happened. After a brief pause, she tried again. Still nothing.

"There doesn't seem to be any link attached to it," she said. "I don't think it's going to take us anywhere."

"Have we lost the connection?" asked John.

Nadera brought up a window showing the website of a different company and began to navigate through the site. No problem.

"OK," said John. "Now, can you go back to the contact page?"

"I'll try one of the other sites," she said.

She did, found the little book icon and clicked on it. Nothing happened.

"Could the website it's linked to be offline for some reason… … maintenance perhaps," asked John

"Perhaps, or maybe it doesn't exist anymore," sighed Nadera. "I'm hungry. Let us have some lunch and try again later."

She pushed back her chair and stood up.

"Come on, John. We need a break. Let's eat."

Sixty-Four

Aullton House –Lunchtime

I could see why Abby loved the house. To her child's eyes, it must have seemed the most idyllic and enchanting place imaginable. The stone mullions, pointed turrets, ancient timbers and brilliant-white rendered walls created just the fairy-tale castle she had described. As we slowly circled the buildings, we were treated to a view of the formal gardens that few people would ever get the chance to see. There was perfect symmetry in the geometrically shaped beds and paths extending from the rear of the house. The colours were probably not yet at their best, but the late morning sun was working hard to do them justice. It was easy to see why they appeared so immaculate. Three people in green coveralls, girls I thought but couldn't be sure – long hair is no give-away these days – paused in their work on the beds to look up at us. One of them waved. I imagined for a moment what it must be like to walk those narrow paths between the tiny hedges delighting in the myriad tints and shades while breathing in the delicate scents. Maybe I would do it, if I got the chance. Maybe one of those girls would even tell me the names of the flowers.

To one side of the house, about one hundred yards distant and set back from the line of the front of the house, was a large square garden bounded by a high wall. As we passed over the wall, it looked as though the inside faces were made of brick with the outside rendered brilliant white to match all the rest of the buildings. The land within the walls seemed to be given over to vegetables and fruit trees. At least, I assumed the trees were some kind of orchard from their relatively low height and the regularity of their planting.

Balancing this, on the other side of the residence and similarly set back, was a block of buildings forming an open square, with an entry arch topped by a clock tower on the side facing the house. Yes, brilliant white again, and I assumed these were the stables, though I could see no sign of horses or the usual evidence of their passing. Beyond the formal gardens, and extending around both sides of the house to encircle walled garden and stables, were shaved lawns dotted with sculpted flower beds, carefully trimmed shrubbery, and the occasional specimen shrub or tree. As we swung around the front of the house, Mike had to take care to avoid a well-spaced pair of beautifully spreading cedars which cast huge shadows over the front lawn. I smiled, pleased that I was able to identify them. I would never have been able to do so before Abby introduced me to the ones at the Dower House.

From the front of the castle ran a double avenue of trees, which I was not yet knowledgeable enough to identify, and which focussed attention on an ornate stone bridge which spanned the river about half a mile distant. Beyond the well-tended lawns, the grass grew darker and coarser as pleasure gardens merged into sparsely- wooded parkland which eventually blended into denser woodland and the bluish-tinted slopes of distant hills.

I could hardly bring myself to believe that I was actually going to spend some days living in these beautiful surroundings. And that was the problem. It didn't look the sort of place where any real people lived, or even ought to live. In that moment, from my temporary bird's-eye view, I wondered how anyone could live at ease in surroundings like these when, down in Birmingham and, as far as I knew in every major city, there were people living amongst dustbins, down grimy alleys and under bridges. Girls who I actually knew personally were surviving in small, damp, lifeless rooms which would have disgraced the hovels of nineteenth century mill workers. The girls I knew, mostly trafficked from Eastern Europe, were forced to keep their rooms superficially clean enough to satisfy the more fastidious punters, but anyone not totally given over to the urges that brought him there couldn't mistake the taint of mould and mildew wafting in the air.

I looked down on the rounded turrets with their conical roofs protruding from the corners of the house, and acknowledged that the prospect was enchanting. It just didn't seem right that people who'd done nothing to deserve it should be surrounded by such a wealth of beauty when others lived day after day in fear and pain and abject poverty. But what did *right* have to do with anything? It's just the way things are, that's all. No-one's ever been able to change things, and I guess no-one ever will. I smiled as Abby caught my eye. Might as well just get on and enjoy it while I can. No point kidding myself I'd be here for long. I just didn't belong. This wasn't my world and, sooner or later, I'd have to leave and find myself back on the dung heap. A different dung heap maybe, but the same crappy world.

Or maybe, somehow, I really would make it back to St. Helena. Dream on!

Mike was hovering now, preparing to land. We were over rougher grass on the stable side of the avenue of trees. I could see now how the smooth lawn in front of the house ended abruptly at a long ditch faced on the side away from the house by a low stone wall which had been invisible until we circled round this side of it. As we settled down, I saw a golf buggy emerge through the stable arch and head towards us, at first along the tarmac drive and then bumping over the uneven grass.

Andy was the first out of the helicopter, and I watched him through the window of the Grand as he carefully scanned the approaching buggy and the several figures who had gathered in ones and twos to watch us land. Most of them seemed dressed for work in the gardens, but on the drive in front of the house stood a couple whose work obviously didn't require the protection of overalls. I had seen them emerge from the front doorway as we hovered just before landing. These I took to be our reception committee.

Cherry climbed down and turned to hold open the cabin door of the Grand and helped Abby and me as we climbed out. For the first few minutes his eyes were constantly on the move as he watched carefully every new individual who appeared. I think he knew there was no real cause to be worried, but he just couldn't help himself. I didn't have time to think about it since the driver of the buggy, who seemed to have passed Cherry's inspection, was calling to us. He was an elderly gentleman with a shock of white hair who looked as if he should have given up driving several decades earlier. He beckoned us to climb aboard.

Abby rushed to obey shouting, "Hello, Mr Mac."

I waited to give Cherry a hand with our bags, but I was near enough to hear the old man's gravelly reply. "Hello yourself, Lassie. Now don't be bouncing all over me. These bones are nay so young as they were."

The reception committee had moved forward onto the lawn and was now standing quietly watching, waiting patiently. For the moment I decided to ignore them as I tossed my bag and Abby's onto the rear seat of the buggy. It wasn't the sort I'd seen before but was a kind of long-wheelbase version with plenty of seats for all of us. I sat with Abby behind Mr Mac – proper name Angus MacInnes, as I read on his name badge – while Cherry sat behind us. There was no conversation as the buggy navigated its way through an open gateway and around the end of the walled ditch which I now learned from Mr Mac's unceasing commentary was called by the ridiculous name of ha-ha.

The reception committee moved to meet us as we pulled up on the drive in front of the house. In the lead was a tall lady who I could now see was slender to the point of being angular, and whose pleasant face was topped by dark hair cut in a bob. Teeth gleamed in a wide smile as she crouched down, arms widespread, to receive the eight year old tornado which leapt from the buggy. A few feet behind the ecstatic pair, a red-haired, stocky man in plaid work-shirt and blue jeans came to a halt, hands in pockets. I climbed down from the buggy and his eyes met mine above the two heads locked together and there was a question in them, as though he didn't know quite what to make of me.

I didn't know what to make of him either. I was unsure of myself, feeling very much out of place in these magnificent surroundings. It took a nudge from Cherry to get me moving.

"Come on, Lizzie. Say hello to Mr & Mrs Elliott."

He led me towards the little group and introductions were made. The lady, "call me Freddy", turned out to be the housekeeper, whose given name according to Abby was Frederica, a name which its owner clearly despised. She was friendly enough, and obviously doted on Abby, but the way she told us to follow her into the house and leave our bags for someone called Billy to fetch suggested that exercising authority was second nature to her. Her husband, of the red hair and plaid shirt, allowed his wife to organise us while he brought up the rear with Cherry and Andy, leaving Mike to see to the Grand.

Cherry had obviously been here a number of times before. I could hear him asking questions about the estate, which clearly showed a fairly detailed knowledge of it, and he asked about progress on some project called *Moving On*. Freddy's husband, Gil, began talking about loans and grant-funding and other complicated stuff, and then I didn't hear any more because we were in the entrance hall of the house and Freddy was telling us which bedrooms in the private apartment she had had made up for us.

I tried to follow her instructions but more than half my mind was given over to trying to appreciate the almost overpowering grandeur of the hall. I wasn't sure I liked it. The Dower House was big, and old, and impressive, but it was comfortable and felt like a home. Aullton House was bigger, older, and much more impressive, and felt rather like a museum. Freddy was pointing up the grand staircase which faced the still-open doorway through which we had come in. It was wide, with red carpet over what looked like white marble and, even to my inexperienced eye, it seemed to be not as old as the rest of the house. The stairs led up to a huge painting on the rear wall which was full of sailing ships, and flashes of flame and smoke. Quite striking if you liked that sort of thing, which I'm afraid I didn't. The stairs then branched to right and left to continue their ascent before doubling back on themselves to reach the floor above. I could see the underside of the third flight from where we stood in the hall and, amazingly, it was quite unsupported.

Freddy must have noticed my open-mouthed stare.

"Yes, it is rather splendid, isn't it?" she said. "The 7th Marquess had it put in after the restoration."

That didn't really date it for me, though I had some vague idea from school history that the Restoration had something to do with Charles II. I learned later that, in the Montrayne family, the term *restoration* referred to the handing back in 1783 of lands that had been unjustly seized by the Crown under George II. Something to do with Bonnie Prince Charlie, apparently.

I didn't have to answer her because just then Andy and Cherry strolled in with Gil, chatting in a friendly way. Abby, who had obviously listened to Freddy's instructions far more closely than I had, grabbed my hand and told me she would show me to my room.

We set off up the stairs and Abby led me to the left branch where I paused at the sight of a notice three of four steps up. It was about three feet long and maybe four inches high and said *Strictly Private – No Public Access.* I looked behind me at the other flight which was totally free of any similar warning. Abby, two steps up now and pulling on my arm, understood my hesitation.

She said, nodding across to the other stairs, "That's where everyone goes. This side is just for us."

"OK," I said. "Lead on Macduff."

We were in Scotland after all, so why not a reference to the Scottish play. Three years and a lifetime ago, I had studied Macbeth for GCSE, and I remembered how I used to pride myself on being one of the few who realised how those challenging words of Macbeth were so often misquoted.

Abby rushed off up the stairs, but I paused for a moment thinking of something else and wishing I hadn't remembered it at all. As I recalled it, the play was all about death, the ultimate consequence of selfish ambition being subjected to the evil influence of external forces. I knew all about the kind of selfish ambition that gave no thought to the needs and welfare of others, and I knew about being in the clutches of external forces I couldn't resist. Lots of people died in that play, some of them maybe deserved it and some probably didn't. I thought of the people who'd become involved in my little drama and hoped desperately that none of them would die who didn't deserve it.

"Come on, Lizzie. What are you waiting for?"

I looked up into Abby's smiling face and prayed to the God I didn't believe in, "Please don't let anything happen to Abby or her Dad."

Maybe if I believed in him I'd be able to stop worrying, but then again maybe not.

Sixty-Five

Newcastle – Lunchtime

It was about a three and a half hour journey up to Newcastle. Using the M18 to keep well clear of Sheffield and Leeds, James had intended to go all the way without a stop. His bladder, on the other hand, had different ideas and, by the time he was approaching Scotch Corner service area on the A1, he accepted that a break was inevitable. It was some time now since he'd spoken to Cherry on the helicopter, so it would do no harm to check in again. They should have landed at Aullton House by now, though Angie would still be up in the air somewhere above him. Instinctively he glanced upwards wondering if it was possible that she might have recovered enough to remember what had happened to her, maybe even who had drugged her.

By the time he had paid the necessary visit, grabbed a sandwich and a bottle of water from the shop, and made it back to the Maserati, he was actually feeling quite hungry. Leaning against the car to eat his sandwich, he had tried Cherry's mobile, and was almost surprised to get through with no problem. Reception around Aullton House could be OK, but was known to be quite erratic at times. A quick word with Cherry informed him that Andy had brought in some outside help from Edinburgh to make it easier to keep an eye on things. At first, James wasn't sure he liked the sound of that. Cherry didn't know the two newcomers or the firm they worked for, but he told James that Andy vouched for them and their presence would certainly ease the pressure. Anyway, if all went well, James would be there in another five hours or so and not much could be expected to happen in that time.

Wanting to get on his way, he didn't speak to Abby, asking Cherry to pass on his promise that he would call and talk to her before leaving Professor Walcott's.

While speaking, his eyes had been roving around the car park. Being around lunchtime, it was relatively busy, with people walking between their cars and the service area buildings, but there were plenty of empty spaces particularly further away from the buildings. About five spaces down, across the lane from the Maserati, was a black BMW X5. He noticed it only because it had followed him in off the A1, pausing briefly in front of the buildings, presumably to set down a passenger with urgent business inside. James hadn't seen anyone get out because he was then too busy deciding on his own parking space. As he nosed into his chosen spot, to give a clear lane in front to allow for an easy departure, the BMW slowly passed behind the Maserati to pull round in a wide loop across two lanes of empty parking spaces to end up facing into the Maserati's lane about fifteen yards distant. James now watched the car as he spoke into his phone, curious rather than worried. Although it was a reasonably bright day, he found he could not see past the BMW's tinted windows and so had no idea if the car was occupied.

Before he said goodbye to Cherry, he noticed a man stroll past the rear of the Maserati. He wore a dark suit but with no tie and his top shirt button was unfastened. Unsurprisingly, he was wearing dark glasses. He sipped coffee from a cardboard cup as he walked by without so much as a glance in James's direction. He was clearly a man with a thirst, since he was carrying a second cardboard cup down by his side. This one had a plastic cover over it. Or maybe he was just being considerate and was bringing coffee for a companion who hadn't left his vehicle. As he reached the BMW he turned heading straight for the driver's door. Perching his second coffee on the roof he reached for the door handle. With the door fully open, he stared just for a moment across the roof of his car directly back at James. Then he plucked the coffee off the roof and climbed in. It all looked natural enough and could have been nothing at all, but it left James wondering as he closed his phone and climbed back into the Maserati.

Heading for the exit, he glanced in his rear-view mirror. The BMW hadn't moved. Then, just as it was about to pass from sight, he saw it begin to edge forward.

On a busy road like the A1, James knew it would be near impossible to check whether he was being followed. Over long distances it was not in the least unusual to spot the same vehicle many times, and it meant nothing more than the drivers were heading in the same direction at the best speed. The BMW was probably perfectly innocent, but he might as well do what he could to find out.

The BMW kept its distance as James followed the curve of the roundabout to the top of the on-ramp. He let his speed creep up to fifty and held it there as he filtered back on to the A1. The BMW eased on behind, matching his speed. A small truck which had pulled over to allow them to filter on soon drifted back into the nearside lane occupying the space between them. For some distance they travelled like that, keeping pace with the general flow of traffic. Eventually James noticed a long gap opening up in the outside lane so he floored the gas pedal and the Maserati's twin-turbocharged V8 engine pushed the car rapidly up to eighty. The BMW responded but rather more slowly. James saw it pull out from behind the truck and he kept glancing in his mirror as it gradually closed the distance until once again it settled down to match his speed. *Must be only the three litre version,* he thought. Which gave it a top speed of about one hundred and thirty, compared to the Maserati's one hundred and sixty plus. He eased back down to seventy and looked for a gap in the nearside lane. When it appeared, he eased in. The BMW did the same two cars back.

Well, that settles that, he thought. *But why?*

It really didn't seem to make sense. If they'd been told he was using this road, they must also know he was heading for Scotland. But not many people knew that, and the ones who did were all folk he trusted. And why would these people be following him anyway? Unless they wanted to prevent or delay his arrival at Aullton House so that Lizzie and Angie could be dealt with more easily. But even that didn't make sense. These were just two frightened girls, wounded and scarred by the experiences they'd been subjected to, who only wanted to be left alone.

Heading north, checking frequently in his mirrors, James continued to puzzle over what it was about the two girls that made them worth all this trouble. There had to be something more than Lizzie had been able to tell him. Having learnt something of his pursuers' ruthlessness, he couldn't risk leading them to the person he planned to visit. He had to get rid of them, and quickly.

With Durham now behind him, he wondered briefly about pulling into the Washington service area and waiting for them to follow him in. He had no doubt about being able to deal with his trackers, but there was no telling what state they might be in when he'd finished, nor whether some innocent bystander might choose foolishly to get involved and possibly hurt. And in a public area like that, the whole thing would probably be caught on CCTV anyway. With Chester-le-Street coming up, another plan began slowly to materialise in his mind.

About three miles short of Junction sixty-three, with traffic significantly thinning out, he decided this was his best shot and floored the gas pedal. As before, it took a few seconds for the driver of the BMW to react and, by the time he did, the Maserati was powering up to one hundred miles per hour.

James flicked on his xenon headlights to warn other motorists to keep out of his way. He wanted no unwary driver wandering into his lane. Fortunately this section of the A1 was designated motorway, so the lanes were wide and the surface was good. The BMW was easily two hundred yards behind now and the gap was widening. The one mile sign for Junction sixty-three flashed by and James began to ease off the gas. At his present speed, he would cover that mile in less than half a minute. Fifteen seconds later the half-mile sign flashed by and he eased off some more. He needed to take the exit slip road as fast as possible without getting creamed. He eased left and here it was. Three hundred yards, two hundred, one hundred, and with nothing to get in his way, he swung left and powered up to the roundabout.

The BMW had not reached the exit slip road before James was on the roundabout. The plan was going to work. From here, there were too many directions he could go and, unless they had placed a tracker on his car, they wouldn't know which way to take. A167 south-west, A693 west, A183 south-east, or maybe back onto the A1 north or south. It would even be possible he had taken Picktree Lane north, which was a road James had found himself on many times with Sarah when visiting former college friends of hers in Picktree village.

He swung the Maserati into a right-hand turn, leaving a certain amount of rubber on the road, and ignored the first three exits off the roundabout. Arriving at the fourth, Picktree Lane, he veered left and headed north. Traffic was light and he headed up the lane as fast as he could, overtaking whenever possible. As soon as he reached a junction on his left he turned in and, finding the cul-de-sac divided into two arms, did a quick three-pointer at the end of the right-hand one, to finish up facing back towards the lane.

He waited five minutes. A shadow appeared in the window of the house over to his left. A vigilant home-owner wondering if a visitor was about to show up on his doorstep? When James glanced round, the shape at the window drew back as though it didn't want to be caught peering nosily into the street. He turned forward again to watch the lane at the end of his road.

Occasionally a vehicle passed by, and the view was clear enough and their speed slow enough to be certain that none of them was a BMW X5. No tracker on his Maserati then.

Unless his followers had realised that he had stopped and decided to pull up somewhere down the lane. What was the range of these tracker devices? James realised that he had no idea. They could be sitting down the lane, just waiting for him to set off again. Or they might have assumed that he had arrived at his destination and were closing in on foot to check it out. Or there was no device fixed to his Maserati and he had well and truly lost them. He had no way of knowing without getting out of the car.

He got out and walked down to the corner.

And there they were. The BMW was parked with its wheels up the kerb something over one hundred yards short of the junction. Its windows were just as opaque as before, but this time it didn't matter. About twenty-five yards ahead of the BMW two men were walking steadily towards him. Or they were, until they saw him appear and stand watching them. They stopped at the same moment, the taller man glancing quickly at his companion, and both began reaching beneath their jackets. Then, like James, they looked up and down the lane, taking in the passing vehicles, a mother pushing a child in a buggy, an elderly couple walking a large but nondescript hound, and a group of teenagers in uniform, presumably out of school on their lunch break. Too many eyes for what they had in mind, whatever that was. They stared at James for several moments before retreating back to their car.

He watched them go, wishing he knew what they were up to. The taller man he recognised from the parking lot at Scotch Corner but the second man also, in spite of having been concealed in the car at the service area, was oddly familiar. And it was he who seemed to be in charge. It wasn't much, a slight gesture and inclination of the head, but James was sure it had been his decision to return to their car. Were they just checking on where he stopped and who he spoke to, or were they really intent on preventing him from reaching Aullton House? Whatever their motive they were becoming a serious nuisance and needed dealing with.

Assuming they would now stay put until the Maserati began to move, he decided to risk a few minutes to try and find the tracking device which had kept them so closely on his tail. Under the watchful eye of the nosey neighbour, he crawled around the car feeling the underside wherever someone could have quickly and easily have placed the device. The trouble was that he didn't know exactly what he was looking for. He didn't know its size or shape or how it might be fixed, but in the end it didn't matter. Being unsuccessful on his first scrabble around the car, he opened the passenger door and reached into the glove box for the flashlight he habitually kept there. He didn't need it for, as he leant in, he noticed the upward curve of the bonnet edge behind which sat the windscreen wipers. Between the bonnet and the windscreen there was a gap, not much but enough. At the extreme left hand edge, where it could not impede the travel of the wiper arm, he found it. Stuck to the underside edge of the bonnet with double sided adhesive tape was a small, thin, grey box that was definitely not Maserati standard issue.

He pried it loose and weighed it in his hand. It was easily concealed, both in his hand and also in the spot where he had found it. How many people could have had the opportunity to attach it to his car? He remembered the times recently when it had been left in the hospital car park. He'd seen the movies and knew the standard places to look for tracking devices planted on the outside of a vehicle. The hero crawls around on hands and knees feeling under front and rear valances and up into the wheel arches. He'd just done it himself. But he'd never seen one planted like this in a movie. Of course, the job was made a whole lot easier because the device was so small and slim, and fitting it meant nothing more than a casual touch. No suspicious bending down and pretending to tie shoe laces while feeling underneath the car. Anyone could have done it.

He walked around the front of the car and climbed in, tossing the tracker into the glove box. He gave a brief wave to the shadow in the window and smiled as the figure once more backed away. Too much interest was being taken in him here. It was definitely time to move.

Deciding it might be best to keep clear of the A1 for a while, he resumed his journey north up Picktree Lane intending to make his way round Washington using minor roads. There were any number of industrial estates in the area and he hoped to use these to elude his pursuers and then keep them lost by tossing the tracker in the back of some handy truck or van heading in a completely different direction. If that didn't work, he'd just have to lead them to some secluded area and deal with them the old-fashioned way.

He was still on Picktree Lane when he saw flashing blue lights somewhere up ahead. Certain they could have nothing to do with him, he carried on, keeping within the speed limit, his eye on the approaching police car. No siren suggested stealth rather than urgency. Wondering why it slowed as it passed him, he watched the police car curiously in his mirror. An impressive turn swung the lights through one eighty degrees and the police were right behind him, a sudden blast of siren demanding that the Maserati stop immediately.

Curious but not worried, James eased to a halt, lowered his window and waited. The BMW, which had been in sight but some way behind, had slowed noticeably in the face of the police car's sudden manoeuvre. That in itself was quite natural. Motorists do the oddest things when confronted by fast vehicles with flashing blue lights. To stop and watch or make a U-turn and retreat would not have been natural. As the policemen emerged from their vehicle, the BMW cruised steadily past keeping scrupulously to the speed limit.

One officer stopped at the rear of the Maserati speaking into his radio while the other approached the driver's door. James looked up to see a face shadowed by the peak of the officer's helmet. Sergeant's chevrons gleamed on his shoulders.

"Good afternoon, sir. Could you turn the engine off please?"

Then, after James had complied, "Is this your car, sir?"

Polite, no nonsense, straight to the point, and with a definite Geordie accent.

"Afternoon, sergeant. It is mine, yes."

"Can I see your driving licence, sir?"

James reached for his wallet, extracted the plastic photo-card, and offered it to the policeman who took it and held it up for scrutiny. The officer read it carefully, studied James's face and then looked back to the card. Still holding it, he called his colleague to join him, and held the card so the other officer could read it. He looked from the card to the notebook he held in his hand.

"Hmmm. This car is registered to Aullton Estates," he said slowly, his own accent less pronounced. "Your name is ... ..." he looked again at the licence card ... ... "James Alistair Christopher Montrayne. How do you explain that, sir?"

James began to reach across to the glove compartment but then, seeing both officers stiffen suddenly, thought better of it.

"Is it OK if I reach for my passport?" he asked.

The officer with the notebook said, "Just keep your hands on the steering wheel, sir. I'll get it. In that glove box, is it?"

Going round to the passenger side, he opened the door and reached in. The glove box light came on as soon as he opened it and the burgundy passport was immediately visible where James had tossed it on top of sundry odds and ends. The tracker device was also clearly visible, but the officer paid it no attention.

Both officers studied passport and driving licence. There was silence for a moment, before the sergeant looked in at James and said slowly, "So you are the Earl of Aullton."

It wasn't really a question, but James answered anyway.

"It would certainly seem so."

"Might I ask where you're going, sir... ... er... my Lord?"

"To Aullton House, my estate in Scotland. Do you mind if I take my hands off the steering wheel now?"

"Oh... ...er, yes... ... I guess."

James still hadn't a clue why he'd been stopped. He knew he hadn't been driving erratically, not for the last few minutes anyway, and neither officer had produced a breathalyser kit, or mentioned any other violation such as a dud light. Maybe a camera had caught him topping a hundred on the A1 and the Maserati's number had been circulated. Maybe all sorts of things.

"So," he said politely, "how can I help you, gentlemen?"

The sergeant looked at his colleague as though he was no longer quite so sure of himself.

"Well sir," he said. "This vehicle has been reported as being parked suspiciously in Lintfort."

James had never heard of it, but believed he knew what the officer meant.

"Is that so?" He thought of the shadow at the window. "May I ask who reported it?"

"That's not relevant, sir. Can you confirm you were there?"

"If you're referring to that cul-de-sac back down the road a bit, then yes I was."

"May I ask what you were doing there, sir?"

"Indulging in a brief fit of nostalgia."

The sergeant's mouth dropped open slightly and he glanced back at his colleague. James smiled but decided he needed to move things along a bit.

"Are you married, sergeant?"

As a devoted husband approaching his twenty-fifth wedding anniversary, Sergeant Jim Preston found himself well able to imagine the heartache in the brief story James told him. He heard how James and Sarah had often visited friends in Picktree in the short years of their marriage, the last time being just before Abby was born. After that, there had been no more Sarah, so no more visits. Until today. With an appointment to see a professor at Newcastle University – the constable checked this while James finished his story – it had seemed natural to drive up through Picktree village, remembering all those earlier visits when he'd had Sarah beside him. Already late for his appointment, it would not have been appropriate to call on those friends, particularly as they were Sarah's old college mates not his, but he could not begrudge himself a few minutes pause for nostalgic reflection in a road near to where they lived.

"And why not stop in their road, sir?"

"I didn't want them to see me, sergeant. I'm sure you can understand that."

"Indeed, sir. And could you give me their name and address?"

Something else for the constable to check. James hoped these friends of Sarah's hadn't moved without telling him. But a few minutes later the constable's radio crackled and he nodded to the sergeant.

"It looks as though we've delayed you to no purpose, sir," he said. "I'm sorry about that, but we do have to follow up on these reports."

"Of course you do, sergeant. Now perhaps to make up for it, you'll do me a small favour."

The sergeant looked doubtful. James reached across to replace his passport in the glove box and then opened his car door. As he emerged he looked back towards the police car.

"That's an Evo you've got there, isn't it?"

"It certainly is, sir," replied the sergeant. "A Mitsubishi Evolution VIII. We've got it on loan for a month's trial. Mostly motorway patrol duties. In fact, that's where we were headed when we got the message to... ... er... ... check you out."

"Yes," said James. "I hear they're pretty good for that. Do you mind if I have a quick look?"

When Sergeant Preston hesitated, he continued, "Our Chief Constable down in Staffordshire was telling me how good they are. He's … … er… a good friend of mine."

He smiled briefly but otherwise ignored the constable's muttered, "He bloody well would be."

"Yes, it was only recently that he was telling me about this motor. It's a real beast of a car, isn't it? I think he's wondering whether we ought to introduce them to our force."

"Ah well. As to that, sir, I really couldn't say. We're only just beginning our trial up here, but I'm sure we'd be happy to pass along our conclusions."

James walked slowly towards the police car, drawing the two officers along with him. He made no attempt to open the door, but looked inside taking in the radios, radar camera, computer and a whole range of controls he couldn't identify. He was sure the sergeant was anxious now to be on his way, but he was equally sure that neither officer wanted to offend an innocent member of the aristocracy who clearly had friends in high places. Resting his hand on the light bar, still flashing alternately blue and red, he said, "Thank you so much, sergeant. And please accept my apologies for delaying you."

"Not at all, sir. Have a safe journey."

Removing their caps, both officers climbed back into their vehicle. With the sergeant driving, the Evo executed a neat 3-point turn, and headed south to join the A1 motorway. James hurried back to the Maserati, watched them out of sight in his rear-view mirror and, as soon as they disappeared, pulled a similar 3-pointer to follow a short distance before turning right into the cul-de-sac he had so recently vacated.

Less than a minute later, a black BMW X5 shot across the entrance to his street heading south down Picktree Lane at rather more than the posted speed limit. He wondered if his followers would ever realise that they were now pursuing a high-performance police patrol car with their tracker attached to its light bar.

Twenty-five minutes later, having skirted the city and crossed the River Tyne, he began looking for the A696 to Newcastle airport. The person he needed to see lived in the village of Ponteland about a mile or so past the airport. It was quite handy really, as the A696 would then take him up to the A68 and on to the Lammermuirs and Aullton House. In fact it was this very convenience that had encouraged him to consider calling on Dr Zena Walcott in the first place. That, and the fact that she was a recognised authority on sex trafficking and forced prostitution, particularly when it involved children. Unlike Sarah, with whom she had once shared a house as students, she had never used her teaching degree, but had continued to study, first an MA and then a PhD in *Child*

Protection and the State. Since then, she had contributed to reports for both UNICEF and the Council of Europe.

From soon after meeting Lizzie, James had been aware of a growing suspicion that he was becoming involved in bigger issues than simply keeping her and Angie safe. Now he wanted some facts, and Zena was just the person to provide them.

Sixty-Six

Aullton House – Lunchtime

Abby led on, and I soon found myself in a completely different world, cut off from the rest of the house by a solid, highly-polished, oak door. There were still plush carpets, and paintings, ornaments and expensive looking furniture, but this was a home. People lived here, and relaxed, and played games, and watched TV. Abby whisked me off straight away on a quick tour. There was a large dining room, an even bigger drawing room, a small sitting room, a kitchen as fully equipped and modern as any I'd seen, a cloakroom with plenty of hanging space plus a toilet cubicle and washbasin, and a bathroom fully equipped with shower cubicle, bath, bidet, toilet and two handbasins. On the floor above, there was another bathroom, and five en-suite bedrooms not counting Abby's room in the turret.

I might not have been very impressed with the museum below, but I loved the family apartments. Having discovered my bedroom, formerly Suzanne's, and dumped my small case on the bed, peeped quickly into the back stairs which extended from attics to basement, we retired to the kitchen.

I was suddenly aware, as I searched through the cupboards for something to drink, that there were still just the two of us in the apartment.

"Will any of the others be staying up here?" I asked, thinking of Cherry and Andy. I knew Mike would be leaving soon to pick up some dignitaries from a conference in Glasgow to ferry them back to London.

"Cherry will," said Abby. "He always does when Dad's not here and, last time, Suzanne was here as well. I expect Andy will stay in the guest apartments over the stables. That's what usually happens."

She reached into a cupboard that I hadn't yet ransacked and extracted a carton of fruit juice.

"You can try this," she said. "Mango and apple. It's my favourite."

She poured us both a glass and we retired to the comfort of the drawing room. There must have been seating for up to a dozen people scattered around the room and among them were two large settees, one facing an impressively ornate fireplace, and the other a wall-mounted flat-screen TV. The windows all had wooden shutters, folded to each side, emphasising the thickness of the walls. Set into the embrasure beneath each window was a padded seat.

We opted for one of these, and sat huddled side by side with a view of the whole room so that Abby could point out various portraits and photos, explaining who was who. I was happy to let her chatter on, as long as she didn't ask the one question I was beginning to dread hearing. Why had her dad sent her up here in term time when she should have been in school? I didn't know what James had already told her, or what he would want me to say in response to that or any similar question. I hated the thought that I might say something that would scare her. I'd nearly made a mess of things at breakfast and I didn't want to do it again. I had known her less than a week and already I knew I would do anything to keep her from being hurt.

Just around the time I was starting to wonder what we were going to do about lunch, I heard a noise from the door the end of the corridor.

"Hey guys. Where are you hiding?"

It was Cherry. We told him, and he followed our voices to appear a moment later with backpack over one shoulder and holdall in his hand.

"Well, Lizzie. How do you like it?" he asked, dumping his bags and making for the kitchen.

"A lot," I said to his disappearing back.

"Thought you would," came the slightly muffled reply.

"Course she does," chipped in Abby. "What's not to like?"

I turned and smiled down at her.

"You are one lucky little girl you know," I said.

"I know," she replied, smiling back with her eyes firmly locked on mine. Then the smile faded as she said, "But sometimes, it doesn't feel like it."

I thought of her growing up without her mum, of being kidnapped and traumatised for months, of Suzanne earning her trust and then leaving her, of having a stranger thrust on her out of nowhere, and I realised that although she had everything money could buy, she didn't have everything a child needed. I wondered how she would take it when the time came for me to leave.

I didn't know what to say to her, but she saved me the trouble of struggling for a reply by punching me lightly on the arm and saying, "And I'm not so *little* if you don't mind."

"Oh dear, has Lizzie been insulting you?"

Cherry emerged from the kitchen with a large glass of something dark and amber. Lager maybe. He took a sip.

"Now then, ladies. We have a choice. The tearoom here isn't open since the house is closed today, so it's either the restaurant up at the golf club, or we raid Freddy's freezer and make ourselves something here. What'll it be?"

Abby pouted as she weighed the choices. I sat quietly, leaving it up to her. According to a brochure I'd glanced at, there was another option but, since Cherry hadn't offered the Aullton Garden Centre restaurant, I decided not to mention it.

"Couldn't we go down to the pub in the village," she asked eventually. "They do wicked fish and chips, and they don't give you those horrid mushy peas."

Cherry wasn't keen.

"Lovely idea, sweetie," he said, "but I think your dad wanted us to stay on the estate until he gets here."

"But the village is on the estate," she argued, adding as a clincher, "Daddy owns it."

My mouth dropped and I couldn't help blurting out, "Your dad owns a village."

"Well," she said, temporising a little, "not exactly all of it. Some people wanted to buy their houses and Daddy let them. But he still owns a lot of it... ... including the pub." She looked triumphantly at Cherry, "So it is on the estate."

I thought I could see Cherry's point. The golf club was presumably on the estate somewhere, but its restaurant would have a more restricted clientele than the pub in the village. That was probably why he hadn't mentioned the garden centre. I couldn't believe we were still in danger so far from Birmingham, but Cherry obviously preferred to take few chances. There was also another reason for not going too far from the house, a reason which I thought Abby would probably understand better.

"We really ought to stay close to the house because we don't know just when Angie will get here. It wouldn't be nice for her if we weren't here to meet her."

Abby gave a quick pout, and then shrugged. She got the point.

"So when will she get here?" she asked Cherry.

Before he could answer her, we were disturbed by the sound of a phone ringing.

He put down his glass on a low table and reached for his mobile. It was obviously James, but we couldn't learn much from Cherry's end of the conversation since, apart from confirming that we were safely settled and that Andy had secured some extra help, he spent most of the time just listening. Abby reached out for the phone asking to talk to her dad, but Cherry appeared not to notice and kept it glued to his ear. Eventually, he placed it on the table next to his glass without offering it to Abby.

She put on her sulky look which, I was beginning to learn, was usually just an act, but she dropped it as soon as Cherry began to speak.

"Your dad's going to ring you after his lunch with Professor Walcott. After that, it'll take him about a couple of hours to get here."

"That's great," squeaked Abby in excitement. "He can take us to see the llamas before dinner."

"He certainly can," replied Cherry. "But we could take Lizzie to see them ourselves, if you like. Pass the time while we wait for your dad to get here."

Abby pondered this, weighing the benefits of waiting against the pleasure of seeing her favourite animals sooner.

"We might miss daddy calling me."

Abby had already told me that cell phone reception was usually OK around the house but could be a bit erratic on certain parts of the estate, so James would almost certainly try ringing the landline to the house.

"No," said Cherry, "because we won't go 'till after he's called."

That seemed to satisfy her, but I thought back to her original question.

"So when will Angie get here? Did James say? Did he know?"

Cherry nudged a chair round so it was facing us and settled himself down.

"The air ambulance James hired is already on its way. I don't know just how Angie is, but she's obviously fit enough to travel. I guess, by the time we've had lunch, she should be here. Which reminds me. We haven't decided yet what we're going to eat."

I thought it was about time I contributed something.

"Well, we seem to have decided we're going to eat in so why don't we go and see what we can scrounge from Freddy?"

There was no argument. In the light of James's phone call the three of us were content to settle for whatever we could find in Freddy's freezer.

That turned out to be salmon fishcakes and spicy potato wedges, all baked in the oven, and served with various salad trimmings and coleslaw. Andy didn't join us, as I'd thought he might, but Cherry said he was going to meet someone. Before we knew that James would be joining us so soon, Andy had phoned a contact in Edinburgh who was in a similar line of work. It seemed he wanted someone else on hand to help out, "just in case" as Cherry put it. "We do have to sleep, you know."

We ate with trays on our knees in front of the television. We couldn't agree on which channel to watch so Abby was allowed her choice of DVD. It was a film called *While You Were Sleeping* with Sandra Bullock playing a young woman whose parents were dead, living on her own, and desperately wishing she could be part of a family. A bit too close to home for me.

We were just getting to the weepy bit where Sandra Bullock, as Lucy, was spending a belated Christmas with the family when we heard the sound of a helicopter approaching. Relieved, I got up and walked quickly to the window overlooking the front lawn. Angie was here. We were together again, and safe.

Except that we weren't.

The danger was probably greater than it ever had been, because we had not the remotest inkling where it would come from.

Sixty-Seven

Lichfield Tube – Lunchtime

Gordon Russell had not been at home when Joanne Hayford called at his stone-built detached home in Elmford Cross the previous evening. His wife Judith had answered the door with a glass in her hand and Joanne was fairly sure that the clear liquid it contained was not water. This impression was enhanced by the way Mrs Russell's dark blue evening gown was slipping from one shoulder thus diminishing some of its elegance. Since this visit was definitely off the books, Joanne had not introduced herself as a police office. She had simply enquired if Mr Russell was home.

"Chance 'd be a fine thing," slurred Mrs Russell, waving her glass vaguely. "Hardly ever see him these days. If it's not work, it's school. And for weeks now it's been thish shod… … sodding election."

Joanne looked puzzled.

"I didn't know he was a candidate."

Mrs Russell looked at her blankly for a moment, and then when she did reply the words came out slowly as though she was trying very hard not to slur them.

"He isn't. But he likes to think he's a good little party member, so he's got to do his bit to get super-boss into parliament."

"Super-boss?"

"Lord High-and-Mighty Laycock. Owner of all he surveys, including my husband. And a future Prime Minister. Least… … that's what Gordie says."

"Is that where he is tonight? Out campaigning?"

Mrs Russell took a long drink from her glass and then looked at it frowning as though she wondered where the contents had gone.

She waved the empty glass at Joanne and asked, "Are you thirshty?"

"Er… … no, thank you, Mrs Russell."

"Hmm… … Good thing. Bottle's empty… … Must find a new one."

She turned away to begin her search, took two steps and then slowly twisted round, reaching out for the hallway wall for support.

"Did you ask me something?"

"I just wondered if your husband was out campaigning."

"Oh no… … No… no… no. Tonight's the school's turn. Emer… … Emerg… … Emergency governors' meeting… … Headteacher's been a naughty boy… … Do you want to help me find that bottle?"

Joanne was beginning to wonder if she was safe to be left on her own so, with some reluctance, she followed her tottering hostess into the house closing the substantial front door quietly behind her.

It was over two hours later that she finally emerged, her brain buzzing with what she had learnt. She had discovered far more than she could ever have expected. The only trouble was she didn't know what to do with it. Interrogating a potential witness while that person was drunk, and while she herself was officially on leave, and without formally identifying herself to the witness at the outset, was not likely to win her any brownie points, in spite of the fact that what she now knew could blow the whole case wide open.

Joanne had salved her own conscience by persuading Mrs Russell let her make a pot of coffee instead of opening a new bottle, but she couldn't deny that Judith's relaxed and confiding frame of mind was very much alcohol induced. Her revealing confidences were also prompted by resentment at the fact that she had been stood up on the evening when she and her husband were supposed to be dining out in celebration of their wedding anniversary.

Glad to escape before Mr Russell returned from his governors' meeting, Joanne suggested to Judith that it might be better if she didn't mention to him that she'd had a visitor that evening.

"He won't ask... ... Won't tell him 'cos not interested... ... Never is... ... You... you good listener... ... good friend... ...very good friend... ... Wash your name again?"

Joanne had told her, but with every confidence that she would have totally forgotten it by morning. She had left Mrs Russell curled up on the sofa which she had occupied all evening, drifting into what promised to be a sound sleep. Moving away from the sofa anything that might cause injury if Judith should happen to roll off, Joanne had crept away.

She hadn't gone far.

She parked her car a short distance away, on the opposite side of the street, where she could watch the driveway of Russell's house. She had barely begun to review all that she had been told, when Russell's Mazda 6 cruised past her and swung sharply into the drive entrance. She breathed a heartfelt sigh of relief that she'd left the house when she did. There was barely time for Judith to have stirred. No need to hang around longer.

Returning home, it had taken Joanne well into the early hours of the morning to record, review and collate everything she now knew about all the circumstances surrounding Phil Simmons' death. Once that was done, she was still left with the problem of what to do with it. Even if she were able to get Morrissey to listen to her, he would just rubbish the information as the unsubstantiated ramblings of a drunk which, to some extent, they were.

There was no help for it but to try for some form of corroboration which meant making another attempt to interview Gordon Russell. She just hoped that Mrs Russell had stuck to what she had said about not telling her husband about her visit.

Deciding not to set her alarm, she slept for seven hours, waking a little after nine o'clock. She treated herself to an unhurried shower before dressing in the jacket and skirt which she'd had dry cleaned after her romp in the woods on Saturday. They had actually recovered rather well and, accompanied by a faintly-patterned, pale blue blouse, looked rather good on her that morning. She took care over her makeup, something she was often a little careless about on a normal workday. She didn't know whether this would carry any weight with Gordon Russell, but there was no harm in trying. Finally, realising that it was a long time since she'd last eaten anything, she made herself some scrambled egg on toast and sat on the bar stool at her kitchen counter to eat it.

All through these preparations, her mind was busy trying to formulate a plan of action which might have some chance of success. Everything was a risk. Continuing on her own while on enforced leave in direct contravention of Morrissey's orders could ruin the possibility of a successful prosecution. Any evidence she obtained would be tainted and probably inadmissible in court. Going to Morrissey with what she had would probably result in her being hauled up on disciplinary charges for disobeying his direct orders. Going over his head, maybe to Detective Chief Superintendent Hilton, might get a result while at the same time putting a complete blight on her further career chances. Nobody liked a maverick who couldn't be trusted to be loyal to the team.

But there was another possibility. Still a risk, but one that might just come down on her side. Slowly she pushed her empty plate away and reached for her coffee mug. As she drained the now lukewarm brew, she again reviewed her options, and came to the same conclusion. She picked up her mobile phone which was lying on the counter and began to scroll through its directory. She found the number she needed and paused, holding her breath while she thought through her opening words. She pressed the call button.

ACC Fletcher was in his office and, yes, he would take her call. She let out her breath in a rush, not realising she held it so long, and waited for him to come on the line.

"Sergeant Hayford. I heard you were on leave. What can I do for you?"

She heard the coolness in his voice and was very much aware of how many levels in the hierarchy she had leapfrogged to come direct to him. He probably thought she was now presuming too much on his friendly manner the previous day.

It took a while to take him through everything that had happened since she had left his office. He asked a number of questions and twice put her on hold for several minutes. His tone of voice warmed as he became intrigued by her theories but this did little to reduce her level of anxiety. He held her career in his hands and they both knew it. When she had finished, he put her on hold again, this time for so long that she began to check her battery level and wonder where she had hidden her charger.

Eventually, she heard a click and he came back on the line.

"Sergeant Hayford, you are no longer on leave. I have told DCI Morrissey that, since he has no need of you at present, you have been seconded to my office for liaison duties. He was wise enough not to ask what that meant. Now, you will go and talk to Mr Russell as soon as possible, but you must take another officer with you. If you run into any difficulty over that, have a word with DCS Hilton. I'll let him know you're working for me. If you think you find grounds for a search warrant, let me know. If you want to bring Russell in for questioning, talk to me first. Remember, this is a fishing expedition, not a bust. OK? And, Sergeant... ... you'd better be right. There's going to be an almighty stink however this plays out, so don't let me down."

She didn't intend to, so she thought very carefully about whom to take with her. Young PC Mayblin would have been her first choice. She knew she could trust him, if only because of how much he fancied her. But he was tied to Morrissey and there was no getting round that. In fact, everyone she thought of, and there weren't many, came under someone else's authority, and she couldn't just borrow them without explanation. Except... ... She reached for her phone.

They arrived at the gates of Lichfield Tube Company just before twelve, hoping to catch Gordon Russell before he stopped and maybe left for his lunch break, assuming he ate lunch. The security guard on the gate couldn't take his eyes off Joanne's companion as they flashed him their IDs. They could have been waving Blockbuster membership cards for all he knew. His directions to visitor parking were almost inarticulate, and his eyes continued to linger on the passenger seat of the Focus as he regretfully raised the barrier to let them through.

Georgie Baxter could have strutted the catwalks or topped the bill at a pop concert – she had the looks and the voice – but she wasn't interested. Her dad had been a police superintendent with the Met, and she had never wanted any other life than to follow in his footsteps. She had sailed through the police college at Hendon to the frustration of less talented trainees who convinced themselves that her flawless skin and perfect figure were the currency of her success. They were wrong, but she hadn't cared enough for their opinion to try and persuade them of that.

Now she was a newly appointed detective constable in her first year of the High Potential Development Scheme, which is how she had crossed paths with Joanne Hayford, also an HPDS candidate. After her dad suffered his first heart attack while she was at Hendon, her parents had decided to move to Lichfield where they had spent their early years of married life. When a second attack left her mum a widow, Georgie had decided to apply to the Staffordshire force so she could take care of her mum in her old Georgian house on the outskirts of the city. It turned out that Mum didn't need as much looking after as she had thought, so Georgie was now taking a week's annual leave to decorate and move into a new apartment not too far from where her mum was living. Since she had been painting since Saturday, and the new carpets weren't due until Friday, Georgie was glad of the chance to put down her brushes and get back to something normal for a while, like chasing down villains.

The matronly lady guarding the Reception desk was clearly unimpressed by either their charms or their identity. However, the young man sent down to escort them to Gordon Russell's office could not disguise his awe and admiration. Georgie wasn't officially on duty so she had gone for a fairly relaxed dress code. She was wearing a black pant suit which would normally be fine for a female detective constable except that this one featured a soft drape tailored jacket with a waterfall front. The matching trousers ended in a wide floating flair which almost hid her shoes, and sported small velvet covered buttons all down the outside seams. Her blouse was a luxuriant scarlet whose wide lapels overflowed her jacket, being open at the throat, and for some distance below that.

The young man, after swallowing several times, introduced himself simply as David. *Don't people have last names anymore?* Joanne didn't warm to this modern trend for informality. David was Gordon's personal assistant. He made it sound as though he was so much more than general dogsbody, which Joanne might have believed if he hadn't looked as though he was still waiting to buy his first razor.

His drooling admiration of Georgie gave Joanne an idea, but she was unable to pass this on to her colleague with David sticking so close, presumably intoxicating himself with her perfume. He opened a door for them to pass through and, when Georgie brushed against him as she entered, Joanne could have sworn his legs actually wobbled.

It was obvious that David would have dearly liked to remain with the visitors but Mr Russell swiftly banished him from the office. He seemed less impressed than his young assistant, but nevertheless he smiled as he invited them to be seated.

"I wasn't really expecting another visit from the police," he said, settling himself on the other side of his desk. "I'm sure I've already told your colleagues everything I can."

"Thank you for seeing us, Mr Russell," said Joanne as she sat down, taking her notebook from her bag as she did so. She wriggled slightly when she discovered that the office chair was not as comfortable as it looked. Her mouth twitched as she noticed Georgie doing the same.

"Er… …yes," replied Russell with a smile of apology. "Sorry about the chairs. I just had them brought up from the canteen. The offices have been redecorated, and we're still waiting for some of the new furniture to arrive."

The two police officers looked around, as it seemed they were expected to do, taking in the canvas block prints on the freshly painted mushroom coloured walls. The only one she could identify was a submarine. All the others seemed to be industrial sites of some sort.

"All installations which use our products," said Russell. "That's HMS Vanquish, currently at Devonport for a refit, and over there is one of the early desalination plants in Abu Dhabi. We're hoping to be successful with our tender for the new one planned for Dubai. 9000MW capacity power and desalination, producing 600 Million gallons of desalinated water per day. And there… …" He paused and pursed his lips. "Well… … that's not what you're here for is it?"

"No, sir."

Joanne had been scribbling as he was talking but now she stopped and passed the sheet of notes to Georgie.

"I should tell you, Mr Russell, that I called at your house yesterday evening but, unfortunately, you were out at a meeting."

"Really?" he replied. "Well… …yes, I was out. School governors' meeting. It's all very unfortunate, James Montrayne getting mixed up in this Phil Simmons business. My house, you said? Strange. Judith never mentioned that anyone had called."

Breathing a quiet sigh of relief, Joanne said, "Not too surprising, sir. I didn't even have time to say I was from the police before your wife told me you were out at a meeting."

So far as it went, that was perfectly true, and fortunately Russell seemed to accept it without question.

"Ah, I see. Well, you're certainly persistent so perhaps you'd better tell me how I can help you."

"Thank you, sir. But before I do, perhaps I can help you. May I suggest that you don't believe everything that you read in the papers?"

Joanne wondered if there was anything more than surprise in that widening of the eyes. Had Riddings been right after all.

"The papers," said Russell. "I assume you mean the Lichfield Daily News? Well, I don't believe everything, of course. Are you referring to the stories about James?"

"I can't really comment on Mr Montrayne, sir, as I'm sure you'll understand. I would just advise caution until all the facts are known."

She knew this was coming out as rather pompous police-speak, and decided to try and tone it down a bit as she changed tack.

"I was wondering just what Mr Simmons was involved in during those last few weeks before he died?"

Russell frowned.

"Involved in, sergeant? I'm not quite sure I know what you mean. Unless you're thinking of the school visit."

From the blank look on her face, he guessed that wasn't it, but he went on to explain anyway.

"It was only a few days before he died. He arranged for James Montrayne and a party of children to look around the works."

Joanne hadn't heard about this.

"Did he, though? Was there anything special about that?"

"No, not at all. It's become a regular thing, since I joined the board of Governors, for the Year Sixes to come and have a look round at some point in the year."

"I see. Well what I was really asking about were the projects Mr Simmons was working on? Anything secret or … …"

At this point, Georgie butted in, uncrossing her legs and addressing herself to Russell.

"Excuse me, Mr Russell, but I wonder if your assistant… … er… … David, was it? Do you think he might be persuaded to give me a quick tour? Just so I can get a feel for the place where Mr Simmons worked. Would that be OK, Sarge?"

Joanne was just nodding her consent when Russell asked, "A tour of the works? Would that help, do you think?"

Georgie gave him her best pearly-white smile.

"We can never be sure what will help, sir. Until it does."

As Georgie disappeared to find David in obedience to the scribbled note that Joanne had passed to her, Russell watched her go. Joanne tried to read the expression in his eyes but, in the end, couldn't make her mind up whether it was admiration of Georgie's rear view or anxiety about what she might find out.

"Mr Russell, I was asking about the projects Mr Simmons was involved in. Was there anything of a… … sensitive nature?"

He seemed to think about this for a while, making a show of looking at a large wall-planner to the left of his office door. Slowly, he shook his head.

"Not really. I mean, there's the usual business confidentiality… … we don't tell everyone what we're working on or what we're tendering for… … especially what we're tendering for. And it's true we do some work for the MOD or, occasionally, even foreign governments, but we're not building secret weapons or anything like that."

Joanne glanced at one of the photographs on the wall to her left.

"I think you said something about tendering for a new project in Dubai. I assume that would be worth a great deal of money to your company."

He gave her a look which she'd seen countless times before. It was the eyes, she thought, always the eyes that gave it away. Good liars could hide it, but most people were not good liars. Russell was wondering whether to spin her a line or come clean and his hesitation served only to draw attention to it with several exclamation points.

"Actually, sergeant, it is our parent company, Ferro-Tech, who are submitting the tender. We are down as a subcontractor for the supply of the tubes, particularly the seamless copper-nickel." He smiled. "And yes, the contract will mean a great deal of money for Ferro-Tech, and a not insubstantial profit for ourselves."

Joanne smiled back. It wouldn't have been a big lie then, just the slight blurring of the truth by someone who wanted to appear more significant then he really was. Ferro-Tech were the big boys and Lichfield Tube the also-rans, not nearly as high in the power stakes as Russell would like to be. It wouldn't do any harm to butter him up a little.

"Mr Russell, I'm just a lowly copper, so I don't know much about the business world, but it seems to me that it must take a high degree of shrewdness and expertise to make a company like Lichfield Tube a success these days. I mean, even I've heard about tube mills closing down – a friend of mine used to work for one in Birmingham – and the news talks about metal prices going up and cheap imports coming in from India and China. I admire you, I really do. Making a success of manufacturing in these difficult times."

Russell sat a little straighter in his chair. Every middle-aged man liked to be admired, especially when the admiration was coming from someone who looked like Joanne Hayford.

"I suspect, sergeant, that you're not quite the lowly copper you make yourself out to be."

"Well, time will tell on that one, sir. But I wonder, and I hope you'll forgive me asking this, with all the pressure there has to be on you and, of course, on Mr Simmons as well until recently, to keep your business going… … well, what I'm wondering is whether anyone has tried to push you into… … shall we say, going down paths you would not naturally choose?"

She deliberately phrased the question as vaguely as possible since Judith Russell had not been able to tell her who had been pressuring her husband, or why. Only that somebody was, and it had been causing Gordon some sleepless nights.

"I'm not sure what you're getting at, sergeant."

His tone was still amiable, and it seemed as though he was making light of her question, but she had been watching his eyes. And there it was again. She would be hard put to describe what she saw, but she knew he was getting ready to lie.

"Sir, you've just told me that some of the deals you make are worth a lot of money to the company. If profits are good, then I assume dividends and bonuses are also good. But you and I both know that where there's money to be made, there are also corners to be cut, sometimes corners that shouldn't be cut. So… …"

When Russell interrupted, all trace of amiability had gone."

"Are you trying to accuse my company of some kind of fraud?"

"No, sir, I'm not. But if someone who might stand to gain was trying to put pressure on Mr Simmons, and yourself, and maybe others, and if Mr Simmons was refusing to cooperate, and if this someone thought that Mr Simmons had learned more than was good for him, then it might give a reason for having him killed."

Russell's eyes wandered to the pictures on the wall as he thought over what she had said. Joanne continued to look at him steadily, but his gaze remained fixed on the desalination plant. Eventually, and still without looking at her, he said, "There are a whole lot of *ifs* in that, sergeant."

"Yes, sir, there are," replied Joanne candidly. "But am I right?"

His chair swivelled slightly as he turned to face her. *Is this going to be his honest and earnest look?* thought Joanne.

"You could well be right, sergeant. Unfortunately, I have no way of knowing one way or the other. If Phil Simmons was being pressured… …blackmailed… … threatened… …whatever, I have to tell you that I knew nothing of it. However, I can tell you definitely that no-one has tried to threaten or pressurise me."

Although his mouth twitched into a smile, it didn't climb far enough up his face to take away the hooded wariness in his eyes.

"Does that answer your question, sergeant?"

Joanne returned his smile and said, "Yes, sir, I think it does."

To herself she thought, *This creep is lying through his teeth.*

Sensing that there was nothing more to be gained from pressing him further, Joanne closed her notebook and replaced it in her bag.

"I wonder if you could find out where David has taken my colleague and have her meet me in reception?"

Trying hard, but not entirely succeeding, to hide his relief, Russell stood and came round the desk to shake her hand.

"I'd be glad to, sergeant. Er... ...can you find your own way, or should I get someone to take you down?"

Don't want to take me yourself in case I put you on the spot again.

"I'll be fine, sir. I'm sure I can remember the way."

She could hear him trying to get David on the phone as she closed his office door behind her. She hoped she had given Georgie enough time. In the end, she assumed she hadn't since she was kept waiting in Reception for nearly fifteen minutes before the pair of them appeared. She spent the time sitting at a low table whose surface was covered by a variety of trade journals scattered rather haphazardly, presumably due to the browsing of previous bored visitors. She started browsing herself, idly flipping pages while she waited. There was nothing in the magazines to interest her so her mind drifted back to the interview with Russell. Had she been right not to show him the photograph from the rifle club? She might have learned something but, on the other hand, if Russell had recognised the man, there was a good chance he'd deny it, and she would have shown her hand to no advantage. She tossed the magazine back on the table to join the others, and as they moved slightly something caught her eye.

It was different from the rest. It was spiral bound, with a clear plastic sheet for its cover. She realised that it was Lichfield Tubes' company brochure. She glanced around to see whether there was any sign of Georgie yet and, when there wasn't, she reached to pick it up.

Under the plastic cover, the first page showed the company name, as though formed from brass-coloured tubes, emblazoned across a photo-mosaic of what Joanne assumed were the company's prestige customers. She recognised some of the pictures from Russell's office. She began to turn the pages and then her fingers froze. She stared unblinking for several seconds before a slow smile began to lift the corner of her mouth.

She was looking at the page which introduced the company's senior personnel, and there he was, staring up at her from the bottom left-hand corner beside a caption which read *Senior Field Inspector – Mitchell Portess*. It was not a large photo, but the image was sharp and clear. Even before she pulled the rifle club photo from her bag, she had no doubt it was the same man.

She and the matriarch at the desk, whose nameplate read *Mrs Roberta Driscoll,* were still the only occupants in Reception, so Joanne stayed in her seat as she asked her question, making her voice sound as casual as possible.

"Do you know if Mitchell Portess is here today?"

A raised eyebrow accompanied the tapping of a keyboard before Mrs Driscoll replied.

"I'm sorry. Mr Portess has been out of the country for the past few days."

Damn! thought Joanne. *Maybe he's not our guy after all. But where was he on Saturday?*

Still trying to sound casual, she said, "I suppose his job must take him all over the place."

"It certainly does, but Lithuania is one of his regulars."

"Is that where he is now?"

"Yes. He flew out to Vilnius first thing on Monday. Should be back later this afternoon, but I don't think we'll see him in the works today."

Joanne smiled her thanks and reached for her mobile to call Georgie and tell her to get a move on. No need. The phone was hardly out of her bag when Georgie appeared with David panting hard on her heels.

Spotting Joanne, she turned to her worshipper and held out her hand.

"David, you're an angel. I've learnt so much, and you explained it all so clearly."

Mrs Driscoll's eyebrows suggested surprise that David could explain anything.

Joanne knew that Georgie could gush flattery with the best of them, but it was almost embarrassing to watch the young man lingering over the handshake and mumbling incoherently.

"Georgie, let's go."

It was time to compare notes, and maybe prepare a reception for Mitchell Portess – Senior Field Engineer.

Sixty-Eight

Thurvaston Arms – Mid-afternoon

Apart from the young couple whom John had seen crossing the lawn earlier in the morning, there was no-one else in the bar when they entered. Not a great surprise really, as the grandfather clock in the corner showed it had already gone two o'clock. They decided on a table by the window overlooking the front lawn and sat to examine the lunch menu. Fortunately, they hadn't left it too late this time. Lunch was served until two-thirty. They made their selections, ordered at the bar, and then sat sipping their drinks thoughtfully while they waited for the food.

Their relationship had changed, they both knew that. A line had been crossed and there was no way back, and each was utterly content. Their hands were on the table, close but not touching, holding glasses and fiddling with beer mats. Alone, they would have reached out, clasping, caressing, but they were not alone. The young couple from the morning were finishing their lunch at a table nearby.

John and Nadera were both wondering what they should do next in their search for Raymond Mellisse, when suddenly John stiffened. His gaze had drifted momentarily out to the garden and his eyes were resting on the statue in the lawn. At first it had seemed like just another Greek god in a fountain but then its shape gradually made a connection with something in his subconscious.

"What is it, John?"

It was her hand reaching out to rest on his which drew his attention, rather than her words.

"You see that statue?"

She looked across the grass, still failing to see what had excited him.

"It's Pan, Nadera… … Or, at least, I think it is. Those are horns on its head, aren't they? And I'll bet you anything those things in his hand are pan pipes."

She was totally confused, and the waiter arrived to find the pair of them gazing out through the window. As he set their plates on the table, John looked up at him.

"The fountain out there… … It is Pan, isn't it?"

The waiter tried not to look bored. It was coming to the end of his shift.

"I really couldn't say, sir. Would you like me to find out?"

"Yes… … Oh, hang it. No. It doesn't really matter."

The waiter left, but the male half of the young couple turned to face them.

"Sorry. Couldn't help overhearing, but you are right. It is Pan. Horns, pipes, goat's feet, and all."

"Oh, thanks," replied John, a little disconcerted now to have attracted such attention. He glanced once more out of the window.

"John."

Nadera squeezed his hand, and a slow smile began to crease his eyes as he turned back to her.

"The Wind in the Willows, Nadera. That gold design on the cover… in the icon. It was Pan, I'll bet you anything."

"So… …" She clearly wasn't following.

"Pan," he explained, "was the Greek god of the countryside. Shepherds, shepherdesses, all that sort of thing."

"OK, but… …"

"No, hang on. Just listen… … Pan was famed for his sexual prowess, and in pictures and… …" he glanced out of the window again, "er… … statues he usually has a rather large… … well, you know… …"

"He does, too." Their helpful fellow guest was still watching them. "We noticed it this morning, didn't we sweetie?"

Sweetie grinned but said nothing.

"And did you know," he went on, with a smile and a wink at Sweetie, "there's a statue somewhere, Naples I think, which shows our friend Pan with his big… … you know… … enthusiastically rogering a goat?"

"No," said John, "I didn't know that, and I almost wish I still didn't."

Nadera frowned at him across the table, and began picking at her salad. He took the hint, nodded to the couple, and began tucking into his fish and chips. The other two left the bar a few minutes later, Sweetie winking at John as she passed their table. He tried to ignore her, but couldn't help turning to watch her progress out of sight.

He turned back to find Nadera watching him quizzically, a slight smile curving her lips.

"I was just watching to make sure they'd gone," he said defensively.

"Of course you were," she said, her smile widening. "Now, tell me more about this Pan, and I don't mean the statues."

As they cleared their plates and progressed to cups of coffee, John developed his theory. He could be wrong, of course, as he said several times until Nadera threatened to pour the cooling contents of her cup over his head if he didn't get on with it.

The icon that led nowhere was Pan, he was sure of it, and if it was Pan then it had to have been chosen for a reason. Whatever else the god Pan was renowned for, sex was well up the list, and made complete sense in the context of what they had already learnt about Raymond Mellisse. Those icons were almost certainly not the dead-ends they appeared to be, and every one of those businesses where one appeared was probably a means of laundering the money he made from the sex business. Not the legitimate clubs, of course, since that income was kosher and didn't need laundering. But the trafficking and the pimping and the prostitution were definitely not legal, and the money had to go somewhere.

"Now," said John, "last night you heard Montrayne say something about some kind of dirty dealings going on at Lichfield Tube?"

Nadera nodded. "Dirty financial dealings, I think he said."

"Yes… … Well just suppose it wasn't financial. Nothing to do with fraud, or dodgy accounting, or bribery or anything at all like that. Suppose Lichfield Tube is that Lithuanian pipeline he was talking about. You know. Girls coming for office jobs and ending up in brothels or whatever. And suppose Phil Simmons found out about it. I knew him. He was a good lad. He'd never have stood for anything like that."

"That's a lot of supposing, John."

"I know. But if it's true, it gives Mellisse one hell of a motive for getting Phil out of the way."

Nadera pushed back her chair.

"I think we need to have another look at those websites. And then, perhaps, we should pay Mr Mellisse a visit and ask him a few polite questions."

As they got up to leave the table, Nadera paused, her brow creasing, and she turned for one last look at the statue in the garden.

Still gazing out of the window, she smiled as she said, "John, what was the name of that company Mellisse has based at Birmingham airport?"

He thought for a moment as his eyes followed hers, and then he too began to smile.

"Pan bloody European Solutions," he said. "Pan… … The cheeky bastard advertises his sordid business to the world, and nobody takes a blind bit of notice."

"Except us," said Nadera, turning away from the window.

"Yes," replied John. "Except us."

Sixty-Nine

Scottish Border – Late afternoon

Dr Zena Walcott had been taken quite by surprise when James had asked if he could call in for a visit. It was unusual, it was impulsive and it was inconvenient, but there really was very little she would not choose to cancel to make time for him. Her enthusiasm had dipped slightly when she learnt that the reason for the visit was not entirely social, and she had been wondering all morning why James had suddenly developed an interest in sex trafficking. It couldn't have been Sarah's doing as she had died some years ago now, and James had never raised the matter in the years since.

Although, after training to be teachers, her career path had veered away from Sarah's, the two of them had continued to remain firm friends. Sarah had always shown interest in Zena's work, even to the extent of proof-reading her report to UNICEF while she was pregnant with Abby. Their rapport had faltered briefly following Sarah's engagement to James, because of what Zena later admitted to be her own unfounded prejudice. He was a member of the military which, in one respect at least, she could not hold in high regard. She knew only too well from her research studies into the abuse of women and children, just how frequently military personnel of all countries made use of the services of prostitutes, especially when serving abroad. What angered Zena was that these servicemen, for the most part, seemed unconcerned about how many of the girls who serviced their needs were coerced, threatened, or even beaten into submission. And how many of them ever wondered whether the girls were under age? How many of them even preferred it if they were?

She had met James determined to dislike him, but her disapproval had failed to last even half way through the meal that Sarah had prepared for the three of them. Her attitude had changed so radically during the course of the evening that, after James had left and the two were preparing for bed, Sarah had teased her about how quickly she had developed a soft spot for her fiancé. She wished she hadn't when she saw the vivid blush creep over Zena's face.

Nothing more was ever said, but over the years Sarah became convinced that Zena's regard for James was more than just a soft spot. She even began to wonder whether this was the reason why her friend never married, although Zena herself always put it down to her rather jaundiced view of men acquired through her work.

Whatever the reason, Zena seemed comfortable with her singleness and threw herself heartily into her work. When she needed a change of scene, or some peace and quiet to write up her research papers, she would come to visit for a day or two or even a week or two, with never a trace of awkwardness in her manner. After Sarah's death, her visits continued their erratic pattern. James was aware of Sarah's thoughts about Zena, and had been a little concerned that she might try to take advantage of Sarah's disappearance from the scene. She never had, and his uneasiness about her continued visits gradually died away. Eventually he began to look forward to her coming, for Abby's sake more than his own, because he saw how much his growing daughter loved to play and talk with her "Aunt" Zena.

So it was that Zena, though slightly puzzled, had been pleased to see him, until he had begun to explain more fully exactly what had prompted this sudden visit. Then she became fearful for his and Abby's safety, and she begged him to take care what he was doing. She warned him that he had no idea what he was getting mixed up in and when he willingly accepted this, she began to go into great detail which was exactly the reason why he'd come to her in the first place.

At first, the name Alexei Borisov had meant nothing to her. She was, however, meticulous in the storage and presentation of her records which extended back over many years and were all fully cross-referenced. It didn't take much searching for the Russian's name to popup in a footnote to an Interpol report on Trafficking in Human Beings. The note was not part of the official report, but had been added by a former colleague of Professor Walcott's who had been working for Eurojust at The Hague since 2003. A quick phone call had discovered Sally Hacker in her office. She had been following Borisov's activities ever since he flew into Vilnius in 2003, a few months after she had taken up her post with Eurojust. She had been more than happy to give the professor a quick summary of her knowledge of him.

Borisov was always described as Russian, although he might just as well be referred to as Lithuanian since that was the country of his birth. He had never been charged by officials of law enforcement in either country, nor was there a record of his ever having been interviewed, in spite of there being weighty suspicions of his being involved in all manner of illegal activities usually involving the exploitation and trafficking of women and young girls. No witness had ever been persuaded to testify against him. Those who were unwilling had never been persuaded to change their minds, and those who might have been willing simply disappeared. He was not a brilliant schemer, as others in the so-called Russian mafia were known to be, but he was a cunning pragmatist, more ruthless than he was courageous.

When James eventually drove away some three hours later, he knew a lot more than he really wanted to about the world Lizzie was trying to escape from. He knew, for instance, that over twenty-five thousand women and girls had already been trafficked into the UK to service the booming sex trade, with at least two thousand new victims arriving every year. He knew that the trade world-wide was estimated to be worth at least £5.5 billion a year to the many gangs and individuals running the business. He could see where the money came from when Zena told him about the case of one girl whom she had interviewed only two months earlier. The girl was only fifteen and she had come to England from Lithuania after being promised a holiday job the previous summer. She had hoped to work as a waitress in a hotel restaurant, but as soon as her new boss had confiscated her passport, she was taken to an entirely different sort of establishment where she was forced to have sex with as many as thirty men a day, seven days per week. She had been sold on for four figure sums at least five times – the girl was so traumatised she had lost count – eventually ending up in Newcastle where she had at last escaped to seek refuge in a church, the only place where she felt safe.

As James left Ponteland behind and headed north up the A696 he thought about what he'd do to any man who dared to subject his precious Abby to such torment. He wasn't sure the Bible was nearly as clear-cut on such issues as many folk seemed to think it was. He knew all about the gospel of love and forgiveness, and he fully believed it. But he also knew about justice, and caring for the weak and helpless, and he failed to see how love could allow a sexual monster to go on roaming the streets simply because the rules of evidence did not allow the law to touch him. Didn't someone once say that all that is necessary for the triumph of evil is that good men do nothing?

Six miles up the road he entered the village of Belsay but he scarcely noticed the old stone cottages to his left or the freshly trimmed hedge bounding open fields to the right. Fortunately, he was concentrating sufficiently on his driving so as not to approach the sharp right hand bend too fast, otherwise he might have found himself making an unplanned visit to Belsay Castle gardens. The trouble was he couldn't get out of his mind the picture of another scene described to him by Zena.

Once again the teenage girls had come from Lithuania. That had surprised him until Zena had assured him that it was by no means unusual for girls to be trafficked from the eastern Baltic states. The two girls, aged eighteen and nineteen, had been sold in full public view in a coffee shop at Gatwick airport in November of the previous year. After a brief bartering session, the pair had been bought for £3000 each, one destined for a brothel in London and the other for Sheffield. Zena had pulled no punches in her descriptions of the horrors each had suffered in their lives as sex slaves. Thankfully, in entirely separate incidents only a few days apart, the pair had managed to escape their captors, eventually finding themselves in the hands of the police.

And that was another problem. Zena had discovered that the police had not so far adopted any consistent protocols for dealing with the victims of trafficking. Officers in some forces were highly sympathetic to the plight of the girls and equally aggressive in their pursuit of the gangs responsible. In other forces, a different approach was taken. The girls usually had no passport or other means of identification, and so were often treated simply as illegal immigrants. Zena had written to the Home Secretary on several occasions requesting the government to consider drawing up a national action plan on human trafficking. On the seat beside him, James had copies of all the evidence she had submitted in support of her request. He had promised to ask his father if there might be some way of encouraging a little more haste in government circles.

As he continued up the A696 through countryside that was largely fields and woodland, the skies became heavily overcast and before long huge drops of rain were bouncing off the bonnet of the Maserati. While the wipers struggled to keep the windscreen clear, the sudden gloom rather matched his mood as he wondered how to tackle the problem of Raymond Mellisse. Zena had confirmed that Birmingham was rapidly achieving the status of sex capital of the UK particularly with regard to the exploitation of teenage girls but the name Mellisse meant nothing to her. On the other hand, she had picked up on a rumour, through police contacts, that some eastern European mafia types were looking to muscle in on the market. This caused James to wonder if Mellisse was looking to turn respectable and pull out of the sex business, maybe selling off his enterprise to Alexei Borisov. Or maybe Borisov was just planning on an aggressive takeover without the usual financial considerations. Whatever the case, Zena had no doubt that these men were incredibly dangerous, something which James already had good cause to believe.

Ahead was the village of Otterburn, site of the battle where the Scots had trounced the English back in 1388, an event so astounding as to be commemorated in *The Ballad of Chevy Chase.* James remembered having to learn this during his schooldays at Gordonstoun up on the Moray Firth. As he entered the village, just a few miles south of the point where he would join the A68 to head north for the Scottish border, he became aware of a black Mercedes saloon coming up fast behind him. He had noticed its lights earlier glinting through the rain as it kept pace with him, but hadn't paid it much attention until it quickly closed the distance as he approached the village.

At first, he thought it was simply his own reduction in speed as he adjusted to the thirty mph limit through the village that had allowed the

Mercedes to draw so close. More out of curiosity than because he was worried, he was slow to accelerate out of the speed limit, allowing the Mercedes plenty of opportunity to overtake him. It didn't, and a few minutes later he passed through the junction with the A68 at about fifty mph with the Mercedes having dropped back about a half-dozen car lengths.

James frowned as he wondered what to make of this. He had once known an elderly peer who drove his CL600 as though it was a Morris Minor on tranquilisers, but no other Mercedes owner he'd ever known would drive as this one was doing.

After the events of the morning, his mind suddenly began toying with a range of possibilities none of which were very encouraging. In his rear-view mirror he had spotted at least two occupants in the Mercedes as they had passed through Otterburn. If these guys belonged to Mellisse or Borisov, they must have picked him up at Zena Walcott's house in Ponteland. And they had done it without the help of a tracker on his car, he was sure of that. The behaviour of the BMW in charging after the police car that morning had assured James that he had dealt with that problem. No, these guys could only have found him if they knew exactly where he was going, which again brought someone he trusted into the frame.

Many people could have had opportunity to place the tracker on the Maserati, but only someone close to him could have told his trackers where he was heading. But if they knew his destination, why had they needed the tracker at all? It only made sense if they wanted to know exactly where he would be throughout his journey, which meant that they intended to intercept him somewhere short of his destination.

He glanced in his mirror for the tenth time in the past minute. The rain was still falling, huge drops bouncing up from the road's slick surface but, for the tenth time, the Merc was still there about thirty yards back. It made no move that was overtly threatening; just one car following another at a safe distance on a murky day along a country road. But still, there was a coldness growing in his gut that told him something was not right, and experience had taught him not to ignore such feelings.

The A68 crossed the Scottish border about twelve miles up the road at Carter Bar. On any normal day, each layby on the north and southbound sides of the road would be littered with a fair scattering of vehicles. People stopped to picnic, to admire the spectacular views, to take photographs, or just to enjoy a break from their journey. Oftentimes, James had noticed some kind of 4x4 with a catering trailer attached, offering food and drink for those unfortunate enough to have forgotten to bring their own. But that would not be the case today. There was a glimmering of lightness in the sky far to the north, but overhead the unbroken grey clouds continued to feed the heavy downpour. There would be no views to admire, no picnics on the grassy verges, and no cameras exposed to the harsh raindrops.

Carter Bar was the obvious place to stop him, and it was only minutes away. If the BMW X5 was waiting up ahead, then the Mercedes was tailing simply to make sure James was heading to the right place. It was obvious now that its occupants had instructions to stay behind him so, whether they belonged to Mellisse or Borisov, that's exactly what they'd do. James could not be sure exactly how these criminal overlords enforced obedience, or how they dealt with any deviation from their instructions, but he had little doubt that it was both unpleasant and painful.

Through trees to his left he could see the slate grey surface of the Catcleugh Reservoir. Up ahead, perhaps half a mile or so, a service road led off on the left to double back around the end of the reservoir and head into the forested area on the far side. He had no time to formulate any sort of a plan, but he knew that if he was to avoid becoming the meat in a very nasty sandwich, then that road would be his best bet. If the guys in the Mercedes followed him, they would have only themselves to blame for whatever happened next.

The only trouble was that he had no weapon of any sort, or at least nothing that he could use that was readily accessible. The belt of trees to his left was coming to an end a couple of hundred yards ahead and the turning he needed was about the same distance beyond the limit of the trees. He eased his foot on the accelerator to begin slowing for the turn. He seemed to remember that the shoulders were cut away at the junction to ease the turn off the main road, but even so he didn't want to swing in too quickly with the road surface slick with rain and possibly mud from farm or forestry vehicles.

The Mercedes closed the gap slightly. James touched his brakes to let them know he was slowing and, as expected, they too slowed and the gap once again remained steady for about a hundred yards. A crash barrier was set back a little from the road's edge to stop cars drifting off into the open scrub land which extended down to the river about a couple of hundred yards away to his left. On the right, a low wire fence bordered similar scrub pasture which rose gently to disappear into the murk of rain-soaked clouds. As he drew closer to the road on the left, James readied for the turn but, once he began to ease the wheel over, he knew immediately that he was in trouble.

About twenty yards in from the main highway, access to the forest road was completely blocked by a wooden five-bar gate. If the rain hadn't made visibility so poor, and if he hadn't been concentrating so much on the Mercedes behind, he might have noticed the obstacle sooner. Now it was too late to change his plan.

It flashed across his mind that he'd no idea whether the gate had always been there and he'd just never noticed it, or whether perhaps it had been recently installed. Not that it mattered now. Pulling to a stop a yard or two short of the barrier, he could see that it wasn't one of those gates that were meant to be easily opened by hikers or horse riders. A stout chain secured it to the gatepost, and a substantial padlock ensured that only drivers who were authorised – or those who had no regard for their vehicle's bodywork – had any chance of access.

Even if he'd had a key, James could not have been through the gate before the occupants of the Mercedes reached him. A glance in his mirror showed the black saloon easing off the highway to glide to a stop sideways on to the rear of the Maserati, effectively cutting off any chance of his getting back onto the main road. Its two occupants were visible through his rain-splattered rear window, peering at him through the side window of their car. So much for his plan of being able to deal with the threat from the Mercedes in the seclusion of the woodland.

He was trapped, unarmed and outnumbered and there was every possibility that the best thing that would happen in the next few minutes would be that he got very, very wet.

Seventy

Aullton House – Mid-afternoon

It was gone three o'clock by the time Angie was comfortably installed in the bedroom next to mine on the upper floor of the family apartment. Doctor Harwood had originally wanted to place her in one of the guest rooms in the stable block because it was nearer to the spot where the air ambulance had landed. I didn't like that idea because if I was going to be staying in the main house then that's where I wanted Angie to be as well. I was dithering about whether to speak up when Mrs Elliott, who had come out to see what was happening, told him that the main house had a lift to all floors which the stables did not. I hadn't known that, or I'd have mentioned it myself, so I was really pleased when Doctor Harwood immediately changed his mind.

While Abby and I helped him to make her comfortable in a room which only the most demanding of celebrities could have found fault with, he told us that Angie had been awake for much of the journey although she had said very little. She had smiled at us, rather woefully, but she was still very confused and unable to remember much at all of the past few days. Once she was settled, Doctor Harwood just wanted her to rest quietly so, in spite of our protests, Abby and I were gently but firmly ejected from her room.

On our way back to the drawing room, I thought about the level of care Doctor Harwood was giving Angie. Not that there was too little, in fact, just the opposite. He seemed far more concerned for her, more protective even, than I would ever have expected, so it had me wondering. Had Angie, unknowingly and without even trying, actually made a conquest here? And if she had, what could possibly come of it?

Abby pushed open the door of the drawing room and broke into my thoughts with a complaint that her Dad had not phoned yet. Cherry looked up from the newspaper he was reading and suggested that we all settle down to watch the end of the DVD while we waited. I didn't have a better suggestion and nor, it seemed, did Abby but we didn't even get as far as turning on the TV.

The phone rang. It wasn't a long call but it was enough to satisfy Abby who told us, as she replaced the phone on the table, that James was about to leave Aunt Zena's and would be home in time for dinner.

"So," she said, with all her usual sunniness restored, "now we can go and see the llamas."

Cherry used the house phone to track Andy down and let him know what we were doing so, by the time we got down to the main hall, he was there waiting for us. He was not alone. There were two other men hovering behind him, men whom I had never seen before. Not surprising perhaps, since I had only been here a few hours, but there was just something about them which made me think they belonged to Andy rather than to the house. They were similar to each other in appearance, both being a little above medium height and wearing sports jackets and slacks which didn't quite seem to suit them. Although they were both smiling, there was a hardness to their faces that made me think they would be more at home in muscle-shirts and jeans than the smart-casual wear they had chosen. I guessed these were Andy's colleagues called in from Edinburgh and that he'd told them to dress appropriately for the job he needed them to do.

One of them, a little broader across the shoulders than his colleague, had adopted the Bruce Willis shaven-head look, presumably to hide the fairly obvious fact that, unlike Willis, he was going very thin on top. The other guy had a full head of gingerish hair above a heavily freckled face. I was thinking of christening them Bruce and Freckles when Andy called them forward to be introduced.

"I've borrowed these gentlemen from a firm in Edinburgh," he said to Cherry. "Lucky to get them at such short notice. This here's Carl… …" The guy with the shaven head nodded but didn't offer to shake hands. "… …and his friend there likes to be called Ginger."

The guy with the freckles grinned.

"If folk call me Ginger 'coz I tell 'em to, it's my choice not theirs."

I wondered if he'd been nicknamed Ginger as a child, and decided just to accept it rather than resist. Somehow, it didn't make me like him any better despite the smile.

I noticed Mrs Elliott come into the hall through a side door and hesitate, frowning as though she didn't quite like what she was seeing. I was sure she wanted to ask what was going on, but I couldn't blame her for seeming a little intimidated by the group of men at the foot of the staircase. I touched Abby's arm and held out my hand to lead her over to where Mrs Elliott was standing. I had no idea what James had told her but clearly something needed to be said.

"It must seem very odd," I said to her, "having so many strangers suddenly thrust at you."

"Well, it does rather," she replied. "Is there something going on I don't know about?"

"I shouldn't think so," I answered, looking down at Abby and giving her hand a squeeze. "What do you think, Abby?"

She looked surprised to be asked but spoke up promptly enough.

"Nah… … Everything's cool. And Dad'll be here soon."

"That's right," I said, "which gives us a bit of a problem. This has all come about very quickly, and the kitchen upstairs is … … well, we don't have much food. I was wondering if there's anyone who could do a bit of shopping for us. It doesn't seem right for us to keep on raiding your freezer."

"Ah," said Mrs Elliott with a smile. "This young lady and her father are always welcome to anything they need from my kitchen." I noticed she hadn't included me in that, but didn't take offence. "But," she went on, "I understand what you mean. I'll make out a list and have Gil send someone off to the supermarket for you… … Unless you'd like to make out your own list."

"Thanks," I said. "I'm sure you'd make a better job of it than I would. I'd be sure to forget something important." I slowed as it suddenly dawned on me that she might expect me to give her the money to pay for the shopping. She seemed to read my mind.

"I'll tell Gil to keep an account and settle it with James later. But… …" She nodded over towards the others. "What about them? Do they need feeding?"

I hadn't thought about it, but said, "I don't think so. At least, they'll need to eat, but I expect they'll grab something down in the village."

"Hmmm… …" She lowered her voice. "But who are they? Why have they come?"

Very conscious of Abby standing right beside me, I answered cautiously.

"Well… … I assume you know Andy."

"Yes, of course."

"These other gentlemen are in the same line of work, come down from Edinburgh to meet with him."

"I see… … So will they be here long?"

"I'm really not sure… … but James will be able to tell you once he gets here."

She nodded but I could see that she still wasn't happy. I couldn't really blame her since I was more than a little wary of them myself. These newcomers were a type I'd seen before too many times in the past three years and in places I doubted Mrs Elliott could even dream of. Still, I understood why security firms needed guys with muscle from time to time and, if things turned bad, I'd rather have these two on my side than a couple of upstanding gentlemen from the church social.

We stood together for a moment just watching the four and waiting for them to finish their discussion. It gave an indication of the size of the hall that we couldn't quite make out what they were saying, though it was obvious they weren't entirely in agreement. At least, Andy and

Cherry weren't. The two newcomers simply stood quietly by and listened, glancing round occasionally at the artefacts displayed on the walls. They seemed particularly interested in the antique weaponry, some of which I couldn't even put a name to.

I was trying to think of something else to say which would give Mrs Elliott's thoughts a new direction when Abby spoke up and did it for me.

"I'm taking Lizzie out to see the llamas," she said.

The housekeeper drew her gaze away from Andy's group, looked down at her and smiled. "What a good idea. You might even have time for a trek."

"A trek?" I asked, not sure I warmed to the idea. "What, me as well?"

"Yes, of course, you as well. You don't have to go far, you know. People come here from all over the place specially to go llama trekking."

I found I was actually becoming quite curious about the creatures and, as Freddy continued to enthuse about them, was almost as impatient as Abby to make our way out to find them. We didn't have to wait much longer.

Cherry came across the hall with Ginger trailing behind him.

"You girls ready?" he asked, more for something to say than because he was in any doubt. "Ginger here is going to come with us while Carl stays with Andy." He looked at Mrs Elliott. "They won't be getting in the way, Freddy. They'll just hang around upstairs and get on with some work. Then they'll be available in case Dr Harwood needs any help or anything."

As an explanation it sounded a bit lame to me, as I'm sure it did to her, but she didn't say anything, just raised her eyebrows in an *if you say so* gesture, and watched as we made our way out to one of the estate Land Rovers which Gil had brought round to the front of the house.

Ginger slowed to look around as we came out through the main doorway, so I took advantage of the distance between us to say quietly to Cherry, "Do you know those two? Have you met them before?"

Abby had opened the rear door of the Land Rover and didn't appear to be listening.

"No. Never come across them before."

"So what were you arguing about?"

He glanced back towards Ginger who seemed to have adopted a lord-of-all-I-survey stance at the top of the steps.

"We weren't arguing," he said. "Just a slight difference of opinion, that's all."

"Yes, sure," I replied thinking, or maybe hoping, that I deserved a little more honesty. Cherry seemed to think so too, since he quickly relented.

"Andy wanted me to stay with Carl while he and Ginger came with you. No idea why. Technically he's my boss but in the end I told him straight, *When James isn't around, where Abby goes I go. That's the deal.* He didn't argue after that, and made out like it was no big deal. Anyway… …"

He broke off as Ginger started to come down the steps. I nodded towards him as I asked Cherry, in a lowered voice, "What do you think of those guys?"

Abby was settling herself in the rear of the Land Rover now, on the opposite side from us, fiddling with her seatbelt.

"They're OK, I guess."

"So," I said, lightly grasping his arm. "Do you trust them?"

"Andy does," he replied. "And that's always been good enough for me."

I watched Ginger approach and wondered why it wasn't also good enough for me.

Seventy-One

Bosnia – September 1995

James's eyes were fixed on his rear-view mirror. The guys in the Mercedes were just sitting still, as though they weren't quite sure what to do. He dropped his gaze to the gate which had so effectively ruined his plan, and immediately his mind jumped back ten years, to Bosnia in the summer of 1995. He was in a French VAB armoured personnel carrier travelling the road from Kiseljac to Sarajevo. In spite of the heat, all the hatches in the three vehicle convoy were closed up tight. The convoy commander, Capitaine Davout, was in the lead VAB and James was sitting beside the driver of the rearmost vehicle.

A newly promoted major in the Royal Marines, he had deployed there as a member of the staff of Major General David Pennefather attached to the UN protection Force at Kiseljak. Their arrival coincided with the Serb massacre of over seven thousand Bosnian Muslims at Srebrenica, supposedly a safe area under UN protection. James very quickly discovered that "safe" as defined by the UN was a far cry from the definition of the Oxford English Dictionary.

The road he was travelling that day in early September 1995 was supposed to be "safe", a protected corridor agreed by all combatants and guaranteed by the UN. Unfortunately, it didn't seem to occur to anyone that the Serbs might have second thoughts about this when NATO started bombing the hell out of them as part of Operation Deliberate Force. Completely ignoring all UN resolutions, the Serbs had continued a vigorous campaign of ethnic cleansing culminating in the mortar attacks on Sarajevo on August 28th. This triggered a NATO air campaign which had been sitting in readiness for several weeks and which ultimately would drive the Serbs to consider a negotiated peace.

Operation Deliberate Force was only a few days old when James was ordered to join a French contingent heading off for Sarajevo. An Aérospatiale Gazelle helicopter had come down in a wooded area to the north east of Sarajevo, and the French crew who had apparently all survived were in the hands of a group of highly volatile Bosnian Muslims. The French platoon, commanded by a Capitaine Davout, had been given the task of retrieving the crew, and James had been attached to them at the last minute. He couldn't see a reason for it other than a lack of trust by the British commander that the French would actually pass on whatever intelligence they might gather in the course of their mission.

They left Kiseljac early on September 5th in three French VABs painted all-over white with the letters UN big and black on the front, sides and rear. This version was basically an armoured personnel carrier, with wheels not tracks, fitted out for two crew and ten fully equipped troops. In recognition of the fact that he was theoretically the senior officer on this mission, James travelled up front with the driver of the third vehicle, while Capitaine Davout took the lead.

In his few weeks in the country James had not travelled this road before so the passing landmarks meant nothing to him. His driver, whose young world-weary eyes had seen more of human brutality in the past few months than most people ever see in a lifetime, tried to pass the time by pointing out scenes of interest. Since these mostly referred to scarred and lifeless tanks, ruined villages, battle sites and scenes of alleged atrocities, James tried to pay attention, never knowing when he might actually learn something useful.

Passing through a lightly wooded area, his driver told the guys in back to hang on tight as the road was about to climb up through a series of four sharp hairpin bends. They were through two of them when the lead VAB suddenly braked hard and stopped. James, sitting in the right-hand seat, was about to stick his head out of the side hatch to see what the problem was when the driver grabbed his arm to hold him in place. His dark eyes were calm and steady, and James was reassured to see there was no sign of fear or panic. The driver just shook his head again and released James's arm as his eyes narrowed slightly in concentration. He was wearing a helmet with integral mike and headphones and was clearly listening to instructions from up ahead. He nodded as he replied, peering forward through the narrow window. It appeared that a tree was blocking the road. Whether it had simply fallen on its own or been felled deliberately was unclear.

With the VAB's Renault-built diesel engine now idling, James could just make out the low growl of another vehicle approaching from the rear. In the large wing mirror bolted to the side of the VAB, he caught a glimpse of a battered truck with an open load-bed on which there seemed to be mounted something which looked suspiciously like a browning M2 50 calibre machine gun. He couldn't be sure of course because of his limited field of view, but he saw enough as the truck swung round the second of the hairpin bends to be reasonably sure. He told the driver what he'd seen and waited to learn what Capitaine Davout intended to do.

Nothing, it seemed. At least, nothing that could be construed as an offensive action, but the men were instructed to be alert and ready to deploy the moment the French officer gave the word. James had seen no insignia markings to show whether the truck belonged to Bosnian Muslims or to the Serbs, both of which were known to be in the area. He hoped for the Muslims. The Serbs would certainly not be very happy with the UN just at present. It was certainly not unknown for UN troops to be captured and held hostage, to be fired on and even killed by combatant forces.

James might be the senior officer present but it was Capitaine Davout's mission so, although his mind was churning with possibilities, he waited patiently for the Frenchman to make his move. When he did, it was quite unexpected. He came strolling down past the middle VAB, rubbing at his chin and looking quite bewildered. Worriedly James turned to his driver, and his anxiety level immediately dropped when he saw that the man was actually smiling.

As Davout drew level with James's VAB he winked at him, but so briefly that James couldn't be sure he hadn't imagined it. Then the Frenchman raised his arm to wave to the men in the truck behind as though to a friend across the street. He called out to them in a language that James was beginning to recognise but hadn't yet learned to speak.

His driver nudged him and pointed to the hatch in the roof above James's head. This gave access to the 7.62mm machine gun mounted on the roof. He knew James could handle it. It was the first thing he'd asked when he discovered James was going to occupy that seat. James loosened the catches to the hatch but didn't open it. He could see Davout in his mirror approaching the truck. The 50 calibre was tracking him all the while and the thought crossed James's mind that he was seeing bravery that he would never have credited to the young officer, and a Frenchman at that. Not that Davout looked the least bit threatening. His manner and tone of voice were completely disarming.

Then the 50 calibre couldn't track him anymore. Its barrel had depressed as far as it would go and was now aimed into empty space above his head. It was the man in the passenger seat of the truck who was speaking to Davout and James assumed that he was the leader of the group. The man opened his door and climbed down addressing Davout in a loud commanding voice. James's driver was listening over his headset. He told James they were Serbs, demanding that Davout surrender his vehicles to them. Still watching in his mirror, James saw Davout slump as though in utter defeat.

Then the driver yelled for him to go and pointed upwards. In two seconds James was through the hatch and traversing the machine gun. He was amazed to see the Serb leader face down on the ground with his arm twisted up behind his back and Davout's automatic pistol in the nape of his neck. Ten soldiers had deployed from the rear of the VAB to the side of the road, crouched low, and scanning the trees and scrub. James risked a quick glance behind. The machine guns on the two VABs up front were manned, one aiming off the road at 11 o'clock and the other at 1 o'clock.

The troops were still inside their vehicles. No point in risking more lives than you need, thought James.

And that was it. All over. Bravery, cunning, and a fair amount of luck and not a shot had been fired. It was the Serbs who had blocked the road and a bunch of them had been hiding in the trees to cover the head of the convoy. The truck had been concealed off the road ready to close the trap from the rear. With their leader down, their main armament pointing the wrong way, and all covered by a suddenly aggressive and menacing band of professionals, the Serbs were in no mood for a fire-fight. It had been a bold move on their part, perhaps prompted by the ease with which the Serb commander Ratko Mladic had manipulated the Dutch UN peacekeepers prior to the Srebrenica massacre a month or so earlier. But Capitaine Davout was no Colonel Karremans, and unlike the Dutch commander he was perfectly prepared to blow the Serbs to hell to protect his men.

Then suddenly it appeared that not all the Serbs had read the script. One of them who had been crouching on the bed of the truck stood up slowly. He was not particularly tall, but impressive enough in a bulked out sort of way. He wore the usual scruffy camouflage jacket and pants of so many of the combatants, but with no badges of rank or unit that James could see. He was clearly anxious not to provoke any shooting but there was a confidence about him that James didn't like. At that moment, he was the only man moving in the stillness of the tableau.

Before he was fully upright, James realised that there was another figure rising with him. The second man was small in comparison. In fact, as the little figure looked around and James caught a glimpse of terrified eyes, he realised that it was not a man at all, but a boy no more than eleven or twelve years old. The first man was using his left hand to hold the boy by his shirt collar bunched up at the back of his neck, and now James could see that the lad had his hands tied behind his back.

The reason for the boy's terror was now obvious. The big guy's right hand held a pistol pointed at the lad's head.

He called down to Capitaine Davout in that language James did not understand, but the meaning was clear. It was what they call a Mexican stand-off. There were more words, but Davout didn't move. He still had his man on the ground, and his pistol still ground into the back of his neck. The other Serbs were beginning to fidget, as though getting ready to make a move even if they weren't sure what that move should be.

More words as the big Serb's left hand twitched to force the boy to hold up his head as if to emphasise the importance of his hostage. James had no idea who the boy was, but the way Davout glanced back at the convoy of VABs convinced James that the boy's identity meant something to him. Their advantage was slipping away.

James had held the 7.62mm machine gun on the Serb ever since he first stood up, but he had never fired this particular weapon and could not be certain of bringing down the Serb without touching the boy. Slowly he reached for his sidearm. Thankfully, the focus of the drama was the truck and all eyes were turned that way. His personal weapon was a Sig Sauer 9mm and at that distance of fifteen yards James was sure of putting a round in the Serb's left ear and blowing his brains out through the right. All he needed was … … …

The Serb shouted down at Davout, leaning forward slightly, and his pistol moved with him, no longer aimed directly at the boy. James's shot missed his ear but took him in the left temple knocking him sideways causing him first to stumble and then to topple clean off the bed of the truck. The way he struck the ground head first would probably have killed him if he hadn't been dead already.

This time, it really was all over. The boy turned out to be the son of the local Muslim commander, which was the only reason the Serbs had kept him alive. Gratitude is a wonderful thing, so the crew of the helicopter was recovered to the accompaniment of exuberant thanks and vows of undying friendship from the overjoyed commander and his men.

He had shaken James's hand warmly and kissed him on both cheeks.

"Anything you need, anytime. Just ask and it's yours," he had said. At least, that's how Davout had translated what had been a long and emotional speech.

James had never believed he would need to take up the offer, but then you often don't until circumstances drive you to it.

Seventy-Two

Scottish Border – Mid-afternoon

James continued to watch the Mercedes in his rear-view mirror. The rain seemed to be easing a little and, helped by a brightening of the sky, he could just about make out the shapes of the two men in the front of the car. Yes, he thought, just like Bosnia. The road blocked to the front, and hemmed in from the rear. The only thing different, thought James, was that they didn't have a 50 calibre trained on him, ready to chop him to pieces. Not that they were defenceless, he was sure of that, which meant that he had to move very carefully indeed. Neither of them showed any sign of wanting to emerge from the Mercedes so, with no other plan to hand, he decided it to give Capitaine Davout's approach a try.

He opened his door and stretched out his hand slowly, palm upwards, as if testing the strength of the rainfall. He was right. It was easing off. There was even a hint of blue sky appearing up to the north. A glance in his mirror showed no movement from the Mercedes, but the guy in the passenger seat was looking his way apparently listening to the mobile phone clasped to his left ear. James was sure they had intended to follow him down the service road, but his sudden stop had forced them into a quick decision which he suspected they were now having second thoughts about.

Deciding there was really nothing to be gained by sitting still, James pushed the door open to its fullest extent and climbed out. He gave a friendly wave in the direction of the Mercedes and gestured upwards to the heavy overcast as though complaining to fellow sufferers about the bad weather. Believing they were working to the pre-determined plan of someone senior to them, a plan which would see him disposed of in a sophisticated manner worthy of the inconvenience he was causing, he was able to be reasonably sure that they wouldn't just shoot him without provocation. The trouble was that he wasn't entirely sure just what these guys would consider to be provocation.

Moving slowly, with gestures as non-threatening as possible, he turned up his collar against the slight rain that was still falling and ambled towards the gate. He laid his hand on the upright nearest the gatepost and shook it. The chain and padlock that secured the gate to the post rattled dully. He heard a door open behind him and turned slowly. If there were weapons in sight, he was ready to fall flat in front of the Maserati and roll into the ditch beside the track. There was no need. The passenger was climbing out, watching him cautiously but both his hands were empty.

Under his bulky leather jacket he could be hiding an arsenal, or maybe it was just a well-stuffed wallet.

There was traffic noise along the road in both directions, which might have explained the absence of weapons. The passenger looked left and right, as if checking what was coming and how far away it was. James waved again as the passenger turned back to face him, and began to walk slowly towards the Mercedes. He stooped a little and hunched his shoulders to try and minimise his height and bulk. He wanted these guys to see him as an amiable giant whom they were easily capable of taking down if they needed to.

The passenger was still standing close to the open door of the Mercedes, arms hanging loosely by his sides. He looked ready to move quickly if need be.

James approached slowly, shuffling and ungainly.

"I'm sure glad you guys stopped by," he said. "Some gremlins must have got in my satnav 'coz it was telling me to turn off here and then go straight ahead down this track."

He had reached the rear of his Maserati now, leaving about two yards between himself and the passenger. He looked into dark eyes beneath heavy brows topped by a thatch of thick black hair.

"Well," went on James, undeterred by the lack of response. "Just look." He glanced back over his shoulder. "That gate's all chained up. There's no way I'm getting through. And that track's just stones and dirt. Ahh, this satnav's useless. I don't know why I bother with it, I really don't. Give me an old fashioned map anytime."

A huge truck thundered south on the far side of the Mercedes and a moment later a white van belted past travelling north at well over the posted speed limit. The traffic sounds gradually diminished to leave a silence which hung heavy in the damp air. The passenger glanced quickly left and right, confirming the total absence of traffic in both directions. Then his gaze returned to James, his mouth twisting slightly into what might have been intended to be a reassuring smile, but his eyes remained dark, hooded and guarded.

Almost imperceptibly at first, his right hand started to move slowly under his jacket and James knew that his soft approach had run its course. He lunged forward at a speed not much slower than he had shown on the rugby field at Gordonstoun. Grabbing the passenger's right wrist with his left hand, he swung his own right violently upwards, palm open, to smack viciously under the passenger's chin, smashing his teeth together and snapping his head backwards. He followed this immediately with a punch to the guy's midriff just below the breast bone. He had swung his shoulder back to get as much of the force of his own two hundred and forty-five pounds behind it as possible.

As the passenger slumped, James grabbed his hair to haul him back upright and twisted him around to face the car before smashing his face onto the top of the door frame. It had the same effect as a vicious head-butt but without any pain to himself. He reached under the guy's jacket for the weapon he hoped was there. He hoped for the weapon partly because he was sure he was going to need it, and partly because he didn't like the thought that he could have inflicted such damage to an unarmed man.

There it was, suspended in a fancy sling under the left side of the passenger's leather jacket. James knew what it was as soon as his fingers closed around it, but he was surprised to find it on this guy. He'd expected some kind of automatic pistol not a Heckler & Koch MP5K submachine gun. Even as he hauled the gun free, he felt the passenger buck against him as though trying to throw him off. Twice he did it, slumping down after each attempt, surprising James for a moment since he'd thought the guy must be unconscious after the beating he'd taken. Then he realised that the jolt was not caused by the passenger at all, but by the driver who was firing wildly trying to hit him with some kind of silenced automatic but only putting bullets into his accomplice instead.

Keeping the passenger upright in the car's open doorway, James thumbed the selector on the MP5K to three-shot burst and fired twice into the car. The driver was going down and, as far as James was concerned, he'd asked for it. Turning the other cheek was OK, and usually James was all for it, but not when it meant running the risk of turning your little girl into an orphan.

There was silence, so James risked ducking his head to look into the car. The driver was slumped against the steering wheel, blood oozing from several wounds to the upper body. As James relaxed his grip on the passenger he felt the man's dead weight crumple. He turned him to see where he'd been hit and immediately saw two small holes, one directly over the heart and another high on the right shoulder. Surprisingly, for shots delivered at such close range, there were no exit wounds so there was little blood. The guy's heart had stopped. James opened the rear door and heaved him in, positioned so no blood would get on the upholstery, and closed it again just before a staggered convoy of several cars passed by in the wake of a large truck.

He kept his head down so no-one should see his face, always assuming they might be looking and when the road was quiet again, he took the MP5K along to the gate to unlock the padlock with two single shots before pushing the gate wide open. He then took a pair of work gloves from the boot of the Maserati, kept there against the possibility of having to change a wheel. He also removed the shooting-stick which had been in the car ever since it had belonged to his aunt. Returning to the

Mercedes, he sat in the passenger seat and hauled the driver back from the steering wheel. Using the shooting-stick to press on the brake pedal so he could put the gear selector into drive, he eased off the hand brake and allowed the natural tendency of the automatic gearbox to creep forwards to take him around the Maserati and through the gate. It was awkward steering from the passenger side, but the pace was slow enough that he was able to manage.

The crawl down to the bridge over the narrow, winding River Rede was easy enough, but the gentle gradient on the far side required more pressure on the accelerator from the shooting-stick awkwardly placed between the driver's lifeless legs. In places the track was deeply rutted and several times the underside of the Mercedes scraped the top of the ridge between the ruts. Once, the jolt of the car hitting the ridge was so severe that the tip of the shooting-stick slipped off the accelerator pedal, but James quickly corrected and kept the car moving. He wondered about the possibility of the impact cracking the sump but figured that at this stage it didn't really matter. It took only a few minutes before the track levelled out and entered the woodland. He was confident now that the Mercedes was hidden from the main road by the increasing density of the trees. The problem now was to find a place to hide it.

To his right the tree growth seemed relatively young and was inaccessible due to a shallow ditch running alongside the track. To his left, he could see through the old woods right down to the surface of the reservoir which glinted silvery grey between the trees. No way of hiding anything larger than a wheelbarrow in that. Maybe this hadn't been such a great idea after all. He kept the car moving, hoping to find an opening wide enough to ease the big car through. Still nothing to the right, and on the left, even where there was a space, the ground was littered with moss-covered tree stumps, long-fallen rotting logs and grassy hummocks.

When it finally appeared, he almost missed it. Long green grass sloped gently downwards through a gap about eight feet wide between the trees bordering the track. The surface of the reservoir no longer provided a backlight to illuminate the ground cover between the closely-packed trunks of the old trees. This would have to do. He steered the heavy car off the track heading for the opening between the trees. It needed frequent use of the stick now to get the car over the rough ground. Before long the gloom was intense enough that he was satisfied that it was sufficiently off the track not to be easily spotted by passing vehicles, walkers or riders. Before extracting himself carefully from the car, he checked the driver's pockets for anything that might suggest who these two were working for. He wasn't disappointed. Along with a nicely tooled leather wallet stuffed with cash, the driver's inside jacket pocket yielded a Russian passport and driving licence in the name of Arseny Trakhirov.

So Mellisse really has got Borisov doing his dirty work. But why is the Russian so keen to help. Was Zena right? Is some kind of takeover being planned?

James stood up and slowly turned a full three hundred and sixty degrees. Trees all around, and there was no-one in sight in any direction. The only sounds he could hear were the occasional drip from leaves stirred by the light breeze and a faint, infrequent hum of traffic from the main road. So far this had been a clean operation but James knew he needed to remove himself from the scene as quickly as possible. Now for the tricky bit. He rubbed down any surface he thought he might have touched before putting on the gloves, mostly around the door frame. Then he carefully hauled the passenger out of the back and positioned him in the front seat, turned slightly towards the driver. He then wiped over the MP5K very carefully to remove his fingerprints from the gun before putting the passenger's right hand on it in several places to cover it with his prints. He then positioned it in the passenger's right hand, pointing over towards the driver whose automatic was still in his lap where it had fallen, its silencer resting on his thigh.

Unsure of what lay further up the road, James would have liked to keep the MP5K with the two spare fifteen round magazines which the passenger had in a clip on his belt, but it wouldn't work. The bullets which would eventually be found in the bodies would have to match the guns found at the scene if his carefully contrived scenario were to be believed. No-one would ever know what had drawn these guys into the woods, or why they had chosen to have a shootout in the front of their Mercedes, but James was confident that a little checking by the police would reveal that both had rather unsavoury pasts which would diminish any enthusiasm to look beyond the obvious.

Surveying his handiwork, his gaze lingered for a moment on the two figures crumpled in the front seats of the Mercedes. He wondered about these men he'd just killed. They had both been babies once, innocent and untainted by the world, so what had occurred on their path to manhood to turn them into these ruthless predators. He knew there were plenty of others out there, willing to kill or torture as long as someone paid them enough. And that was without the religious zealots, and those who would destroy the lives of others just for the fun of it. He shook his head sorrowfully, not so much over the plight of these two, as over the appalling wickedness that could dart out from the dark places of the world to invade the lives of innocent people.

He didn't understand it. How could the world be as it was, and God still be God? His faith hadn't yet offered him any answers that made sense. He wished he hadn't had to kill these men, but told himself that by their own actions and lifestyle they had brought their fate upon themselves. And there was no arguing against the fact that the world would be a better place without them.

Just on the off-chance, he decided to check in the boot of the Mercedes and, when he flipped the lid, he smiled with satisfaction. An Adidas holdall sat to one side, its zip partly open. James could already smell the gun oil even before he pulled the zip fully open to look inside the bag. In it lay what appeared to be a laptop case, but when he zipped it open he discovered another MP5K with five apparently full magazines. He thought about simply taking the bag but then decided it might be best to leave it. The gun, however, was a different matter. He zipped up the laptop case and removed it from the holdall. If he didn't need it, then he could dispose of it later, but these guys and whoever they worked for had already shown they were playing for keeps, and James didn't want the dice stacked too heavily against him.

He looked carefully at the ground alongside the Mercedes, aware that his scenario made no allowance for footprints. He need not have worried. The ground under the trees was damp from the rain but it was firm and uneven, with a covering of twigs and leaves. He pulled up a small sapling and carried it back up towards the track. At the edge of the trees he paused and looked carefully left and right to check for hikers, bird-watchers or anyone else daft enough to brave the recent horrible weather. The track was clear. Slowly and carefully, he brushed the sapling over the grass to disguise the evidence of the car's passing. If you knew where to look, faint signs were still there, but otherwise anyone passing wouldn't give it a thought. Returning to the Mercedes, he disturbed one or two slightly flattened areas with the sapling before gathering up gun and shooting-stick and backing away into the trees careful to leave no further marks of his passage.

The sound stopped him cold. There was a rustling behind him which had nothing to do with the breeze through the treetops. Nor was it gentle enough for a ground foraging bird or small animal. This was something heavy enough to crack a twig. Someone was moving around behind him. And whoever it was, was not alone. There was another sound off to his left. A foot stirring dead leaves; a body brushing against a tree trunk.

Could it possibly be Borisov, come down with his crew from Carter Bar to help out his friends? Did he see the Maserati parked by the gate and decide to come looking for them? Or were these just innocent bird-watchers, or even forestry workers? He couldn't just shoot them and find out later. But he couldn't wait for them to shoot him first.

Spinning around, he flung himself down behind a rotting tree stump, fingers fumbling for the zip on the laptop case. Two pairs of eyes flashed in the gloom followed by the sound of feet crashing through bushes and scrub. Dark shapes flitted through the trees. Low, compact shapes. Four-legged shapes. With slender, curving, pointed horns. James breathed slowly, in and out, calming the adrenalin rush. He'd heard about the feral goats of Redesdale Forest, but he'd never made their acquaintance before. He replaced the gun which he'd partially extracted and zipped up the case. Slowly he got to his feet, wondering who had been more scared by the encounter.

He didn't want to walk back up the track from the Mercedes for fear of leaving footprints on the soft dampness of the verge, so he continued through the trees angling back to join the track just before it sloped down to cross the river by the narrow bridge. From there it was just a couple of hundred yards back to the gate which he hauled closed before wrapping the chain loosely around the post. The Maserati was exactly as he'd left it, all alone and apparently unnoticed by the occasional passing vehicle whose occupants were intent only on getting to their various destinations.

He was about to get back into the car when a thought struck him. It might be helpful at some time in the future not to be found to have any trace in the Maserati of the type of leaf mould and other detritus which now surrounded the Mercedes in the woods. So James went round to the boot of the Maserati and unzipped his suitcase to retrieve the spare pair of shoes which he probably wasn't going to need but had decided to bring anyway. Having found them, he then rummaged around in the canvas Marks and Spencer shopping bag in which he habitually kept his walking boots. Inside the bag, together with the boots was a plastic carrier bag, useful if the boots happened to be particularly muddy after a long hike.

Changing quickly at the front of the car where he wouldn't be easily seen, James put on the clean shoes and placed his slightly grubby ones in the plastic bag. He'd have to dump them which was a shame because he hadn't had them long and they'd been really comfortable. Still, there was a Salvation Army shoes and clothing bank at the supermarket in Hawick where he could dispose of them safely and give someone else the opportunity to wear them out.

This was always assuming he managed to get across the border. The turn for Hawick was just north of Carter Bar and he still had no idea what awaited him there. Whoever it was, Borisov or someone else, he'd have to confront them. If he didn't, and doubled back to Otterburn to pick up the Rothbury road across to the A697, he would certainly avoid Carter Bar, but would leave the possibility wide open that whoever was after him would eventually turn up at Aullton House. He couldn't let that happen, not with Abby and Lizzie there. It never occurred to him to call the police. He'd never had much confidence in them where his daughter's safety was concerned, and what could he tell them without landing himself in deeper trouble than he already was?

Settling back into the Maserati, he lay the laptop case on the passenger seat and opened it. Removing the MP5K, he released the magazine and checked the load. Satisfied, he reinserted it, and placed the gun back in the case on the passenger seat. He flipped the lid closed but left it unzipped. He then reversed onto the main road and pointed the nose of the Maserati in the direction of Carter Bar.

Seventy-Three

Aullton House – Mid-afternoon

Andy stood at the foot of the staircase, watching as Cherry led the others out through the main door. His eyes lingered on Abby, still holding onto Lizzie's hand. He was amazed at the bond that seemed to have grown up so quickly between the two of them. He saw them start to descend the steps and was about to turn away and take Carl upstairs, when he noticed Ginger pause and begin to look around. He was wondering what was going through Ginger's mind when his view was cut off by the closing of the door. Mrs Elliott stood with her back to it, her eyes moving between him and Carl, and an expression on her face that he couldn't quite interpret.

"Are you not interested in the llamas then, gentlemen?" she asked.

The tone of her voice made the question more probing than simply curiosity, but Andy decided to try and turn it away with a smile and an innocuous answer.

"I'm sure we could be, Mrs Elliott. If we had the time."

Because of what was about to happen, he was glad he didn't feel comfortable enough with her to call her Freddy, as Cherry did. It was all going to be messy enough without having to deceive and hurt people he cared about or, at least, any more than he had to.

"No," he continued, with an irony that wasn't lost on Carl. "A quiet afternoon with the llamas would probably be far more preferable to what we have to do, but work beckons I'm afraid."

"I see," she replied, although she really didn't. "If you need anything, I'm going to be in the library… …" she pointed to a door on her left "… … with some of our house volunteers. Nothing exciting, I'm afraid. I'd probably rather be out with the llamas myself."

Andy smiled and nodded, thinking that was an end of their brief conversation, but there was more to come.

"Oh, and I'd be grateful," Mrs Elliott went on, "if you and your friend could keep to the apartments if you're going to stay indoors. All the house alarms are off as we've got volunteers working in several rooms today, but … …"

"I know," interrupted Andy. "You don't want clod-hopping oafs like Carl here wandering around knocking over priceless Ming vases."

She smiled. Carl didn't seem to mind the slur, but it was hard to be sure from his stone-faced expression.

"Well, something like that," she admitted, "though if you're still here tomorrow and decide to take the tour, you'll discover we don't actually have any Ming vases. None of their lordships seem to have liked them... ... I'll see you later perhaps."

As she walked over to the door of the music room through which she would have to pass to reach the library, she glanced back at Andy and Carl, now ascending the staircase. They were speaking quietly, and she had the impression from the way Carl was nodding that Andy was giving instructions. Well, whatever they were up to, it wasn't any of her business. Except that she had been housekeeper at Aullton for so long that it was hard not to regard anything that went on in the house to be her business.

Andy let the two of them into the family apartments using the keypad code given to him by Cherry. The code was changed regularly, and it was seldom necessary on his infrequent visits that he needed to know what it was, since he was nearly always accompanied by James or Cherry. In fact, there was only one occasion that he could think of when he had let himself into this part of the house, and that was over a year ago.

He held the door as it closed so that it shut behind them without a sound. Assuming nothing had changed, and Cherry had assured him that it hadn't, then he was confident that he'd be able to find his way around the apartment. He knew which room Angie had been given, again courtesy of Cherry, and Carl was now waiting for him to lead the way to her. The big man wasn't here to organise anything. He was just the hired muscle sent along to help finish a job that should have been completed long ago. It had been Andy's decision to opt for the *divide-and-conquer* routine, and in his original plan it would have been Cherry here in the house with Carl. At this moment, in this hallway, Carl would have shot Cherry with the silenced Smith & Wesson .357 which he had tucked away in a specially designed holster under the left side of his jacket. Cherry would have led the way, just as Andy was about to do, and would have died without even knowing it was coming.

Next it would have been Doctor Harwood, as he was mobile and a potential threat whereas Angie was bedridden and harmless, except of course for the information tucked away in her befuddled brain. So she would have been last, with no pretence this time that it was anything else but an unprovoked and brutal murder.

But it wasn't going to be like that now. It wouldn't exactly be true to say Andy had a new plan since he was now making things up as he went along. Maybe Angie would still be dead. He wasn't sure he could avoid that, but Doctor Harwood needn't die. In fact, it would be far better if he didn't.

Standing with his back to the door and looking down the length of the hallway, Andy reached into his jacket pocket and removed the Beretta Bobcat which Ginger had surreptitiously handed to him before the three of them had entered the house a short while previously. The small Italian pistol was a pocket-sized semi-automatic chambered for 0.22LR ammunition, and was loaded on this occasion with subsonic rounds to assist noise-reduction. Ginger had assured Andy that the gun had not been previously used in any crime and was untraceable. Andy hoped he could believe him.

As the two men moved slowly down the hall, their silent footsteps perfectly cushioned by the thick pile of the carpet, their ears searched for any hint of sound that might warn them of Doctor Harwood's presence on this level. Andy didn't expect to find him here. He assumed, and hoped, that he'd still be on the upper floor keeping an eye on Angie. How ironic it would be if the sun finally chose this moment to shine through her clouded thoughts enabling her at last to explain to the doctor exactly what had happened to her in his hospital, who it was who had shoved in the needle that had poisoned her mind. It would be a deadly irony since, if that happened, the best way for Andy to secure his future would be for both of them to die.

The last few hours had stretched Andy's nerves to their limit. It had been almost beyond bearing, never to know at what moment James might learn that it was one of his oldest friends who was responsible for Angie's current wretched condition. He could imagine all too easily the sense of betrayal which James would inevitably feel if the truth should ever be known, and in his troubled mind self-loathing battled with his instinct for survival. If he couldn't make this turn out well, there would be no going back to RRISC, and that hurt. With James's backing he had built the company up from nothing to a position of international respectability. He hated the thought that he might lose it.

On the other hand, he did have a bit of leverage which might just save him even if his revised scheme failed. Although he hadn't been present, he knew the full details of the battle at Heighley Grange Farm on Saturday night. He knew about the bodies hidden in an old warehouse in Birmingham. Ironically, it had been James himself who had told him. It would be another betrayal of course, and not just of James. If he made this information known, people he had served with, fought beside, commanded and defended would probably end up in jail because he'd forgotten how to be loyal to the folk who trusted him. But he wouldn't really have to reveal what he knew, only threaten to do so if he couldn't salvage this mess and bring himself clear.

Andy had reached the end of the corridor, and now stood in the archway which gave access to what had originally been the servants' stairs. Straight ahead of him was a large plain window which looked out onto formal gardens at the back of the house. It had originally been a small window above head height designed to allow light into the stairwell without permitting the servants to look out and watch their betters at play.

It had been converted to its present size when the house had been remodelled to create the family apartments. At the same time, the stairway going down had been sealed off by the installation of a substantial door, now to Andy's right, secured by an electronic lock whose combination he did not know as it was not the same as the one he'd just used. To his left, the stairs ascended to the upper floors where his desperate plan for survival would either succeed or damn him forever.

Pausing at the foot of the stairs to listen for any sound from the rooms above, he sensed Carl's impatience as the big man moved alongside him. Not wanting to lose control of the situation, he placed his foot gently on the first stair and started upwards, gun held low at his side, any potential sounds muffled by the rich pile of the stair coverings. After two steps he stopped so suddenly that Carl, behind and to his right, nudged the hand holding the pistol. From somewhere, both behind and up ahead, cutting through the stillness like a bolt of lightning, came the sound of telephones ringing. Andy's heart was already pounding but this jolt sent it into overdrive. He stood frozen, waiting for the noise to stop.

Seventy-Four

Scottish Border – Mid-afternoon

With the Catcleugh Reservoir behind him, James reckoned that Carter Bar lay only about three miles ahead. He couldn't be sure exactly what or who might be waiting for him there, but he knew he wasn't fully prepared for it. He needed time to think this through, to consider his options, but he'd been in a hurry to move the Maserati. He felt he had to get it away from the gate to the track by the reservoir. The skies were clearing now and, with visibility improving every minute, it was more than likely that the car could be noticed by someone who, if they were ever asked, might recall having seen it there. Somewhere ahead, he was almost certain, there were at least a couple of pull-ins where he might pause and try to develop some sort of strategy.

    The road was still not busy so, with the improved driving conditions, he was able to think as he continued north up the A68 at a fairly sedate pace. He wondered briefly whether he would still have decided to help Lizzie if the inherent dangers in such a course had been more obvious from the beginning. He hadn't expected that keeping her safe from a Birmingham thug would turn into a shooting war, in spite of the build-up Lizzie had given to Mellisse's reputation. Nor had he expected to find a hopeful offshoot of the Russian mafia bringing his team on board to bat for Mellisse with such gusto. Most of all, he hadn't expected that helping a teenage girl in trouble would bring the threat of danger once more into the life of his precious Abby.

    He had thought that sending his little girl to Scotland would keep her safe, but he'd been wrong. It wasn't surprising that Mellisse or Borisov should have discovered that he had an estate somewhere in the Lammermuir Hills. That information was freely available to anyone curious enough to look for it. The deeply unsettling aspect of it all was that they seemed to know for certain that this was where he was heading. He could have put it down to a good piece of deductive reasoning on someone's part once Borisov had trailed him to Newcastle using the tracker planted in the Maserati but, even after the game he'd played with the police car, they seemed to have known exactly where to pick up his trail again. They had known that he was going to see Zena Walcott, he was sure of it. There just wasn't any way they could have covered all the possible routes that he might have taken to get from Newcastle to Aullton House, and he didn't believe they had picked him up by blind chance.

    This led to the even more unsettling thought that it might have been someone he knew and trusted who had placed the tracker on the

Maserati. He didn't want to believe it and, of course, it need not necessarily be true, but the villains in this little drama seemed to know just a bit too much about his planned movements. He immediately felt a need to warn Andy about this possibility, and began looking for somewhere to pull off the road.

Up ahead, though he couldn't see it yet because it lay in a dip around the bend, he knew there was a wide driveway where he could pull in. The entry gave access, through a wide double gate, to a large barn-type structure which he thought had something to do with the Whitelee Fell National Nature reserve which he could see rising high up to his left. The important thing was that the gate was set back from the road by at least two, maybe three, car lengths, giving plenty of space for him to pull in and turn ready for an easy departure. The Maserati would not be easily noticed, partly because of the bends in the road and partly because the barn was at a much lower level than the road surface due to the slope of the ground down to the river.

Slowing as he came around the bend, he saw that there were no vehicles in the driveway or in the yard in front of the barn, and nor did there seem to be any walkers in the vicinity using the public footpath which led down to the river. He swung in and turned the car so it faced back out towards the road, and then he allowed it to trickle back until almost touching the gate. Turning off the engine, he reached for his phone.

He wasn't really surprised to find that he couldn't get through to Andy's mobile. Cell phone reception was notoriously unreliable in the area around Aullton House. He gave up and pressed the speed dial for the family apartment in the house. After several rings, his call was answered by a voice he recognised saying tentatively, "Hello?"

"Hello, Barrie," he replied. "It's James. Everything OK up there?"

"Oh, hello James. Yes, sure. Everything's fine. We've got Angie settled down comfortably, and I rather think she's going to be OK. Not talking much at the moment, and her memory for the last few days is still pretty much a blank, but she's stable and... ... well, she doesn't deserve what happened to her so I'm going to stick around and do everything I can to make sure she pulls through."

"Glad to hear it," said James, wondering whether he was hearing a bit more emotion in those last few words than he might have expected. He dismissed the thought and asked, "Is Andy up there with you?"

"Yeah, he's around somewhere... ... Meeting with some Scottish chaps, I think. Extra help, he said. Why, do you need him?"

"Well, I can't get him on his mobile so... ... Yeah, I know, I know. Signal's horrible up there. Anyway, when you see him, can you get him to give me a call from the landline?"

"Sure, no problem"

"Great, thanks. Is Abby there at the moment?"

"No, you've just missed her. Cherry's taken her and Lizzie off somewhere to look at llamas of all things."

"Ah… … No point in trying their mobiles then. Signal's even worse out there."

He paused for a moment, wondering whether he should tell Barrie about the events of his journey and his suspicions, but decided in the end that it would serve no useful purpose. It wasn't as though Barrie could do anything that Andy would not already be doing.

"OK, Barrie. I should be seeing you before too long. You just go on taking care of Angie."

"Yeah, I'll certainly do that."

Emotion again? James began to wonder about his doctor friend. Maybe he wasn't going to be quite so wrapped up in his work in future.

He shut off his phone and sat staring through the windscreen, over the road towards the narrow lane leading steeply up to the buildings of Whitelee Farm and its holiday cottages. It was here that some friends of his had been staying when they made the acquaintance of the Redesdale Forest goats. They had subsequently told him about their surprise encounter, with some excitement, when they called in at Aullton the following week on their journey up to Edinburgh. He'd forgotten all about it until… … was it really less than an hour ago? He shook his head and his mouth twisted in a smile which had little humour in it.

He wanted to see Abby, to wrap his massive strength around her and keep her safe. He had no reason to believe she was in any immediate danger, but just the merest possibility was enough to settle an icy coldness in his stomach. He needed to get to Aullton House, and quickly, but he was now as sure as he could be that Borisov was somewhere in between, possibly at Carter Bar, but definitely somewhere on the road up ahead. What would Borisov be thinking, now that his two henchmen in the Mercedes had gone quiet? Would he be planning some sort of simple ambush? Brute force on the public highway in broad daylight? Or would he have in mind some sort of subterfuge, a deception that would hopefully lure James into a situation where he could be quietly overpowered and disposed of. As he considered the possibilities, James became gradually more certain that Borisov could no longer be hoping that he would not be alert for anything the slightest bit out of the ordinary. No, by now the Russian would probably be improvising like crazy, and improvisation was not the easiest thing to plan against.

He was just thinking that he needed another Capitaine Davout inspired plan, when the most outlandish idea leapt into his mind. What he needed was the leverage to make Borisov turn tail and run. Nothing James could threaten would scare the Russian off. That seemed clear enough and, capable as he was of resorting to violence against anyone who threatened the safety of people he cared about, he couldn't bring himself to coldly arrange the death even of someone like Borisov. Retaliation when threatened was one thing, but pre-emptive murder was something else entirely. So, even if he could not intimidate Borisov sufficiently to cause him to back off, was it possible that someone else might? Someone who, though now respectable, once enjoyed a reputation that Genghis Khan would have envied. Someone who owed James the biggest of favours, a fact which he had not so long ago been reminded of at an embassy dinner in London.

James lifted his phone and checked its contact book for the number of an oddly modern-looking building set amongst the mostly-white columns of early Victorian grandeur in Lexham Gardens, London. He selected the number and pressed the call button. A short wait and then his call was answered by a female voice speaking perfect English, pleasingly tinged with just a hint of Eastern European.

"Good afternoon. This is the embassy of Bosnia and Herzegovina. How may I help you?"

"Good afternoon," replied James. "Is it possible to speak to Osman Izetbegović, please?"

There was a slight pause. The Bosnian security attaché did not receive many phone calls from unknown members of the British public.

"I do not know whether he is in his office at this moment, sir," came the eventual reply. "If you can give me your name and the reason for your call, I will see if I can find him for you."

James needed her to apply rather more effort than seemed at the moment likely, so he allowed a veneer of icy formality to overlay his words.

"My name is James Montrayne, Lord Montrayne if you will, Earl of Aullton and Laird of Ewesley. Whether he is in his office or not, Mr. Izetbegović will take my call."

"I see, sir. Er… … my lord. Please wait while I try to connect you."

James had no idea whether his name meant anything to her or not. There was no reason really why it should, although he had met Osman Izetbegović on several occasions since that gentleman's appointment to his country's London embassy. Each time the Bosnian had made sure to remind him of their encounter in the summer of 1995 in the woods north of Sarajevo. He would remind James of his son, taken by the Serbs in a skirmish, and held hostage until James had blown out the brains of his Serbian guard and tormentor. He would remind him of a favour owed and assistance offered if ever it should be needed. Every time they met,

Osman never allowed them to part before he had expressed again his eternal gratitude for the life of his son, restored when he'd been given up for dead.

"James... ...James," a powerful voice boomed suddenly in his ear. "How are you my friend? And that so charming little girl of yours, she is well, I hope?"

"Indeed she is, Osman," James replied. "But I'm afraid her continued good health may rest in your hands."

He knew that a potential threat to his own child would pique the Bosnian's curiosity and guarantee his determination to honour the debt which he had so frequently acknowledged.

"What are you saying, my friend?" the Bosnian asked, his voice sounding genuinely concerned. "How is this?"

James knew it was more than likely, in spite of his protestations of friendship, that Osman would be recording their conversation – such a move would be almost second nature to him – so he had decided to be very circumspect regarding the details of the story which he needed to tell.

Osman listened with great attention and few interruptions to the account of a young woman's escape from sexual slavery in Birmingham, of her encounter with James and his family, of the attempts on the life of her and her friend, of her growing relationship with Abby, and the potential threat that brought to the little girl. James finished his interpretation of events with an explanation of the involvement of the Russian mafia in the person of Borisov, or as much as he'd been able to deduce from what had happened so far.

In the short silence that followed his account, James sensed rather than heard the click and brief hiss which, he was almost certain, indicated that Osman had stopped recording their conversation. Maybe he didn't want enduring evidence of their discussion any more than James did.

"So what is it that you want, my friend? Can you not deal with this vermin yourself?"

James had already anticipated the question and he had his answer ready.

"I seem to remember a little while ago that the Russian Ambassador Grishenko denied quite strongly that the Russian mafia had any influence in Bosnia-Herzegovina."

He paused to give Osman time to respond to this sudden change in direction. He wasn't disappointed.

"That is true, my friend. At least, it is true that he denied it."

"Was it then not true in fact?"

"There were many rumours. Who knows if they were true?"

"OK," said James. "I believe the Ambassador was upset about a number of unexplained attacks on Russian businesses."

A long sigh came down the phone, so deep James almost felt it vibrating in his ear. The silence which followed dragged out for so long that James found it a real struggle not to jump in and fill it with words.

"It was a difficult time," said Osman eventually. "Those years after Dayton were full of opportunity for the wrong sort of people. Giving us a Federation with a rotating presidency may have stopped the fighting, but it also gave us a political system with no central authority. And then when you start pouring in billions in aid for reconstruction... ... well, it created some tempting opportunities. My job was to make sure the wrong people didn't succumb to those temptations."

"And," replied James, "if my memory serves, your methods were most effective."

"Indeed."

"So much so," James went on, "that some Russian mobster called Ivankov actually put out a contract on you. Then he disappeared, and others like him in the Russian mafia decided to pull back from Bosnia. There were rumours that too many were ending their dubious careers in the foundations of new bridges or office blocks."

"Ah, my friend. These rumours. What can I say?"

"Well now," replied James. "I can tell you just what I'd like you to say."

Seventy-Five

Tamworth – Mid-afternoon

Thanking whatever lucky stars might be lending their support, Sergeant Hayford and DC Baxter had left the offices of the Lichfield Tube Company with stony faces entirely at odds with their inner elation. Not revealing the photo of the man they now knew to be Mitchell Portess had been absolutely the right thing to do. For the first time since she had found herself enmeshed in this case four days ago, Joanne believed she had a solid lead that was actually going to take her somewhere. Returning to the Focus ST, the two officers climbed in without a backward glance towards the offices they had just left.

Joanne drove out slowly through the gates in the green, metal-post fencing that surrounded the Lichfield Tube site. The same security guard was on duty and although he gave them a cheery wave, his face fell when he realised they were not this time stopping for a chat, however brief. The ST kept going until a large hangar, left over from the time when this whole area was an airfield, hid the car from any curious eyes in Lichfield Tube's premises. Then Joanne braked to a stop and turned to grin at Georgie.

"First thing," she said. "Let's check what flight he's on and when it's due in."

"And where," replied Georgie.

Joanne grimaced. "Hell yes. I just assumed it would be Birmingham, but I suppose it needn't be. Second, we need an address. And third... ...."

"I know," interrupted Georgie. "Check if he's got any form."

"OK. You get on with that while I check flights."

Both women set to work, Joanne on her phone and Georgie on her laptop. It took several minutes and Georgie finished first because Joanne had to go through various levels of identification and authorisation to get what she wanted from the airlines. While she waited for her friend to finish her calls, Georgie continued surfing as she tried to chase down a vague idea glimmering in her mind.

"OK", said Joanne as she put away her phone. "It looks like we have a few hours to kill. There's no direct flight into Birmingham from Vilnius, but there is one from Kaunas."

"Never heard of it. Where's that?"

"Also in Lithuania apparently, but it's some distance away from the capital so probably not likely. There is a direct flight from Vilnius to Luton but that landed early this morning, so almost certainly not that one.

The one I put my money on was from Vilnius with a change in Frankfurt and, guess what?"

"He's on it."

"Landing at Birmingham at 17:45 this afternoon."

"Wonderful," said Georgie, as she took a quick peek at her watch. "Now listen to this. I've got an address on the outskirts of Tamworth which is pretty handy. We could be there in half an hour tops. It's also handy for him too. Easy to get over here to work, and it's straight down the M42 to Birmingham airport."

"Any previous?"

"Nothing to speak of." She was looking at her laptop screen. "Just speeding. He's got six points on his licence. Can't find anything else. Except... ... ..."

She paused and glanced at Joanne with a teasing smile on her provocatively sculpted lips.

"Well, go on then," urged her colleague.

"Well... ... it could be nothing really, but I was just Googling a bit while I waited for you, and I came up with this."

She turned her laptop slightly so Joanne could see the screen. Across the top was a picture of a battle-grey warship cruising across a slightly choppy blue sea. Below it the page was split into two columns. The upper part of the left-hand one was filled by another picture, this time a group of naval officers and ratings apparently taken on board the same warship. The lower part of the right-hand column showed a third picture, a group of civilians on the quayside with the warship towering up behind them, her pennant number clearly visible. The remainder of both columns was filled with text. Above the top picture, the page was headed *Unsung heroine of the Falklands slips quietly into mothballs.*

Joanne studied the page for a moment before looking back to Georgie, her raised eyebrows asking the question. Georgie smiled. She was obviously enjoying herself.

"That's HMS Selkirk, a Type 42 destroyer that was decommissioned in February this year. This report appeared in the local paper."

"So?"

Georgie zoomed the page and then scrolled to centre on the civilian group.

"Recognise anyone?"

Joanne leaned over to look more closely at the picture as Georgie lifted up the laptop. At first she just stared, then her mouth opened in surprise before her lips pursed in a silent whistle.

"OK," she said, sitting back in her seat. "Tell me."

Georgie resized the page so all the photos and text were visible.

"The sailors were serving on HMS Selkirk at the time of her decommissioning. The civilians had all served on her at some point, and they came to Portsmouth to pay their last respects, as it were. Some of them were interviewed for the paper, and that's how their names got into the text, and that's how I managed to pick them up."

She turned the screen again and used her right index finger to point at figures in the civilian photo.

"Our friend Mitchell Portess here was a petty officer aboard the Selkirk until he left the Navy in January '96 during her refit at Rosyth. Gordon Russell, over… … ah, just here… …was a lieutenant, some sort of technical specialist, and he left at the end of '94. The real surprise was this one." Her finger lightly brushed the screen. "Sir Vernon Laycock. Apparently, his company Ferro-Tech was a big supplier to the naval dockyards and there was a lot of his stuff in HMS Selkirk."

She settled the laptop more comfortably on her knees before delivering her final thought.

"Gordon Russell is now the MD of Lichfield Tube, but guess who gave him a job when he left the navy? And who in turn did he give a job to? And… … if he and Portess both served together, and now work together, can it really be possible that one doesn't know what the other one is up to?"

Joanne looked at her for a long moment, thinking it over. Eventually she said, "Russell and Portess. I'll give you that, especially if Simmons was killed to cover up something going on at Lichfield Tube. But Laycock? Our budding MP? It's a bit of a stretch to think he could be involved."

Georgie shrugged. "No, I must admit I can't really see it myself." Her long, carefully-manicured fingers stroked the laptop's touchpad and brought up another screen. "Now, do you want to check out this address for Portess?"

Twenty-three minutes later they entered a small village on the north-west outskirts of Tamworth and they found the house without too much difficulty. It was actually on the main street, opposite the church, and turned out to be a large, double-fronted structure, built to look old using recycled bricks to blend in with the older cottages that lined the street. A low wall made of the same type of brick bounded the front garden, and a paved drive swept up to the front door and round to a detached double garage off to the right. The rear of the house was invisible from the road.

Joanne stopped a few yards past the driveway entrance and the two women turned in their seats to look up and down the street. There was little activity as it wasn't yet time for children to be coming home from school. Neither of them was worried about their enquiries alerting the curiosity of neighbours, as the cat would be out of the bag anyway as soon as they intercepted Portess at the airport. As they sat in the Focus wondering just where to start, Joanne noticed an elderly lady in the garden of the cottage next to the church. She seemed to be pottering about, tending to her plants in a rather haphazard fashion whilst leaning heavily on a walking stick.

Deciding that she was as good a place to start as any, the two police officers crossed the road and entered her garden through a rickety wooden gate. The old lady watched them approach and smiled a greeting. When they introduced themselves, she said she was perfectly happy to stop and chat for a while as it would give her an excuse to rest her ancient bones. Inviting them into her ivy-clad cottage she insisted on making them "a nice cup of tea." Her name, it turned out, was Jane Ampler, and she had lived in the village all her life. As she chatted while the kettle boiled, and then while the tea brewed, it soon became apparent to both police officers that, however frail her body might now seem, her mind was equally as sharp as theirs, which made Joanne wonder just how formidable she must have been in her younger days.

Once settled with their china cups and saucers, and a plate of rather good chocolate chip cookies, Joanne turned the conversation to the old lady's neighbour across the street. Jane – she insisted they call her Jane – frowned at the mention of his name and the natural cheeriness went out of her face.

"Well, I don't know dears," she said. "With a bit of imagination, and I do assure you I have more than most, I could make up no end of stories based on some of the things I've seen, but I don't really *know* anything."

It turned out that she was underselling herself and actually knew rather a lot, which Joanne and Georgie carefully extracted from her over the next half-hour. It was the unknown girls that caused Jane's frowns. There seemed to have been a constant stream of them, always arriving with him in his "big silver car."

"It's the one with the four rings on the front, dear."

"Audi," said Joanne and Georgie, almost together.

"That's right, dears. I don't know a lot about cars, but I think it might have been the four point two litre S6."

They stared at her and her eyes definitely twinkled.

"I watch Top Gear, you see. And I can't help remembering things."

After that, they began to place a lot more reliance on her observations and recollections, and their confidence in her as a possible witness increased enormously. Usually, Portess only brought home one girl at a time, but occasionally there were two and, at least once, three.

"It's not that I mind him having girlfriends, dears. Well, one can't mind these days, can one? It's just that they often seem… … well, scared. As though they don't want to be there."

Joanne wondered if this was a bit of her imagination at work.

"And you can tell that from here, can you?"

"Oh yes, dear. No problem at all. Nothing wrong with my eyes, you know."

"So," said Georgie, feeling that this needed to be established beyond doubt. "You'd be able to read our car number plate without having to go outside."

"Of course," said Jane, adding with another twinkle, "I suppose you'd like me to demonstrate?"

And she did, heaving herself to her feet with the help of her walking stick so that she could look out of her front window, down her garden and across the road to the rear of the Focus.

"Impressive," said Georgie. "I'm sorry but we had to be sure."

"Of course you did, dear. Now where were we?"

After getting Georgie to note down everything Jane could remember about the girls, especially how many and how often, their behaviour and demeanour, Joanne moved the conversation on to the morning of the previous Saturday.

"Yes, of course I remember Saturday," replied Jane in answer to her question. "But whether I noticed anything you'll be interested in is another matter."

"Can I ask what time you got up that morning?"

"Four o'clock, dear. Maybe a few minutes before. My arthritis was being a bit of a nuisance you see, so I hadn't been sleeping very well. I thought I'd get up and make myself a nice mug of drinking chocolate."

Joanne's mouth was open to ask her next question but, before she could get the words out, Jane spoke again.

"And you want to know if I saw Mr Portess that morning. Well, I did… … He came out of his house soon after I got up. I was just standing here waiting for the kettle to boil, you see."

"And the curtains were drawn back?"

"Oh yes, dear. How else could I have seen out of the window? I don't often close them but, if I do, I always draw them back before I go up to bed."

"And you saw Mr Portess quite clearly, even though it was still dark?"

"Well, he has these lights, you see. You know the things. They come on if anything moves in front of them. As soon as he came out of his front door, the whole front garden lit up. Oh yes, dear. I saw him very clearly. It was quite odd, really. He looked rather military. It was his clothes, you see. Some sort of camouflage jacket, and trousers as well now I come to think of it. And he was holding something loosely in his hand. Maybe pair of gloves, or maybe a balaclava, like those IRA men used to wear. He went into his garage. The car backed out and he drove away."

"I don't suppose you noticed what time he came back?" asked Georgie.

"My dear, in this village I have a reputation for nosiness that is perfectly well-founded, I assure you. Of course, I know when he came back. It was a little after seven thirty. In the morning, that is."

Joanne watched Georgie's pen scribbling away for a moment before she asked, "Can I ask you, Jane, and please don't be offended by… …"

"That's all right, dear. I know you have to be sure. You want to know whether I can really be certain that this happened on Saturday morning and not Friday or Sunday, don't you?"

Both police officers smiled. Neither of them could remember the last time questioning a witness had been such a pleasurable experience.

"Yes, Jane," replied Joanne. "We do have to be sure."

"Well, it was the DVD, you see. I was watching this Jason Bourne movie, Supremacy it must have been because Identity was the first one. I do hope they make another one because the story isn't finished yet, is it? I do so love it when the baddies get blown up, don't you?"

Joanne shook her head in amazement and grinned at Georgie. This old lady was truly wonderful.

"And it had to be Saturday, you see. My neighbour got it for me from the library – it's so much cheaper than Blockbuster, you know – and it was due back on Saturday. She was going to drop it off at the library when she went into town that morning."

She nibbled at a biscuit and the two police officers waited patiently for her to resume.

"I had started watching it on Friday evening with my supper. I got over half way through but then I started feeling sleepy and I didn't want to miss anything. It's too complicated for you to miss anything you know. You'll never understand what's going on."

She reached for her cup to take a sip of tea but then realised it was empty.

"So I decided to save the rest to watch with my breakfast on Saturday. Except that I watched it with my mug of drinking chocolate instead. And I started again at the beginning, just to make sure I got the story straight. It was good… … Well, that Matt Damon is quite a hunk, isn't he? It's worth watching just to see how easily he wipes out all the baddies. But how could they leave it with him telling her she looked tired and then just walking away? I was still thinking about that when I saw Mr Portess come back."

She looked at them while she quietly munched the remains of her biscuit.

"So you see, my dears, I can be absolutely sure it was Saturday that I saw Mr Portess go off very early in the morning and come back about three hours later. And very muddy he was too."

That more or less clinched it, and the interview came to an end shortly afterwards. After thanking Jane for her hospitality, and being invited to come back for another cup of tea anytime, the two officers returned to Joanne's Focus. As they walked down Jane's garden path, they couldn't help looking across the road at the large empty house and wishing they had a search warrant. Perhaps, if they'd been looking harder and wishing less, they might have seen the eyes watching them from behind the curtains of an upstairs window. Then again, perhaps not, since the movement of the curtain was barely more than a twitch of the edge. But it was just enough to allow the eyes to follow them across the road to the car and to study them for the next ten minutes as they sat there working their laptop and phones.

The eyes did not withdraw until the car drove away and only then did a small, delicate hand reach for the bedside phone and begin to dial.

Seventy-Six

Aullton House – Mid-afternoon

Andy and Carl waited to see if the phone would be answered. The marble figures in the small alcoves which graced the stairway could not have been quieter or more still. Though they listened with the utmost concentration, neither could hear any sound of footfall or creaking boards above the sound of the phone. Then suddenly the ringing stopped, and they heard the gentle voice of Doctor Harwood as he answered it. From his opening words, they knew he was speaking to James which probably meant that it would be some time before James actually arrived.

Andy nudged Carl, put a finger to his lips and nodded in the direction of the upper floor. They moved together, as quickly as their attempt at silence would allow.

At the top, they emerged through an arch onto a corridor running left and right. There was a door at both ends, and several more at intervals along the length of the inner wall. Most were shut, but the one at the far end to their left stood wide open while another along to their right stood ajar. It was from the door to their left that they could hear the doctor's voice explaining how Angie's memory of the last few days was still pretty much a blank.

Andy pointed at himself and then towards the door from which they could hear the doctor speaking. Then he pointed at Carl and the slightly opened door along the corridor. Carl nodded and moved in that direction. Andy watched him for a moment and then strode down the corridor in search of the doctor. Although he was no longer making any attempt at silence, his feet made no sound on the rich pile of the carpet. Just before he reached the door, he slipped the Beretta back in his pocket. He didn't want the doctor to see it. Not yet. He risked a quick glance behind him and saw Carl, paused outside the other open door trying to peer through the crack into the bedroom beyond.

He licked his dry lips and took a deep breath, knowing that nothing could calm the pounding of his heart at that moment. His whole future hung on what happened in the next few minutes. He just hoped that Carl wouldn't botch it. He wasn't a callous person, just desperate, so he hoped that Angie could die without ever knowing it was coming. After that, well it was up to him.

He heard the doctor say with strange emphasis, "Yeah, I'll certainly do that." Then the phone was hung up just as Andy entered a bedroom which seemed at first glance bigger than the whole of his apartment. There was door in the far corner, leading presumably to the en-suite bathroom. The doctor had obviously allocated himself this room since a suitcase lay unopened on the king-size bed, and two other more business-like cases stood on a table in front of the window. A jacket was draped over the back of a chair.

"Hello Barrie," Andy said, hoping his voice sounded calm and relaxed.

Barrie looked around from where he had just replaced the phone on an ornate bedside cabinet.

"Oh. Hello Andy. You've just missed James. He was asking for you. In fact, he wanted you to call him back."

He reached for the phone again. "If you do it now you might catch him before he sets off again."

His hand hadn't even touched the phone before there was loud crash from down the hall. For a fraction of a second, the two men's eyes locked, and then they were both rushing for the door and the corridor beyond. Andy was in front, as he'd been nearest the door. He was halfway along the corridor when there was a second crash. With Barrie on his heels, he didn't hesitate though he couldn't understand what was happening. The metallic clack of a silenced gunshot which he'd expected to hear was actually sounding more like someone throwing furniture about. Heavy furniture, thrown hard.

Before he reached the wide-open door of Angie's room, the Beretta was back in his hand. He entered, arms outstretched, the gun at eye-level in a two-handed grip. Since the door was hinged on the left, and was fully open, the whole room was laid out before him. His eyes rapidly took in the scene and his experienced mind interpreted it more quickly than words could express it.

The duvet on the bed to his right was thrown back and Angie was nowhere in sight. Carl was standing in front of the door to the bathroom, gun in hand, gathering himself for another kick at the firmly closed door. When the rooms on this floor had been converted and bathrooms inserted into each one, everything was in keeping with the original structure, which meant that every door was of substantial oak with locks to match. Angie must have been in the bathroom when Carl entered, and the fool had been in too much of a hurry to wait for her to emerge in her own good time. Or maybe she had emerged, at least enough to see him, and slammed the door and locked it before he could get to it.

However it had happened, Angie was not dead, and Andy was amazed at the flood of relief that rushed through him. She had never deserved to die, not like Carl did. The thug was a killer for hire and, in Andy's original plan, he was going to die anyway after he'd done the job on Angie. Maybe it was better this way.

"Carl," shouted Andy, sensing Barrie now at his shoulder.

The third kick at the door was already underway, and landed even as Andy shouted. Nevertheless, Carl heard him call and swung round, slightly off balance, instinctively bringing up his own gun. He probably wasn't going to fire it at Andy but no-one would ever know since he was flung backwards by three bullets striking the centre of his chest.

Andy lowered the Beretta and watched Carl stagger before crumpling to the floor, knocking over a small table as he went down. Barrie pushed past Andy and strode over the where Carl lay. He knelt and checked for breathing and a pulse. He wasn't really surprised to find neither. He turned to look up at Andy who had advanced into the room.

"Did you have to shoot him three times?" he asked, in a tone full of a doctor's natural abhorrence of violent trauma.

"Had to," replied Andy. "This is only a .22 and I've never fired it before. I wanted him down."

He peered at Carl's chest.

"Looks like it pulls a touch to the left. I was aiming for his heart."

Barrie looked back at Carl's body. He rubbed at his forehead, looked up at Andy, and then back at the body. He seemed profoundly shocked at what had just happened.

Andy touched him on the shoulder.

"Barrie."

He waited for a response, and when he didn't get one he repeated the doctor's name.

"Barrie. I know this is a bloody awful mess, but I need to find Cherry. These guys are obviously not who they said they were, and Cherry doesn't know that. I'll go find him."

He bent to scoop up Carl's Smith and Wesson from beside the upturned table and pointed to the still-closed bathroom door.

"You look after Angie. She's probably terrified in there."

Assuming that would kick-start Barrie into action, he turned for the door but paused as a thought struck him.

"Whatever you do, don't call the police. This is over in here, and they're too far away to help Cherry. I'll go and find him. Just wait until James gets here and then do whatever he thinks best. Have you got that? No police."

He waited just long enough to see Barrie's slow nod before leaving to make his way out of the house.

Seventy-Seven

Birmingham Airport – Mid-afternoon

Sitting in her Focus outside the house of Mitchell Portess, Joanne tried to contact ACC Fletcher while Georgie checked the latest flight information. When Fletcher was finally able to take her call, she quickly ran through the developments since her conversation with him earlier that day. She was a little nervous about what would happen next. Fletcher might decide that the proper course would be to pass the information on to DCI Morrissey since he was still the officer in charge of investigating Simmons' death. When Fletcher put her on hold and the seconds of waiting expanded into minutes, she found her nervousness mutating slowly into resentment as she thought of Morrissey getting the credit for all her work.

While Joanne waited in growing frustration, Georgie's slender fingers were flying over the laptop's keyboard as she progressed from checking flights to generating their official report on the day's events so far. She was still typing when Fletcher came back on the line and her fingers paused in their frantic dance as she listened to Joanne's end of the conversation. She smiled when she saw her friend begin to relax as the tension slowly bled out of her.

"So what's he going to do?" she asked.

"He wants that report as soon as you've done it," replied Joanne, "and he'll pass it on to Morrissey in due course. He emphasised that – *in due course.* I think he's going to sit on it for a bit."

"Why?"

"Because he got in touch with West Midlands to make sure that their officers at the airport would be expecting us and he found out they were already interested in our friend Portess. They were asked to look into the apparent disappearance of several young women, girls really, who flew from Lithuania to Birmingham at different times over the past year. They were supposed to be coming over here to work, and did actually let their families know they got here OK, but after that first text or phone call… …nothing. Eventually… … well, you can imagine. Families got worried and reported them missing. There's a lot more to it, obviously, but the bottom line is… …when West Mids eventually began taking this seriously they found that each of the flights used by these girls had something in common."

"Don't tell me," said Georgie. "Portess."

"You've got it. He was on the plane every time."

"So West Mids are wondering about trafficking... ... maybe sexual exploitation?" asked Georgie.

"Got it again," replied Joanne. "Which means that our dear ACC can let us pursue this with West Mids because it's a completely separate investigation from Morrissey's."

"So who gets him, them or us?"

"We do. They'll help with the arrest but we get first crack at him. He may be flying into Birmingham but he mostly lives and works in Staffs. The ACC's organising a warrant to search his house."

Joanne's face was illuminated by a beam of unholy satisfaction.

"Morrissey will go ape," she said with delight. "Only trouble is... ...I probably won't be there to see it."

"Probably just as well," said Georgie, and the two of them sat there smiling.

As Joanne started the car, Georgie asked thoughtfully, "What do you suppose that business with the poisoned dart was all about?"

"How do you mean?"

"Well, it's pretty obvious that Portess is well in the frame for killing Simmons, but why go all Agatha Christie about it? It's your case not mine, so I know I'm not fully in the loop, but it just seems so... ... clumsy, and... ... well, stupid and unnecessary."

"Funny you should say that about Agatha Christie," replied Joanne. "I had the same thought. Poisoned darts is just so... ... cliché. In the end, I think he was just trying to muddy the waters, throw as much confusion around as possible. Mayblin found out that Montrayne did serve in Belize for a while. Not exactly common knowledge, but easy enough to find out. He could have brought some curare back from there, though we haven't found any."

"But it wasn't curare that killed him, was it?" asked Georgie.

"No," answered Joanne. "It was succinylcholine. Different substance, similar effect. More muddying of the waters I suppose. The dart suggested an airgun; curare would have pointed towards the Americas; and if Portess realised toxicology would show up succinylcholine, he may have thought that we'd suppose Montrayne got it from that hospital of his."

"Yeah... ... Maybe... ... I guess. Can you get enough of the stuff smeared on a dart?"

"Forensics say probably not, but from the way Montrayne described the scene, Portess could have jabbed Simmons with a hypodermic, and pushed the dart in afterwards, just for effect."

"But why the effort to implicate Montrayne? Was there any special reason, apart from mud and confusion? And that stuff in the paper. Was that him as well?"

"I guess those are things we shall be asking Mr Portess, when we finally get hold of him."

It took just over three quarters of an hour to travel down the M42 to Birmingham airport, in which time Georgie finished off her report and emailed it to the ACC. By the time they arrived, there was quite a party waiting for them on the concourse outside the Arrivals Lounge. Three uniformed officers stood in one group, two constables led by a sergeant, all of whom were armed with some sort of shoulder slung carbines whose make Joanne neither recognised nor cared about. Slightly apart from them were two plain clothes officers who introduced themselves as DI Cobham and DS Sidebottom. Joanne had never actually met anyone called Sidebottom before and she couldn't help wondering, as she shook hands with the grim looking young man, whether constantly having to admit to such a name was the reason for his sour expression.

Apparently not. The two detectives were thoroughly pissed at having to surrender their potential prize to some Johnny-come-lately pirates from a neighbouring force. It was, as always, all about who was going to get the credit. DI Cobham was more civilised about it than his sergeant, and he demonstrated his superior self-control by inviting his two female colleagues to take a coffee with him while they waited for the flight to land. Unsure whether or not he really meant it, Joanne decided to accept anyway. According to Cobham, the flight from Frankfurt was on time but they had nearly forty-five minutes before it was due to touch down.

The uniformed sergeant sent his men back to their normal patrol duties with instructions to be in the Arrivals Lounge five minutes before the flight landed. Cobham then led his own sergeant, the two women and the uniformed sergeant inside the building to find their coffee. The café on the ground floor didn't seem too busy so Cobham headed towards it asking the others what brew they would prefer. The two ladies opted for cappuccinos but the uniform shook his head.

"Not for me, thanks," he said. "Wouldn't look right."

Cobham just nodded and went off with Sidebottom to get the drinks leaving the others to sort out the seating arrangements. When Georgie was about to commandeer a fifth chair from another table to drag across to theirs, uniform stopped her.

"You lot sit," he said quietly, looking around. "I'll stand. Odd, I know, but to everyone else it'll look more natural that way."

Georgie looked at him, her eyebrows raised questioningly.

"As far as the public's concerned," he explained, leaning slightly towards her, "uniformed officers carrying weapons are always on their feet."

Georgie thought, nodded, and then smiled before taking her seat at the table. She didn't have time to respond because Sidebottom arrived just then with his own drink and hers. Cobham placed Joanne's cappuccino on the table in front of her and sat down in the chair next to her.

"So, tell us," he said, trying hard to keep the edge out of his voice. "What was it that put you onto Portess, and why are we only just hearing about it?"

Everyone looked at Joanne, but she wasn't going to be intimidated. She glanced around to make sure no-one was close enough to overhear the conversation at their table, but she needn't have worried. The nearest table was occupied by a couple who had their hands full coping with two tired and fractious primary-age children and a squawling baby.

"Same reason we only just heard about your interest over possible trafficking," she said calmly. "And, just so we're clear, we're not looking at Portess for that. We've got him lined up for a murder last Saturday morning."

"And I suppose you think that gives you priority with him?"

Joanne smiled, still forcing herself to stay calm.

"I think we both know it does," she replied. "But you're welcome to come along and make sure we don't do anything to sabotage what you've been doing."

Her offer didn't exactly break the ice, but it seemed to be enough to start a slow thaw. Having settled to everyone's satisfaction exactly how the arrest would be carried out, they began to share information from their respective investigations. The minutes ticked by. Occasionally, one or other would glance up at the flight information board and then at his, or her, watch. The uniformed sergeant kept one ear tuned to the conversation and both eyes scanning the arrivals concourse. He was the only member of the group to notice the large, bearded figure mingling with the waiting herd of friends, relatives, business colleagues and hire-car drivers. The man stood out partly because of his height, his bulk and his bushy beard, but also because of the petite, blond, young woman who shadowed his every movement as he eased his way through the crowd.

It was unfortunate that no-one who knew had thought to warn the sergeant that the presence of this man might be significant.

It was also unfortunate that no-one among the police personnel noticed how closely they were being scrutinised by a gentleman in a long waxed drovers coat. Had they been able to see the dark, unblinking, wide-set eyes under the shadow of his broad-brimmed hat, they might have paid him more attention, and a murder might have been avoided.

Seventy-Eight

Carter Bar – Mid-afternoon

The road climbed steadily up to the border at Carter Bar. Reaching the crest, just before the panorama of the Scottish Lowlands broke open under a hazy blue sky to the right, James turned into the northbound viewpoint layby. On the passenger seat, still in its laptop carry-case, lay the MP5K with its selector set to single-shot. As the Maserati crawled past the blue and white flag of Scotland, James very much hoped that the gun would not be needed. Already he could see that the brightening sky was encouraging passers-by to pause for a while to take in the view. Three cars, a VW camper-van, and a motor-cycle were scattered through the parking area, their occupants wandering about with cameras and binoculars.

One vehicle stood apart from the rest, down at the far end of the parking-area. It was a black BMW X5 with tinted windows. James recognised the number of the vehicle from Picktree Lane down in Newcastle. If Borisov wanted to be unobtrusive, he really should have resisted the urge to put a personalised plate on his car. There were plenty of spaces and few vehicles, so James ignored the bay markings and eased to a stop about three car lengths short of the BMW. Both cars were facing the direction of the exit.

What would happen next was anybody's guess, but James was hoping that whatever the Russian had planned, witnesses did not figure in the scenario. At that moment, the expanding views lit by the clearing afternoon sun ensured there were several scattered about, with more joining. Borisov should really have left this sort of dirty work to lesser villains. He obviously hadn't yet fully mastered the gangster's skill of leading from the rear.

There was no movement from the BMW and James couldn't see inside because of the tinted glass. It suddenly occurred to him that he couldn't be sure that there was anyone actually in the vehicle and he looked rapidly to left and right. Just for a moment he was conscious of being a sitting target for a long-range rifle, but then he smiled to himself at the thought. There were trees some distance up the rising ground to his left, but he was shielded from that direction by the bushes that bordered the parking area. A shot from the right would have to come across the A98 and the ground on that side was open and falling away from the road. In any case, Borisov would hardly have placed himself, or an underling, to lie in wait just on the off-chance that James might decide to stop here.

"So what was the plan if I hadn't stopped?" said James to himself as he turned his gaze back to the BMW. And then he realised.

Borisov never had assumed that James would stop at the viewpoint. All he would have been expecting was that the Mercedes would follow close behind James's Maserati as it came over the hill at the border. Phone communication should ensure they got the timing right. Borisov could pull out ahead of James to put the Maserati like meat in a sandwich as the three vehicles descended the northern slope. With a little ruthless manoeuvring, a fatal accident on one of the hairpin bends would not be too hard to manage, the unfortunate result of a wet and slippery road surface.

But James *had* stopped at the viewpoint, and the Mercedes was *not* following. As he wondered what options were available to Borisov now, James saw an ageing Honda Accord pull into a parking bay over to his right. Two boys and a girl, primary school age, immediately erupted from the rear to run over to the low wall that bordered the road. The girl jigged around excitedly pointing at something in the distance. She was about the same age as Abby. The adults exited the car more slowly than the children. All the twisting and stretching to ease their older muscles suggested they were cramped from a long journey. James had no reason to believe that Borisov was stupid, but he was definitely ruthless, and probably extremely angry. He wondered if he should just drive on. At least that way he could ensure these unsuspecting sightseers would be safe.

No time. The front passenger door of the BMW slowly opened and the Russian emerged, leisurely, unhurriedly, as though aware that any sudden movement might precipitate something he wasn't prepared for. He stared back at an angle across the roof of the BMW to where James sat watching and waiting. Slowly, without taking his eyes from the Maserati, he backed away from the BMW, far enough for James to see his hands hanging empty at his sides.

James waited, his left hand reaching into the gun case beside him, needing to feel the security of the MP5 while hoping desperately not to have to use it. He stiffened as he heard a faint electronic chirping sound break the stillness. There was little doubt where it was coming from when he saw Borisov reach slowly inside his jacket and then withdraw his hand equally slowly gripping a small mobile phone. He looked at the display to see who was calling before deciding to answer. He then spent several minutes, listening more than speaking, before ending the call.

He then stood motionless, phone in hand, just watching James as the seconds ticked by. No-one else emerged from the BMW. Cameras clicked and children laughed while adults stood at the viewing board and tried to identify the distant hills. Eventually, Borisov turned to watch them, his gaze passing briefly over each of the nearby sightseers, before turning back to the Maserati. His head tilted somewhat, his gaze intense, as though trying to focus on the face staring back at him through the windscreen. Then he shrugged, arms lifting outwards slightly, as if to say *What can we do?*

James felt the tension of the last few minutes begin to ease and his grip relaxed around the stock of the MP5. He didn't withdraw his hand completely because the driver of the BMW was still nowhere to be seen. He *could* just be sitting in the car waiting patiently for Borisov to complete his business. But he could just as easily be watching the Maserati, holding ready his weapon of choice, prepared to fire as soon as James stepped clear of the car.

No, James told himself again. Borisov was not stupid. The place was too public; too many people, too many cameras. The mother of the three children who had just arrived – James assumed she was their mother – had now extracted a video camera from their car and was slowly turning, eyes glued to the tiny screen, capturing a three hundred and sixty degree panorama. Quite unintentionally, she now had a record of every vehicle in the parking area, and she would probably not be the only one. Clearly Borisov's best option was to leave without fuss but, for some reason, it looked as though the Russian wanted to talk.

As James withdrew his hand from the gun-case, a slight smile appeared on his lips. This was actually going to be easier than he'd had any right to expect.

He climbed out of the Maserati and stood to rest his forearms along the top of the still open door, watching Borisov carefully. No-one took any notice. Still facing the Russian, James nodded in the direction of the driver's side of the BMW, his eyes flicking to the door and back to Borisov's face. The Russian's eyebrows lifted slightly, and then he shrugged and said something in what sounded to James like Russian, but could actually have been any of the Eastern European languages. James knew none of them, apart from a little Serbian which he could speak but not write. He had never taken the trouble to try and master the strange mixture of Cyrillic and Latin scripts that was unique to the Serbian language, and felt none the worse for it.

He tensed as the driver's door of the BMW opened. Unhurriedly, the driver emerged and turned to face him. The same dark suit, still with no tie and the top shirt button still unfastened, dark glasses in place; there was no doubt about it. James was looking at the same impassive face that had stared at him over the roof of the BMW in the parking lot at Scotch Corner. James pointed towards the viewing board, ahead and to his right on the other side of the driveway through the parking area. The driver looked at Borisov who spoke a couple of words and nodded. The driver shrugged and strolled away to admire the view from a point which James could keep constantly in sight while hearing what Borisov had to say.

Closing the car door, James moved towards Borisov but stopped while he was still well out of reach. Even from that distance, the Russian had to tilt his head up to look James in the eye but he gave no sign of resenting it, as though he had grown perfectly comfortable with his own moderate height. It was only two days since James had first seen him in Andy's office at RRISC, but so much had happened it seemed an age since.

"Mr Montrayne," said Borisov in his deep, slightly accented voice. "I congratulate you. Truly, you are very hard man to be rid of."

"And you are very persistent, Mr Borisov."

"So, you know then who I am. That is good."

"How so?"

"Because, Mr Montrayne, if you know who I am you will also know I am very… … er… … persistent, in getting what I want. And you do have something that I want."

"What would that be?"

"Oh, I think you know, Mr Montrayne, and I am willing to be reasonable. You are surprised? Yes, I see that you are, but I have great gift of… … ah what is your word? It is beautiful word. Ah, yes. Magnanimous. I have great gift to be magnanimous. Strange is it not. You cause me great trouble. You kill my men. You did kill them, did you not?"

He looked around the parking area, as if to emphasise their absence.

"I can't think what you mean, Mr Borisov," said James.

"Ah," the Russian shrugged. "No matter. What is done is done. Bygones, that is what you say, is it not? I am reasonable. You are reasonable. We can deal."

"So what are you suggesting?"

"I am suggesting, Mr Montrayne, that you have three packages in your possession. One is small. Not too small, you understand, that I could not make use of it, but it is I think more valuable to you than to me. The other two packages are bigger, much bigger, and only recently come into your possession. They, I most certainly can make use of. I suggest that you hand them over to me and, in return, I will guarantee that no-one in my organisation will attempt to gain possession of the smaller package. It will remain solely yours, ah… … unopened, shall we say."

James felt the cold fear settle in the pit of his stomach. It was not something he had ever felt on his own account, but neither was he a stranger to its sensations. His mind flashed back to the time when Abby had been taken from him, and he thought that he had lost her forever. He knew exactly what Borisov was talking about, with his scarcely veiled threat that the nightmare could begin all over again. His instinctive response was that of any father faced with a threat to his daughter and, in his quiet rage, he wondered briefly what it would be like to feel the bones of Borisov's neck grate, and twist, and snap, and pull apart under hands which he knew were capable of making it happen.

Fortunately for the Russian, and ultimately for himself, James had sufficient control over his rage to let the moment pass. There was a better way.

"Do not look so shocked, Mr Montrayne," said Borisov, breaking into the extended silence. "There is no need. Did I not tell you? We are reasonable. We can deal."

In spite of his anger, James sensed that there was something wrong here. If Borisov really thought a deal would be so easy, and he wanted those two girls so much, why had he apparently gone out of his way to try and have James disposed of before he had actually got his hands on them? Or was the Russian now just trying to make the best of things since his original plan had been shot to hell? Literally.

Pushing his nagging questions aside, James pressed ahead with his own plan.

"Yes indeed, Mr Borisov," he replied in a voice of such controlled calm that he surprised even himself. "We can deal. And I will now tell you how this deal will work."

Borisov frowned as he tried to retain an initiative which he felt might be slipping away.

"No, Mr Montrayne. I will tell you… … …"

"Hold up your cell phone," said James, uninterested in what the Russian was about to tell him. Borisov's frown deepened as he felt the initiative slip a little further. Nevertheless, after a brief pause, he raised his hand and looked at his phone.

"Dial enquiries," said James, "and ask for the number of the Bosnian embassy in London."

Borisov's eyebrows shot up and his mouth dropped open in surprise.

"Directory enquiries," said James again. "You do know their number?"

The Russian looked down at his phone, and then glanced away to where his driver stood admiring the Scottish hills and trying to keep his face averted from the many cameras still in evidence.

"You don't need him," said James in the voice he once used to bring recalcitrant NCOs to order. "Just dial, and ask to be put through."

Eventually, after another pause just long enough to maintain some self-esteem, Borisov dialled and asked for the Bosnian Embassy.

"Ask for Osman Izetbegović. He's waiting for your call."

"Osman... ...?"

"Izetbegović."

Borisov spoke into his phone, waited, and then looked at James.

"He just said to hold."

"Then we hold," said James.

A moment later, James's own phone began to ring. He pressed the answer button.

"Hello," he said, and then, "right...... Yes, he's listening."

Keeping the phone to his ear, James said to Borisov, "You're now on a conference call with the head of Bosnian security in London."

The Russian's hand twitched, pulling the phone away from his ear. His eyes were dark, but not unfathomable. In their depths was a hatred mixed with frustration that the balance of power in this meeting was swinging inexorably away from him and, for the present, he had no idea how to pull it back. James heard Osman asking if the Russian was still listening, and it seemed that Borisov heard him too for he slowly returned the phone to his ear, and growled something James didn't catch.

The call took a little under ten minutes. Osman had clearly rehearsed what he was going to say, and he delivered it perfectly. By the time the conversation ended, Borisov fervently wished he'd never heard of Osman Izetbegović, or Bosnia, or even James Montrayne. He had long since been a man who understood fear, but usually from the perspective of someone who instilled it rather than experienced it. He gave no sign even now of being afraid but, alongside the anger that still sparked in his eyes, his expression suggested a kind of settled pragmatism.

He was breathing hard as he returned his phone to his pocket without speaking. He allowed his gaze to wander over the sightseers gathered at the boundary wall where they could look out at the increasingly impressive view. Finally, his eyes settled on his driver on whom the distant vistas had already ceased to work their magic. It was no good. The ruthless obedience of his henchman, usually so effective, would not serve him here. As he watched his driver pacing impatiently around the viewing area, he remembered an old dictum carefully instilled in him by his father at an early age: ***If you meet a situation you have absolutely no power to change, accept it, work around it, and move on without regrets.***

Often easier said than done, it was nevertheless a useful maxim which had served him well in the past, and now seemed wholly appropriate to the present. He knew of the Russian mafia's attempts to exploit the economic potential of Bosnia following the Dayton Accord in the mid-nineties, and he knew how often they had been thwarted by a shadowy figure high up in the Bosnian security services. He had heard of Oleg Ivankov's attempt to deal with the threat by putting a price on the security chief's head. He had also heard, as so many in the Russian mafia had been intended to hear, of the sudden disappearance of Ivankov and the subsequent speculation about which newly constructed bridge, office block, hotel or roadway hid the Russian's remains in its concrete foundations. Russian mobsters disappeared and Russian businesses burned as Osman Izetbegović had ruthlessly set about protecting his fledgling country from outside predators. It became known that it would serve no purpose to target him personally, as Ivankov had done, since Izetbegović had a powerful and widely spread team of equally dedicated operatives whose retaliation would be as brutal as it would be coldly efficient. Borisov understood now why, for a time at least, the Russians had largely withdrawn from Bosnia. He wondered also whether their current resurgence was in any way linked with the Bosnian's posting to London.

Not that it mattered. It was just his bad luck that he had decided to extend his enterprise into a country inhabited by Osman Izetbegović. He had been left in no doubt about the consequences of any move made against James Montrayne. If the meddling English lord were to die, or be harmed in any way, then Alexei Borisov would be dead within days, if not hours. If any member of Montrayne's family were threatened or harmed, Borisov was dead. If the two troublesome young women were harmed, he was dead. If accident or illness should carry any of them off, he was dead, unless it were clearly evident that he could not have been responsible, and maybe not even then.

Borisov resented being manipulated, and even more did he hate being threatened, but pragmatism was always his bottom line response. The more he thought about the situation, the more he realised that there was little downside. He was only involved as a favour to Mellisse, to lubricate the merging of their business interests, and already that decision had cost him dearly in personnel. Perhaps it would be better to step back and simply allow matters to take their course and, if those wretched girls truly were the threat to Mellisse that he claimed they were, maybe the merger could instead become a takeover.

And then his heart gave a little lurch as he remembered events already in motion to the north, up at Aullton House.

He turned back to face James rather more quickly than was consistent with the calm and untroubled demeanour he was trying to portray.

"You have interesting friends, Mr Montrayne. You are fortunate. The situation is now clear to me. I will interfere no further in your journey. But... ..."

He paused, his eyes locked on James's with an intensity that was no longer fuelled by anger.

"… … things are happening which I did not order and which I do not control. Might I suggest that you waste no time in reaching Aullton House? No time at all, Mr Montrayne."

Seventy-Nine

Aullton Estate – Mid-afternoon

I didn't like Ginger. He wasn't rude or impolite. That would be hard for a guy who hardly spoke, but I noticed the way he looked at me when he thought I wasn't watching. I was used to the kind of look I'd get from guys who were wondering how much fun it would be to get in bed with me, but this wasn't it. There was something different in his eyes, and I couldn't put my finger on it. Maybe that's what worried me.

I thought we were going to walk to find the llamas because, from the way Abby talked, it didn't seem as though they were that far away. I was wrong, but not about the distance. Ginger suggested to Cherry that we should take one of the estate Land Rovers so we could spend more time at the llama farm and get back quickly when James arrived. It seemed a reasonable idea. Abby was OK with it, and I didn't mind one way or the other. There was one parked handily near the entrance to the stable courtyard, so Cherry said he'd go and check whether anyone else was planning to use it. Apparently nobody was since, a few minutes later, we were all safely belted into the Land Rover and ready for off. Cherry insisted on the seat belts being fastened even though we were not on a public road and would not be travelling at any great speed. I wasn't surprised. I'd learnt by now that he would take no chances when it came to Abby's safety, and she wouldn't want to buckle up if no-one else did. He drove with Ginger up front beside him and Abby next to me in the rear. We cruised sedately along a narrow road that curved between two enormous fir trees.

"Those are Noble Fir," said Abby. "We have a little one in the house at Christmas. The needles don't drop off so much."

"Really?" I said, thinking back to the artificial tree that my aunt and uncle used to put up for a couple of weeks around Christmas. They had always been adamant that they would never have a "proper" tree dropping its needles all over the carpet to be constantly reappearing for the rest of the year.

"Oh, yes," replied Abby, so confidently that I assumed she knew what she was talking about. "Pine trees aren't much good for keeping their needles, but Nordmans are fine. Nobles are even better."

We passed between her giant Nobles to loop around a lake, and then follow the road through woodland in the direction of the clearly sign-posted Llama farm. I was listening to Abby with genuine interest as she explained what we were going to see there. She was both animated and knowledgeable, and had clearly spent a fair amount of time among the llamas during her school holidays. She was describing the difference between the long-haired woolly llamas and the shorter-haired Ccaras when I felt the car begin to slow down. I looked up and, peering between the front seats and through the windscreen, I saw a track leaving the road up ahead on our left. Opposite the track, on the right-hand side of the road, another sign pointed straight ahead for the llamas.

The Land Rover continued to slow, edging slightly to the right as though preparing to swing off the road and onto the track. This seemed strange, as it was obvious even to me that we needed to drive straight on. Abby was still talking and didn't seem to have noticed.

And then I saw the gun.

I had no idea what make it was or what calibre. I had no idea how many bullets it could fire, or what its range was. But I didn't need to know any of those things. All I needed to know, I could see right in front of me. It was an automatic and it was big. It was held low, gripped firmly in Ginger's right hand and the end the bullets came out of was tight up against Cherry's left side. Ginger was turned to his right and he was whispering which was why I hadn't heard him above the noise of the engine and Abby's chatter.

It would be foolish to say my heart stopped, because it didn't. I didn't freeze either, or stop breathing, but my mind was suddenly racing as questions and possibilities tumbled over themselves. I had no idea what was going on but, when all the whys and whos and hows were boiled down, the only question that really mattered was **Will Cherry be able to get us out of this?**

The way things were looking at that moment, I wasn't entirely confident that he could, so I was scared. After all of James's efforts, there was a good chance my life was going to come to an end here in these woods, and I was so desperately sorry that Abby had to be here to see it.

And then my heart did stop, and my stomach felt icily cold. If Abby was allowed to see what happened to me, then these woods would be the end for her too. And Cherry.

Following Ginger's whispered instructions, Cherry turned off the road and onto the track which led away through a forested area over ground that rose gently upwards. It was the turn that stopped Abby's flow.

"This isn't the way, silly." And then, when he didn't reply, she leaned forward to speak around Cherry's right shoulder. "Cherry, you know this isn't the way."

She didn't sound worried or frightened. Just puzzled that Cherry had forgotten a route which he must have taken many times before.

With the Land Rover now bouncing up the track, Cherry spoke.

"Just you sit tight, honey. It seems there's a group out trekking up by the Cantle Burn. We'll go and see if we can find them."

I knew this was nonsense, but it wasn't a bad response for the spur of the moment, and it seemed to reassure Abby. She sat back in her corner and started to tell me how the Cantle Burn got its name. For a brief moment, my eyes found Cherry's in the rear-view mirror and he knew I was not reassured.

"You too, Lizzie," he said. "Just sit tight."

I didn't want Abby to be frightened before she needed to be. I didn't want her to be frightened at all, so I sat back and pretended to listen to the history of the burn. She was tucked back in the corner of her seat behind Cherry, half-turned towards me, and I realised that her line of sight between the two front seats was too narrow to allow her to see the gun in Ginger's hand.

Suddenly, I had a thought.

"Ginger, why don't you let Abby out? She doesn't need to come any further. Let her go. She can find her way back from here."

Abby stopped in mid-sentence. Her mouth was still open and she was frowning.

"Lizzie? What do you mean? Why should I get out? I want to see the llamas."

Ginger turned to look at her, and I had a vision in my mind of Cherry leaning forward in his seat, pinning the gun to the back of it with his left arm, and reaching for Ginger's throat with his right. It never happened, and I wondered if he too was scared.

"Of course you want to see the llamas," Ginger said. "So, you just sit still and we'll be there in no time."

She sat still. She looked at me hard for a minute; puzzled, questioning, thoughtful. Then she looked at Ginger and noticed for the first time how his right hand seemed to be reaching down behind Cherry's back. She leaned sideways to look, and her eyes opened wide.

It was a half-whisper, half-sob, but I still heard the word clearly.

"No...o...o...o."

She started to shake, so I reached down to unbuckle her seat belt and pull her close. She didn't resist, but she didn't help either. As she slid across the seat, I heard her whimper, "They're doing it again. Don't let them take me. Lizzie, don't let them take me."

She thought it was all about her. She thought she was about to be kidnapped again. Holding her tight, I stared at Ginger over her head. We couldn't quite see eye-to-eye as I was sitting directly behind him, but his head was turned enough so that he could see what was happening on the back seat.

"It's OK, sweetie. Ginger doesn't want to take you anywhere. Do you, Ginger?"

He wasn't stupid, and he didn't want a hysterical child on his hands.

"That's right, little lady," he said, in a tone which I assumed he intended to be reassuring. "There's nobody wants to take you away from here. That's the truth."

It was too, and I knew exactly what he meant. Fortunately Abby didn't, and I felt her relax ever so slightly.

"What's happening, Lizzie?"

"I don't know, honey. So let's just do what Ginger says, and everything'll be OK."

She said no more, but I felt her arms reaching around me and she snuggled in close.

Ginger nodded slightly, and his gaze shifted back to Cherry. I was disappointed. Everyone had seemed to put so much faith in Cherry but here we were being carted off at gun-point and he seemed powerless to do anything. Apart from telling us to sit tight, he had nothing to say. I would have sworn he'd give his life to protect Abby, but maybe I was wrong. Maybe people didn't really do that sort of thing outside of the movies.

So I sat tight, and hugged Abby, and waited.

Eventually, the track emerged from the woodland quite suddenly. One minute we were surrounded by trees and the next minute we weren't. We were bumping across an open meadow Ahead, maybe a couple of hundred yards away, was what looked like a log cabin. There were trees behind it and on the far side, but beyond it the land rose steeply in a series of rocky slopes. We were approaching the cabin sideways on. To the front of it the meadow sloped gently away down to a broad stream, or maybe a narrow river. Our approach brought us in parallel to the stream which rippled and sparkled down to our right.

And we were not the first to arrive.

Some kind of SUV was parked in front of the cabin. It was at a slight angle, but I could tell nothing more apart from the fact that it was dark in colour and appeared to be empty. Ginger seemed to be expecting to see the SUV because he told Cherry to pull up close behind it. As we got closer, I could see that the bottom couple of feet of the cabin walls were made of stone. Or maybe they were the foundations since I could see a couple of steps at the front leading up to a veranda enclosed by a wooden railing. The front door of the cabin opened out onto the veranda. The wooden walls and the veranda railings glowed a beautifully warm honey-gold in the afternoon sunshine. Another day, another time, and I'd have loved it here.

As the Land Rover eased to a stop behind the SUV, which I now saw was a Jeep because it said so on the back panel, two men stepped out through the cabin door. The first to appear was not especially tall, but his wide shoulders, stubbled chin and shaved head would have people crossing the street to get out of his way. Even without the heavy automatic he was carrying low beside his right thigh. The second man was even more menacing: black boots; black leather trousers; black silk shirt; and a black Armani leather jacket. Startlingly at odds with his chosen colour scheme was the heavy white bandage which engulfed his right hand, though his left was fully in keeping with the rest being encased in a black glove and gripping some kind of small black machine-pistol.

It was Laddy, the same as always, apart from the hand which James had mangled that night in the hospital. His white teeth sparkled in a grin of pure delight, and I knew now that this was the end for all of us.

I fought back the prickles of moisture welling up in my eyes. I wanted to weep, to break down and let out all the anger, disappointment and, let's be honest, genuine terror. But I couldn't. Not in front of them. Not in front of Abby. I would have been weeping for myself, it's true, but far more would those tears have been shed for Abby. Somehow, it seemed as though the path of my life had brought me finally to my inevitable destination, but Abby's path shouldn't end here. Her path should take her to find all the happiness and joy in life that I had lost ten years ago. She was a beautiful child, as I think I had once been, and she deserved better than this.

I blinked hard as I held her tight. If I could find a way to get her safely on that path, at whatever cost, then I would.

Eighty

Aullton House – Mid-afternoon

Leaving Doctor Harwood to take care of business upstairs, Andy left the house via the back staircase and the old kitchens. Getting through the stairway door on the lower floor had been no problem as the code for the electronic lock was only needed to enter the apartments, not to leave them. Once outside, he hurried along the rear of the house in the direction of the stables, aiming not for the courtyard where the information centre, shop and restaurant were situated, but for the garages at the rear where the estate vehicles were kept. On his last visit, he and James had taken quad bikes up into the hills to a fishing cabin near a remote but well-stocked trout stream. The approved route for reaching the cabin was to go north up one of the estate roads by Land Rover, and then veer off along a track which led up through woodland to reach an open area of meadow beside the stream. He and James had chosen quad bikes just for the fun of getting there cross country.

As soon as he became aware of James's plan to relocate temporarily to Scotland, it had not taken Andy long to decide that it should be the fishing cabin which would provide the setting for the final act of his drama. It should all have played out so smoothly, the last scene recorded in high quality video, exactly as he'd been instructed. He had planned that scene carefully, hiring the extras and giving them their parts and now, at the last minute, he was trying to rewrite the script. However it played out, it would be at the fishing cabin where all this would finally be resolved.

Two things were driving him now. The possibility that he might still emerge with life and career intact, and the need, discovered in some deep part of himself only that afternoon, to protect Abby from the horror which he knew had to come. He had watched that little girl struggle through the aftermath of her kidnapping trauma. He knew how long it had taken for her to learn to trust, and laugh, and play again. He had no children of his own and he often found himself envying James for having a daughter as cute as Abby, to love and take care of, and protect. Especially protect. That was a father's job, after all. But James wasn't here, so it was up to him. So now he had to find a quad bike.

"Hey, Andy. What's the hurry?"

For a moment he was tempted to ignore the voice behind him, but he knew that would look wrong as it was obvious that he must have heard it. He slowed and turned to see Gil Elliott, the estate manager, watching him curiously. His hand was reaching for the knob of the door through which Andy had exited only moments before. Gil must have come around the corner of the house and seen Andy emerge in obvious haste, and wondered at the reason for it.

"Oh, hi Gil. I... ... er... ... fancied a bit of air, so I was thinking I'd take one of the quads and go and join the llama group."

Gil let go of the door knob, and started towards him.

"OK, no problem. I just wondered if there was something wrong. You seemed in such a hurry."

He left it hanging out there as a question, and Andy let it dangle while his mind raced through various courses of action. If he told Gil that the estate had recently acquired a dead body, he could be sure that the estate manager would waste no time in taking charge of the situation. In which case, he could be equally sure that Gil would shuffle off responsibility as quickly as possible into hands more official and more capable than his own. The situation would then spiral rapidly out of control and Andy's life would crash and burn. That might happen anyway, but there was still a chance it might not, if only he could keep control of things. If it all worked out right, Gil would never need to know what had been going on in his domain.

"Nothing wrong, Gil. I was only thinking the quicker I set off, the quicker I'll find them."

"You know where they are then?"

Another sodding question. Of course he bloody knew, and it wasn't going to have anything to do with llamas.

"I thought I'd start at the centre. I don't think they were going trekking. Just looking. Maybe stroke a few of the babies. I take it there were some young this year?"

"Sure," said Gil, standing quite close now. "They'll be a couple of months old now. It's been a good year so far."

"Great," replied Andy, backing away. "So... ... if you don't mind, I'll be on my way."

But Gil was not to be so easily put off.

"Look," he said. "You don't need a quad to get to the llama centre. Take Freddy's Sportage. She won't be needing it this afternoon."

The robust Kia was a four wheel drive, but something a bit more nimble was better suited to what Andy had in mind.

"Thanks, Gil. Kind of you. But I thought afterwards I might come back across country, just for the hell of it, you know."

Gil frowned which made Andy wonder if he was offended that his offer had been turned down. But the estate manager had something else in mind.

"Well, if that's what you want, Andy. But you'll have to let me check you out on the quad before you take it."

"Check me out? What the hell do you mean? James and I took them out last time without any fuss."

"Not exactly," said Gil, a harder note coming into his voice. "After you got back that time, I gave James a right royal bollocking. He's trained and insured for using those things on the estate. You're not. He should never have taken you without getting the formalities sorted. So, if you want one of my quads, you do it my way or not at all."

"I never knew you were such a tight-arse," growled Andy, his patience eroded by his sense of urgency. Still, common-sense told him that arguing was only going to make things take longer. So, short of clouting Gil round the head with his Beretta, the easiest thing would be to let him have his way and get the business done as quickly as possible.

"Sorry, Gil," he said, before the estate manager had time to recover from the insult. "That was uncalled for. I... ...er... ..." Then inspiration struck. "I've been feeling the stress a bit lately. That's why I fancied getting out into the country."

Gil allowed himself to be mollified.

"OK, but if you end up flipping over and breaking your neck in a gully, it's my neck the health and safety folks come after."

"Yeah, yeah, I understand. Er... ... Look... ... I'll take the Sportage, OK? And thanks."

It was, after all, a four-by-four SUV and should be able to cope with any off-road work that might be called for. In fact, it looked as though it had done a fair bit already, judging by the mud that streaked its silver-grey paintwork.

"I'll find the keys for you," said Gil, apparently relieved that the awkwardness of the last few minutes seemed to be over. "And, er... ... try not to bend it. It may look filthy, but Freddy's not had it long and it's a bit of a pride-and-joy thing."

As he drove away, Andy could see what Gil meant. Whatever the outside looked like, apart from a bit of dirt on the driver's floor-mat, the inside was immaculate and still retained a hint of that new-car smell. He hoped it would still be like that after he'd finished with it.

He ignored the road that led around the side of the house and then to the main gatehouse in the village two miles away. Instead he followed a narrower road that curved between two enormous specimens of Noble Fir to loop around a lake, and then meander through woodland to the clearly sign-posted Llama farm just over a mile away. In the height of the season, a shuttle-bus ferried less energetic visitors to this and other more distant locations on the estate.

Andy knew he wouldn't find Cherry and the girls with the llamas. Ginger's job was to get the little group up to the fishing cabin as quickly and as quietly as he could, and the llama farm was not exactly on the way.

That he would manage this, in spite of Cherry's competence as a bodyguard, Andy had no doubt. Cherry would be slow to react, partly because he had no reason to mistrust Ginger, but mostly because he would do nothing hasty that could lead to Abby being hurt. He would protect her, if necessary, by doing exactly as he was told.

Cherry would die to keep Abby safe. Andy knew him well enough to have no doubt of that. He smiled at the irony of it. She was only in danger now because of him, so it was up to him to sort it out. The smile faded as he thought of the mess he had created and the harm he had so nearly done. He knew he was a fool, snared by fear, and pride, and greed, but in knowing it lay the seeds of his redemption.

He passed the turn to a narrow logging track off to his left. It was about three miles up the track to the cabin, over ground that became increasingly rough the further it got from the road he was on. He didn't make the turn, but carried on another quarter of a mile to the llama farm. The detour was costing him time but, if he didn't try the llamas first, it would be obvious later that he had known all along exactly where Ginger was headed, and there would be only one explanation for that. He couldn't risk it.

Eighty-One

Scottish Borders – Mid-afternoon

The journey from Carter Bar up through the Scottish Borders to Aullton House would normally be expected to take around an hour and thirty-five minutes. Speed cameras dotted along the A68 hindered attempts to achieve a better time than this, and usually James didn't bother to try. It was a good road, and the scenery was definitely worth looking at.

Unfortunately, scenery of any kind, even spectacular Scottish scenery, had not been uppermost in James's mind for several days. With the sun now unobscured in the west, a gloriously undulating panorama lay revealed all around him, but his visual attention was focussed entirely on the road ahead. In recent years, he'd had neither the need nor the opportunity to discover whether the Maserati's three-point-two litre, twin-turbocharged V8 was still good to top one hundred and sixty mph, but then no Russian mobster had previously told him to get home as quickly as possible. So, he was pushing the car hard up the A68, as fast as safety and speed cameras would allow.

He wasn't worried about the cameras because of the possibility of picking up a fixed penalty or two, although the extra points on his licence could end up being rather a nuisance. He watched out for them because he didn't want a photographic record of his dash up the A68 to end up on police records. Fortunately, he'd made the journey so many times that he knew every twist and turn of the road and the position of every camera, even the ones partly obscured by roadside foliage. He was also very much aware that he would be no use to anyone if he wrapped the Maserati around a tree, or crunched into a truck on a sharp bend. So, he thought about safety, at least a little.

With Jedburgh behind him and Melrose still some way up ahead, he came out of a left-hand bend at seventy-five mph and entered a long straight bounded by hedges, occasional trees and green grass verges. Three cameras coming up. Brake, accelerate; brake, accelerate; brake, accelerate. As he passed the third camera, clearly visible just past a pull-in on his left, his phone rang. There were several hundred yards of straight road ahead so, as he pushed down with his right foot, he glanced at his phone to check the display. It was the number for the private apartment at Aullton House. A quick glance at the dashboard clock showed him that it must be at least half-an-hour since he had last spoken to Barrie. He'd tried to call the house before leaving Carter Bar but found his phone had lost the signal, and he didn't dare wait for the bars to reappear. Maybe this was Andy at last.

Without lifting his foot, he pressed the hands-free button, and cruised into the sweeping right-hand bend at a touch over seventy mph.

"James, here. Is that you Andy?"

"No, James. It's Barrie again."

"Oh, right. Look… … is everything OK up there?"

"Well… …actually… …"

"Hang on, Barrie. Bit of a problem."

Coming out of the bend, James saw a left-hand turning up ahead. Emerging from the side road was a big eighteen-wheeler truck, painted in Sainsbury's orange colours. It had turned to head north, the same direction he was going. The truck was doing about fifteen miles per hour. James was doing seventy. Braking was not an option. The distance was too short. Just coming out of the bend at the end of the straight and heading south towards him in the opposite lane was another truck, slightly smaller maybe, but equally deadly in a collision at speed. Calculating quickly, James dropped a gear, flashed his headlights, and floored the accelerator. Even at seventy miles an hour, he felt the power of the sudden thrust in his back and smiled. By the time he pulled alongside the eighteen-wheeler, he was up to ninety mph and the on-coming truck began flashing its lights. Then he heard the hiss of air brakes to his left as the Sainsbury's driver slowed to give him room to pull back into the left-hand lane. It was a thoughtful move, which spoke of the trucker's alertness and competence, but it was also unnecessary. The Maserati swung safely back into its proper lane, and James was already braking for the next upcoming bend as the oncoming truck swept past to his right. Its driver made a gesture in passing which James was fairly sure did not represent a tribute to his driving skills.

The next stretch, approaching Newtown St Boswells and another speed camera, was surprisingly busy with traffic which gave little opportunity for overtaking for several minutes. Time to find out what Barrie wanted.

"You still there, Barrie?"

The response came clearly through the car's speakers.

"Still here, James. Are you OK."

"Fine, Barrie. I'm just short of the Melrose turn. Now what's going on?"

A short pause, and then, "James, did you actually know these fellows Andy brought in from Edinburgh?"

"No. Andy just told me he was bringing in some temporary help."

"Well they're not exactly helping. One of them was up here in the apartment just now and was all set to have a go at Angie. Looked like he was trying to kill her. Andy had to shoot him."

"Dead?"

"Of course he's bloody dead! He's got three bullets in him... ... James, what the hell have you got me mixed up in?"

It was a good question, and James wished he had a clear answer. He avoided replying directly by getting Barrie to relate exactly what had happened. That took a couple of minutes or so and by the time Barrie finished he still had no answer. Just more questions. ***Who were these guys from Edinburgh and how did they end up at Aullton House?***

"Barrie, where are they now?"

"No idea. Andy went charging off a while ago to find Cherry and the girls and this other bloke from Edinburgh. I've spent most of that time trying to settle Angie down – you can imagine the state she was in – and get hold of you."

"Yes, but does Andy know where they are?"

"They were supposed to be going to the llamas, but who knows now? If that other guy is as much a villain as this one was, he could be taking them anywhere."

James thought about that, and didn't like it. Not one bit.

"Do me a favour, Barrie. Call the llama farm – the number's listed in the phone – and find out if Cherry & the others are there. If they are, tell him what's happened and have him sit tight 'til Andy gets there. Then call me back."

"And if they're not there?"

"Call me back."

The turn to Melrose with its fine old Abbey ruins was behind him now, with the small town of Earlston up ahead. Another long straight gave him a chance to overtake a caravan pulled by an ageing Jaguar, and then he was flashing past the count-down signs to the thirty mph speed limit through Earslton. Bypassing the town's centre, he was just clearing the built-up area on the north side when his phone rang again.

"Sorry it took so long, James," said Barrie, his words tumbling out in an uncharacteristic rush. "No-one at the farm's seen Cherry or the girls. They never got there. Apparently some girl called Susan and one or two others have been out repainting the railings at the farm entrance. According to them, no vehicle had passed there since lunchtime. Andy was there a few moments ago, and they were absolutely certain he was the first since lunch. He went into the farm office to check they hadn't walked in the back way, but no-one had seen them. They told him all this and he'd left just before I called. The girl I was speaking to ran off to see if she could catch him, but he was already out of the gate."

James let that sink in. He had vowed after the last time that Abby was taken from him that he would spare no effort and begrudge no expense to ensure that she never had to face such trauma again. Yet somehow, in spite of all his efforts, he had failed. His grip on the steering-wheel tightened as the anger built up inside him. He could feel it coursing through him. He was sick with fear for his little girl's safety, and consumed with rage towards these strangers who threatened her. He should be there with her himself, ready to protect her, not delegating that responsibility to Cherry or Andy.

Andy?

It was Andy who'd brought in these guys from Edinburgh, strangers whom he alone could vouch for. Andy had access to his car and could easily have planted the tracker. Andy knew Borisov, and had obviously been developing plans for a long-term working relationship. And Andy had visited Angie just before the attack in her hospital room.

If all of that really added up to what it seemed, why had Andy defended Angie from the Edinburgh thug who was trying to kill her? And why was he, even now, rushing around trying to find Cherry and the girls and the second thug?

None of it made sense.

"Hello... ... Are you still there, James?"

"Yes... ... just thinking."

"Well, what do I do? Andy said not to call the police but... ... James, this is a mess. We can't keep it secret."

"Just hang on. I'm almost at the Lauder turn. I'll be there soon. Don't do anything. You hear? Nothing. Just sit tight and take care of Angie, and call me if you have any word from Cherry or Andy. You got that?"

There was a short pause before Barrie said, "Got it." His tone was subdued, almost resentful, but not panicking. James was confident he could trust him to hold fast for a while longer.

At least he knew where to go now. If Cherry's party had set out for the llama farm, but hadn't actually got that far, there was only one other place they could have headed for. The fishing cabin up by the Cantle Burn. It was on the other side of the house from his direction of approach and he knew he couldn't normally hope to reach it in much under an hour.

And all that time his baby would be scared and in danger.

So this wasn't normal.

He prayed he would be there before the worst of his imaginings could happen, and pushed his foot hard to the floor.

Eighty-Two

The Cantle Burn – Late-afternoon

I should have had more faith in Cherry. He was sitting perfectly still with Ginger's gun nuzzling his waistband while Laddy came down the steps of the veranda, white teeth gleaming all the way. I hated that smile. I hated Laddy. I hated everything that his presence here made me remember. He took up a position by Cherry's door, gun held in his left hand, the stubby barrel resting on his right forearm, but just enough back from the vehicle that he couldn't be caught off-guard by the sudden opening of the driver's door. Once he was in position, and the other guy had moved to cover me with his pistol, Ginger finally climbed out of the front seat.

It was then that I saw the second gun. Ginger was holding it in his left hand and both weapons were pointed at Cherry. He never really had any choice but to do exactly what Ginger had told him. One gun he might have knocked aside, but not both of them. And if he'd tried and stray bullets started bouncing around in the Land Rover someone could easily have ended up dead. I felt guilty for doubting him.

I was also scared, more than I'd ever been since that night they came and told me my Mum and Dad would never be coming home again. Then, I was only scared for me. Now, I was scared for Abby and for what this repeated trauma would do to her. Would it scar her permanently, emotionally or psychologically? I'd seen enough and heard enough to know that it could.

I was still holding her tight, huddled together in the back of the Land Rover, my right arm around her shoulders. Her face was snuggled down onto my right breast. Her cheek seemed dry and warm. Her right hand reached for my left and gripped it firmly. She wasn't crying or shaking, just hanging on tight, and it suddenly dawned on me that the last time she'd been kidnapped she'd been alone. This time she had Cherry, and she had me, and I determined there and then to make that count.

Once the three of them had taken up their positions, Ginger pulled a strip of black plastic out of his pocket and made it into a loop. I'd seen something like it before. It was a cable tie. He tossed it onto Cherry's lap.

"Put that on," said Ginger. "And pull it tight. You know the drill."

Cherry hesitated. He glanced out of his side window towards Laddy and then back to Ginger. I could tell he didn't want his hands bound, but he really had no choice, as Ginger pointed out.

"I don't actually need you, mate. Put that on or I'll finish you right now."

Cherry put his hands through the loop and pulled on the free end with his teeth to tighten it. Ginger watched carefully, and wasn't satisfied.

"Tighter," he said, "or I'll get Jonno here to do it and we'll watch your hands turn blue."

Cherry tugged again. After that, it was no trouble at all for them to get us safely out of the Land Rover and into the cabin. There was a brief pause when Ginger decided that we should all be searched before going inside. Cherry was obviously their main concern, but I already knew he didn't carry a weapon on his person. The rifle and shotgun for which he held licenses were both securely locked in his own SUV back at the Dower House. At Laddy's urging, Cherry raised his hands above his head so Ginger could pat him down, but he wasn't going to try anything, not with Jonno's pistol just inches from the back of Abby's head. After Cherry, it was my turn, and this was obviously to be Jonno's treat. With Laddy watching Cherry, Ginger pointed his pistol at me, then changed his mind and switched aim to Abby. That's when Jonno moved in close.

I could smell him just behind me. The aroma of cigarettes and stale sweat wafted around me as his hands ran over my body. Abby stood stock still, making no sound, her eyes locked on Cherry, the one whose job it was to keep her safe. He smiled at her, trying to reassure, but I caught no response from her. She moved slightly when Jonno made me lift my arms so his hands could slide under them and round onto my breasts. They lingered there, just as they lingered moments later on the inside of my thighs, creeping up towards my crotch.

"She's clean, Jonno. Leave it," said Ginger with the kind of edge to his voice that left us in no doubt, if we'd ever had any, as to who was in charge.

"Just funning," replied Jonno. "Now shall we give the little lady a turn?"

The thought of his filthy hands touching Abby caused me to swing around and pull her in close. I glared at him venomously over her head.

"Don't you dare lay a finger on her," I warned, not knowing what I could possibly do to prevent him.

"Or what?" he asked, his mouth twisting in a lecherous grin.

"Or I'll blow your kneecap off," said Ginger calmly. "You know the rules. We leave the kid alone."

I stared at him struggling to keep a blank expression, but he didn't seem to realise he'd given anything away. Someone higher up the food-chain had given instructions that Abby was not to be harmed. Which meant that the pistols pointed at her was all a bluff simply to make sure Cherry and I did exactly as we were told. I felt an enormous relief for her sake, because it meant that whatever they had in mind they were not going to hurt her if it could possibly be avoided. At least, not physically.

I kept hold of Abby's hand and we walked up the steps together. As we did so, I looked around thinking how unreal it all seemed. The green of the meadow shimmered as the light breeze wafted across it. I could hear water rippling over stones in the burn. The blue sky was streaked with wisps of white cloud and a pair of buzzards circled lazily over the trees across the burn. This was a place for quiet contemplation or peaceful solitude. It was not a place for threats or violence or pain, or whatever other nastiness these thugs had in mind for us.

I felt a sharp jolt as Laddy jabbed me in the back with his gun.

"Keep moving, bitch. And remember, you and me got business together when this is over."

What? When what was over? I had no idea what he was talking about. In fact, the whole situation made no sense at all.

I entered the cabin with Abby at my side. My right arm lay across her shoulders keeping her close. Her left hand reached up to hold my left. We were a unit, tight together. Was it really all about her? Could this be another kidnap? If it wasn't for Laddy's presence I'd have been sure of it, but his being here meant Mellisse was involved, and Mellisse suggested it was about me. Maybe. The only thing that seemed certain was that it wasn't about Cherry. Ginger had said he didn't need him, and I believed it.

It still didn't make sense. This was a huge amount of trouble for Mellisse to go to just to get even with me for running away. There had to be something else going on.

I was about to find out that there was.

The door from the veranda led into some kind of living room with a wood-burning stove set against the far wall. A flat-screen TV was mounted on the wall to the right of the stove at about head-height. Against the left wall of the room was a three-seater settee in what looked like cream coloured soft leather. A large patterned rug occupied the centre of the wooden floor, and the space to my right was taken up by a two-seater settee of similar design to the one opposite. Behind the smaller settee was a granite-topped counter, perpendicular to the front wall of the cabin. This served to separate the living-space from the kitchen and dining area which together occupied the right front corner of the cabin.

My eyes lingered for a moment on the kitchen. Normally, kitchens had knives, and this was a normal kitchen. There they were. Five black handles poking out of a wooden knife-block sitting peacefully beneath the window in the far right-hand wall. I looked away quickly, wondering how I could manage to get close to them. And wondering too if

I could actually bring myself to stab one into Ginger or Jonno or Laddy, and watch the life go out of them as their blood ran over my hand.

Feeling Abby close beside me, I decided I could. For her, I'd do it as many times as necessary, and consider it a job well done.

I turned my attention back to the living space, hoping no-one had noticed my glance at the knives in the kitchen. Around the walls were framed pictures of the estate at different times of the year. On the wall in front of me, to the left of the stove was a distance shot of Aullton House set in a snow-covered landscape. I wondered whether I'd ever see snow again.

A firm hand grasped my left arm and pulled.

"You sit there," said Ginger. "And let go of the kid."

Abby held me tighter as I was hauled over to the big settee. It was an awkward move and we stumbled. The settee caught the back of my calves and I collapsed onto the centre cushion pulling Abby down after me. As she fell, the guy called Jonno tried to pull her away from me by grabbing her hair. So much for not hurting her! The sound of her squeal enraged me and I twisted round to dig my nails into Jonno's wrist to force him to let go. He did, but immediately drew his arm back to swing a blow at my face. It didn't land. Ginger caught his wrist and moved between us.

"Don't forget why we're here, Jonno boy," he said. "We don't want any marks on her before the job's done."

He released Jonno and stepped back, glancing round to check on Cherry. There was no problem there. Laddy had pushed him down onto the other settee and was covering him with his machine pistol. I had no real idea what an Uzi looked like, but I'd heard it was sort of short and squat with a long magazine sticking out of the bottom and could fire lots of bullets very fast. Since that was a pretty good description of what Laddy was holding, I wasn't surprised to see Cherry sitting very still.

Ginger turned back to look down at us. I returned the look. My heart was pounding and there was a coldness in my stomach, but I was determined not to let him see how scared I was.

"What job?" I asked, not really expecting an answer.

He grinned. "You're going to be a movie star."

The coldness in my stomach deepened and my skin began to crawl. I had good reason for knowing very well the sort of movies Mellisse was interested in, and I knew I couldn't do it. Not again. Not for anything. Not with these animals.

Ginger seemed to know what I was thinking, and his grin widened.

"Now, don't you worry, princess. You've got me all wrong. Not that I wouldn't mind... ... Still, maybe later, eh?"

Checking again that Jonno and Laddy had us all well covered, he went into the kitchen area, picked up a large holdall from off the table, and turned to face us over the counter. Reaching into the bag, he came out with a video-camera mounted on a small tripod which he set up on the counter. He focussed it directly at me.

"Now listen, princess" he said. "You get to keep your clothes on for this. Just talk to the camera, calm and natural. OK?"

I didn't get it. "Talk about what?" I asked.

"This."

He held up a sheet of white A4 paper.

I still didn't get it. "What is it?" I asked.

"Take a look."

He came around the counter and handed me the sheet.

"You're going to learn it bit by bit and say it to camera. It doesn't have to be word for word. Just get the gist of it. And we'll do as many takes as it needs to get it right."

He looked down at Abby, still snuggled in close beside me.

"Now we can't have the kid in the shot, so I want you to get her to move away a bit. You know... ... tucked into the corner... ... You can still hold her hand if you must, but she doesn't move and she doesn't speak. OK?"

I nodded. At least he had the sense not to try himself to force her to move. She would have resisted. No question of it.

I spoke quietly to her and eventually she moved away enough to satisfy Ginger who watched on the display screen of the camera.

She still held on to my right hand, so I held the paper in my left and began to read silently.

I was five lines in before I began to have any idea what Mellisse was trying to achieve. Another five lines and I was sure of it. By the time I reached the end, the whole scheme was as plain as day. I knew at last why Mellisse needed me, why only I could do what he wanted. Everything made sense because Mellisse was playing for the jackpot, and I was his winning token. Or, at least, this video was, and no-one else could make it but me.

But once it was over, the story told, and the video recorded to Ginger's satisfaction, there was no need for any of us to be kept alive. In fact, there was every need to ensure that none of us would ever be seen again.

I had to spin this out as long as possible. And hope for the best. And, yes, maybe even pray. It couldn't hurt, could it?

Eighty-Three

Aullton Estate – Late afternoon

As Andy was driving away from the llama farm, he caught a glimpse in his door mirror of someone running out onto the road behind him. He saw her wave and call out but the voice was faint above the sound of the Kia's engine, and he ignored it. Whoever it was would think he simply hadn't heard. He knew very well that Cherry and the others were not there. Right at that moment, they should be up at the cabin by the Cantle Burn, just as he'd planned they would be. He watched for the turning to the forest track. It would be coming up on his right at any moment.

The track appeared, and he made the turn. Soon, the going became rougher as the trail climbed up through the trees, but the Kia's suspension and four-wheel drive coped with the ease for which it was designed.

He hoped that Barrie would not have panicked and made a call to the local police, but as he thought it over he decided it was more likely that the doctor would try and call James. Andy knew James wouldn't want the police involved, and he'd know what to say to calm Barrie down. He found himself wishing he knew just where James was at that moment, and how much he understood of what was going on. He shrugged it off. Wishing got you nowhere.

When he'd last come up to the cabin with James, they hadn't approached it using this track. They'd used the quad-bikes to take a short cut around the hill and come at it from the other side. Nevertheless, he was fairly certain that he must be nearing the meadow. The trees seemed to be thinning out up ahead, and blue sky was visible directly in front of him. He slowed the Kia to a crawl since he didn't want to actually break out from the treeline. Nor did he want to get so close that the sound of the Kia's engine would be heard by those at the cabin.

He watched for a space among the trees where he could pull off the track. He wouldn't be able to completely hide the Kia, but he could at least make sure that it wouldn't be visible to anyone peering down the trail. When he found the space, it was perfect. It had obviously been the site of some logging operations since there was a sizeable stack of timber on the upward side of the clearing. He turned in and found he had enough space to manoeuvre the Kia so that it was close up to the stack and facing out to the trail. He wound down the windows, switched off the engine and listened to the silence, hoping that he'd not driven close enough for the Kia to be heard from the cabin.

As he waited in the stillness, he realised that the forest wasn't actually quiet. There were rustlings on the ground from animals or birds foraging. There was the occasional beat of wings as some larger bird weaved its way through the trees. There was a strange creaking which he assumed was caused by branches rubbing against each other as the trees swayed a little in the breeze. There was the sound of an aircraft up above, probably heading for Edinburgh airport. And there was the ticking of the Kia's engine as it began to cool.

Still listening carefully, he checked his armoury. First there was Carl's Smith and Wesson. It was the M&P .357 Sig model with a 4.25 inch barrel and a fifteen round magazine. Carl hadn't fired a shot but Andy was careful so he counted the rounds anyway. Carl had been careful too. There were sixteen rounds, a full magazine and one up the spout. Laying it back on the passenger seat, he extracted the Bobcat from his pocket. Beretta had produced a fine little pistol but the magazine only held seven rounds and its effective range fell far short of the Smith and Wesson's fifty metres.

Andy carefully opened the Kia's door and climbed out. The Bobcat went back into his jacket pocket and he reached in for the Smith and Wesson. He removed the silencer and slipped it into another pocket before tucking the pistol into his waistband. He would have loved an H & K MP5 or even a Steyr TMP which would push his effective range out to over one hundred metres. But he couldn't use what he hadn't got and he was soldier enough to press on and make do with what he did have.

Skirting the log pile, he headed up through the trees in what he imagined was the direction of the cabin. Once he could see the green of the meadow between thinning tree trunks, he slowed and proceeded with a great deal more care. His sense of direction had been spot on and he was soon able to see the cabin and the two vehicles parked out in front. If he kept well back among the trees, it would take about fifteen minutes to circle around to the rear of the solitary building where he would have much less open ground to cross.

He had thought about his approach very carefully. He could have driven, slowly and unthreateningly, straight up to the front of the cabin. That was the straight-forward approach. Once recognised by the crew inside, he would have been accepted and welcomed. Once inside, it wouldn't really have been too difficult to take down three unsuspecting, untrained and inexperienced villains. The trouble with being straight-forward was that Cherry, Lizzie and Abby could scarcely help but notice the friendliness with which Ginger and his team would welcome him. Even worse, he would be accepted not as an equal, but as the man in charge, the guy running the show, the one from whom they were taking their orders. Whatever he did after that, their initial reaction to him would be very hard to explain away.

So, straight-forward wouldn't do. It had to be a stealthy approach, followed by a quick take-down before they had a chance to recognise him. That way, it would seem like a rescue, pure and simple.

There was a good bit of debris on the forest floor, but he made his way from tree to tree without too much difficulty. He moved slowly to keep the sounds of his passage as quiet and as few as possible, especially as he got closer to the cabin. All the time, he was trying to imagine what would be going on inside. What stage would they be at with the video? He thought of Lizzie and the little he knew about her. He was reasonably confident that she would be trying to spin things out as long as possible, maybe insisting on rehearsing the words. He hoped she succeeded.

It was all about the video. If he could time this right and step in just as it was completed, and if he could then get the video to Borisov without anyone knowing, then his debt would be paid. He didn't know why the Russian needed the video and he didn't care. He'd been a little curious about where the hired help had come from, since he'd thought Borisov only employed Russians. But then, the guy had suffered a few losses recently which was probably why he'd been forced to recruit locals to help out.

Andy was optimistic. If no-one suspected the scope of his involvement with the Russian, and if all the dead bodies could be effectively tidied away, then he might, just might, be a free man once again. A lot of ifs.

He pressed on through the trees until he was about twenty yards from the rear of the cabin. He could see the windows of the two back bedrooms and two smaller windows with some kind of patterned glass for the en-suite bathrooms. He would have about eight to ten yards of open ground to cross, and most of that was grass. There was a narrow strip of paving about a yard wide bordering the stone foundations of the cabin. He was thankful that they were paving slabs and not gravel or stone chippings which would crunch underfoot.

He knelt at the foot of a substantial spruce and leant against its sturdy bole. He studied each of the windows in turn. There was no sign of any movement in the darkness behind the glass, and the fact that rooms appeared dark suggested that the doors into the main room of the cabin were probably closed. Was that a good thing? Probably. The fact that he could hear no sound made him think the bedrooms were not being used. There was no reason why they should have been, if Ginger and his team had stuck to their instructions, but Andy was well aware that villains like these could easily develop ideas of their own, especially when pretty girls were involved.

He realised at that moment just how little he knew of these men. He thought of Abby. Were any of them the type to interfere with little girls? He'd told them she wasn't to be hurt, but he really had no idea what they were capable of. Then he thought of Lizzie. Would they be interested in her? That one was a no-brainer. Of course they would, and there was no reason why they shouldn't enjoy a bit of fun once the video was completed.

He shook his head and wondered how he could possibly have been so stupid as to have taken money from Borisov. He should have gone to James as soon as his investments in Eastland River Securities went bad. The mint his broker had promised had turned into a bottomless pit when the performance of ERS turned out to be the exact opposite of what he'd predicted. On the crucial Friday morning when Andy could have cut his losses and run, he'd broken a tooth and spent hours at the dentist so that he hadn't heard the disastrous news until late in the evening. By then, his broker was inconveniently absent for a weekend's golf.

Since he'd used most of his assets to finance the purchase, and had also, with his broker's help, negotiated a substantial short-term loan, his personal finances were now in complete disarray, and all set to get substantially worse if he failed to repay the loan. Going to James was a possibility, but it would also have been embarrassing. He couldn't bring himself to take the money out of the company, and anyway the loss would have been noticed by RRISC's auditor.

And then Borisov had turned up. A minor player amongst the wealthy Russians currently residing in the UK, Borisov had ambitions. And, in some way that Andy was only now beginning to understand, those ambitions were dependant on a deal with Raymond Mellisse. And that deal somehow depended in turn on the video now being filmed only yards from where he was kneeling.

Andy knew it had been both stupid and cowardly to have contemplated even for a minute the offer Borisov made. He still couldn't be sure whether the Russian had engineered his financial difficulties, learnt of them by chance, or maybe he'd just been chancing his arm. It had all been so delicately phrased; a civilised chat over a quiet drink; a suggestion of attractive business contracts for RRISC together with a little sweetener for himself. Borisov had understood exactly how to reel him in, and Andy hadn't been able to help himself.

So what if Borisov needed him to breech company protocols and divulge information about Anatoly Ilyumzhinov, yet another Russian oligarch newly arrived in London. It seemed that Ilyumzhinov was not very trusting of his fellow Russians and so had engaged RRISC to provide a full close-protection service while he established himself in his new country. Borisov hadn't wanted much, just details of his journeys. Who drove him? Where to? At what time? Which car did he use? How many security personnel? It was easy enough to provide that from the daily reports. And then Borisov had asked for up-front information on what Ilyumzhinov would be doing two days ahead. Another sweetener got him what he wanted, and two days later Ilyumzhinov lay dying in hospital after a road accident on the way to Newmarket.

At least, that's how it was reported in the papers, a road accident, but the police and security team knew different. And so did Borisov. And so did Andy Graham. After that, he'd been hooked, with no choice but to dance to Borisov's tune. Up to now. This time, the price was too high. Borisov was asking too much. Andy had thought he could go through with it but, now it came down to it, he found he couldn't.

Angie had been a stranger. Even though he knew he was betraying the trust of colleagues and friends, he had convinced himself he had no choice. He had believed himself capable of dealing with Angie, until it came to the point only a short while ago when his personal morality, temporarily suppressed, rose up to convince him not only that he shouldn't, but also that he couldn't.

On the flight up to Aullton House, he had been battling with his anxiety that Angie would recover sufficiently to be able to give a lucid account of what had happened to her. In the midst of that, he had called to mind a story which James had once told him. The story was usually attributed to the Cherokee nation, and it involved an interaction between a young Indian brave and an elder of the tribe. The brave was troubled with bouts of violent aggression and sought help from the elder. He was told that he, like everyone, had two wolves inside him, one black and one white. The black wolf was evil and violent, while the white one was good and peace-loving. The two were of equal strength, but constantly fought against each other. The brave asked the elder, "If they are equal in strength, which one will win?" The elder looked at the brave and told him, "The one you feed will win."

Andy had realised he had been feeding the wrong wolf and it was time to change.

So Carl had died instead of Angie. And now he had to protect Abby. She called him Uncle Andy. He had known her all her life. He'd seen what the trauma of the kidnapping had done to her. It had never been part of his plan to hurt her, or even Lizzie once he'd seen how attached to her Abby had become. His plan had been simple. Stupidly naïve perhaps, but simple. In his original plan, Ginger's team was supposed to make the video and depart leaving Cherry and the girls stranded at the cabin.

As he stared through the trees at the rear wall of the cabin, ears straining to catch the slightest sound from inside, Andy Graham cursed himself for a fool. Whatever the instructions he himself had given to

Ginger, it was obvious to him now that Borisov would want no-one left alive who could testify as to how the video came to be made. He thought about that as he pushed himself away from the spruce and inched forwards to the cover of another, slightly more slender trunk. He could barely hear himself move, so he was sure that he had made no sound to alert the folk in the cabin. But he couldn't hear anything from them either, and he told himself that was a good thing. No gunshots, no raised voices, no screams. Yes, that must be a good thing.

He crouched motionless. For several minutes, he watched and listened before being finally convinced that everyone must be together in the main room at the front of the cabin. In the silence, he also became convinced of something else.

He wasn't supposed to leave here alive either.

He might not know why the video was so important, but he certainly knew only too well how it had been made and by whom. He would be seen as a risk, and there was only one way to deal with risks. He would probably have been left in the apartment with Angie and Barrie, three tragic victims of a murderer who then vanished without trace.

In which case, it would be Carl whom Ginger would be expecting to join them, maybe at the cabin, maybe somewhere else. He would not be expecting to see Andy.

Andy was supposed to be dead.

Andy thanked his lucky stars that he had decided against the simple frontal approach. It would never have worked.

He began to think through the moves he was going to have to make, and then his brain froze up. From somewhere, above the natural sounds of the woods, his ears had picked up something else. It was the sound of an engine, faint and muffled by the trees. He couldn't make out whether it was something big far away or something small closer to him. He was still trying to pinpoint its direction when the sound died away. For several minutes his ears strained to pick it up again, but there was nothing. The trees still whispered in the breeze, branches creaked and other natural sounds intruded on his senses but no engine sound was mingled among them.

Then he remembered the flocks of Scottish Blackface sheep on the exposed, brushy hillsides to the west of the golf course in the northern part of the estate. The shepherd used a quad bike to get out among them and make sure all was well. That probably accounted for the sound he'd heard, carried along to him on the breeze. No-one in the cabin seemed to have heard it or, if they had, they weren't taking any notice. No doors opened and he heard no sounds of alarm.

He turned his thoughts back to the matter in hand. He had trained for situations like this, but then he'd been a member of a team. If it came to a take-down, he would usually know the location of the bad guys in the interior of the building. It would be assumed that anyone sitting or lying on the floor would be a hostage, and anyone standing would be a target. He would only have one sector to cover. Other team members would deal with the rest. Maybe the targets would be disorientated by flash-bangs or smoke grenades. He'd be carrying his MP5 and he'd be wearing body-armour.

But that was then, and this was now.

He had to find out what was happening inside the cabin, and that meant crossing the open ground to get alongside. He wasn't sure he dare risk a peek through a window of the main room, but he ought to be able to hear voices. He did know the layout of the room, assuming it hadn't changed from his previous visit. He didn't think it would have, since there weren't too many options about how to arrange the furniture in that space.

He decided to keep among the trees and move across the rear of the cabin so he could come up to it on the kitchen side. He thought it fair to assume that everyone's attention would be on the main room of the cabin and, if the slatted blind in the kitchen was down but not fully closed, he might be able to get a look inside. He couldn't see very far through the trees in the direction he would have to move since the view was obscured by a pile of cut logs. The pile extended from the edge of the treeline back into the woods, and seemed to be held in place by living trees on either side. Presumably this was the fuel for the wood-burning stove in the cabin, and it was inside the treeline so as not to mess up the clear grass around the outside. He thought it was new. He couldn't remember it being there when he'd come up here with James. Whatever, it would be the ideal place to start his break for side wall of the cabin.

There was still no sign of light or movement through the rear windows as Andy moved cautiously through the trees in the direction of the log pile. Drawing closer, he suddenly realised that it wasn't a log pile at all, but a U-shaped hide made out of logs with the open end facing out to the grass. Ideal for someone wanting to observe the natural history of the forest without being seen. He drew alongside and crouched down to check his weapons for the last time.

The Bobcat was back in his pocket and the Smith & Wesson snugly in his right hand when he heard it.

The twig snapped right behind him immediately followed by the press of cold steel against the back of his neck. Crouched as he was, no matter how suddenly he moved, he couldn't be sure of knocking his assailant's weapon aside and bringing his own pistol to bear before getting a bullet in the back of the head. So he froze and waited for the next move, wondering how he could possibly have missed it. How could someone have come from the cabin and he not noticed? Or maybe they'd had a sentry posted by the hide all the time, just in case. He was slipping, and he knew it was going to cost him.

"Don't even twitch, Andy. I'm not in the mood for it... ... Good... ... Now reach out to the side and put that down, slow and careful."

He recognised the voice, and wasn't surprised. It was clear now, however it played out, for him the game was lost. He did exactly as he was told, carefully. With a bullet up the spout and no safety, the Smith & Wesson wasn't a gun to mess with. And anyway, he still had the Bobcat in his jacket pocket.

"Now take off your jacket and let it drop."

So much for the Bobcat.

He felt the jacket scooped away behind him, and then the pressure against the back of his neck withdrew. He wondered if he dared risk turning his head to look at his assailant, but decided it was safest not to.

So he crouched, not speaking, waiting again for the next move.

It came a moment later in the form of an agonising jolt to the centre of his spine which sent him crashing forward face down in the dirt.

Eighty-Four

Aullton Estate – Late afternoon

The Maserati was normally a beautiful and forgiving car to drive, but today she was taking punishment, and she protested loudly. For twenty-five minutes the engine growled, the exhaust roared and the tyres squealed. Other motorists also protested with wild gestures, honking of horns and flashing of lights. Fortunately for James, once he left the A68 at Lauder, there were no more speed cameras to trouble him. Not that he would have taken much notice of them. By this time, he was past caring.

The roads now were narrower, with many twists and turns, but James knew them well, and he used that knowledge to the full.

At the end of that twenty-five minutes, James found himself driving in a northerly direction alongside a high stone wall to the right of the road. Although this stretch of road was dead straight, he began to ease off the accelerator. About half-way along the straight, there was a break in the wall bounded by stone pillars. The ends of the wall curved back slightly from the road, and provided a perfectly acceptable entry point for the coach and horses for which it had been designed over two hundred years previously. It was, however, far too narrow to be taken at speed, as one golf-club member had discovered to his cost when the front near-side wing of his Mercedes SLK 230 open-topped roadster had clipped one of the pillars causing the ball on top to fall, bruising the immaculate leather of the, thankfully unoccupied, passenger seat.

James took the turn a little slower than the Mercedes had done, though not much, and as soon as he was through the entry he floored the accelerator once again. This was a single track estate road with passing places and a posted ten mph speed limit. To enforce the speed restriction on independent-minded golfers who chose to ignore it, Gil had recently had road bumps installed at hundred metre intervals. James hadn't entered the estate this way since they were laid down and, although Gil had told him about them, he'd completely forgotten. He saw the first one too late and hit it at a little over fifty. The jolt to the suspension sent a shockwave through the car followed by a screeching crunch as the underside scraped over the hump. James slowed and listened for any sounds indicating damage down below. He heard nothing apart from the quiet purring of the engine so he carried on, but with a little more vigilance. He accelerated hard and braked hard for about half a mile until he saw a break in the bank of rhododendrons to his right. It wasn't a road, or even a track. It was just a short pathway, easily wide enough for golf buggies, which led out onto the ninth fairway.

The Maserati just fitted between the bushes and would have emerged onto the grass unscathed had it not been for the two-seater electric buggy which had just turned in at the far end to head up the middle of the path towards him. James braked hard and gestured through the windscreen for the buggy to reverse out onto the fairway. Unfortunately, the buggy's sole occupant turned out to be of a determined and belligerent disposition. She climbed out and stood glaring at the Maserati. She probably stood a little over five feet in her golf shoes and wore wide-checked tartan trousers topped by a heavy woollen sweater. Her greying hair was almost covered by a rather jaunty tartan cap.

James lowered his window and leaned out.

"Would you mind backing up so I can come through?" he asked, politely but with an edge of urgency.

"Yes, I bloody well would mind," replied the elderly tartan tigress. "What the hell do you think you're doing, bringing that bloody monstrosity down here?"

James took a breath to reply, but then decided against it. He eased the Maserati forward until its nose just nudged the front of the buggy and, under his tartan tormentor's furious and speechless gaze, he pushed the buggy backwards onto the edge of the fairway. Speechless she may have been but paralysed she was not. Taking advantage of the fact that his window was still down, and with impeccable timing, she thumped him hard on the ear as he passed her. It was a meaty fist with a golfer's swing behind it, and it stung like crazy, but he was through and clear.

Turning aside from the buggy, James accelerated down the fairway. Although the Maserati's suspension wasn't built for this, James managed to keep up a good speed over the smooth grass, fishtailing slightly as he steered to avoid a pair of golfers apparently looking for a ball on the edge of a bunker. They looked up as he approached, too stupefied to hurl the insults which he felt he probably deserved. He had to slow as he cut through some rough to get to the sixteenth fairway but then picked up speed again to head for a bank of trees at the south end of the course. Some golfers shook their clubs in the air in protest as he passed but none were in any real danger of being mown down.

The blur of the forest ahead began to take on definition, and when James found he could make out individual trees along the edge he began to slow down. Somewhere along here was a track through the forest which he'd used before. He knew it was good for the quad bike which he'd then been using, but whether the Maserati could take it he had no idea. Even if the surface was too rough for the car, he had to drive into the forest as far as he could. This was partly because it would take him nearer to the fishing cabin, and partly because, if the car was seen to drive into the forest, all the irate golfers would do was to complain at the clubhouse. If the car was left by the trees on the edge of the fairway, the more curious, or more angry, among them might come to investigate.

The track was certainly worse than he remembered it, and he hated to force this beautiful thoroughbred over a course for which it was never intended. Still, as long as it was coping, he had no choice.

It couldn't go on forever, of course. He saw the sheen of dampness on the uneven surface of the track some distance ahead. The patch of mud was several metres long and extended across the width of the track. It was rutted from the forestry vehicles which regularly used it. He sped up with the intention of getting across it as quickly as possible and thought, for a moment, that he'd succeed. Then the slippery, cloying mud closed around his wheels slowing them down until eventually they began to slip. The wheels kept turning, but forward motion stopped. The mud was too thick, the car too heavy and the tyres just too smooth.

James switched off the engine, grabbed the bag off the passenger seat, got out of the car and began running through the trees.

He was a big man, not built for speed. On level ground, he was better than most for his age, but he was no sprinter. And this ground was not level. The uneven surface was made worse by grassy tussocks, nettles, occasional brambles and the odd small branch broken off by strong winds. Nevertheless, he was determined and highly motivated, so he barged on through the trees, falling a couple of times as brambles grabbed at his ankles. His progress wasn't quiet, but it didn't need to be. Not yet.

He was running in the general direction of the meadow by the Cantle Burn, and realised that he would likely emerge from the trees at a point where he could be seen from the front of the fishing cabin. So, after several minutes, he slowed and veered to his right. His route would now take him round to the rear of the cabin. He knew he was getting close when he left behind the firs which extended up to the golf course, and found himself moving between larger and older spruce.

He needed to proceed more cautiously if he was going to approach unobserved. It was no good charging in on an emotional high, pumped up by adrenalin. He had to set aside his instincts as a father, and fall back on his training as a marine. Slow and stealthy was what was needed here.

He was close enough to the meadow now to see the grass through the trees off to his left. A few moments more and he could make out the cabin and the two vehicles parked in front. He was hugely relieved to see them. In spite of the fact that no vehicles had driven out past the llama farm, as Barrie had told him, and the only other place to go was the cabin, he could think of no good reason for them to be here. If this was all about killing Lizzie and Angie, why had they just not done it and left? Why had Andy seemed to think he could catch them?

And how would he have known where to look?

All of James's previous suspicions of Andy, repressed in his haste to reach the cabin, now came flooding back. He had no idea what Andy's objective might be, but he was now convinced that his friend was playing a devious and very dangerous game.

As he circled round through the trees, he remembered the hide at the rear of the cabin. It had actually been Abby's idea. She liked watching the wildlife in the area and had no problem spotting the brown hares in the meadow, but trying to look out from the cabin into the gloom between the trees was utterly hopeless. Too much ambient light prevented a watcher's eyes from adjusting to the impenetrable darkness of the forest. Abby had learnt that if you actually stood among the trees you could see much better, and so the idea for a hide at the forest's edge had been born.

He was moving through the trees about ten yards in from the edge of the meadow. He knew from experience that, at this time of day, he would be completely invisible to anyone looking out from the cabin. He wondered how many pairs of eyes there could possibly be, looking out of the cabin's windows. Was Andy inside? Was one of those vehicles out front his? It would make sense. One vehicle to bring Andy, and one to bring Cherry and the girls with that other guy from Edinburgh.

He wished he knew what he was dealing with. If the guy in the apartment had been trying to kill Angie, then he had to assume that the other one was after Lizzie. So why had they ended up here? The group had gone off to look at the llamas, Barrie had been sure of that. So coming up here to the cabin had to be the Edinburgh guy's idea, which meant that Cherry and the girls had come under duress. So … …

He stopped trying to work it out. There was too much he didn't know, and guessing wasn't helping. He had to get close enough to find out.

There was the hide. He could see it now, reaching up well over head height. He knew there were small holes cut in each of the sides at varying heights so that those using the hide could look out in any direction. He closed in on it, but cautiously since he had to move nearer to the edge of the trees to do so. When he reached the side nearest him, he lowered his bag of weaponry to the ground. Still keeping a close eye on the cabin, he reached into the bag for the MP5K. The pre-loaded, slightly curved magazines were all there, and could be useful, but James was a little worried about them. He had no idea when the magazines had been loaded, or how old the springs were. If springs were kept in the compressed position for too long, they could become weak and lose their power to consistently feed well. Still, he couldn't do much about that now.

Once he'd stopped making noise himself, he'd become conscious of the usual soft forest sounds, and he recognised them for what they were. But there was something else out there. He stood up slowly, gun in hand, ears straining to catch the sound again. It was close. Very close. The soft footfall of someone trying very hard not to be heard over ground littered with forest debris. He looked back the way he had come, and then away into the depths of the forest, but the sound had come from the other side of the hide. Someone was approaching from that direction. Someone who was taking just as much care as he had himself. He bent a little to peer through one of the peep holes in the wall of the hide.

Nothing.

He tried to look across the hide and out through the holes in the opposite wall.

Still nothing.

And then he heard the sound again. It was like a soft brushing, as the forest floor compressed to take the weight of a man's stealthy footsteps. Not wanting to be heard himself, James kept still. He tried to gauge the man's position from the sounds he could hear. Then, suddenly, there was no need.

Peering through the hole, across the hide, and out through a long slit in the back wall, James saw movement. Someone had closed up to the far, back corner of the hide. He had no idea who it could be, unless it was Andy. But wasn't Andy inside the cabin? He had to know.

More movement, and this time James was fairly sure that whoever it was had his back to him, and was looking along the far wall in the direction of the cabin. Moving as little as possible, and taking care not to brush against it, James leant to peer around the corner of the hide. The figure had indeed got his back to him. James watched him crouch down and lay a weapon on the ground. At that moment, as the figure's head turned slightly, James realised who it was.

Only days ago, Andy would have been the one person above all others who James would have wanted beside him at a time like this. Now, too many unanswered questions had eroded his trust. He had no idea whether the next few minutes would see him embracing Andy as a friend or shooting him as a threat to the safety of his daughter. He longed for the one, but prepared himself for the other.

Without taking his eyes off Andy's back, James slowly raised the MP5K. Andy had taken something from his jacket pocket, something which James couldn't see, and he appeared to be inspecting it. After a moment, he replaced it in the same pocket and James caught the glint of metal. Then Andy reached to pick up the pistol which he'd laid on the ground, his shoes or his knees making a slight scuffing sound on the forest floor.

James moved. He tried to be quiet but, so close to his quarry, it was hardly possible. He heard the twig snap under his foot, so he thrust out urgently the hand holding the MP5K and it ground, harder than he'd intended, into the back of Andy's neck.

Eighty-Five

Aullton Estate – Late afternoon

Andy tried to turn his head to the side, but it wasn't easy. He couldn't lift his chest from the ground because of the MP5K pressing firmly down between his shoulder blades. He wanted to speak but needed to empty his mouth of the muck and decaying needles which his sudden lurch forward had forced between his lips. His chin scraped on the ground and he spat, working his tongue to expel the foul mixture.

"You didn't have to do that, you idiot."

He spat again.

James heard him, but his only response was to kick Andy's legs wide apart.

"Bloody hell, James," Andy hissed, keeping his voice low in spite of his anger.

"Clasp your hands behind your neck," responded James, his own voice soft, almost a whisper, as he glanced up towards the cabin to check for any sign that they'd been spotted.

Andy was a little slow so James leant harder on the MP5K.

"OK, OK," muttered Andy, though he was fairly sure James wouldn't shoot him, if for no other reason than it would toss away any possibility of surprising those in the cabin.

As soon as Andy had complied, James stepped back. The jacket with Andy's second gun was round the back of the hide. The Smith and Wesson was tucked, rather uncomfortably, in James's waistband and the MP5K was trained on the back of Andy's head.

"Keep your hands where they are and get up on your knees."

James knew this wasn't an easy manoeuvre and watched as Andy used his elbows to push himself up from the ground to end up sitting back on his heels, hands still clasped behind his neck. Andy's left elbow brushed the side wall of the hide. He was facing out towards the cabin and he too, with as much interest as James, looked for any indication that those inside had heard the disturbance in the woods.

There was no movement at the windows; no sound from inside.

Then James spoke again.

"Now shuffle back on your knees. Back round the corner here."

James wanted them both to be out of sight from the cabin while he himself would have that slit in the back wall through which he could keep it under observation. With Andy on his knees and with his back to him, James knew he could risk frequent glances through the slit.

"Can I put my hands down now?"

Andy's voice was still low and soft, and James began to wonder if his former friend was just as reluctant as he was himself to attract attention from the cabin.

"No. Stay as you are."

James knew that being on your knees, hands behind your head, and unable to see your assailant was both humiliating and intimidating, and he was very much in the mood for intimidating Andy right now. Whatever information he had, James needed it. He also needed to decide how far he could believe what Andy told him.

"I trusted you with my friends and my little girl, and you betrayed me."

Andy said nothing. He wasn't going to deny the truth.

"It was you that tried to kill Angie with those drugs. You put the bug in my car. You told Borisov that we were coming to Aullton. You even told him I'd be calling at Newcastle on my way up. You brought those thugs down from Edinburgh, or wherever it was they came from. And it's because of you that my little girl is in that cabin with a gun at her head... ... Now tell me I'm wrong."

James's anger began to burn more fiercely with each accusation until, like the flick of a switch, his training kicked in and professionalism pushed back the rising passion. The heat of emotion was no aid to clear thinking.

Andy seemed to sense danger in that moment, and spoke hurriedly.

"No, James. You're not wrong. But I can explain, if you'll just give me two minutes."

James glanced through the slit. No change. He felt calmer now, fully in charge of himself, but this was already taking too long. On the other hand, if Andy was here at the cabin trying to redeem himself... ...

"Two minutes, Andy. And I really can't spare them, so get on with it."

Andy did and, as it all came out, kneeling seemed like an act of contrition. He still felt vulnerable, but also immensely relieved to finally bring it all out into the open. He spoke so quietly that James found himself leaning down to catch his words.

"It started last year. I got in a financial mess... ... don't worry how. I'll tell you later. Borisov offered me a way out. But there were strings. Then somebody died and it was my fault... ... I didn't do it. Didn't intend for it... ... But it was my fault. Then Borisov began turning the screw. Wanting more favours. And I got in deeper... ... He had this deal going with a guy called Mellisse. This Mellisse needed Lizzie for something, but then she ran away. I don't know what it was all about but it must have been bloody important because he went totally apeshit.

Borisov was on the phone but I could still hear Mellisse ranting at him. I think killing Angie was just spite… … or maybe he thought she knew something… … I don't know. Borisov was doing a deal to take over Mellisse's operation, but for Mellisse to step aside, he needed this other thing to work. That's when Borisov started pressuring me to help. I had to do it. I did do it… … Then I felt so bloody awful about it… … I wanted Angie to live, but knew I was finished once she explained what I'd done. So I ended up doing what Borisov wanted, but I was trying to find a way out at the same time. In the end I realised that whatever happened I was totally screwed… … so when this guy Carl was supposed to kill Angie, I knew I had to stop him. It felt good to be doing the right thing again, so then I came up here to try and take care of Abby and Lizzie… … And Cherry. And, yes, it was me that told Borisov about this place. There are three of them in there. One is Borisov's though he's on Mellisse's payroll. You've met him before… … bust his hand. The other two, I don't know. Borisov told me to use them but I think they might belong to Mellisse… … I don't really know them, but you can bet your life they're as ruthless as they come."

Andy's back seemed to straighten as he came to the end of his story, and his head was up, eyes no longer focussed on the ground. James watched him warily. It wasn't that he didn't believe Andy. The trouble was that he did believe him, and the extent of his friend's treachery only served to fan the embers of his earlier anger.

His instinct was to treat Andy to another vicious kick in the back, and to stamp his head into the dirt. But, once again, he held himself in check. Giving vent to his fury would be no help to anyone just now.

"My little girl is only in this mess because of you."

He forced himself to keep his voice low, though he felt like yelling. He ended his words by jabbing the muzzle of the MP5K hard into Andy's neck. He wanted him to know just how close he could be to dying at that moment.

Andy turned his head slowly to the side.

"I know, James. I know… … But if it means anything, I did tell Ginger that Abby was not to be hurt. They weren't to lay a finger on her. I made it sound as though the order came from higher up than me. Like maybe Borisov had something else planned. I don't know if it worked, but it was worth a try… … Look, whether you believe it or not… … I'm here right now to take those guys down and get Abby, Lizzie and Cherry out… … It's the only reason I'm here. And that's what I think you're here for too."

James was watchful, but he thought he was beginning to understand what was going on in his friend's troubled mind. It felt strange. He was still angry but, for the present at least, the two of them were on the same side. He could easily believe that Andy had been an unwilling player on Borisov's team, especially over the last few days, but he was also aware of a strong sense of disappointment that his friend should have preferred to turn not to him but to the Russian when he first found his back against the wall. But there was a greater disappointment even than that. He had now discovered that there was a streak of ruthlessness in Andy which could lead him to consider killing an innocent girl in order to protect himself. That could prove a difficult revelation to deal with in their future relationship. But that was for later. Right now, that ruthlessness might just come in handy.

"OK, Andy. You can put your hands down and get up."

James stepped back to give him plenty of room. Andy turned as he stood, all very slow and unthreatening. He had forgotten what an impressive sight James could be when the fury gripped him. The extra three inches in height and maybe twenty pounds in weight was probably enough on its own, but put that with the H&K MP5K in his hand and the Smith and Wesson in his belt, he seemed to Andy quite formidable.

"I really am on your side, Boss," he said. "Believe it. Now can I have my gun back?"

He sounded, as he'd intended, just like a child asking for a confiscated toy to be returned.

James's grim expression softened slightly. After all, in spite of his friend's recent failings, he was a man whom James had previously trusted with his life. And there was business to be done. He drew the automatic from his belt and handed it over.

"You'd better have your jacket too," he said, bending to pick it up. He hefted it as though weighing it. "What have you got in there? It doesn't seem very heavy."

"Beretta Bobcat," replied Andy. "It may be small, but… …"

He stopped. James had turned to glance through the slit, but then leant forward as something caught his attention. Andy joined him to peer at the cabin.

Through the window of the right hand bedroom, a shadow could be seen moving. Then they heard a faint cry; definitely female but, whether it was Abby or Lizzie, Andy couldn't tell. James ears were more finely tuned.

"That's Lizzie. Time to move."

"Right, Boss. So tell me quick. Just how are we going to do this thing?"

Eighty-Six

Thurvaston Arms – Late afternoon

Nadera had tried for over an hour, but the icons of Pan had led nowhere. The time, however, was not entirely wasted. It suddenly dawned on her, after all that fruitless surfing, that each of the four websites where the icon appeared had a section that was password protected. The other sites all appeared, as far as she could tell, to offer complete public access to all areas. Only the icon sites needed a Login to access certain pages. By the time she was finished Nadera was certain that, once the correct password was entered, the Pan icon would become live and lead to… … … wherever.

It was frustrating but, in the end, they decided that it didn't really matter. They were convinced that their assumptions were correct and it had never been their intention to uncover proof that would stand up in a court of law. Whatever needed doing to ensure justice for Phil Simmons, they would attend to themselves. They just needed to be absolutely certain they had found the man responsible.

John eased himself off the end of the bed where he had been sitting watching Nadera at work. He walked over to the window, scratching his head in thought. Before he got to the point where he could see down into the garden, he suddenly stopped and turned.

"Nadera love," he said. "Haven't you got any contacts over here; someone who would do you a favour; find out what we need?"

She smiled at him and shook her head.

"John… … John… … What did I tell you? We must cut ourselves free of everyone we knew in the past. You know what will happen if we don't."

"I know… … I know. Al-Mubarak will get us both."

His lips compressed in a grim smile.

"Just for a moment, back here in good old England, I'd completely forgotten about him."

"Well I hadn't. At the moment, the Italians think you are dead, and so will he. The body they found had a smashed up face and no fingers to print. Remember that propeller?"

John nodded and gave a theatrical shudder.

"I know. And if they try to match dental records, they'll hit a brick wall because thanks to you my dentist's surgery went up in flames."

"Exactly," said Nadera emphatically. "And no-one has any idea where I am. No-one will even be looking, except Al-Mubarak. And even he has no way of knowing if I am alive or dead. I do not think he will look too hard, or for too long."

"OK. Got the message. Low profile. Nothing to draw attention to ourselves."

He looked at Nadera intently from his position by the window.

"But I still want to deal with this bastard who killed Phil."

"I know you do," said Nadera. "So we have to find some way of getting under the skin of this Mellisse." She pushed her chair back from the dressing table on which they had set the laptop. She leant back and closed her eyes which were feeling the strain of staring at the computer screen. She gently massaged her forehead with her fingertips.

"There could be a way," said John. He was still at the window of their room gazing out at the statue in the garden. "I was thinking… … there must be some sort of charity trying to help girls who've got caught up in the sex business… … in Birmingham, I mean."

Nadera dropped her hands and opened her eyes.

"Probably… … but… … what are you getting at?"

John came away from the window to perch himself on the edge of the dressing table.

"Look. We know Mellisse owns at least two of these lap-dance clubs, or whatever. Or at least he owns the holding company which owns them. That's all legal. It's on record. We believe he's involved in the dirtier stuff… … illegal stuff… … trafficking… … you know. But we can't be certain, and even if we were, we can't link him to Phil's death. Now, just suppose we're right, and I'm sure we are, there must be whispers about him somewhere, even if nobody can prove anything."

Nadera rested a hand on his knee and smiled.

"Hmm. I see what you're thinking. Maybe someone who works for a charity like that could have heard something. Or even one of the girls themselves… … if we could get to talk to them. I'll Google it and see if one of these charities pops up."

"No, no," said John. "Don't look for the charity. Try the Birmingham newspaper. The Mail or The Post or something. If the charity exists, I bet someone's done a story on it… … which means someone else will already have talked to the charity workers, and probably some of the girls. There'll be a load of info in the story… … if we can find it… … but I'll bet there's a ton more that didn't get printed because it couldn't be substantiated, or because the paper was afraid of legal repercussions."

"So, what you really want is the reporter who wrote the story."

"If there is one."

"Right. If there is one."

She leant forward again and began tapping away at the keyboard. It didn't take long. She found an archived story in a Birmingham paper dated just over a year previously.

New life for Birmingham sex-workers!

The by-line told them the story had been written by someone called Shay Johnston.

"Shay?" queried Nadera. "What sort of name is that? A man or a woman?"

"A woman would be my guess," replied John. "The charity... ... the girls... ... they'd talk more easily to a woman. Google her. See what comes up."

Shay Johnston, following the trend of many serious journalists, had her own website which appeared on the first page of Google's umpteen million results. As John and Nadera scanned the pages of her website, they learned little about her personal life, but a great deal about her writing career. One page highlighted particular articles of which she seemed to be especially proud. One of them was about the Birmingham sex-workers, and included a little more information than had been in the newspaper story, but not much. Her contact page offered nothing more than the opportunity to send her an email.

"Look up the phone number of the paper," suggested John. "Let's see if we can track her down there."

The number was easy to find, but then they realised that they hadn't worked out which one of them should make the call, and what kind of approach they should use if they were fortunate enough to speak to her.

"It had better be me," said Nadera. "My accent will be good... ... and I can make it more... ... erm... ..." She smiled. "More foreign."

John leant forward and kissed her on the lips, a gesture which she willingly received.

"I think your accent is very sexy," he said. "So, you're going to pretend to be a prostitute... ... trafficked and forced into it."

"It should work, I think," she said, speaking slowly, her accent more pronounced. "I forced here... ... I made work... ... I escape... ... I hide... ... Friend tell me of newspaper writer... ... I call... ... Ask for help... ... But say I know who made me come here."

Setting his gender aside, John knew he could never pull off anything like this. His thought processes moved too slowly. Nadera, on the other hand, had both an agile mind and a fertile imagination which made for a powerful combination when linked with her ability to lie with total sincerity.

He looked down at her a little wistfully.

"Whatever made you hook up with a staid old codger like me?" he asked.

"Old! You're not old," she exclaimed, her eyes sparkling. "And what is this codger?"

"You make me feel old."

"I didn't make you feel old last night."

"Hmm. That's true. Almost young, in fact."

"And anyway, it was your money I really wanted."

"Ah, well. That won't last forever."

"I know where to invest. It will do very well, so I might even let you spoil me a little. Now, do you want me to make you feel young again, or shall we get on with this?"

She pointed at the laptop screen which was displaying the contact details of the newspaper.

He pulled a face at her.

"I guess I'd better put off feeling young until later. Let's get this done."

In the event, what could have been a tedious and drawn-out business, turned out to be remarkably simple. As a backup, Nadera had used BT's directory enquiries to find a private listing for a Shay Johnston which, since it was the only one in the area, they assumed to be the one they wanted. After a mental coin toss, she had used her new mobile to phone the private number first, but only got through to an answering machine. Hoping the elusive reporter wasn't just out shopping, she had then phoned the newspaper offices and asked to be put through to her extension. After a tense few seconds, the phone was picked up and Nadera slipped seamlessly into her role.

John looked on, listening in amazed fascination to a young prostitute on the run from sex-slavery seeking help from an unknown journalist. The wonder of it was that it actually seemed to be working. In spite of his growing excitement, he kept very still, not saying a word, since Nadera had the phone on speaker so that he could hear both sides of the conversation. The most crucial part of the exchange came after several minutes in response to a comment from Nadera about a man called Raymond Mellisse being behind the trafficking ring that had brought her into the UK.

"Sod the bastard! I knew it," exclaimed Shay Johnston. "I knew it, many of those girls I talked to knew it, even the charity workers suspected it, but there was sod all we could do about it."

"What was it you knew?" asked Nadera in an unnaturally subdued tone.

"Exactly what you know," was the reply from the speaker. "He's been behind the trafficking of girls for years, but the word is that he's now trying to get out of the business and turn respectable."

"Can you help me?" asked Nadera.

"Course I can, love... ... Look, we need to meet up. Where can I find you? Just tell me and I'll come and get you right now."

They had already considered this, so Nadera was able to provide a location in Birmingham that John knew would sound right to the reporter. He felt a moment's guilt when he thought of raising this stranger's hopes, and of her disappointment at finding no-one waiting at the appointed rendezvous. The feeling soon passed as he thought of the hand of justice soon to land with crushing force on Raymond Mellisse; not the reporter's hand but his own. She would still have a story to write, just not the one she was expecting.

Eighty-Seven

The cabin – Late afternoon

Once I had skimmed through the script I'd been given, there was no way I wanted Abby sitting there while I read it out loud. There was stuff in there that no-one should have to hear, let alone an eight year old child. Holding the papers in my left hand, I waved them in Ginger's general direction, while glancing down at Abby.

"Can't we do something?" I asked. "Abby shouldn't have to listen to this."

Ginger smiled from the other side of the kitchen counter.

"What's up, princess? Getting squeamish are we? Worried about tarnishing your good reputation?"

His eyes then settled on Abby, huddled in the corner though still holding tight to my right hand. The eyes in her pretty face were wide with fear, glistening with the tears she was fighting to hold in. Whether he was swayed by these or by some other calculation, I couldn't tell, but he beckoned Jonno from his corner.

"Take the kid in there."

He nodded to a door to my right, near the front of the cabin. I assumed it was a bedroom running behind me along that side of the cabin.

Abby wriggled closer and clung to me as Jonno approached her.

"Hold on a minute."

The voice was firm, authoritative, and unexpected. It was Cherry, and he was speaking to Ginger.

"Can't you see it's no good? She won't go with him. Not on her own. Not without a lot of fuss and bother."

He gestured towards her with his bound hands.

"Look… … she's terrified. But she'll go if I go with her. Won't you sweetheart? You'll come with me, won't you?"

Abby had turned towards him as soon as he spoke. She heard the words, and seemed to respond to the quiet confidence of their tone. But she didn't reply.

Cherry smiled at her and lifted an eyebrow in query. This time she nodded ever so slightly.

"There's a good girl," said Cherry encouragingly. "Now come on, Ginger. What do you say?"

We all looked at Ginger, and I decided to try and help things along.

"We'll probably get this finished more quickly if there are no distractions," I said. "I'll be able to concentrate better."

Once I'd said it, I wished I'd kept quiet. I was sounding far too helpful, but Ginger didn't seem to notice anything strange.

He was quiet a moment longer, and then he nodded.

"OK, Jonno. Take the both of them in there. Sit them down and keep your eyes open. And don't get too close."

At that, Cherry stood and reached out his bound hands towards Abby. I squeezed hers gently and let go.

"It's OK, honey. I'll be here. You just go and keep Cherry company for a bit."

She seemed inclined to hang on for a moment but then, as I nudged her lightly with my shoulder, she eased away from me and stood to take Cherry's hand.

Over her head, Cherry winked at me. It was only the merest flutter of his eyelid but I recognised it for what it was. Whether he was just trying to be encouraging, or whether he was trying to let me know there was an idea forming in his mind, I had absolutely no idea. I smiled anyway, and watched them leave followed by Jonno.

Now it was just Ginger, Laddy and me. Divide and conquer. I wasn't sure it would help but you can always hope.

I began reading through the script again, but stopped after a few words. I looked up at Ginger.

"What's going to happen when we've finished this? I mean, to us. Cherry, Abby and me."

Ginger shrugged.

"Don't you worry, princess. You do the job right, and we're done. No need to hang around. We'll… …er… … tie you up and leave you to enjoy the peace and quiet. Somebody'll find you before too long."

I didn't believe a word of it, but I had to act as though I did. I had to seem cooperative while at the same time spinning this out as long as possible. I'd no idea where James was, but he surely couldn't be far away by now. And then there was Andy. What was he doing? Was Carl part of this set-up? Was Andy even still alive? Or Angie? I'd forgotten about Angie. So much I didn't know.

The inside of my mouth was dry, and I don't know what expression came over my face but Ginger noticed something.

"Are you OK, princess? Need a drink or anything?"

A drink, preferably in a glass. Might be useful.

"Water would be good, thanks."

Ginger searched the cupboards and came up with a pint-sized glass which he filled from the tap.

"Wonder where they get the water from," he mused as he brought the glass over to me. It was a little over half full.

I took it and sipped a little, letting it run around my mouth. Then I placed the glass on the floor by my feet.

"Ready now?" asked Ginger.

I nodded slowly as another idea formed.

"Could I just try reading it through without the camera? Try and get the feel of it."

Laddy was sitting now, on the settee opposite, in the corner where Cherry had been. He was still watching me but seemed relaxed now, to the point of laying down his gun on the seat beside him. Ginger was back behind the counter, facing me. I tried not to look at the gun resting so casually on the settee, just an inch or so from Laddy's thigh. If he was distracted, for just a couple of seconds, I could grab it.

But could I use it? Sure I could point it at Ginger, or Laddy, or Jonno, and pull the trigger, and keep on firing until it ran out of bullets and they were all dead. But I wasn't sure it was that easy. In the movies I'd seen, they have to pull levers at the side, and flick off safety catches, and I had no way of knowing if you needed to do that with Laddy's gun. If I did grab it, I could be fairly sure that before I had time to find out, Laddy would be beating me over the head with it.

On the other hand, given the right moment and a lot of luck, I might just pull it off.

"Don't even think about it, Babe." Laddy must have been reading my mind. "You're not quick enough. All I gotta do is pick it up and pull the trigger, and you're dead. Just like that. So stop jerking us around and read the damn script."

Thanks, Laddy. Just what I needed to know. Not that I believed he would pull the trigger. Not until I'd completed the video, at least.

I looked down at the script and began reading.

This wasn't going to be a long recording. I reckoned maybe ten minutes at most. But then, it was obvious from the start that this wasn't the whole movie. The finished product would have extra segments of video footage edited in, and I didn't have to work hard to guess what they might be. I'd always known that Bruno tried to get film of his girls in action whenever possible, but sometimes the location worked against him. In the early days, I'd not been able to do much about it, but then my talents and my looks got me moved up-market. Not quite the high-class call-girl yet, but that's the way Mellisse had me headed. My guys now tended to be more discreet, possibly because they had more to lose if their extra-curricular activities came to light. It had usually not been hard to encourage them to pick a venue of their own choice for our assignations. We might be followed to the house, hotel, boat or whatever, and we usually were, but at least our activity was out of range of pre-installed recording devices.

I was forcefully reprimanded by Bruno on several memorable occasions for not bringing the guys to a rendezvous of his choosing. Not obeying was my way of fighting back and, though the consequences were usually painful, it was oddly satisfying.

Unfortunately, there came to be one person whom Bruno seemed especially interested in. He was a businessman at the pinnacle of his career, but a disobliging wife had driven him to seek an alternative outlet for his sexual needs. Eventually, about six months ago, our paths crossed and Bruno began to pay serious attention.

And that, since Bruno never acted on his own account, meant that Raymond Mellisse himself was somehow interested in the behind-the-scene activities of the client I was told to refer to only as Michael.

However, my client was not particularly discreet over the use of his credit card, and it wasn't long before I discovered who it was that made use of my services with increasing regularity. We had become quite at ease with each other by then, so he didn't seem to mind very much that I had found out who he was. If anything, he seemed rather pleased that he didn't, any longer, have to be wary of what he said when we were together. I became interested enough to follow his activities in the newspapers since it gave me things to talk to him about, or at least ask him, on our dinner dates or excursion to the theatre.

He had been so candid in telling me his hopes for the future that, when Tony Blair announced the date of the General Election last month, it came as no surprise to discover that Sir Vernon Laycock was standing as a Parliamentary candidate for his local constituency in the Midlands. Opinion polls were forecasting another five years of Labour government, and Vernon was confident – if elected – of a post in Cabinet.

And the power behind Sir Vernon Laycock MP would be Raymond Mellisse, respected businessman and entrepreneur. I had no doubt that Mellisse would be subtle in his manoeuvring, silky tongue and velvet glove, but always in the background would be a threat of exposure in the tabloid papers of Vernon's sexual activities. Extra-marital affairs among politicians no longer raised many eyebrows, but this would be different. This would be sex with a call-girl or, to be brutally frank, a prostitute; a low-life sex-worker is probably how the tabloids would describe me. And, according to my script, it wouldn't be just common-or-garden sex either. Exotic and experimental, bordering on the extreme, is how the tabloids would see it as they rejoiced over the potential for increased sales.

And this video would be the proof.

Extracts from Bruno's previously-recorded videos would be intercut with my narrative to portray Vernon as some sort of depraved monster. The script I held in my hand was what would do the most damage. According to this, Vernon forced me to perform weird and degrading acts with him, beating me savagely if I showed any sign of resistance.

And the whole thing was a complete pack of lies.

I had no way of knowing how much video Bruno already had, or how explicit it was, but I was sure that on its own it would be damaging to Vernon. However, my narrative would turn this gold-plated club into pure, solid platinum.

I finally realised why Mellisse couldn't just let me go. He hadn't been trying to find me simply to punish me. He needed me for this. His hold over Vernon would be absolute. If I had learnt anything about Vernon during our meetings together it was that he valued enormously the esteem of his society friends and business colleagues. He would be mortified at the prospect of seeing details of his private life so grossly distorted for public edification. I was sure he would do anything to prevent it.

"OK, princess, you've had enough time. Now, let's get this recording done. I got some business should be flying into London about now. Wouldn't want to keep the little ladies waiting."

Little ladies? Of course. The new batch of girls would be flying in from Lithuania this afternoon. I'd completely forgotten. Not that there was anything I could do to help them. They were going to have to fend for themselves, and it looked as though Ginger was planning on joining their induction programme.

He was behind the counter, looking down at the camera's small screen. My eyes had jerked up from the papers I was holding, which seemed to prompt his own eyes to lift up to meet mine. I tried to hold his gaze, to stare him down, but couldn't help feeling intimidated by the hardness in his glare. I didn't want to give them anything on video which they could use, partly because I liked Vernon, but mostly because I hated Mellisse. The trouble was that I couldn't think of a way to stall any longer short of an outright refusal to cooperate. That would delay things for as long as it took them to beat me into submission, which I suspected might not be all that long.

I gave up on the staring contest and looked back at the top paper. The first paragraph was quite short and didn't really say anything very much. It was a sort of introduction, explaining more about me than it did about Vernon, presumably to show just how low he had sunk. It wasn't an entirely true picture, but then it wasn't all lies either.

"Right," I said. "Could we just try this first bit. Then you can tell me how it looks. See if I'm doing it right."

Ginger's glare relaxed, just a touch.

"That's the way, princess. Look straight at the camera. The mike's picking you up. Start when you're ready."

I started, but Ginger interrupted almost straight away.

"What did I just say? I don't want you looking like you're reading a script. Look at the camera. Improvise if you want, but get the gist of it right."

I dropped my eyes again, and tried to look as though I was memorising the words. I waited a little too long. It was Laddy who showed his impatience this time.

"This is taking for ever. Come on, Ginger. Let me soften her up a bit. I won't mark her face, honest. I'll just fool around with her other bits. Then, if she still won't play ball, you can have a go."

"I'm ready," I said quickly. I looked straight at the camera, exactly as I'd been told, and began. It was true to the text, but it was the most stilted and unnatural speech I could produce. I knew immediately that I'd gone too far.

Ginger slammed his fist down on the counter so hard that the camera wobbled on its mini tripod.

"Ok, Laddy. She's all yours. Take her in that back room. I'll try and raise Carl. See how things are going at his end. Now hurry up so we can get this thing done and get out of here and go and have some real fun."

It was the smile on Laddy's face, rather than the gun now in his hand, that sent an icy shiver coursing through my stomach. I felt sick and knew it was fear of being at Laddy's mercy. I knew what he was capable of, and cringed at the thought of him grasping and groping, forcing his way into my most intimate places. Even in my fear, I was surprised at my reaction. His attentions probably wouldn't be worse than anything that I'd experienced before, but something had happened to me in these last few days. Something about how I viewed myself, probably because of how I was viewed by those who had so recently burst into my life and suddenly become so important to me. Whatever it was, it had changed me, and now it seemed as though Laddy would defile the sprouting new life before the bud had a chance to break into flower.

Laddy was standing over me but, with the gun in his good hand, he could hardly haul me to my feet, which is what I was sure he would have liked to have done.

"On your feet, darlin', and let's you and me go and get cosy."

I didn't want to go, but I knew their patience had run out. The only good thing I could see in this was that the enemy would now be truly divided, one in each room. The dividing part had gone great, but how that could lead to any conquering I had absolutely no idea.

Laddy pointed to the door leading to a back room, presumably another bedroom.

"On your way, girl."

I went. We were through the door and I saw I was right; double bed, pine wardrobe, pine dressing table, mirror above.

Mirror!

In the glass I saw Laddy glance back as he pushed the door closed with his right elbow. Without thinking, I turned suddenly and kicked him hard in the groin, slightly off-centre but enough to do damage. At the same time, as he grunted and doubled forward, I aimed a kick at his face. The toe of my shoe connected with his nose and slid off into his left eye. He staggered and I kicked him again. He tried to reach for me with his bandaged right hand. I grabbed it and pulled him off balance so he fell to his knees. He didn't try to use his gun, which meant I had probably been right about his unwillingness to kill me before I made the video. Mellisse would not be kind to him. He was trying to push himself up with his bad hand so I jumped forward and landed hard on it with both feet. He yelled but I doubt if it was heard over my own screaming.

I was a raging fury, avenging years of appalling abuse, and Laddy was taking the brunt of it all. I wasn't thinking clearly. I was swept up in a stampeding rage and I stamped down again, once, twice, three times. Somewhere in my stamping I grabbed Laddy's gun, surprised at the ease with which it came away from his hand. I swung it like a club at his left ear and he collapsed to the floor just as the bedroom door was flung open.

Eighty-Eight

The cabin – Late afternoon

I glimpsed the movement of the door before I heard it crash back against the wall. Turning from Laddy, I was horrified to see Ginger framed in the doorway, pistol in his right hand, his left palm flat against the still-vibrating door. His eyes went from me to the unmoving heap that was Laddy. His expression said that he could scarcely believe what he was seeing. Surprise made him sloppy. His pistol was wavering as though he wasn't quite sure just where he should point it. He was clearly not quite the seasoned professional he liked to think he was.

Laddy had said his gun was ready to simply aim and pull the trigger. I hoped he was right.

I gripped it with both hands and aimed.

I pulled the trigger.

I think I expected the gun to jump around a bit as it spat out several bullets, but there was surprisingly little recoil.

Ginger disappeared from the doorway, but whether I had hit him, or whether he was simply ducking for cover, I had no idea. I glanced down at Laddy but he was still lying motionless. I noticed that the gun in my hands was quivering. I hadn't realised until then that my whole body was trembling. I had been frightened before and I'd been angry before, but never until today had I held in my hands the means of killing someone and been fully prepared to use it. I took a deep breath to steady myself and looked up through the open doorway.

I could see the whole length of the front room, along the settee on which I'd been sitting as far as the main entrance. I could see the door to the bedroom where Jonno was guarding Cherry and Abby.

The door began to open just as Ginger spoke. I still couldn't see him, but his voice sounded strained. I thought at least one of the bullets must have hit him.

"You stupid cow… … Can't you see how this is going to end? … … Think you can take us all out do you? All on your own."

The bedroom door beyond the settee opened wider and Jonno stuck his head out for a quick look. I lifted the gun but he'd ducked back before I could pull the trigger.

"Hey Ginger," he called out. "What the hell's going on?"

"Bloody cow's got hold of Laddy's gun, that's what… … Now just keep those two quiet while we sort this thing out."

I wondered how he thought he was going to do that. I guess he was wondering the same, as he was quiet for a moment.

I sensed rather than heard Laddy stir behind me. I glanced round nervously and saw his left hand moving slowly towards his head which he was trying to lift from the floor. I loathed him but, in spite of that, I couldn't bring myself to shoot him as he lay there. I shifted slightly and drew back my right leg to kick him with as much force as I could manage right under his chin which he had so conveniently raised into position. I was glad I was wearing trainers, not open-toed sandals. His head jerked back and flopped down. I watched carefully, but he didn't move.

"Lizzie," called Ginger. I was glad he'd stopped calling me Princess. "Why don't you put down the gun, and we'll forget all about what just happened? ... ... All we want is the video. Finish that and we can be on our way. No-one'll hurt you. Any of you."

"Laddy will," I said, knowing that he'd never forgive me for taking his gun away from him. I'd been going to say more but the words choked off in my throat as I sensed something move behind me. It wasn't that I heard anything. It was more like a change in the light as when a bus or lorry would drive past the front windows of my apartment in Birmingham. I swung round but whatever it was had gone. There was nothing outside the window and Laddy was still flat out on the floor.

"Laddy's a randy Russian sod," said Ginger. "I'll take care of him. Now be a good girl. Put the gun down and come in here."

I didn't know what to do next. I certainly wasn't going to put the gun down and walk tamely into the next room. Once I did that, we were all dead. Ginger's assurances were about as kosher as a bacon sandwich. I didn't believe a word he said.

But I still didn't know what to do. Cherry was bound, and in the other room where he couldn't see what was going on. I wished with all my heart that James was here. He'd know exactly what should be done, and would have no hesitation in getting on with it. It was a kind of Mexican standoff, but it wasn't going to last forever. The only thing I had going for me was the fact that Ginger wasn't going to shoot me if there was any possible way to avoid it. Maybe if I agreed to what he said, apart from the bit about putting the gun down, I could walk into the front room and shoot him before he shot me. It might take him by surprise, especially if he was wounded, as I thought.

Then Ginger spoke again, but not to me.

"Jonno."

Jonno's head appeared again at the bedroom door.

"Yeah?"

"Grab the kid and take off her panties."

My heart lurched and I could feel the blood pounding in my ears. I knew Ginger was just using the threat of hurting Abby to get to me, and I didn't really think he'd go through with it. But I couldn't be sure, and I daren't take the chance of being wrong. Perhaps better than anyone, I could imagine what it would be like for her. Not Abby, I thought. I can't let them do that to Abby. I started to raise the gun, wondering if I had any sort of chance of hitting Jonno as he stood in the doorway.

Jonno didn't notice my movement. He was looking towards the kitchen area, so I wondered if Ginger was leaning against the counter. It seemed that Jonno wasn't sure he'd heard right.

"What d'you say?"

When Ginger replied, his voice was harsher. Maybe he was losing patience, or maybe he was really hurting.

"Take off her bloody pants, and find something to shove up her. Do the job yourself, if you've a mind, but don't stop unless I tell you... ... Did you hear that, Lizzie? It's your choice. Get in here now or that kid'll never be the same again."

Jonno looked my way and I saw his eyes widen as they took in the gun pointed, perhaps a little waveringly, in his direction. Feeling I had nothing to lose, I pulled the trigger.

I dared to hope that Jonno might collapse to the floor, hit by one or more of my bullets, though I more than half expected to see him duck safely back out sight. He did neither.

He lunged forward into the sitting room with Cherry on his back. Cherry's bound hands were around Jonno's throat and he was hauling back as hard as he could. I wondered how my bullets could have missed the pair of them. They surely must have scorched Cherry's back, so close must they have been. I could see wood splinters on the edge of the doorframe where the bullets had hit.

Jonno was thrashing about trying to get free of Cherry, who was struggling to get enough leverage to cut off Jonno's air supply. Cherry also seemed to be trying to keep Jonno's body between him and Ginger.

Ginger. I had to do something about Ginger.

Abby was shouting out from the bedroom. Alternately she called for me and for Cherry. There was a huge amount of fear in her voice, but it wasn't hysterical. Not yet.

I took a deep breath, steadied the gun in both hands, and stepped through the door into the sitting room. Ginger didn't immediately see me and for a moment I hesitated, taking in the scene.

Ginger was on the kitchen side of the counter, leaning hard against it. His left hand was resting limply on the surface, and the left sleeve of his shirt was red with blood. Unfortunately, his right hand was unaffected. It held one of his pistols and was pointing it at the pair struggling in the centre of the sitting room. Obviously, he was trying to get a clear shot at Cherry, but didn't trust himself to move. I wondered whether he'd been hit somewhere else, as well as the arm.

Jonno also had a gun in his hand, and he was trying to twist his arm around to put a bullet in Cherry, which Cherry was trying equally hard to avoid. I thought Jonno should be weakening, but it was Cherry who seemed to be losing strength and moving more slowly. Then Jonno saw me, and swung his gun in my direction. I couldn't fire for fear of hitting Cherry. Then I shuddered as I saw a spreading patch of red on Cherry's back.

At that moment, I heard the sound of movement behind me and I knew it was all over.

I was just starting to turn when there was a huge crash and the tinkle of breaking glass. I thought Ginger or Jonno must have fired at Cherry and I turned back to see, forgetting Laddy behind me. But it hadn't been a gunshot.

The front door had been smashed in. The glass pane in the upper section of the door was shattered as the wooden frame around it splintered under the force of a mighty kick. James had finally arrived. He stood in the doorway, his massive form filling the entry. I had never been as glad to see anyone as I was to see him at that moment.

Before I could call his name, the gun in his hand spat twice and Ginger's head snapped back. The ruthlessness faded from eyes suddenly blank, and Ginger's body collapsed to the floor behind the counter.

Jonno had frozen as soon as the door crashed open, and Cherry slowly moved his hands away from Jonno's neck and lifted them over his head. Then I remembered Laddy and swung round to face him, gun levelled.

There was no sign of him. My eyes searched the room frantically, but there was no doubt. He had vanished. I wondered about the wardrobe. I'd seen a movie once where someone was hiding in a closet, and the villain had just fired a burst through the door. I was tempted, but decided instead to pull the door suddenly open and jump back. I needn't have bothered. It was empty. I was similarly tempted to fire a few bullets under the bed, but contented myself with twitching up the corner of the bed cover and taking a peep. Nothing.

Then suddenly it was blindingly obvious. There was a door in the corner of the bedroom, in the alcove formed by the en-suite bathroom, which must lead into the adjoining bedroom. Laddy must have gone through there, scared off by the clamour in the main room. I wondered whether he had another weapon on him. I knew he was always armed, but he could hardly walk the streets of Birmingham carrying a machine gun. The odds were that he had another gun hidden under his clothing, and he was now planning to break into the kitchen unexpectedly from the other bedroom.

I rushed to the open door of the sitting room to shout a warning to James, and was surprised to see Andy had now arrived. He had moved through the room to lean over the counter so he could look down at Ginger. James was standing in the doorway where Jonno had been. He was trying to reassure Abby while at the same time keeping a careful eye on Jonno who had dropped his pistol and was standing perfectly still. Cherry had sunk down onto the settee and now sat hunched exactly where I had been.

Ignoring everything, I called out, "James. There's another one." I pointed. "In that room through there."

Andy immediately raised his gun and pointed it at the door in the far corner of the kitchen. For a moment, there was complete stillness, and the only sound we could hear was Abby's crying. My heart went out to her. The poor kid had no idea what was going on, except that her dad was now here but unable to give her the hug she so desperately needed. She must have been scared out of her wits.

James moved, only slightly, so he could get a better view of the room where Abby was now alone. Seeing I had my gun pointed at Jonno, he risked a quick glance through the doorway. He raised a hand and said something which I didn't quite catch, and then he touched a finger to his lips. Abby's crying stopped. It was a bad mistake.

Jonno saw that Andy was watching the door at the rear of the kitchen, and James was looking into the side bedroom. I kept glancing from James to Andy, and then back at the door in the corner of the back bedroom. For a second or two, most of us were taking little notice of Jonno. Only Cherry was watching him, but he was too weak to move. Suddenly, Jonno saw an opportunity and dropped to his knees, snatching up the pistol which he had previously let fall to the carpet. Keeping low, he spun and fired. He managed to get off two shots before a burst from my gun blew his head apart. Blood and other stuff spurted out, staining the side wall of the counter and the settee where Laddy had been sitting. My stomach heaved. The acrid smell of gunfire was now joined by the sickly aroma of bodily fluids. I breathed hard, fighting the urge to vomit.

I won, but only just.

My aim was clearly improving, but it was no consolation as I glanced to my left and saw Andy crumpled over the counter. At least one of Jonno's bullets had found its mark.

From the moment when Cherry had leapt onto Jonno, everything had happened faster than I could think. Action followed by reaction, over and over. Now all was still and quiet, and I tried to ignore the nasty tang in the air.

I turned from Andy to watch the door to the other bedroom where Laddy must be hiding. James was watching from the door to Abby's room. Cherry had managed to lean forward to pick up Jonno's gun which he was now holding ready in both hands. We were as ready as we could be, but Laddy was both cunning and vicious, which made for a dangerous combination. I was sure he was going to die that day, but I couldn't be certain he wouldn't take one or more of us with him.

It was still less than a minute since the front door crashed in, and James spoke to me for the first time.

"Are you OK, Lizzie?"

His eyes were constantly moving; Abby, me, Cherry, Andy, the kitchen.

"Did they hurt you? Did they do anything to Abby?"

Without taking my eyes from the door behind which I believed Laddy was hiding, I shook my head. They had done a great deal to terrify that child, but they hadn't actually molested her in any way.

"No," I said. "She's scared, but they didn't hurt her."

"OK." He spoke to Abby now. "I want you to just stay in there, sweetheart. This is nearly finished, but I don't want you to move until I tell you."

"Daddy."

It was just one word, but the fear wrenched at my heart almost as much as it must have torn at his. I glanced in his direction.

"It's OK, sweetheart," James said. "I just have to move, but I'm not going away. I promise."

He caught my eye and jerked his head to indicate that I should join him. I took a last look at the door in the corner of the bedroom. It was still shut fast so I hurried into the sitting room. I stepped over Jonno's legs and tried not to step in any of the messy bits that had leaked out of his head.

James came towards me and whispered as he passed, "Stay in the doorway where she can see you. She needs to be able to see someone she can trust." He squeezed my arm gently. "And she needs to see you're OK."

I nodded and whispered, "It's Laddy in there. That guy from the hospital... ... with the hand."

James's eyebrows rose slightly, then he nodded and I took his place in the doorway. I looked into the room. Abby was sitting cross-legged on the bed, her back against the headboard. Her arms were folded over a pillow which she hugged tightly to her chest. Her eyes glistened and I could see dampness on her cheeks but, when I smiled and gave her a little wave, she was able to summon up a faint smile in return. I held Laddy's gun in my right hand down by my side, where I hoped she wouldn't be able to see it.

James was now where I had been, just inside the doorway to the back bedroom. Andy was still propped against the counter with his pistol pointing at the door in the corner of the kitchen. Cherry was holding Jonno's pistol with both hands resting on his knee. If one of them had been more mobile, I guessed that James would have sent him round the outside to take a shot at Laddy through one of the back windows, but that was clearly not an option. I was about to ask if James wanted me to have a go at that when he moved from sight, preparing to kick in the adjoining door in the corner of the bedroom.

The gun felt warm against my thigh, but I could also feel a draught coming in through the demolished front door just a couple of feet to my right. I glanced that way, and felt an icy hand grip my chest as I stopped breathing.

Eighty-Nine

Birmingham Airport – Late afternoon

He looked around the room. It wasn't much different from most other hotel rooms he'd stayed in, but it would do just fine. He had no need of the many features which the hotel boasted of in its brochures. He would not be lying on the Queen bed, nor would he be making use of the en-suite bathroom. The flat-screen TV with its multiplicity of channels held no interest for him. He would certainly not risk making phone calls from his room, and he would not be here long enough to consider utilising the free WiFi connection. His eyes passed over the tea and coffee making facilities but lingered for a moment on the mini-bar. He mustn't have a drink, he knew that, not before the job was done, but it was a temptation nonetheless.

Tearing his eyes away, he moved across to the one feature of the room which made it ideal for his purpose.

The window.

It had been left slightly open. In the days when smoking was still permitted in hotel rooms, cleaners often left windows open to allow the air in the room to clear. When the girl on reception had asked whether he preferred a smoking or non-smoking room, he had said it didn't matter. He had no intention of lighting up anyway.

The preference he expressed had been for a room on the second floor on the south side of the hotel. He claimed that the quality of sunlight coming through the windows was much better on that side. The receptionist who had booked him in only minutes earlier had heard guests make requests far more strange than this, and had been happy to oblige him. He had settled his bill up front, claiming that his flight left very early the next morning and he didn't want to risk being held up.

He had carried his own bag up to the room. He only had the one item, and it was more of a holdall than a suitcase, but the hotel staff were used to their temporary residents arriving with all kinds of luggage, or even no luggage at all, and no-one gave it a thought. One or two were mildly curious about his long drovers coat and waxed Aussie-style wide-brimmed hat and wondered vaguely where he had flown in from, or what kind of climate he was travelling to, but it was only a passing thought. Had it been anything more they might have noticed how he always kept his head down so the shadow of the brim made his face hard to see.

Gently, he lowered his holdall to the floor and took a quick look out of the window. The view was perfect. He could see clearly down to the paved area in front of the doors through which the newly-landed arrivals would emerge from the main airport building. He glanced at his watch. When he had received the phone call a little under an hour ago, he had known that the timing was going to be a little tight, but his natural tendency to ignore speed-limits had got him here in time. He had been fortunate to find an empty bay for his car near the exit of the short-stay car-park which meant that the stolen Mazda 3 was less than three minutes' walk from where he now stood.

He had considered the possibility of taking care of the problem confronting him by employing a daring technique of which he had become rather proud. It involved a simple walk-by shooting using his Makarov PB silenced pistol. It maybe wasn't the best handgun in the world, but he'd had it since he was fifteen and he'd grown attached to it. To date, he'd walked away from five such killings in three different countries, and no-one had yet come close to catching him.

Unfortunately, as soon as he'd entered the main concourse, it had been obvious that, although a simple walk-by might get the job done, he'd have little chance of getting away afterwards. He had been warned in the phone call that there would be police around, also watching out for his target, and a quick reconnaissance had confirmed that there were too many, too close. He would have to resort to Plan B for which, happily, he had come fully prepared.

Plan B was in the holdall which he now bent down to unzip. First thing out was a pair of latex gloves which he quickly put on before extracting a number of components of varying shapes and sizes all carefully wrapped in pieces of felt-like fabric. He unpacked each one, laying it on the carpet on top of its wrapping. That done, he moved the one and only coffee table over to the window and knelt to peer along its surface through the open window towards the exit from the terminal building. He pushed the window as wide as it would go. The gap was possibly wide enough for a well-fed monkey to wriggle through, but no child was going to fall out through the narrow aperture – which was probably what the designers intended. He adjusted the table slightly and peered along it again. He nodded to himself, sat back on his heels and gave a grunt of satisfaction.

He glanced at his watch. The display board in the terminal had told him that the plane was expected to land on time which meant that it would be on the tarmac in three and a half minutes. Adding on time for clearing customs and getting through the baggage hall, he knew he'd be ready well before his target appeared.

Patience was not a virtue he had ever felt the need to cultivate so it was fortunate that he had plenty to occupy him while he waited. One by one he picked up the components he had laid out on the floor and, with the expertise of long practice, he assembled his German manufactured DSR-1 sniper rifle.

He liked the DSR mainly because, no matter how many times you took it apart and put it back together again, the point of impact of its bullet would remain unchanged. In his line of work, that level of reliability was worth its weight in gold. He was confident of a lethal shot at anything up to three hundred metres using subsonic 7.62 ammunition. What was the use of a suppressor on your rifle, if your bullet generated a sonic crack as it sped towards its target? As he placed the assembled weapon on top of the coffee table, he was confident that no-one would be able to say where his shot had come from. Detailed forensics might eventually be able to suggest a direction and trajectory, but by then he would be long gone.

He wasn't a sniper by training, but he knew enough not to project the barrel of his rifle through the window aperture. The DSR rested sedately on the coffee table, supported by its integral bipod with the end of the muzzle just over three inches inside the window frame. The gap was wide enough to allow him all the latitude he might need to zero in on his target, whichever door was used to exit the terminal building.

He looked at his watch. His target should have disembarked and be making his way through customs which, if experience were anything to go by, would probably take less time than his wait in the baggage hall. Not long now.

He stood up and looked around the room. He had touched remarkably little, and everything he no longer needed he packed back in the holdall. Once his target was down, he would disassemble the DSR sufficiently to fit back in the holdall, replace the coffee table in its original position, and exit the room. In less than five minutes after that, he would be in his car and heading for the airport exit. He should then be back at the safe-house in plenty of time to meet the latest consignment of girls.

He hoped they wouldn't get caught up in the chaos that his bullets would inevitably precipitate, but he trusted Bruno and the new girl, whose name he couldn't remember, to get them safely through it. Under his breath he damned the stupid bitch who'd run away. She should have been meeting the new lot with Bruno and, up until a few days ago, she'd seemed entirely trustworthy. No. Trustworthy wasn't the quite right word; more like cowed into a subdued reliability. And then she'd run off, resulting in her mate getting a sound thrashing before being tossed onto the Aston Expressway.

As he knelt once again at the end of the coffee table and tucked the stock of the DSR into his shoulder, he wondered briefly what had happened to Angie. Was she still alive? He gave a kind of mental shrug. Who gives a toss? He certainly didn't. He focussed his attention on the job in hand.

There were a few people just milling around in front of the Arrivals' exit doors, but most who came into his sights were clearly moving purposefully towards some destination known only to them. Some were moving laterally across the space in front of the doors, but most who appeared were exiting the Arrivals concourse in search of taxis, buses and car parks.

He sighted on the face of a young woman who came through the exit pushing a baby-buggy. She was accompanied by a slightly older-looking man awkwardly manoeuvring a trolley loaded with baggage. He tracked her through his rifle sights as she moved forwards several paces before turning to her left, his right. He smiled in anticipation of seeing a red mist cloud her head as his bullets tore into bone and flesh. He licked his lips but waited, his finger not yet on the trigger.

After that test, he reckoned he had a window of about seven seconds minimum in which to take the shot. Tight, but doable. The DSR moved slightly as he sighted again on the exit doors, the young woman and her baby now forgotten.

He was ready. His laser range-finder had given him the distance and he'd made the necessary allowance for the drop in elevation. Wind was almost non-existent and humidity was low. He expected a kill with one shot but was ready to follow up with a second for good measure. If anyone blocked his view at the crucial moment, he was fully prepared to take them down and follow through with a kill-shot to the target.

He settled down to watch the doors knowing that, from now until the job was done, he couldn't afford to take his eyes off them. Men women and children appeared in his sights, some singly, some in groups. They hovered there with perfect clarity for a moment or two before drifting away to right or left. A group of five girls appeared, pretty girls in their late teens, maybe twenty. They hesitated in front of the doors looking around uncertainly as though waiting for someone to tell them what to do. The sniper licked his lips as he took in every detail of their eager and excited faces. So this was the fresh meat, due to make his acquaintance later that evening. His assumption was confirmed when Bruno appeared at the side of the group and pointed, showing them where to go.

The sniper frowned. There should be… … Ah, yes. There she was. Another young woman, showing less animation than the group of five, drifted up to Bruno's side, looking quite tiny in comparison to his huge bulk. Philippa was already a good little earner with plenty of potential, but she'd never be a patch on that bitch of a runaway whom she was now having to stand in for.

He watched the group move away and knew the moment was nearly here. His target usually allowed the girls to exit the terminal first, hanging back to keep a good distance from them, but ready to step up if, for some reason, Bruno didn't show.

He could feel his heart rate picking up and he forced himself to breath steadily, in and out, trying to relax.

The uniformed sergeant appeared first, his weapon slung at rest across his chest. He was speaking into his radio and, as he finished, a police squad car eased in from the left of the sniper's view, siren off but with blue lights flashing. It stopped at the kerb maybe twenty yards from the terminal's doors. It didn't matter. Wherever it had stopped, it wouldn't have obscured much of the view of the target.

The sergeant looked back at a group emerging from the exit. Three men and two women, all in plain clothes. The men walked in line abreast, the women following close behind. The man in the middle had both hands behind his back.

Handcuffed, thought the sniper as he focussed on the target's head. It wasn't exactly a full-frontal shot, and he allowed for the slight lateral movement before squeezing the trigger. He prepared for second shot but, even as he did so, he knew he wouldn't need it. The first one was good.

The target's head snapped backward before his body twisted and crumpled to the ground, the only still form in the midst of sudden panic.

Thirty seconds later, the sniper left the hotel room satisfied that Mitchell Gareth Portess would never be tempted to give up the secrets the police so desperately wanted from him.

Ninety

The Cabin – Late afternoon

I'd been wrong. Laddy didn't have another gun. If he had, he wouldn't have been crawling along the veranda, keeping down below window height, as he tried to make it to the front door.

I realised immediately what had happened. Being without a weapon, he had decided not to hang around in the bedroom where he had hidden, but had left straight away through one of the windows. Coming along the side of the cabin, he had climbed between the rails at the end of the veranda and peeped in through the front window of the kitchen. He had either been very careful, or we had all been so engrossed in what was happening inside the cabin that none of us noticed him. He would have seen my attention switching between Abby in the side bedroom and James in the back, and he would have seen Andy and Cherry fully focussed on the rear door of the kitchen. With his two mates out of the game, his only chance of turning the situation around would be to come up on me from behind and get hold of my gun, formerly his gun.

He aimed to be the only one leaving that place alive. I was sure of it.

He was almost at the front door, readying himself for the final lunge that would send me to the floor and place his gun back in his own hands.

He was still crouched low at the moment I saw him. His mouth was open in an almost animal-like snarl, and his eyes were wide and staring, filled with hate. He sprang up at the very same moment that I swung the gun up from my side. I didn't have time to fire. The combination of his movement and mine caused the end of the muzzle to rake across his face, the sights gouging at those eyes. I hadn't intended it, but the result was very effective.

Laddy fell back on the wooden boards of the veranda, his good hand clutching at his eyes. Behind him, the green of the meadow stretched away to the stream and beyond, in a scene of such tranquillity that for a brief moment it tugged my mind away from the madness inside the cabin. It was an ephemeral flashback that didn't have time to become fully formed in my mind before Laddy's moans and curses thrust it away. I stood still, watching him, the gun heavy in my hand. I heard a crash from inside the cabin, but didn't turn my eyes from the writhing piece of vermin which, in that moment, represented everything bad that had happened in my life. Part of my mind registered that the crash must have been James breaking through into that last bedroom, but I didn't care.

Laddy was such a mass of rage that if he once got to his feet he would overpower me in no time. I couldn't let that happen.

But I couldn't bring myself to pull the trigger. He was a useless piece of shit who deserved to have done to him what he had inflicted on so many others.

But he was an unarmed useless piece of shit and shooting him as he knelt there was too much like an execution.

I just couldn't do it, so I stepped back a pace to increase the distance between us. I called for James, who must by now have found that last bedroom empty.

"James. Get back here. Laddy's here at the front."

Stupidly, I glanced sideways to see if he had heard, and that's when Laddy made his move.

He leapt up, his left hand reaching for my gun, his right forearm aiming to crush my throat. What he would have done to me with his legs and feet I never found out.

Two shots crashed out, close together, but distinct.

Laddy fell against the doorframe as though hurled there by a sledgehammer. His head thumped against the wood before his body slid slowly down onto the veranda. I watched him crumple, my mind not thinking quickly enough to wonder who had fired the shots. I saw blood on the left shoulder of his shirt, and a red stain down the doorframe caused by the exit wound produced by the bullet which had entered his left temple.

Left shoulder. Left temple.

Those shots could not have been fired from inside the cabin. As the realisation hit me, I became aware of James standing beside me, his weapon pointed down at Laddy's quiet and inert form. Then I felt his arm go around my shoulders and pull me in close. I leant into him but then drew back as I heard his words.

"It's OK, Lizzie. You did what you had to do."

He thought I'd shot Laddy.

"James, it wasn't me. I didn't shoot him."

He stiffened and then I saw him bring up his gun to aim in a new direction out over the meadow. I looked to where it was pointing.

Coming out of the trees on the other side of the Cantle Burn were two figures, too far away to be recognised. They walked slowly, several yards apart, one slightly ahead of the other. The man in the lead was medium height and stocky and he seemed to be carrying something slung from his right shoulder. It wasn't until they reached the stepping stones to cross the stream that I could make out what it was. It swung away from his body as he jumped from one stone to the next and I realised that this must have been the rifle used to shoot Laddy. He was carrying it inverted on its sling, barrel sloping downwards with the stock up behind his shoulder.

"Hmmm," said James, still holding me close. "He's holding it so we can see it, but trying to make sure it doesn't look threatening."

I didn't have time to answer because I was suddenly aware of a little body pushing itself between us.

"Daddy," it said, and I looked down to see Abby's huge tear-filled eyes staring up at James. "Is it over?"

He let go of me and rested his gun against the doorframe to scoop up Abby to his chest. She tucked her face into his neck and burst into tears.

"It's all over, sweetheart," he said. "All over."

He stroked her hair to reassure that it really was, and to let her know that she was safe again. I wanted comforting too, and felt very alone in the knowledge that I had no-one to hold me, and probably never would have. It sounds a bit pathetic, but that's how I felt.

But then, as we watched the distant figures draw steadily closer, I felt James's arm around my shoulders again, drawing me close and holding me beautifully tight. I let myself lean into him, and this time didn't pull away when he spoke.

"Cherry, Andy. Can either of you get over to the front window?"

The replies came almost simultaneously.

"OK, Boss."

"Sure, Boss."

I knew they were both wounded, but their replies suggested that neither was in immediate danger. I heard them moving behind me, slowly, one of them dragging his leg, but they were both in position by the time I could recognise the man coming towards us with the rifle.

"James," I said, my body going tense. "Do you see who that is?"

"I do, sweetheart. I do," he said, and it took a moment to dawn on me that he had used the same term of endearment with which he spoke to Abby. Was it just a slip of the tongue? I really did hope not, but didn't dare to hope too much.

As we stood waiting for the men to approach, I was glad to know that James still had his gun nearby. I made to draw away so that his hand would be free to pick it up, but his arm around me tightened and he wouldn't let me.

"It's OK, Lizzie," he said. "Mr Borisov and I have already had words."

Then I heard Cherry's voice.

"What do you want us to do, Boss?"

"Just hold tight," replied James. "Keep him covered, and be ready to take him down, but only if I say so. And let him see you're there."

"Right, Boss."

Alexei Borisov and the guy with him came forward slowly until they were about twenty yards from the veranda. I was surprised to see that their line of approach had kept them well clear of the vehicles parked out front. They stopped and stood there out in the open, completely exposed, like ramblers coming up to ask the way.

"Good day again, Mr Montrayne," called Borisov.

"Good day to you, Mr Borisov," James answered, in the same mocking polite tone. "And… … I think… … thank you."

"You most welcome, Mr Montrayne. This was messy business. Best to end it."

"I agree," said James. "But… … how did you know to come here?"

Borisov gave a small shrug. "Not difficult. We follow after you, and… … er… …I know that this place was where things were planned to happen, so… … Anyway, we find your car in trees but we lost you. I not know woods like you, so we keep on along track and we end over there."

He gestured behind him, back over the burn, and then lightly tapped the telescopic sights on his rifle.

"We were far away, but these sights are good. I see you break in. We hear the shots, and then this young lady come to the doorway."

His left hand made a slight movement in my direction, and he spoke as though he had no idea that we had met before. Maybe he'd forgotten. Or maybe he thought it simply didn't matter.

"She not looking out, so she did not see that thing… …" he pointed at Laddy, "… … until it almost too late. Suddenly she turn and he fall down. She could shoot him, but she does not. I am ready. I do not hesitate. As I say… … it is time to end this thing."

I didn't understand why Borisov had shot Laddy and not me. I thought the two of them were both on the same side. James was curious about that too.

"You could have ended it differently, Mr Borisov," he said. "Isn't he one of yours?"

"Sadly, I have to tell you, yes, he one of mine. On loan, as you might say, to Mr Mellisse. I am… … er… … unfortunate man, Mr Montrayne. It seem I surround myself with… … ah, what is that word you have?"

"Incompetents?" offered James.

Borisov beamed. "Indeed, yes. Incompetents."

"So you punished him for his incompetence," said James.

"Partly," replied Borisov. "It is good for reputation. You understand?"

James ignored Borisov's question.

"You said *partly,* Mr Borisov. So what was your other reason?"

Borisov spread his hands, palms open, his eyebrows raised as though the answer was obvious.

"But Mr Montrayne, you have short memory. I do not wish to die so soon in my new and beautiful country."

He looked around him as he spoke, gesturing to the woods and hills.

"And I do not wish to be chased out of it by your mad Bosnian."

His voice was hard now, the bantering tone completely gone.

"I do not forget your promise, Mr Montrayne. I know what will come to me if you or your girls are harmed."

He carried straight on, so I almost overlooked the fact that he'd spoken of girls, plural. Then I assumed he must have misspoken. James only had one girl, didn't he?

"I will tell Mr Mellisse that this little game of his is over. I will go and … … now, what do you say? Yes, I have it. I will go and fry some other fish. We will not meet again, I think."

"Without wishing to seem impolite," said James, "I really do hope not."

Borisov nodded and turned to leave, then seemed to reconsider. He stood still, half-turned away, thinking. His man just watched him, patient, unmoving, ready to do whatever his boss told him.

"Almost, I forget," said Borisov, still looking away. "I do not like loose end. There is another of my men here, I think."

I thought he must mean Ginger or Jonno. Didn't Borisov know there had been three of them, not two? Then James's reply set me wondering again.

"I know about that one," he said, slowly and firmly. "That loose end has been firmly tied. I think I'll keep him, if it's all the same to you."

Borisov seemed to understand, though I certainly didn't. He was looking towards the window where Andy still stood with Cherry.

"He is yours, then," he said. "But there is still a matter of… … debt he owe me."

"Invoice me," replied James.

Borisov continued to stare at the window. After a moment, he pursed his lips and shrugged.

"No need," he said. "We call quits. He very fortunate man to have you for friend."

I hadn't a clue what he was talking about, but then I felt James turn his head and I twisted round to see where he was looking. Cherry was nearest, and he was still looking out through the window, ready to fire on Borisov if necessary. Andy had propped himself against the further side of the window. He was staring straight at James, eyebrows slightly raised, mouth open. James gave a quick nod and then turned back to face Borisov. I continued to stare at Andy, and his eyes held mine for a long moment before he looked away. I was wondering what to make of that when I heard James speak again.

"Anything else?" he asked.

Apparently, there was. Borisov pointed towards the Jeep parked in front of the Land Rover.

"I think that belong to Mr Mellisse," he said.

"Maybe," said James. "I really have no idea."

"Yes," continued Borisov, ignoring James's comment. "That Mr Mellisse Jeep. I return to him. He like to get his property back."

He pointed to his silent henchman. "My associate can drive."

"In that case," replied James, "since you're concerned about loose ends, perhaps you'd like to return the rest of his property to him."

There was a long silence. Borisov seemed at first not to understand James's meaning, and I wasn't sure I did either. Did he mean the camera, or maybe the guns?

"You ask big favour, Mr Montrayne."

So, he did understand after all.

"Not really," said James. "After all, they're his men. His and yours. And I'm sure you can think up a satisfactory story to explain their … … condition. A story that will convince him that you are a man to be to be feared."

Borisov thought it over.

"You would not rather bury them in woods?"

"Not really," said James again. "My land is not a rubbish tip."

"Ah," responded Borisov, and thought again. Eventually his lips began to expand into a slow smile.

"A story, you say. I have good story… … So, yes, I will do it. But tell me, please. What happen to other men? They follow you up road."

I looked up at James, wondering who these other men were. He smiled, but there was no humour in it; just a grim twist of the lips.

"Well, Mr Borisov, if you want to know about them, you'd best go talk to the Redesdale goats."

Ninety-One

Pan European Solutions – Late afternoon

Raymond Mellisse looked up from his desk, and frowned. Although the offices of Pan European Solutions were some distance from the airport's terminal buildings, he knew something significant was happening. The wail of sirens was not entirely unknown within the precincts of the airport, but not usually this level of activity. They were police and ambulance, he thought. He could usually tell the difference. No fire trucks, as far as he could make out.

On any other day he wouldn't have been worried, but today wasn't any other day. Today was import day. Mitch Portess was due back with another consignment of girls from Lithuania, and he was due about now.

He stood and walked over to look out of his prized picture window. In the distance, he could see a number of aircraft scattered about the runway and taxiways with the usual collection of fuel trucks, stairways and baggage carts. Everything seemed normal. He could see no sign that anything untoward was going on. As he looked through the glass and wondered, the wailing of sirens gradually tailed off. The commotion seemed to be coming from the other side of the terminal buildings, with its entrances and exits for arrivals and departures. He could make out the upper stories of the hotel on the far side of the terminal, but he couldn't see what was going on at street level.

He returned to his desk and pressed a button on the intercom.

"Roger," he said abruptly. "Find out what all those sirens were about. The action seemed to be somewhere near the terminal entrance. And do it now."

The chances were that whatever was going on had nothing at all to do with Mitch Portess, but he just wanted to be sure. He sat back and thought about the five girls coming in. Each of them could bring in anything between £35,000 and £50,000 in one year. Multiply that by all the girls they'd brought in over the years, and pretty soon you're talking real money. A number of them were no longer working, of course, but then there was always going to be a certain amount of natural wastage. Some just had to be taught a lesson *pour encourager les autres.* Some succumbed earlier than expected to the drugs used to keep them under control. Some became diseased to the extent that punters simply wouldn't pay for them anymore. One or two silly cows had even committed suicide. Still, there had been cash and to spare to provide the crucial investment capital for the strongly-developing legitimate aspects of his business enterprise.

The fact that he was now trying to change the direction of his business had little to do with some deep shift in his moral compass. His priorities were what they had always been: himself first, family second, and third? Well, there was no third. Everyone else was there to be used, and he didn't care in the slightest how they were used as long as he got what he wanted.

He'd been working on the details of a new contract when his train of thought had been disturbed by those damned sirens, and now he found that he just couldn't settle back to it. The deal involved working with the city council to develop a number of brown-field sites in Birmingham, covering them over with low-cost housing and small industrial units. He didn't give a toss for the families who desperately needed that low-cost housing, and nor did he have any interest in developing enterprise and helping unemployment in the city. His only concern was the bottom line of his balance sheet and, in this case, it was going to be very healthy indeed.

He glanced at the papers on his desk, shuffled them into a pile, and replaced them in the folder from which he'd not long removed them.

He stabbed at the intercom.

"Roger. I'm still waiting."

There was an immediate response.

"Sorry, Mr Mellisse. I've asked a guy I know in the airline to check and I'm still waiting for him to get back to me."

"Tell him to pull his finger out if he wants to keep it."

"Sir."

Mellisse was sure that Roger knew exactly what that meant and would pull his own finger out with a vengeance. He thought about phoning Bruno who, as usual, was in charge of receiving Portess's cargo, but decided to wait until he could be sure that Bruno was not himself in the middle of whatever was happening over there.

The intercom buzzed.

"Well."

"Sir, the arrivals area is swarming with police, and it seems someone has been shot."

"By the police? Dead?"

"Don't think so, and yes. Word is that the police arrested some guy and were taking him out of the terminal when he was shot by someone else. Guy bled out on the pavement."

"Do they know who?"

"Steve didn't know who was arrested or who shot him."

"Steve?"

"My contact."

"Was it just the one guy they arrested?"

"So far as Steve can tell, it was just that one guy."

"Did the shooter get away?"

"Not clear at the moment, but Steve thinks so."

"OK. Keep digging. I want to know who it was that got shot."

"Sir."

Knowing what he now did, Mellisse thought it should be safe enough to call Bruno, which he did using a disposable phone which couldn't be traced back to him. All being well, he knew that Bruno would now be in the minibus with the cargo, so he kept his voice low to be sure it couldn't carry beyond the Bluetooth device which Bruno kept clamped in his ear.

"You OK?" he asked when Bruno answered.

"No problems. Clockwork, same as usual."

"Not quite. I think the clock just got busted. Did you see any police at the airport?"

"Sure, there's always some. Much higher profile these days. Guns and all."

"But nothing out of the ordinary?"

"Not really. So what is it you're not telling me?

Mellisse filled him in with the sketchy information he had so far.

"If it wasn't Portess," he concluded, "no worries. It's business as usual. If it was him, then you'd better keep low while we find out what put the police onto him… … and who wasted him and why."

"Any reason to suppose it really was him?" asked Bruno.

"Only my gut feeling… … and the timing of it."

Bruno thought for a moment or two before asking, "Is it still safe to use the house?"

"Don't see why not," replied Mellisse. "That was a side of the business Portess wasn't involved in. Compartmentalising works, that's why we do it."

Switching off the phone and placing it in a drawer of his desk, Mellisse thought over the little he knew. It wasn't enough, so he decided to take a chance. Retrieving the phone he dialled Portess's mobile. It rang for so long that he thought it would switch to voicemail, but then a rather breathless voice answered.

"Hello?"

The voice was female so it definitely wasn't Portess. He improvised quickly.

"Is that Mr Portess's secretary?"

There was a pause before the same female voice answered him.

"No, sir. My name is Joanne Hayford. I'm a police officer. Did you know Mr Portess?"

Did you know… …Not do you know… …

Mellisse closed the connection and removed the SIM card and battery from the phone. It was time to get rid of it, but it had told him what he needed to know.

Somehow the police had got onto Portess, and apparently felt they had enough at least to arrest him. Taking him out before he could tell them anything wasn't actually a bad idea, but it hadn't been his idea. Which meant there was only one other person who could have ordered it.

"That bloody Russian!"

But how? How did he even know that Portess was about to be lifted when Mellisse himself hadn't picked up even the slightest sniff of trouble? In that moment, it dawned on him that Borisov must have a more thorough understanding of his organisation than he'd given him credit for. In view of the planned transfer of power from himself to the Russian, it had seemed a natural move to allow Borisov to put some of his men into the business. They would learn the ropes and enable a smooth transition, in so far as such a thing was possible given the ruthless ambition of the various individuals involved. He had accepted Oleg and his cousin Ladislav, the one they all called "Laddy", but only on the condition that there was no direct link between himself and them. Bruno would oversee their activities, and therein lay Mellisse's layer of protection. Except that it was a fairly flimsy layer since the Russian cousins would no doubt report directly to Borisov, who definitely did have a direct link with himself.

There was no question. The sooner he was out of this business, the better. He'd made his money and he'd discovered better ways of growing it than staying in the grubby business he was handing over to Borisov. On the surface, their deal had been amicable enough. Borisov had agreed to take care of certain loose ends, and to obtain for him the leverage he needed for his new enterprise, plus a meagre one million pounds, and all for a business which was grossing a cool £4.5M every year.

Mellisse sighed and nodded to himself. There'd been a time when he would have laughed at anyone who said money wasn't everything, but now he had the money he knew that power was what he really craved, and power at the highest level. Sir Vernon Laycock had no idea of the size of the thunderbolt that was about to descend on him once he'd been elected to Parliament and given a seat in Cabinet. Mellisse would have his very own puppet in the highest echelons of government, not a willing puppet certainly, but one who would do anything to avoid public exposure as a sexual pervert.

As long as the men who'd been sent up north came through with the video. He knew he probably had enough material already, but that video would most certainly be the clincher.

He sat back suddenly in his chair, mouth open, eyes staring, as a new thought struck him. Then his fist slammed down on the surface of his desk.

"Bloody hell!"

Copies of all the video material that Bruno had used to blackmail numerous individuals were held on several USB pen-drives in a safe-deposit box in a bank in Birmingham. They were perfectly safe. He, Mellisse, alone had access. But the originals, every single one of them, were stored somewhere in the memory systems of a sophisticated computer suite in the specially constructed basement of Mitch Portess's house near Tamworth. It was a perfectly natural arrangement given that it had been Portess's technical expertise and equipment that had made so much of the videoing possible. After all, someone had to be the caretaker for this inflammatory material, and Mellisse didn't want it anywhere near his own premises, home or office.

He stood up, his mind now in overdrive.

If Portess were dead, and it now seemed more than likely, then it wouldn't be long before the police were crawling all over the house at Tamworth. So many thoughts came tumbling into his mind all at once. He found it hard to keep track of them, to follow one train of thought to its conclusion before it was interrupted by another one. This was an unusual experience for him. He was used to methodical planning, ruthlessly applied, but always carefully thought out. He was used to being ahead of the game, always in control, but right at that moment it looked as though the game was getting ahead of him.

The house. He needed the address of that house.

"Roger," he shouted at the door to the outer office.

Roger's head appeared round the door almost immediately.

"Get me the address of Mitchell Portess, somewhere near Tamworth."

He paced over to the window while he waited, trying to get his thoughts in order. What could he do at the house, even if he could get there before the police? The place would be unoccupied, all locked up and alarmed.

He stood stock still, arms outstretched, palms flat against the glass, eyes staring out but seeing nothing.

The last piece of the puzzle had just fallen into place.

The house, of course, would not be unoccupied. Hadn't Borisov told him that his sister… … no, not his sister… … a cousin of some sort… … had taken a fancy to Portess and had become quite cosy with him over the past few weeks. So cosy, in fact, that she'd actually moved in with him.

Suppose the police had gone to the house looking for Portess, and found her instead. Her instinct would have been to alert Borisov and Portess ASAP. Depending on the timing, Portess would probably have been in the air with his mobile turned off. Borisov, however, would have been easy to get hold of, and Borisov had obviously decided what action needed to be taken... ... ... without consulting him.

He was jerked out of his thoughts by the buzzing of his intercom.

"Mr Mellisse, I have that address you wanted... ... but... ..."

"Stop pratting about, Roger. But what?"

"I Googled it, just to get a feel for the local area, and a breaking news report flashed up. The house has been burning for about an hour. Police and fire appliances are on the scene. A little old lady who lives across the road has just been interviewed. She called it in, and she's saying it was started deliberately. She's convinced she saw flames in one of the downstairs rooms before some woman left via the front door. There's nothing official yet, but that's what she says."

For the first time in many years, Raymond Mellisse had no idea what he should do.

Ninety-Two

Thurvaston Arms – Late afternoon

"So," said Nadera, "what do we do now, John?"

She lay on her side, John on his back with her right arm draped over his chest. Even after such a short time, it seemed natural that she should occupy the right side of the bed and he the left. Probably it would always be that way.

It hadn't taken much for John to be persuaded that they needed to step back a moment from their investigation and give their brains a rest. Of course, that didn't mean that they needed to rest everything, and the bed was so inviting. In the course of Nadera's highly successful efforts to make good on her promise to make him feel younger, the duvet had become displaced and was lying half on the floor. Although this had the advantage of allowing plenty of freedom of movement earlier, John now felt a little chilly. He pulled the duvet up to cover them both. For the best part of an hour, he had given no thought to what their next move should be, but her words dragged him back to the reason for their presence in England.

He knew that the reason for her asking the question was not because she had no idea what they should do. Her mind, always quicker than his, already had every option covered. She asked because she wanted to know how far John was prepared to go. He had come to England because his friend had been killed and because he doubted the ability of the British criminal justice system to seek out and identify the murderer. And if the police actually did get someone into court, and secure a conviction, how long would the killer actually spend in jail? John knew that if he himself were brought to justice, he would probably end up serving a longer sentence than Phil Simmons's killer. Under British law, a person's life often seemed to have less value than someone else's property.

So, John had come seeking justice, but how far was he prepared to go to get it?

"First thing, I suppose," said John after a moment's thought, "is to be clear about what we know, as opposed to what we're assuming or just plain guessing."

"Makes sense," replied Nadera, "so go ahead."

He turned his head to look into her eyes only inches from his own. He knew why she was tossing it back to him; making him think. It was because this was his show, and if it was to be played out to its end, he had to be convinced in his own mind of the rightness of what they were doing.

He turned back to stare at the ceiling and she snuggled in close curling her right leg over his own.

"Raymond Mellisse is a louse," he said. "Specifically, he's the boss of a holding company which owns or controls many of Birmingham's sex clubs. That's legal, and it's public knowledge if the public know where to look for it."

"Point one," said Nadera, and she nibbled his ear in encouragement.

"Mmmmmm," muttered John, momentarily distracted.

"I'm waiting for point two," said Nadera.

"OK, I'm getting there... ... Point two. He's on the board of several other companies which gives him a profile of respectability in Birmingham's business community."

"Good. Point two," acknowledged Nadera, resisting the temptation for another nibble.

"He's trying to become more respectable by backing the campaign of Sir Vernon Laycock to become MP."

"Point three."

"Right. Now underneath that respectable sham, he's got his hands in some pretty dirty stuff. Shay Johnston turned up women who knew this for sure, but none willing to go on the record. There's plenty of rumour in certain places, but no evidence. People know, but no-one will talk."

"Point four, I think. Do we know this, or are we just guessing?"

"We know," said John firmly. "We know it, just like others do. We just can't prove it."

"OK. Point four, then."

"If we can believe what you overheard at that minister's place, with Montrayne and that girl, then Mellisse was behind some blackmail attempt to try and get that vicar, or pastor, or whatever to point the finger at Montrayne for Phil's murder."

"We can believe it. Remember what that reporter, the Rigby girl, told us. Point five."

John lay quiet for a moment, staring at the ceiling but not really seeing it. Nadera waited for him to move on. When he did speak, it was tentative and thoughtful.

"If Mellisse was prepared to use blackmail to point the police the wrong way, that surely proves he was behind Phil's murder."

"Behind it, almost certainly," agreed Nadera. "But did he pull the trigger?"

John pursed his lips as her considered the question.

"We could always ask him," he said at last. "Pressure him a bit, like we did with the Rigby girl."

Then, before Nadera could comment, he sighed and shook his head.

"No, it wouldn't work. From what we know so far, he's not the sort of guy who'd crack that easily… … But then, he does have a wife and kids. Maybe we could… …"

He stopped, not even prepared to complete the thought.

"No."

"No," agreed Nadera. "The wife… … maybe, if she's anything like him. But not his kids."

John pursed his lips and stared at the ceiling, trying to clutch at something hovering in his thoughts, but not yet tangible enough to grasp.

"So, what does that leave us?" he asked.

Nadera stroked his stomach in a circling motion feeling his muscles quivering under her touch.

"Aren't you forgetting Gordon Russell?" she asked.

John's stomach muscles tensed as he began to sit up.

"That's it," he said, adjusting the pillows so he could lean back against them. "Russell's MD of Lichfield Tube. Mellisse is on the board, and the company is owned by FerroTech whose chairman is Sir Vernon Laycock. Mellisse and Laycock were both at that same dinner… … the one in the photograph. Remember? And Montrayne thinks Russell's dirty. Or, at least, some department his father is head of seems to think so."

He paused as different thoughts began to slot together in his mind.

"Go on," Nadera prompted. "Work it through."

"OK," said John. "Try this. The dirty business at Lichfield Tube might have been financial, like Montrayne thinks, or it might have something to do with bringing in girls from overseas. That must be a possibility with Mellisse on the board. Either way, if Phil found out about it, he wouldn't want anything to do with it. And he wouldn't be prepared to keep quiet. So Russell must know why Phil was killed, and who did it. Maybe he even did it himself."

"Maybe," said Nadera. "And how do we find out?"

"We put a gun in his mouth and threaten to cut his balls off if he doesn't tell us what we want to know."

"He might lie."

John thought for a moment.

"Yes, he probably will. But if I think he was in any way involved in planning Phil's death, or even knew it was going to happen and didn't stop it, I'll blow his head off. And, if he points the finger at someone else, then we'll go after them as well."

"Messy, John."

"I know, but in the end, it was always going to be, wasn't it?"

Ninety-Three

Aullton Estate – Late afternoon

I fought hard to stop them, but the shakes just wouldn't go away. At first, I'd been trying to appear brave for Abby's sake, and later I kept it up because I didn't want Laddy or the others to know how scared I was. Then, when the fighting erupted and bullets started flying, I was so pumped up with adrenalin that I did what had to be done without really thinking about it. But the cabin now was quiet, and the scene in front of us was tranquil and, in an odd way, reassuring. The grass of the pasture shimmered to the teasing of a gentle breeze, the distant treetops shivered and white cotton-wool clouds drifted lazily across a blue sky.

At James's urging, I had walked with Abby over to the stream while the bodies of Ginger, Laddy and Jonno were being loaded into the vehicle Borisov was taking. She hadn't spoken as we picked our way through the grass and around clumps of wild flowers. She had held my hand tightly all the way and hadn't once looked back. I asked her about the burn, the birds we could see darting low over the water, the llamas, in fact anything I could think of to take her mind off what had just happened, but she seemed to be in some sort of daze. I desperately hoped it wasn't the beginning of the same type of trauma shock that she'd experienced after the last kidnap.

We had come to the edge of the stream and sat down on the bank, our legs overhanging and our feet almost touching the water. Abby let go my hand and snuggled close, eventually laying her head down in my lap. It was while we sat there in the quietness that reaction to the last few hours began to take hold of my mind and my body, and my hands began to shake.

For the second time in my life, I had actually killed someone. The first time, I hadn't really meant to do it, but I couldn't say that this time. When I'd fired those first shots at Ginger, I'd fully expected, even hoped, to see him fall dead in the doorway. When I pulled the trigger and released a burst that blew Jonno's head apart, I was glad of the certainty that his lifeless body was no longer a threat to Abby or to me. Even so, as I clasped my hands together over Abby's head, trying to stop them trembling, I wished with all my heart that it hadn't had to come to this.

I don't know how long we sat there. Abby's breathing was slow and steady and she seemed so peaceful that I didn't want to disturb her. For a while, I wasn't much aware of anything but Abby, and a cold sickness deep down inside me. Then, slowly, I became aware of the warmth of the sun on the side of my face, and I began to look around. As I did so, the quivering tension which had gripped the muscles of my back from shoulders to waist began to ease. I took a deep breath and let it out so very slowly.

A dark shape flashed in front of me, only a few feet away. My eyes followed it. There were birds darting around, some of them passing very close. I've never been very good at sorting out swifts from swallows and martins, but their swooping flight brought several so close that I could make out the pale underside and reddish throat and decided, with no great confidence, that they must be swallows. I breathed deeply once again and my mind and my emotions began to respond to the calming beauty of the scene laid out in front of me.

I thought Abby must have fallen asleep but, as I continued to breathe deeply, she stirred and said, "They're so pretty."

She must have been watching the swallows, just as I was, concentrating on their twists and turns, allowing the beauty of the birds in their setting to displace the ugliness of the scene behind us.

"They are," I agreed, relieved that she was ready to talk again. "Do you always get them here for the summer?"

She was quiet for a moment, and then I heard her mumble, "I think so."

Behind us, I heard the sound of a vehicle's engine coming to life, and I felt Abby tense. My hand shivered as I stroked her head and took a quick glance over my shoulder.

"It's OK, Abby," I said. "It's only Mr Borisov getting ready to go."

She didn't try to look up, but I felt a bit of the tension ease out of her. I looked back again and saw the Jeep turning across the grass to head for the track by which we ourselves had first arrived. I couldn't see whether it was Borisov or his man who was driving, but I didn't really care. He was going, and that was all that mattered.

I heard Abby mutter something else, but it was so quiet that I couldn't make it out.

"I'm sorry, love," I said. "What was that? I didn't quite hear."

"I didn't like him," said Abby, a little more loudly. "I think he came to help us, but I didn't like him."

"Neither did I, sweetheart," I said. "Neither did I. But you're right. In the end, he did help us."

We could still hear the faint sound of the Jeep as it disappeared into the trees, but then it was masked by the noise of the Land Rover starting up. I turned to see it set off across the grass towards us.

"I think your dad's coming for us," I said.

She reacted immediately and sat up to take a look for herself. Uncertain at first, she squealed with delight when she saw that it was

James behind the wheel. She pushed herself away from me and stood up. She took a couple of steps towards the Land Rover and then stopped, perhaps realising that it wasn't a good idea to get in the path of an oncoming vehicle. James pulled up several yards short and when he got out Abby raced up to him to fling her arms around his waist.

She wasn't crying, which I took to be a good sign, so I got up slowly and started towards them on legs which felt decidedly wobbly. Conscious of the quiver in my hands, I folded my arms tightly across my chest and tucked my hands into my armpits. As I drew close, I could see that there was no-one else in the Land Rover, and I began to wonder about Cherry and Andy. It was Abby though who got the question out first.

"Where's Cherry?" she asked, tilting her head right back to look up into her father's face. "Is he OK?"

"He's fine, sweetheart," he said, his right hand gently caressing the back of her head.

"Really?"

"Really. He's got a cut across his back which hurts a bit because it's into the muscle. But Mr Borisov's friend was able to stop the bleeding, and he's fine now."

"Good," she sighed, apparently unconcerned about any damage to Andy. Not too surprising, I thought. It didn't seem as though she spent as much time with Andy as she did with Cherry. I thought I'd better ask.

"What about Andy?"

James looked at me, and a slight frown appeared on his forehead but, before he could answer, Abby piped up.

"Oooh, I forgot. Is Uncle Andy OK?"

Cherry was just Cherry, but Andy was Uncle Andy, and that I supposed summed up the difference in the way she regarded them.

"Nothing that won't mend," said James. "So, no need to worry."

"Did Mr Borisov's friend mend him too?" asked Abby.

James smiled down at her. "He did quite a good job actually. He used to be a soldier a few years ago, and was trained as a medic. I think that's why Mr Borisov likes to keep him handy."

Andy had looked to be in a bad way the last time I'd seen him, with blood down his trousers and on his back and chest. I learned later that the leg wound had been high up in the thigh, apparently what those in the trade call a *through and through*. Fortunately for Andy the bullet had missed both artery and bone, otherwise he'd probably have bled out on the cabin floor. The other wound had been in the shoulder, also through and through, entering low at the back and exiting higher at the front. Borisov's man had warned that the bone and muscle damage may not put itself right without help, if he wanted to keep full use of his arm. But that was something to be dealt with later. There were more pressing matters to attend to.

"We'd better get back down to the house," said James. "Dr Harwood's got a bit of a problem which needs sorting pretty smartish."

"It's not Angie, is it?" I asked, suddenly anxious.

James shook his head.

"She's fine. But we do need to get back there, or we may have a problem we can't talk our way out of."

Ninety-Four

The Green Man, Elmford Cross – Early evening

John didn't want to waste any time, so he and Nadera had decided to try and track down Gordon Russell that evening. They had left the Thurvaston Arms after an early dinner, setting off for Elmford Cross more in hope than with any real expectation of success. One of their problems was that they didn't actually have a great deal which they could use to pressure him. All they really had was that snippet of conversation which Nadera had overheard at the minister's house when Montrayne had made it sound as though Lichfield Tube was being quietly investigated by a government department over irregularities with some defence contracts. It didn't seem much but, with careful handling, it might just be enough to get Russell talking.

Their other problem was that they didn't know what kind of man they'd be dealing with. When pressured, would he fold or would he fight? Many men, when threatened, would eventually fold out of fear. Not necessarily physical fear, but fear for their loved ones, or their reputation. Sometimes it was fear of financial loss, or being put out of work, but in the end it was fear that did it. Other men fought back when threatened, sometimes violently, sometimes deviously, because it was somehow in their nature to resist. It was as natural to them as the lion turning on its hunter.

What sort of man was Gordon Russell? His naval service suggested more likely the fighter, but that had been a long time ago and things, and people, change.

They decided that Nadera should handle it. This was not because John didn't have the stomach for it, but because they had recognised early on that she could spin a web of deceit far more quickly and confidently than he could. Thinking on her feet with lightning speed, she could fabricate entirely credible, thoroughly convincing, scenarios while eyeball to eyeball with her victim. There was also the fact that, while John was reasonably sure that he and Russell had never met, he couldn't be absolutely certain. It wouldn't do for him to be recognised now that they had built the illusion that he had died in a Venetian canal.

Finding a convincing reason for approaching Russell proved a little tricky until Nadera remembered that Lichfield Tube proudly portrayed on their website some of their more prestigious customers. One of these was Aquaheatex, a company also owned by FerroTech, who regularly supplied military-grade heat exchangers as replacement parts for military vehicles in several Middle-Eastern countries. If Montrayne was right, there was a high probability that Lichfield Tube had supplied substandard tubes to Aquaheatex in order to get the price low enough to win the contract. This was a practice of which John had experience, and it had to be something like that for the DTLO to be interested. Lichfield Tube's website listed no significant overseas customers so, for a problem to have caught the attention of the DTLO, it had to have something to do with material they supplied to UK companies that did boast export defence contracts.

Feeling that she had enough to work with, Nadera found herself a little after eight-thirty that evening walking up the drive of Russell's house in Elmford Cross. John was parked a little way down the road where he could see the entrance to the drive straight ahead of him. Neither of them had any idea whether Nadera would have to deal with Russell inside his home, or whether she would be able to entice him out, perhaps on the pretext of needing to visit his works. Looking the way she did tonight, John had little doubt of her being able to entice Russell anywhere.

His fingers drummed lightly on the steering wheel. Waiting, especially when he couldn't see what was happening, was not easy. Even the best of plans could be knocked askew by the unexpected. He peered through the windscreen, ears tuned for the slightest sound that might give him an indication of what was happening.

Nadera knocked on the door and waited. After a few moments, in which she heard nothing more than the muffled sound of a radio or TV, she banged the knocker again, with a bit more effort. This time it worked, but not quite as she'd intended.

A female voice called from the other side of the door, "Bloody go away! And you can take your leafy… … leaflets and shove them up your candi… … your candid… … candidate's bloody arse."

The voice definitely sounded drunk, and Nadera struggled to know what the woman could be referring to. Then she remembered that tomorrow was the day of the General Election. Putting her face close to the door, she spoke loudly but without shouting.

"I'm sorry to trouble you, Mrs Russell. I am not part of the election. I just need to talk to your husband. Is he at home?"

"Doesn't bloody know where home is these days," came the reply through the door. "What d'you want him for?"

"It's to do with work," said Nadera, her face close to the door. She was beginning to think this was a complete waste of time.

The silence that followed drew out just long enough to make her wonder if the woman had disappeared to replenish her drink, or maybe sunk to the floor in a stupor. Then there was a faint grating sound and the door opened. The woman, who Nadera assumed was Judith Russell, peered out.

"You're not the other one," said Judith inexplicably, lurching slightly and catching at the doorframe for support.

"No, probably not," replied Nadera, wondering who the woman was talking about.

"Always want him in the evening, you fancy women. Don't know what you see in him. Not much of a catch. I should bloody know."

Nadera was close enough to smell the drink on her breath. This was definitely a waste of time. Apologise and go, she told herself, but the woman hadn't finished. She staggered as she spoke, but managed to remain upright.

"It was always bloody work before… … then it was bloody work and bloody school… … then the bloody election… … now it's bloody women as well. Can't a girl be left alone to have a drink in peace?"

Nadera thought, from the sound of it, she'd probably been left alone too much. Judith let go the doorframe to place a hand on Nadera's chest.

"I'll tell you what I told her, then you can all bloody sod off."

With exaggerated caution, she looked to her left and then to her right before peering over Nadera's shoulder, as though she expected to find eavesdroppers hiding amongst the rhododendrons of the front garden. Apparently satisfied, she finished the contents of her glass in one swallow, and leaned forward lowering her voice to a whisper.

"We were right," said Nadera, a short while later.

Her voice was tinged with excitement as she climbed back in the car beside John.

"Along the road here, take a left and then we'll find The Green Man."

"And why do we want him?" asked John, teasing her in his relief that she seemed to have found out something useful.

"It's a pub," she said, fastening her seatbelt. "You drive and I'll explain."

Somewhere in his distant past, Gordon Russell had made a mistake, a serious mistake the memory of which had been eating away at him over the years. Judith Russell had not been able to say what the mistake had been because, even after his most disturbing of nightmares, her husband always refused to say. All she had been able to prise out of him was that his mistake – and he always used that term, never theft or fraud or corruption – had been observed, and the witness had been blackmailing him ever since.

It was no distance at all to the pub, so Nadera was still explaining when John pulled into the car park and found an empty space not far from the entrance.

Judith had been unable to name this blackmailer, but she did know that his demands never involved money. It was always favours, often involving Gordon closing his eyes or looking the other way while the blackmailer went about his business. Whatever that business was, it involved Lichfield Tube, or *that sodding company* as Judith had called it. More than that she wouldn't say and, after pressing her a little, Nadera concluded that she really didn't know. Pressing her had been a mistake. Judith had resented it.

"Too bloody nosey you are," she had said. "Not good lishner. Not like that other one."

And with that she had retreated into the house slamming the door in Nadera's face.

"So why are we here?" asked John, gesturing towards the pub entrance.

"Because earlier on, before she decided she didn't like me, Mrs Russell said that her husband usually comes here with his fellow… … er, what do you call them? Campaign people. They come here after they have been knocking on doors."

John glanced at the dashboard clock.

"We may have to wait a bit then," he said. "So, how about we wait inside and grab a drink?"

The Green Man turned out to be busy without being overly crowded. It was obviously a popular eating place as most of the clientele were seated at tables neatly set for dinner. Some had already been served, others were still waiting, but John and Nadera found themselves a corner table in an area that seemed to be reserved for those who were not there for food. They also had the privilege of a large-screen TV which the diners did not have. John glanced at it from time to time, but it was tuned to some kind of reality TV show which wouldn't have held his attention even if he hadn't had other things on his mind.

Nevertheless, during a break for advertisements just before eight o'clock, the opening words of a news bulletin brought his head up and both he and Nadera stared transfixed at the screen.

A dark-haired, female reporter was standing in front of what she referred to as the arrivals terminal at Birmingham airport. She described how, only hours before, a man had been gunned down not far from where she stood. She allowed a touch of incredulity to creep in to her voice as she explained how the victim had been in police custody at the time, placing more of her emphasis on the question of how this could have happened, rather than why it had happened.

It was how she had referred to the victim that had grabbed the attention of John and Nadera. He was, or had been, a senior employee at the Midlands-based firm, Lichfield Tube Company, returning from a business trip to Lithuania. According to the reporter, his name was Mitchell Portess and the police had been wanting to speak to him in connection with the murder of another employee at the company only a few days earlier.

John looked to Nadera, his mouth half open. He had to lick his lips before asking, in a low voice, the question that was in both their minds.

"What the hell is going on?"

Nadera didn't answer. She laid a hand on his arm to quieten him and continued to watch the reporter until the bulletin ended. Then she turned to John, frowning as she tried to fit this new information into what they already knew. In the end, she gave up. There were too many pieces of the puzzle missing. One thing she did know. The nature of their meeting with Gordon Russell now had a completely unexpected twist, especially if he hadn't yet heard the news.

"We still need to talk to Russell," she said eventually. "We have to know who has been blackmailing him, and what their hold on him is."

"It wasn't Phil," said John quickly, knowing that blackmail provided a good motive for murder.

"No, of course," replied Nadera. "I wonder if it could be this Mitchell Portess who is now dead. If perhaps he blackmailed Russell, he may have also blackmailed someone else. Someone a little more... ... violent than Russell."

They mulled that over for a while, wondering how they might use this new information. Their eyes kept flicking over to the entrance with every new arrival until, finally, their waiting was rewarded.

A group of half a dozen came in together, four women and two men. One of the men was carrying a backpack which he slung off once he was through the door and held it open for the others to deposit leaflets which several had been carrying in their hands. One of the women, young and eager, let her gaze wander around the tables of diners as though searching for a potential recipient of her political charms.

"Remember," said the second man, noticing her scrutiny, "no canvassing in the pub. These folk have come here for a peaceful meal out and they won't thank us for interrupting."

"Shame, though," said the woman. "It's not as though they're going to get up and run off, is it?"

"No," said the man, "but you could always make them vote for the other side."

He shrugged out of his coat while he was speaking and, in doing so, turned his face full on towards John and Nadera. John immediately looked down into his drink but Nadera, catching the man's eye, stood and walked over to him.

"Do you mind if I have one of those leaflets?" she asked, treating him to her most dazzling smile.

He looked surprised but smiled back at her and said, "Of course."

He reached for his friend's backpack and took out an A4 tri-fold flyer and a thin booklet. As he handed them to her, Nadera dazzled him again.

"Thank you," she said. "My name is Suleima Hassan. I haven't had chance to look at one of these yet."

"Gordon Russell," replied the man. He hesitated, as though weighing his opportunity, but then bowed to the fact that she already had company and said merely, "If there's anything else you'd like to know, come and find me. I'll be here for a while yet."

"I expect there will be a great deal I would like to know," responded Nadera. "I will look at these and then, as you said, I will come and find you."

Satisfied that she had not only positively identified their man, but that she had also paved the way for another approach, Nadera returned to her table but took a different chair. Now, for John to be facing her, he almost had to have his back to Russell's group, whereas Nadera could watch them easily as they gathered themselves around a larger table close to the bar.

For ten minutes or so, she made a show of studying the papers Russell had given her, pointing out different passages to John and talking to him so quietly that only he could hear. Eventually, John stood and made his way to the exit. Nadera noticed that Russell's eyes settled on John's back as he left. Gathering up the documents and her handbag, she also stood, hesitated a moment, and then made her way to Russell's table.

"You said I could find you if there was anything I needed," she said to him.

"Quite right," he replied, politeness bringing him to his feet.

"Well, my friend has had to go to work – his shift begins at ten o'clock – and I was wondering if you would like to walk me home and answer one or two questions as we walk."

"I'd be delighted," said Russell.

"Too right," said the other man, still seated at the table, between the young eager canvasser and an older woman. The smirk on his face made it clear what was going through his mind, until it suddenly disappeared to give way to a pained look. The older woman, perhaps his wife, had kicked him under the table. Nadera caught the movement, but gave no sign of having done so.

It was all so easy.

Russell slipped on his coat, which he'd previously draped over the back of his chair, said goodbye to his friends and escorted Nadera to the door.

It was not yet fully dark, but the street-lights had come on so the parked car was clearly visible as they walked towards it. Obedient to instructions, John had turned left out of the pub car-park and pulled up about a hundred yards along the street, midway between two street lights. The car's engine and lights were off. There was nothing to draw attention to it.

As Nadera and Russell came alongside the rear of the rented Ford, she drew aside from her companion and reached into her handbag. When Russell turned to see what had caused her to slow down, his eyes widened as he took in the heavy automatic pistol in her right hand. This was not the micro-Uzi replica which had so terrified Corrina Rigby, but a similarly heavy, all-metal replica of a Glock 18 purchased at the same time. John now had possession of the Uzi which he held loosely on his lap waiting to play his part.

It was not to be expected that the reporter would have easily distinguished a replica from the real thing, but an ex-serviceman such as Russell was a different matter. Which was the reason Nadera had decided on the Glock. In their efforts at realism, the manufacturers had constructed the slide as a working mechanism which produced a very satisfactory sound of oiled metal parts clicking together as it was pulled back. Nadera demonstrated this causing Russell's mouth to drop open. Whether this was from amazement or because he was about to speak, Nadera didn't wait to find out.

"We do not intend to harm you Mr Russell, but we will if you do not do exactly as you are told. Now, turn around and put your hands behind you."

Russell looked past her, down the street, but there was no help there. He saw a car pull out of the pub car-park but it turned right to head off in the other direction. He risked a quick glance the other way but, as Nadera had already seen, the street was empty.

Before his eyes turned back to her, Nadera launched a vicious kick at his groin. As he doubled up groaning, she kicked him in the side of the head. She took no pleasure in what she did, but Russell had to learn quickly that she was serious, and not to be messed about with. Stepping back just out of his reach or kicking range, Nadera raised the gun.

"Stand up and turn around, Mr Russell. Now!"

She didn't shout the last word, but hissed it with such vehemence that he instinctively complied, though his hands still clutched at his groin.

"Lean forward and rest against the car."

He did so, resting his chest against the top of the door, supporting himself with one hand while the other continued to sooth the damage to his privates.

"Spread your legs, and put both hands behind you."

In this ungainly position, struggling with the fiery ache between his legs, he felt something loop around his wrists and be hauled tight. He knew straight away what it was. He'd had to cut plastic ties off enough tube bundles in the past. He flexed his wrists, but there was no movement. The plastic tie had been pulled so tight it would probably cut off his circulation.

"Move to your right. Lean on the trunk."

As soon as she saw he was clear of the door, Nadera grabbed the handle and hauled it fully open.

"In," she said. "Now!"

The manoeuvre is not easy to accomplish with your head throbbing, your hands fastened behind you, and your groin on fire, but with enough incentive it's doable. Russell did it, and found himself looking into the barrel of the Uzi held in the steady hand of the driver.

"Now sit still," the man said, "and nothing else will happen to you. Mess us about and you're dead. Understand?"

When Russell didn't respond, John repeated, "Understand?"

Russell nodded and then glanced to his right as the woman got in the car behind the driver. It was a good position, for them, not him. Both of them could aim their guns at him, which wouldn't have been the case if he'd been positioned behind the driver.

Nadera looked at her prisoner and wondered if he had any idea why this was happening to him.

Apparently he did.

"Mellisse sent you, didn't he?" said Russell, his tone resigned, as though he'd been waiting for this to happen.

Nadera ignored his question.

"Who do you think killed Mitchell Portess this afternoon?" she asked.

The look of amazement and horror which came over Russell's face showed that this was the first he'd heard of events at the airport. His eyes closed, licked his lips and swallowed. Tears glistened between his closed eyelids.

"Is this true?" he asked. "Because if it is, you've done me a huge favour."

Nadera smiled as John started the car. This was going to be easier than she'd expected. Gordon Russell was a folder, not a fighter.

Ninety-Five

Aullton House – Late evening

It was nearing midnight and I was feeling completely drained. At least, that's what my body was telling me, but my mind didn't seem to want to shut down. My limbs felt heavy, all energy completely sapped away but, in my head, I was awake and alert. I just couldn't stop replaying everything that had happened in those few, short, fear-filled hours. Every minute remained stark and clear; the sounds, the smells, the colours. Even after a long and comforting shower, the crash of the gunfire was still echoing in my head; the acrid tang of the smoke lingered in my nostrils; and the scarlet splashes of blood were still there even when I closed my eyes.

How could I ever have foreseen that my mad dash for freedom would lead to something like this? Would I still have run away if I had known? Probably. Anything was better than life as one of Mellisse's girls. I settled back against the cushions of the settee and wished I could be sure that this was the end; that now it really was all over.

"Still awake?" asked James, as he came back into the drawing room after checking once again on Abby.

"Is she asleep?" I asked in return.

"Seems so, at last."

"She's had a rough day," I offered, as some kind of excuse for Abby's restlessness as she struggled to settle in her bed. She had wanted me to stay with her once she'd snuggled under her duvet, so I'd lain down beside her for a while, only leaving when I thought her steady breathing indicated that she was asleep. I had hovered nearby just in case, and it hadn't been long before I heard her tossing and turning, eventually calling out for her dad.

I watched James from my position at the end of the settee where I sat curled up with my legs tucked under me. He looked around the room as if unsure where to sit. Like me, he had showered and changed and was dressed now in jeans and reddish check lumberjack shirt with the cuffs turned up. He was, as always, a powerful presence but the strain of the day could be seen in the tiredness of his eyes. Some, perhaps, would not have noticed. But I did.

"Do you need anything?" he asked.

A home, I thought. ***A family. A place to feel safe.***

"I'm fine," I said.

"OK."

He nodded and took in a deep breath, letting it out slowly. Then he came over and sat down at the other end of my settee, half-turned so that he could see me without having to twist round. I was glad. It wasn't exactly intimacy, but it showed he didn't feel a need to keep a formal distance even when I wasn't upset or in danger. When we'd sat together before on another settee, I had been crying and he had held me. It had been pure reflex on his part of course, the adult male comforting the weeping child, but it had felt so comforting, so reassuring, that I knew I wouldn't mind if he did it again.

I also knew I was not a child. But did he, I wondered.

"Maybe we should think about turning in," he said. "Everyone else seems to be settled."

Once we'd got back to the house, James had sent Dr Harwood up to the cabin to take care of Andy and Cherry, after warning him quietly what sort of condition they were in. When the doctor had reappeared with them, stitched and bandaged, he had insisted that they both needed hospitalisation. He had insisted so forcefully that James offered to arrange for Mike Colman to fly them back down to the Aullton Foundation Hospital with Dr Harwood himself in charge of their care. That had seemed to put the doctor in a strange quandary, and it soon became obvious that he was very reluctant to leave Angie even though she was getting stronger and more lucid by the hour. I was beginning to wonder about the good Doctor Harwood.

In the end, a compromise had been reached. Andy and Cherry had been tucked up in a twin-bedded room upstairs, their pains eased a little by a couple of injections. Doctor Harwood himself was ensconced in the room next to Angie, no doubt trying to reconcile his troubled conscience with all the events of the day. Abby was in her own turret room, which meant she was further from James than he would have liked, but it was her own private space and it was there that she felt comfortable.

That left two bedrooms. One was James's own room, and the other had been Suzanne's but, for tonight at least, it would be mine. They were next door to each other. I liked that. Again, not exactly intimacy, but the comfort of closeness.

I wondered if I should go up and look in on Angie, but she would probably be asleep. I had sat with her for a short while after we had got back from the cabin, and I thought then that Barrie had done a great job of settling her down after what must have been a terrifying experience for them both. She seemed willing to place a huge amount of trust in him. I hoped he wouldn't let her down.

The body of the guy who'd tried to kill her had been removed while Abby was taking a shower and getting changed for bed. James had told me to take her up to her room immediately we got back. He hadn't wanted her to know anything about the danger to Angie. The cabin was, in a sense, remote, up in the forest hills, but this was home, and he wanted Abby to feel that home would always be safe. Neither of us knew whether it would work, but we had to try.

I didn't know what sort of deal James had made with Borisov, but the Russian had been waiting for us down at the house. James had shown him where to bring the Jeep so that it was as close as possible to the door of the apartment's back staircase. I didn't see how they got the body down to the Jeep since I was up with Abby, and it was all over by the time the two of us came down to the drawing room.

So maybe it really was all over. If Borisov could be trusted. Hope on the one hand, uncertainty on the other. Not the best recipe for trying to settle down to sleep.

And then, there was Andy. I didn't know what to make of him. He was supposed to be one of the good guys, but Ginger and the others up at the cabin had spoken as though he was one of them. I had even wondered at one point if he was giving them their orders. After all, it had been he who had brought them to Aullton House. But then he'd come with James to rescue us. It was confusing, and my brain didn't really want to struggle with it, but it was too unsettling not to mention it.

"James," I said. "Is Andy... ..."

I trailed off, not knowing quite how to put my uncertainty into words. Thankfully, I didn't have to.

"It's OK," he said, his lips twisting into a grim smile. "I know all about Andy. He's been a total idiot. Recklessly, dangerously so. But, in the end, he was there when we needed him. I haven't decided what to do about him yet. It's difficult, but it's going to be hard to trust him again." He sighed. "Tell you what, I'll give you the whole story, and what I've decided, once I've had chance to sleep on it. That do?"

I nodded and smiled. It was a relief, as always, to know that James was in charge and that he would sort it out. I could let go of my uneasiness.

Until another thought struck me.

"James, can we really trust Borisov? I mean... ... he knows so much now. What if he... ... ..."

This was another uncertainty I didn't know how to express, but James seemed to understand my anxiety.

"In most things, I wouldn't trust him an inch," he said. "But in this one instance I think we're on the same side."

He could obviously see I wasn't convinced.

"Borisov knows that if any harm comes to me or anyone I care about, then trouble will descend on him so heavily and so fast that he'd be totally finished in the UK, always assuming he manages to get out alive."

He said it so calmly and with such certainty that I could only wonder what lay behind it. I was about to ask when he continued.

"One day," he said, "I'll introduce you to a good friend of mine but, for now, just be assured that he is watching our backs, and Borisov knows it."

"What about Mellisse?" I asked.

"Borisov will convince him that it's in nobody's interest, least of all his own, to bother us any further. Whatever Mellisse's scheme was, it no longer includes you. Or Angie for that matter."

"Can he do that?" I wondered. "I mean... ... does Borisov have so much control over Mellisse?"

"Well, it seems Mellisse was wanting to step aside for Borisov anyway. He has plans to turn respectable, and you were part of the leverage he needed, or thought he needed, to make it happen."

Leverage, I thought. That would have been the video. Mostly lies, of course, but when mixed with the footage Mellisse already had, it would prove a weighty blackmail weapon. I felt sorry for his victim, and then immediately wondered what had happened to the script for that wretched video. Not much of it had found its way onto the camera, but the paper must still be lying around somewhere.

I wondered whether James had seen it. Had he read it?

"James... ... you know they were trying to get me to make a video... ..."

"I know."

"Did you... ...?" I dropped my eyes, unable to hold his gaze, but when I looked up again after a moment's silence, I saw he was calmly watching me.

"There was a script," I said.

"I know," he said. "I found it. I didn't plan to mention it just now but, since you ask... ..."

"Did you read it?"

"Yes," he said. "And I expect you're going to tell me it was all a pack of lies."

And you're not going to believe me, I thought. That script may not be used against its intended victim, but it certainly wasn't going to do me any good.

I looked into James's eyes, trying to tread their expression, but there was nothing there. Or, at least, there was something, but I couldn't make it out.

"No," I said and, resigned to being disbelieved, went on slowly. "It wasn't all lies. But most of it was... ... I didn't want to say it, to read it... ... I delayed as long as I could but, in the end... ... they just ran out of patience. That's why Laddy took me into the back bedroom... ... to soften me up... ... And then you came and... ... They *were* lies, James. Most of what they wanted me to say... ... it never happened."

I wanted to say that all of it had never happened; that I'd never been a person who would do such things; that it was all a huge mistake and that sort of life had nothing to do with me. But, much as I wished otherwise, that really would have been a lie.

James was watching me, his expression still unreadable. Whatever he was thinking, whatever he was feeling, was very much held in check.

"Lizzie," he said quietly. "I want you to listen carefully. What your life has been like up until now, I can scarcely begin to imagine. You can tell me one day if you want to, but it's not important to me right now. The life you've been living these past few years is not the real you. I know I've said it to you before, but I don't think you believed me. And you really must, you know. For the sake of your future."

What did he mean? How could he possibly know the real me? I wasn't even sure that I knew the real me anymore.

"The real you, Lizzie, is the girl I've come to know in these past few days. You're young, but you're resilient and highly resourceful. I've seen you scared and I've seen you brave. I've seen you struggling against the odds to do the right thing. But... ... more important maybe than all of that is the way I've seen you taking care of Abby. And... ... do you know something? I really think you'd defend my little girl with your life, if it ever came to that. So I don't care what your life was like before, except to wish that you'd never had to endure it. I care about what your life is going to be like from now on."

I didn't know what to say. I thought I understood him, but wasn't sure he could really mean it. Only a week ago, I'd never heard of him, but now, after knowing him for only a few days, I wanted never to leave him. Or Abby. They had become the most important people in my life. Along with Angie, of course.

He sat very still, watching me. His head was tilted slightly and his eyes seemed to have lost their tiredness. His expression had scarcely changed, but his eyes were now smiling.

"James," I said. "I'm not sure just... ... ..."

He interrupted the question which I scarce knew how to ask.

"Lizzie," he said. "You mentioned at some point that you'd quite like to go back to St Helena... ... to where you were a little girl and were happy."

I know my shoulders slumped as I sank back against the cushion. Now I understood. He was going to send me away, though I was sure he didn't mean it quite like that. He probably thought he was giving me the opportunity to fulfil my dream. He meant it to be kind but it was like a knife thrust into my heart.

He must have seen the change in me for his eyes narrowed in a slight frown.

"If that is what you still want, Lizzie, then I'll make sure you get there with enough money to buy a home and to live on for the next ten years. I've already checked and there'll be no problem. You were born on the island and have a right to live there as long as you can support yourself."

I heard myself thanking him, but the words sounded hollow and he seemed to pick up on that. His eyes were smiling again.

"On the other hand," he said, a little tentatively this time, "if Mellisse and Borisov between them haven't entirely put you off a life in the UK, then Abby and I would quite like it if you decided to stay with us. You could take Suzanne's place permanently, and… … …"

He gave up trying to explain any more when I flung myself against him, my arms struggling to encircle his massive chest. I couldn't help myself. His words were just such a relief.

"I didn't think it was that bad an offer," he said, in response to my sobbing into his shirt. "But if you don't like the idea… …"

"Oh, I do, I do," I sobbed, feeling his shirt growing damp from my tears.

His hand gently patted my back in a ***there, there*** sort of way, and he waited without speaking until I'd cried myself out.

How long we sat like that I have no idea. Even after the sobs had finished, I was reluctant to pull away and bring to an end the comfort of his embrace. The dampness of his shirt against my cheek reminded me of how my dad had comforted away my tears with his tender hugs, but in that moment I knew that this was not the same. At least, not for me it wasn't.

For years now, I had learnt to distrust almost every man I had met. Experience had taught me how depraved they could be, and my instinctive response had been to become cold and withdrawn. I hadn't intended to become that way; I just couldn't help it. In the same way now, I just couldn't help the upwelling of emotion as I sat within James's embrace. I cried because I loved him, and because I knew I could never have him. It had been growing on me, but now there was no denying it. I loved him in a way I had never loved anyone before, and if the only way I could have of showing it was to take care of Abby then so be it. That little girl would never have to suffer the loss of innocent childhood as I had done. She would never… … …

"Oh, no!"

I sat back abruptly, my eyes wide in horror, showing dismay that I could ever have been so stupid as to let such a thing slip my mind.

"What is it?" James asked, frowning in sudden concern.

"Those girls... ... they were supposed to arrive today."

"What girls?"

"They were coming from Lithuania... ... this afternoon."

I pushed myself away from James, horrified at the thought of what lay in store for them. About my own age, they were set to become what I had been, and I felt sick with guilt that I was supposed to have been the one who introduced them to it.

I forced myself to look into James's eyes as I explained.

"Someone went to Vilnius and promised them good jobs if they came to the UK. It was just a trick. There were no jobs... ... not what they were promised anyway. They were flying into Birmingham this afternoon and I was supposed to be there with Bruno to meet them. I was supposed to... ... to reassure them... ... to make them feel safe until the softening up started."

"Softening up?"

"You really don't want to know," I said, standing up and beginning to pace around. I imagined what might be happening to them – what almost certainly was happening –and I wondered if it was too late to help them.

I didn't hear James stand but suddenly he was there right behind me. I felt his hands on my shoulders gently turning me to face him.

"Do you know where these girls were going to be taken?" he asked.

I nodded.

"Well then," said James. "We'd better get a move on."

Thursday

5th May 2005

Election Day

Aushra Paulauskaitė – Day Six

Birmingham, England – 6:00 am

Aushra lay still, staring in utter despair through the gloom of her bedroom at the cracked and peeling ceiling above. Warm, salty tears trickled silently down her cheeks as she held Jolanta close to her. They lay together, side by side, on a dirty mattress covered in stains whose origin Aushra hadn't liked to think about. There was no bed. The mattress lay directly on the bare boards of the room. On the other side of the room, beneath a window with bars cemented in place across it, was a second mattress where the other three girls lay huddled together sobbing quietly.

Aushra still wore most of her clothes, but Jolanta had been stripped naked. She had been so hysterical that Aushra's efforts to coax her back into her tattered clothing had been totally useless, and in the end her friend had to settle for just pulling her in close to hold and comfort and hopefully calm her. It had taken a long time for the wails to die away to subdued moans, and even longer for the heart-rending moans to subside to a pitiful whimper.

It was a nightmare beyond anything Aushra had ever experienced, and she knew with stone-cold certainty there would be no waking up from this one. It had begun less than twelve hours ago, within minutes of their arrival at this beautiful house.

The flight from Vilnius had been wonderful. With the connection in Frankfurt, she had seen three airports in the space of a little over five hours. For a girl who had never before set foot outside Lithuania, the airports had been magical places, vibrant with life and activity, and the planes breathtaking in size, beauty and power. On both flights, Aushra had found herself in a window seat just behind the wing and she had watched mesmerised as the flaps extended and retracted during take-off and landing. All that business about oxygen masks and life-jackets during the preparation for take-off had at first slightly alarmed her, but that initial thrust in her back to the accompaniment of the throbbing power of the engines as the plane strained to lift into the air thrilled her soul.

Everything had happened just as promised. At Birmingham airport, where they had landed just after five forty-five in the evening, a smartly dressed young woman – remarkably young, Aushra had thought – had met them in the arrivals hall. She had introduced herself to them as Philippa, personal assistant to Mr Portess, who must have been one of the last to leave the plane since Aushra could see no sign of him. Philippa had been accompanied by a very large man whose white teeth smiled at them through his bushy beard giving him the appearance of a benevolent teddy-bear. She had introduced him as Bruno, their driver, and together they had led the five girls out to a minibus parked nearby.

Aushra wasn't really sure about the length of their journey in the minibus since she hadn't taken any notice of the time after they had landed, but she guessed it had probably been a little over half an hour. The girls had chattered excitedly all the time but Philippa and Bruno had been remarkably quiet. They had answered any questions the girls put to them, although their answers were not always very informative, but otherwise they had remained silent. The other girls hadn't seemed to notice, but the silence troubled Aushra, especially when she remembered that it was Philippa who was supposed to provide them with their briefing packs on the company, and neither Philippa nor Bruno had been carrying anything – handbag, holdall or briefcase – which could have contained these documents.

When she had asked about them, it had been Bruno not Philippa who had told her that the packs were waiting for them at the house where they would be staying. It had been a reasonable response, but Aushra's sense of unease had stayed with her until finally in an explosion of violence it had been made clear to her, albeit far too late, how justified her uneasiness had been.

That was later, however. For now, from her seat behind Bruno, Aushra watched Philippa out of the corner of her eye, and wondered how a person so young, and apparently so lacking in vitality, could have risen to become personal assistant to someone as important as Mr Portess. It seemed so odd, but at the same time strangely encouraging as it gave her hope for her own future.

When the other girls noticed the brown road signs pointing the direction to Cadbury World, they became very excited. They had all heard of Cadbury's chocolate and the prospect of maybe soon having a chance to see the world-famous candy being made started all their mouths watering. Their excited chatter almost drowned Bruno's low mutterings as he answered a phone call via the Bluetooth device in his right ear. His Birmingham accent and quiet tones ensured Aushra could make out little of what was said and she would probably not have given it much thought had she not noticed Philippa suddenly become anxiously alert.

She was still wondering what this could have meant when their journey ended among large houses down tree-lined avenues. When the minibus turned into the driveway of a large, double-fronted Victorian house set well back from the road in its own landscaped grounds, the girls become almost ecstatic. This was luxury beyond anything they had imagined.

While they were still seated, Philippa suggested that now would be a good time for them to call home to say that they had arrived safely.

She explained that their phone signal might not be quite so good inside the house. There followed a few moments of excited chatter before Bruno told them it was time to go and find their rooms.

Ushering them quickly inside, Philippa told them they could explore the grounds later, as soon as they were settled. Once the front door had closed behind them with a very solid thud, Bruno told them to leave their bags on the beautifully tiled floor of the hallway and led them through to a room at the rear of the house. It was a surprisingly spartan room for such an impressive property. The walls, from the deep skirting board to the decorative cornice, were a plain magnolia colour completely unadorned by pictures or mirrors. The curtains hanging part-drawn across the tall windows were of a dark, unimpressive fabric. In front of them was a huge wooden desk which looked at least as old as the house. Slung across it was a long, waxed drovers coat on top of which lay an Aussie-style wide-brimmed hat. Standing behind the desk, facing them with his back to the window, was a young man whom Aushra had taken to be not much older than herself. With his black hair and dark, unblinking, wide-set eyes, he looked intimidating enough, but taken with his black leather trousers, black silk shirt and black leather jacket the whole effect was horrifyingly sinister.

Two other men, both young, had obviously been standing in front of the desk talking to the man in black, but as the girls entered they turned round and stood aside to take a good look at the newcomers. One was tall, with gelled blond hair, and looked as though he'd stepped out of the men's pages of a clothing catalogue. The other was more stocky, of medium height, with a shaven head that reminded Aushra of a turnip. The way they licked their lips as their eyes roved over the girls made it perfectly obvious what thoughts were fermenting in their minds.

As the man in black stared at them across the desk, Aushra felt an icy chill invade her stomach. Feeling a nudge in the small of her back, she looked round at the other girls crowding in behind her. Although there was plenty of clear floor-space in the large room, some instinct seemed to be causing them to huddle together. Behind them, Philippa looked small and scared standing to one side while Bruno's massive frame blocked the door. The four other girls were not yet looking frightened, that would come later, but their pale faces showed puzzlement, and a hint of anxiety.

Sensing that none of the other girls was in a hurry to take the lead, Aushra stepped forward, doing her best to offer a smile to the man in black, politely giving her name, and asking if they could please be given the briefing packs they had been promised and then shown to their rooms.

Blondie grinned hugely at this while turnip-head continued to leer and lick his lips. The man in black stared at her for a moment before he explained in clear, but heavily accented English that there had been a change in plans. There were no briefing packs, and no jobs, or at least not the kind of jobs they had been expecting. But, he informed them with a smile, there were rooms, to which they would be shown immediately.

It wasn't quite as immediate as he suggested because, in spite of their objections, the girls were first thoroughly searched. Jolanta dared to protest, actually slapping turnip-head when his hands lingered on her breasts, thumbs teasing her nipples. His response was immediate and overwhelming. A sharp jab to her stomach doubled her over and he then grabbed her hair with his left hand to haul her upright so he could slap her across the face, forehand and backhand, with his right. When he let her go, she collapsed weeping to the floor. There were no more protests, even when Blondie's and turnip-head's hands searched caressingly in places where nothing could possibly have been concealed.

The man in black watched it all impassively, Bruno with interest, and Philippa fearfully, while the two men carried out their search of the girls. All their jewellery was taken, apart from the rings in their ears, together with money, credit cards and mobile phones. Particular importance seemed to be attached to the mobile phones. One of the girls didn't have one. She said it had broken before she left Lithuania and she hadn't replaced it as she hoped soon to have the money to buy a really nice one in the UK. At first they didn't believe her, and it was only when a severe beating from turnip-head failed to encourage her to change her story, that it was accepted that she was telling the truth.

Then they were led away to their rooms. Turnip-head took away Jolanta while Bruno, Blondie and the man in black, took the three other girls. Aushra had been locked in the room where she now lay trying to comfort Jolanta who, she knew without being told, had been savagely and repeatedly violated.

Aushra had been told that her turn would come but, for some reason, it never did. The sounds of rape and beating drifted to her faintly through the solid old walls, and she suffered agonies of anticipation while she waited for the scrape of the key in the lock to announce that her turn had finally arrived. Alone and in the dark, her imagination fuelled by the sounds of the ruthless assault on her friends, Aushra hugged her knees to her breast in misery and despair. When at last the door did crash open, with darkness having long since fallen, she scrabbled across the mattress to huddle in the corner of the room, but none of the tormentors came in. Only Jolanta, stumbling, weeping and totally naked. Her clothes were tossed in after her, but she seemed not to notice. She just stood, swaying and moaning, in the dim moonlight.

At first she resisted, keeping up an anguished wailing, as Aushra tried to pull her down onto the mattress, but gradually her friend's soothing words managed to penetrate her traumatized mind and she subsided. From time to time the door would open again to allow one of the other girls to be thrust into the room. They were in no better state than Jolanta. Aushra wanted to reach out to them to comfort them, but Jolanta clung to her tightly and wouldn't let her go, so Aushra did her best to talk to them calmly and quietly, trying to give them hope when really she was sure there wasn't any. She knew they weren't actually listening to her, but she kept talking to them anyway.

And then, finally, Aushra sensed the darkness beginning to fade, and she wondered what fresh traumas the new day would bring.

Outside their room, the house had been still and quiet for some time, but now Aushra could sense a strange throbbing in her ears. She struggled to sit up and, this time, Jolanta let her go. She shook her head slowly and the throbbing increased. She stood and the throbbing changed to a pulsing whine. It was not inside her head. It was coming from outside. She narrowed her eyes, trying to identify the sound which she was sure was familiar to her. And then suddenly, with a clattering roar, a shadow flitted across the window.

Aushra stumbled forward, accidently knocking over the bucket which she herself had made use of when she had still been all alone in the room, in the dark of the previous night. She barely noticed the spill of yellow liquid onto the grimy floorboards because she recognised the sound and now, against all the odds, the faintest glimmer of hope was struggling to surface in her mind.

Ninety-Six

Lichfield – 12.05 am

Joanne Hayford groaned.

It had been one hell of an evening. Her debriefing after the murder in custody of Mitchell Portess had been a gruelling interrogation. The only thing that could have made it worse would have been the gloating presence of DCI Morrissey. Thankfully, this was not his jurisdiction and, since he had been off duty for most of the time, he probably hadn't heard about it yet. Nobody wants the kind of fallout that follows when the prisoner you've just arrested is shot dead right in front of you. The only thing that had so far saved her and Georgie had been the fact that the killing had not taken place on their turf. Birmingham Airport was the territory of the West Midlands force and, technically, Portess had been in their custody. It still left a lot of questions to be answered, and Joanne had done her best to satisfy a very suspicious West Midlands DCI, but the fact was she had no idea who had killed Portess or how they had learnt of his impending arrest. The general assumption seemed to be that he had been killed to keep him from talking, but the information he might have disclosed had now died with him.

Frustration and buck-passing was rife and, by the time she was done in Birmingham and had returned to her home in Lichfield, Joanne felt totally wrung out. At some point during the evening, she had been told that Portess's house near Tamworth had gone up in smoke before a search team had arrived on the scene. More accurately the property had, according to neighbours, turned from a desirable residence to raging inferno so quickly that there was little doubt that it was arson. Some neighbours even claimed to have heard something like small explosions. Of Portess's live-in girlfriend there was, so far, no sign. Someone was tidying up with drastic, even lethal, efficiency and Joanne was too tired to even begin to work out who that someone might be. There was not a drop of logical thought or physical energy left in her. She had slipped off her shoes and, without undressing, flopped onto her bed. Within minutes she had been fast asleep.

And now her phone was ringing.

In a daze she struggled to reach for the cordless phone on her nightstand. She put it to her ear, but the ringing went on. It must be her mobile. She had hardly begun to wonder where she had left it when the ringing stopped. She lay back, still clutching the cordless, and closed her eyes. She didn't care who it was, or what they wanted. The only thing that mattered was that they had gone away.

Except that they hadn't.

The ringing began again. Joanne reached for the switch to the light on her nightstand, and turned it on. She saw her handbag on the floor near her bed. That was where the ringing was coming from. She tried to reach it but it was just too far and she rolled off the bed to land heavily on bare boards, unfortunately just missing her deep-pile Afghan rug. She groaned again, and again the ringing stopped.

Opening her bag would take less effort than climbing back onto her bed so she eased herself onto the rug, snapped the clasp of her bag and reached in for her phone. She checked the call log but the number displayed meant nothing to her. The only thing she was sure of was that it wasn't a local area code. Suddenly the phone vibrated in her hand and the ringing began again. It was the same number.

She looked at the screen, bemused and exasperated. Why couldn't whoever it was just go away and leave her alone? Still, she was a police officer, and this sort of thing was par for the course, so she pressed the receive button and raised the phone to her ear.

"Who is this?"

"James Montrayne. Are you awake now?"

"I wish I wasn't, but yes. What can I do for you?"

"Have your enquiries into Phil Simmons' death taken you anywhere near the Lichfield Tube Company?"

"It's possible," said Joanne guardedly. "Look… … do we need to talk about this now? Can't it wait until morning?"

"It's already morning," responded James, who sounded infuriatingly awake. "And no, I think you'll agree it can't wait."

"OK," she replied, heaving herself around into a more comfortable position, her back resting against the side of her bed, legs stretched out in front of her. "What is it?"

"Did you know that Lichfield Tube is involved in trafficking girls into the UK?"

Joanne's back straightened as her brain kicked into gear. More alert now, she wondered how she should play this.

"I'm not really able to say," she ventured, hoping to draw information rather than to give it.

"Bollocks," came the undiplomatic reply. "We've no time for messing around. Did you know or not?"

Joanne wondered where this was heading, but decided to play along. "Yes."

"So, did you know Mitchell Portess is involved, and he was due to bring another five girls in from Lithuania yesterday afternoon?"

So that was it. "Shit!"

"What's up? What bit didn't you know?"

"I knew about Portess but not the girls."

"Well, if you move quick, I've got someone here who can give you Portess and the girls."

Joanne sighed. "If only they could."

"Oh but she can. I guarantee it."

"The girls maybe, but not Portess. Not now."

The was a momentary pause before James replied.

"What is it I'm missing?"

"Haven't you seen the news?"

"Not since yesterday. I've been a bit busy."

It was public knowledge now so Joanne had no reason not to tell him.

"Portess was arrested at Birmingham Airport late yesterday afternoon. Five minutes later, he was shot dead just outside the building."

There was a longer pause this time.

"And the girls?"

"We didn't see them. He was clearly on his own when he came through customs. We didn't even know to look out for any girls."

"I guess you're not flavour of the month at the moment."

"Far from it."

"So maybe it's time for you to redeem yourself. You can take it from me the girls came in on the same flight. They're still in Birmingham, and I can tell you exactly where they are and who, most likely, is with them. Are you interested?"

"As long as you're not going to tell me they're at Portess's house."

There was a pause and Joanne thought she could hear conversation at the other end of the line. Then Montrayne was back.

"I don't know where Portess lives, but no. The girls were not going to his house."

It was odd but, suddenly, Joanne didn't feel tired anymore. Excitement flooded through her, followed immediately by suspicion.

"How do you know this?"

"Because I have someone with me now who is running away from the same gang which took delivery of those Lithuanian girls."

Suddenly, the penny dropped. Joanne reached for her handbag and scrabbled in it for her notebook. She flipped through the pages until she found what she was looking for.

"It's Elizabeth Burleigh, isn't it," she said. "The girl at the farm. That's why she was there. She was looking for somewhere to hide."

"Elizabeth Burleigh is employed as a nanny… … no, wrong word… … companion to my daughter."

James's reply deliberately avoided answering Joanne's question. She thought she understood why, and didn't press it.

"OK, but if I'm going to do something with this, I have to know the information's good."

"It is. My word on it."

Joanne hesitated. From what she had learnt of him, her gut told her that his word was good. But she wasn't convinced that it was good enough to get any action out of the West Midlands police just coming on her say-so. As he had already pointed out, she wasn't flavour of the month.

But then she wasn't the only one, was she? DI Cobham and DS Sidebottom were deep in the mire in their own West Midlands force and might just be willing to grab hold of it if she could throw them a rope.

"Tell me everything you know, names, addresses, everything. I think I know who to call to get things moving."

It didn't take long and, when he'd finished, Joanne didn't feel the least bit tired. The flow of adrenalin filled her with a sense of urgent expectancy as she pressed Georgie's speed dial number.

Ninety-Seven

Birmingham – 12.30 am

The middle of the night was not the best time for getting things organised, especially when the people you needed belonged to a different force. Joanne had no authority to plan a raid on the address which James had given her. Even if it had been within her own force's jurisdiction, she had used up all her credit with her superiors. After today's fiasco, no-one was going to go out on a limb just on her say-so, certainly not within the timescale that was needed.

DI Cobham was her only hope of getting to these girls before they became lost in the bowels of Birmingham's seedy underbelly. After she had woken Georgie and told her to be ready to be picked up in ten minutes, Joanne searched in her purse for the card which Cobham had given her when they first met at the airport. From the speed with which he answered his mobile, she assumed he was still wide awake, maybe even working.

"Sir," she said in response to his weary greeting. "It's DS Hayford... ... er... you know... ...from yesterday..."

"It's OK, sergeant. I haven't forgotten you. I've just finished writing up my report and your name cropped up several times. Now I've finished it, I was hoping to get to bed and forget all about you, so can we make this quick?"

She made it quick, concisely setting out the details without any embellishment.

Once she had finished, there was only the briefest pause before Cobham asked, "Who is this Montrayne? Why do you put such store on what he's told you?"

She wondered whether to lay it on thick. Cobham needed to be persuaded because without him she was sunk. But then, he wasn't a DI for nothing and would see through whatever bullshit she tossed him. So she settled for the simple, honest truth.

"I've met him," she said. "I trust his word. If I was in trouble, he's one person I'd want on my side."

"So you're asking me to go with your gut instinct."

"Yes, sir."

She almost felt the sigh breathing into her ear.

"My career's hanging by a thread and I can't tell if you're offering me a lifeline or a pair of scissors... ... Give me his number. I want to talk to him."

While she waited, she quickly changed her clothes and grabbed a drink of water. She was on her way down to the garage for her car before Cobham called her back.

"OK, I'm convinced. I'll get things moving and hope to hit the house at dawn, say around six. I suppose you want in?"

"Yes, please," she replied, a little breathlessly. It had never occurred to her that she wouldn't be allowed to take part.

"OK, I'll clear it with my people. You'll have to take your chance with yours but, if this works out right, I don't suppose anyone will mind."

Clearing it with her superiors would involve waking them up in the middle of the night, which wasn't likely to get her the answer she wanted. Better just to hand them a successful operation.

She started her car and went to collect Georgie.

For most of the journey down to Birmingham she used her blue lights so from Georgie's flat to the rendezvous point took a little over forty minutes. They didn't talk a great deal on the way down. There wasn't much to be said that hadn't already been covered that evening, and they were both tired. Joanne hadn't told Cobham that she was bringing Georgie for the same reason that she hadn't contacted her superiors. She didn't want to be faced with a negative response. If this operation worked out OK, then Georgie deserved a share of the credit. If it all went belly-up, Georgie wouldn't be tainted. Joanne had made sure of that by keeping her name out of it so far.

Three streets away from the house where it was believed the girls were being held, there was a row of shops. It was the usual sort of thing; a newsagents and card shop, a bakery and deli, a drycleaners, a greengrocer and general store, and a nearly-new clothes store run by a local church. There were parking bays out front for customers, and a service road leading to a large area at the back for delivery vehicles. It was to this area at the rear of the shops that Joanne had been directed by DI Cobham. As she drove carefully down the service road to turn into the large space that would normally be empty at five in the morning, she saw in her headlights a number of vehicles scattered at the far end. Some were obviously police vehicles, though without any flashing lights, while others were unmarked. From a group near one of the unmarked cars, DI Cobham approached Joanne's Focus as she pulled to a stop.

Near darkness descended once she turned off her headlights, and the only illumination was that provided by the interior lights of several of the cars. Getting out of her car, Joanne assumed that they were keeping their lights to a minimum in an effort not to draw attention to their presence in the yard. She looked around. It shouldn't be too difficult. There was a high wall on three sides, the shops on the fourth, so they weren't easily overlooked. The floors above the shops were given over to office space rather than dwellings so, all in all, it seemed like a well-chosen location.

"You'll remember DC Baxter," said Joanne, as she shook Cobham's outstretched hand.

His eyes flicked across to Georgie's shadowy form on the other side of the Focus, and Joanne felt a momentary tightening of his grip. That was the only sign he gave of any irritation he may have felt at having Georgie thrust into the scene.

"I remember," he said. "Her name was in my report as well as yours."

"She's only here to observe," Joanne said quickly, hoping this would not be an issue.

"As are you," replied Cobham, just as quickly. "Let's be clear about that. You're here as a matter of courtesy, with permission to observe. You don't get involved at any stage. My people will do the business."

Joanne bridled at that. Without her information, this operation wouldn't even be happening. She felt a moment of anger even though she knew he was right. It passed quickly, but only to give way to a strong sense of disappointment. She'd hoped to be allowed to play a role, any role, in the planned operation but knew now that she'd have to settle just for the credit for providing the intel that sparked it off. That was always assuming that DI Cobham didn't try to keep all the glory for himself. He had, after all, spoken directly to Montrayne and taken action in response to that conversation. It wouldn't be the first time that a more senior officer had taken credit that more properly belonged to someone lower down the totem pole.

Cobham led the newcomers over to the group gathered near to an unmarked Jaguar. Their eyes adjusting to the gloom, both women were surprised to see a uniformed ACC at the centre of the group. They were even more startled to see that this most senior officer present was a woman. Joanne cast a quick sideways look at Georgie and knew she too had taken note. They both knew that women were still, even in this age of equality, severely under-represented among the higher ranks of most forces.

Joanne was ashamed of herself for hoping that this particular Assistant Chief Constable had gained her appointment on merit and not as a result of some politically motivated attempt to fill a quota.

"DS Hayford, ma'am," said Cobham by way of introduction, pointedly ignoring Georgie.

"Ma'am," said Joanne, not knowing if anything else was expected of her.

"So this is all your fault," said the ACC. "Those poor sods over there... ..." she nodded towards a group of black-clad officers clustered near the open rear door of a white Audi A6, "... ... would far rather be huddled up with their wives and girlfriends than sneaking round here in the middle of the night. Isn't that so, Rodgers?"

"Quite so, ma'am," replied a tall, heavy-set officer who Joanne now saw was wearing body-armour over his black uniform. His tone suggested an amused respect which Joanne found reassuring.

"Still," went on the ACC, "we do pay our heavy mob good money for the privilege of buggering up their fun every now and then."

She looked directly at Joanne and took a step closer.

"Your source is good?" she asked, showing that Cobham had been completely open about the source of the intel. If all went well, Joanne thought, she must remember to thank him for that.

She licked her lips, realising for the first time how many careers might be on the line that night. And more than careers, if James Montrayne had been right about the men they were after being armed, as he had assured her they would be.

"Forgive me, ma'am, but I don't think we'd all be here now if there was any doubt about my source."

There was a slight pause before the ACC nodded. "Fair enough," she said. "OK, Rodgers, take us through this once again while your guys finish getting kitted up. I want us all out of here before the bakers arrive at half-five."

The briefing was exactly that – brief – but it covered what they knew and what they needed to know. Joanne was sure they'd already been over it before she got there, and that Rodgers' men knew exactly what they had to do.

A short while later, the yard was empty as everyone converged on the target house.

Dawn wasn't very far off and, low down near the horizon, the sky was already lightening. The big Victorian house was exactly as Joanne had expected. On their way down, Georgie had managed to find an estate agent's image from when the house had last appeared on the market. She was very much looking forward to the release of the new Google Earth, due in just a few weeks' time, which would make the whole business of reconnaissance so much easier.

They were at the tail-end of the convoy which entered the street right on the dot of six o'clock. Seconds later, a marked police car turned into the drive of the target house followed by the black van, a second marked car and the ACC's Jaguar. The other vehicles all followed instructions to park on the street, obstructing both the entrance and exit to the house's U-shaped driveway. The driver of each vehicle was to stay with his or her car, so Joanne told Georgie she was elected.

Even as she got out of her Focus, the target house was suddenly bathed in the bright beam of a search light. An MD 902 police helicopter, summoned from its base at Birmingham airport, settled into a hover immediately above the house. At the same moment, there was a loud crash repeated several times as Inspector Rodgers' heavy mob effected their entrance through the front door. Joanne knew there would now be others in position at the rear. She stood beside a stone pillar in the right-hand one of the two drive openings. Letters carved in the stone informed her that this was officially the EXIT.

She tried to remember the layout of the house from the plan which Rodgers had spread out on the bonnet of the Audi. Where he had obtained it, she had no idea, but she did know that it was inconceivable that he would send his men into a building containing armed suspects and potential hostages without knowing the arrangement of the rooms. As he said in his briefing, he would have liked to know the precise location of the suspects and the girls, but the decision had been taken to back surprise against more detailed intel.

Looking across the lawned area inside the curve of the drive, Joanne could see the ACC and DI Cobham standing, partly shielded from the house by the bulk of the Jaguar. The ACC had a hand up to her ear and Joanne assumed she was listening on a headset to Rodgers' progress inside the building.

She saw both figures jerk at the sound of gunfire from somewhere inside the house. The door was wide open and the lights in the hallway were on but Joanne could see no movement. She knew there were armed officers positioned at the corners where each could watch two sides of the house, and she wondered how hard it was for them to hold their position when their mates were being fired on. She edged cautiously up the drive careful not to intrude so far as to get between armed officers and the house.

In mid-stride Joanne froze at the sound of a shotgun blast followed by the crashing tinkle of shattered glass. It had come from the left-hand side of the house, visible to Cobham and the ACC but not to her. She looked for them and, when she couldn't see them, hoped it was simply because they had ducked behind the car. There was another crash from the shotgun, then another, this time followed by a cry. Joanne realised from the rate of fire that the gun must be magazine-fed rather than the double-barrelled type. Unless there were two of them in use.

In front of her, a black-clad figure in helmet, visor and body-armour raced across the front of the house. He must be assuming that his mate on that side, or maybe the ACC herself, had been hit by the blast.

For a moment he was caught in the light of the hovering chopper and then he disappeared into the shadows behind the Jaguar.

Joanne looked along the right-hand side of the house. This should still be covered by the officer stationed to watch the rear corner, unless of course he too left his position for some reason.

Then a movement caught her eye. It was high up, above the large bay window that looked out from that side of the house. It was hard to make out what was happening because the chopper's searchlight was now temporarily focussed on the other side where the shotgun had been fired.

Ninety-Eight

Birmingham – 6.02 am

As Aushra kicked aside the bucket in her struggle to reach the window, she heard a loud crash from somewhere in the house.

Downstairs, she thought, *maybe near the front.*

At the same time, the gloom outside the window was brushed aside by a sweeping beam of light shining down from above. Though she had never been a great one for saying her prayers, the thought flashed into her mind with heartfelt sincerity, *Dear God, let it be the police.*

Although the drifting light gave some illumination, there was little to see that helped her to understand what was going on. Her window looked out from the rear of the house presumably so that its temporary occupants had no chance of attracting the attention of passers-by in the street. Nor was there much chance of being seen by neighbouring residents as the property was screened on all sides by tall conifers. As she peered over to the right, she thought she spotted movement low down at the base of the trees. It was outside the beam of light coming from the hovering chopper, but she was sure there was a figure crouching down in a position to watch the rear and one side of the house.

She didn't have time to wonder about her discovery because her attention was snatched by the sound of gunfire from somewhere inside the house.

Upstairs, she thought, *just down the hallway.*

Her back to the window, she listened to the confused shouting that followed the gunshots. Somewhere amid the noise, she thought she could hear someone shouting *Armed police* and then something about weapons. She tried to imagine what was happening, but the sounds were all so confusing. Hope and fear battled inside her, neither gaining the ascendancy until the door to her room suddenly burst open, and fear robbed hope of victory.

The man in black stood in the doorway. She had thought about him many times during the night, wondering if it would be he who came to fetch her. Of all the men in the house, this was the one she feared the most. His black clothing had been chosen, she was sure, to project that darkness in his soul that drove him into the shadows of society to do the evil things he did and, in her mind, that's what she called him – **Shadow.** Somehow the impeccable neatness of his black attire was more menacing to her than the casual thuggery of his associates. Why she dreaded his appearance more than that of the others, she could not have said. It was an emotional response, not logical, but for all that it was very real.

She watched warily as the figure hesitated in the doorway. With his shirt cuffs flying open, buttons undone all down the front and shirt-tails only half tucked into his trousers, his appearance was no longer impeccable. Dishevelled and panting, some sort of automatic pistol in his right hand, he strode forward. His staring eyes searched the room, settling briefly on the girls huddled together in the corner, then on Jolanta curled into a terrified ball on the mattress. Finally his gaze settled on Aushra. She probably seemed to him to be the only one capable of responding to him.

"Come," he shouted, gesturing with the pistol that she should go to him. Petrified, she just stared at him, so he raised the gun and pointed it directly at her face.

A thunderous crash pierced her brain before she collapsed to the floor.

Two more loud booms followed in quick succession.

Aushra was vaguely aware of them as she was roughly hauled to her feet and dragged from the room. Shadow was surprisingly strong and well fuelled up with adrenalin. He dragged her along the upstairs landing away from the stairs and towards the front of the house. She struggled to keep upright but had difficulty persuading her legs to obey her. Behind her, crouched at the head of the stairs, Turnip-head and Blondie directed occasional fire into the hall below. Through the open door of a room on her right she caught a glimpse of Bruno silhouetted against the bright light now directed on that side of the house. He was pointing a shotgun out through the shattered panes of the window. Then there was a clatter and a faint hiss behind her followed by coughing from Turnip-head and Blondie.

Aushra wondered if Shadow was heading for the big stained glass window at the end of the upstairs landing but, when they drew level with the last room on the left, he shoved open the door and thrust her into the room. Her struggles didn't seem to impede him in the slightest as he kicked the door shut behind them and hauled her over to the large sash window in the side wall of the house. Flattening her chest against the wall to the right of the window, he jabbed his pistol painfully into her lower back.

"Keep still," he hissed. "I'll shoot you if you don't."

She wondered why he hadn't shot her already. She couldn't see that she was much use to him in the middle of this fire-fight. And then it struck her. Somehow he was going to try making his escape, using her as a hostage if he could. She felt an increase in the pressure of the pistol in her back as she heard the lower window of the sash sliding upwards. The cool air of early morning drifted through the opening and she felt the chill of it on her bare arms.

Keeping her body still, Aushra slowly turned her head so that she could see Shadow. He was looking out of the window and appeared to be hesitating. She wondered whether he had any sort of plan, or was just making it up as he went along. She saw him lean forward slightly peering out into the gloom. He glanced left and right but seemed to be mainly interested in what lay directly below the window.

The sound of scuffling somewhere near the head of the stairs made him straighten suddenly. He reached across with his left hand to grasp Aushra's left wrist and drag her in front of the window.

"Get out," he said, his voice low and urgent.

Aushra stood frozen, wondering if he'd gone mad. They were much too high to jump.

"I said get out," he repeated, more forcefully this time, and jabbing her with the pistol to emphasise the point. "You can die in here, or take a chance out there."

Aushra was so sure she was going to die that she wished he'd just get on with it and bring the nightmare to an end. Then she looked out through the window and saw a ledge a few feet below the opening. They were above a ground floor bay window. She shook her arm free of his grasp and put both hands on the window sill to support her while she swung her legs over. She eased herself gently down until she felt her feet touch the roof of the bay.

She wondered if there was a chance of being shot by mistake by one of the police stationed outside the building. Then again, it was quite dark on this side of the house with all the attention temporarily focussed over the other side where Bruno wielded his shotgun. She heard it fire again as she crouched there, and it occurred to Aushra that Shadow might have posted Bruno there for the precise purpose of causing a distraction while he made his escape on this side.

"Over you go," said Shadow. "Lower yourself down, like you just did, and then drop. But you do anything I don't tell you to do and I'll kill you."

She had no doubt that he meant it so she sat herself down on the edge, fingers curled over the lip. The she realised she couldn't manage it from this position and she twisted herself around so that she was kneeling with her back to the edge, palms flat on the roof.

"Hurry."

She heard his voice hissing above her so she inched back to lower herself over the edge. Immediately, she was aware of him doing the same thing beside her. He dropped first, then grabbed her ankle to yank her down. He lay on top of her crushing the plants in the flower bed. His hand was clasped tightly over her mouth.

The shotgun fired again, and was followed by two sharper cracks in quick succession. After that, the only sound from the house was men shouting and doors slamming. For the moment at least, this side of the house remained relatively dark and quiet. Seizing his only opportunity, Shadow pulled Aushra to her feet and dragged her across a path and over a strip of grass into the bushes that fronted the conifer hedge.

A thorny twig scratched her leg and Aushra would have cried out had it not been for the pressure of the gun jammed into her side. The weight of Shadow's hand on her shoulder forced her onto her knees and the two of them crouched side by side, shielded from inquisitive eyes by the leafy shrubbery.

Aushra shivered but, even as she trembled, she knew it had nothing to do with being cold. She knew she was going to die that day, maybe here in this garden, maybe someplace else, but as soon as Shadow had finished with her he would kill her. No question. And, because she didn't want to die, she shuddered as waves of fear coursed through her.

"Keep down, and move quietly."

As Shadow whispered the words, Aushra felt him move behind her and push her in the direction of the front wall of the garden. How did he expect to get through the driveway entrance without being seen? She was sure the police would have that spot covered which set her wondering if she'd end up the victim of a nervous or over-zealous police marksman. And then she remembered the gate in the corner. She had noticed it when they arrived. A branch of the path that Shadow had hauled her across a few moments before wound its way between lawn and shrubbery to a gate in the front wall by which pedestrians could enter the property without using the vehicle entrance. That must be where he was directing her, which meant that the gate was either kept unlocked or Shadow had the key. Either way, there was a good chance that they would make it because, for the moment at least, hidden as they were by the bushes, they were invisible to the police whose entire attention was focussed on the house they had just left.

Ninety-Nine

Aullton House – Early morning

I couldn't sleep. After James had finished his call to Sergeant Hayford, there hadn't much else we could do so I'd gone to my room to try and settle down. The house was quiet, the bed comfortable, the duvet soft and warm without making me too hot, but I hadn't been able to sleep. I couldn't help thinking about those girls from Lithuania. They had been promised so much – I didn't know exactly what, but I knew how the scam worked – but all that hope and excitement would now have been brutally crushed. I knew how that worked as well.

I had tossed and turned for hours, going over and over all the different things I could have done, should have done, that might have prevented what I was sure must now be happening to them. Would the police get to them before the damage became irreparable? Would the police even find them at all? Would Bruno or Mellisse have changed their plans after I ran away? Could they be using a different house?

So many haunting questions, whose answers only time would reveal, but I kept asking them anyway. And there was another question that troubled me probably more than all the others. Would James really want me to stay and take care of Abby once I told him the whole truth? Not the truth about my life for the past three years. He seemed to be able to understand that and, wonderfully, to accept it without judging me. But what would he do when I told him I was wanted by the police for murder? I couldn't not tell him, not now. And then I realised that the decision about whether I stayed or not might no longer be his to make. The police might have ideas of their own if someone somewhere had worked out who I was.

When troublesome ideas take a hold, especially in the middle of the night when there are no other distractions to soften their grip, sleep – comfortable though it would be – eventually becomes impossible.

At that point, I got up and crept downstairs to make myself a drink. I didn't have to put any lights on until I reached the kitchen because there were soft red bulbs glowing dimly at intervals along the ceilings of corridors and stairs. As my mug of hot chocolate turned lazily in the microwave, it actually crossed my mind that I could simply sneak away while everyone was asleep. I shook my head and tossed the thought back where it had come from, not because I had no idea where I should go or what I should do, but because I couldn't bring myself to display such ingratitude in the face of James's kindness and generosity. At the very least he deserved an explanation… … … which he was going to get rather sooner than I'd expected.

The lights came on in the hallway outside the kitchen just at the moment that the microwave pinged to announce that my chocolate was ready. I spun around, heart pounding, but it was only James who came through the door.

"Oh… … You made me jump," I said, my left hand pressed hard to my chest, my right held up to my mouth.

"Sorry," replied James smiling. "I thought I heard someone up and about. I wasn't sleeping so I thought I'd take a look… … Is that hot chocolate you've got in there?"

I nodded, relaxed, and allowed my hands to drop.

"Hmm," he said. "I think I'll join you."

"I'll do it," I said quickly. "Look, you have this one and I'll make myself another."

A few minutes later, we were settled in the sitting room, back on the same settee, him in one corner and me in the other, both clutching our steaming mugs in a warming two-handed grasp.

"What was keeping you awake?" asked James after taking a sip of his drink.

"Oh… … stuff," I answered noncommittally.

"What sort of stuff," he asked, not giving up.

I almost told him then, but I couldn't quite get the words out. After a pause which made him frown, I took an easier route and explained about my concern for the girls.

"I can't help worrying that the police might not find them. I mean… … it's been hours and we haven't heard anything."

"And we probably won't for an hour or two yet," he said, twisting round to look at the clock on the mantelpiece. "It's just after five, so my guess is that they'll be going in about now. They'll have had time to get their people together, and to come up with some sort of plan. Just before dawn is a good time. Your targets are generally sound asleep and any sentries are usually tired. You can go in quick and quiet or you can use the shock and awe approach. They both work."

"So… … what do you think the police will do this time?"

"No idea," said James with a shake of his head. "I guess it depends who's in charge, and what they think will be safest for the girls."

Safest, I thought. They hadn't been safe since they got off the plane. By now they were probably terrified and traumatized and wouldn't care whether the police came as silent wraiths or raging bulls as long as their torment came to an end.

"Why don't they tell us what's happening?" I asked, frustrated with the silence.

"They can't," said James. "Once the operation is underway, they won't be talking to anyone on the outside until it's over. Sergeant Hayford will call as soon as she can."

I nodded and raised my mug in both hands to take another sip. James did the same and, in the silence that fell momentarily between us, I knew it was time to tell him why I would not be able to stay with him and Abby. I lowered my mug, took a deep breath and began.

"When my Mum and Dad died back on St Helena, my uncle – that's Dad's brother – came to fetch me to live with him and my aunt in Ashbourne."

James inclined his head slightly and looked at me intently as if he knew that something significant was coming.

"When I was twelve, my body began to... ... fill out. It was about that time that my aunt got sick and she and my uncle stopped sleeping together. She had her room, I had mine and he had his."

I paused a moment as I thought what should be said and what could be left out, and in that moment James asked, "What was wrong with your aunt?"

"I don't know. They might have told me but I don't remember. It was some kind of degenerative thing. Some days she was good; some days not so good. She died when I was fifteen."

James leaned forward to rest his mug on a glass coaster on the coffee table. He'd only drunk about half of it. It seemed like he didn't want any more.

"Is that when your uncle began to abuse you?" he asked quietly, sitting back in his corner.

I stared at him. How could he know? Ever since I left... ... that place – I could never bring myself to call it home – I hadn't said a word about this to anyone. As I continued to stare wonderingly into his eyes, I could see only kindness and sadness and somehow that made it easier to tell the story.

"No," I said. "He started coming into my room when I was twelve. It was our secret, he said. Our own private way of loving. Just touching at first... ... you know... ... and then he wanted to do more. That's when I found out what a condom was... ... He was always very careful about that... ... always using one... ... except when he wanted me to... ..."

James raised his right hand off the cushion where it had been resting. His forefinger was stretching upwards as though he was going to bring it to his lips to tell me to hush. Then his fingers clenched into a fist as he spoke.

"Lizzie," he said. "You don't have to tell me... ... the details of what happened. I understand, and it wasn't your fault."

Julie had said that. My best friend at school was the only person I had ever told about my uncle. I had sworn her to secrecy. She had wanted me to tell my form teacher, or the school nurse but I had always felt too ashamed and could never bring myself to do it. How could James know that I'd always blamed myself? Uncle Graham said I teased him. He said I was too pretty. He said I encouraged him. He said he needed me and I mustn't let him down.

"If you'll listen to me, James, I think you'll see that it was. Everything that happened, I brought it on myself."

He frowned as though he couldn't understand what I was saying, but he didn't speak so I steamrollered on.

"I should have run away after Aunty died, but I'd worked so hard for my GCSEs that I wanted to take them. I often did my homework at my friend Julie's house. We studied together. We revised for our exams together. She was the only person I ever told about my uncle. When I was at her house, he couldn't touch me. I thought that if I got good grades, I could find a job and get away from him. After the exams were over, Julie's mum and dad were going to take us away for a weekend break… … to kind of celebrate. It was Friday and I was packing my case for the weekend and my uncle came back early from work. He'd been drinking and he wanted me to take my clothes off and get into bed with him."

I closed my eyes as I remembered the scene. Uncle Graham had been angry one minute and pleading the next. As clear as if it was yesterday, I saw him unbuttoning the waist of his trousers and unzipping his fly. Then I was lying on the bed, arms flung wide, and he was coming at me.

"I didn't plan to kill him," I said. "It just happened. I honestly didn't mean to kill him."

James mouth looked grim and his eyes were blazing with anger but his voice was soft and tender.

"Of course, you didn't mean to," he said, and he stretched out his hand.

"If you want to, Lizzie… … only if you want to… … come here."

So I came, and once again allowed myself to be wrapped in his arms. He believed me, and I hadn't even told him yet what had happened. So then, with his arm around my shoulder and my cheek snuggled down against his massive chest, I told him the rest.

It was the table-lamp that did it. It was on the nightstand by my bed and, after Uncle Graham had pushed me back onto the bed, my right hand was brushing against its marble stem. At least, it looked like marble and it was so heavy that I'd always thought of it as marble but, in the end, it didn't matter what it was made of. It was there; it was available; and my hand could grasp it.

As he leant over me, his trousers now discarded, I swung that lamp as hard as I could. Its solid base hit him square on the side of his head. He groaned and toppled sideways off the bed ending up on his knees. At the same time, I rolled off the other side, still clutching the lamp. As I turned to face him across the bed, he began to struggle up, his right hand on the bed to push himself up and his left holding his head where I'd hit him. I just wanted to get away but when I began to sidle along my side of the bed, he did the same at the other side. He seemed dazed but whether it was from the drink or the blow from the lamp I couldn't tell. We each made it to the end of the bed and he lunged at me. His foot caught in the duvet which had slid partly off the bed, and I swung the lamp again. This time he fell back against my dressing table, his head bouncing off the corner before he slid down to the floor and lay still. That's when I knew I'd killed him.

I had to get away but I had very little money. I needed the cash from his wallet and, thankfully, I didn't have to touch him. His jacket was on the floor where he'd dropped it so I reached in the inside pocket for the wallet. It was there, and it was full. That was quite normal because he always said he didn't like using plastic.

I was in a mad panic and definitely not thinking straight, but I knew I had to get away. I couldn't tell anyone what had happened. Who would believe me? They would just think I'd killed him for his money.

So, I ran.

I ended up in Birmingham, and changed my name so the police wouldn't be able to trace me. I'd been sure that I'd find a job before the money ran out but I didn't. So I ended upon the streets where Ray Mellisse found me. I was one of his girls for almost three years, until the day came when I had the chance to run again. And I took it. Could that really have been less than a week ago?

One Hundred

Birmingham – Early morning

Joanne stared at the bushes which lay to the right of the path that snaked around from the rear of the house. She was sure she had seen something flit across the path from the base of the house wall. The shape had been indistinct, low and broad. She couldn't be certain but it could well have been two figures crouching as they moved, and keeping very close together. She wished she hadn't looked so long and hard at the beam of light from the chopper. That mistake had played havoc with her night vision.

Because she was present simply as an observer, Joanne hadn't been issued with any communications gear. This meant that not only could she not hear what was going on with the assault team inside the house, she had no way of communicating what she had seen, other than by shouting which was probably not a great idea. She risked a quick glance behind her to see if she could attract Georgie's help but her friend was out of sight. Joanne thought she was probably behind the right-hand pillar of the driveway exit where she could obey her orders to stay with the car but also have a clear view of the side of the house where all the action seemed to be focussed.

Joanne wasn't a great one for cursing. In her mind, things happened or they didn't, and bitching about it got you nowhere. She wondered briefly about edging quietly back to the gateway to alert Georgie to what was happening, but decided against it. For one, she might be seen by the suspects in the shrubbery; two, she might lose track of where they were; and three, one of them could well be a hostage rather than a suspect, which meant a terrified girl in great danger. There was no time to waste. Joanne was the only one who had seen them. She had to move.

Smiling ruefully at the thought that this was not exactly what DI Cobham had meant by "observing", she sidled slowly into the bushes to the right of the path. The earth was soft and damp under her feet which meant that moving quietly was no problem. In fact, until she came within a few feet of her quarry, any slight rustling she might make would be effectively masked by the throbbing of the chopper's rotors.

Then the sound of the rotors changed as the chopper lifted a few feet while at the same time edging towards her side of the house. It resumed its hover in the new position its searchlight now sweeping the grounds to the rear of the house. Joanne wondered if someone had tried to escape out the back. If so, they wouldn't get very far. From her recollection of the plan she had been shown, the grounds to the rear were bounded by a high stone wall.

Anyway, that wasn't her problem. But something else might be.

There was a high possibility that the searchlight was not the only way of showing the crew of the chopper what was happening on the ground. Many of them these days were fitted with infra-red cameras which, by utilising temperature differences, can identify objects in situations where a searchlight is all but useless. The kind of situation, for instance, where a suspect is hiding at night in thick undergrowth which a searchlight beam cannot penetrate.

If that was the case here, which might explain the slight repositioning of the chopper, not only would the suspects be showing up on the screen mounted on board, but so would she. And probably, at that very moment, the camera operator would be asking her, over the communications net to which she had no access, to identify herself.

Although she was, by now, deep in the bushes and actually brushing against the high conifer hedge that bordered the property on that side, she would be glowing like a beacon on the operator's screen. If she didn't respond to a request to identify herself, she would risk being taken for one of the bad guys and could end up getting shot. She had to act quickly.

So she stood perfectly still.

She stood straight and tall with her hands by her sides and then raised her arms, crossing over her wrists above her head and then lowering her arms so they extended horizontally. She did this twice more before lowering her hands to her sides again. She had no idea whether it would work but it was all she could think of. She stared up through leaves and twigs wondering how the chopper's crew could signify that they had spotted her. Always assuming that her strange gestures had been understood.

As she watched, the searchlight blinked off briefly and then on again. Then twice more, before resuming its sweep of the rear garden. Joanne didn't realise that she'd been holding her breath until she felt her lungs deflate. Assuming that she was still under observation, she lifted both arms above her head to point vertically upwards before lowering them to point towards the spot where she believed the two suspects – or one suspect and one hostage – to be. She intended to repeat this twice more but, before she had completed her gesturing, the searchlight blinked off and on again.

So, what should she do now? The chopper's camera operator must have alerted Inspector Rodgers to the presence of the bodies in the bushes, so common-sense and training told her that she should hold her position and wait for his team to round up the two suspects.

But all the action still seemed to be in the house and away to the rear. She flinched at the sound of two shots which she thought came from inside the building, and another which she was sure was some way off behind the house. She was glad this operation wasn't hers. The follow-up enquiries and paperwork work would take until Christmas and beyond.

She held still, but could feel the frustration mounting. Her training told her to hold her position and allow those dedicated to the task to wind it up. They clearly weren't having an easy time of it and her getting in the way could make things a great deal worse.

But because they weren't having an easy time of it, there seemed to be no-one available to deal with her suspects only yards away in the bushes. And those suspects were starting to move.

She heard a faint cry followed by a sharp intake of breath, and the sounds were much closer than she would have expected. All the time she had been thinking, the two unknown subjects had been making their way stealthily towards the gate at the front corner of the garden. One of them must have been jabbed by a thorn or sharp twig causing an involuntary, suppressed cry. The sound had been soft, but high-pitched; a girl, almost certainly. Joanne weighed the possibilities.

Her first thought was that these were a male suspect with a female hostage, but it suddenly dawned on her that these could be two of the Lithuanian girls trying to escape in all the confusion. They would have no idea what was going on and might not even speak English.

What a mess! She would just have to wait and hope to be able to react effectively to whatever confronted her.

She had no idea how many seconds passed but they were, without doubt, the longest in her life. Every sense strained to snatch some clue from the darkness, but she could pick up nothing more but the odour of moist earth and the scent of conifers.

Then, out of nothing, her senses were bombarded with stimuli: a dark shadow moving to her right; a faint whiff of body odour mixed with aftershave; and a voice, whispering indistinctly, but definitely male.

That settled it, and she readied herself to move. The two figures – she could clearly see now that there were only two – evidently had no inkling of her presence. Not a surprise, really. From the movement of their heads, particularly the taller one, they seemed to be alternating between studying the ground in front of them and glancing back at the scene of activity to their rear.

Joanne was not supposed to attack a suspect without warning. Procedure dictated that she would not clout him over the head, kick him in the balls, gouge at his eyes, belt him in the kidneys or chop him back-handed across the throat without first offering him the opportunity to give himself up peacefully. Procedure was not going to work here, so to hell with it.

When the taller figure next looked back, he was only about four feet away, and the girl was between him and Joanne. He was gripping her arm with his left hand and his right held a gun. Joanne couldn't make out what type it was but it was bigger than a pistol, smaller than a rifle.

With a brief nod at procedure, Joanne yelled, "Police" at the top of her voice. Two startled faces swung round towards her, but she was already moving.

She kicked out to sweep the girl's feet away from under her so that she fell flat on her back tearing herself free from her captor's grasp. He tried to twist around but there wasn't much space. Because he'd been looking backwards, his gun hand had to swing through over one hundred and eighty degrees and, in swinging without care, it snagged on a branch of rhododendron. Joanne had followed through her kick to the girl, allowing her body to twist to the left, keeping her right hand down low in preparation for a move that she hadn't practised in years. With all the speed and strength she could summon up, that right hand now swung upwards in a flashing arc that ended in a vicious flat-handed chop to the man's exposed throat. In some sort of reflex, his gun fired three shots as he crumpled choking to the ground. He must have had the weapon set on semi-auto, but the bullets came nowhere near to Joanne or the girl.

As the man writhed on the ground, struggling to get breath past his shattered larynx, Joanne looked for the gun. It had fallen close beside him, so she kicked it out of reach before turning her attention to the girl who had squirmed away, as far as the hedge would allow, from the man on the ground.

Not knowing whether she would be understood, and keeping one eye on the man who seemed to be losing his battle to breathe, Joanne said, "I'm with the police. I'm Detective Sergeant Hayford."

She saw the girl's wide eyes dip as she nodded slowly at the words. Encouraged, Joanne asked, "What is your name?"

For a moment there was no reply, and Joanne began to think that perhaps the girl had not understood after all. Then there was a sob, and a quavering sigh, and the girl spoke.

"My name is Aushra… … … Thank God… … … Thank God you came."

One Hundred and One

Aullton House – Early morning

James didn't interrupt to ask a lot of questions but seemed content just to let me rest against him and tell my story. When I finally ran out of words, he asked me how I knew my uncle was dead. Had I checked his breathing or his pulse?

"No," I told him, my cheek still pressed against his chest. "I didn't want to touch him. I just wanted to get away. But he was dead… … no question. Afterwards, I kept going to the library… … I don't know… … several days anyway… … checking the local papers, and eventually there it was. **Graham Burleigh found dead at his home in Ashbourne.** Something like that anyway."

James shifted in his corner and eased me gently away from him so he could see my face.

"Now I'm not an expert, Lizzie, but soon I'll be talking to someone who is… … and I think she's going to tell us that this is a clear case of self-defence."

I looked into his eyes, willing him to be right, but not knowing whether I dared believe him.

"Lizzie, if the police did their job right, I really don't think that the CPS would even have let this go to court."

I frowned. "The CPS?"

"The Crown Prosecution Service. It's their job to decide whether prosecution is in the public interest and whether there is enough evidence to take it to court."

I could feel my eyes welling up with tears.

"Do you mean I needn't have run away?"

"I can't be sure, Lizzie. I think so, but I promise you this. If some over-zealous, misguided twerp decides to bring charges against you, I know a barrister who can virtually guarantee that no court will ever convict you. And while we work this out, you stay with us. OK?"

I can't describe how it felt to have that burden lifted, to have shared it with someone who was on my side and would stand with me come what may. Unsurprisingly, I burst into tears again and found my face buried in the same patch of wet shirt that I had created last time. I didn't mind and it seemed that James wasn't too worried either.

I was still sobbing when the phone began to ring. It was the landline and the handset was lying on the sideboard where James had placed it after speaking to Sergeant Hayford earlier on. It took him several seconds to disengage himself from me and get over to the sideboard.

I looked at the clock. Ten minutes past six. There was only one person likely to be ringing at this time in the morning?

"Sergeant Hayford," said James. "Good of you to call."

I listened but there wasn't much to hear because James wasn't saying much and the call was very brief. Part way through the conversation, he swung around to face me, his eyes alight with pleasure. He nodded and gave me a thumbs-up sign which could only mean one thing. I stood and walked over to him. He reached out to put his arm around my shoulders and draw me in close. Then the call was over and he put the phone down.

"They've got them, Lizzie. All of them. It seems they've had a rough time but they're OK now and on their way to hospital to be checked over."

I closed my eyes and my body sagged as relief flooded through me.

"Who's this then?" asked a deep voice from behind us and we turned to see Cherry standing in the doorway.

"Cherry, you idiot," exclaimed James. "What are you doing up?"

"Interrupting you two, by the looks of it," replied Cherry with a grin.

"Nonsense," said James. "Come over here and sit down."

We sat, James and I back in our respective corners of the settee, and Cherry in one of the big armchairs. He explained that he was already awake when he heard the phone ring and got up to see what was happening. James told him what the call had been about.

"So, all's well that ends well," said Cherry, and then winced. "Wasn't comfortable in bed. Can't get comfy down here either."

We watched as he rearranged himself in the chair.

"How's the little one," he asked, after making himself as comfortable as was possible.

"Surprisingly good," replied James. "I thought I'd be up and down to her all night… … bad dreams and so on. But once she finally settled, we've not heard a peep from her."

The two of them looked across to a small device on the sideboard near the phone cradle. It had a small flashing blue light on it. I suppose I'd assumed it was something to do with the phone system.

"Baby monitor," said James, turning back to me. "Started using it after the kidnap… … just to be sure she was OK. I was actually on the point of putting in CCTV but in the end that seemed… … well… … just a bit too intrusive."

"Too right," said Cherry. "We all need our own private space… … You want to know what I think?"

He looked from one to the other of us, including us both in the question.

We both nodded.

"I think this will be different. Last time, she was away for... ... what... ... several days? Cooped up in a crate? She came up here this morning thrilled to be having a little holiday in a place she loves. She had a bit of adventure... ... didn't last long... ... and she went to sleep safe in her own bed. And don't forget this... ... Lizzie or I were with her all the way through. She may have been scared, but she was never scared on her own. And you, Dad, did what you promised. You turned up when she needed you. So, I think she'll be OK."

He shrugged and then winced.

"I'm no child psychologist, but that's what I think."

I looked at James to see what he thought.

"I hope you're right," he said, uncertain but wanting to be convinced.

"Which brings us," said Cherry, "to our loose end... ... What are you planning to do with Andy?"

James and I looked at each other. We were both of us wondering how much Cherry knew, and what had alerted him to Andy's betrayal which had landed us in our current mess.

"Tell you what," said Cherry, "I don't feel like moving so, if one of you will make me a cuppa, we'll have a chat and see what's to be done."

I'd learnt by now that Cherry's "cuppa" meant strong tea so I hauled myself up and trotted off to the kitchen leaving the two of them to talk. After all, Andy's fate was not really my concern, which isn't to say I didn't have a view but I didn't feel it was my place to get involved in that kind of decision.

It seemed I was wrong.

When I returned with Cherry's mug of tea I found them talking about Borisov. That was when I first heard the name Osman Izetbegović and, having listened for several minutes, tucked up once more in my corner of the settee, I understood at last why James was able to be so sure that Borisov would keep his word.

"OK," said James, indicating a change of subject. "Back to Andy. How did you work out he was involved with the other lot?"

Cherry grinned as he lowered his mug.

"Not exactly rocket science, Boss. There was something not right about those guys taking us up to the cabin. If Andy brought them in, he had to know who they were. He's not the sort of guy who'd trust blokes he didn't know in a tricky situation like this. And if he knew them, he must also have known they weren't kosher... ... Then there were just one or two things they said up at the cabin... ... like they were told they mustn't hurt Abby. Not much on its own, but they all added up. And then there was that odd reference to a loose end when you were talking to Borisov. You said you knew about him and were keeping him."

He paused for a sip of his tea, and then grinned again.

"The stupid sod was a bit dopy upstairs so I chatted to him like I knew all about what he'd been up to."

He shrugged.

"He filled in the rest. Glad to get it off his chest, I think. I wondered for a bit what was going on when he turned up at the cabin batting for our team but ... ... all makes sense now."

James nodded and took a deep breath which he let out slowly as his left hand tapped against the arm of the settee. Then he turned to me.

"You're part of this, Lizzie. He definitely tried to kill Angie and he tossed you to the lions before he had his change of heart. He might have told those guys not to hurt Abby, but he doesn't seem to have been too worried about what they did to you. What happens to him now is as much your decision as ours."

I was surprised and felt rather daunted by the idea. I wasn't sure I wanted that responsibility. James must have seen something in my face.

"Don't worry, Lizzie," he said. "We're not thinking of blowing his brains out."

I relaxed just as he'd meant me to, and for a few moments we all thought about the problem.

"I might be wrong here," I said, "but it seems he betrayed your trust far more than he did mine. I never knew him before all this, but he's been your friend for... ..."

I trailed off.

"Fifteen years," supplied James. "He was best man at our wedding."

"Twelve years," said Cherry. "And we both served with him."

"There... ... you see," I replied. "He's really let you down big time, and I think you're both wondering whether you can trust him again like you used to."

James and Cherry looked at each other, and I saw James's clenched fist rubbing against the bottom of his chin in the way it does when he's thinking hard.

"Spot on there, love," said Cherry. "I think we both know that trust is out the window, so where does that leave us?"

That was something I didn't know the answer to, so I offered instead, "I know he drugged Angie and nearly got her killed, but he did save her from that guy upstairs. He came through for us in the end, which ought to count for something. Couldn't we just let him get better and then go find himself another job?"

It was a simple solution, probably too simple, but it was all I had to offer. Again James and Cherry looked at each other, both apparently struck with the same thought, but it was James who put it into words.

"He can have the Gulf job."

"Keep him out of our hair," agreed Cherry. "And it'll get him well away from Borisov and that guy Mellisse. Mind you, he'll have to buy a ton of suntan cream. Serve him right, the silly sod."

I'd no idea what they were talking about until James turned to me to explain.

"Some of the shipping companies are getting a bit jittery about sailing through the Gulf. It's all to do with pirates out of Somalia. The perception is that it's the oil and gas carriers that are at risk because of their value. RRISC was approached last month after the MV Feisty Gas was hijacked. We've been asked to carry out a risk assessment and make recommendations about providing on-board security for ships passing through the Gulf."

"Bit of a crap job really," put in Cherry. "Assessing the risk is the easy part. It exists and it's going to get worse. But how do you convince governments in that area that it's a good idea to let armed private security bods traipse around on their turf? And if you can't convince them, and you have to put your security team on board at the port of embarkation and leave them in place until the ship gets to where it's going, then a three-day job turns into a three-week job."

"Cherry's right," said James. "Andy filled me in on it, but said he was thinking of turning it down." He smiled grimly. "I think he's about to have another change of heart."

"He might even make a proper job of it," said Cherry. "Old Tosser from the SBS is on the loose. If Andy can sign him up, we could be getting ourselves a branch office in Dubai. Now there's a thought."

And so it was that Andy's fate was decided, along with that of the unsuspecting Sergeant David Toseland, formerly of the Royal Navy's Special Boat Service.

One Hundred and Two

Birmingham – Early morning

"Didn't I say you were just here to observe?"

Joanne nodded. She accepted that, from his point of view at least, DI Cobham had a right to be angry. They were standing in a front room of the house, the one with the bay window at the side.

"You do know what observe means, don't you? I mean, they do teach you that out in the sticks?"

She looked him straight in the eye, knowing full well that he didn't expect an answer, though she was sorely tempted to give him one. The adrenalin boost generated by her encounter in the bushes hadn't entirely faded, and she resented being reprimanded for doing something which needed doing. An armed man has escaped from the house with a terrified girl as a hostage and was all set to break out of the police cordon. Although the helicopter crew seemed to have spotted him, there was no-one near enough on the ground to stop him getting out of the garden. Except for Joanne. If she wanted to be certain of the girl's safety, she'd had no choice but to act as she did, and she knew it.

She also knew that, although it had turned out more messy than planned, the operation had been largely successful. Cobham's anger wouldn't last. She suspected that it was fuelled largely by his frustration at having to spend all his time with the ACC while occasionally being shot at, while she had been able to sneak in and get her hands dirty and make an arrest.

She rather hoped that the man she'd apprehended would survive, in spite of the obvious concern of the paramedics. She'd never been responsible for anyone's death before and she didn't want this to be the first time. While he fumed in front of her, she silently praised Cobham's forethought in having an ambulance on hand, primarily for the girls, but also ready for any other injuries that might arise. She knew the regulations, and death following police contact was about as serious as it gets. Even if the guy survived, there was bound to be a Critical Incident investigation because it was clear to everyone that, without the speedy intervention of the paramedics, he would now be on his way to the morgue rather than the A & E department at Selly Oak Hospital. Although trained in the procedure, neither of the paramedics had performed an emergency tracheostomy before, but both knew it was the victim's only hope. The senior, a competent woman in her mid-thirties, had unhesitatingly grasped the nettle and got the job done. It had been a tense few minutes, but Joanne had known immense relief when the ambulance had left with the guy still breathing.

Cobham stopped his rant and looked past Joanne through the front window. She turned to watch a second ambulance setting off down the drive, blue lights flashing, as it led its police escort on another dash to Selly Oak. This one, summoned once gunfire had broken out, contained the two occupants of the house who had resisted the police invasion from the top of the stairs. For their stupidity they had received respectively a bullet through the shoulder and one through the lower abdomen. They had already received treatment at the scene and, short of any complications arising, were both likely to survive to stand trial. Joanne didn't know their names. She wasn't really interested. Her guy had ID on him that showed his name to be Oleg Berezin though whether that could be believed was, for the moment, anyone's guess.

Berezin had been carted away by ambulance some time previously, his case being far more urgent, and the girls had been taken in police cars, also to Selly Oak hospital. Georgie had been sent with them as a hopefully reassuring female presence. Selly Oak A & E were going to have a busy time that morning. Still lying in a room upstairs lay the only fatality so far. Joanne hadn't seen him but she'd heard one of the assault team describe him as a "great, hulking brute with a beard like Pat Roach." This was the one who'd been trying to hold off the police with a pump-action shotgun until one of the team took him down with a bullet in his chest.

The Pat Roach reference had caught Joanne's attention. Her dad could remember when wrestling was a sport regularly televised on Saturday afternoons. Pat Roach had been one of his favourites, even after he left wrestling and turned his hand to acting. Joanne doubted whether there was anyone else on site besides herself, maybe in the whole force, who could have known that Roach was the only actor, apart from Harrison Ford, to appear in all three Indiana Jones films. If they ever made another one, they'd have to do without him as he'd passed away the previous year. Joanne had been home for a visit the weekend after Roach had died, and her dad had made quite a thing of it, though he'd given more attention to Roach's **Bomber Busbridge** character in Auf Wiedersehen Pet than he had to Indiana Jones.

So the guy upstairs looked like Pat Roach, which meant he was well over six feet, and wide to match. Put that with his full beard and curly hair and… … …

"Sergeant, are you listening to me?"

She wasn't even aware that Cobham had spoken again. Her mind was back in the airport where they had sat together watching and waiting. She remembered a figure who had stood out from the throng because he was a good head taller than most folk around him. She remembered the width of his shoulders and his bushy beard, and she cringed inwardly at the thought that, if only they'd known who he was, maybe those girls could have been spared the horror of the previous night.

"What's the matter, sergeant?"

Cobham was sounding concerned now. He reached out to touch her lightly on the arm, to get her attention. She looked at him.

"Sorry, sir... ... I was just thinking... ... Could I take a look at the guy upstairs?"

She took her look, and knew she was right, and she added another piece to the many that were going to fall into place that day. But in spite of all their efforts, one piece was destined to elude them.

While Joanne recounted her part in that morning's events, once informally at the scene and again for the record at Lloyd House police HQ in the centre of Birmingham, scene of crime officers made a thorough search of the house. They ranged from mildewed basement to cobweb-strewn attics but found nothing to lead them to the next rung up the chain. They found ample evidence of beatings and sexual assault. They found a safe containing records, photos and digital video, not just relating to the girls found in the house, but to others going back several years. They found assorted unlicensed weapons which they had high hopes of linking to other criminal activity. They found a girl hiding in the basement among some mouldy mattresses. After crying hysterically for several minutes, she had calmed enough to tell them her name was Philippa and to plead with them to take her away from that awful place. They even found a rifle which they suspected had been used to kill Mitchell Portess, complete with Berezin's fingerprints.

What they did not find was anything to tell them who owned the house or who the men living there were working for. Reports were coming down the line from the forensics team sifting through the remains of Mitchell Portess's house near Tamworth. Diligent though they were, they were struggling to come up with anything useful. Cobham had hopes that something would eventually turn up at one of the sites, or that maybe one of the survivors would be persuaded to help them with their enquiries. With the ACC on his back, he had to have faith in something.

Joanne, however, had another idea, one which had escaped her in the busyness of the morning, but which was now beginning to germinate. Her stomach was beginning to tell her that it was way past lunchtime, and it suddenly dawned on her that she hadn't actually had breakfast. You could only go for so long on nothing but coffee. What she needed now was a Costa. One of their strawberry coolers with a panini, or maybe one of their wraps, would do the trick. The trouble was she'd been told not to leave the station, just in case she was needed again. So she went in search of DI Cobham to see if she could be let off the leash, at least as far as the Costa, which she knew was just around the corner in Colmore Row.

When she found him and told him what she wanted, his eyes took on a far-away look before he gave her a tired, slightly crooked, smile.

"Tell you what. I'll come with you. That way we'll both get a breather and no-one can accuse you of slipping away without permission. Not that it really matters now." His smile widened. "I've just heard from the hospital and Berezin's going to make it. The pressure's off."

Over a cooler and wrap for her, and a latte and panini for him, Joanne explained to him where he might find the information he wanted. And since the person they needed was on her turf not his, she would have to go with him.

One Hundred and Three

Thurvaston Arms – 9.30 am

It had been a long night and Nadera was dog-tired. She looked over at John, fast asleep beside her. They had returned to the Thurvaston Arms just after sunrise, eventually strolling in through the front door as though they had just been out for a breath of fresh air before breakfast. Since the hotel served breakfast up until ten o'clock, they had decided to try and catch an hour or two of sleep before eating. John had dropped off almost immediately, but Nadera had lain awake, her mind buzzing with all that they had learnt from Gordon Russell, and the action John wanted to take on the strength of it.

They had eventually dropped Russell at his home, more or less unharmed, somewhere around three o'clock in the morning. The staff at the Thurvaston Arms would have long since packed up by that time, so they wouldn't be able to get back to their room until the place woke up around six-thirty. With time to kill, they had driven over to the motorway services at Donington Park where they could be sure to find clean toilets, somewhere to sit, and maybe something to drink and free Wi-Fi. Over drinks from a machine, they discussed Russell's information, with Nadera making notes on her laptop to add more detail to the picture they were uncovering. Making sure they didn't overstay their two hours free parking, they left just before a quarter to six and headed at a moderate pace back to their country hotel.

If, when he woke up, John was still determined to go ahead, there would be a host of arrangements to be made. She went over the details in her head to make sure that the job, if it had to be done, would be done efficiently. There would be an element of risk but she'd do her best to minimise that so they ought to be able to extricate themselves without too much trouble. If all went well they would be leaving the country as the sun came up the next morning.

If only John weren't so stubborn they could be flying out today. She'd try again to persuade him once he woke up but, in her heart, she knew it had to be his decision. Phil Simmons had been his friend.

She closed her eyes and tried to sleep, but it was impossible. Just as well really, because it wasn't long before the alarm on her phone buzzed and she felt John stirring beside her. He reached for her but his hand only brushed her back as she sat up and swung her legs out of the bed.

"Hey," he said in mock disappointment.

"Hey yourself," replied Nadera, jolted a little by the time showing on her bedside clock. "If you wanted to play games you shouldn't have gone to sleep."

"OK. OK. What time is it?"

"Nine-thirty, so come on. There's no breakfast if we're not down by ten."

After each had paid a necessary personal visit to the en-suite facilities, they left the bathroom door open, sharing the space as they each showered and dressed as quickly as they could.

The bar was empty when they arrived at two minutes to ten, and most of the tables had been cleared but there were still two with undisturbed cutlery, napkins, small pots of jam and pats of butter. Selecting the one furthest from the bar counter, John and Nadera sat and studied the menu.

"I don't know why you do that," said Nadera. "You know what you are going to have."

"Just making the most of it while we're here," John smiled.

After they had both been served – full English for John, and almond croissants for Nadera – she asked him again whether he really wanted to go through with it.

Although there seemed to be no-one within earshot, they kept their voices low.

"Not much option really," said John, dipping a portion of sausage into the soft yolk of his fried egg. "Not if we want justice for Phil."

"Not if *you* want justice, you mean," replied Nadera, making it clear that this was John's quest not hers. "And what do you mean by justice anyway?"

John chewed on his sausage and thought. Then he glanced around before replying.

"Justice is making sure the guy behind Phil's death doesn't get away with it."

"Even if that means… … murdering him?"

"You weren't worried about dumping that guy in the canal," he said. What's the difference?"

"The difference is that he was out to get us. It was him or us. Self-defence. This Raymond Mellisse doesn't even know we exist. He is no threat to us."

John scooped up some baked beans and followed them with a wedge of black pudding. He looked at Nadera as he chewed slowly, a sure sign that he was thinking hard.

"Did you believe what Russell told us?" he asked eventually.

Nadera sighed.

"We talked about this last night," she said. "Yes, I believed him. Look… … You were listening… … He seemed… … relieved to be able to tell someone. I don't think he was bullshitting us. I don't think he was hiding anything."

"Yes," said John. "Me too."

It was the turn of the hash browns to get a thorough chewing, along with a portion of bacon and egg. Nadera sipped her coffee, and waited patiently while he thought.

"Do you think the police are going to be able to pin anything on Mellisse?" he asked finally.

Nadera shook her head.

"Not likely. Not if they need Russell as a witness. You heard him. He knows what happened to Portess when he became a threat. He doesn't want the same thing happening to him. He's not going to tell the police what he told us. He only opened up to us because he needed to be able to tell someone… … and we were quite obviously not the police. You could see how it's been eating away at him, ever since that business years ago when Portess first got his claws into him. He's not a villain… … not really. He did what he did because he had to, because Portess had a hold over him. He didn't want to and, if we believe him, he never profited from Portess's side-line."

"I believed him all right," said John. "That's why I had no problem letting him go… … But it means the police have no way of getting to Mellisse. Hell, they probably haven't even got a clue that he's the guy they should be looking at."

He speared the last piece of fried bread with his fork and used it to scoop up the final remains of his breakfast. Nadera picked up some of the larger flakes that had fallen from her croissants and slipped them delicately into her mouth.

"You're going to do this, aren't you?" she asked.

"Like I said… … We don't really have a choice."

In spite of the determination in his voice, Nadera believed that, if she tried hard enough, she could persuade him to change his mind. The trouble was that John would always regret not having followed through on what he saw as his obligation to Phil Simmons… … And he would always blame her for having dissuaded him… … And she didn't want that hovering like a brooding vulture over the start of their new life together.

Having so unexpectedly fallen in love with him, she had gone to a lot of effort to ensure John had a future and that she would be able to share it with him. She had travelled to England to destroy his dentist's records so that no identity checks could be made via that route. When John's safety had been threatened by Dave Talbot, the ex-para in the pay of her boss Al-Mubarak, she had come up with a way of disposing of

Talbot in a way that would lead the authorities to identify his mangled remains as those of the Englishman, John Salisbury, for whose arrest there was a European warrant outstanding. She had looked out for John while he tried to uncover the truth about Phil Simmons' death, and she would look out for him still while he worked it through to its only logical end.

She took a deep breath and let it out slowly. Decision made.

There was a moment's pause in their conversation as a waiter appeared from the kitchen to refill their coffee cups. Job done, Nadera watched his back until he was out of sight again.

"OK. Did you check whether that licence is still valid?"

Among the documents with his brother-in-law's passport, John had found a shotgun licence, renewed only a couple of months before the fatal crash. He had no reason to suppose that it would come in handy, but he hung onto it just in case. Today it would be put to use.

"It's fine. The photo's the same one he used for his passport and that's served me OK so far."

Nadera nodded.

"OK… … after this, I think we had better get ourselves some new documents. I know how to find people who can do that. But now… … where do we go shopping?"

"Shopping's the easy bit," replied John. "It's getting close enough to Mellisse that's going to be the problem."

Nadera looked at him over her steaming coffee, her eyes crinkling with the beginnings of a smile.

"Not too much of a problem," she said. "I think I have an idea."

One Hundred and Four

Aullton Estate – Mid-morning

Abby slept until gone ten o'clock. We heard her stir briefly around eight and I went straight up to her room but, by the time I got there, she'd settled back to sleep. She didn't stir again until after the clock-tower above the stables sounded ten. Since Cherry had decided he'd rather be with us than upstairs with Andy, I eventually got around to making us some breakfast. It was nothing exciting, just scrambled eggs on toast, topped with rashers of crispy grilled bacon. We sat around the breakfast bar in the kitchen to eat, and washed it all down with mugs of the most amazing St Helenian coffee. I couldn't believe it when I saw the label on the brown paper packet it was stored in, but James told us he'd bought it on a whim the last time he'd taken Abby to Betty's Tea Rooms in Harrogate.

While I was cooking, Barrie appeared and told us Angie was awake and felt like eating something. I got some more eggs and bacon on the go, and used some of the first batch to make a bacon sandwich for him and scrambled eggs without the toast for Angie. He poured out a couple of large glasses of fruit juice and took the lot up to Angie's room on a tray. I began to hope that his attentiveness meant what I thought it did. Angie deserved to have some good come into her life.

As we ate, we talked about the various things that needed doing, not least clearing away all the mess up at the cabin. There were no bodies, but there was plenty of broken glass, splintered woodwork, blood stains, bullet holes and cartridge cases. James hadn't liked to leave the place unattended for so long, but there had really been no other options, short of bringing Gil Elliott and others into a scenario they so far appeared to have no inkling of. In the early part of the previous evening, James had Borisov to deal with, and then he wanted to see Abby comfortably settled. After that, there was nothing that could be done in the dark, and he wasn't going to leave the house this morning until Abby had woken up.

Still, waiting for Abby did allow time to think about what was best to be done. We were all agreed that it would do Abby no good to see the cabin at the Cantle Burn ever again, and in the end it was Cherry who offered a simple but drastic solution.

"Burn it and clear it," he said, after a few thoughtful moments of corporate silence.

"I can't," replied James instinctively.

"Course you can," said Cherry. "What's the fuel up there? Propane isn't it? OK, some folks went up there yesterday – Andy, me, you, Lizzie – and like the total wally that I am, I forgot to turn the gas off properly when we left. There was a build-up overnight, and this morning – boom. Not worth rebuilding so you decide to level it and let it grass over. If you still want a cabin up there, you can build something completely different on the other side of the burn."

James frowned and looked doubtful.

"What about the trees? The last thing we want to do is start a forest fire up there. No telling how far it'd spread."

"No worries. If you hadn't been snoring your noble head off last night, you might have noticed it's been tipping it down from about midnight onwards."

He peered out of the kitchen window at the solid mass of unbroken cloud. The leaden skies were heavy with rain. James followed his gaze and nodded.

"And it doesn't look as though it's going to stop anytime soon."

I kept quiet. Burning down houses was not one of my strengths.

When Abby finally emerged, none of us heard her until she appeared at the door of the kitchen wrapped up in her fluffy, pink Tatty Teddy dressing gown. We hadn't heard her stirring because James had forgotten to bring the baby monitor through from the sitting room. I noticed her first as I was facing the door, more or less, whereas James and Cherry had their backs to it. She paused in the doorway and looked at each of us almost warily, as though trying to reassure herself that everything was OK, normal, just as it should be.

I smiled at her, which made James twist round on his stool.

"Hi, sweetie," he said, reaching out his hand towards her.

I was relieved to see her smile back as she came forward to wrap both arms around his waist and snuggle in tight. Cherry turned as well, rather more slowly than James, and I could tell it hurt. There was a flicker in his eyes before a broad grin took hold. He was obviously determined not to let Abby see there was any problem.

"Hey, girl," he said. "You're a real sleepy-head this morning."

He reached out to stroke the back of her head. She eased away from James enough to turn her face to Cherry and I saw the smile had gone and there was a serious look in her eyes.

"Are you OK, Cherry?" she asked, in a quiet uncertain voice.

"I'm fine baby, especially now I've finished off one of Lizzie's great breakfasts."

He was smiling, but her serious look remained.

"I thought something happened to you."

Above her head, his eyes caught James's briefly. Then he brushed her cheek with the back of his hand.

"Well you just take a look, baby. Here I am, fit as a fiddle."

I could see it in her eyes. She wanted to be convinced, but her fragmented memories of yesterday belied what she was seeing and hearing. A bit more normality was called for.

"We've all had scrambled egg and crispy bacon," I said. "So, what would you like?"

She pulled away from James, frowned and wrinkled her nose as she looked at all our empty plates. Distaste was it, or savouring the smell, or just thinking hard.

"Have we got any of those chocolate Danish?" she asked at last, dismissing the bacon and egg in spite of the lingering aroma.

I wasn't sure what she meant so I raised my eyebrows in James's direction.

"Go check the freezer, sweetie," he said, giving her a pat on the behind as she turned away.

I went to help her search and we were soon engrossed in preparing a couple of Danish pastries with chocolate sauce centres and chocolate chips scattered throughout. I began to wish I hadn't eaten quite so much scrambled egg. I offered the microwave, but Abby told me they were much better heated in the oven since this gave them a crispy outside which she liked.

While they were warming, James explained that he needed to go and rescue his Maserati from the mud where it had got bogged down. Cherry was going to help him, and James assured Abby that they'd be back in time for lunch. I wasn't surprised when she asked them to wait so she could go with them.

"It's not very nice out there, love," said James reasonably. "I don't really want to go myself, but the ground's only going to get boggier with all this rain."

"Sooner it's done, the better," agreed Cherry. "You stay here in the dry and help Lizzie get a tasty lunch ready for us. We'll be back before you know it."

You won't, I thought, since retrieving the Maserati was probably the easier of the jobs they had in mind. Still, recovering the car gave them a good reason for being up in the area of the cabin in a heavy downpour.

"Tell you what," said James seeing, as we all did, the troubled look on Abby's face. "Before we leave, I'll get you one of the sat-phones from the office. I'll take one with me and that way you can talk to me any time you feel like it. How's that?"

"You've got sat-phones?" I said, not quite believing it. They were just things I'd heard about on TV.

"The estate has," said James. "Folk working in the more remote areas usually take one with them. Just in case, you know. Ordinary cell-phone coverage is so diabolical around here."

"I can show you how to use it," said Abby, perking up. "It's dead easy."

I grinned at her. She was half my age but was at least twice as competent when it came to technology.

"A deal," I said, "but you've got to help me with lunch."

Everything settled, the morning then proceeded smoothly and unhurriedly, at least for Abby and me. Once she'd waved off James and Cherry, she wanted me to keep her company while she showered and dressed. It was no hardship, and she reciprocated when it was my turn to get dressed. All the while, she chatted on without ever mentioning the events of yesterday. Occasionally, she paused and a distant look came into her eyes, but she quickly picked up the thread of what she was saying or jumped to some entirely new topic. She talked about her favourite toys, the pictures on the walls of her room, and then my room, the clothes she always kept here ready for when she visited, the things she enjoyed doing with Freddy the housekeeper, horses, her pony and how much she was missing her best friend, Debbie.

Not once did she enquire about Andy, where he was or how he was. I wondered about that.

Once we were back in the kitchen, she showed me how to use the sat-phone to speak to her dad. I was amazed at the sound quality. Above his voice, I could hear the rain pattering on the roof of whatever vehicle he was sitting in. They had driven round to the golf club and borrowed some sort of tractor, a cat he called it, and they were just about to pull the Maserati backwards up the track, Cherry in the car and James in, or should it be on, the cat. I just couldn't imagine what that looked like and Abby, for once, couldn't explain. Of Borisov's BMW there was no sign. The Russian had obviously made his own arrangements.

Satisfied that all was well, Abby suggested a hot chocolate before we started thinking about lunch.

"Hot chocolate sounds good," said a voice which caused Abby to swing around in alarm, until she recognised the man entering the kitchen.

Barrie placed a tray containing empty glasses and plates on the counter.

"Do you want me to wash these up?" he asked.

"I'll put them in the dishwasher," said Abby, having recovered from her surprise. "Sorry Doctor Harwood, I'd forgotten you were here."

"That's OK, Abby. People forget about me all the time."

She smiled up at him.

"No they don't."

He returned her smile, and I was glad to see that his face, if not his mind, had shed the worry and anxiety of yesterday. I suspected that he knew as well as I did that the last thing Abby needed to see around her was uneasiness and fear. He caught my eye and gave the briefest of nods.

"You did mention chocolate, didn't you?" he asked.

"Sure," said Abby. "Do you want some?"

"Not just me," said Barrie. "I think Angie might be persuaded to take some as well."

That gave us something else to think about. Leaving Abby to show Barrie how to make four mugs of drinking chocolate in the microwave, I nipped upstairs to see Angie. She was still in bed, but she looked so much better I could scarcely believe it. I was all set to reassure her, but it seemed that Barrie had already done a good job. She still couldn't remember what had happened at the hospital, which I suspected was no bad thing, but she knew very well what had happened in her room the previous afternoon. She asked me if the man had been sent by Mellisse, so I told her he had but that it had all been sorted now, and Mellisse wouldn't be bothering us anymore. Barrie had told her that already, so she accepted what I said without further questions, except for one.

"Lizzie, what's going to happen to us?"

"Well," I said. "I'm going to be looking after Abby for a while, but… …" and I smiled down at her, "… … if you're worried about what's going to happen to you, I think your good doctor might have some ideas."

Puzzlement flashed across her face, but it disappeared when she noticed what I'm sure was a definite twinkle in my eyes. Realisation dawned.

"No, Lizzie… … Do you really think so?"

I hoped I hadn't spoken out of turn and raised hopes where there was no hope, but the look on Barrie's face when he came into the room with two steaming mugs of hot chocolate told me I needn't have worried. I happily left them to it.

When I reached the top of the stairs, Abby was standing at the bottom waiting for me. I suddenly wished Barrie hadn't left her alone, even for such a short time. I wondered if she'd asked him anything about yesterday. What might he have said?

"Hey Abby," I said, starting down. "Missing me already?"

She smiled, as I hoped she would, but didn't answer. When I reached the bottom step she took my hand and we walked side by side to the sitting room. She'd placed our mugs on the coffee table near the settee. We sat, still side by side. I reached for the mug nearest me and took a sip. It was hot and strong.

"Taste's good, Abby. Just what I needed."

She left her mug alone, and turned sideways so she could see me better.

"Can I ask you something, Lizzie? About yesterday?"

I set my mug down and took her hand.

"You can ask me anything you want, Abby. Anything. Anytime. I'll try and give you a straight answer, and I promise I'll never lie to you. But before you ask your questions, let me just tell you this."

I paused for a moment to sort out what I wanted to say without breaking the promise I'd just made to her.

"The thing you need to know, Abby… … those men who were such a nuisance yesterday… … it was nothing to do with you, or even your dad really."

Her eyes narrowed and her forehead creased. She was listening but not quite understanding.

"It was about me, Abby. Those men wanted me to do something… … something bad… … and I really didn't want to do it… … They pretended to be cross with you to try and force me to do what they wanted, because they knew I'd never let anyone hurt you… … never. If your dad hadn't come, with Andy, I would have done what they wanted. It was all a kind of a game really… … I don't know whether you remember this, but one of the men said that the person who'd put them up to this had told them not to hurt you."

Her eyes drifted off as she thought about that, and then she nodded.

"But who told them to do it, Lizzie?"

"It started with someone I used to know. He was not a nice man so I ran away."

"And came to us."

I smiled at that. She said it as though it was the most natural thing in the world.

"Yes, I came to you. And your dad tried to help me. Then these other men got involved and it all got very complicated. That's why your dad wanted us to come up here. So we'd be safe, out of the way."

"But we weren't."

"No… … but it's all OK now. Your dad sorted it all out and the bad men have gone away. You'll never see any of them again, and neither will I."

"Hmmm." She thought that over.

"But what about the man who sent them?"

I wanted to close this down if I could, to reassure her without having to go into too much detail.

"Do you remember that man who came at the end?"

She nodded. "I didn't really like him."

"Sensible girl," I said. "But he actually helped us. He agreed with your dad to see the man who started this and to make sure he doesn't bother us anymore."

"Can he do that?"

"Your dad thinks so, and so does someone else... ... with a funny name that I can't quite remember... ... er... ...Begovitch, maybe."

Her face was immediately transformed into one huge smile.

"Uncle Osman!" she exclaimed. "Silly... ... It's not Begovitch. It's Izetbegović. Does he know about this?"

I nodded. "So your dad says."

"Oh well... ... That's all right then."

I had, it seems, finally spoken the magic word. Abby relaxed, and so did I. For the last few minutes, I had been horribly afraid of saying the wrong thing, of sparking a memory that she would find upsetting, even frightening. My back actually ached from the tension, but that now began to ease.

Abby reached for her mug and sipped tentatively, testing the temperature. Then her face drew back sharply and she peered at the mug her face clearly expressing distaste. I laughed. She had a brown smudge on her lips. She had left the hot chocolate just long enough for it to form a skin on the surface. That skin now dangled across her mouth.

"Ugghh," she said, looking around for a tissue. She found one in a box on the narrow shelf below the coffee table, did the job and then, because I was still smiling, threw the crumpled tissue at me.

We both laughed and I knew she was going to be OK.

One Hundred and Five

Hunter's Court –Lunchtime

Sir Vernon Laycock was indulging himself with a late lunch away from the press and the voters. Hunter's Court was quiet, his wife having taken it into her head to assist the campaign by offering elderly ladies a lift to the polling station in her new Bentley Continental GT. Promising her husband that she wouldn't actually offer them bribes, she had cruised off to enjoy herself.

Laycock wasn't the kind of man who craved attention, but nor was he usually fazed by it. He had long since mastered the skills for controlling wayward boards of directors across the wide spectrum of FerroTech companies, and delivering a speech in a packed auditorium held no terrors for him. Early morning appearances on Breakfast TV were never a chore.

Today, however, was different.

Earlier that morning, while being interviewed by a reporter from the local TV news, his mobile phone had vibrated in his pocket. When he had finally been able to turn away from the camera and read the message, the screen said simply, ***Can't find her. Call me.***

Canny enough not to risk being overheard in public, Laycock had waited until the convenient excuse of a lunch break gave him opportunity to make the call. In the seclusion of his library, with a plate of smoked salmon sandwiches in front of him and a bottle of Principessa Gavia Gavi at his elbow, he scrolled down the list of contacts in his mobile phone. He was looking for the number of a highly efficient, extremely exclusive and inordinately expensive private detective agency.

"Omega Personal Consultants, Mandy speaking. How may we help you?"

The voice in his ear was quietly seductive, the words clearly enunciated, their tone filled with echoes of Cheltenham Ladies' College.

"Michael Haslam, please," said Sir Vernon.

"May I ask who is calling, sir?"

"Laycock. Tell him I'm returning his call."

"Thank you, sir. Please hold for one moment."

And one moment was all it took before Omega's CEO came on the line.

"Sir Vernon. Thank you for getting back to me."

Laycock wasted no time in coming to the point.

"What do you mean, you can't find her?"

"Just that, I'm afraid. We've used the photograph you gave us in all those locations you mentioned, but nothing came up."

"You were discreet, I hope."

"Very, Sir Vernon. Trust me, you have nothing to worry about. The problem is… … Diane Thomas is a very elusive young lady and she doesn't show up in any official records. Which is to say… … there are any number who do show up, but none are the one we're looking for… … Erm… …"

The pause suggested more bad news was coming, and Laycock braced himself.

"The thing is," Haslam continued, "we tried that contact number you had for setting up your… … meetings. Every time it just kept going to voicemail which, of course, we ignored. Anyway, this morning one of our people tried it again and she actually got through. The phone was answered… … by an officer of the West Midlands Police."

Haslam waited to give Laycock time to react.

"Go on," was all he said.

"The police can't trace the calls back to us. The phone we used was a throwaway. The officer wanted to know who we were and why we were calling, but wouldn't give anything away about why he was answering this Thomas girl's phone… … But… … I wonder if you've been watching the news lately."

Laycock was puzzled.

"I have, but what in particular?"

"The shooting at Birmingham airport and that raid on some brothel, also in Birmingham, early this morning."

Laycock remained quiet, thinking hard. He had heard both reports but hadn't made any connection between them.

Haslam broke into his thoughts.

"We've… … er… … developed a source in the local news networks and our information is that the police are linking the two events."

"Are you certain about that?" Laycock asked in a voice that suggested he already knew the answer.

"As far as we can be. Should have confirmation before the end of the day."

That might explain why Gordon Russell wasn't answering his phone. Laycock had tried to get hold of him several times since he caught the item on the news about the shooting of Mitchell Portess. Occasionally, an employee of a FerroTech company working in less well policed environments might fall victim to some form of local violence, but never had one been shot dead in the UK, in broad daylight while in police custody. Laycock was looking to Russell for some answers, but so far he hadn't even been able to ask his questions.

"Are you thinking that Diane Thomas might have been rounded up in this morning's raid?"

"Unlikely, Sir Vernon, but it is possible. First indications seem to be that most of the girls found in the house were recent immigrants from Lithuania, but there was another who hasn't been identified and who we don't know anything about."

"Could that be Diane?" asked Laycock.

"We're trying to find out."

Laycock wondered about the girls rounded up by the police. Russell had been developing contacts in Lithuania and Portess had been his man on the ground there. So what the hell had been going on at Lichfield Tube Company? He made a mental note to send one of his trouble-shooters over there as soon as this phone call was over.

"Look, Michael," he said, returning to the issue of Diane Thomas. "The deal is still the same. I've given you the money, so find Diane and make the offer. She's to go back to that island she was always talking about and stay there. It seems it's what she always wanted to do, so there shouldn't be any problem. As I said before, I'll leave it to you to sort out the details but make sure she signs that non-disclosure agreement about what she did and who she met while in the UK. And she's not to know that this comes from me."

"I understand that, Sir Vernon. We'll keep on it, and I'll be in touch as soon as we have anything more."

The call over, Laycock leant back in his chair and thought about what he'd been told. He had always believed Diane Thomas to be a fairly high-priced escort, but she'd always been good company and the cost never interested him. He had never associated her with any kind of sex-trafficking operation. He had assumed she enjoyed what she did, or at least tolerated it as a means of earning enough money to go back home to St Helena.

But maybe he'd been wrong. Maybe he'd completely misread the situation which unsettled him because he wasn't used to making such mistakes.

It unsettled him also because he liked Diane. He hated the thought that she'd met with him under duress, and had done what she did out of fear. He hated the thought because, if true, it meant that he was an exploiter of a vulnerable young woman, purely for his own gratification, and that was going to be hard to live with.

But maybe it wasn't true. Maybe Diane had nothing to do with these recent events in the news. Maybe Omega would find her and offer her the opportunity she said she always wanted.

Sighing, he reached for a sandwich and took a small bite as his brain changed gear.

Now who should he send to check up on Gordon Russell and avert a potential screw-up at Lichfield Tube?

One Hundred and Six

Elmford Cross – Early afternoon

Joanne Hayford, driving her own Focus ST2, drew up at the kerb behind DI Cobham's Volvo. Before leaving Birmingham, she had phoned Lichfield Tube to discover whether Gordon Russell would be in his office that afternoon. Not wanting to give him a heads-up on the impending interview, she hadn't identified herself to the lady on reception who had taken her call. She'd been told that Russell had booked the day off weeks earlier, in order to help with the election, transporting old ladies to the polls, that sort of thing. Turning down the offer of speaking to David, the personal assistant with no surname, Joanne had hung up.

If he was driving around the neighbourhood giving people lifts, Russell might be hard to track down, but Joanne wondered whether his wife might know which polling station he was taking them to. It was worth the try, as she explained to Cobham, but this time they decided not to phone ahead. As it turned out, that was probably just as well since, when they turned in at the gate, they saw Russell's Mazda sitting on the drive in front of the garage

As she followed the DI up the drive, Joanne wondered whether Mrs Russell would remember her last visit. If she did, things could get awkward. Joanne had interviewed her without identifying herself as a police officer and at a time when she was officially on leave. Cobham would certainly take a dim view of that if he were to find out. Joanne found herself praying, to a god she didn't believe in, that Mrs Russell had been so tanked up that she would remember very little of their previous meeting.

At the door, Cobham hesitated briefly as he chose between pressing the bell-push and using the knocker. The knocker won and he rapped loudly. Joanne waited as calmly as she could to see who answered the door. She wondered if this little trip was going to open up the case, or whether it would turn out to be a fruitless dead-end.

Mrs Russell, elegantly dressed in a pale mauve blouse and a patterned skirt several shades darker, opened the door slowly. She rested one hand on the edge, but today did not look in need of its support. Her eyes were bright and alert with makeup carefully applied. Joanne wondered if she were dressed for the jamboree that usually accompanied the declaration of election results.

"Mrs Russell?" asked Cobham, and then went on in response to her nod, "I'm Detective Inspector Cobham and this is Detective Sergeant Hayford."

While speaking, he held up his ID and Joanne did the same. Mrs Russell paid little attention to the IDs but fixed her eyes instead on Joanne's face.

"We've met before, I think?" she said slowly, the words coming out more as a question than a statement.

"That's right, Mrs Russell," replied Joanne, with more confidence than she actually felt.

"Hmm … … You were… … kind to me, I think."

"I… … er… … well, I tried to be, Mrs Russell."

Cobham looked from one to the other, momentarily curious, but not enough to follow it up.

"We'd like to talk to your husband, Mrs Russell. Is he at home?"

As if on cue, they heard a male voice from inside the house.

"Who is it, Judith."

"It's a lady and gentleman for you, Gordon," she called over her shoulder, opening the door wide. "They're from… …"

She was interrupted by the sound of glass hitting a hard surface. This was followed by a strange scuffling, and the sound of something like a heavy book falling to the floor. Russell appeared through an open door on the right of the hallway. His face was white and full of apprehension as he peered at his visitors.

"Are you all right, darling?" asked his wife, looking slightly puzzled.

Joanne was puzzled as well. There was no reason for him to be nervous. His wife had referred to them only as a lady and gentleman. She hadn't got as far as mentioning the police. And why was he at home when he was supposed to be ferrying old ladies about?

Russell stared at them wide-eyed before appearing to relax slightly.

"Er, yes… … yes, I'm fine. Ask them to come in."

Mrs Russell did so and showed them into the room to which her husband had retreated. They found Russell in front of a settee bending to pick up a largish book whose colourful dust jacket said something about the East India Company. He straightened one of the inside pages which had become bent over when it fell.

"You're interested in maritime history," offered Cobham in a friendly tone.

Russell closed the book and placed it on a nearby coffee table. Before answering, he reached down towards the fireplace to retrieve a heavy whiskey tumbler which lay on its side on the stone hearth. Joanne noticed that he had regained some of his normal colour, and his eyes were no longer wide-eyed with anxiety.

"I served in the Royal Navy for a while," he said, straightening up. "The sea... ... it kind of sticks with you."

He placed the tumbler on a coaster next to the book.

"I'm sure it must, sir," said Cobham, once again holding up his ID. "I'm Detective Inspector Cobham and this is... ..."

"I know. I know," interrupted Russell. "Sergeant Hayford, isn't it? Do you know... ... I've been half expecting you."

He gestured at Cobham. "This is your boss, I suppose."

"Not exactly, sir," replied Joanne. "DI Cobham is a colleague from another force. We're working together. Actually we weren't really expecting to find you at home. Your office said you were... ... er... ... involved in the election."

"I see. Well... ... the fact is, I had a rather rough night so I opted to do the six until ten shift this evening. Give myself a bit of a break. So, is it me you want, or Judith?"

"You really, sir," said Joanne. "Since you're here."

"Right," said Russell, frowning a little as his eyes flicked to and fro between his visitors. "Look, won't you sit down. Judith will make us a cup of tea and you can tell me what this is all about. And then... ... there's something I think I need to tell you."

That sounded interesting so, when they were comfortably seated, with Joanne and Cobham in easy chairs and Russell at one end of the settee, Cobham tried to jump straight in with his questions but Russell cut him off.

"I *will* answer your questions, Inspector, but I'd like my wife to be present. It's time... ... past time... ... that she heard the full story."

Cobham nodded as if he understood, but then glanced towards the door as though willing Mrs Russell to appear with the tea so that he could get on with his questions. To avoid the silence prolonging to the point of embarrassment, Joanne decided to make a harmless enquiry.

"Is the East India Company a particular interest of yours, sir?"

Russell glanced at the book lying on the coffee table and smiled, grateful it seemed to have something innocuous to talk about.

"It is, it is. Did you know that the Honourable East India Company ruled India for over a hundred years before the Crown took over in 1858?"

He seemed to savour giving the company its full name, and Joanne wondered if she detected some slight emphasis on the word **honourable.**

"No, I can't say I did know that, sir," said Cobham in a tone that suggested he wasn't particularly interested. Joanne ignored her colleague and kept the conversation going for the few minutes needed for the tea to appear.

It was served in Denby mugs and poured from a matching teapot. Once she was happy that everyone was satisfied with the colour and sweetness of their drink, Mrs Russell joined her husband on the settee. The little interlude seemed to have settled him down so that he was much more like the confident executive whom Joanne had met at Lichfield Tube.

"OK, Inspector, it's over to you now. Ask away."

"Thank you, sir," said Cobham, glancing at Joanne to make sure her notebook was out.

"Can I ask first of all whether a Mitchell Portess is a colleague of yours?"

"Indeed he is... ... or was."

"I see, sir. So you are aware that he died yesterday?"

"Shot whilst in police custody was how the TV news put it," replied Russell. "Careless of somebody, wasn't it?"

Cobham winced.

"That's something which is still being investigated, sir. Did you know that Mitchell Portess was involved in the illegal trafficking of young women into this country?"

There was a pause and Joanne noticed Judith Russell's free hand reach along the settee towards her husband, her face showing no surprise at the question.

"I was aware of that, yes."

Cobham sat up, surprised. He hadn't expected it to be this easy.

"So, when did you become aware?"

Russell's hand now crept towards his wife's and covered it in a light grip.

"It was about six months ago, when Phil Simmons told me about it."

Cobham turned to look at Joanne.

"Isn't that... ...?" he began.

"Yes, sir," said Joanne. "Phil Simons is my case."

She glared at Russell, angry that this was only now coming out.

"So Simmons knew about Portess and the trafficking?" she said, as evenly as she could.

"Yes."

"Before you?"

"Yes."

"And you've only just decided to tell us. Why is that?"

"Because Portess is dead."

"That makes a difference?"

"Of course it makes a bloody difference."

Joanne glanced at Cobham, but he seemed content for the moment to let her run with it.

"Why does Portess being dead make a difference?"

Judith Russell slid along the settee right up close to her husband. She lifted his hand and held it in her lap.

"Tell them, Gordon. It's time you got it off your chest."

Russell gave her a tight smile, and sighed.

"I know." He looked from Joanne to Cobham and back again. "Judy knows some of this, but not everything. It all began some years ago when Portess and I were serving on the same ship. He happened to see me do something… … actually, fail to do something… … which gave him some hold over me. Oh, it wasn't illegal; nothing like that. Just cowardice really. I behaved badly and he knew it, and threatened to report it to the captain. He was coming out of the Navy about the same time as me and knew I had an engineering job lined up with FerroTech. He wanted me to see him right. That's how he put it. *See me right.* It really didn't seem a big thing so I managed to get him a job in the group."

Joanne was frowning.

"Was this with Lichfield Tube?"

"Not at first, no. I went to Lichfield as MD about five years ago and Portess came with me. I didn't want him, and I'm sure he knew that, but I was stuck with him."

He turned to his wife, but continued to address Joanne.

"He'd met Judy at some event or other and he came to me one day soon afterwards and said what a shame it would be if some pervert were to break into the house while I was at work… … and have some fun with her. I knew he had some dodgy friends. It was obvious what he meant and… … I couldn't let it happen. Until this minute, Judy didn't know about that. I never told her."

His eyes flicked to Joanne and then back to his wife.

"I didn't want you to be afraid of being in the house on your own. I was sure nothing would happen as long as I did as he wanted."

Judith reached out and pulled his head in close until their foreheads touched. They stayed like that for a long moment and neither Joanne nor Cobham interrupted. Then Judith pulled away and looked at Joanne.

"I may have told you, the other night, that Portess had some hold over my husband."

Joanne nodded.

"It was the nightmares that gave it away; he'd be tossing and turning, crying out in the night. Then one night he told me it was Portess forcing him to turn a blind eye to… … well, to stuff he'd found out. That was it. He never told me what it was that Portess was threatening him with. Until now, I never knew what it was."

She pulled her husband close again.

"I wish I'd known... ... I've been stupid... ... I ended up starting to despise you... ... thinking you were weak, and all the time you were trying to protect me. And then I found that bank book... ..."

Cobham seized on that.

"What book would that be?" he asked quickly.

The couple on the settee looked at him, frowning as though angry at his intrusion into their private moment.

"It's not relevant to Portess," said Russell at length. "But I will tell you about it later."

Cobham hesitated, allowing them their moment, but then went on to ask the question that had been hovering on his lips.

"Why was Portess so keen to come to Lichfield Tube?"

Russell eased away from his wife and sat up straight.

"At the time, I didn't know. Later, it turned out that it was our Lithuanian business that interested him."

"And what sort of business would that be, sir?" pursued Cobham.

Russell hesitated for a moment and Joanne wondered if there was some prevarication coming, but it turned out that he was just pausing to get his thoughts in order.

"You have to understand," he said, "that, in the run-up to 2000, LTC was one of the worst performers in the FerroTech group. I had a plan for restructure and development to take the company forward which I put to the chairman of the group and... ..."

"That would be Sir Vernon Laycock," said Joanne. "Is that right?"

"Absolutely," replied Russell. "He put me in as MD and gave me five years to turn the business around. Part of my plan involved getting hold of machine tools from Lithuania. Good quality, low cost. I'd also discovered that the machine-tool company also had a nice line in couplings and fittings – brass and copper – you know what I mean?"

"Yes, I think we get the picture, sir," said Cobham. "But why did this interest Portess?"

Russell smiled. "I wondered that, but I didn't ask. All he wanted from me was to be given control of the Lithuanian imports. Whenever there was a deal to be done, he was the guy who got on a plane to Vilnius. To be honest, he was pretty good at it. He made some sweet deals, and business was definitely picking up. We were on a roll and I almost forgot about his threats... ... until about six months ago."

He paused and reached for his mug of tea. There was silence while he sipped at it thoughtfully. Cobham tried to keep the momentum going.

"What happened six months ago, sir?"

Russell lowered his mug and let it rest on his thigh.

"Phil came to me one day… … He chose his time well… … Portess was out of the country… … Anyway, he said that one of our customers wasn't happy with the quality of the tubes we'd supplied for a new range of heat exchangers they were building. Up until then, we'd been getting our copper from Finland and the brass from Germany, but Portess had found a new source which claimed to be able to supply all our copper and copper alloys to the highest spec including NES and ASTM… … And, as you've probably guessed, it was a good deal cheaper."

He took another sip of his tea.

"I wasn't a fool. We didn't rush into it. Just a few sample orders to start with. Our buying team were happy, and the quality guys did their tests and were satisfied. We insisted on original mill certificates and everything seemed OK so eventually we increased the orders."

He turned to his wife and gave her a rueful smile.

"I should have known something wasn't right when Portess insisted on visiting this new mill on his own. Our chief purchasing officer wanted to go as well but Portess told me he didn't want him, and made it clear that's how it was going to be. I let him have his way… … as usual."

Cobham interrupted the flow.

"I'm afraid you're losing me a bit here. What has this to do with Phil Simmons?"

"Phil used to work for a company called Salisbury Marine. The company folded a while back and that's when Phil joined us. Salisbury went under because of a massive fraud dreamt up by its MD John Salisbury. I don't remember all the details except that it involved buying cut-price tubes from places like India or Brazil and passing them off as top-notch gear from Finland or the US. Phil had spotted something was dodgy and then when it all came unravelled he was able to make sense of what had been going on."

He paused for a breath and to make sure his listeners were still with him.

"Phil told me he suspected the same thing was happening at LTC and it worried him because we had some big overseas contracts coming up. I told him not to worry and I'd look into it… … which meant asking Portess what the hell he thought he was playing at. It had to be Portess and his new friends in Lithuania."

Joanne was just about keeping up.

"You mean Portess was importing low-grade stuff from this Lithuanian mill and then… … what? Falsifying documents to make it look as though it came from somewhere else?"

"Yes and no. He was falsifying documents, yes... ... but the tubes weren't made in a Lithuanian mill. They were coming into Lithuania from India, and then they were just re-crated and shipped on to us. The price was good for the high-spec tubes we asked for, but way over the top for the rubbish they actually were... ... I confronted Portess, of course, and that's when he told me what was going on. He made no bones about it... ... seemed actually quite proud of it. He claimed he'd put LTC back on the map and I was just as much a party to it as he was."

He licked his lips and looked a little sheepish.

"The thing is... ... well, my name was on some of the false test certs. That was Portess's doing. Insurance to make sure I wouldn't be able to talk if I found out what he was up to. That's when I asked him about the girls. Phil had been trying to track down the tube fraud but he'd dug up some other stuff as well. It was well buried but Phil was a bright lad. He found computer files with employee records for girls who didn't work for us and... ... well a whole load of stuff. Your tech guys shouldn't have any problem finding it... ... assuming Portess hasn't wiped the lot. I didn't mention Phil to Portess. I pretended I'd found the files and asked him straight what was going on. He said it was private business and I was to keep my nose out if I didn't want something nasty to happen to Judy."

He looked down at the carpet and shook his head.

"I was appalled, but there was nothing I could do. Portess said if I mentioned to anyone else what I'd found out my career would be ruined and I'd end up in jail as an accessory... ... which would pretty well finish my marriage since things hadn't been going too well for a while anyway. If I wanted to keep Judy safe, I was to forget about the girls. It wasn't that hard. I hadn't actually seen them. Portess told me all I had to do was look the other way when necessary, and he'd sort it."

He continued to look at the carpet while his wife put her arm around him and leant her cheek against his shoulder.

Cobham jumped in quickly.

"Who was Portess working with? Not the tube business... ... the girls. Who was he importing them for? Where did he take them? Who paid him?"

The questions seemed to batter Russell, and from the slump of his shoulders, Joanne sensed a breakthrough coming.

"I really can't tell you," he said finally, disappointing both police officers. "I wish I could, but I was never involved in that side of things."

"Are you sure you don't know," Cobham persisted.

"Absolutely," said Russell, and Joanne wondered whether she believed him. Maybe he was just keeping quiet to protect himself and his wife. Owning up to fraud in his company was one thing, but spilling the goods on importing girls for the sex trade was something else entirely. If he was hiding something, she wasn't sure she could blame him. Then Mrs Russell spoke, quietly, just for her husband.

"You should have told me, Gordon," she said. "Everything. I would never have left you. Not if I'd understood."

"I couldn't," he said, in a very low voice. "I've been ashamed for too long… … so ashamed it hurts."

There was silence for a moment. In the quiet, Joanne and Cobham looked at each other. In the end, it was Joanne who asked the next question.

"Are you saying, sir, that you knew that Portess was going to kill Phil Simmons?"

He looked up, his eyes wide open in surprise.

"Good Lord, no! In fact things seemed to settle down over the next few months. Nothing more was said, except… … Phil seemed a little cagey around me. Anyway, he never mentioned the quality of the tubes again, or the other records he'd found. I assumed Portess had sold him some story, or maybe threatened him. Whatever… … it all went quiet."

The room was so quiet, Joanne could hear Russell's breathing. It seemed laboured and uneven, but she had to persist.

"You mentioned feeling ashamed, Mr Russell. Ashamed for a long time. Is there something you still haven't told us?"

Russell looked straight at her, and she saw sadness and pain in his eyes. He took a few slow breaths to calm himself before speaking.

"That, Sergeant Hayford, is quite another story. It began ten years ago on a small island in the South Atlantic… … and it's haunted me ever since."

One Hundred and Seven

Aullton House – Early afternoon

Lunch was a bit of a problem at first, mainly because we had no idea what to make. The first task was to search around to see what we had available. There was plenty of stuff in the freezer, but not so much in the fridge. At least, nothing that really took our fancy. Next stop Freddy.

We tried phoning her office and then her cottage, but with no success. I didn't think the mobile would be much use but Abby said if we used the house phone we might get her on her mobile if she was off the estate. She was right. Freddy explained that she was down in the village visiting one of the estate tenants. We had the phone on speaker so we could both hear. Abby pulled a face.

"They don't sell much in the village."

Freddy overheard.

"Don't worry," she said. "I think the fish van's still here. I'll nip out and see what he's got. Oh… … how many is this for?"

"Four," said Abby.

"Five," I said, thinking about Barrie. "No, six."

Mustn't forget Angie. She might be ready for something tasty.

"Is that for Andy?" whispered Abby.

"OK," I said to Freddy. "Better make it seven."

"Any advance on that?" asked Freddy, and we heard a chuckle at the other end of the line.

"No," said Abby and I together.

"OK, I'll see what I can get and have it there in… … say, half an hour."

Once we'd rung off, I turned to Abby and said, "Fish van?"

She looked as puzzled as I felt.

"Dunno," she said. "Probably a man who drives around the villages selling fish… … in a van."

We both laughed. I was so pleased to hear that sound. Earlier that morning, I don't think James or I expected to hear Abby laughing at anything that day, maybe even for some days to come.

"OK," I said, hoping to keep the mood going. "Apart from chips, I've no idea what to do with fish, so you'll have to cook them."

The result of this was a search through the kitchen cupboards for any cookbook that might have something helpful to say about fish. We didn't find many… … books, that is. Of the few there were, the most promising was a big, brown-covered, rather heavy volume that had obviously had some use.

"This was Mum's," said Abby, opening it up very carefully on the kitchen counter. Written by a lady called Delia – her first name was in much bigger letters than her very common surname – it had been published years before Abby was born, and turned out to be a real treasure-trove. While we waited for Freddy, we learnt how to marinate kippers, bake cod, souse herrings, deep-fry sprats and grill trout. The only trouble was... ... we had no idea what sort of fish we'd be given to cook.

Still, we wouldn't be able to start cooking whatever it was until we knew what time James and Cherry expected to get back. I was reluctant to let Abby use the sat-phone again in case we interrupted them in the middle of blowing up the cabin, or burning it down, but it was a needless worry. The phone rang just before Freddy turned up with the fish.

The conversation was brief but apparently everything had gone well and they expected to be back with us inside half-an-hour. They were as well, arriving just before two o'clock, thoroughly soaked but pleased with themselves for a job well done. The Maserati, it seemed, was none the worse for its brief burst of off-roading.

While Abby and I prepared the dining table for lunch, James and Cherry went off to change out of their wet clothes. The meal turned out to be a leisurely affair. None of us was in any mood to hurry, and we had no deadlines to drive us. Conversation was generally light-hearted, and we found no end of things to talk about, including the many and various ways of cooking fish. In our case, the fish we'd practised on was trout. Freddy had provided seven good-sized rainbow trout from the man with the van, a couple of onions and green peppers from her own vegetable store, and a crusty bloomer loaf which she'd baked early that morning. We supplemented that with chips and peas from the freezer and were really quite proud of the result. Whether Delia would have been proud of our grilled trout stuffed with onions and peppers is, perhaps, in doubt, but it went down well with everyone but Angie who only managed about half of hers.

For those still hungry, the men rather than us ladies, there was a blackberry and apple pie from the freezer with vanilla ice-cream for those who fancied it. Of course, we had to wait for the pie to cook which meant that it was just gone four o'clock by the time we were done. Barrie stayed to have coffee with the others in the sitting room while I went up to check on Angie.

I paused in the corridor outside her room and looked along to where the door to Andy's room stood slightly open. Barrie must have left it like that when he nipped up to collect Andy's tray after lunch. He was the only one of us who seemed to be giving our wounded friend any attention and I wondered whether he knew that it was Andy who had wielded the needle that had reduced Angie to her current condition. Maybe, given his doctor's ethics, it wouldn't have made any difference to his care for Andy, but I knew I wasn't ready yet to face the person who had been ready to kill Angie, and put Abby's mental and emotional health at risk.

I opened Angie's door and left Andy to his suffering, rather pleased with myself that I didn't actually hope that he was suffering.

"Hey, girl," said Angie, trying to push herself upright against the pillows.

"Hi," I said. "Here, let me help you with those."

I helped her ease forward so I could adjust the pillows, fluffing them up a bit to give her more support as she sat up in bed. She wasn't looking bad. No makeup of course, and her hair could do with a wash but, after all she'd been through, she looked a whole heap better than she had any right to expect.

"You're looking good," I said, perching myself on the edge of the bed. "How do you feel?"

"I'm fine now, just sitting here… … a bit wobbly though if I get out of bed… … I can just about take myself to the bathroom if I take it steady and hold onto things."

I nodded. "That's good."

She shivered and pulled the bedclothes a little higher.

"I was in there when that bastard came to get me yesterday. Thank God Andy was here."

So maybe Barrie didn't know about Andy's treachery or, if he did, he hadn't let on to Angie. She clearly hadn't remembered yet what had happened at the hospital, and I was beginning to think it might be better if she never did.

"Thank God," I echoed, and realised that I actually meant it. "Look Angie… … we're not telling Abby about that guy yesterday. She knows about the others but… …"

Angie laid a hand on mine. "It's OK, Di – or should I call you Lizzie now – anyway, Barrie told me about keeping quiet. I won't say anything. No point in upsetting the kid."

Barrie told her. Not **the doctor** or **Doctor Harwood.** Barrie.

"Thanks," I said. "And, yeah… … it is Lizzie. Elizabeth Isobel Burleigh. Looks like I'm back to being my real self again."

Angie was quiet and I felt her grip on my hand tighten. I looked closely at her and was surprised to see her eyes glazing over with tears.

"I always was my real self, Lizzie," she said quietly. "I don't have anyone else to be."

I didn't know what to say, and was quiet as I tried hard to think of something. Then it came. Maybe because I'd just told her my real name.

"Angie, my mum used to tell me a story. She didn't read it. She knew it so well she could just tell it to me. It was about a lady called Elizabeth – Mum said they named me after her – and this Elizabeth Bennett met a man she didn't like. Do you know the story? It's been on TV."

"I think so. You mean **Pride and Prejudice?**"

"That's it. Have you seen it?"

"Once," she said, and frowned. "But it must have been about ten years ago. I can't remember it all."

"Doesn't matter," I said. "But here's the thing. This man who Elizabeth – Lizzie –met was called Darcy. In the story he changed. My mum used to say he didn't really change… … but the good part that was always really there was able to come out, all because he met Lizzie."

She looked at me searchingly, her mind ticking over slowly. I realised she didn't get it. She used to be a lot sharper than this.

"Angie," I said, trying to find the words to explain. "I've only known you for three years, but I can see there's always been good in you. Now you've met someone, that good is going to have a chance to come out. You can be the person you were meant to be… … if you want to."

I watched her closely to see whether my words were having any effect and, for a moment or two, I wasn't sure. She still held onto my hand, but her gaze was now fixed on a hump in the duvet, right where her toes would be. I couldn't make out whether her mind had just gone blank or whether she was thinking hard about what I had said. Eventually she sighed and turned her head slightly. Her eyes were still downcast so that it seemed as though she was looking at the duvet but I doubted she was actually seeing it.

"Are you going to stay with them, Lizzie?"

It wasn't quite what I'd expected.

"With James and Abby?" I asked. "Yes, I think so."

Now she lifted her eyes and looked at me directly.

"So what will happen to me? Where will I go?"

Her voice was quiet but insistent. These were questions she really needed an answer to.

"Who can I stay with? And don't go talking about Barrie. He hardly knows me."

"I think Barrie would like to get to know you and while he does that… … you can stay with us. I know James won't mind."

I was going out on a bit of a limb here, but I'd seen the way Barrie looked at her and was as sure as I could be that there was a growing attraction there. It wasn't as if he didn't know her background, but he still seemed to be taken with her. As for where Angie would stay, I hadn't asked James about it but I couldn't believe he'd mind if she stayed on while she sorted out what to do next. Assuming Barrie didn't sort it out for her.

"It wouldn't work, Lizzie."

She was obviously getting used to my new name, but I thought she meant that staying with us wouldn't work. I was wrong.

"He's a doctor and I'm a... ..."

She searched for the appropriate word.

"I'm a sex worker," she said at last. "Isn't that what they call us these days?"

She shook her head.

"Even if he likes me... ... ..."

She trailed off.

"It wouldn't work, Lizzie."

I realised that I didn't know Dr Harwood well enough to be able to convince Angie, or even myself, that he had the strength of character to be able to live with the knowledge of her past, and to love her in spite of it. I was still trying to find some words that would reassure her, when she spoke again, her voice calm and resigned.

"He will always know what I was and, even if he tries, he'll never be able to forget it."

That jolted me. Would James ever be able to forget what I had been?

I had no time to ponder on it because a new voice spoke from the doorway.

"You're quite right," said Barrie as he came into the room, and I wondered how long he'd been standing outside the door. We both watched him as he walked slowly over to the bed. Neither of us knew what to say while he stood looking down at us, his face giving nothing away.

"I'm really sorry," he said, "but I have to confess I was eavesdropping." He smiled, ignoring me, his eyes fixed on Angie. "And I'm glad I did, because you haven't asked one important question... ... Will it matter?"

We both frowned but kept quiet, and I felt Angie's hand grip mine tightly.

"I don't hold with all James's religious views," he said, "but there is one aspect of them where he and I do agree. It really doesn't matter who you *were*. What matters is who you're going to be."

I didn't realise Angie had such strength in her, but my hand suddenly felt crushed.

"Oh, Lizzie," said Barrie, his smile fading as his eyes locked on mine. "I came up to tell you you're needed downstairs. There was a phone call."

I managed to disengage my hand without any damage to my fingers.

"Thanks," I said, looking up. "Who was it? Do you know?"

"Some female detective," he said. "It seems she's been digging into your past and needs to talk to you. Fairly urgently, I think."

I stood up slowly. I wasn't sure Sergeant Hayford would agree with James and Barrie over what really mattered.

One Hundred and Eight

Aullton Estate – Late afternoon

James told me not to worry about the police, but I knew it wasn't going to be an easy interview. In fact, I was dreading it.

Sergeant Hayford had wanted to see me so urgently that she was willing to travel all the way up to Scotland that very evening. Just to make me even more jumpy, she was bringing someone with her who, she had told James, really needed to speak to me without delay. My mind was in turmoil as I thought about all the laws I must have broken in the past three years, but I couldn't believe that it was any of those that was filling the police with such urgency. I was sure it had to be something to do with the death of my uncle that was bringing them racing northwards.

And racing they were, at around one hundred and fifty miles per hour.

Once James realised that Sergeant Hayford intended driving up almost immediately the phone call was ended, he told her he had a better idea. He thought five hours was a long time for me to be anxiously waiting to find out why I was suddenly of such interest. He had spoken to his father to track down the whereabouts of the helicopter, and discovered that both he, and it, were at Thurvaston Priory for the start of a long weekend. Thankfully, Mike Colman had more than enough flying hours left that day to make the trip to Aullton.

James had made a snap decision and, after telling me about it, confided that he was now wondering whether it had been the right one. Perhaps, having a little more time to prepare would have been helpful but, in truth, there was very little we could have done. We were in the drawing room, at opposite ends of the settee where he'd sat me down to tell me the news. Abby was in the kitchen with Cherry trying to decide which of the freezer's many offerings could be combined to make a decent dinner.

James wasn't feeling happy about the police coming to his house after what had taken place in the last twenty-four hours, and I wasn't happy that he was helping the police arrive quicker than they would have done under their own steam. Oddly, it never seemed to occur to either of us at the time that I should leave Aullton and try to dodge the police altogether.

"I know there isn't anything much for them to find," James told me. "And I don't suppose they'll be looking for anything suspicious way up here. Sergeant Hayford only seemed interested in you."

"The trouble is," I offered, "we don't know what they know."

That was it in a nutshell. And it wouldn't change whether they came to us or we went to them. All we could do was wait. And wonder.

And what I was beginning to wonder was whether the police were coming to ask me questions that I really couldn't answer. What if it wasn't about my uncle after all? What if they wanted to ask me what I knew about the trafficking, and how it was run, and who was behind it? No matter what deal James had made with Borisov, if I were to help them break through the firewall with which Mellisse surrounded himself there really would be little chance of seeing my twenty-first birthday.

As I pondered these things, Abby's voice drifted through from the kitchen.

"We don't all have to have the same, Cherry. Some can have fish and chips and peas, and others can have chicken pie with roast potatoes and peas... ... and gravy, I suppose... ... if they want."

I saw James smiling.

"She's just like her mum," he said, and then the smile faded. "I wouldn't have hesitated to drive you down myself, Lizzie, and whisk Abby away from here, except... ... she seems so happy. I don't understand it. It's as though yesterday never happened."

"Maybe Cherry was right," I said. "But... ... you may not have noticed with being out quite a bit... ... she hasn't wanted to go out of the apartment all day. I don't know if that means anything or not... ... and I didn't like to ask her."

The fingers of James's right hand gently massaged his chin while he thought.

"Let's wait 'til tomorrow," he said at last. "See what she's like then."

"OK," I agreed. "But about the police. I could have gone to meet them on my own, you know."

I didn't really want to meet them at all, let alone on my own.

"You can't drive," he said.

"There are trains."

"No, Lizzie. It wouldn't have done. And in any case, it's all sorted now. They'll be here in a couple of hours. Time enough for a good dinner."

Abby danced through the door right on cue.

"OK," she said in her best don't-mess-me-about voice. "Who's for fish and chips, and who wants chicken pie?"

We gave her our orders, and she skipped off back to the kitchen, from where we could faintly hear her issuing instructions to Cherry.

James's eyes lingered on the doorway through which Abby had disappeared and we sat in silence for a several moments, each of us lost in our own thoughts. Occasional snippets of conversation drifted through from the kitchen. Mostly, it was Abby's voice we heard since she was speaking more loudly than Cherry. Her chirpiness made me think again of her Uncle Osman, whose name alone had seemed to give her such confidence.

"James," I said, more tentatively than I intended. "This guy Abby calls Uncle Osman… … you and Cherry were talking about him this morning… …Who is he?"

James turned to look at me, but then his eyes drifted off as though his mind were floating far away. I wondered what he was thinking.

"James?" I prompted.

His gaze came back into the room and eventually his eyes settled on mine.

"His name is Osman Izetbegović and he's the security attaché at the Bosnian embassy… … I should say Bosnia and Herzegovina. He's very meticulous about that. He's… … well… … I met him some years ago when I was serving in Bosnia with the UN. We… … met and became friends. He's a good man to have on your side."

He smiled.

"He's known Abby all her life and I think he rather likes being called Uncle Osman."

"Hasn't he any children of his own?" I asked.

"A boy," replied James. "Well, actually he's a grown man now. I… … er… … helped him when I was out there."

I remembered what I'd heard about the Bosnian conflict; the atrocities, the horrors, the war criminals.

"Was it really bad out there?"

James didn't answer immediately, and his gaze drifted away again. I decided this time not to prompt him. He'd tell me if he wanted to.

"Whatever you've heard, Lizzie… … it was worse."

His eyes were on mine again now.

"I told Sarah what it was like when I came back. We'd not been married long, and I wanted her to know the things I'd had to do… … the things I'd seen… … and the things we couldn't do because the wretched UN wouldn't let us." He sighed. "Maybe I'll tell you one day, Lizzie, but for now I think you've got enough nightmares of your own to deal with without taking on any of mine."

I nodded but didn't press him even though I wished he would tell me. It wasn't because I was keen to hear about wartime atrocities, but because I was more than willing to share the burden of his nightmares. Perhaps, as he said, one day he would let me.

All this put me in mind of something else which I was becoming increasingly curious about. I glanced towards the door, checking that Abby was still engrossed in preparations for dinner.

"I've been wondering," I said, and then stopped, not quite sure how to phrase my question. It was now James's turn to do the prompting.

"Go on," he said.

"Well… … over the past few days, people have died… … been killed. I've been part of that… … So have you. I know we didn't ask for it to happen, and I know we didn't have any choice but… …"

James features seemed to relax a little and he smiled slightly as he sensed where my question was going. Even so, he didn't prompt me, but simply waited patiently as I stumbled over my words.

"You're… … a Christian… … I guess. I mean… … you pray and go to church and stuff. Now… … Look, I'm not saying what you… … we… … did was wrong but… … well, isn't there this commandment about not killing and such? How does that work, with you being a Christian? I mean… … being in the army, and Bosnia, and then all that's just happened."

James shifted in his seat, not uncomfortably, but just as though he was giving himself time to think through his answer. His expression didn't give the impression that he was at all fazed by my questions.

"First off, Lizzie, I was Royal Marines, not army."

"There's a difference?" I asked, realising there must be.

"You bet your life there's a difference. But that's not really what you want to know about. Your question… …about standing up for what's right even if people might get killed… …it's a good one… … a tough one as I think I said to you once before, but a good one. In fact it's such a good question that loads of people over the years have written a ton of books trying to answer it. And the trouble is… … they don't all tell you the same thing. So, you either pick the answer that suits you best, or you try to work it out for yourself."

I was puzzled.

"I thought the Bible was pretty clear on stuff like that."

"Have you read it lately?"

His voice was gentle, so I knew he wasn't trying to have a go at me, to put me on the defensive. I shook my head.

"Not since Sunday school on St Helena. But I still know stuff… … about the commandments and such."

"The commandment you're talking about actually says that you're not to murder anyone. Murder, you see; not simply kill. It makes a difference."

I thought about that, but not for long. The Bible seemed to have another card that trumped that.

"But what about Jesus telling you to love your enemies?"

I was sure I'd got that one right.

"Yes, he did say that. Which means that you don't deliberately set out to do them harm, or even think badly towards them, simply because they have made themselves your enemy. But the Bible also tells us to protect the weak and fight injustice. And don't forget, when Jesus was preparing his disciples to go out into a hostile world, he told them to sell their cloaks and buy swords."

Now I was really confused.

"So you're saying… … killing people is OK, even if you're a Christian?"

James shook his head, and there was no hint of a smile now.

"Killing people is never OK, Lizzie. It's just that… … we live in a world where there are far too many evil people all hell-bent on doing bad stuff… …all of which leaves other people… … good, well-intentioned people… … with a choice. You sit back and let the bad folk get on with it, or you do what needs to be done to stop them."

He paused for a moment, and I could sense that he was just getting into his stride.

"Look Lizzie, where we live… … in our western democracies… … people can think about these issues, what's right and wrong, and they can talk about them, and write about them because they're free and safe to do so. But they're only free and safe because there are others in the police and the armed services, even the security services… … maybe especially the security services… … who are fighting hard to keep them that way. And I mean fighting hard. It's always been easy to pontificate from inside your citadel while others outside have to square up to the bad guys, face the tough situations and make the difficult decisions just to make sure you stay safe inside. But get outside yourself, meet the bad guys yourself, face the situations yourself, make those decisions yourself… … well, then it's a whole different ballgame, and it's no longer easy."

And now the smile came back.

"That's why there are all those folk writing all those books. They try to work it all out for us, so we can have a rule to follow, to guarantee we're doing the right thing. We want them to make it easy for us, so we don't have to think."

I was certainly thinking. It seemed to me that James was making sense, though I hadn't expected my tentative query to get him started on a lecture.

"So," I said, as he took a breath, "what I think you're saying is that what's written in the Bible isn't easy and we have to work out for ourselves what it means for us today."

Even as I spoke the words, I was amazed at myself. *We, ourselves, us?* What on earth had made me include myself in this search for truth?

"That's right, Lizzie. The Bible isn't easy. Some Christians will tell you it's a... ... a whole unit, the inspired Word of God, every single word of it. Inerrant is the word they use. And then there are other Christians who will tell you that it's a collection of books, written by different people, in particular circumstances, at different times over a span of a thousand years or more. And then there's... ... ..."

He stopped and shook his head ruefully.

"Sorry, Lizzie. Didn't mean to get carried away."

"That's OK," I said. "So forget them... ... what do you think about the Bible?"

"Ah," he said, with something approaching a twinkle in his eyes. "I'm still working on that one. And when I do work it out, some Christian folk will agree with me and some won't. That doesn't matter... ... Sarah and I didn't always agree on everything. Being a soldier and having to fight was one of them. But we always tried to talk it through, so each of us could understand where the other was coming from... ... Ultimately, I think all the Bible asks of us is that we think about it carefully and then do the best we can, wherever we can, and make the best choices we can, even when the going gets tough... ... The only guarantee is that we will all of us, at some point, face tough times. I think we can both of us testify to that."

I nodded and sat quietly, pondering on what James had said. I suspected that there was a whole load more that he could have added, and that this was not the first time he'd discussed the matter. As it happened, we didn't have a chance to take it further since Abby appeared in the doorway to break into our thoughts.

"Dinner's ready. Time to come through to the dining-room." And then, as an afterthought accompanied by a beaming smile, "Be good and go and wash your hands."

With a chuckle she disappeared, leaving us to answer at a more leisurely pace her summons to the table.

One Hundred and Nine

Aullton House – Early evening

I thought we'd have managed perfectly OK in the kitchen, as we had for lunch, but Abby insisted that we eat her dinner properly. We were rather a small group for such a large table – it could seat a dozen comfortably – but the four of us gathered at one end where our place settings were neatly laid out. Abby sat next to her dad, with me opposite him and Cherry next to me. Barrie was eating upstairs again with Angie, and Andy remained in solitary isolation in his room. His prolonged inactivity seemed to suit both him and us. James had visited him earlier and now offered to take up his chicken pie and chips, but I couldn't bring myself to face him... ... not yet, and maybe not ever. Even though he'd helped us in the end, I couldn't forget what he'd tried to do.

There was a jolly banter throughout the meal, with plenty of compliments to Abby on her cooking, especially her competent way of extracting the chicken pie from its box. I think I made a pretty fair attempt at joining in but my thoughts kept drifting towards that helicopter drawing two-and-a-half miles closer every minute. While the other three debated the merits of shortcrust pastry over puff pastry for a chicken pie, I came to a decision.

My decision was that I didn't really have a clue what I should do.

If Sergeant Hayford wanted to try and use me to find out who was behind the trafficking of girls into the UK, then I ought to do what I could to help. With Bruno and Mitch Portess both dead there was, as far as I was aware, no-one else who knew what I knew, or had seen what I'd seen. Not even Angie. If I wanted to see Mellisse brought down, I would have to give the police what they needed. But could I do it?

It wasn't that I was scared, although I was. Who wouldn't be? Whatever deal James had made with Borisov would crumble to dust the moment I started singing to the police. So, yes I was scared. But my biggest fear was for Abby. I knew that James would try to protect me, and he wouldn't go back on his word to let me stay with him and be a companion to Abby. But if I stayed, and did what I could to help the police, that would put his little girl in danger again. I could leave, of course, but if I ran again, James would come looking for me and he would find me. Of that I was certain.

So, the arguments chased each other around in my head. Speak up and bring Mellisse down, or keep quiet and ensure Abby was safe. I couldn't sit back and see Mellisse go free, but I couldn't possibly risk Abby being caught up in whatever method he might choose to try and get rid of me. It was stalemate, but only temporarily. In less than an hour, I'd be put on the spot and I'd have to choose.

Keeping quiet maybe had a slight edge, as it still held out the possibility that perhaps, in time, James might find a way to give Mellisse what he deserved for all the misery he'd caused.

I stole a glance at the long-case clock standing in the corner. Since we began eating, Sergeant Hayford had travelled about sixty miles. I looked around at the faces smiling and chatting happily, and I shivered.

Abby caught my eye at that moment and frowned.

"Are you OK, Lizzie?"

"I'm fine, sweetie," I said, with an attempt at a smile. "I was wondering if you'd like to watch a movie after tea since we've got some visitors coming."

Straight away, I wished I hadn't mentioned them, although she'd have to know some time. She'd hear the noise of the helicopter if nothing else. Her face froze and, in a very quiet voice, she spoke a single word.

"Who?"

James came to my rescue.

"It's that nice police lady who came to visit the farm last weekend when there was all that fuss," he said.

Lines creased Abby's brow for a moment as she tried to remember. Then they cleared.

"She told me you'd soon be home," she said, seeming reassured.

"That's the one," said her dad, smiling. He then gave her a little nudge. "And it looks as though she'll have to stay the night, so you'll be able to give her a sample of your cooking at breakfast."

A good ploy, and it worked. Abby immediately began planning a breakfast menu, working out what would need to be taken out of the freezer to thaw overnight. James caught my eye and winked.

At that moment, the house phone rang and James stood to go and take the call in the drawing room. We chatted on for a moment or two about the possibilities for breakfast and then, when he still hadn't returned, began to clear the table. We had everything cleared away and the dishwasher stacked before he appeared in the kitchen doorway, his brows creased in thought.

"That was Katie," he said, as the three of us turned to look at him. "Miss Cooper to you, Abby. Look… … er… … come into the drawing room and I'll fill you in."

Abby hung back as Cherry and I began to follow him, but he turned and smiled at her.

"You too, sweetheart, if you're not too busy with menus."

She wasn't, and she bounced along after us to find a place next to her dad on the settee. Once we were all settled, James began.

"I think we're going to have something to tell our police sergeant when she gets here. I'd actually forgotten, with everything else going on, but the school was closed today for the election."

I must have frowned at that because he went on to explain.

"We're used as a polling station, so we always close on Election Day. Katie was in because she wanted to change one of her classroom displays. The mother of one of the Year Six boys came along to vote and spotted Katie through her classroom window. Anyway… … cut the story short… … her lad, Wayne, came on that visit Mr Russell arranged for the Year Sixes to visit Lichfield Tube just after Easter. We were divided into three groups with Russell taking one, his assistant … … David something or other… … he took the second group, and Phil Simmons took Wayne's group which happened to be the one I was with. Now Wayne's mum told Katie that she found some pictures on her lad's computer which he says he got from a computer at Lichfield Tube. Now, if I remember this right, Phil took us to a room where there was a huge map on one wall showing where all LTC's raw materials came from. It was obviously someone's office, but I'd no idea who's. I suppose I just assumed it was Phil's until some guy cruised in and seemed all set to lose his rag until he realised he wasn't the biggest guy in the room."

"Few blokes are when you're around," said Cherry, and Abby chuckled and snuggled up closer to her dad.

"Yes… … well… …" said James, "the thing is, before he came in, we were all so busy looking at the map and listening to Phil, that I never noticed what Wayne was up to. We all knew he was a computer geek, so I suppose I should have watched him more carefully since there was both a laptop and a PC on the desk in the office. According to his mum, Wayne spotted that the laptop was on and sneaked round to have a look. There were large photos of girls with all sorts of info about each one. Wayne wasn't interested in the info, but he liked the pictures. Guess what the monkey did."

I don't think James expected a response but I thought I could see where this was going.

"You said he was a geek," I said. "I bet he had a memory stick on him and … …"

James was smiling, so I knew I had it right.

"… … when he saw no-one was looking he slipped it into the laptop and downloaded the files."

"Spot on," confirmed James. "Wayne's mum says he just managed to whip it out of the laptop before the new guy spotted it. Anyway, this chap was in a right paddy, and he slammed the laptop shut and told Phil to get us all out of his office. Phil seemed a bit stunned, but he apologised and shooed us all out. By the time we got back to school, I'd forgotten all about it."

"So who was this guy?" Cherry asked.

"Phil might have told me his name. I can't remember, and I wasn't really all that bothered. But I'm pretty certain, now I think about it, that it was Mitchell Portess."

"The airport guy?" asked Cherry again.

"The airport guy," James confirmed.

My mind was already churning away, feverishly examining a possible new theory about why Phil Simmons had been killed in a way that could potentially implicate James.

Cherry, it seemed, was on the same track.

"So what you're saying is that you and Phil Simmons were both in Portess's office … … unexpectedly, I assume… … at the very time when his laptop was displaying information about his… …"

He trailed off, suddenly realising that Abby was still sitting there, listening to everything and understanding a good bit of it.

"… … his other activities."

James nodded.

"And he would have no way of knowing for certain whether you'd seen it or not?"

James shook his head.

"No, and the mum is worried now that this business with young Wayne might have something to do with Phil getting killed. Katie, bless her, told her not to worry but to hang on to that memory stick in case the police wanted to have a look at it."

At that moment, my ears picked up the distinctive sound of rotor blades close by. That ended our discussion.

To get Abby's mind thinking about something else, I helped her choose a DVD while James went off to meet the newcomers.

We watched the Swiss Family Robinson get shipwrecked while we waited for James to come back upstairs with our visitors. It took a while, so I assumed that he was telling Sergeant Hayford about Katie's phone call.

I totally lost interest in seeing how much John Mills and his family could salvage from the wreck. If this visit was about my uncle, these next few minutes were not going to be pleasant. If it was about Mellisse, then I had a decision to make. If it was about both, then I was in deep trouble. I strained to hear the sound of the apartment door opening. My heart was pounding so much I could hear it in my ears. Then I felt Cherry's hand on my shoulder. I hadn't even noticed him leave his chair.

"Hang in there, girl," he said, giving my shoulder a gentle squeeze.

I nodded, unable to speak. My mouth was too dry.

I got up and went to the kitchen to get a glass of water. I was just returning through the kitchen door when James appeared from the stairway. Behind him was Sergeant Hayford, looking even more tired than when I'd first seen her less than a week ago. As they walked towards me, a third figure turned into the corridor. I didn't recognise him, not at first, even though it was only three days since our paths had last crossed. I sensed a vague familiarity, but that was all.

James smiled at me and told me to hang on a minute while he poked his head into the drawing room to tell Cherry and Abby that we'd be in the sitting room. Logically, it would have made more sense for them to move to the smaller sitting room to finish the DVD while we, the bigger group, met in the drawing room. That James didn't suggest it was, I was sure, due to his desire to let Abby stay where she obviously felt comfortable.

We followed him to a room at the end of the corridor, which I had peeped in when I first arrived but had since ignored. I was puzzled by the looks I was getting from Hayford's companion who, strangely I thought, had not been introduced. He allowed me to enter the room ahead of him with a polite "After you."

His voice jolted me into recognition and I remembered where I'd seen him. It was in James's office at the school last Monday morning. Everything was suddenly flipped upside down. This was Russell somebody, or somebody Russell, the Chair of Governors, so was it really James he was here to see after all and not me? And if so, why was Sergeant Hayford here? I was still struggling to make sense of it when James invited us all to sit down.

The room by most standards was a decent size with, amongst other furnishings, four easy chairs grouped around a coffee table. We each selected one and made ourselves comfortable. Not that I felt in the slightest bit comfortable, and I was surprised to see that Russell didn't seem at ease either as he kept fiddling nervously with his tie, and glancing at me when he thought I wouldn't notice.

As host, James kicked off the proceedings.

"Now, housekeeping first. You've had a long journey so would anyone like coffee or tea? Something to eat, perhaps. And if anyone needs the bathroom, it's the door opposite this one."

Orders were placed and James asked Cherry to do the honours while Russell disappeared into the bathroom.

"Why's he here?" I whispered to James thinking that Russell may have explained the reason for his visit on the way up from the helicopter.

"I really don't know," he replied in a thoughtful tone, showing that he was as puzzled by this turn of events as I was. He raised his eyebrows in Hayford's direction inviting her to enlighten us.

"I'm going to leave it to Mr Russell to explain," she said. "It's his story, so he should tell it."

So we waited. Eventually, both guests had made use of the bathroom and Cherry had produced two coffees, one tea, a hot chocolate and a plate of Scottish shortbreads. After that, we were all set.

"Well, Gordon," said James, "according to Sergeant Hayford, this is your show, so tell us… … what's it all about?"

Hayford sat back in her chair nursing her coffee mug as Russell began speaking. I was looking at him but, out of the corner of my eye, I could see she was watching me. Russell's tea sat on the table untouched.

"I'm not sure how to start," he said. "I suppose the beginning would be best."

He licked his lips and his eyes flicked away as he tried to find the words he needed.

"I met you first when you were a little girl and I was in the Royal Navy. My ship visited St Helena, and your dad invited me for tea… … Back then, everyone called me Gordy."

My eyes grew wide and my stomach lurched as I stared at the man who had been with my parents when they died. I couldn't speak. I felt bile in the back of my throat. I thought I might be sick. The memory of that appalling night was suddenly so vivid.

"I'm sorry, Lizzie. I can see you remember, and I wish with all my heart that I didn't have to bring this up, but it's right that you know what happened."

I didn't know what he was talking about. I did know what had happened. My dad's car had crashed and blown up and my parents had died, and with them so had my happy carefree childhood. That was it. What more was there to say?

"I think one of the front tyres blew out."

He was talking again but his voice sounded distant… … muffled somehow. Then James's chair was very close, and his hand grasped mine. I forced myself to concentrate.

"The car spun and bounced between the rock face on one side and the stone wall on the other… … I don't know if you remember that road, but it's not all that wide. On the other side of the wall the cliff drops down into Upper Jamestown. Part of the wall was weak and the car broke through… … It hung there… … balanced. I was in the back and your mum and dad in the front."

He stopped and took a deep breath. His right hand was over his mouth and his eyes closed. James and I were watching him, but Sergeant

Hayford still had her eyes on me. It dawned on me then that she already knew the story and was concerned about my reaction. I had none... ... unless you call numb a reaction.

Russell's hand dropped and his eyes opened.

"What should have happened was that your mum and dad should have joined me in the back. They couldn't get out at the front because your mum's door was over the drop and your dad's door had jammed. The rear window had smashed... ... we could get out that way. Your mum needed to be the first to move and she tried to get between the seats but the car started rocking... ... we sat still, hardly daring to breath."

At that moment, he looked me in the eye, directly, for the first time since we'd sat down.

"Your dad was very calm and very brave... ... I don't know if you've ever wondered about that... ... your dad never panicked... ... He quietly told your mum what to do and she did her best, but every time she moved the car rocked. In the end, he told us just to sit still and wait for help to come."

I tried to picture the scene. In my head it was clear, but Russell was now rather fuzzy as I stared at him through my tears.

"Why didn't you get out? Get help?" I asked in a voice that sounded very croaky

He shook his head slowly but I didn't know why. My question didn't seem that stupid.

"My weight was needed in the back of the car," he said. "To keep it balanced. Maybe if we'd stayed like that, and just waited, everything would have been all right."

I didn't quite see where this was going, but James apparently did.

"So, why didn't you?" he asked.

Russell sighed. "I don't know."

He shook his head again and rubbed his hand over his forehead. His tea was still untouched. He looked as though he needed something stronger.

"I don't know," he said again. "I tell myself that I thought... ... I thought if I could get my weight just a bit further back, we'd stop rocking and we'd be safer. So I began to ease myself over the back of the seat and across the parcel shelf... ... and it was working. The back of the car began to tilt just a little towards the road... ... but then there was a grating sound from underneath... ... the car jolted, and I didn't know what was happening so I let myself roll out of the window and down onto the road... ... I was scared shitless... ... totally pulverised... ... but so relieved to be out on the ground. I heard your dad yelling for me to stand on the back of the car... ... to get the balance back... ... I staggered and tried to reach it but it was too late. The car toppled over and I heard your mum scream before it crashed into the bottom. Then the fuel tank exploded and… …."

He stopped speaking when I began moaning. I clasped my hands across my chest and rocked in my chair as I remembered standing in my pyjamas on the veranda, looking down the road along which my parents would return. Instead, I had heard an explosion and, in a flash of childish fear and insight, I had known they were never coming back.

One Hundred and Ten

Aullton House – Evening

For several minutes none of us spoke. At some point, I became aware of James sitting on the arm of my chair. I was leaning into him and slowly I grew conscious of his hand gently caressing my back. There were tears in my eyes but I wasn't crying. I was stunned by what I'd heard. My brain had quite simply seized up. For a brief period there was no conscious thought. Just blankness. Then suddenly, the blankness became a turmoil as a host of different thoughts began tumbling around in my head. Eventually, one of those thoughts extracted itself from the rest.

"Are you telling me… … my parents needn't have died?"

When Russell didn't reply, I turned my face towards him so I could look directly into his eyes. He was watching me and his mouth was working as though he was having difficulty getting the words out.

I eased myself away from James and sat up straight in my chair. I don't know what expression Russell saw on my face, but I could feel the fires of anger beginning to burn inside me.

"Did my parents die because of you?" I asked, each word spoken separately and deliberately.

"I… … I don't know."

I was on my feet now, with James beside me, holding me, as though he feared I would launch myself at Russell.

"What the hell do you mean, you don't know?"

It felt like a scream, but James told me later it came out more like a whisper.

Russell didn't answer, and Sergeant Hayford decided it was time to come to his rescue.

"It's one of those things, Lizzie, where no-one can know for sure."

"How can you know?" I said, turning to her. "You weren't there. He was."

"I know," she replied, unfazed by my response. "But I've now heard that story twice, and I've had time to picture it in my mind twice. Let's just think about it for a minute."

I let James guide me back into my chair. He sat on the arm, his arm around my shoulder as before. I didn't want to think about it for a minute, or even a second, but the reasonable part of my mind was telling me just to shut up for a bit and let her speak.

"This accident was simply that, an accident. A tyre blew… …No-one's fault. But the result was a very dangerous situation. The car was finely balanced on the edge. It was hard for anyone to move without upsetting that balance. The only one who could move safely was Mr Russell here, and the only direction he could go was backwards. He tried that, and it seemed to help the car's balance, to make it safer. Then something started to give under the car. This made the sound Mr Russell heard and the car lurched. If he'd stayed where he was, it's possible, maybe even likely, that all three of them would have gone over the edge. Maybe, he was right to roll out."

"You can't know that for sure," I said reasonably.

"Nor can you know for sure that it was Mr Russell's action that led to your parents' death… … It's just one of those situations where we simply don't know."

We were quiet again, just sitting while they gave me time to come to terms with what I'd heard. Then it suddenly dawned on me. This had all been pointless. It hadn't changed anything. The accident was still an accident and my parents were still dead.

"Why did you come all this way to tell me that?" I asked, curious but in a strange way also accusing.

"We came, Lizzie," said Sergeant Hayford, sitting forward in her chair, "because the consequences of what happened didn't just affect you."

I frowned. My eyes were clear of tears now. I was confused and, yes, still angry, and I let it show in my voice.

"What do you mean? This isn't making any sense."

"There was someone else on the road that evening. Someone who saw what happened. That person was Petty Officer Mitchell Portess."

I felt James's arm tighten around my shoulders, as he spoke for the first time since this began.

"Are you talking about the guy who was shot yesterday?"

Sergeant Hayford nodded. "One and the same."

"So how does he fit in to this?"

I don't know what James thought was coming, but I certainly couldn't guess. When Russell didn't respond, Hayford continued the story.

"Portess had been visiting some… … ladies… … up country somewhere, and was on his way back to the ship. He had turned when he heard the car coming down the hill, hoping to get a lift back to the seafront. He saw it all. The blowout, the crash, and Lieutenant Russell, as he was then, scrambling out of the back. Portess, it seems, was never one to miss a chance, so when he found his officer, dazed and in a state of shock, he spun the story to make it sound as though Mr Russell had acted to save his own skin at the expense of your parents."

"But he did," I protested.

"I don't think so," she replied in a reasonable tone. "The way Portess told the story didn't match Mr Russell's memories of what happened, but he was confused and couldn't be sure what was really true."

"And you believe this?" I asked.

"Actually, I do."

She looked over at Russell who shook his head slightly, but his eyes never left my face.

"She's right," he said. "I let Portess help me back to the ship and I accepted that it all happened the way he said it did. I had no reason not to believe him... ... not until he came to me one day on our way back to Portsmouth... ... he asked me to guarantee him a job... ... His term in the navy was nearly up, like mine. When I told him I wasn't sure I could, he said he'd have to report what had happened... ... with the accident. He said I had acted in a cowardly manner and I had failed to rescue the other people in the car when I could have got them clear before it went over. In my head, I knew it wasn't true, but I couldn't argue with him because there was the question of why I hadn't stayed around to explain to the police what had happened... ... But that was his doing. I was in shock and had just let him take me back to the ship. He made it sound as though I'd coerced him somehow into keeping quiet. As if anyone could coerce him into doing anything. Ruthless bastard."

I thought I was understanding things a little more clearly now, and this story certainly tallied better with my memory of the man who'd shared our tea table that evening.

"Did you get him the job?" I asked.

He shrugged.

"Well, it didn't seem such a big thing really. I'd been offered a job by FerroTech. I was Chief Engineering Officer and we'd been trying out some of their new systems in the Selkirk which is how they knew me."

He glanced at Hayford in a way that made me wonder if he was about to say something that she didn't already know.

"The thing is... ... we had a bit of a problem with the bimetallic leak detector tube. It was only minor, but it could have caused trouble for FerroTech if it had been formally reported. I got it sorted with the help of Portess and his crew. As soon as I got a chance, I reported it to FerroTech and let them know that I hadn't logged what we'd done. This was the start of an on-going contract with the Navy dockyard so they were very grateful."

Hayford was watching him as though she was trying to work out whether a crime had been committed.

"Obviously, it didn't take much to get them to let me bring Portess along with me and put him on a pay-grade substantially higher than anything he'd have got for himself in Civvy Street."

James interrupted now, for the first time.

"Didn't the St Helena police ever want to talk to you?"

"Yes, they did eventually. I don't know why they took so long but they didn't contact the ship until after we'd sailed. By then, Portess had this story that we met up with him on the road and I'd got out to walk with him back to the ship. Mr and Mrs Burleigh had continued down the road to find a place to turn round. By the time we passed, the car had already gone over the edge. We didn't see it happen… … At least, that was his story, and that's what was radioed back to the St Helena police. I went along with it because if I hadn't he'd have told his other version which would certainly have raised questions, if nothing else."

"The police didn't question it?" asked James.

"No… … That was the end of it… … Except, for me, it was just the start of one piece of blackmail after another, and… …apparently… … a whole mess of dirty dealings, most of which… … and this is God's honest truth, I knew nothing about."

The room fell quiet as James and I thought about what we'd heard, and Russell and Hayford waited to see how I was going to respond. The truth was I didn't know how to respond. If everything I'd heard was true, then I did at least know exactly how and why my parents had died.

But it didn't change anything. They were still dead. I would still have had to go and live with my aunt and uncle. He would still have done what he did, and he was still dead. And I had run away and become what I was.

"Nothing's changed," I said at last. "You tell me all this, but… … really… … nothing's any different. Nothing could have been different."

"Oh yes it could," said Russell wearily, but with quiet firmness. "Very different. You never got my letters did you?"

"Letters?"

I had no idea what he was talking about.

"They were found after your uncle… … died," said Hayford, and she obviously noticed the change in my expression. "Yes, I do know about that, and I'll get to it shortly. But I'll tell you straight, right now, there's nothing for you to worry about."

Could she really mean what I thought she meant? James seemed to think so. I sensed it in the gentle squeeze of his arm which still lay around my shoulder.

"I wrote to you, Lizzie," said Russell. "Quite a few times. At first to tell you how sorry I was about your mum and dad… … later, I just wanted to let you know that I was now permanently in the UK and, if you ever needed... ... a friend... ... anything, to let me know."

"Feeling guilty?" I asked, and straight away wished I kept my mouth shut, but Russell didn't seem offended.

"Not so much that," he said. "Mostly it was sympathy with an eight year old kid who was going through what I'd gone through at thirteen when my own parents died."

"Your uncle kept the letters," put in Hayford. "The early ones had been opened, but the later ones were still sealed."

"I actually had a visit from the police about three years ago when they were trying to find out where you'd gone, but there was nothing I could tell them. Naturally, they wanted to know how I knew you, so I told them how I'd met your parents when my ship visited the island. That was all I told them, nothing about the accident, and they went away."

"Tell her what else you didn't tell them," said Hayford, a strange smile softening her eyes.

Russell pursed his lips and treated her to a sidelong glance.

"Go on," she said, still smiling. "She can only say no."

This was it, I thought. This was what had brought them up to Scotland to see me. Or, at least, it was what had brought Russell. Hayford had obviously come about my uncle.

"I did a bit of checking about your uncle, but I swear I had no idea what sort of person he was. I only learnt that from Sergeant Hayford last night. I never knew what you were going through... ... What I did learn was that your uncle wasn't especially well off and wasn't going to be able to do much to provide for your future... ... University, maybe. That sort of thing."

He paused, watching to see if I was following.

I was.

Intently.

Satisfied, he went on.

"I had a good job with FerroTech. My wife and I... ... well, we don't have a particularly flashy lifestyle, so my salary was a good bit more than we needed. We never had any children of our own, you see. So, with the help of a friend of mine, I set up an investment fund for you. Your uncle knew about this and sent me your birth certificate so we could get it done. Very cooperative at the time, but I thought later that all he was bothered about was finding a way he could get his hands on the fund. Anyway, forget about him. The point is that I've been putting £5000 a year into the fund, which is now coming up ten years."

He was smiling now.

"My friend knew what he was doing. The fund has done well. As of right now, your trust fund is worth a shade over £85,000."

One Hundred and Eleven

Aullton House –Evening

I was still reeling from the shock of what Russell had just told me when, on the edge of my vision, I noticed the door nudge open just enough to allow Abby's face to appear. She remained like that, peeping in, obviously unsure whether it would be OK to intrude. I turned my head so she would know I'd seen her, but none of the others seemed to notice her.

"Hey Abby," I said, trying to keep my tone jolly and upbeat, which was a far cry from how I was feeling.

She pushed the door open a little further, and other heads turned to watch her.

"You OK?" I asked, when no-one else spoke. "Has your DVD finished already?"

"Nooo," she said slowly, "but I needed a bathroom break so I thought I'd go up and get changed."

She grinned.

"I think Cherry needed a break too, from the movie. He's catching up on the news now. News! Yuk!"

James smiled at that. "Was there anything you wanted, sweetheart?" he asked.

"Not really," she replied. "I just wondered if you were nearly done yet."

"Not quite, sweetheart, but I don't think we'll be too much longer."

Disappointment clouded her face and my heart went out to her.

"Tell you what, Abby," I said, "why don't you get changed and finish your DVD and, as soon as you're done, come and get me and I'll come up to your room with you and we'll have some time together before you settle down. How's that?"

"What if you're still not finished?" she asked sceptically.

"Then our visitors here will just have to wait for us, won't they?" I replied, and got the smile I wanted.

Abby left, seemingly content, and I turned my thoughts back to Russell and his incredible announcement. He had remained quiet during that little exchange, his eyes flicking between Abby and me. His frown made me wonder whether he was puzzled by the obvious bond of affection between Abby and me. It was as though he didn't know what to make of it.

I didn't know what to make of this fund he'd spoken of. I could see no reason for him to give me all that money, unless it was guilt, and I hadn't made my mind up yet whether he had any need to feel guilty or not. There was so much to think about.

Then Sergeant Hayford tossed something else into the mix; something she had told me not to worry about, but which had kept gnawing away at me anyway.

"You and Mr Russell here clearly have a lot to talk about," she said, "and none of that is police business. But this is, and I thought we should get it cleared up."

I watched her, trying to appear more calm that I felt, and wondering whether it was about my uncle or Mellisse.

"I think we now have the full story about your uncle… …"

So that was it. Was I going to be charged with anything? Her earlier reassurance made me think not, but I'd learnt you can never be sure with the police. They use whatever tactics they have to in order to build their case.

"… … and I've looked at all we have on record about his death." She smiled, which I took to be a good sign. "You really shouldn't have left a used tampon in the middle of a crime scene. If that had not been found in the woods, I'd never have made the connection."

Everyone was silent. James looked at me, puzzled. Russell's expression was unreadable.

"Your uncle's body was found because when you left in such a hurry – quite understandable, I might say – you didn't close the front door properly. A neighbour spotted it and went in to check if everything was OK."

"Mrs Herbert," I said, thinking of the nosey-parker who used to live next door.

"It was a Mrs Herbert, yes," confirmed Hayford. "According to the report, there was a good deal of evidence, forensic and otherwise, but there's only one thing which I think will interest you."

I reached my hand up to James and he took it and gave it a squeeze.

"There was some skin and hair under the fingernails of his right hand which it was assumed got there during the struggle when he tried to rape you."

She was watching my face for a reaction. I don't know what she saw, but it seemed to satisfy her.

"So, he did try to rape you?"

I nodded.

"The first time?"

I shook my head.

"No. That's what your friend Sonia told the officers who spoke to her."

She'd been a good friend, Sonia. She'd listened and sympathised, even telling me to go to the police or, at least, my form teacher at school. She hadn't ranted at me when I refused, afraid of all the fuss it would cause, afraid of being known as the victim of abuse. And she'd kept my secret, just as I'd begged her, never telling another soul about the horrors of my home life. Not until the police came calling.

"So, she finally told them," I said, glad that she had.

"Yes, she told them. But what I was coming to was this... ... They were able to get DNA from the samples under your uncle's nails, and they matched them to other items from your room... ... hairbrush, dirty clothes, that sort of thing... ... and gradually they pieced together what had happened. It was assumed that your uncle was trying it on again... ... you defended yourself... ... somehow, almost certainly accidently, he died in the struggle. But, without you there to ask, there was nothing more to be done... ... until your DNA turned up in that wood. Of course, I didn't make the connection until the match with your tampon came through yesterday, but as soon as I saw your picture in the file everything fell into place."

I looked up at James. He knew all of this. I'd told him myself, after all. Yet, somehow, it seemed so much worse hearing it from the police. But he was still holding my hand, so I gripped it tightly. He didn't look at me. He was watching Sergeant Hayford.

"So," he said. "What happens next?"

"The Derbyshire police want to talk to Lizzie, to get her side of things on record. But I spoke to the officer dealing with this before coming up here, and I can promise you there is no question of bringing any charges."

I think there was a sigh of relief all round which was quickly overwhelmed by Sergeant Hayford's next words.

"However... ... you, Lizzie, provided us with some very useful information earlier today, so the other reason I'm here is to ask you how you came by that
information, and what else do you know about this trafficking business? Who else is involved, and who is running it?"

So there it was, at last.

Decision time.

But before I could get even part way to making a decision, the door of the room was flung open. I looked across, expecting it to be Abby, but was surprised to see Cherry stride in, not bothering to close the door behind him. He seemed to hesitate when he saw the expression on my face, but it was only momentary. He continued across the room to the corner on my left, propelled by an urgency which the rest of us failed to grasp. Turning on the flat-screen TV mounted high across the corner, he fiddled for a moment with the remote. We were all watching him, our faces showing various shades of puzzlement and incomprehension.

BBC News 24 flashed up on the screen to show presenter Jane Hill running through the top news stories of the day. Cherry stepped to one side so we could all see the screen.

"I just caught the headline," he said. "Keep watching." So we did.

We had to sit through some boring stuff about the election, with various pundits waffling on about the turnout and likely outcome. I wasn't much bothered. I was now old enough to vote but I hadn't registered anywhere. Watching the talking heads droning on, I realised that I had no idea how to set about getting on the electoral roll, but that didn't bother me much either.

"Keep with it," said Cherry, sensing that our attention might be wandering.

After a few moments patience, we eventually got there.

It was a stretch of dual-carriageway which a box in the corner of the screen identified as the A38 Bristol Road, Birmingham. As the camera stopped panning around, the screen was filled with a head and shoulders shot of the roving reporter sent to the scene. It was easy to see why she was there. Behind her, sealed off by police crime-scene tape, was a large car, something like a Rolls Royce or a Bentley. Its nose was wrapped around one of the trees that lined the central reservation along the straight stretch running down by Edgbaston Pool. There was something about the car that seemed familiar. I was willing to bet on it being a Bentley. Excitement began to grow inside me, but I hadn't forgotten that there was a police officer in the audience so I prepared to hold myself in check, whatever news unfolded.

Earlier this evening, the car behind me, a blue Bentley, was travelling south along this dual-carriageway stretch of the A38, when a vehicle following pulled out to overtake it. According to witnesses, the second car was a blue Ford Mondeo and had what looked like a rifle or shotgun sticking out of the front passenger window. As it drew alongside, two shots were fired at very close range into the Bentley which immediately swerved. The shooter's car drove away fast and, I understand from the police, has not yet been identified or located. It appears that the Bentley initially struck a tree on the nearside, but this caused it to spin completely around before lodging as you see it now. The two passengers in the rear of the Bentley were pronounced dead at the scene, having suffered multiple wounds to the head. Their identity was initially withheld until next of kin could be informed, but in the last few minutes I have learned that the victims are local businessman Raymond Mellisse, and Russian entrepreneur Alexei Borisov. Two photographs appeared side by side on the screen while the reporter's voice continued in the background. *They were being driven by Mr Mellisse's chauffeur, Jim Large, who has been taken to hospital though his condition is not thought to be serious. Also in the car, occupying the front passenger seat, was a man thought to be Mr Borisov's bodyguard. So far, he has not been named, but police have confirmed that he was pronounced dead at the scene. There is speculation that he was not wearing his seatbelt. According to police, there is no apparent motive for this shooting, but it is clear that these two men were deliberately targeted for some reason as yet unknown. Police have also confirmed that several firearms have been recovered from the wrecked vehicle. In a few moments… … …"*

"Daddy, isn't that… …?"

Abby's voice came from behind us where she stood unnoticed in the doorway.

"Yes, it is, sweetheart," said James quickly as Cherry clicked the remote and the screen went blank. "Nothing for you to worry about though. I thought you were going to finish your DVD."

"I was, but Cherry wasn't there so I came to find him."

"Well, now you have," said James. "Why don't you go and finish your DVD and I'll be along in a minute."

"Do I have to watch on my own? Can't Cherry come back. Or Lizzie?"

"Sweetheart, we'll all come in just a minute. Why don't you go and get started?"

Abby hesitated, and I could see signs of distress bubbling to the surface. The picture of Borisov had obviously triggered memories.

I stood up to go over to her. As I did so, James's mobile buzzed to show a text had been received. That would happen sometimes. Texts would somehow manage to get through even when voice calls couldn't be made. I glanced at Abby and gave her a smile but paused while James looked at the message. He stared at it for a moment and then turned the screen so I could see it.

The message was from Osman Izetbegović and it said simply *It wasn't us.*

I nodded to James before saying to Abby, "Let's go finish your movie."

As I walked over to her I passed Sergeant Hayford. Pausing, I looked down at her and said, "I've given you all I can. There's no-one left now for you to go after. No-one that I know of anyway."

I glanced back at the blank screen, and then down into her eyes where I saw a tiny flicker of understanding.

I took Abby's hand and together we walked down the hallway to the drawing room to join **The Swiss Family Robinson.** James could sort out the others. I'd had enough of them for one night.

And anyway, I had someone far more important, certainly far more precious, to be giving my attention to.

Someone who needed me almost as much as I needed her.

Epilogue

The Dower House

10 days later

Epilogue

The Dower House

I didn't keep Russell's money. I accepted it and, since I'd had so little for so long, the temptation to hold on to it was very strong. In the end, though, I decided to give it to Angie. She's come along really well but, amazingly, still can't remember what happened at the hospital. Barrie thought it best not to tell her, so we all went along with that. Anyway, Andy will soon be out in the Middle East and a danger to no-one but the Gulf pirates. I don't know if the thing between Angie and Barrie will actually develop into something tangible and long-lasting, but I didn't want her to feel it was her only option. If she and Barrie end up an item, the money will be a bonus. If not, having the money will open up a range of possibilities for her, and I reckon she deserves it.

And there was the fact that I didn't want to feel beholden to Russell. His story could well be true, but I just have the strangest sense, based on nothing in particular, that there was something he was holding back about the way my parents died. I remember that my dad helped him send a message to some people in the UK, and I think I now understand why Russell didn't want to send it from the ship. Not if it was to FerroTech about covering up the fact that they'd supplied defective tubes. James and I have talked about this a little, and he has come up with a theory. James doesn't believe that Russell would ever have had any intention to kill my parents, but he does think that Russell may have been glad they died or, at least, that my father did. If he's right, this fortuitous accident meant that no-one, other than its recipient, would know that Russell had sent that incriminating fax. So James believes that Russell is so confused emotionally, that he doesn't even know himself whether he could actually have saved them, and the guilt is eating him up.

It's all speculation, of course, so James and I agreed to let it rest. Nothing was going to bring my parents back, and I just want to leave the past behind and move on.

James has the same thoughts about that reporter, Corrina Rigby. He could have made life very difficult for her, and probably her paper as well, but he just sees it as water under the bridge. Her editor made sure she wrote a retraction, clearing up the innuendo of her previous articles, and James sent a copy to his father. To give her credit, Rigby did phone James, after we got back from Scotland, to offer a personal apology. I was with him when he took the call, and it was no surprise to hear him tell her to let it go. Bearing in mind what she'd been through, losing her fiancé like that, he thought she didn't need any more trouble in her life.

Abby's been back at school for the past week. I've been going in as a volunteer, but mostly I've been helping James get everything in order for his successor, whoever that will be. I'm even having a CRB check done, now that I know that the Criminal Records Bureau won't turn up anything nasty about me in police files.

James has decided that teaching, as a long-term career, is not for him. He went into it on leaving the Royal Marines because it had been what Sarah wanted, and it had offered him a rewarding job with time available to spend with Abby. That decision had been made before he received such an immense inheritance from his Aunt, and before the plane crash killed so many members of his family. He had already begun to put the money to good use, but hadn't the time to manage everything himself. Recently he's become convinced that the various trusts that he established were not being managed as efficiently as they could be. There were going to have to be changes so James decided to begin with himself.

He handed in his notice to Gordon Russell once we'd travelled back down to the Midlands, and accepting it was probably the last thing Russell did before stepping down as the Chair of Governors. The police and CPS don't seem to have made up their minds yet whether it's in the public interest to charge him with anything, but I think he decided to jump ship before he was pushed. He's probably finished at Lichfield Tube as well. Sir Vernon Laycock is now an MP, so he'll probably have a load of other things needing his attention, but James has heard that someone from FerroTech has gone in along with Paul Riddings to see if anything of the company can be salvaged from the mire.

Obviously, there are no jobs at Lichfield Tube for those girls from Vilnius, but James offered to help them find work if they wanted to stay in the UK. Some sort of charitable trust of his called **Moving On** would deal with it, helping with training, accommodation, even grants if necessary. I wasn't surprised that only one of them wants to stay. Her name is Aushra Paulauskaitė, and she seems determined to try and make a new life for herself over here. She did, though, want to see her mum which I think we all understood. So James is arranging for her mum to come over for a holiday and the two of them can work out together what they want to do next.

According to Sergeant Hayford, quite unofficially, there is still no information on the killers of Mellisse and Borisov. What few leads the police had at first have taken them nowhere, and the trail is virtually stone cold. A witness claimed to have seen a man, the shooter, and a woman, the driver, in the blue Ford and, although roadside cameras seemed to confirm this, no clear images could be recovered. The car, which turned out unsurprisingly to have been stolen, turned up on a housing estate some miles away in Marston Green, near Birmingham airport. It was, as

Hayford said, totally sanitised. After that, all trace vanished. The only tangible clue left to follow remained so far unexplained, and I couldn't help. On the front seat of the Ford, tucked into a large brown envelope, was a photograph run off on an inkjet printer. It showed the brown, front cover of a first edition of **The Wind in the Willows.** On the back of the picture were the words **Follow Pan.** It meant nothing to me and the Birmingham police are still working on it.

I met with the Derbyshire police last Tuesday. James had to be in school, so Cherry drove me over to Ashbourne. I hadn't seen the place in three years and wasn't at all sure I wanted to visit it this time, but the lady officer who led the interview couldn't have been nicer. Sergeant Hayford had been right. They already had a fairly clear idea of what had happened on the afternoon my uncle died, pieced together from evidence found in the house together with what Sonia had told them. The story I told exactly fitted the facts as they knew them. When we were done, the lady inspector smiled and told me I was free to put it all behind me, but she gave me a card in case I found I needed help in doing that, counselling and suchlike.

I don't. Need help, that is. Living with James and Abby is all I need. For the first time in a lot of years, I feel totally safe and secure. I have a job and a salary with board and lodging thrown in. Abby seems to think of me as a big sister, and James treats me like a grown-up daughter. Sometimes, when I catch him looking at me, I allow myself to hope that there's more to it than that. Soon, perhaps, I might find the right opportunity to tell him how I really feel because I doubt whether he'll speak first. I think it might be partly due to age difference, but I also think it's about the burden of trust. This can be such a fragile thing, so easily shattered and so nearly impossible to restore. He knows at the moment that I trust him implicitly and absolutely, and I wonder if he's shy of putting that at risk by an unwanted declaration.

There's always the problem of the Marquess, of course. We have met only once since returning from Scotland, and his opinion of me doesn't seem to have changed. Still, James did tell me that his father has stopped trying to persuade him to cut me loose, which I suppose is a start. Whether he'll ever stop thinking of me as some sort of gold-digging slut, I guess we'll just have to wait and see.

I can be patient.

The chains of my past have been broken, and the same, I think, is true for Angie. We still have memories going back through the years that occasionally surge up from the darkness to haunt our dreams, but they will fade with time. We are both of us, for now, happier than we have any right to be.

Whatever the future holds for me, I can face it.

For now at least, I have a family again.

Acknowledgements

Thanks to my wife, Jan, without whose support and encouragement this story would never have emerged from its chrysalis.

Also to Dr Ruth Fish for her advice on medical matters. Any errors in this area are the result of my not paying sufficient attention to her comments.

Thanks also to my daughters, Becci and Rachel, whose enduring interest helped me to press on to a conclusion.

A debt is also owed to my long-time friend, Richard Ayres, who took the time to proof-read the almost-final draft of the manuscript, noting errors and inconsistencies, and offering suggestions.

Finally, a hearty thank you to Katie Cooper who allowed me to borrow her real-life character for my story. While all other characters are creations of my imagination, intended to bear no resemblance to any person living or dead, Katie truly lives and breathes and really does love her car.

Care Farming UK

Some readers may be intrigued by the notion of a farm dedicated to helping young people from troubled backgrounds. The concept is not new, and I hope I may be forgiven for so blatantly borrowing the idea for the purpose of developing my story. Heighley Grange is not modelled on any particular farm, nor are its managers, Chick and Rachel Childers, anything other than creations of my imagination.

However, farms such as this do exist throughout the UK. They provide an environment where young people, who have been damaged by early life experiences, can learn and develop skills while building up confidence and self-esteem. I have taken the liberty of giving Heighley Grange a faith-based foundation, but this is by no means an essential component of care farming. If anything could be said to be a pre-requisite for becoming involved in such an enterprise, it would probably be a durable blend of patience, compassion and goodwill.

Anyone who is interested in learning more should visit **www.carefarminguk.org.**

Printed in Great Britain
by Amazon